Judith MacNaught

Coena Domini: An essay on the Lord's Supper

Its primitive institution apostolic uses and subsequent history

Judith MacNaught

Coena Domini: An essay on the Lord's Supper
Its primitive institution apostolic uses and subsequent history

ISBN/EAN: 9783337202897

Printed in Europe, USA, Canada, Australia, Japan

Cover: Foto ©Andreas Hilbeck / pixelio.de

More available books at **www.hansebooks.com**

AN ESSAY ON

THE LORD'S SUPPER; ITS PRIMITIVE INSTITUTION, APOSTOLIC USES, AND SUBSEQUENT HISTORY.

BY THE

Rev. JOHN MACNAUGHT, M.A.,

EX-INCUMBENT OF ST. CHRYSOSTOM'S, LIVERPOOL; OF LAURA CHAPEL, BATH; AND OF TRINITY CHAPEL, CONDUIT STREET, LONDON.

LONDON:

C. KEGAN PAUL & CO., 1, PATERNOSTER SQUARE.

1878.

PREFACE.

By way of preface a few words only need be offered.

As to the matter of this essay, the thoughts have been culled where they could be found, from sources too numerous to be named. If there is anything original in the essay, it may be in the thoroughness with which, in the first book, the Scripture narratives have been allowed to tell their own story, going counter, as they do, to many of those preconceived notions which have been inherited from mediæval writers. This probably holds good, in an especial degree, with reference to the words of Christ in the administration of the Supper.

And, again, the same line of Biblical instruction has led the author to be very free and very earnest in applying the Scriptural principles of the first book to the exposition of the Reformed Liturgy in the third book.

From the nature of the subject, not a little reiteration has been necessary. If unfamiliar truth is to be brought effec-

tually within the cognizance of the popular mind, it must be
set in many lights, illustrated in diverse applications; and
this involves the frequent reproduction and enforcement of
such truth.

If the writer has erred on the side of being too explicit, or
of too often repeating important principles of interpretation
or essential truths of primitive teaching, he craves the reader's
forbearance.   His object has been, above all things, distinctness and such emphatic statement as should make the simple
and wise teachings of the apostolic Church, on the subject of
the Lord's Supper, prominent and conspicuous.

TABLE OF CONTENTS.

BOOK I.

THE INSTITUTION AND APOSTOLIC USE OF THE LORD'S SUPPER.

CHAPTER I.

CHAPTER II.

BOOK II.

POST-APOSTOLIC USES OF THE LORD'S SUPPER.

CHAPTER I.

CHAPTER II.

BOOK III.

THE LORD'S SUPPER IN THE REFORMED CHURCH OF ENGLAND.

CHAPTER I.

CHAPTER II.

CHAPTER III.

CONTENTS. xi

CHAPTER IV.

INTRODUCTION.

§ 1. *The Central Act of Christian Life and Worship.*

WHAT is the central and highest act of Christian life and worship ? We unhesitatingly reply, Such an act can only consist in the soul's inmost union with God and Christ, in its devotion to Him who, on the cross of old, and in heaven now and always, devotes Himself to procure for us His Spirit and all good things in accordance with the beneficent will of the Father.

The central and highest act of Christian life and worship must thus have its root in God and Christ; but, as there is no selfishness in God, whose centre has been described as everywhere and His circumference nowhere, or in Christ, who pleased not Himself, but gave His entire life a sacrifice of obedience and love for the redemption of the world from sin and self, so, when a man enters into union with this God in Christ, though the first vow may be registered in the depths of affection and thought, where holiest resolves are formed, yet from this unselfish and world-redeeming religion the early and continuous outcome must be love and sympathy and help and blessing for every child of man on whose behalf Christ once died and now lives for ever.

Union with God in Christ implies communion and co-operation with every man,—with the king who is to be honoured, with the lowliest who is to be reverenced,—as having in him, despite the wounds and scars of sin, such a mind as can study and discover, or else can comprehend, the works of God in nature and in grace ; or, better still, as having such a heart and spirit as can sympathize with the sorrowful like God, love the generous and the good even in its embryonic imperfection like Christ, or yield an admiring approval to suffering heroism as did the voice of Him who was well pleased with the crucfied One.

Union with God in Christ, though its root may be hidden in the secret place of strongest resolutions, yet must show itself in love and beneficence towards all men, specially towards brothers in Christ, and more specially still towards the nearest and dearest in one's own house.

Thus the central and highest act of Christian life and worship must be devotion, however secret, to God and Christ, and devotion, open, active, unmistakable, to the dear ones of home first, then to those with whom we are at one in the love of Christ, then to those whose wants and weaknesses are like our own, while their minds and hearts are grand with all the stamp of the divine upon humanity, and interesting with all the infinite capacities to become like Newton or like Paul, like one of the spirits of the just made perfect, even like Christ.

Clearly, such union with God in Christ, such helpful fellowship with man for Christ's sake, may be originated in the sacrament of baptism, or may be sustained by the sacrament of the Lord's Supper; but it would be hard to say it could not have its origin in the joy and thankfulness of the bridegroom, in the broken heart of the disappointed and bereaved, in the mind and affections of man under any of the countless appeals of Him who, by His Spirit, ever stands at the door of man's heart and seeks for admission that, out of whatever may be the source and occasion, He may bring forth the sanctifying results of union with Himself as God and of fellowship with men as His beloved.

However, whenever, wherever, this divine union, this humane fellowship, be originated or enhanced, we hold it to be the central and highest act of Christian life and worship.

This, however, and not the occasion out of which it springs, is the highest act alike of conversion and of sanctification.

We cannot tie this central and highest act to any outward rite; neither can we divorce it from any. The lightning flash on the road to Damascus, the moral reaction from some hideous sin, the pious resolves of her who confirms of deliberate choice that wise step taken for her in her unconscious infancy, the breaking of bread in some unadorned tabernacle or in some gorgeous cathedral, the appeal of the preacher, the example of the Christian, the horror of some crime in others or in self—these and a thousand other occasions may be the ground and medium of the union and the fellowship, but its root is deeper down in the heart of man and in God's secret dealings with that heart; and its growth and manifestation are vaster, more constant, more catholic and world-embracing, than any or all of these the surroundings and occasions of its emergence.

If one may borrow an illustration from the structure of a suspension bridge, these occasions are but the ground through which the mighty chain passes ere it becomes visible to man. The union and source of strength for that chain are deep down in the solid rock; its great work is not in or on the surrounding soil, the decorative forms, or the beautiful flowers; its work is far and wide over the hideous chasm which it bridges for the good of every man who needs a passage from earth to heaven, from the temporal to the eternal, from the human to the divine.

Still it will be urged, This central and highest act of Christian life and worship, what is it? And not a few, in the present day, are ready to reply that it is the sacrament of the Lord's Supper, neither more nor less; this and nothing else.

If they are right, it must be well to know the truth; but if they are wrong, no small misconception, no unimportant misdirection of energy, must come out of such an error.

This inquiry, this question of the day and of the Church, engages us in the following pages.

Connected with this inquiry are wellnigh countless issues. The true nature and aim of the Christian sacrament; the mode and comeliness of its celebration; the line of feeling, and thought, and belief to be cultivated therein; the results to be expected therefrom; with what results we ought to be disappointed at the Lord's Supper; with what we should be thankfully and humbly satisfied;—all these issues, and many besides, lie in the investigation; and they all impel us to a study of the matters dealt with in the following pages.

§ 2. *The Use of this and other Books in Preparation for the Lord's Supper.*

One word should be said with reference to this work as a manual to be used in preparation for the Lord's Supper; and this word is, we believe, only the echo of that which has been said by Bishop Wilson and almost every writer who has been engaged in a similar line of thought.

Let the reader who, apart from the mere critical study of a very important investigation, wishes to prepare himself to be a guest at the Lord's Table, master the subject as well as he can before taking part in the sacred rite itself. Let him make up his mind whether he is to look for a vision of Christ there present to the senses, or for a sanctifying memory of Christ once in that upper chamber in Jerusalem, once on that dreadful cross, now, bodily, at God's right hand in heaven, and, spiritually, in the heart of every man on earth.

Let the reader intelligently and piously comprehend the Liturgy[1] of his Church, and have a distinct impression in his own mind of all its important thoughts and phrases— especially, let him be clear in his judgment as to whether he will understand the service generally, and its parts in detail, in accordance with the mediæval Mass and its sacrifice of the host or victim, its altar for that sacrifice, and its corresponding priest; or whether he will understand the entire service, in its general spirit and in its details of expression and act, in accordance with the precepts and intentions of the Reformed, Protestant religion as by law established in England, and as brought back, three hundred years ago, into closer harmony with the Church of Christ and the apostles, as represented in the pages of the New Testament.

---

[1] It may be well to remind the unprofessional reader that "Liturgy" is the appropriated name for the Communion as distinguished from other Church services.

Let the reader, and especially the communicant, clear up these points thoroughly in his own mind by the help of God. Let him familiarize himself with every important term of the Liturgy, with every pregnant phrase—like those, for instance, that deal with self-examination, with "mysteries," with eating the flesh of Christ, with being one with Christ, and the like ; and when he has thus reasonably and devoutly studied the service, fixed his principles, hallowed his convictions, ripened his anticipations, then let him lay aside every book of instruction, and let him give his whole heart and mind to the important act he is about to perform.   The confession and prayers and thanksgivings and joy of the Liturgy will give ample scope for all the activity of the most brilliant imagination or the most loving heart.

At any human banquet, in memory of noble acts and more noble men who wrought the acts, how unseemly would it be if the guests were engaged with books, at the table or in the assembly, for the purpose of then studying the achievements they were met to celebrate, or for the purpose of directing their thoughts and feelings into certain well-worn channels of routine as to the meaning and interpretation of what the president should say to them.

No, if the Liturgy is fit for its work, it is the best and only book that should accompany the communicant to the Lord's Table ; and all his thoughts and feelings—informed and cultivated to the utmost in the periods of preparation—should now, under the guidance of the Liturgy, be full of Christ,—the Christ of the Supper Table in Jerusalem, the same Christ once upon the cross, the same Christ now ever living to intercede for us "according to God ;" the same Christ who is "in us" always, unless we fall short of His standard ;[1] the same Christ of whose divine presence we become conscious in prayer, in praise, in breaking of bread, or on any occasion of spiritual awakening,—with this Christ the mind and heart should be full throughout, alike when we deplore sin, when we triumph in faith, when we ask pardon, when we hear the promise and the prayer that insure its

[1] 2 Cor. xiii. 5.

bestowal, when we take the bread and the wine, when we join in the hymn that glorifies our God and His Christ, and when the final blessing sends us home to show forth, in ordinary conduct, the Lord who is ever with us, the light of our life in the mean while, the hope of glory for the great hereafter.

With these preliminary remarks we proceed at once to those investigations which constitute the main topic of our essay.

THE LORD'S SUPPER.

BOOK I.

THE INSTITUTION AND APOSTOLIC USE OF THE LORD'S SUPPER.

CHAPTER I.

THE INSTITUTION.

§ 1. *Investigation of the Subject especially needed at present.*

In this first book an attempt will be made to examine what is taught in Holy Writ concerning the divine institution and apostolic practice of the Lord's Supper, and concerning the benefits to be derived therefrom.

At all times such an inquiry should be of deep interest to Christians, who know that the earliest and purest information, with reference to their religion, as it issued from its divine Founder, can only be obtained in the writings of the New Testament. But, in the present day, when clergymen of learning and position declare in the most public manner —for instance, in the famous correspondence of the *Times* in January, 1875—that unless there be an *objective* presence of Christ in the consecrated elements of the Supper, there is no use whatever in receiving those elements, and all plea for the continuance of the sacrament has vanished, it is more than interesting, it is absolutely necessary, to refer to the original records of our religion, as it came from the hands of the Saviour and His apostles, in order to ascertain what may be the truth on this momentous question.

§ 2. *The Terms " Objective," " Subjective," and " Real."*

It will be well now, at the outset, to try and explain, once for all, what is meant by the words " objective " and " subjective," in the above-named correspondence, in this our essay, and in general discussions of the question. " Subjective " denotes something existing in the mind or heart of him who thinks. " Objective " denotes something which has an independent existence separate from his thoughts. An illustration may here assist us. At the Lord Mayor's banquet there is an objective presence of the Prime Minister and certain other guests, quite irrespective of what men think or feel about that presence. At the poor man's breakfast-table there is no objective presence of the late Mr. Cobden ; but if, at any time, the poor man gratefully remembers that it is to Cobden he is indebted for his cheap loaf, then, and so often as the man's mind and heart thus recall Cobden, there is a subjective presence of the great statesman. He is present to the mind and feelings of the poor man ; he is subjectively present in the man's memory and affections. The sign or channel of association by which Cobden is recalled to the man's memory is the bread. But yet Cobden is not present in the bread ; that would be an objective presence : but he is only present in the mind of the thoughtful man—that is, he is subjectively present. What is objectively present in the bread—for example, the baked particles of wheat and such-like materials—is received and eaten by the child at the table, who knows nothing of Cobden and his history. With that child there is no presence of Cobden.

The objective presence of anything is independent of man's consciousness.

The subjective presence of anything depends wholly on man's mind realizing it.

The line of distinction between a material or corporeal presence of anything, and its objective presence, is thus perceived as too fine for recognition by any but the subtlest of metaphysical fancies; and no less fanciful, if not fictitious, is the distinction between spiritual presence, or presence in memory and affection, and subjective presence.

To all intents and purposes, and in all plain and intelligible use of words, an objective presence is the same as a material, corporeal, substantial presence; whilst a subjective presence is equivalent in meaning to a spiritual and ideal presence, a presence in the mind or heart of its subject.

" Real " presence, it is worth remembering in this line of remark, is an ambiguous phrase. It sometimes denotes objective, material presence; and at other times it signifies true presence, though only to the mind of the subject, and not at all in the matter of the object.

It is well to try and obtain clear views on these and kindred questions of the day. Definitions may be useful at a time when the desirableness of the Lord's Supper, as a perpetual memory of Christ's death and of its blessed effects, is made to depend on an objective presence of the Saviour's body in the bread, as contrasted with a subjective presence of His Spirit in the heart of man.

§ 3. *Neglect of the Question, What says Scripture ?*

Definition and investigation are needful, at a time like the present, when it is debated, even in the columns of the daily press, what Cyprian said in the African Church; what Gregory taught in his Sacramentary; what Aquinas wrote for the schools; but, meanwhile, there is a portentous ignoring of that which is prescribed in those sacred Scriptures which, for English Churchmen at all events, are authoritatively described as containing "all things necessary to salvation: so that whatsoever is not read therein, nor may be proved thereby, is not to be required of any man, that it should be believed as an article of the faith, or be thought requisite or necessary to salvation " (Article VI.).

It is to these Scriptures that we propose to make our present appeal.

§ 4. *Metaphors connected with the Question.*

On approaching the subject, however, of the institution of the Lord's Supper, there are certain preliminary points which demand attention.

It can hardly have escaped the reader's observation that metaphors like those which speak of " food for the mind," not only of reading, marking, learning, but also of "*inwardly digesting*" truth, " devouring an author," " drinking in thoughts," " imbibing principles," being " satiated " with a style or a subject,—metaphors like these abound in our English language as they do in all tongues.

§ 5. *Old Testament Usage.*

Not otherwise is the usage of the Hebrew Scriptures. Isaiah refers not to material nourishment for men's bodies when he exclaims, " Ho, every one that thirsteth, come ye to the waters, and he that hath no money; come ye, buy, and eat; yea, come, buy wine and milk without money and without price. Wherefore do ye spend money for that which is not bread? and your labour for that which satisfieth not? " It is here some food for the soul which is indicated by the prophet: and for that nourishment he not only describes men as thirsting, but the means of supplying their spiritual appetite are themselves portrayed under the figures of " bread," " milk," " water," and " wine," the chief and typical supports of strength and instruments of refreshment.

Perhaps the most striking employment of this common metaphor, in the pages of the Old Testament, is that in Proverbs ix. 5, where Wisdom is represented as having built her house, furnished her table, and sent forth her maidens to cry upon the highest places of the city, " Whoso is simple, let him turn in hither: as for him that wanteth understanding, she saith to him, Come, *eat of my bread, and drink of the wine* which I have mingled." Here it is obvious that to eat Wisdom's bread, and drink her wine, is to learn her lessons and act upon her principles. This is a forcible metaphor, to denote union and incorporation between wisdom and man ; but still it is a metaphor, and, in this and similar passages, no reader presses it further.

No man, for instance, who reads another verse of the Book of Proverbs (iv. 17) will be in danger of believing in an objective change of elements, when he is told that evil men " eat the bread of wickedness, and drink the wine of violence."

§ 6. *New Testament Usage.*

From this general usage of the metaphor in common language, and from its frequent employment in the Hebrew Scriptures, and especially from its remarkable adoption by Wisdom, personified in the Book of Proverbs, let us proceed to notice some parallel expressions in the New Testament. We will not dwell upon the beatitude which declares, " Blessed are they which do hunger and thirst after righteousness, for they shall be filled," though this is based upon the idea that righteousness is meat and drink to the soul of man, and that, if we would find satisfaction for the infinite cravings of our spiritual nature, we must so incorporate ourselves into right, and right into us, as if it were our very meat and drink.

In a similar manner our Lord, in the conversation with His disciples springing out of His instruction of the woman of Samaria, declares He has *meat to eat*, that they know not of ; and that this *meat* consists in doing the will of Him that sent him and finishing His work. Here, again, observe the figure. To confront this poor woman with herself ; to awaken conscience in her to the recognition of her life and its guilt ; to show her God, the Spirit God, who seeks men to worship Him in spirit and in truth ; to make known to her the Messiah of this God, His Anointed One, who unveils Him as the Father ; this work—this absorbing, satisfying work—is meat and drink to Jesus Himself ; it satisfies and strengthens His whole soul and spirit.

§ 7. *John* vi. 26–63, *as bearing on our Investigation.*

Evidently our Saviour was no stranger to this forcible mode of expression. He used it frequently and in many applications. Among the most remarkable instances of this figure's employment by Jesus is that in the conversation recorded in the sixth chapter of St. John's Gospel; and to this notable passage of Scripture we must now give a somewhat close attention.

At the outset, let it be borne in mind that the occurrences here narrated by the Evangelist preceded the crucifixion and the Last Supper by twelve months, as appears from John vi. 4; and, moreover, what is described in this portion of the fourth Gospel took place, not at Jerusalem, but on the shores of the Lake of Gennesareth, and especially at Capernaum and in its synagogue. This appears irrefragable from verses 1, 17, 24, 25, 59, of John vi. and from the opening words of chapter vii. Whereas *Jerusalem* was the scene of our Lord's *Last* Supper, *Capernaum* was the place which witnessed the conversation we are about to examine; and the date of this conversation was prior, by some twelve months, to the closing days of suffering at Jerusalem.

St. John's sixth chapter opens with an account of the five thousand being fed with five barley loaves and two small fishes. This was a work which delighted the multitudes. It was just what they expected and desired from their Messiah. They were ready to take its beneficent achiever and make Him their king by force. Such a bestower of material boons they would watch for, seek, and follow, with all the zeal which characterizes the seed of Abraham. In spite of the Saviour's only performing such a deed when it was needful, when He knew that it was right; in spite of the Master's withdrawing Himself and seeking seclusion, the people, in their ecstasy, sought Him out and found Him.

The twenty-sixth verse shows us how little Jesus was misled by their delight and apparent devotion to Him. "Ye seek Me," are His words, "not because ye saw the miracles, but because ye did eat of the loaves and were filled." It was not the thing signified—God and His continual working with them and for them, and His manifestation to them in the man Jesus; it was not this which drew the stiff-necked multitude. No; they had eaten of the loaves, and they longed for more. The spiritual, the religious, the soul-touching was nothing to them. It was after the carnal, the material, the worldly that they hankered. Still there was a zeal in them, and though it was far from being perfectly informed, yet it brought them, for the time, to Jesus; and He was more than willing to try and lead them on and up towards the higher, the better, and the more abiding.

Accordingly, the Saviour's words to them are (ver. 27), "Labour not for the meat which perisheth, but for that meat which endureth unto everlasting life, which the Son of man shall give unto you: for Him hath God the Father sealed." Food for eternal life through the Son of the Divine Father! And this attached to "working the works of God" (ver. 28)! Here were words not so acceptable to the crowd as more loaves and fishes would have been. But still they remembered His former feeding of them, and they did not despair. What "work of God," they asked, was required of them? "Believe on him whom God hath sent," was the reply (ver. 29). Believe, indeed! Have faith and trust; and, probably, as they might think, let faith work by love and kindness! This was a demand upon their minds and hearts. It even looked as if it would involve them in work and labour for God and not for pelf; and this earnest self-abnegation, this devotion to humanity and to God, were the last things they wished, the furthest from their contemplation. Still they were Jews, and could not help persevering in pursuit of their own ends. The loaves were yet in their thoughts. Could they not bring back the miracle-worker to their views? Thou askest faith; well, what sign showest Thou (verses 30, 31) as a warrant for our believing Thee? Something akin to Moses' old gift of the manna; more "bread from heaven" canst Thou give us "to eat"?

Not Moses, but God, bestowed that gift, replies our Lord (ver. 32); "but My Father giveth you the true bread from heaven. For the bread of God is He which cometh down from heaven, and giveth life unto the world." Then the better side of the Jewish character shows itself, even in this hungry multitude. They exhibit a susceptibility to be affected by sacred things. Jesus recalled to their minds "the bread of

God';" assuredly, no strange idea, but one which the manna of the wilderness, and probably the "*lekhem*," or "shewbread," and other offerings to Jehovah (*vide* Exod. xxv. 30, and Lev. xxi. 6, 8, 17, etc.), had made familiar to their minds in connection with the religion of their fathers, and with the Temple and its holy usages. Was He, thought they, about to give them "manna," or "shewbread," or some other "bread of God," and to endow it with a new potency, with some Messianic charm against death? Was this the meaning of what He had said about the "bread of God" and "eternal life?" "Lord," is their exclamation (ver. 34), "evermore give us this bread."

Then follow the momentous words of the Saviour's reply (verses 35—40) : "I am the bread of life : he that cometh to Me shall never hunger ; and he that believeth on Me shall never thirst." Distinct is this utterance of Jesus. The bread of God, the bread of heaven, manna in the wilderness, shewbread in the Temple, or any other kindred ideas which, in the God-ward instincts of your souls, or from the sacred teachings of your religion, you have learnt and now experience—these are all foreshadowings only of Him that is to come. They are the shadows ; the substance is He on whom you now look. I am the bread, the food, the meat and drink of life. Are you at a loss how you can eat Me, or how you can drink Me ? Coming to Me, entering into My society and fellowship, learning of Me ; this is eating Me : and recognising My trustworthiness, knowing that you may safely confide all to Me, believing in Me so as to give up all and follow Me, having faith which worketh by love ; this is drinking Me. I am the bread of life ; the reality, and more than the reality, of all your best dreams about a bread of God. He that so cometh to Me, as disciple and follower, eateth Me, and shall never feel the disappointment that makes men crave for a better and a higher. He that so trusts and devotes himself to Me, alike for action and for suffering, drinks Me, and shall never find his hope make him ashamed, but shall be satisfied and shall never thirst, or wish to exchange for something else the true and only wells of salvation, the waters of eternal life, which are in Me.

Before we pass from this verse, let us notice distinctly that, according to our Saviour's own definition, eating Christ denotes *coming to Him*, and drinking Christ denotes *believing on Him*.

After our Lord has shown the multitude that it is only by recognising and feeling the tender love of God as their *Father*, who draws and urges them towards Jesus, whom He has sent and sealed as the Messiah; and that, for any and all who will thus yield themselves to the Fatherly drawing and influence, there shall be perfect security, no such thing as being lost, but a certainty of being raised up, even at the last day, and of receiving the gift of eternal life;—after this lofty train of thought had been touched by the Master, we find a reaction of doubt swaying the minds of His audience (verses 41, 42) : "Is not this Jesus, the son of Joseph, whose father and mother we know? how is it then that He saith, I came down from heaven ?"

In reply to this doubt, and the consequent murmuring of the audience, Jesus repeats His teaching as to the necessity of men feeling God to be their loving Father, if they would recognise His Son, the Messiah, in a gentle and true carpenter from Nazareth. The possibility of this recognition of the Father is enforced on the attention of the people by an appeal to their own prophets (Isa. liv. 13 ; Jer. xxxi. 34 ; Joel ii. 28, etc.), whose testimony was that a time was coming when all men should be taught to know God as their Father.

In ver. 47 this teaching is followed up by the emphatic assertion, " Verily, verily, I say unto you, He that believeth on Me hath everlasting life." The metaphor is dropped for a moment, and that action and movement of the mind and affections, which is faith in Jesus, is said to put a man instantly into the present possession and growing enjoyment of the true and eternal life.

Then (verses 48—50), there is a repetition of the Lord's assurance, " I am the bread of life," and a contrast between the transient effects of the manna in the wilderness and the imperishable results produced by Christ as the bread from heaven. In this passage is introduced the truth that eating Christ, or coming to Christ, will abolish death. For the disciple of Jesus, the change from existence in this world to existence in the eternal shall be so lighted up with faith, and hope, and joy, that they who thus eat of this "living bread" shall never die, but live for ever.

Observe this modification of the metaphor. It is the *living* bread, the *living* Jesus, with whom we must be incorporated in order to obtain this deliverance from the fear of death. Manna and material bread, or any lifeless object, will not suffice. Types and figures they may be, and they are—signs of something signified; but the reality is Jesus, "*living* bread."

And here (ver. 51) the insufficiency of the figure, suggested by the Jewish desire for more loaves and fishes, is made apparent; and, accordingly, our Saviour proceeds to employ a new and even more striking metaphor. "The bread that I will give is My flesh, which I will give for the life of the world." However surprisingly these last pregnant words, "My flesh for the life of the world," may have failed to carry to the minds of those who heard them a distinct instruction concerning the Lord's redemptive suffering, we have here a momentary abandonment of "bread" as the figure representing Christ; and we are introduced to the remarkable ideas which the Saviour proceeds to associate with the phrase, "My flesh," and its equivalents. My flesh, He says, I am going to make a sacrifice for the world; and as the flesh of your Paschal lamb and other sacrifices is partaken of by you Jews, in order that you may become incorporated into the system of sacrifice, self-denial, and devotion before God, so in like manner must be your incorporation with Me, the perfect sacrifice, who give My flesh for the life of the world.

Over these words arose a great strife amongst the multitude (ver. 52, they "strove among themselves;" literally, they "fought or battled with one another"). "How," they asked, "can this man give us His flesh to eat?" The earnestness, as well as doubt, implied by this vigorous questioning among His hearers calls forth from the Saviour an emphatic and reiterated enforcement, by different figures, of the same truth He had been urging on them throughout His conversation, namely, their need of being incorporated and united with Him.

You ought, He implies, to have been familiar with the idea of eating the flesh of a sacrifice; but I am more to you than any of your sacrifices. Their blood, indeed, you shed and sprinkled, but you did not drink it. With Me, however, so entire must be your union, that it must not only be an eating of My flesh, but a drinking of My blood. " Verily, verily " (verses 53—55), " I say unto you, Except ye eat the flesh of the Son of man, and drink His blood, ye have no life in you. Whoso eateth My flesh, and drinketh My blood, hath eternal life; and I will raise him up at the last day. For My flesh is meat indeed, and My blood is drink indeed." All other meat and drink are for a time only, and minister primarily to the lower and animal life of man. This eating My flesh and drinking My blood, this " coming to Me " and " believing on Me " (according to ver. 35), is food for the mind and the affections, and is for eternity.

Then (ver. 56) the metaphor is varied and explained: This eating My flesh and drinking My blood is an abiding of the disciple in Me, as in a shelter and home; it is an abiding of Me in him, making him a very temple and shrine for My indwelling. As I live through the Father, so (ver. 57) shall he who is thus united with Me, eating My flesh and drinking My blood, coming to Me and believing on Me, abiding in Me and I in him,—so shall he live the higher life of the soul and of eternity through this union with Me. And this (ver. 58) is what I meant and said, at the outset of this discourse, when I told you, in contrast with the perishable manna after which you hungered, of the bread which came down from heaven and fed man with eternal life.

Thus ends this marvellous and beautiful address. Its text might well be, Man doth not live by bread alone. His spirit hath its hunger and its thirst. The bread, the flesh, the wine for those cravings of the eternal in man, am I. Whoso, then, hungereth and thirsteth after righteousness must come to Me, must believe in Me, must abide in Me, and I must abide in him; he must live engrafted into Me, as I live in very union with the Father. This, and this only, is bread, and flesh, and wine—in a word, food—for the soul.

To many of our Master's disciples this was a "hard saying." To help them in their difficulty; to aid them in solving their remaining doubts as to, "How can this man give us His flesh to eat?" the gracious Teacher tells them how He will *not* give them His flesh and blood, that so, being excluded from false ideas, they may be, as it were, constrained to ascertain and recognise the truth.

Do not think, He proceeds (ver. 62), that it is My *material body* which constitutes the "flesh and blood" you are to eat and drink; for that body shall pass away out of your sight into heaven. Reflect, what will be the form of this your doubting question, "if ye behold the Son of man ascend up where He was before." Get rid, He urges (ver. 63), of the idea that I referred to anything material, or corporeal, or objective, when, under the figures of bread and flesh and blood, I taught you of the intimate, abiding, and living union of believing and loving discipleship that must subsist between you and Me, in order to your entering into man's true and eternal life. "It is the spirit," not matter of any kind, "that giveth life. The flesh profiteth nothing."

Were it even possible for you to eat with the teeth the flesh of Me, your Lord and Teacher, it would injure and not advantage you. Could you even lacerate the flesh of the Son of man, and suck from His veins and arteries the stream of His life's blood, the practice would be abhorrent, the idea detestable. In very deed, "The flesh profiteth nothing." It is the *words*, which I speak unto you, which are spirit, and which quicken unto eternal life. Feed your souls with My words of truth, and love, and self-surrender. Devour these. Imbibe the principles embodied in them. Drink of My Spirit. So shall you eat of the bread from heaven; so shall you be incorporated into Me, through My words, spirit into spirit,

with a union a thousand times more intimate and abiding
than any that can be brought about by material and objective binding of flesh to flesh. This spiritual engrafting is
that to which, by the figures of bread and flesh and blood, I
tried to lift your minds and hearts from the flesh-pots and
the manna after which ye hungered.

Such is a brief comment upon this wonderful discourse of
our Saviour's, delivered, be it remembered, at Capernaum
long prior to His closing visit to Jerusalem, twelve months
before the events which then and there occurred. Of course,
we know how apt is the human mind to mix up all the
language and all the metaphor of this discourse with the
Lord's Supper; but it is very desirable we should at least
occasionally clear up our conceptions on this subject, and
bear distinctly in mind that, long before the Saviour conjoined these metaphors with symbols, He used them as metaphors, insisting on their force and guarding against their
misconception and abuse.

If, as some say, in spite of the apostles and other listeners
at Capernaum having no idea of the Lord's Supper which
was to be instituted in the future; in spite of such an idea
being impossible for them at the time, yet Jesus spoke
" proleptically " or prophetically, intending His words to have
a double meaning, one figurative and significant at the time,
the other non-significant at the time, but capable of becoming
significant a year afterwards,—if this explanation be offered
or adopted by any, we can only say it is opposed to all our
convictions as to the simplicity of the Saviour, alike in words
and in character.

But, for the argument's sake, let us concede the possible
truth of this " proleptic " theory : and what will follow ?
Why, in this " proleptic " reference to the Lord's Supper,
we shall have one of the most spiritual and anti-objective
interpretations of that institution. It will protest to us
against expecting any profit from the carnal and material
elements of that holy rite. It will insist for us that only
when we approach the God who is a Spirit, in spirit and
in truth, through His life-giving words and not in the flesh

or through the flesh, do we rightly or truly eat the flesh and drink the blood of the Son of man. It will show us that the validity of our communion depends on no objective presence even of Christ in the flesh, but depends entirely on the state of our minds and hearts and lives, and on Christ's consequent spiritual presence with us. Are we coming to Christ and believing on Him? Are we feeling and acting as He felt and acted? Is this our mental attitude, our lifelong habit? Then, we are satisfying the hunger of the soul, we are drinking for the refreshment of the soul in its thirst. With or without the subsequently enjoined intervention of bread and wine, we are, in our several respective measures, eating the bread and flesh of Christ and drinking His blood, not in the flesh, which profiteth nothing; not in the letter, which killeth; but in the spirit, which giveth life.

Thus, understood proleptically, or understood naturally and simply, the sixth chapter of the fourth Gospel makes equally against the notion of any material, corporeal, or objective presence of Christ in the sacrament. All depends upon the mind of the believer, and upon its acceptance and use of the Divine Spirit and His aid.

§ 8. *Narratives of the Institution.*

And now, from this consideration of metaphors, common to all languages, concerning "meat and drink" for the mind, concerning the "bread and wine" of Wisdom, concerning the "bread" from heaven, and the "flesh and blood" of Jesus required to be eaten and drunk by all His disciples long before they could have any idea of the Lord's Supper and its institution, let us pass on to observe the Last Supper itself, and the important points connected therewith in Holy Writ. For this purpose, it will be necessary to examine and collate the narratives of the Synoptists and of St. Paul.

A. *St. John's Silence, and the Light thrown by him on our Subject.*

St. John, as is well known, supplies no record of the institution of the Supper as a rite to be repeated and per-

petuated, but he tells us not a little that is important, relative
to the Last Supper and the blessed words and acts of Jesus
on that occasion.   The lesson in humility and ministering
one to another, given by our Saviour in washing the disciples'
feet, is set forth in the thirteenth chapter of the fourth
Gospel.   Then, in the three following chapters, we find the
words of warning by which Jesus strove, even at the last, to
awaken the conscience of the traitor to a wholesome horror of
the deed of treachery, which was already begun, and for whose
completion Judas was eagerly seeking an opportunity.   In
those chapters, too, we have the consolation left by our Lord
with His chosen ones, who were so soon to need comfort, not
only because He would be taken from them by a cruel and
ignominious death, but still more because that treatment
would be embittered a hundredfold by their denial and
desertion of Him.

   And how was this comfort to be provided?   How were
these bereaved ones to be consoled?   After a little while,
they should see Him no more in the flesh: and that was
for their good, for they were too apt to cling to whatever was
material and objective about Him, whereas He had taught
them, and still taught, that even *His* flesh could profit them
nothing; but when that was gone away into heaven, then the
Father would send to them the Spirit of Jesus, the Spirit of
His truth, the Spirit of His comfort and exhortation:[1] and in
that Spirit all His instructions would flow back into their
memories with a new force and a new life.

   In this Spirit let them keep His new commandment to
love one another.   In this Spirit let them be one in Him,
as fruitful branches in the vine.   In this Spirit let them
teach others also that they likewise might believe on Him
through their words.   In this Spirit let them all be one in
union and communion with each other and with the Lord,
even as He was one with the Father: and so, by the
union of love and by the fellowship of service, which this
Spirit of the Father and of the Son should bestow upon the
apostles, and on all who should believe on Jesus through

τὸν παράκλητον, the Exhorter and Comforter.

their words, let it be brought about that even "the world" (John xvii. 21) "may believe" that Jesus was sent by the Father.

Such is the strain of thought which runs through these four exquisite chapters of St. John; and if there be in them no categorical mention of the institution of the Lord's Supper, there is, assuredly, most distinct and abundant illustration of the manner and temper in which alone any holy and religious union and communion between the Lord and His people, and between His people among themselves, can be established or maintained. It must be, say these chapters, in perfect harmony with the sixth chapter, not in or by the material flesh of Christ, which profiteth nothing, but by the absence of that flesh, and by the working of the Spirit of truth, and energy, and love, which giveth life, that such union and communion must be established and maintained.

B. *St. John and the Synoptists on the Date of the Last Supper.*

From this notice of St. John's teaching as to the spiritual, in opposition to the carnal and material, presence of Christ in all communion amongst believers, and especially in the Lord's Supper, let us proceed to observe one matter of detail which is supplied to us by the fourth Gospel. From the expression of the Synoptists it might be inferred that the meal which Jesus kept, or "made"[1] (according to St. Matt. xxvi. 18), as the Passover or Paschal Supper, was the veritable Jewish feast of the 14th of the month Nisan. This, however, would be, according to St. John, a misconception, and might mislead some into the idea, entertained indeed by the Ebionites of old, that our Lord's Supper was a precise and formal *annual* feast to be celebrated by Christians neither more nor less frequently than once in each year, and that exactly at the time when the Jews keep their festival of the Passover. Such a misconception, however, is rendered next to impossible, one would think, for the readers of St. John, inasmuch as he pointedly and repeatedly intimates that the Last Supper took place on

[1] ποιῶ.

the evening *before* the Passover.   On this point nothing can
be more definite than the representations of St. John.

In the opening words of his thirteenth chapter, the date
of the Last Supper is fixed as "*before* the feast of the Passover;" and, similarly, in the twenty-ninth verse, some of the
disciples are represented as thinking that words, addressed by
our Lord to Judas, had reference to his buying the things they
had need of "against the feast," on the obvious assumption
that the feast, though at hand, was yet future.   To the same
effect it is recorded in St. John's eighteenth chapter, ver. 28,
that when the Jewish authorities led Jesus from Caiaphas to
Pilate's Prætorium, they would not themselves enter that
Gentile "hall of judgment," "lest they should be defiled; but
that they might eat the Passover."   And, again, John xix. 31,
we learn that "the Jews, therefore, because it was *the preparation*, that the bodies should not remain upon the cross on
the sabbath day (for that sabbath day was an high day),
besought Pilate that their legs might be broken, and that they
might be taken away."

The day of the crucifixion was the day of preparation
for the Passover, whose occurrence that year on the sabbath
day would make that day doubly important and sacred.
The crucifixion being ended and the bodies removed before
the arrival of that evening when, in Jewish reckoning, that
"high day" of sabbath and Passover commenced, it is
evident that our Saviour's Last Supper, however much He
treated it in Passover fashion and kept it as the Passover,
must have been twenty-four hours previous to the beginning
of the strict, legal festival of the Passover.

Here, then, is a point noticeable in the institution of the
Lord's Supper.   It was a feast like the Passover, and adopted
instead of the Jewish Pascha, but it was not held on the exact
day of the Jewish feast, and no imitation of the first institution, however literal or narrow, can bind men to its celebration only on the 14th of Nisan, or only as an annual solemnity.

Thus have we set forth an explanation, which has been
thought to be admissible, of the day on which the Saviour
instituted His Last Supper; but if any reader should chal-

lenge this explanation, and persist in bringing into view the
fact that the Synoptists seem to fix the 14th of Nisan as the
date of the Last Supper nearly or quite as definitely as the
fourth Gospel fixes it on the 13th of Nisan, then we cannot
claim to settle absolutely this long-debated point, but, for the
purposes of our present investigation, the logical result must
stand thus ; namely, that on the evening of a certain day,
whether Paschal or pro-Paschal being left uncertain and
unascertainable by the indefiniteness of Holy Writ, Jesus
instituted the Lord's Supper. The fair inference from this
condition of things we take to be, that it is not essentially
important that the Christian Supper should be celebrated on
the 14th of Nisan only or at any other particular and definite
time. The sequel may throw greater light on this subject ;
but, even at the outset, we are taught, with some distinctness,
that our holy Supper is not a rite to be necessarily observed
at some precise moment or hour of *time* and at no other.

C. *The Place of Institution.*

As to the *place* in which the Supper was instituted, it is
interesting to observe that, whereas questions have been raised
concerning the preliminaries in arranging for that place, there
are certain points connected with it which remain beyond the
reach of question. We learn (Mark xiv. 13, etc.) that our
Saviour bade two of His disciples go before Him from the
neighbourhood of Jerusalem, where He then was, "into the
city, and there shall meet you," were His words, "a man
bearing a pitcher of water : follow him. And wheresoever he
shall go in, say ye to the goodman of the house, The Master
saith, Where is My guestchamber" (τὸ κατάλυμά μου, according to the oldest manuscripts), "where I shall eat the Passover with My disciples ? And he will shew you a large upper
room furnished and prepared : there make ready for us."

What is the purport of this narrative ? it has been asked.
Did Jesus, out of His miraculous prevision, know that the
water-carrier's labour would synchronize with the arrival of
the two disciples ? And did he similarly foreknow that the
goodman of the particular house, to which was attached this

water-carrier, would be willing to lend his guestchamber as asked ? Is all this, as it might be by possibility, a stupendous miracle ; or have we here an ordinary, though important, instance of the wisdom and mercy of our Master ?

To this it may be answered that we have here, as usual, a simple and unexplained narrative of what Jesus did to prepare for the much-desired Last Supper, and yet to avoid putting temptation in the way of the traitor. Judas had been with the Jewish authorities, and was now watch-ing for an opportunity to deliver Jesus to them quietly, away from the crowd and the possibility of popular dis-turbance. If he should know that, at such an hour of the evening, his Master would be supping in a private house in Jerusalem, here would be the very means of secret betrayal and apprehension for which he longed. How much safer and more opportune this, than for him to proceed with a band of soldiers to Gethsemane, on the mere probability of finding Jesus there, in a haunt which he loved and to which he oft resorted. From the temptation of such an opportunity Judas would be screened, if Jesus did not divulge His intention as to the whereabouts of the coming Supper.

Besides, the disciples, like Nicodemus or Joseph of Arima-thea, who were likely to have such houses in Jerusalem as that here indicated, were, up to the time of the crucifixion, not avowed followers of our Lord, but attached to Him secretly, for fear of the Jews.

Taking into view, then, the proper desire of self-preser-vation which would be felt by our Lord, and His righteous wish to shield the traitor from facilities which would enhance his frightful temptation, and considering, moreover, the secrecy of discipleship on the part of any who might be the Saviour's host on this occasion, it seems likely—especially in view of the reading, "Where is My guestchamber?"—that Jesus had made arrangements with His contemplated entertainer, whether it were Nicodemus, or Joseph of Arimathea, or some one else, that a water-carrier should await the arrival of James and John, and then conduct them to the appointed but undivulged resort in which the pro-Paschal Supper was to be eaten. The importance which our Lord attached to this feast, and His vehement desire for its safe and peaceful celebration, render this explanation the more probable. Nor is it at all strange or unusual for the Evangelists to omit such details while recording events that tally with and suggest, if they do not absolutely require, such a comment.

Thus proceeds the simple and exquisite history of redemption as it presents itself to our minds; but let it be observed that, whether the designation of the place were miraculous, as is possible, or natural, as we have represented it, one point is clear: the *locale* of the Last Supper was a "guest-chamber," or entertaining room, in some private house in Jerusalem. It was like hundreds of other "upper rooms" in the Holy City, which were wont to be placed by their owners at the disposal of families or parties who had come from the country to keep the feast in the place which Jehovah chose to set His name there. There is no trace of the exact locality; we can only guess at the owner's name. The scene of so august a rite is not represented as set apart in any special manner. Neither before nor after the Last Supper is this "guest-chamber" marked off or consecrated as materially different from any other. In the ordinary upper room of some private house the Saviour partook, with His disciples, a meal which He substituted for the precise and rigidly defined supper of the Passover.

D. *The Paschal Supper.*

And here it may be well to describe, in words borrowed from Neander's "History of the Church" (vol. i. p. 449, edit. Bohn), the mode of celebrating the Paschal Supper among the Jews:—

"The Jewish Passover was a feast of thanksgiving for the grace which the Almighty Creator, who causes the fruits of the earth to grow for the service of men, had bestowed on His people when He honoured them with His *especial guidance*; after delivering them from the Egyptian bondage. Every father of a family, who kept the Passover with his household and distributed wine and bread among the guests, praised

God, who had bestowed these fruits of the earth on man, for the favour He had shown to *His own* peculiar people. For this reason the cup of wine over which the giving of thanks was pronounced was called the cup of praise or thanksgiving."

It is alleged that, in the course of the ordinary Jewish Passover, three or four cups of wine were passed round for the guests with blessing and thanksgiving similar to that described above.

And now, keeping this idea of the Jewish Passover in mind, and remembering that Jesus was keeping a feast either identical with that Jewish rite, as some say, or in lieu of it, as others say with perhaps greater probability, let us proceed to observe the several particulars as recorded in the sacred narratives of the Synoptists and St. Paul.

E. *Simple Introduction of the Subject by the Synoptists.*

The first point which calls for attention is the simple, natural way in which the history of so solemn an event as the institution of the Lord's Supper is introduced. The two earliest Evangelists agree in their very words, " as they did eat," as they were eating, in the course of their meal, the institution occurred. Whether a lamb was part of the meal we know not, nor whether the bitter herbs and all the characteristics of a normal Passover were employed; but we are told that there was a supper. Something they ate ; and, in the course of the eating of that meal, over and above the other words and discourses recorded by the four Evangelists, certain events took place which have been the root and origin of what is deemed the holiest part of later Christian worship.

One particular, antecedent, according to St. Luke, to these events, is mentioned by the third Evangelist alone. At some comparatively early point in the Supper, if St. Luke's narrative is precise in arranging the series of occurrences, Jesus (Luke xxii. 17) " took a cup and gave thanks, and said, Take this, and divide it among yourselves: for I say unto you, I will not henceforth drink of the fruit of the vine, until the kingdom of God shall come." Subsequent, according to St. Luke, upon these words, with their solemn intimation that a great crisis in the development of the divine kingdom was at hand, came the first part of the words of institution.

F. (a.) *Parallel Histories, by St. Paul and the Synoptists, referring to the Bread.*

Before comparing them in their fourfold form, let it be observed that what the sacred narrative sets before us is a very general sketch of a domestic meal, in *lieu* of the Passover, in an upper room of a private house in Jerusalem. That such a meal was being partaken of by the apostles with our Saviour, is all we learn with certainty up to this point.

And now let us compare the four histories of what followed :—

MATT. xxvi. 26.	MARK xiv. 22.	LUKE xxii. 19.	1 Cor. xi. 23-24.
" But as they were eating, Jesus took bread,	" And as they were eating, He took bread	" And He took bread,	" The Lord Jesus, in the night in which He was betrayed, took bread,
and blessed, and brake, and gave to the disciples, and said,	and blessed, and brake, and gave to them, and said,	and gave thanks, and brake, and gave to them, and said,	and gave thanks, and brake, and said,
Take, eat; this is My body."	Take : this is My body."	This is My body which is being given for you; this do for My remembrance."	This is My body which is for you; this do for My remembrance."

(b.) *Comments on these Histories.*

In these parallel columns we have the most reliable readings of the several passages quoted. They are given as Tischendorf gives them, upon the authority of the Sinaitic, Vatican, and Alexandrine manuscripts. They are translated as literally as possible, and are so arranged as to show their substantial agreement in the points common to more than one narrative.

Wholly unimportant is the usage of "but" by St. Matthew, instead of "and" by St. Mark, and, perhaps, equally unimportant would be the introduction of the definite article by the Alexandrine copy of the first Evangelist, "the bread," in place of "bread" in the other three histories.

(i.) *" Blessing," or " Giving of Thanks."*

More interesting is the variation between "blessing" the

bread mentioned by St. Matthew and St. Mark, and " giving thanks " for it as described by St. Luke and St. Paul. The Alexandrine manuscript of the first Gospel reads, indeed, " gave thanks " instead of " blessed ; " but the other two most ancient manuscripts agree in reading " blessed." Whether our Lord both gave thanks and blessed, or whether His blessing was identical with His giving of thanks, we have here one of the merely verbal variations which are chiefly useful as teaching us how remote are the sacred writings from giving a precise literal transcript of the very words employed by our Saviour.

(ii.) *The Words, " Take, eat."*

It is not a little striking that the greatest variations in the naratives are found just in those words of institution which, from certain points of view, men would be prone to regard as most important, and as requiring to be handed down with most literal exactness.

There is a *consensus* of the three oldest manuscripts in omitting the word " eat " in St. Mark ; and they are similarly agreed in omitting the words " given " and " broken " in St. Paul's narrative. Only the Alexandrine manuscript inserts the word "Take " (in St. Luke) before " This is My body," etc.

(iii.) *The Body "given," etc.*

Very pointed is the significance of the words in which St. Luke alone tells us that our Lord described His body as " being," in the then present time, " given "[1] for man. It is no declaration as to the past, as if there had already occurred on earth any realization of the eternal purpose of God concerning the "Lamb slain[2] before the foundation of the world."

In our Saviour's flesh " being given," in that then present

---

[1] διδόμενον.

[2] ἐσφαγμένου. *Vide* Rev. xiii. 8, and Rev. xvii. 8. This last passage makes it highly probable, as De Wette long ago observed, that the words, " from the foundation of the world," in Rev. xiii. 8, belong to " written " and not to " slain." In this view of the expression, it would contain no difficulty for our consideration in this essay. We have, however, preferred adopting the prevalent and popular translation in our text above.

time, there is no intimation that His sacrifice was often, or perpetually, to be repeated or continued in the future. Here, on the contrary, is a record that, in the then present time, was realized, once for all, the eternal purpose of God : Christ appeared (Heb. ix. 26) now once in the end of the world, and gave His flesh to be, in that then present time, a " full, perfect, and sufficient sacrifice, oblation, and satisfaction for the sins of the whole world." Surely, we should miss much if we had not this portion of our Lord's utterance ; and yet it is only from one of the four histories that we learn it, St. Paul's parallel expression, " being broken," being of less than doubtful genuineness.

(iv.) " *This do for My Remembrance.*"

Similarly, if it were not for the records of St. Luke and St. Paul, we should be without those words, " This do for My remembrance," which, to the vast majority of believers, make the participation of bread, at least, in memory of Christ, of abiding and perpetual obligation. So important and instructive are the fuller forms of the words of institution.

(v.) *Omissions instructive.*

We should notice, before quitting for a time this first part of the institution, that the actual and obvious omissions, occurring in the briefer forms of institution, render it conceivable that even the fullest of the four existing records may be an abbreviation of our Saviour's entire words. As St. Matthew and St. Mark obviously epitomize the words narrated by St. Luke and St. Paul, so these two last-named writers may possibly have given only an abbreviation of our Saviour's full utterance. They *have* omitted the " Take, eat," of which St. Matthew tells us. They have omitted to mention that the memorial rite was instituted in the course of the pro-Paschal meal. They *may have* omitted other words of which neither of the two first Evangelists supplies a record. How important is this line of observation, and how far it is confirmed and justified by indirect evidence of a very forcible character, will become apparent as we proceed in our study of the subject.

G. (*a.*) *Parallel Histories of St. Paul and the Synoptists, referring to the Wine.*

And now let us set forth in parallel columns the four narratives of the second part of the institution :—

MATT. xxvi. 27, etc.	MARK xiv. 23, etc.	LUKE xxii. 20.	1 COR. xi. 25.
"And He took a cup, and gave thanks, and gave to them, saying, Drink of it, all of you; for this is My blood of the covenant, which is being shed for many for remission of sins.	"And He took a cup, and gave thanks, and gave to them : and they all drank of it. And He said unto them, This is My blood of the covenant, which is being shed for many.	"And in like manner the cup after supper, saying, This cup [is] the new covenant in My blood, which is being shed for you."	"In like manner, also, the cup after supper, saying, This cup is the new covenant in My blood.
			This do, as oft as ye drink, for My remembrance."
But I say unto you, I will not drink henceforth of this fruit of the vine, until that day when I drink it new with you in My Father's kingdom."	Verily I say unto you, I will never drink again of the fruit of the vine, until that day when I drink it new in the kingdom of God."		

(*b.*) *Comments on these Histories.*

(i.) *Epithet "New" before "Covenant."*

In closely examining these histories, it will be noticed that before the word "covenant," in the narratives of St. Matthew and St. Mark, the epithet "new," to which the received version has accustomed us, is omitted. This omission, unimportant to the signification, has been made in accordance with the text of the oldest manuscripts, the Sinaitic and the Vatican, although it is not sanctioned by the Alexandrine.

(ii.) *The Blood-shedding once for all.*

In this part of the institution, as in the former, the shedding of the Saviour's blood, like the giving of His body, is described as an event occurring, once for all, in that then present time. The one act of sacrifice, once offered, is detached from the divine idea, intention, or purpose, in which the Lamb had been slain from the foundation of the world. The blood was being shed in Jesus' devotion of Himself, in that wicked deed to which Judas and the Jewish authorities had already set their hands. It was a present action, being once performed without any hint or intimation that its repetition in time to come was possible. Blood which is "being shed" is spoken of, but all allusion to future reiteration of the sacrifice, or to continued offering up of the blood, is as completely absent from this historical narrative, as it is pointedly excluded by passage after passage in the Epistle to the Hebrews, where we read (ix. 12), "By His own blood He entered in *once* into the holy place;" "Nor yet" (ix. 25, 26, 28) "that He should offer Himself often . . . . for then must He often have suffered since the foundation of the world : but now *once* in the end of the world hath He appeared to put away sin by the sacrifice of Himself;" and again, "Christ was once offered to bear the sins of many;" and yet again (x. 10), "We are sanctified through the offering of the body of Jesus Christ *once for all;*" and (verses 12, 14) "This man, after He had offered *one* sacrifice for sins for ever,[1] sat down on the right hand of God . . . . for by *one* offering He hath perfected for ever[1] them that are sanctified."

So completely was the blood-shedding and offering of our Lord an act present in the time of that one terrible Passion, and never to be repeated. He, the great High-Priest, would plead for us, and intercede according to the will of God, at God's right hand. What part in that pleading should be borne by the Saviour's making mention of His blood and His life as the ransom for all men (1 Tim. ii. 4), we may thankfully and piously imagine. Nay, we may plead for mercy through that blood ourselves; but the shedding of it —that terrific sacrifice—was an act once witnessed in the world and never to be repeated. Thus entirely does the record of the Evangelists, "blood *being shed*," harmonize with the general teaching of Holy Writ in excluding all idea of a recurrence or perpetuation of that blood-shedding, as of that giving of Christ's body, either by man on earth or by the Lord Himself in heaven.

(iii.) *The Wine "after" the Supper.*

To return, however, to another point in the comparison of our records. It is very interesting to observe, in the words

---

[1] εἰς τὸ διηνεκές.

of St. Luke and St. Paul, that whereas the bread had been broken and distributed *during* the Supper, it was "*after*" the Supper that the wine was given in the cup of blessing.

(iv.) "*Drink of it, all of you.*"

Curiously interesting and instructive in the face of mediæval superstition, which, for fear of spilling a drop of the wine, withheld the cup from the laity, is the precept in St. Matthew, "Drink of it, all of you," and the record in St. Mark, "They all drank of it." Of course, those who, in the teeth of these passages, withhold the cup from the laity, make a distinction between *all* the apostles and *all* believers; and, upon this distinction, they say that Christ enjoined participation in the cup to all the apostles, but not to all Christians. If this line of argument were valid, it would prove too much, for it would make the entire duty of celebrating the Lord's Supper obligatory on the apostles only.

For the lay people there would be no duty, nor any right, to perpetuate the Lord's Supper until His coming again. And thus it appears that if the Supper be in any part for *all believers*, as the withholders of the cup agree with us in teaching, then the words, "Drink of it, all of you," are addressed as much to all Christians as is any other portion of the institution; and, in this point of view, they form a notable comment on the manner in which mediæval superstition has defied alike the letter and the spirit of our Lord's command, while yielding to the dictates of its own fanciful scrupulosity.

(v.) *Catholicity of Redemption.*

In connection with this width and catholicity of the intent of our Lord, alike when He gave the bread and the wine, should be noticed the variations of our first three columns— "Blood which is being shed for you" (St. Luke); "Which is being shed for many" (St. Mark); and "Which is being shed for many for remission of sins" (St. Matthew). If the mediæval superstition, which attempts to narrow the recipients of the cup to the circle of the apostles only, were

right, the "you" of St. Luke would similarly denote the
limited body of the apostles. This idea is in itself abhorrent
to every scriptural and catholic conviction regarding God's
love for "the world," His unwillingness that any should
perish, His wish that all should be saved; but, moreover, if
St. Luke's "you" be thus meant to include only the apostles,
it will become diametrically opposed to the "many" for whom
St. Mark and St. Matthew agree in representing our Saviour
as declaring that His blood was being shed.

Here, then, is proof, if proof were wanted, that the cup
of blessing, like the precious blood-shedding itself, was intended "for you and for many," as the happy words of
the Liturgy express it. And, indeed, the loving heart that
has been touched with even a spark of the divine philan-
thropy must, at the sound of this word "many," crave to
learn, How many? Nor is the answer far to seek. Immediately after these words were spoken, the blessed Lord Himself, in His great prayer (John xvii. 20), expands such apparently limited terms by His supplication to the Father,
"Neither pray I for these alone, but for them also which
believe on Me through their word."

Here is the means of harmony and reconciliation supplied to us by Christ Himself, between the "many" for whom
He was shedding His blood, the "many" (Matt. xx. 28) for
whom He came to minister and give His life a ransom, and
the statement of St. Paul (1 Tim. ii. 6) that Christ was "a
ransom *for all men*." God, says the same apostle (1 Tim.
iv. 10), "is the Saviour of all men, specially of them that
believe." This is the measure, the only measure, of the
"many" for whom Jesus shed His blood. In the divine
wish the "many" are "all men." Only by abusing our
tremendous responsibility of freedom, in opposition to that
wish of God, can we limit this multitude of the "many"
so that it shall be less than equivalent to "all."

(vi.) *Frequency of Celebration.*

Akin to this divinely intended catholicity of participation
in the wine of the Lord's Supper, no less than in the redemp-

tion wrought by our Saviour, is the instruction as to the frequency of the Supper's celebration according to Christ's purpose and injunction. "This do, as oft as ye drink, for My remembrance." That St. Paul should have recorded this part of our Lord's institution is a fact no less happy and momentous than his being its sole reporter is curious and pregnant with instruction. In the latter aspect of the matter, how striking is it that words of such grave importance should have been omitted by three out of our four histories of the event!

What a clear intimation is here afforded us of the summary and suggestive sketch of all our Saviour did and said which is supplied to us in the narratives of the New Testament. A spirit is in those sketches that marvellously touches and convicts and elevates our human spirits; but if any reader neglect or lose the clue supplied by this spirit of Christ, the spirit of truth and love and freedom—if any reader surrender himself to the mere letter even of this holy record—especially if he attempt to construct out of the letter of this blessed book, apart from its holy and glorious spirit, precise, logical, and penal definitions which shall enslave his own thoughts or curtail the liberty of other men—let him beware lest the word or text, possibly the isolated word or text, on which he depends and which is out of harmony with the general analogy of Holy Writ, may have been surrounded, on its utterance by the Lord, by other terms and other phrases such as would have softened down the hardness with which our supposed literalist is inclined to invest it.

So true is it, in this sense as in all senses, that the letter killeth and the spirit giveth life. This lesson of charity and wisdom we may well learn from the proved and important omissions occurring in some portions of the sacred volume, from the various readings and various arrangements of words to be met with so frequently in other portions, and not least in the history of the institution of the sacred Supper.

Without St. Paul's Epistle to the Corinthians, we might, in spite of what has been noticed above, have supposed that the Supper of the Lord was, after the manner of some

Ebionites, to be commemorated as only an annual Christian Passover. Or it might have been regarded as a monthly, a weekly, or at most a daily celebration that was alone befitting. No, says the apostle, "This do, as oft as ye drink, for My remembrance." Whenever thirst oppresses you and you are refreshed by any beverage, "*as oft as ye drink*," be it by night or by day, be it seven times in the twenty-four hours, be it when it may, where it may, and (apparently) of whatsoever beverage it may chance—"as oft as ye drink," do this for My remembrance.

"Do this:" do what? Assuredly, thank God and bless Him for His gifts of nature and of grace; assuredly, impart to others of the cup of wine, the spring of water, the wells of salvation, the bread that nourishes man's body and the living bread that feeds his soul—impart of all to your fellow-men; "this do," all this, in the humblest and yet most bounteous spirit, do it; and do it "for My remembrance," recollecting how I broke the bread and shared it with you, how I took the cup and gave it to you all, how I gave Myself, My life, My will, My all, a sacrifice and a ransom to redeem you and all men.

In whatever special manner you may do this, at the family meal, or in the friendly gathering, or in the congregation (ἐκκλησία) of believers, yet forget it not; even in the solitude of your journeying through unfrequented places, forget it not: "Do this, as oft as ye drink, for My remembrance." Well might St. Paul exclaim (1 Cor. x. 31), "Whether therefore ye eat, or drink, or whatsoever ye do, do all to the glory of God." So, ceremonially or unceremonially, are we to remember Christ and His sacrifice and His blessed salvation; so to cultivate helpfulness and fellowship with our fellow-men; so to live in a spirit of thankful blessing of God for all His gifts and all His inestimable grace.

(vii.) *Error of "Fasting Communion," etc.*

What a wealth of truth and piety is in the few words which, but for St. Paul's Epistle to the Corinthians, would have been lost and forgotten, like so many of the precious sayings that fell from the lips of Him who spake as never man spake. What a grafting is here enjoined of all our life, day by day, hour by hour, into oneness with God in Christ and into communion with all men, specially with them that believe. "This do, as oft as ye drink, for My remembrance." What a correction for the error and superstition of those who, leaning on the decisions of a handful of men assembled in one city or another as councils, not of the whole Church, but of some portion of it, have said, Do this only when you have placed an interval of sleep, or of night, or of so-called "fasting" between your last meal and your participation of the Lord's Supper.

Of such "fasting communion," or such exclusively early communion, the sacred volume of the New Testament knows nothing, either in the letter or the spirit of it. These traditions are of men, and, like others of older date, they make the commandments of God of none effect; for, whereas He, in whom the Father was manifested, said, "Do this, as oft as ye drink, in remembrance of Me," the traditions say, Do this only before midday, and after ye have fasted awhile.

Surely, in face of the attempt to resuscitate such a dream of mediæval darkness, we may well be reminded of Scripture teaching and divine appointment in this matter.

(viii.) *The "New" Fruit of the Vine.*

In looking over the narratives of the institution, as set in parallel columns above, it will be observed that the first two Evangelists append to their record a solemn statement by our Lord, to the effect that He would not again drink of the fruit of the vine, till He should drink it new with His disciples in the kingdom of God. Here is a declaration which might well prepare those who heard it for the near approach of some great crisis in their relationships, and in those of the world, with Jesus and the Father. Such a change was imminent as would revolutionize every detail of life. Old things would be passed away; behold, all things would be new.

The whole creation, travailing in pain together, would put on a fresh phase in its subjection and subserviency to the sons of God. The very fruit of the vine would henceforth be surrounded by such novel association of thought, of gratitude to God and Christ, and of fellowship amongst men, that it would be "new" in the kingdom of God, which itself, by the death and resurrection of the Saviour, would be advanced by a new and unique development; and all this was so near at hand, that this was the Last Supper, the last meal, the last drinking of the cup with the Master, ere it should come to pass. "Verily I say unto you, I will never drink again of this fruit of the vine, until that day when I drink it new with you in My Father's kingdom."

These important words are altogether omitted in St. Paul's description of the Last Supper; but St. Luke, though he fails to place them *after* the institution, as do St. Matthew and St. Mark, has recorded them, as we have seen, with variations and additions, as having been spoken *before* the institution. In the third Evangelist, they bear this form (Luke xxii. 15—18): "With desire have I desired to eat this Passover with you before I suffer: for I say unto you that I will never eat of it again, until it be fulfilled in the kingdom of God. And He took a cup, and gave thanks, and said, Take this, and divide it among yourselves: for I say unto you, I will not drink henceforth of the fruit of the vine, until the kingdom of God shall come."

The different position occupied by these words in the third Gospel, as compared with the two first, is full of instruction for those who, in their devout adoration of the Saviour, wish to learn as much as possible of the principles and method on which the evangelical histories were constructed and composed. If Jesus spoke these words both before and after the institution—a supposition which is possible, but surely in the highest degree improbable—then each of the three historians omits one of the repeated utterances, and we are shown an instance of evangelic condensation of our Saviour's words.

But if, as is more likely, the words were only spoken once, and that in the fuller form indicated by St. Luke, with reference to eating the Passover as well as drinking the wine; then, in the displacement by one or other historian, and in the abridgment by the two later Evangelists, as well as in the variations between the phrases, "until I drink it new with you in My Father's kingdom," "until I drink it new in the kingdom of God," "until it be fulfilled in the kingdom of God," "until the kingdom of God shall come"—in such displacement, and abridgment, and variations we are again taught how the Gospels are the sacred instrument for awakening and sustaining the spirit of Christianity in all devout and earnest students, but are not a literal transcript of words and sentences out of which, by the mere formularies of logical definition and inference, apart from the temper of beneficence, love, and salvation, sentences may be constructed which shall be reliable dogmas of the faith.

These displacements, variations, and abridgments show how necessary it is that, whenever two or more versions of any event can be found in Holy Writ, we should place them in juxtaposition, and, instead of converting an isolated passage from one version into some formulary and "shibboleth" of party, we should diligently endeavour to ascertain as nearly as possible the true teaching and the sanctifying spirit of the Saviour in the fullest statement.

An illustration of the manner in which different records of the same divine utterance throw light upon one another is afforded to us in the several expressions which, as set forth above, go to confirm the view we have given of the sense in which Jesus would drink of the fruit of the vine "*new*" in the days when the kingdom of God should be come, and when, therefore, the Passover feast and its cup of blessing, hitherto associated chiefly with Jewish rescue from Egyptian bondage, would be *fulfilled*, and so would be replete with new associations touching deliverance from the servitude and selfishness of sin into the glorious liberty of righteousness, into the holy brotherhood of men, into the blessed sonship with Christ unto the Father.

"New," indeed, would be such a fulfilled Passover; "new," indeed, such unleavened bread of sincerity and truth;

"new," indeed, such a cup of blessing; "new," indeed, the Lamb without blemish, the Lamb of God which taketh away the sin of the world, the Lamb slain from the foundation of the world, Christ our Passover, who is sacrificed for us; "new" indeed, each part of the sacred rite, the fulfilment, the perfecting, the substance of that which had only been foreshadowed in the weak and beggarly elements of the law; "new," indeed, and in marked and glorious contrast with that which waxed old and decayed, and was ready to vanish away; "new," indeed, this substitution, by Christ, of the spirit of righteousness and life for the letter of condemnation and death.

But this, full as it is of the "new" spirit of Christ, remote as it is from any teaching of a material presence of Jesus in each repeated commemoration of His Last Supper, is very far from being all that we are taught by a careful collation of the several histories of the institution.

(ix.) *St. Luke's Notice of Wine given before the Bread.*

We have seen that whilst St. Luke gives us, in some respects, the more complete statement of our Saviour's words as to His not again eating and drinking till all was "fulfilled," and so made *new* by fresh and ennobling associations in the kingdom of God, that Evangelist stands by himself in contradistinction from the two who place their representation of those words after the institution. As we accept St. Luke's fuller statement, so we yield our judgment to the testimonies of Matthew and Mark on the point in which they are agreed, namely, that those words of Jesus were spoken *after* the institution.

And, in this line of thought, it is not unimportant to observe how, subsequently to our Lord's blessing and thanksgiving over the bread and wine, and subsequently to the disciples' partaking of those elements, one of them is still designated "the fruit of the vine" (St. Luke), and "*this* fruit of the vine" (St. Matthew). Surely, if it had been intended by Jesus, or by the Evangelists, to teach us that the wine had undergone an objective change, and was now

become His blood, objectively or materially, words could
hardly have been less happily chosen than these, " This fruit
of the vine." If language on the lips of the Saviour or from
the pens of the Evangelists have any definite and intelligible
meaning, here is an indication that the wine was still the fruit
of the vine, and nothing more and nothing less *objectively*,
whatever, *subjectively*, might be the association of thought
and emotion rightly and piously to be connected therewith.

(x.) *Christ's Participation in the New Fruit of the Vine.*

But even this is not the only warning against materializing spiritual things, furnished to us by an attentive study of
the primal records of our Lord's institution of the Supper.
For this passage of those primal records represents Jesus as
implying that He would participate with His disciples in the
drinking of the fruit of the vine, new, in the kingdom of God.
If the Master had said He would give His disciples of the fruit
of the vine, new, in His Father's kingdom, it would not have
countenanced the belief that wine, in the Supper, became
objectively differentiated, or materially changed, from the
fruit of the vine ; but what the Saviour intimates is, I will
drink of this fruit of the vine, new, with you in the kingdom
of God.

Let any man, who is not revolted at the abhorrent idea,
image to himself Jesus drinking, not the fruit of the vine, but
His own blood, *objectively*. So repulsive a thought finds no
place in Scripture, and might well forbid our interpreting
literally any isolated passage, if such did exist, which would,
when so literally interpreted, lead directly and inevitably to
results intolerable, as a matter of taste, and impious in connection with God and Christ. When we meet with precepts
enjoining or seeming to encourage the hatred of our parents,
the mutilation or dismemberment of ourselves, or the perpe-
tration of aught that is abhorrent, we pity the error of Origen,
and feel that metaphors must not be pressed to absurd and
wicked lengths, lest here again the letter be found to kill just
as truly as the spirit giveth life.

If, then, there even were any text which taught that the

bread in the Supper became objectively changed into the flesh of Christ, and the wine into His blood, this portion of the Gospel narrative would compel us to interpret that text as metaphorical on pain of becoming blasphemous and cannibalistic.   But we have seen thus far, alike in examining the general usage of all languages and the phraseology of the Old and New Testaments, that there is distinctest instruction given us that Wisdom's bread and Wisdom's wine, the flesh of the Son of man, and His blood, are metaphors enjoining the union or embodiment which is to be effected between us and Wisdom, between our spirits and the Spirit of our divine Master.

In the institution of the Supper, we have also seen these metaphors conjoined with symbols : the symbol of bread with the metaphor of Christ's body, so that as often as we partake of the former we may thankfully remember the latter, and more nearly come to Christ our Saviour ; the symbol of wine with the metaphor of Christ's blood, so that as oft as we drink we may thankfully remember the Lord's dying for us, and, more vividly realizing and believing on Him, may be more thoroughly in union with Him, and in communion with our fellow-men and fellow-believers.

All this has been clear enough as the sacred records have been investigated ; but instead of showing us any trace of a material transformation in the elements of bread and wine, they have warned us that all our advantage is to be drawn, not from any flesh, not even from the flesh of Jesus Himself, but only and solely from the spirit which breathes through His divine words of comfort, love, and truth.   Each particular of time and place and detail, in the narrative, has, thus far, made as strongly against any literal, and material, and objective interpretation of the figures and symbols in the Supper, as it has made distinctly in favour of their subjective and spiritual exegesis.

H. (a.) *Christ's Words in Administering the Bread and Wine.*

It remains, however, for us to examine carefully the very core of this matter—the words, namely, with which our

Saviour gave the bread and delivered the cup : and in these words men have sometimes thought there was to be found justification for a belief in such objective change in the bread and wine, as is designated at one time " transubstantiation," at another time " consubstantiation," and yet again " insubstantiation." At this point it will be useful to refer to the words of institution, as given in parallel columns on pages 22 and 25 of this essay.

(b.) *Comments on the Administration.*

(i.) *From briefest Forms, what follows ?*

At the outset, the two first Evangelists inform us that Jesus said, " Take " (Mark), or " Take, eat " (Matthew); " this is My body." Now let us suppose, for instruction's sake, that which is only an hypothesis, however, and does not, happily, hold good in fact. Let us suppose that these briefest words of administration were all we knew of what Jesus said as He administered. And let it be, moreover, supposed, contrary to the facts again, that on our Lord's giving the cup, it was only recorded that He said, " This is My blood." From this hypothesis, what would follow as to the necessity of believing in any objective change in the bread and wine ?

If we were to forget all that has hitherto been adduced against materialistic tendencies in the worship of Him who is a Spirit, and seeks to be worshipped in spirit and in truth, there would still remain the Saviour's declarations that He is " the good shepherd " (John x. 11), that He is " the door of the sheep " (John x. 7), and that He is " the true vine, and His Father is the husbandman " (John xv. 1), or that He is " the vine, and ye (His disciples) are the branches."

There would remain these and not a few other like employments of metaphor by the Master: and until interpreters shall be prepared to insist that Christ's disciples are objectively changed from men into sheep; that the Eternal and Unchangeable is objectively changed into a " husbandman " (γεωργός in the Greek); that our blessed Lord is objectively changed into a " shepherd " of real sheep, and not of men ; or that He is objectively changed into the " door," or gate, of a sheepfold; or He into an objective vine, and we into objective branches;—until interpreters are prepared for these extravagant and well-nigh, if not quite, blasphemous and unnecessary courses, they must, to be consistent, confine metaphoric and symbolic language to figurative, prudent, and pious significations, alike when it is said, "This bread is My body," or "This wine is My blood," or "I am the door," or "I am the good shepherd," or "I am the true vine," or "Ye are branches," or "Ye are sheep," or "My Father is the husbandman."

Against a literal, and objective, and materializing interpretation the special senses testify; for there was the body of Jesus visibly and tangibly present with the disciples, apart from both the bread and the wine. The dictates of common sense and good taste and piety bear similar testimony against any objective interpretation, as may be perceived the moment we apply such interpretation to any of the metaphors in connection with which familiarity has not blunted our sense of the indecorous and the impious.

Faith, likewise, bears testimony to the same effect against any objective or material presence of Christ's body and blood on earth, for it is guided by the teaching of Holy Writ, that Jesus, with His glorified body, has ascended to the Father's right hand, and there sitteth awaiting the subjection of His enemies, and interceding for us. Faith bears this testimony as to Jesus being absent, objectively and carnally, from all bread and wine and other things on earth. Faith apprehends the truth that it is good for us Jesus should thus go to the Father and leave us, and send us, instead of His bodily or objective presence, the blessed and abiding Spirit, the Guide and Comforter, to be ever present with us, to knock at the doors of our hearts, to sup with any who will open to Him, to be present with each and with all till the end of the world.

Thus would faith and common sense and piety combine with the dictates of a consistent exegesis in forbidding us to interpret, objectively or materially, the phrases, "This is My body," "This is my blood," even if they stood—as, however, they do not stand—absolutely and by themselves in the sacred narrative of the Lord's institution and administration of the Supper.

(ii.) *Four Records of the Administration.*

But these important phrases do not so stand, absolutely and by themselves, and without limitation or definition in the narrative of the Apostle and Evangelists. For the sake of distinctness, let us reproduce the words of administration of the bread and wine by the Lord in their fourfold form :—

MATT. xxvi. 26–28.	MARK xiv. 22–24.	LUKE xxii. 19, 20.	1 COR. xi. 23–25.
"Take, eat; this is My body.	"Take: this is My body.	"This is My body which is being given for you. This do for My remembrance.	"This is My body. which is for you. This do for My remembrance.
Drink of it, all of you : for this is My blood of the covenant, which is being shed for many for remission of sins."	This is My blood of the covenant, which is being shed for many."	This cup [is] the new covenant in My blood, which is being shed for you."	This cup is the new covenant in My blood. This do, as oft as ye drink, for My remembrance."

To several points in connection with these solemn words, our attention has already been directed. Of the extent of the "many" for whom Christ suffered, and of the divine mercy as wishing that "many" to be equivalent to the "*all* men" for whom Christ gave Himself a ransom (1 Tim. ii. 6), we shall at present say no more. Neither need we add anything concerning the precept that *all* should drink of the cup. Nor will we further insist on the frequency, the constantly recurring frequency, with which our blessed Saviour ought to be remembered and sympathized with, and communion with Him and His people participated in by us all.

(iii.) *Phrase " For Remission of Sins."*

St. Matthew's mention of Christ's blood being shed "for remission of sins" calls for the remark that "remission" (ἄφεσις in the Greek) signifies *putting away*, and denotes not only God's putting away, or remitting, or forgiving sins, but also signifies man's putting away, dismissing, or desisting from sins. When, here or elsewhere in the New Testament, we read of the remission of sins, and of Christ dying for that object, let it be borne in mind that Christ died that God might put away sin by remitting it, and that man might put away sin by dismissing it.   God in Christ has done everything for the remission of sins ; but unless man responds to this divine inception of grace, by dismissing sin, and abandoning it on his part, the sin must remain, and man's guilt will be that he nullifies and frustrates God's merciful wish and the gracious work of Christ and the Holy Spirit.

(iv.) *Variations in the Records.*

This pregnant truth, concerning "remission of sins," we could not fail to offer to our reader on the suggestion of St. Matthew.   But, once more, how striking is the fact that only St. Matthew records our Lord's introduction of these words into the institution and administration of the Last Supper ! And, in a similar vein of instruction, how noteworthy is it that, as becomes conspicuous in the parallel columns just employed, in so solemn a matter as this, of the Lord's Supper and its institution, no two of the evangelic records are entirely agreed. · Even in the briefest form of administering the bread, where St. Matthew writes, "Take, eat ; this is My body," St. Mark, as shown by the three oldest existing manu- scripts, omits the word " eat." So true is it, as should ever be borne in mind, that in the Lord's Supper, as in everything connected with the Gospel narratives and with the entirety of Christianity, it is the spirit that giveth life, and to depend on the letter is fatal.

(v.) *Habit of abbreviating the Words of Christ's Administration.*

Few passages of Scripture more need, and few will better repay, a minute and careful study and comparison, than those which record the words of our Saviour in administering the Last Supper, and, strange as it must seem, few passages appear to have received so little diligent and thorough examination.

"This is My body," and "This is My blood,"—these are the words which ring in men's ears, and cleave to their memo- ries, and are conspicuous in their controversies, as if they were the sole words of Jesus at the Supper, or, at least, were the centre and core and essence of what was spoken by the

Lord, as if all His other sayings on that occasion were inci-
dental and of less moment.

(vi.) *St. Luke and St. Paul on the Administering of the Wine.*

Let us now collate the parallel histories given above, and
ascertain what they may teach us. From the popularly
quoted and almost exclusively remembered phrases, " This is
My body" and " This is My blood," the point of widest
divergence, and therefore, probably, the point of best illustration and most useful instruction, is to be found in the
histories supplied by St. Luke and St. Paul with reference to
the wine. These histories inform us that our Lord's words,
in giving the wine, were, " This cup is the new covenant in
My blood." St. Luke adds, " which is being shed for you."

Here is a statement which looks, at the first glance, very
different from that which is all but exclusively quoted and
relied upon in support of the notion of an objective change in
the elements of bread and wine. Instead of " This is My
blood," " This cup is the new covenant in My blood " is our
various reading; and this various reading is furnished to us
by two out of the four historians of the event, those two being
St. Luke the Evangelist, and St. Paul the Apostle, whose
first Epistle to the Corinthians supplies us with what is, as
says Dean Stanley (Cor., vol. i. p. 241), " probably the
earliest record of the institution of the Eucharist."

(vii.) *The Records differing, which is our better Guide?*

The question which must press itself upon the attention of
the diligent and unprejudiced reader of these two representations of our Saviour's words is, What did Jesus say ? Were
His words, " This cup is the new covenant," or were they,
" This is My blood " ?

It is perfectly clear that the two different records of the
Lord's words cannot *both* be literally exact, correct, and
complete. If Jesus said, " This cup is the new covenant," He
cannot also, with the same breath, at the same moment, have
said, " This is My blood." It is to be observed that in each
of the records, looked at in their entirety, both the phrases

occur. From neither of them is the word "blood" wholly absent. In both the term "covenant" is mentioned. In one, Jesus speaks of "My blood of the covenant;" in the other, of "the new covenant in My blood." Which was the precise utterance of Jesus? If we cannot positively decide that question, what a frail basis will be left for the theory of an objective change in the elements, resting as that theory does in the main upon words of institution, which are at least as likely to have been "This cup is the new covenant," as "This is My blood!"

The stupendous miracles of objective change in the elements will rest on the doubtful issue, Did St. Paul and St. Luke more accurately record the words of Jesus on this occasion; or must the credit of greater accuracy in this case be awarded to St. Matthew and St. Mark? Is such dubiety in the evidence a sufficient basis for any miracle? Still more, is it sufficient to uphold a miracle of objective change in the bread and wine against the contravening testimony, as we have seen, of sense, of common sense, of taste, and of faith itself? We will venture to assert, at all events, that no other Christian miracle rests upon testimony so slender and so questionable.

(viii.) *Failing an Answer, what follows?*

Nay, we will acknowledge ourselves convinced that, if it be impossible to decide which is the more genuine and exact record of the words employed by Jesus, the case must stand thus:—The four historians—or two of them, at least— whatever theory of their inspiration may be adopted) cannot have thought it a matter of supreme importance to give their readers the *ipsissima verba* in this matter; they must have attached little weight to the enormous doctrines of objective change insisted upon by certain modern teachers, if indeed they had any conception whatever of such objective change; and, furthermore, if both the discrepant records are to stand as substantially true and historical, then the inference seems inevitable that Jesus, in giving the wine after His Last Supper, spoke something about its being His blood of the covenant in such a sense and with such a meaning that His words could be reported, not as insisting upon an objective change of wine into blood, but as declaring that the cup of wine was, *in some sense*, the new covenant in His blood.

(ix.) *The Cup a "Covenant."*

A covenant is a promise in words spoken or in words written. Obviously and confessedly on all sides, the cup of wine was not metamorphosed, or objectively changed, into a covenant in the sense of the sound of words spoken, or into a covenant in the sense of a piece of parchment or papyrus with words inscribed thereon. No one sets up this pretence of transubstantiation upon the words, " This cup is the new covenant." Then why, or with what appearance of reason or reverence, can the theory of wine being objectively changed into blood be originated and upheld upon the parallel and (at most) explanatory phrase, " This is My blood of the covenant " ?

If the words, " This cup is the new covenant," are, confessedly, a statement that there is a connecting association of thought and memory between the wine and the covenant— that the wine is a token and reminder of the covenant ; by what fair process of interpretation can the parallel utterance be denied the exposition which makes it a statement that there is a connecting association of thought and memory between the wine and the blood of Jesus—that the wine is a token and reminder of the blood of Jesus ?

(x.) *The Simpler Form of Administering the Wine.*

Thus much must be said on the supposition that one of our discrepant records has no greater appearance or evidence of exactness than the other. Now, however, we proceed to inquire into this important point—what may be the meaning of these words, " This cup is the new covenant in My blood which is being shed for you " ? Do they yield any plain and natural signification ? As to the connection between blood and a covenant with Jehovah, the Jewish mind was quite familiar with this. When, for example, Moses had been

called up into the mountain, and had received and written all
the words of the Lord, "he took" (Exod. xxiv. 7, 8) "the
book of the covenant, and read in the audience of the people :
and they said, All that the Lord hath said will we do, and be
obedient.   And Moses took the blood" (of the sacrifice just
slain), "and sprinkled it on the people, and said, Behold
the blood of the covenant, which the Lord hath made with you
concerning all these words."

Besides this historical association of the old covenant
with the blood sprinkled by Moses upon the Israelites, there
was the blood of the Paschal lamb which was to be "struck"
(Exod xii. 7) "on the two side posts and on the upper door-
post of the houses wherein they shall eat it."   This was to
be "a token" between them and the Lord, a token of the
covenant of the Passover.   This was the old covenant in
the blood of the lamb.   Then, in connection with the Passover supper, there sprung up the custom of drinking a cup
of wine with blessing of God for His mercies to Israel, when
He destroyed the firstborn of Egypt and spared Israel, and
delivered them out of the house of bondage.

Thus, without insisting on a reference by Jesus to the
shedding of blood and pouring out libations of wine which so
generally accompanied the ratifying of ancient heathen truces
and covenants, we find the Jews of our Saviour's day familiar
with the idea of their covenant of deliverance from Egypt,
with the idea of the blood of the Paschal lamb particularly
connected with that ancient deliverance, and with the idea
of a cup of wine taken in thankful blessing of Jehovah as
they remembered that Paschal deliverance and the entire
covenant of which it formed an important part.

It only needs to remember how the writer of the Epistle to
the Hebrews quotes the prophet Jeremiah (Heb. viii. 8—12,
Jer. xxxi. 31, etc.) as foretelling the time when Jehovah
would make "a new covenant" with His people, and we have
all the ideas, ready, familiar, and sacred, in the minds of our
Lord's countrymen and contemporaries, only requiring to be
welded together and stamped by Him into the form—"This
cup," analogous to your wonted cup of blessing in the Pass-

over, " is the new covenant," fulfilling the anticipations of
Jeremiah and the prophets, "in My blood" which, much
more than the blood of bulls and of goats, shall (Heb. ix. 15)
"purge your conscience from dead works, to serve the living
God."

Thus naturally and distinctly does the form of administration of the wine, as recorded by St. Luke and St. Paul, yield
a definite and intelligible signification in harmony alike with
the writings of the Old Testament, the usages of the Passover,
and the ideas which were current among the Christian
Hebrews of the apostolic age.

This cup of blessing is the token and remembrance of the
new covenant which is sealed and ratified between you and
God by no less than the shedding of My blood for you. Here
are words entirely free and distinct from any vestige of the
idea of an objective change in the fruit of the vine : and with
these words must be reconciled the others recorded by
St. Matthew and St. Mark.

If our Saviour and the apostles meant to be understood
as teaching the enormous doctrine that, in the Supper, wine
was objectively and miraculously changed, in any way of
transubstantiation, consubstantiation, or insubstantiation,
into the blood of the Saviour, it is inconceivable that two
out of the four historians of that miracle, which contra-
vened the senses of those who looked on Jesus bodily present,
apart from the wine, should have failed to mark pointedly
the sole ground for believing in so stupendous a change ; it
is inconceivable that if Jesus said, "This is My blood," and
was understood to mean, This wine is objectively changed,
and has become materially or objectively My blood, the re-
corders of such words of transformation should have altered
them and toned them down into so beautiful and natural
and non-miraculous an utterance as, "This cup is the new
covenant in My blood."

The historians, being (by the hypothesis of transubstantiation) in duty bound, and intending, to record the most
astounding miracle which rested on no evidence but the words,
"This is My blood"—nay, which was and is controverted by

every testimony of sense and common sense and faith, except those words—would never have substituted for those all-important words a phrase like "This cup is the new covenant in My blood," which must be susceptible of a meaning, and in the natural acting of men's minds must be understood to bear a meaning, entirely different and distinct from any objective and material change in the wine.

But now, accepting these words of St. Luke and St. Paul as having been, thus necessarily, the fuller and more precise utterance and the more exact meaning, of our Lord; bearing in mind what we have already noticed of the sketchy and fragmentary nature of the New Testament records; understanding that the New Testament writers, at the time when they represented Christ as saying, "This cup is," not My blood, but "the new covenant in My blood," could have entertained no idea of a miraculous and objective change by which the wine became blood in the cup;—bearing all this in mind, how easy is it to conceive that, in "the simplicity of the gospel," St. Matthew and St. Mark, having no dream of insubstantiation or any other metaphysical or physical change in the material wine, did, in their obviously fragmentary and summary style of composition, write, "This is My blood of the covenant, which is being shed for many."

So inconceivable a notion as transubstantiation, in any of its modifications, being out of their ken; so incredible and demonstrably false an idea not entering into the apostolic mind (as we have seen is shown by the variations in St. Luke and St. Paul); it is quite conceivable that they wrote, "This is My blood of the covenant," instead of, "This cup is the new covenant in My blood." To St. Matthew and St. Mark, who presently, *after* the participation in the cup of blessing, describe our Saviour as designating the contents of that cup as "the fruit of the vine," "this fruit of the vine," there was no danger imaginable in speaking of that unchanged fruit of the vine as Christ's blood of the covenant, as a cup of wine which was henceforth for ever to be associated in men's minds with Christ's new covenant between God and man, and with the blood of Christ by which that new covenant had been ratified and confirmed.

Thus, on the supposition that Jesus or the New Testament writers believed and intended to teach that there was an objective change in the wine of the Supper, the words of St. Paul and St. Luke, " This cup is the new covenant in My blood," become a perilous and inconceivable deviation from Christ's words of administration ; whereas, on the contrary, if we recognise the fact that no change of substance was known or thought of by our Saviour, or by the writers of the New Testament, in that wine which St. Matthew and St. Mark declare to have been the fruit of the vine after the Saviour's blessing, just as it was before His giving of thanks, then the substitution of "This is My blood of the covenant," for "This cup is the new covenant in my blood," becomes an unimportant and harmless variation of the words.

Between the phrase, This cup is a token and remembrance of God's new covenant with you established in the shedding of My blood, and the phrase, This fruit of the vine is a token and remembrance of My blood, in the shedding of which is established God's new covenant with men, there is no difference of meaning ; but between the sentence, This cup is the new covenant in My blood, and the sentence, This fruit of the vine, which continues to be the fruit of the vine, is, nevertheless, objectively changed into My blood —between these sentences there is all the difference which separates self-contradiction and unmeaningness from an utterance of divine simplicity and wisdom.

Looking thus closely at the four records of our Lord's administration of the cup, we are constrained to believe that the words of St. Paul and St. Luke must necessarily be taken as defining the signification of the parallel expression in the two first Gospels ; and, moreover, the idea of there being any objective change in the wine of the Last Supper appears to be no less utterly precluded by the cup being called the new covenant in Christ's blood by the Apostle and the third Evangelist, than by its contents being designated by St. Matthew and St. Mark, after the Supper, as still the fruit of the vine. So necessarily absent from our Saviour's words, in administering the cup, is all idea of objective change in the wine.

(xi.) *From this is to be inferred the Form, or Meaning, in Administering the Bread.*

And this truth, so established, throws its light upon the four different and obviously fragmentary records of the words spoken by our Master in distributing the bread at His Last Supper. As Jesus said, " This cup is the new covenant in My blood," so it becomes in the highest degree probable that He said likewise, "This bread is the new covenant in My body, which is being given for you." Just as, in your Jewish Passover, you took unleavened bread and ate of it, with thankful remembrance of Jehovah's covenant with Abraham and with Moses, and of His delivering you out of Egyptian slavery, and of His bestowing upon you all the good gifts of His providential bounty; so, in future, break bread, distribute it, and eat it in thankful remembrance, not only of all else which your Heavenly Father bestows upon you for the body and for the mind, but also, and especially, in thankful remembrance of Me, the Lamb of God which taketh away the sins of the world—of Me, who am giving My body to be broken and sacrificed as the propitiation for your sins, and not for yours only, but " for the sins of the whole world " (1 John ii. 2).

(xii.) *Remembrance, not Sight, aimed at.*

" This do," as say St. Luke and St. Paul, "for My remembrance." To recall Me and My sacrifice of Myself to your minds; thus to show, declare, or preach ($\kappa\alpha\tau\alpha\gamma\gamma\epsilon\lambda\lambda\epsilon\iota\nu$) My death until I come again (1 Cor. xi. 26); do this in remembrance of Me. Do what? Change bread into My body? That, if it were objectively done, should produce, not a remembrance, but a vision of the Saviour. But there is no material and objective vision of Jesus even alleged by any one, and therefore the necessary inference is that there is no such objective change. If the bread be associated, subjectively or in the mind of the recipient, with memories and thoughts of Christ's body given for us, then may the doing this be said to be, not for a vision, but for a remembrance of the Lord. Thus, from the terms appended by two of our historians to the administration of the bread, it appears that they believed in no transformation of the bread, either physical or metaphysical, but simply and solely in its serving for a token which should recall the memory of Christ's sacrifice, and thus, reminding us of the benefits resulting from that sacrifice, should itself become a special channel and means of grace. " This do," they wrote, not for a vision of Me, but " for a remembrance of Me."

(xiii.) *Test the Hypothesis of Objective Change.*

This subjective realization of Christ's spiritual presence in the receiving of the bread, tallies with what we have learnt in examining the records of the administration of the cup. But suppose, on the other hand, that Christ and His disciples had understood and taught that, in the Supper, the bread was metamorphosed into the flesh of Christ objectively ; then it would follow, in all probability and consistency, that they must have understood and taught that the wine was similarly metamorphosed into the blood of Christ : and then comes the inconceivable want of judgment and lack of accuracy into which St. Paul and St. Luke must have been betrayed when, believing, by this hypothesis, the bread was become flesh and the wine was become blood, they nevertheless deviated into a needless variation of the Lord's words, and represented Him as saying, " This cup is the new covenant in My blood."

As it is impossible to reconcile these words of St. Luke and St. Paul with apostolic belief in any objective change in the elements, so it is most natural to understand them in their plain grammatical signification ; and then the other texts, relative to the administration of the bread and the wine, are seen to be variations and abbreviations of what our Saviour said, and so the shorter or less definite forms will have their meaning fixed and illustrated by those sacred utterances which, being preserved to us in greater fulness, are recognised as at once more precise, more definite, more simple, and more spiritual.

(xiv.) *Conclusion.*

Thus, then, whether we look at the words of institution and administration by Christ Himself; or whether regard be had to the Master's frequent employment of the metaphors which tell of hungering and thirsting after righteousness, of eating the bread from heaven, and even of spiritually eating His flesh and drinking His blood; or whether we contemplate the scriptural and general usage of similar metaphors in the Old Testament and in all languages, the result is the same. There is no semblance of a belief in any kind of transubstantiation, or in any form of objective presence of Christ in the sacramental bread and wine; but, on the contrary, there is distinctest warning that that which is profitable, particularly in this part of our Christian religion, is not material, fleshly, objective, but is spiritual and subjective.

Such are the results of our investigation of the Saviour's institution of the Lord's Supper. We shall next attempt a study of apostolic usage and belief in connection with that sacred rite.

CHAPTER II.

§ 1. *The Days between Christ's Resurrection and Ascension.*

HAVING, in the previous part of this book, examined the origin and institution of the Lord's Supper, we now proceed to observe the records of its usage in the apostolic histories. And, in this connection, it may be worth while to consider an event which took place in the transition period between the resurrection and the ascension, in the course of those forty days while yet the disciples had frequent intercourse, by sight and touch, with the glorified and spiritual body of the Saviour.

In those days, however changed His external appearance might be, though Mary could mistake His semblance for that of the gardener (John xx. 15); though one of the ancient records explains (Mark xvi. 12) that His appearance was "in another form," [1] in a *different* form; yet there was something in the tone and expression of His voice by which He was unmistakably recognisable. The glory of His different form might fail to strike the Magdalene. She was absorbed in thoughts of Her blessed but lost Redeemer. For any other human form than His she had no eye, no thought. Resplendent that form might be with heavenly sheen; the movement full of divine vigour; the eye beaming with grace and truth; the whole being replete with the gentleness, and power, and spirit of the Lord of glory: but such a form was not like that of the scourged and crucified carpenter, not like that of the exhausted bearer of other men's

---

[1] ἐν ἑτέρᾳ μορφῇ.

sins, not like that of the inanimate corpse which she and death had both embraced and, as it were, contended to retain.

The beneficent victim of the cross was in her mind's eye, and she could not identify Him with the spiritual and glorified body that still bore, indeed, the prints of the nails and the wound of the spear, but was passing to the Father, and receiving the crown of heaven's King, instead of the crown of thorns.

For this "form," so identical and yet so changed, Mary had no eye. He was different from her Saviour on the cross and in the grave. He might be the gardener. Could He tell her where lay the lacerated but beloved remains of Him who had given her deliverance from the seven demons? Then He spoke her name. At the sound of that name, breathed so familiarly, so tenderly, in the very tone and with the very spirit that freed her from the evil bondage, she turned from the sepulchre to the living man, and in His changed form she saw her Master, and fell at His feet with the adoring cry, " Rabboni."

To Mary Magdalene it was thus His words that were spirit and were life, and they revealed to her once more the Saviour, Jesus.

§ 2. (a.) *The Journey to Emmaus and the Meal there.*

But this appearance to the Magdalene was not the only marvel of that first Lord's Day. Two of the disciples were walking to Emmaus, and as they talked with sadness of Jesus and His being lost to them, the risen Lord came and walked with them. His words, as He talked with them and opened to them the Scriptures from Moses and all the prophets, made their hearts to burn within them (Luke xxiv. 32), but still they failed to recognise their Lord. Their own preconceptions and prejudices as to how He should "redeem Israel" with pomp and with the sword, and with a kingdom of this world, held their eyes, so that even in the changed and spiritual body of Him who had been crucified, but now was glorified, they failed to recognise Jesus, the King of

righteousness, the King of peace. Arrived, however, at the
village whither they went, they constrained their unknown
companion to tarry with them, as the day was far spent
and it was towards evening. "And it came to pass" (Luke
xxiv. 30), "as He sat at meat with them, He took bread, and
blessed, and brake, and gave to them."

As the sound of her name upon the lips of Jesus recalled
Mary to her right mind, and led her to turn from the grave
and her own sad imaginings, and to behold and recognise her
Master in His changed form, so this act of Jesus, and these
words of blessing in this evening meal at Emmaus, opened
the eyes of Cleopas and his fellow-disciple : and "they knew
Him" (Luke xxiv. 31); "and He vanished out of their
sight."

Of course, we cannot say positively, in the silence of the
Gospel narratives on the subject, that the apostles had already
communicated to the disciples who were with them in Jerusalem, the manner in which Jesus had instituted the breaking
of bread and the drinking of wine to be done in remembrance
of Him as oft as they should drink. We cannot be sure
that already, in the few hours that had intervened between
the Friday of crucifixion and the Sunday of resurrection,
Cleopas and his companion had learned from the apostles
that, in obedience to one of the latest of the Lord's loving
precepts, they were never to refresh their bodies with bread
and wine without also refreshing their souls by that eating
of Christ's flesh which consists in coming to Him, and that
drinking of Christ's blood (John vi. 35) which consists in
self-abandoning trust in Him. This we cannot say positively ;
but nothing seems more natural or more likely than that, in
those hours of bereavement and dismay and agony, every
memory of the beloved Jesus should be sought for and repeated amongst the apostles and the women, and the others
who were with them. Each would tell the other what he had
learnt of the Master's last sayings and doings ; and it is hard
to imagine that any of the disciples then in Jerusalem, the
little flock who must have been drawn nearer than ever
to one another by the loss of their Good Shepherd, failed to

be informed of that Last Supper, and of the especial and
abiding rite and memorial that had there been instituted.

Not certain, but highly probable, does it thus appear that
the two from Emmaus made a conscious reference to the
Last Supper and its memorial rite when, on their return to
Jerusalem, they "told" (Luke xxiv. 35) "what things were
done in the way, and how Jesus was known of them in the
breaking of bread."[1] Notwithstanding that these two from
Emmaus are said, on their return to Jerusalem (Luke xxiv.
33), to have found "the eleven" gathered together with the
rest of the disciples ; yet this phrase, "the eleven," may be,
like " the twelve " in 1 Cor. xv. 5, and in Matthew xix. 28, a
mere official designation of the apostles generally, without
precise reference to their then exact number. And, if this may
be so, it leaves open for consideration the opinion of those
scholars who have identified the " Cleopas " of Luke xxiv. 18,
with the " Alphæus " of Matt. x. 3—each being a Greek
equivalent for one and the same Jewish name, Khalphai—and
then, as this Alphæus was the father of an apostle James,
the surmise is not wholly without warrant, that the companion of Cleopas, on the way to Emmaus, was his son
James ; and this, these same scholars say, is, in all likeli-
hood, the occasion referred to by St. Paul (1 Cor. xv. 7) in
the words, " After that, He was seen of James."

This chain of scholarlike surmises appears to us far from
being deficient in verisimilitude ; and, if it be true, it will
readily account for the Saviour's words of blessing in "the
breaking of bread" being familiar to the disciples at Emmaus, and serving as the suggestive association of thought
which recalled them from Jesus in His death to Jesus once
more alive, in His changed form and risen body.

Whether James the Less was at Emmaus or not ; whether
or not the two disciples in that breaking of bread had called
up before their minds a vivid recollection of words they had,
within the last few hours, heard from apostolic lips as
amongst the most precious relics of their crucified Master ;
whether with or without any such direct and fresh associa-

[1] ἐν τῇ κλάσει τοῦ ἄρτου.

tion of memory with the Last Supper; at any rate, here, at Emmaus, was an instance of our Saviour using His words of blessing at an ordinary evening meal in a private house, with only two disciples present, as an occasion and instrument for making the scales of ignorance and prejudice to fall from His followers' eyes—an occasion and instrument for enabling them to know and recognise Him as their Master and their Lord.

Whether or not it was a conscious repetition, on the disciples' part, of the scene in that guestchamber before the Paschal feast, this is clear—it was an exemplification of the Lord revealing Himself, at a domestic meal, to the minds and hearts of some disciples, just as to other disciples He made himself known by the name " Mary," or by the " Reach hither thy finger and behold My hands " (John xx. 27), or by the " Peace be unto you " of another occasion (John xx. 19), or by the eating " a piece of broiled fish " (Luke xxiv. 42), or by the " Cast the net on the right side of the ship and ye shall find " (John xxi. 6), or by the thunder and the lightning and the " Saul, Saul, why persecutest thou Me ? " (Acts ix. 4) of yet another occasion.

Many are the ways in which He comes and seeks to save us by constraining us to know and love Him ; and this opening the eyes at an ordinary meal, partaken with only two friends, or this celebration of the Supper with a Church (an *ecclesia*, an assembling of only two), is just one among the many and various methods by which our Lord manifests Himself to us and to all who will receive Him.

But now let us look at the instructions, bearing on our present inquiry, which arise out of this incident at Emmaus.

Whether it be regarded as an ordinary domestic meal, or as a Church ordinance, or as both, what follows ? This, assuredly : that in a house or Church of Christ's own choosing there was an evening celebration, just as the Lord's first institution had been at an evening meal ; there was no altar, but a table ; there were no vestments but the ordinary costume of the disciples and their Master ; there was no trace of an eastward position, nor any sign of the Saviour and the disciples looking in one direction, but, on the contrary, the English rendering, "As they sat at meat with Him," has for its equivalent in the Greek[1] (Luke xxiv. 30), "As He *reclined* with them," in obvious allusion to the then prevailing custom of not sitting, as is the modern practice, but reclining on couches round the table—Jesus, the president in this domestic meal or Church ordinance, on one couch, the two disciples on other couches on either side of Him.

The direction of their three faces would thus be towards three different quarters of the heaven, except in so far as, at any moment, they turned themselves away from the natural attitude as they reclined to look at some momentary attraction; and we can well image to ourselves how, as the Master spoke the words of blessing, their attention would be roused and riveted. They would gaze, not all three towards Emmaus as on their journey, but now the two, with rapt attention, on His face, on His features, familiar though transformed. And thus, when they looked steadily on His glorious countenance, the recognition would grow upon them, as it had done in the case of Mary Magdalene when she fixed her attention on Him who called her by the familiar appellation, "Mary." So was Jesus known of them in the breaking of bread.

Upon the Master and His disciples being thus brought face to face and eye to eye, the recognition followed; and, so far as this precedent is applicable to the uses of a modern Church assembly, it would seem to favour the practice of the clergyman officiating with his face towards the congregation.

It may be urged, however, that the salient point at Emmaus was that both the disciples looked towards their divine Lord in this breaking of bread; and that, similarly, in our Church assemblies, all the disciples, alike those who minister, and those who are ministered to, should look in one direction, towards their Saviour. Let this be granted, and what then? Christ the Lord is in heaven, at God's right hand: and though some may urge that heaven is (in spite of the antipodes) above, beyond the clouds, in the circumambient

---

[1] ἐν τῷ κατακλιθῆναι αὐτὸν μετ' αὐτῶν.

ether, always "above," always "on high;" and though
others may urge that heaven is no locality at all—without
entering into that dispute, it is, we hold, impossible, unless
we go back upon the remnants of some antique worship of
the sun, to show any substantial reason why all men, all over
the world, should look for our blessed Lord in the east, rather
than in the west, or south, or north. By all means let us
look towards Christ with mind and heart, and in whatever way
we can.   But let us not deceive ourselves with the idea that
He is exclusively in Jerusalem, or on Mount Gerizim, or in
any quarter of the horizon.

(b.) *An "Objective" Presence at Emmaus, and its Bearing on
our Inquiry.*

One other point is brought before us by the scene at
Emmaus; and that is, the bodily and objective presence of
our Saviour in that breaking of bread.

True, whether the repast at Emmaus is regarded as a
domestic meal or as a Church ordinance, or whether, as seems
to us the more obvious the more fully we study the entire
scene, it be a happy blending of Church communion with
ordinary family life—on either hypothesis there was, on the
occasion of that breaking of bread, an unquestionable *objective*
presence of the Lord. But then observe, that objective
presence of Christ was manifest to the sight of the disciples,
was ascertained by their sense of hearing as they listened
to His words; and though for once He checked the touch of
Mary when (John xx. 17), in her amazement and delight, she
was too prone to cling still to His bodily presence, yet at
Emmaus, as subsequently in dealing with Thomas at Jerusalem, there is no room for doubt that our Saviour was
palpable to the touch of His disciples.

This is legitimate evidence of objective or corporeal presence. Here is bread present and broken, and given and
received in its objectivity, palpable to the touch, familiar to
the taste, obvious to the eye, distinct upon the table from all
other objects that lie around—distinct and different as the
inanimate from the animate, the merely material from the

divine,—so distinct and so different is that bread that was broken at Emmaus from the blessed Jesus who broke it, and who was there palpably, audibly, visibly present' in His corporeal and objective reality.

Let those who tell us Christ is *objectively* present with the bread on their Communion Tables, give to us the same proofs of objective presence as were manifested to the disciples on that occasion, and they will convince all sane persons that the Lord is corporeally present, and is also corporeally and objectively separate and distinct from the bread which is broken.

In that breaking of bread with the two disciples, Christ was indeed objectively present, but He was there, not by transubstantiation or insubstantiation with the bread, but by juxtaposition.

In quitting the consideration of this interesting episode, we would only further draw attention to the fact that Christ's objective presence with the disciples began, not in the breaking of bread, but in the course of their walk, and while (Luke xxiv. 14, 15) they talked and reasoned together of all those things which had happened to their Master in Jerusalem. If, in the more steady and prolonged gaze as they reclined with Jesus on their couches, His features, even through their new glory, were recognised and became again known, by Cleopas and his companion, it was on the road, while their tongues and thoughts were busy with the things of Jesus, that He came and joined them. And when, after the meal, He had (Luke xxiv. 31) vanished out of their sight, the chief impression left upon their thoughts finds utterance in the words, " Did not our heart burn within us, *while He talked with us by the way, and while He opened to us the Scriptures ?* "

Truly the history connected with Emmaus makes for a distinguishing between the body of Christ and the broken bread ; and it attaches more importance to the burning words of Christ than to any rite, however holy, or any participation of bread, even though it be blessed by His distinct bodily presence.

§ 3. (a.) *"Breaking Bread"* at *Jerusalem*.

But we must now proceed to the next point in the history of the apostles' usage in celebrating the Lord's Supper. The days of transition between the resurrection and the ascension are past. The Pentecostal effusion of the Holy Spirit has been witnessed. St. Peter has given his explanation of that wondrous event. As a skilful fisher of men, he has drawn into the Gospel net "about three thousand souls" (Acts ii. 41); and, moreover (Acts ii. 47), it was a period of joy and prosperity with the infant Church. Not only did the Lord add to the Church, the assembly or *ecclesia*, day by day, them that were in the way of salvation ; not only was the Church occupied in praising God; but, for a longer or a shorter time, the believers even had favour with all the people. The horrid cries, "Crucify him! crucify him!" were past. The persecution of Peter and John and the murder of Stephen were not yet. In the mean while there were halcyon days such as, but for the sins and follies of believers, and but for the outbreaks of unbelieving madness, should oftener prevail. The Church was serving God in righteousness and peace and joy in the Holy Ghost, and accordingly (Rom. xiv. 18) she was not only acceptable to God, but was also "approved of men."

It is of these peaceful days that we are presented with a picture in the closing verses of the second chapter of the Book of the Acts of the Apostles. With most of the points in that picture we are at present only so far concerned as they help to give distinctness and colour to one particular part of that early and apostolic life. What a picture it is, however! The first feature delineated by the historian is that those growing thousands of the primitive Church " continued steadfastly in the apostles' doctrine," [1] in the teaching, that is, of the apostles —not only in the acceptance of some one or other peculiar dogma of the apostles, but in the general instruction of those men who had been most intimately associated with the Saviour, and were now His chief pastors and representatives.

The time might come when some of these very apostles,

---

[1] τῇ διδαχῇ τῶν ἀποστόλων.

pre-eminently St. Peter (Gal. ii. 11, etc.), would depart from
the simplicity of the Gospel, and require to be "withstood to
the face" by those who, like St. Paul, had also seen the Lord
and were jealous for the truth that was in Jesus, and for the
freedom wherewith Christ had made men free. But that time
was not yet arrived. At present Peter and his colleagues
were fresh from companionship with the Blessed One. The
Holy Spirit was bringing all things to their remembrance.
Many a saying of the Lord, that passed unnoticed when He
spoke it, was making itself to be perceived in the strange
treasury of recollection. Misunderstood when first heard
amid Jewish expectations of temporal pomp and power, many
a spiritual promise and hope and aspiration now showed itself
to the apostles' minds in fresh glory and impressiveness.

Was it not through suffering and toil, through watchfulness and anxiety, that Noah, and Abraham, and Joseph, and
Moses, and Joshua had served God and ministered to man?
Was it not through peril and persecution, not seldom through
death itself, that Samuel, and Elijah, and Elisha, and David,
and Isaiah, and Jeremiah, and Daniel, and the other servants
of God had wrought righteousness, and out of weakness had
been made strong? If it had been so with these typical men,
must not their divine antitype, in like manner and still more,
be perfected through suffering? Was not this foreshadowed
in every rite and sacrifice of the Mosaic system? Was not
this plainly portrayed as awaiting the great Servant of God,
the Man of Sorrows (Isaiah liii. 3), who bore our griefs, and
with whose stripes we are healed?

Burning words on these topics Jesus had spoken after His
resurrection, and before it (Matt. xx. 18, 19); and these
heart-pricking words were being brought freshly back to the
apostles' memories. Here was teaching about the woes and
agonies of the Lamb of God, about His taking away the sin
of the world, about His precious blood-shedding, about our
need to be washed in that blood, to enter into those sufferings,
if we would have a share in His glory. Here was teaching
with which the apostles were being filled by the Holy Spirit,
and with which they were replenishing the minds of the

believers. Here was the first noticeable characteristic of the
primitive Church, continuing steadfastly in the apostles' doctrine, laying strong and persistent hold of the apostles'
teaching.

The second point in this historical picture is that the first
Christians adhered with similar persistency to that fellowship
or communion[1] which Jesus and His apostles taught and
exemplified.   No Christian   suffered   without   his fellow-
Christians suffering with him; no Christian rejoiced without
the brethren rejoicing with him.   Nor was it the sympathy of
the heart alone; nor was it with words of kindness only,
however sweet those words, that this sympathy, this fellowship or communion, was shown.   Christ's communion had
consisted in His giving and suffering all that could be given
and suffered for man; and His disciples' communion was of a
like sort.   It is true, to any who would not work, it said
(2 Thess. iii. 10), Neither shall he eat; but, amongst those
who were willing to work, its practice was to distribute to all,
as every man had need.   No man (Acts iv. 32) said that aught
of the things which he possessed was his own, but they had
all things in common; and, so far as it was requisite and as
the owners chose (Acts v. 4), they sold their possessions and
goods (Acts ii. 45), and parted them to all men, *as every man
had need.*   Such and so thorough was the communion of
saints, or of believers, in the spring-time of apostolic days.

The next prominent point in the historic delineation is
that the first Christians adhered with the same persistency to
"the breaking of bread" as they did to the communion or
fellowship, and to the teaching or instruction of the apostles.
This point, as it recurs presently in the history with additional
features, and as it touches the chief interest of this our inquiry, we pass by for the moment.

The fourth trait in the picture of apostolic Christianity is
the steadfast continuance in "the prayers," alike of the assembly, where a few families or individuals might be gathered
together, and of the closet (Matt. vi. 6), where the believer
prayed in secret to his Father, and of the Temple, where it

[1] κοινωνία.

appears (Acts ii. 46) they were still wont to join in some portions of the Judaic service; unless, indeed, this resort to the Temple was for Christian prayer in some of the precincts or courts of that great edifice. However that may be, these Jewish disciples of our Saviour "continued daily with one accord in the Temple," and that is made a special feature in the picture of their early history. It was far from being offensive to their Jewish fellow-citizens. It must, therefore, have commended itself to the unbelieving Jews as a reverent and religious employment of the Temple. It marks a willingness in the first disciples to worship with those who were far from being in entire harmony of religious thought with them. It shows that even from the unbelieving Jews Christ's first followers were far from hastening to rend and sever themselves.

This abstinence from the schismatic temper and practice is quite noticeable in the primitive Church, and beautifully does it combine with their persistence in all Christian devotion and prayers to show us their piety. "In everything," doubtless, as afterwards taught the great apostle of the Gentiles, "by prayer and supplication, with thanksgiving," they made known their requests unto God (Phil. iv. 6); and this, again, was a marked feature in their Church. They persistently adhered to all opportunities for prayer. They daily frequented the courts of the Temple.

Yet another characteristic marked that early Church. "Many wonders and signs" (Acts ii. 43) "were done by the apostles;" and such was the effect of these deeds, that admiration, reverence, even "fear, came upon every soul." Whether this fear was chiefly among the believers or the unbelievers, we are not told at this point; but, doubtless, its general course would be, to begin with the awakening of attention, even among unbelievers, to the great power of Christ, and then to melt, among believers, into love and trust as more was known of the divine goodness and mercy. This fear, this reverential awe, was a conspicuous feature in that age of the Church's history.

And now the course of St. Luke's description brings us back once more to that which he had before enumerated as

the third characteristic of the primitive Christians.   After
mentioning the daily resort to the Temple, the historian adds
that they also, in all appearance *daily* too, broke bread at
home,[1] "from house to house," and "did eat[2] [partook or
ate *together*] their meat[3] [food] with gladness and singleness
of heart."

It will, we think, be perfectly clear to the reader that this
"breaking of bread," which is twice insisted upon by St.
Luke in his delineation of apostolic religion, must have had
some special importance attached to it.   Unless it constituted
a distinctive part of that religion, the "breaking of bread"
would scarcely be twice emphatically mentioned in connection
with the apostolic instruction, the fellowship, the prayers, the
reverential awe, the miracles, the daily gatherings in the
Temple, the praise of God, and the popular esteem of the first
believers.   Obviously, this "breaking of bread" was part,
and no unimportant part, of apostolic religion.

And if we look back over a period of some five or six weeks
only in the history of that early Church and its Saviour, it
will not be hard to find the meaning of this mention of the
breaking of bread in the midst of the solemn and characteristic acts of the first believers.

We have already seen how likely it was that the two
disciples, on their return to Jerusalem from Emmaus, made
conscious reference to the then recent institution of the Lord's
Supper, when they narrated to the apostles what things were
done in the way (Luke xxiv. 35), and how Jesus was known of
them *in the breaking of bread*.   But, morally certain as we
regard the reference to the Lord's Supper in these words of
Cleopas and his companion, it is surely beyond all question
that, even if the disciples had not been acquainted with the
institution of the Lord's Supper up to the time of their
making that announcement to the apostles, that very announcement, connecting their recognition of Christ with the
breaking of bread, must have called forth from the apostles
an explanation of their Master's command, " This do, as oft
as ye drink, for My remembrance;" and this explanation and

---

[1] κατ' οἶκον.   [2] μετελάμβανον.   [3] τροφῆς.

this injunction would naturally and necessarily be spread at once among the hundred and twenty of Acts i. 15, and among the three thousand of Acts ii. 41, as well as among the other new converts of Acts ii. 47. So obviously is this " breaking of bread," mentioned by St. Luke as one of the religious characteristics of the infant Church, to be identified with that commemorative breaking of bread and drinking of wine, whose institution by the Saviour has been our study in the preceding pages.

If, indeed, the certainty of this identification needed or admitted further confirmation, it might be made doubly sure by the manner in which, as we shall in due course be led to observe, the phrase " to break bread " had become, for the writer of the Acts and for the Apostle Paul, an accustomed designation for the communion of the Lord's Supper. We almost owe an apology to the reader for any elaboration of the proof of this identity, but its importance will, it is hoped, hold us excused. And now we proceed to notice the lessons concerning the Lord's Supper derivable from this mention of it in St. Luke's history of the apostles.

The first point that strikes one in this connection is the manner in which the believers' breaking of bread *at home*, or *from house to house*, is contrasted with their resorting to the Temple, and at the same time is associated with their partaking, together with it, of their other food or nourishment. In the Temple, for whatever purpose the Christians went there, they might be assembled in their hundreds or in their thousands " with one accord "[1] (Acts ii. 46) ; but, in any one of their homes, there is nothing to make it probable that more than a few scores at the most, out of the three thousand and upwards, could meet together for such an act as the breaking of bread.

It is true, indeed, that, in some sense, we are told (ver. 44) that " all that believed were *together*,[2] and had all things common ; " and this statement is made just after "three thousand souls " have been named as the number of those already added to the Church in Jerusalem. Some

---

[1] ὁμοθυμαδόν.   [2] ἐπὶ τὸ αὐτό.

interpreters regard the phrase "together" as signifying cordial and affectionate agreement amongst the believers, and not as implying residence or assembly in one place. Other interpreters, pressed by the difficulty of such a multitude being "continually assembled together," minimize it by explaining that, the feast being over, a large portion of the three thousand would by this time have returned to their homes, away from Jerusalem!

Whether the phrase "together" is to be understood of locality or of agreement, it is quite clear that though in the court of a house, or in the street adjacent, three thousand people might assemble to listen to an apostle's discourse, such a vast assembly could not be "continually together," and still less was likely to be accommodated and supplied with bread and wine daily in any one private house in Jerusalem. Yet this primitive "breaking of bread" was conducted in their houses, *at home*. Did two or three families meet daily in one house? And was another private house the meeting-place for several other families? And, so, in a hundred or a hundred and fifty private houses, was the daily "breaking of bread" among the three thousand carried on? Shall we say that only one-third of the whole number were adults, and came to the breaking of bread? There is no ground for such an assertion as a fact; but if, for the argument's sake, it were supposed, there would still be a thousand to "break bread" in, probably, not less than forty homes.

At a later period of the history (Acts xx. 7), it appears that the believers at Troas were wont to meet for the breaking of bread on the "first day of the week." Possibly, they did not also come together for that purpose at Troas, at the date of St. Paul's visit, on the other six days of the week. Shall we suppose that lesser family breakings of bread took place *daily*, but that the gathering themselves together for all the believers in Troas, or for several families in Jerusalem, to break bread in common, was a *weekly* custom? That may be so. But it is impossible to believe that, in any private room belonging to the first Christians in Jerusalem, there were daily or even weekly assemblies of the whole three thousand, or even of the one thousand who *may* have been the entire number of the adults.

Thus, then, by the contrast between the use of the Temple for some purposes and the employment of their private houses for the "breaking of bread"—by these considerations, coupled with all the probabilities that can lead us to a judgment concerning the accommodation likely to be provided by the homes of the first disciples in Jerusalem, we are led to infer that the daily breaking of bread, mentioned in Acts ii. 42, 46, must have been conducted in numerous private houses, and in such manners and ways as would not unduly engage the time, or interfere with the industrial occupations, of a body of believers who, for the most part, belonged to the poorer sections of the community. Does it not thus appear most probable that if, on each first day of the week, each resurrection-day, there may already have been *weekly* groupings of several families to "break bread," the *daily* practice most likely was for each family to "break bread" at its own house? This probability is greatly enhanced when we consider that the "breaking of bread," as a religious ordinance, was closely connected with partaking of their other food together with it.[1] They partook of food, literally *nourishment*, the ordinary meal, together with the broken bread.

Nothing, we take it, can be clearer than the connection, in this history, of the Lord's Supper, the breaking of bread, with the ordinary meals of the first believers in their homes. Such meals and such Lord's Suppers may have been partaken daily by several families in common; but, we confess, to us it seems much more probable they were the practice of each family, ordinarily, by itself in private, however occasionally the family circle may have been enlarged by the presence and participation of friendly individuals or families.

(b.) An Appeal to "Antiquity."

One thing is indubitable—this combination of the Lord's Supper with a domestic meal (known afterwards as the *agape*, or love-feast) could have been no vast aggregate assembling of

---

[1] μετελάμβανον τροφῆς.

the three thousand and upwards. Whether consisting of one
or more families, each of these parties was gathered at a
house, in private, in close resemblance to the original institution by Christ, and only in more remote analogy with the
Lord's Supper, without an ordinary meal, as practised in the
public Christian buildings of later ages. "As they were
eating, Jesus took bread, and blessed, and brake, and gave to
the disciples" (Matt. xxvi. 26). Thus was the breaking of
bread, then, combined with the feast of that sacred party;
and just in the same manner did the early Christians, as we
have seen, combine the common meal with the breaking of
bread in remembrance of the Lord.

The quietness, the absence of pomp and ritual, of form
and ceremony, in this apostolic usage, can hardly fail to
strike attentive and thoughtful students of the best and
purest Christian antiquity, at a time when, as in the present
day, there is a vigorous attempt on foot to add so much of
pomp, and rite, and ornament to the decorous comeliness of
the Reformed Church in England; and this teaching of the
earliest Christian antiquity, speaking through the pages of
the New Testament, should be all the more striking and impressive, inasmuch as the modern upholders of postures, and
vestments, and genuflexions appeal to *antiquity* for the justi-
fying of their strange practices. Antiquity! To what antiquity should the appeal be made? To that of the Middle
Ages, and to that of post-apostolic times? or to the very
actions and customs of the apostles and of the Lord Himself? This is a case, we take it, in which, to any mind of
moderate wisdom and piety, the question asked involves the
certain answer. Better, surely, to follow the precedent and
example of Christ Himself, and of His apostles, than that
of any subsequent teacher.

(c.) *The " Gladness," etc., of the Early Christian " Breaking of
Bread."*

Before we quit this part of our subject, it is most necessary
to observe the frame of mind in which these primitive Christians, just illumined by the Holy Spirit, fresh from intercourse

with our Saviour, undisturbed for the time by persecution and difficulties, partook of the broken bread and of their other food with it.

Instead of any feeling of terror, instead of regarding the sacred Supper as a " terrible sacrifice," instead of approaching it with pallid lips, and half inanimate from fasting—instead of all this, perfect love had cast out the fear in which piety had its beginning (1 John iv. 18), and those earliest followers of the Lord partook of the broken bread and of their other food " with gladness and singleness of heart " (Acts ii. 46).

It would be difficult, if not impossible, to find a word expressive of more exuberant joy than the Greek noun here translated " gladness." [1] Its English equivalent is given, in Liddell and Scott's Lexicon, as " exceeding great joy." In St. Luke's Gospel (i. 14, 44), this same word is used to describe the delight of parents over the best and most blessed of children. In the Epistle to the Hebrews (i. 9), it portrays the divine joy given to the Messiah, " the oil of *gladness* above " His fellows ; and, once more (Jude 24), the same term describes the " exceeding joy " of the Redeemer in His people, when He presents them faultless before the presence of the Father's glory.

Surely, in this word which depicts the gladness, the joy in the Holy Ghost (Rom. xiv. 17), the religious cheerfulness of genuine Christianity, there is something which should sweeten the sour looks of the sullen Puritan on the one hand, and correct the ascetic self-torture of the mediævalist on the other hand. Even at the board where he broke bread in memory of his Saviour, and as a sacred means of grace, the temper and appearance of the believer who had seen Christ, who lived nearest to Christ, were marked by the gladness of exceeding great joy.

Not far removed from this " gladness " was the other characteristic of the primitive believers, " singleness of heart." The " singleness " of this description [2] is a word derived from a piece of ground which is void of stones,

---

[1] ἀγαλλίασις.

[2] ἀφελότης, compounded of ἀ, *not*, and φελλεύς, *a stone*.

smooth, without a roughness to obstruct him that runs. From this root-idea of the word when applied to *places*, it came to signify, when applied to *persons*, plain, simple, unsophisticated; and when applied to *language*, its meaning was simple, not intricate or involved. From these usages of the word and its kindred terms, it is not difficult to perceive what is its meaning in connection with the heart of man. Such "singleness of heart" implies that there was in these early Christians the sincerity that was void of anything which could make a brother to stumble and fall; the smoothness of genuine amiability that, without guile or hypocrisy, would fain make things easy and pleasant with its neighbours; the singleness and simplicity which, amidst many joys and many sorrows, many labours and many distractions, yet had its note of harmony, its bond of union and consistency in utter and absorbing devotion to the once crucified but now risen and ascended Lord.

Whatever forces might at any time be acting from without on these Christian hearts, you might count on this one thing, namely, that within them the loving, self-sacrificing, glorified Christ would be the prevailing force, the one control, the ruling inspiration. Truly, it was no wonder that such "singleness of heart," such absence of all double-mindedness and of all offensiveness, such concentration of thought and energy upon the things which were useful, kind, and of good report, should, through these few halcyon days, win for the first believers "favour with all the people."

And thus we have the picture, set before us in its completeness, of the first recorded apostolic celebration of the Lord's Supper.

Noteworthy are the omissions in this delineation, as compared with the administrations of some later times. Mark, here, in the apostolic age, in the quiet days of the very Church of the apostles, there is no trace of an altar, no sign of a sacrificing priest, no note of peculiar vestment or posture or ceremony of any kind. Doubtless all things were, as they should be, done "decently and in order;" doubtless, too, with a wisely pliant adaptation to the varying circumstances, op-

[Book I.

70   SCRIPTURE TEACHING   [Book I.

portunities, and abilities of the different families or groups of families, who, "breaking bread from house to house" (or at home), "did eat their meat with gladness and singleness of heart." There is no record, nor any room for a surmise, that an apostle was present at each of these numerous breakings of bread. The obvious inference, on the contrary, is that these meals, accompanied by a celebration of the Lord's Supper, were presided over, in the vast majority of cases, by the natural and therefore divinely appointed head of the house, its parent or elder—that is, in Greek, its *presbyter*.

Except the bread, there was only the wine in all cases implied in obedience to Christ's institution; and, besides this, there was the blessing or thanksgiving, Christianized, indeed, among believers, but otherwise common to Christians and all pious Jews. These sacred things, in their private homes, presided over, in the ordinary absence of apostles, by the natural heads of families, and all conjoined and associated with the family meal, but hallowed and refined by the memory of Christ and His sufferings and His triumph—these, as parts of a life whose atmosphere was apostolic teaching, and fellow-helpfulness, and prayers, and signs and wonders, and the loving, reverential fear of not being thorough and in earnest with God and with Christ—these, with Temple worship, and the habitual praising of God, and with a pervading temper of gladness and singleness of heart,—these were the essentials of the Lord's Supper, so far as we have yet been able to learn them from the institution by Christ Himself, and from the history of the earliest administrations. The general life with Christ was all-important; "the trivial round, the common task," sufficed as the occasion to break bread; the sole essentials apparently required for the Lord's Supper were the believer's pious disposition and religious life, and the partaking, as memorials of Christ, bread and wine after blessing and thanksgiving by the head of the family.

§ 4. *St. Paul on the Lord's Supper.*

But from this general description of the pristine habit of

" breaking bread," let us proceed to notice the more definite teaching of St. Paul on this important subject.

In this connection there are two passages, especially, to be studied ; one in the tenth chapter of the first Epistle to the Corinthians, the other in the eleventh chapter of the same Epistle. The two passages, though so near to one another, yet spring out of quite different trains of thought and reasoning in the apostle's mind, and in his dealing with the religious life of his correspondents ; and they may well be expected, therefore, to show us the mind of St. Paul in different and yet mutually illustrating views of the Lord's Supper. In the earlier passage, this holy feast of the Christian is regarded in juxtaposition with the banquets of the unbelieving and idolatrous heathen. In the latter passage, the Lord's Supper, quite apart from unbelievers and their practices, is regarded in two lights—its proper use, and the corruptions of that use which had already crept into the Corinthian Church.

(a.) 1 Cor. x. 16, 17, etc.

Let us examine the first passage, in which St. Paul mentions the Lord's Supper in contrast with idolatrous feasts.

In a mixed and busy population like that of Corinth, where heathen people, and Jews, and converts to Christ from both Judaism and heathenism, were all living near one another, and cultivating one another's society and intimacy for the purposes of that commercial buying and selling which brought them to the city of the two seas, east and west of the Mediterranean, and of the two lands, north and south of Greece, it will readily be understood how great would be the inclination in men's minds to break down all the barriers of caste ; to make friends, for the widest possible spreading of *connection*, by obliterating the party walls of national custom or religious practice.

To the utmost limit of what conscience would permit, and the requirements of national caste would tolerate, the man of the east would in all things cultivate the exchange of intimacy and friendship with the man of the west, and he from the south with him who came from the north.

What Alexandria taught, in her eclectic wealth of speculation, would become intermingled with the stream of Grecian lore and Grecian elegance and subtlety. What the Gaul, or the Spaniard, or the colonist from Southern Italy, or from Sicily or Cyrene, was groping after and blundering over in the dark, was interchanged and became commingled with what the dark and superstitious traffickers from the Phœnician mother-land, or from Crete, or from the remnants of the old Carthaginian stock, could offer as their contribution to this strange intellectual, moral, and religious compound.

Amidst the concessions and soft compliances of these multitudinous thinkers and worshippers, what should the Christians do? Stand stolidly aloof, keep themselves separate, would be the ready answer of the common herd of minds. But St. Paul, with true Christian insight, could see there was more involved in the question than showed itself to the shallow and the superficial. As those merchants desired intimacy in their concessions, with a view to commercial barter and pecuniary gain, so the apostle sought for the widest range of intimacy, even by becoming all things to all men, that he might save some and edify as many as possible.

The question " concerning the eating of those things that are offered in sacrifice unto idols " (1 Cor. viii. 4) had been touched in the eighth chapter of the first Epistle to the Corinthians, and it was then left with two lines of reflection on it : " We [Christians endowed with any strength of mind] know that an idol is nothing in the world;" it has no reality of the divine or spiritual about it; it is a *simulacrum* and a sham; "there is none other God but one." For us, therefore, so far as we ourselves are concerned, other men's inanities and dreams about an idol having power to contaminate sacrifices do not touch us. We may and can harmlessly thank God for food prepared in an idol's temple, and we may and can eat it with an undisturbed conscience.

So stands the case for ourselves; but when the possible effect of such action on the less strong-minded believer is

contemplated, then love for Christ and for the souls He died
to save leads us to pause and stand aloof from meat which,
harmless to us, might raise scruples in their minds, and,
those scruples being roughly set aside in compliance with
our example, their consciences would be blunted; they would
learn to do those things of whose propriety they had doubts;
and so "this liberty of" ours might "become a stumbling-
block to them that are weak."

With these two reflections, and with the glorious resolve,
"If meat make my brother to offend, I will eat no flesh while
the world standeth, lest I make my brother to offend," the
question is left for a time. Then, after a while, the subject is
resumed by St. Paul, in view of so many Israelites having
been overthrown in the wilderness by unbelief and idolatry and
other sins. These things were written, says the apostle, for
our admonition. "Let him that thinketh he standeth take
heed lest he fall." "Wherefore (1 Cor. x. 14, 15), my dearly
beloved, flee from idolatry. I speak as to wise men; judge ye
what I say."

Look, reasons St. Paul, at this subject of participation in
meat connected with idol-sacrifices in the light of our own
breaking of bread. "The cup of blessing which we bless, is
it not a communion [1] of the blood of Christ?" Is it not a
fellowship in the new covenant sealed by the blood of Christ? [2]
"The bread which we break, is it not a communion of the
body of Christ?" Is it not a fellowship and participation in
the new covenant ratified by the body of Christ slain upon the
cross? "For we, the many [3] [the multitude of believers], are
one bread, one body: for the whole of us [4] partake of [5] [out of]
the one bread." Here is the *rationale* of our communion or
fellowship.

Though we are a multitude of separate individuals, yet,
by participation in that one bread of the covenant which
symbolizes Him who is the bread of life, we become incorporated into a fellowship or communion one with another.

---

[1] κοινωνία, without the definite article.
[2] *Vide* 1 Cor. xi. 25, and pp. 39—47 of this essay.
[3] οἱ πολλοί.   [4] οἱ γὰρ πάντες.   [5] ἐκ.

There is a fellowship in the religious commemoration; there is a fellowship of believers among themselves; there is a fellowship of each and all with the Lord. The very aim and object of our Lord's Supper is this pervading idea of fellowship and incorporation of us with one another, and of all with Christ, by means of participation in the one bread. But, is St. Paul's line of thought, before I draw the legitimate conclusion from this view of the matter, "Behold Israel after the flesh;" consider the case of the unbelieving Jews, who still practise the sacrifices of the Mosaic law (1 Cor. x. 18). "Are not they which eat the sacrifices partakers of the altar?" Do not those who eat the Jewish sacrifices enter, by the very act, into a fellowship and communion with the Jewish altar, and its worshippers, and its priests, and its God?

What am I saying then? asks the apostle. Am I forgetting that I before said idols were "nothing," and had no real connection with God or Spirit? Nay (1 Cor. x. 20), I do not forget or contravene what I then said. Idols and their sacrifices have no objective reality at all beyond that of their constituent wood or stone or flesh, but the dream of man gives them a subjective connection with evil, so that, repeating and insisting, as I do, that idols have no *objective* reality, except as stocks and stones, yet I say that, *subjectively*, "the things which the Gentiles sacrifice, they sacrifice [in their thoughts and intentions] to demons and not to God."

And, while it stands true that like as there is, in the minds of believers, communion with Christ and with our fellow-believers in the breaking of bread; while it stands true that like as there is, subjectively, in the minds of Jews, communion with Jehovah in the sacrifices of the Jewish altar; similarly there is the possibility and danger of communion with mischief even in men's subjective imaginings of idols having demoniac reality, "I would not that ye should have [even this semblance of] fellowship with demons" (1 Cor. x. 20).

Indeed, there is an utter incompatibility between the Lord and idols which some may identify with demons, so that the moment one's own scruples, or the reminder of a neighbour, bring the mental association of idols and demons into one's memory, it is impossible (1 Cor. x. 21) to "drink the cup of the Lord and the cup of demons; ye cannot be partakers of the Lord's Table and of the table of demons." Then the apostle repeats his assertion of liberty for the strong-minded believer to go, if he be inclined, to an idolatrous friend's banquet, and eat, without question, of whatever may be provided, whether slain in the idol's temple or not; and this is accompanied by a warning to desist from such strong-minded exercise of freedom, if any weak-minded companion draw attention to the conceivable association of the meat with idolatry.

Such, in brief, is the connection and train of thought in which St. Paul makes this, his earliest, reference to the Lord's Supper; and now let us examine the passage and seek for the instruction it can give us concerning the celebration and use of the Christian breaking of bread.

In the forefront of the scene is mentioned "the cup of blessing which we bless," and presently afterwards is named the inconsistency of believers drinking of that "Lord's cup" and of the cup of demons. Obviously, as the command at the institution was, "Drink of this, all of you;" so now, although the familiar designation of the partaking was "breaking bread," without any specific mention of the wine, yet those who administered blessed the cup, and the recipients drank of it, just as frequently as they broke the bread and ate it.

Blessing the cup and breaking the bread, eating the latter and drinking of the former, were conjoint and associated acts, inseparable one from the other, in the original command of our Saviour, and seen in St. Paul's allusions to be similarly inseparable in apostolic practice. Though " *breaking* bread," and not *blessing* bread or *eating* bread, or drinking wine, had been accepted as an almost technical designation for the Lord's Supper, yet St. Paul and the Evangelists make it quite clear that there was no communicating in one kind only, no withholding of the cup from any section of the believers in those primitive and apostolic times.

Another interesting point which is conspicuous (1 Cor. x. 21), is the mention of the Lord's "*Table*," where the ideas of certain schools of thought would lead us to expect the mention of an *altar*. The Jewish "altar" (ver. 18) is named, and, assuredly, if the apostle had known anything of an altar in connection with the Lord's Supper, he must, in all accuracy, have named or alluded to it here; but no, he mentions the altar of the Mosaic ritual: but it is a "table,"[1] not an altar, with which he associates the Christian communion.

This, of course, we say with a full remembrance that, in a figurative sense, a Christian "altar" is named in the Epistle to the Hebrews (xiii. 10—16); but that "altar" was one "outside the gate," "outside the camp," on which Jesus suffered and, by His own blood, sanctified the people. On what "altar," outside the gate and enclosure[2] of Jerusalem, did Jesus so suffer except upon the cross? Our Christian "altar," in this only[3] mention of it in the New Testament, is thus clearly seen to be the cross; and upon that altar or

---

[1] This argument seems to us to lose none of its force from the fact that in three passages of the Old Testament (Ezek. xli. 22; Mal. i. 7, 12), the word "table" is employed as a designation for the Jewish altar. If St. Paul had adopted that phrase and spoken of the Jewish table, the case would have been different. As it is, he writes about the Jewish *altar* and contrasts with it the Lord's *Table*; and the force of the contrast is very striking.

[2] παρεμβολή.

[3] An attempt is sometimes made to construct a theory of fitness or necessity for a Christian altar upon earth, other than the cross of Jesus, by reason of "the golden altar that was before the throne" in the heaven of the Apocalypse (*vide* Rev. vi. 9, viii. 3, 5, ix. 13, xi. 1, xiv. 18, xvi. 7). It should be remembered, however, that this altar was in front of the throne upon which the Lamb sat. Christ, the Lamb, was on the throne, at God's right hand. He was not represented as being in any sense at or upon that golden altar. Upon that altar not Christ, nor any memorial of Christ, is offered, but (Rev. viii. 3) the prayers of saints or Christians and much incense; and he who offers at that altar is not Christ, but an "angel." Throughout these passages of the Apocalypse it is deeply interesting to observe how consistently the idea is maintained that, although Christ ever retains the dignity of our Priest and High-Priest, yet He is not now engaged in the priestly work of making or offering a sacrifice; but, that work having been once for all perfected and finished on the cross, He reigns a King at God's right hand, and procures (ἐντυγχάνει) for men all good things according to the will of God (κατὰ Θεόν, Rom. viii. 27).

It is worth adding, for those who are capable of drawing inferences from the Apocalypse, that in the perfected ideal of the new Jerusalem (Rev. xxi. 22)

cross the sacrifices we are urged to offer are, not bread and wine, or a repetition or commemoration of Christ's death— not these, but (ver. 13) the "bearing His reproach," and (ver. 15) "the sacrifice of praise continually to God," that is, the fruit of our lips as we confess to His name[1]—these sacrifices of patience, fidelity, and praise, together with (ver. 16) the remembrance " to do good and to communicate"[2]— these sacrifices, offered upon the altar of Christ's cross, are those with which God is well pleased. But, in connection with the "breaking of bread," Scripture knows of no "altar," nor of any " sacrifice."

In connection with the breaking of bread, St. Paul pointedly avoids the word "altar," though it was forced upon his attention and pressed into his employment by his argument from the sacrifices and the altar of Israel after the flesh ; and he as pointedly uses the word " table," "the Lord's Table." Here then, we see, in the apostle's language, not only an absence of sacerdotal and sacrificial terms and thoughts in connection with the Christian breaking of bread, but a pointed and remarkable avoidance of any such term or thought. He, as it were, turns aside and goes out of his way from altars, as a Jewish shadow, that he may attach himself to the Table and communion and fellowship of his beloved Lord. And when another New Testament writer speaks to Hebrew believers of a Christian altar and the sacrifices of Christians, that writer makes it quite plain to every moderately careful reader that, in his figurative language, the " altar " is the cross of Christ, not the Lord's Table ; and the sacrifices

there was "no temple," and, by consequence, no altar ; "for the Lord God Almighty and the Lamb are the temple of it."

In other words, with God and the Lamb present by the Spirit in our spirits, there is in us no room, nor occasion, nor necessity for any material temple or material altar.

It must, surely, be all but needless to remind the reader that the altar named in Matt. v. 24, and some few other passages of the New Testament, is the Jewish altar in the Temple at Jerusalem, and is no more a direct example or obligation for us Christians to have altars in our churches, than is circumcision, or any other rite of that Judaism which has perished and " vanished away" (Heb. viii. 13), an example which it is our duty to copy.

[1] ὁμολογούντων τῷ ὀνόματι αὐτοῦ.

[2] κοινωνίας, fellowship, helpfulness.

are, not bread and wine, but patience, fidelity, praise, well-doing, and fellow-helpfulness.

And now let us look at another aspect of truth presented to us by St. Paul in the passage under consideration (1 Cor. x. 17). The "bread," throughout the Supper, is here spoken of as "bread." No change is hinted at as taking place in its substance or objective character; or, if there be any change of substance, if there be any transubstantiation, observe what is its nature. The statement is, not bread is changed into and becomes Christ, but we, the Christian multitude, the *hoi polloi* of Christendom, "are one bread, one body." It is *we*, believers of every age, clime, colour and sex, *we* are the one bread ; *we* are the one body : and the divinely appointed sign of this, by Christ's grace its instrument, is that *we all* partake of "the one bread." We, by the eating of the bread in remembrance of Christ and in obedience to His command, are one body. If there were any *objective* transformation here implied, it would be of us all into bread and into a body of some kind. Such an objective change of Christian men into bread, or into any living unit which can, without metaphor, be called a body, is contradicted by every special sense and by every other test to which such a question can be subjected.

But this union of us all into one body, the *figurative* body of Christ (1 Cor. xii. 27), in which we are all members in particular, is just the very drift and point of St. Paul's argument. At one time he teaches that, by the Spirit, we are all baptized into this one body (1 Cor. xii. 13). At another time, he teaches that it is in eating the bread we are one body. If, then, any reader wishes to press this language beyond the realm of figure into the literal and direct use of words, so be it, but observe the language and press its letter fairly and truly. It will then lead you to the untenable result that men are objectively changed into a loaf, or loaves, or fragments of bread ; or men are objectively changed by Christian baptism, and by the Christian Supper, into a material body different from that of their own humanity. This, however, is a very different result from that transformation of bread into Christ's body which is the *credendum* of those against whom Scripture bears such striking testimony.

But it may be urged, does not part of this very passage itself (1 Cor. x. 16) designate the contents of the cup of blessing as the blood of Christ? Let us see. What are the precise words? "The cup of blessing which we bless, is it not a communion of the blood of Christ?" In this interrogatory of the apostle, that which is taught is that the cup is, not the blood, but *a communion of the blood*. Just as we have already seen that, in his history of the original institution, St. Paul (1 Cor. xi. 25) represents our Saviour as declaring the cup to be, not His blood, but *the new covenant* in His blood; so now, to say the cup is, in some sense, a communion or participation in the blood of Christ, is altogether different from saying that the cup is the blood of Christ.

If the cup be a token and means by which pious believers pledge and associate one another in the sufferings and benefits of Christ's precious blood-shedding, this is a natural and sufficient explanation, surely, of the words, "This cup is a communion of the blood of Christ;" and yet this plain, grammatical explanation of the words involves no objective change in the wine any more than a parallel interpretation of the words, "This bread is a communion of the body of Christ," involves any objective change of bread into the flesh of our Lord. The bread and wine are a sign and means of incorporation or embodying for the pious Christian; but this incorporation, as we have already learned from ver. 17, is of the multitude into one figurative body, of which Christ is indeed the head (*cf.* 1 Cor. xii. 12, 13, 27; xi. 3; Eph. v. 23), and all we are members in particular.

So, then, this tenth chapter of the first Epistle to the Corinthians teaches us that, in the breaking of bread, Christians are concerned with a "table" and those things which a table implies, and not with an altar and those things which are implied by an altar; and, moreover, this passage teaches us that, in the Lord's Supper, the bread and the wine—which were both enjoined by Christ, and were both administered and received by the primitive Christians—are a sign and means of fellowship and union between all Christians with one another, and with their one common Head and Lord.

In all this there is no trace of "orientation," as turning eastward has been called of late, nor of any special posture or vestment. Neither is there anything that is, when closely examined, reconcilable with the idea of bread and wine being in any way objectively converted into the body and blood of Christ.

(b.) 1 *Cor.* xi. 17—34.

And now we must proceed to study St. Paul's second reference to the Christian "breaking of bread." He no longer illustrates the peril of fancied contamination in a feast of things sacrificed to idols by the union and communion that arise in the Christian breaking of bread. In this second passage (1 Cor. xi. 17—34) St. Paul deals with his correspondents in the matter of certain abuses and corruptions which he hears, and partly believes, have crept into their celebration of the Lord's Supper. In the first three verses of this passage St. Paul alludes to the schisms and heresies which had arisen from different sources among the Corinthian Christians. Whatever good purpose, of testing and making manifest (ver. 19) those who were worthy of approval among them, these divisions might effect, and whether they arose from questions regarding the parts to be enacted, in the assembly of believers, by men and women respectively, or whether they concerned the head-dress of men and women, or whether they related to indecorum and irreverence in the breaking of bread, they sprang out of a contentious spirit which was altogether opposed to the religion of Christ; and the result of this contentiousness, in its various manifestations, was that the Christian coming together in the Church (*ecclesia*, the popular assembling), instead of building up believers in their most holy faith, was "not for the better, but for the worse" (ver. 17).

"When ye come together, therefore, into one place, [1] this

---

[1] ἐπὶ τὸ αὐτό.

is not to eat the Lord's Supper" (ver. 20).   These are most
remarkable words.   When ye come together, in the Christian
assembly, for the very purpose of celebrating the Lord's
Supper, if ye bring this spirit of contention, this mind of
the heretic which will obstinately choose its own way in
defiance of the concessions that should issue from brotherly
love, this heart of the schismatic who will rend the one
body of Christ's disciples in spite of the divine precept that
we should love one another and be one even as He and the
Father are one—if ye come to the Lord's Supper with such
contentious minds and hearts, ye frustrate the holiest of
ordinances; ye make your breaking of bread and drinking
of wine to be no Lord's Supper at all.

So entirely does the validity of the sacrament depend on the
state of mind and heart in which it is approached.   Contentiousness in the recipient destroys union and communion
among those whose oneness among themselves and with the
Lord is essential and indispensable for any real participation
in the Lord's Supper.   As we have hitherto found in the
bread and wine no objective change that was to constitute the
central act, or form any part of the Supper's administration,
so now we are instructed that a particular temper and disposition in the partaker is absolutely the condition, *sine quâ non*,
for that sacred act of holiest worship.

It may be well to observe here that this verse (20) supplies
us with a second Scriptural name for the Christian "breaking
of bread."   It is, in accordance with its first institution, a
supper[1] (as the Germans rightly call it, an *Abend-mahl*, an
evening meal).   Here, in this Scriptural designation of the
rite, we are provided with a perpetual, and assuredly a
sufficient, answer to those who make *evening* communions a
reproach to any who practise them in accordance with apostolic example and in obedience to the Lord's command.
After laying down the general principle that a lack of fellowship and unity in the hearts of communicants frustrates their
celebration, and makes their act to be the eating of something
quite different from the Lord's Supper, the apostle next proceeds to point out some of the particulars in which this anti-

---

[1] δεῖπνον.

Christian spirit was then manifesting itself at Corinth. "In eating, every one taketh before other his own supper: and one is hungry, and another is drunken."[1]

The condition of things indicated is this:—For the Christian Supper each believer, or each party of believers, was wont to bring a portion of meat and drink, such as accorded with the ability of the contributor. These portions were then made into a common stock, out of which the viands for the love-feast and the portions of bread and wine were provided in common for all the communicants alike and equally. None felt he was entitled to one part of the provisions but was debarred from participation in another part of the common meal. Each and all should be satisfied with an ample, but not an excessive, share.

Instead of this, however, what St. Paul blamed at Corinth was that some contributors retained, as it were, a preferential claim upon their own provisions. These they grasped and ate as their own, before any who brought no contribution, or who brought a contribution less in quantity or inferior in quality, could take a share. Such is the force of "In eating, each taketh before other his own supper." Greediness and selfishness and irreverence were the sources of such conduct: and the result is portrayed in the words, "One is hungry, and another is drunken." The fuller phrase would be, One is insufficiently supplied with meat and drink, while another has taken amply and selfishly, or even to excess, of both meat and drink. It was, indeed, time there should be apostolic rebuke and correction of such a state of things; and St. Paul, with all his charity and all his courtesy, has both fidelity and courage for the occasion.

What!—is the purport of his remonstrance, setting aside cases of manifest excess, and looking at first only to those of indecorous greed—have ye not houses, apart from the common meeting-place of the brethren, in which, if uncontrollable and irresistible craving for food be upon you, it may be gratified without the display of haste that waits for no fellow-Christian, without obtruding on fellow-worshippers the

[1] μεθύει.

ravenous appetite of the animal nature that is in us? Or is it so that, although you have such houses, although you can command such privacy for the concealment of the indecorous, yet you are impudently scornful of your brethren, who constitute the Church (the *ecclesia* or assembly) of God, and you are careless of affronting them with your improprieties? Or has your pride of wealth and its ostentation reached such a pitch that you are minded, of set purpose, to put them to shame whose possessions and means are none, or are less than yours? What shall I say to you in such a state of things? Shall I praise you, as I am wont to do, as it is my delight to do? No. In this I praise you not.

Then upon this reproof (ver. 22), upon this exhibition of their conduct before their own eyes, follows the apostle's record of what he had received in the way of revelation from the Lord, of what he had, too, previously delivered to the Corinthians in the way of instruction, as to the Saviour's original institution of the Supper. This record we have already examined, in its immensely interesting details, in earlier pages of this essay, so that it must suffice, at present, to remind the reader of the words, "This cup is the new covenant in My blood," as having been shown to be the most exact—as it is the earliest—record of the Saviour's words; as being the authentic exposition of the briefer form, "This is My blood;" and as throwing light upon the sense of the parallel expression, "This is My body." If "This is My blood" was the abridged form of "This cup is the new covenant in My blood," we can hardly fail to believe that "This is My body" was a similarly abridged form of "This bread is the new covenant in My body;" and these formularies, as we have seen, teach a spiritual lesson without giving occasion, or indeed leaving room, for any doctrine of transubstantiation or objective change in the elements of bread and wine.

In connection with this earliest extant written record of the Saviour's instituting the Lord's Supper, we have also noticed the injunction, "This do"—exercise your minds and hearts in all this fellow-helpfulness towards one another, and in all this loving thankfulness to God for His gifts and graces

—"this do, as oft as ye drink, for My remembrance." In this injunction we observed the perpetually recurring frequency of the communion prescribed, "as oft as ye drink;" and we also noticed that this communion in eating and drinking was instituted by Christ for a "*remembrance*," not for a *vision* of Himself; whereas, on the supposition of the bread and wine being objectively changed into the body and blood of Christ, a vision of Him, and not a remembrance, would be the result.

"For," proceeds the apostle (ver. 26), "as often as ye eat this bread and drink the cup, ye preach[1] [or tell the tidings of] the Lord's death till He come."

In these words, again, as so often in similar passages of Scripture, the mention of "the cup" and "this bread" is most worthy to be noticed; for, assuredly, if St. Paul had any knowledge of an objective change of the cup of wine into a cup of blood, or of the bread into Christ's objective body, so important a doctrine, so stupendous a miracle, could hardly fail to be recognised by Him in some such natural and truthful phrase as, "So oft as ye eat the body of Christ and drink His blood," ye *show* the Lord's death. The absence of these words and the mention of "the cup" merely, without reference to its marvellous contents, and of "the bread" categorically, as the other element still, even after the Lord's words had been spoken over it, are intimations of most satisfactory distinctness that the apostle of the Gentiles knew nothing of any objective change in the elements of the blessed Supper.

But the thought may occur to the English reader of this twenty-sixth verse, if he be unacquainted with the original Greek, that here we find the apostle speaking of the Supper as *showing* Christ's death until His coming; and this obviously bears the semblance of a vision to be *shown* and seen objectively, not of a set of associations to be remembered subjectively. Such a thought, however, rests only on the accident that our current English version has changed the Greek word,[1] and its root-figure of announcing tidings, delivering a message, into the different metaphor of *showing*, with

---

[1] καταγγέλλετε.

its root-idea of something to be seen.   If we keep literally
and faithfully to St. Paul's line of thought, as indicated by
his expressions, we read, "For as oft as ye eat this bread
and drink the cup, ye announce, like messengers, the Lord's
death until His coming."

Thus vanishes even this semblance of a verbal support
for the notion that the bread and wine present a vision of
Christ's body, and not a remembrance of His redeeming
death.   St. Paul's thought is, In the time that must intervene
between this present and that glorious future when Christ
shall come again, as often as, with fitting associations of
thought and with becoming purposes and acts and words,
ye participate in the Supper of your Lord, ye do, by commemorative act as well as by attendant words, tell forth to
men the blessed tidings that God so loved the world that
He gave His son to die as a ransom for all men.   Such is
the purport and meaning of each celebration of the Supper.
In every repetition of the breaking of bread, ye preach to
men that Christ died to save them from sin, that His body
was given and His blood was shed for the remission of sin,
that God might remit and pardon our transgressions, that
we might dismiss and put away our sins.   This, and no
less than this, ye declare, by your every communion in the
bread and wine, is the divine aim and object of Christ's
dying for you, of His giving His body and shedding His
blood for your sake.

Following up this reference to the death of Christ, the
apostle (ver. 27) continues, "Wherefore whosoever eateth the
bread or drinketh the cup of the Lord, unworthily, shall be
guilty of the body and of the blood of the Lord."   The Corinthians had already (ver. 20) been told that unworthy participation of the bread and wine defeated the purpose and
destroyed the nature of the Lord's Supper, made it to be
no eating of the Lord's Supper at all.   Now St. Paul warns
them that such frustration of their communion is not a
mere act of folly and waste of energy.   It is more.   It is a
desecration of holy things.   It is a manifestation of irreverence in connection with symbols which the Saviour has

appointed to be associated, in the minds of His disciples, with the redeeming sacrifice of His body broken and His blood shed for us; and who can irreverently bring acts of greed, and gluttony, and inebriety, and self-seeking, and contumely into such a sacred feast of loving fellowship with God and man, without sin and guilt?

In such unworthy eating of the bread or drinking of the cup—mark, there is no departure from these terms; there is no hint of any objective change in the elements—but he who unworthily eats the bread or drinks the cup of the Lord is guilty,[1] and that in connection with the body and the blood of the Lord. No measure of this guilt in each case is given. According to the profanity and conscious irreverence of every such offender, the guilt will vary from that of being "in danger of" trifling with holy things—so the Greek word for "guilty" is translated in Matthew v. 21, 22—to that of actually "crucifying to themselves the Son of God afresh, and putting Him to an open shame," as is the description of several kinds of conscious and wilful wickedness named in the Epistle to the Hebrews (vi. 6).

The guilt of those who unworthily partake of the bread and wine in the Supper is connected with the Lord's body and blood; but we must no more, on this account, insist on there being an objective presence of the body and blood of Christ in the Corinthian Supper, than on there being an objective cross and an objective Christ in the crucifixion and open shame mentioned by the writer of the Epistle to the Hebrews. In the latter instance no one dreams of Christ as being crucified otherwise than subjectively, in the minds of the wicked; and it is as inadmissible to understand the body and blood, in the former instance, as being anything but subjectively present.

In contrast with this danger of trifling with holy symbols, the apostle lays down an opposite course. "But," he says (ver. 28), to avoid this risk and guilt of unworthy participation, "Let a man examine himself, and so let him eat of the bread and drink of the cup." How strange, if St. Paul

---

[1] ἔνοχος.

believed the bread and wine were objectively changed into flesh and blood, that he should persist, even here, in designating the elements by the same terms as were applied to them before the prescribed blessing and giving of thanks! Even in worthy participation, after self-examination, just as the Evangelist speaks of the cup still containing the fruit of the vine, so the apostle writes of eating the bread and drinking of the cup.

Another point, well worthy of attention in the present day, is here brought under our notice by the apostle's words. To judge from the teaching of some modern Christians, it might be supposed that the injunction in this passage of Holy Writ was, Let an intending communicant get himself examined by a clergyman. Let him resort to a confessional. Let him not quit himself like a man, but let him kneel beside a fellow-being and whisper his every failing, his every sin, into the ear of one whose position bears too much resemblance to that of lording it over God's heritage. Such are the maxims of not a few modern Churchmen; but they are wide as the poles asunder from the teaching of the apostle.

Doubtless, if any believer had wronged his fellow-man, and if acknowledgment of the wrong constituted a material part of just reparation, St. Paul would urge, as did St. James (Jas. v. 16), that we should "confess our sins one to another;" or, in view of the duty and advantage of the prayer of a righteous man accompanied by work,[1] St. Paul, like St. James, would urge Christians to confess themselves sinners in need of such intercession, and to choose confidants, not necessarily officers of the Church, that with such confidants they might exchange the confession of sins. But even this kind and measure of voluntary and friendly confession is not brought into connection by the apostles with the Supper of the Lord, so far are they from the mediæval and modern practice of auricular and sacramental confession.

What St. Paul enjoins is, " Let a man [each man, every man] examine himself."[2] Let a man bring himself to the proof; let him see that he is no reprobate, but is up to the

---

[1] δέησις δικαίου ἐνεργουμένη. [2] δοκιμαζέτω δὲ ἄνθρωπος ἑαυτόν.

mark and standard of Christ; let him compare his thoughts with the mind of Christ (1 Cor. ii. 16); let him ascertain that he has the Spirit of Christ (Rom. viii. 9), and is bringing forth the fruits of that Spirit (Gal. v. 22); let a man thus bestir his own intellectual activity concerning God and Christ and his heart and life; let there be no weak dependance on another, but, only in the strength that comes from God and his Christ, let each man awake and seek for light and purity, and zeal and grace; "let a man examine himself" upon his own tremendous responsibility, as in the sight of God and the Lord, "and so let him eat of the bread and drink of the cup."

In these words of the apostle is wise and much-needed instruction, alike for those who strive to share the labour and responsibility of self-scrutiny with some official partner, and for those who neglect the solemn duty of self-examination in connection, particularly, with the remembrance of Christ in breaking of bread.

This special command, to examine one's self and to keep the mind religiously on the alert, in the Supper of the Lord, is then enforced by another consideration which St. Paul adduces (ver. 29). "For," adds the apostle, "he that eateth and drinketh"—(the word "unworthily" is not given in the best manuscripts)—"eateth and drinketh judgment[1] to himself, if he discern not the body." Such is the most reliable reading here, "if he discern not *the body*." Of course, the *Lord's* body is signified just as in the authorized version it is expressed. And now let us proceed to examine the meaning of these important words.

The apostle teaches that self-examination, in preparing for the Lord's Supper, must include the ascertaining whether we "discern the body," for fear of "eating and drinking judgment to ourselves." What is meant by this "discerning the body," manifestly the body of Christ? The words[2] of the original signify a failure in judging or distinguishing between the body and something else, not discerning the difference between the body and something else.

What is that something else? Is it not obviously the

[1] κρίμα.　　　　　　　[2] μὴ διακρίνων τὸ σῶμα.

bread? And have we not here a distinct and most remarkable intimation from St. Paul that to confound the material
bread with any objective presence of Christ's body, to fail in
discerning between that bread objectively present and the body
of the Lord which can only be mentally, spiritually, and subjectively present, is, by materializing spiritual things, to eat
and drink judgment to ourselves?

Instead of confounding the bread with the objective body
of Christ, present in the bread, or with the bread, or as the
bread, we must, on pain of judgment, distinguish between the
bread, which is one thing—a symbol and material instrument
—and the body of Christ, which is quite another thing, absent
in its objectivity but present subjectively to the mind and
heart of him who, as he looks upon and participates in the
bread and wine, thankfully remembers the one sacrifice of
Christ's body and blood for the sins of the whole world; and
devotedly calls to mind that, with that sacrifice of body and
blood and life, he must be so united and incorporated, that
he would, for Christ, be willing to be offered up as a sacrifice
(Phil. ii. 17), to be poured out as a libation (2 Tim. iv. 6)—
yea, would be willing for the brethren to lay down his life
(1 John iii. 16).

What a difference between the mere material symbols and
instruments of bread and wine—objects which are palpable to
the senses—and the sacrificed body and blood of Christ which
are partaken of by coming to Him and by believing in Him
(John vi. 35), subjects for the believer's mind! Some such
vigorous conception of Christ's body broken and of His blood
shed, as the one sacrifice, quite distinct and different from
the bread and wine which recall these associations, must be
in the mind of the partaker in the Lord's Supper; or, failing
this, he slights a holy commemoration, he materializes a
sacred and spiritual worship, and, so doing, he eateth and
drinketh judgment to himself.

And yet, in another sense, must the body of Christ be
"discerned" by the worthy partaker in the Lord's Supper;
for all we, all believers, are one body, even "the body of
Christ" (1 Cor. xii. 27); and this, with its lessons of fellow-

ship, helpfulness, and love, must be thoroughly and distinctly realized by all who would be meet participants in the breaking of bread.

Thus, if any man fail to distinguish and discern between the objective symbol, bread, and the spiritual reality of Christ's body sacrificed and of His body, the Church, such an one, in proportion to the wilfulness of his negligence, eateth and drinketh to himself judgment.

This "judgment" is, obviously, a result and consequence which must follow upon the profanity of taking bread and presuming that, objectively and materially, that bread must convey to us the body of Christ and incorporation therewith ; and what can be more certain than that, as the scales of culpable ignorance fall from our eyes, as the light of truth increasingly shows all things in their real character, either in this world or in that which is to come, negligence and profanity in sacred acts and holy worship will not only bring upon us the just and merciful and exactly discerning judgment of God, but will disquiet our own conscience and self-knowledge, and so will compel us to judge ourselves ?

Thus do unworthy communicants eat and drink various degrees of judgment to themselves. But, moreover, adds St. Paul (ver. 30), " For this cause many among you are weak and sickly, and many sleep." There is, indeed, no necessity for here supposing reference to some *miraculous* sickness and death that were in operation among the Corinthians. Such may have been the state of things. An unmistakable intervention of the divine power may have been at that time displayed at Corinth ; but such a supposition is not necessitated by the words of St. Paul, for, given, amongst any body of men, such gluttony and inebriety and hunger and want as he depicts, given such greed and such excess, even at the sacred feast of believers, and what would be the general habits of their ordinary and less religious life ? And from such habits of destitution on the one hand, and excess on the other, what result would be more sure to follow than sickness among many, and torpor and even death in not a few ? These consequences of sin and profanity were some of the outward workings of that judgment of God and of their own consciences in which men involved themselves, who exhibited the irreverence and want of self-control which St. Paul describes as discrediting the Corinthian Church when he addressed to them his first epistle.

After this appeal to facts, and the natural sequence and interdependence of facts, which must have been notorious in Corinth at that time, the apostle sums up in words that call back to memory the phrases in which he had been rebuking the Corinthian desecration of the Lord's Supper. "But if," he says, "we discerned[1] ourselves, we should not be judged."[2] As, before, self-examination[3] was made to include "discerning[4] the body" of Christ, so now this verb "discern"[5] is used instead of that previously employed to denote self-examining; and so, with an instance of that playing upon words and their compounds which is quite in accordance with the custom of the apostle, we learn that "If we would judge ourselves distinctly concerning things whose difference is important, we should not be judged subsequently by the judgment of God and of our own consciences." Nay, it is added (ver. 32), "But when we are judged by the Lord we are chastened, in order that we may not be judged to our condemnation together with the world"[6] (another instance of playing upon a compound of the Greek verb used throughout for judging, discerning, etc.).

All this is a clear setting forth of the loving mercy with which our God judges and chastens, with a view to save us from future and more terrible judgment and condemnation. Still, clear as it is, this verse (32) throws no more light upon our present subject. Then (ver. 33) the exhortation is, "Wherefore, my brethren, when ye come together for the eating,[7] wait for one another." Let there be no impatient, disrespectful haste. "If any hunger, let him eat at home, that ye come not together unto judgment."[8] If any man be possessed by uncontrollable appetite, let him, as was implied

---

[1] εἰ δὲ ἑαυτοὺς διεκρίνομεν.   [2] οὐκ ἂν ἐκρινόμεθα.   [3] ἑαυτὸν δοκιμάζειν.
[4] διακρίνειν τὸ σῶμα.   [5] διακρίνειν.   [6] κατακριθῶμεν.
[7] εἰς τὸ φαγεῖν.   [8] εἰς κρίμα.

in ver. 22, eat something at home, and so tame the ungovern-ableness of his hunger before he joins the congregation or *ecclesia* of the Lord. Let this be done to avoid unseemliness and the judgment of God and of our own conscience, that must, in time, sooner or later, follow upon unseemly and unworthy participation in so sacred a duty as breaking of bread in the Christian assembly. "And the rest [any details about which you have consulted me, or about which you may be in doubt] will I set in order when I come."

With these words of decorous common sense, St. Paul takes leave of our subject, and passes to other topics.

A truly interesting and important episode has the apostle thus left us in connection with the Supper of the Lord. He gives the earliest written record of its institution. He points out the frequency of its commemoration. He shows how the communion of the Lord's Supper depends for its validity upon the state of mind of its recipient. He insists upon the necessity of clearly recognising, on the one hand, the objective elements of the blessed bread and wine, and, on the other hand, the subjective and spiritual presence of Christ in the believer's mind.

As of something distinct from the objective elements of bread and wine, there must be a *discerning*, in the mind of the communicant, of that which is subjectively present in the adoring memory and love of the believer, namely, the body of Christ slain once for all, the blood of Christ shed once for all, to put away the sin of the world; nor will this *discerning* between the bread and wine on the one hand, and the body and blood of Christ on the other, be adequate and complete unless, together with the subjective realization of the spiritual presence of Christ the Head, there be also a sympathetic and loving fellowship with all the believers in Jesus who constitute His catholic or universal Church, the members in particular of His figurative body.

Without this *discerning* of the body of Christ, alike in Him-self the head, and in the whole of the constituting parts or members, there can be, says St. Paul, no worthy communion of the Lord's Supper, but only a selfish, careless, stolid, and irreverent trifling with holy things in such a manner as to bring upon men the judgment of God and of their own awakening conscience. Thus definite and important is St. Paul's instruction; but, clear and many-sided as is this passage of the apostle's teaching in connection with the Lord's Supper, it contains no sanction, as must have been observed, of those doctrines and practices which were rife in the mediæval ages, and which it is the aim of some men to resuscitate in the present day.

Instead of auricular and sacramental confession to a Church officer, the apostle urges that a man should *examine himself.* Instead of partaking in one kind only, the apostle enjoins us to eat of the bread *and drink of the cup.* Instead of discouraging and denouncing nocturnal celebrations, the apostle teaches us to come together for the Lord's SUPPER. Instead of individual and isolated administration, the apostle emphasizes the duty of Christians to wait for one another, that there may be a common and congregational participation. Whereas much is said, nowadays, of vestments and postures and priests, the apostle is significantly silent on all these points. Whereas mediævalism speaks of altars, the apostle, of obviously set purpose, names *the Lord's Table.*

While some insist on an objective presence of Christ's body in, or with, or instead of the visible bread and wine, the apostle solemnly warns us against such materializing of things spiritual, and goes the length of teaching that, if any man allows himself to be so superstitiously childish, or so profanely careless, as not to discern and distinguish between things differing so widely as the blessed bread and wine objectively present and the body of Christ spiritually present to the believer's heart and mind, or the same body of Christ metaphorically represented by all members of the Church, then—the apostle teaches—such sinful childishness, or such profane carelessness and confusion of mind in things sacred, make a man guilty in connection with the body and blood of Christ; in other words, they render him liable to the judgment of God and of his own conscience, as one who lightly and irreverently fails to image to himself the saving love of the Son of God upon the cross, who is mentally enslaved by the elements of bread and wine, instead of setting before his memory and his imagination the sufferings, and wants, and joys, and hopes, and capacities, developed and still undeveloped, of the whole body of believers, and of all men for whom the Lord gave His body to be broken and His blood to be shed.

Such is the contrast between the modern and mediæval doctrine of an objective presence of Christ in the bread and wine, and the teaching and admonition of the apostle concerning the peril of confounding things which differ so widely as the mechanical reception of bread and wine on the one hand, and on the other hand the devout and loving and active communion of believers in the memory of Christ and His death, as well as in helpful sympathy with Christ's body, the Church or whole assembly of the faithful.

§ 5. *St. Paul and the " Breaking of Bread" at Troas.*

From this contrast between mediævalism and apostolic truth, whose force comes out the more strongly the more deeply and reverently the subject is studied, we proceed to notice another reference to the Lord's Supper which occurs in the Book of the Acts of the Apostles.

From Ephesus, where St. Paul was when he wrote the first Epistle to the Corinthians (*cf.* 1 Cor. xvi. 8; Acts xix. 1, 10, 21; xx. 1, 2, 3, etc.), he had now passed through Macedonia and Greece, and had returned, eastward, to Troas. These journeys had occupied several months. Some chronologists place an interval of eighteen months or more between the composition of the first Corinthian epistle and the visit to Troas. The exact length of the intervening period is unimportant for our present inquiry. Suffice it to say that there is no question but that, some months after writing what we call the first Epistle to the Corinthians, St. Paul arrived at Troas, as is described in the history of the Acts (xx. 6—12), and there "abode seven days."

On the first day of the week, we learn, there was a meeting of the believers *to break bread*. Whether such breaking of

bread, in the congregation, had now become a weekly observance at Troas, or was still a daily practice, may be questioned.   Possibly, this meeting is named, as taking place on
the first day of the week, only to mark it more definitely as
the last assembling with St. Paul, on that visit of his to Troas,
or to designate it as the time when the fall and recovery of
Eutychus occurred.   This is quite possible.   There *may*
have been a "breaking of bread" every day in the Christian
assembly.   This, however, does not seem so much in keeping
with probability and with the demands that could be made on
the time of a Church consisting mainly of comparatively poor
and busy men, as is the other opinion that, while from house
to house, at each house, there was a daily "breaking of bread"
in obedience to the Lord, the congregational communion had
already become a weekly observance, and was held especially
on that first day of the week which should ever be, to the
Christian, a day of thankful and triumphant remembrance of
the resurrection and all which it implies.

Be this as it may, whether the Troadic Church's "breaking of bread" was daily or weekly, one point is clear—this
was intended to be a *nocturnal* celebration.   Not only were
there "many lights" (ver. 8) in the room where they were
assembled, but the apostle's discourse continued till the un-
usually late hour of midnight: and then it was that the
fall of Eutychus, and his restoration, occurred; and then,
about midnight, instead of earlier in the evening, as had
been expected, St. Paul went up again, and broke bread, and
tasted it.[1]   After that he "talked a long while, even till break
of day."   It was a midnight celebration, after all the
rejoicing and all the ordinary meals of a "Lord's Day"
(Rev. i. 10), or first day of the week.

There is no trace of any fast preceding it.   Indeed, the
remarkable expression, "tasted," which is here employed by
the historian, seems to imply that the recent abuses at
Corinth, and probably at other places, had induced the
apostle to separate, in this his practice, participation in an
ordinary meal from the breaking of bread in the Church

---

[1] γευσάμενος.

assembly. However much the relief of hunger might be still combined with the family breaking of bread at home, the partaking of the Lord's Supper, in the congregation, was, on this occasion at least, only a "tasting" for the apostle.[1] It would be rash to draw too positive conclusions from this single recorded instance; but it may be that we have here an indication of a change, as already practised, which was, in after times, assuredly to become a necessity and a custom —that of separating the Lord's Supper from the love-feast.

It is all the more interesting to observe this possible avoidance of a peril and a temptation for the Church, because it brings out into greater conspicuousness the fact that, even after the abuses at Corinth, and just after St. Paul had revisited that Grecian Church, and doubtless had, as he promised (1 Cor. xi. 34), "set in order" other points besides those named in his letter, he still recognised no demands, of necessity or of propriety, which called for any deviation from the original institution and usage of making the believers' breaking of bread to be at the close of the day and its work and its meals—an evening or a midnight celebration.

It is obvious to remark, in this narrative of what occurred at Troas, how close was the resemblance to, if not the imitation of, our Saviour's institution, even in such an accidental and unimportant detail as the Troadic breaking of bread having taken place in an "upper chamber"—in this case, as we learn, on "the third loft" or storey. In this, almost the latest glimpse given us by the New Testament of the primitive "breaking of bread," or communion of the Lord's Supper, as throughout its Scriptural history, nor time, nor place, nor vestment, nor attitude was deemed essential or important.

What was indispensable was that, in partaking of bread and wine (or apparently of any other beverage), there should be a devout and thankful remembrance of Christ's death and of its redemptive purposes of divine love, a union and incorporation of communicants, in heart and mind and

[1] Unless, indeed, we adopt the unlikely supposition that the verb γεύομαι, I *taste*, is used here in the unusual signification of eating a meal.

act and life, with Christ the head and with all the members of
His body, the Church.   These things being postulated as
essential, and a warning given of the necessity of distinguishing between the elements of bread and wine which are objectively different from the " body," which is Christ and His
Church, all other matters are of minor importance.   They
can be set in order when the apostle visits any Church, or
they can be changed, from time to time, as circumstances
may require, provided only all be done " decently and in
order " and " in charity."

Here we might conclude our investigation of the Scripture
testimony concerning the institution and apostolic usage of
the Lord's Supper, with the remark that not only have the
purest and holiest vouchers of antiquity failed to supply us
with a vestige of proof or apology for the doctrine of an
objective presence of Christ in the elements of blessed bread
and wine, but, moreover, these very vouchers, instead of
witnessing for such an objective presence and for the inferences
and doctrines and practices connected with it by the mediævalists, are plain and emphatic in their statement of the peril
of impiety incurred by careless or profane confounding of the
bread and wine with the body of our Lord.   Strangely enough
—nay, with surpassing wisdom in the merciful providence of
God—Scripture warns us all that our danger lies in the
direction of materializing spiritual things, and drifting into so
degrading a superstition as the belief that while there is a
consubstantiation, or transubstantiation, or insubstantiation
of the elements into Christ, and of Christ into the elements,
there is no need to " discern " and distinguish between the
memorial elements, which are bread and wine, and the " body "
whose head is our blessed Lord and all we its members in particular.   The case, in Scripture, is thus ample and irrefragable
against any objective presence of Christ in the bread and wine.

§ 6. *Scripture Promises of Christ's Presence, not more in the
Lord's Supper than on other Occasions.*

But, as if omission to inculcate this strange doctrine were
not proof enough against it, as if warning against the risk

H

and sin of such a confusion of things spiritual with things material were not enough to make us safe against the danger, we are actually supplied by the primitive writings of Christianity, and by our blessed Saviour's own words, with yet another and a very remarkable safeguard against so serious a peril.

When the question is raised, On what distinct grounds of Scripture proof does the doctrine of Christ's alleged objective presence in the bread and wine rest? we have seen that whereas the support of this doctrine is based on a *"proleptic"* interpretation of the sixth chapter of St. John's Gospel, such *"proleptic"* interpretation implies that Jesus used language in a highly artificial and non-natural manner; and this supposition is so abhorrent to our idea of the Saviour's simplicity, that it could only be admitted under the pressure of such absolute logical necessity as by no means exists in the passage under consideration. There it is a figurative and spiritual interpretation of the phrase, "Eating the flesh of the Son of Man and drinking His blood," which is not only in perfect accord with the metaphors constantly adopted by Jesus and by the Old Testament writers, but which is made obviously appropriate, and indeed alone admissible, in the sixth chapter of the fourth Gospel, by the principle therein laid down, that "The flesh profiteth nothing, it is the spirit that giveth life." And, yet again, the spiritual and figurative interpretation of that phrase, in that chapter, is rendered absolutely necessary, inasmuch as Christ Himself (ver. 35) defines "coming to Him" as that eating Him which satisfies hunger, and "believing on Him" as that drinking His blood which does away with thirst. Thus, as we have seen, the "proleptic" interpretation cannot be relied on as correct; and, if it could be accepted as true, it would yield no support (as we have further seen) to the amazing opinion that Christ's body is *objectively* present in the bread and wine of the Lord's Supper.

Similarly, when we examined the other alleged Scripture proof of the same doctrine, it became apparent that the words, "This is My blood," are only an abridgment of the fuller form, "This cup is the new covenant in My blood:"

and in the same way, beyond a doubt, the words, "This is My body," must be interpreted, "This bread is the new covenant in My body ; " and so, here again, even apart from the light thrown upon the shorter form of institution by such expressions as "I am the door," "I am the vine," and the like, there is no room left for thinking that our Saviour said only, "This is My blood." He is recorded to have said, This cup *is the new covenant*, a very different statement from the sacerdotalist interpretation of the abbreviated formulary.

So have we seen the only two apparent Scriptural proofs of the theory of an objective presence of Christ in the Supper fail to support that astounding opinion of the dark ages. All the other Scripture notices of the Lord's Supper have been strong and direct testimonies against any such erroneous opinion.

But now let us ask, in this absence of all specific Scripture promises of Christ's objective presence in the Supper of the Lord, whether there are not other very definite promises of Christ's presence, His general and His special presence either objectively or subjectively—we say not which at present—to be found in the New Testament, either referring to something entirely different from the Lord's Supper or only, by possibility and inference, referring to it in common with other wholly different practices and occasions.

(a.) *Matt.* xviii. 19, 20.

In this connection of thought, who can fail to remember the words of Jesus as they stand in the Gospel according to St. Matthew (xviii. 19, 20)? ".If two of you shall agree on earth as touching anything that they shall ask, it shall be done for them of My Father which is in heaven. For where two or three are gathered together unto My name,[1] *there am I in the midst of them.*" Here is a most distinct and unquestionable promise that where two or three Christians are assembled, in their Christian character and spirit, to pray for something as followers of Christ—that is, with a condition, an "If it be possible," attached to all earthly boons ; and

---

[1] εἰς τὸ ἐμὸν ὄνομα.

only unconditionally for that sanctification and salvation which we know to be in accordance with the divine pleasure—there, in all assemblies for such common Christian prayer, "I," says Jesus, "am in the midst of them." Here is a promise of the Lord's presence amongst communicants of the Lord's Supper, if they be engaged in united Christian prayer; but then it is a promise of the same presence, on the same condition, with every Church assembly, with every prayer meeting, with every gathering for domestic worship, with every "two or three" disciples who, unitedly, put up their Christian supplications in any place, at any time, and however separately from the Lord's Supper.

This is a clear promise of Christ's real presence, either subjective or objective; but its fulfilment depends not on the intervention of bread and wine, or any other material thing or person, except the mental resolve, the disposition of heart and life, on the part of two believers—it may be, of two who are starving to death in a garret, or perishing shipwrecked on the barren rocks of a desolate and shelterless coast.

(b.) *John* xiv. 23.

No less precise is the promise of our Master as we find it in the fourth Gospel (John xiv. 23). In reply to the question, " Lord, how is it that Thou wilt manifest[1] Thyself to us, and not unto the world?" Jesus said, " If *any* man[2] love Me, he will keep My words: and My Father will love him, and *we will come unto him, and make our abode*[3] *with him*." What—a reader of the least thoughtfulness must ask himself in view of these words—can be a clearer or more emphatic promise of the real and true presence of Christ and of the Father than this? However clearly implied—one cannot help reflecting—may be the assurance of Christ's spiritual presence in the communion of the Lord's Supper, it can convey to the mind nothing fuller or more divine, or more unlimited and unconditional, than that which is here pledged to *any man and every man* who will love Christ, and keep His commands in memory and do them.

[1] ἐμφανίζειν σεαυτόν. [2] ἐὰν τις. [3] μονήν.

To such an obedient and active lover of Jesus, God and Christ will not only come in the observance of some particular precept, but they will make *an abode, a remaining, a continuing residence, with such an one.* They will be with him when he prays, when he visits the sick, when he gives the cup of cold water to a disciple in Christ's name, when he breaks bread, when he is an hungered, when he is asleep, when he is stricken down by sickness, when in death he is carried to the mansions[1] or abodes of the Father's house—at all times, and in all places, and under all circumstances, as long as any man lovingly keeps Christ's words and does them, Christ and the Father will make their abode with any and every man so doing.

This divine presence of Christ is thus to be, not transient and occasional, but permanent. Had such a promise been attached exclusively, or been restricted in any special way, to the "breaking of bread," it might have made in favour of some of the theories of sacerdotalism; but, on the other hand, it would have been a promise of an *abiding* presence, and not of a presence confined to the mere moments during which the bread and wine are received and retained, as seems to be the notion of the mediævalists. This blessed promise, however, is not so tied down to any precise rite or ceremony; it is a general declaration that God and Christ will, in their divine fulness, come and abide with any loving and obedient disciple. This promise applies, indeed, to those who, with fitting conditions of mind and heart, partake of the Lord's Supper in compliance with the Master's word; but this presence is not conjoined, for them or for others, in any manner, with the elements of bread and wine, but with the spirit of loving obedience.

God and His Christ will be as really present with them in every other act of obedience to the Saviour's word as in their participation at the Lord's Table. It is a full, general, abiding presence of Christ which is here promised, and by no means a presence, at the Supper or with the bread and wine, differentiated from the presence vouchsafed where two or

---

[1] μοναί; the same word is rendered "abode" in John xiv. 23.

three are met for prayer, or where any one is assiduously discharging the commonest acts and duties of the life delineated as "faith which worketh by love." It is, we submit, impossible to imagine any promise of a real presence of Christ which could be fuller, more divine, or more continuous and all-embracing than this. However distinctly implied may be the assurance of a presence of Christ in the Lord's Supper, such assurance can only be a promise of the same divine presence in the communion as in all other acts of Christian obedience; but, in face of this promise recorded in the fourth Gospel, it could be no more.

No doubt, participation in the Lord's Supper is, for those who (like ourselves) regard it as of permanent obligation, a part of our due obedience to Christ: and as such it is a channel by wilfully and disobediently closing which we may exclude Christ's presence; and, contrariwise, by obediently opening this channel, we should admit that blessed presence. To this extent, and in this way, one believes the Lord's Supper to be a special and appointed means of receiving the grace of Christ's divine presence; but though the means be special, and in each case of obedience a diverse act is the special means of grace, yet the presence is, in all cases, the same, for it is no less than divine and infinite, the abode of God and Christ in a man.

Before passing from this most gracious and remarkable utterance of Jesus, there is yet another point to be noticed in connection with it.

According to the Lord's words (John xiv. 21, 23), taken together with the apostle's question (ver. 22), this presence of Christ and the Father with every loving disciple was to be a "manifestation," a "seeing" (ver. 19), vouchsafed to those who have Christ's commandments and keep them, but not vouchsafed to the world. Here is a noteworthy distinction. Christ shall be seen by believers, and yet not seen by those who believe not. Why? Will He only come and abide in places and at times where there is an absence of them that believe not? And, so, will His *objective* presence be granted to believers only and exclusively, and be strictly withheld from unbelievers?

If the presence be *objective*, the presence of an object, we can conceive no means by which that object can be present amongst men with eyes of equal power, and yet all who hold one opinion shall see it, and all who hold a contrary opinion, though looking in the same direction, at the same time, in the same place, shall not see it. Thus, the supposition of an *objective* presence of Christ leads us into difficulties and confusion inextricable. But suppose the promised presence of Christ is to be *subjective*—a thing seen by, and manifested to, the mind's eye—dependent, not upon the state of external objects, but upon the condition of mind and heart in the subject by whom the manifestation is to be seen; and then Christ's words are clear of all difficulty. The loving disciple sees with the eye of faith the manifestation of God and his Christ; while to the eye of ignorance and unbelief, there being no object present, and the subjective condition of mind being unattained as yet, there is no vision, no manifestation of the Blessed One.

(c.) 1 *Cor.* xiv. 23.

The truth of this teaching, that the most definitely promised presence of Christ is *not objective* but *subjective*, and dependent on the mental and spiritual condition of the beholder, receives full and highly interesting confirmation from many a passage in Holy Writ. For instance, St. Paul urges the Corinthians to avoid ecstatic exhibitions of their piety, lest unbelievers, if present at such exhibitions, should think them "mad" (1 Cor. xiv. 23). He intreats the Christians of Corinth to be "perfect" in the intelligent utterance of words "with the understanding;" and then, adds the apostle, if all preach in this reasonable and intelligible manner, and there come in an unbeliever, or one unacquainted with Christianity, he is convinced, his moral judgment is set at work, the secrets of his heart are brought unwontedly before his mind's eye, and so he will fall down and worship God, and "report that God is *in you* of a truth"[1] (*vide* 1 Cor. xiv. 19, 20, 24, 25).

---

[1] ὄντως ὁ Θεὸς ἐν ὑμῖν ἐστι

At His first entrance the unbelieving, or the ignorant, could see nothing but the room and its Christian occupants; there was no objective presence of the Deity for him to look upon : but, as his mind opened to spiritual facts, and spiritual convictions, and spiritual wants, and to God's message in Christ for the spirit, his subjective receptivity being thus changed, he reported the manifestation of God in the Christian believers as he saw it in his own changed mind and heart.

(d.) Gal. i. 16, etc.

Just so, whilst the companions of Saul were, with him, on the way to Damascus, they saw no God and heard no Christ in all the brightness and the sound of a voice; but Saul (Acts ix. 4, etc.) not only heard the distinct words of the Lord and communed with Him, but, when he came to write an account of those events (Gal. i. 16), his own description of the matter is, It pleased God " to reveal his Son *in me*." [1] Even this revelation of Christ, however accompanied by external sights and sounds which were objective enough, was not itself objective.   Christ was not seen, His words were not heard (*vide* Acts xxii. 9), by those who were with Saul; and even in the case of Saul himself, on his own direct written testimony, the revelation of Christ, the Lord's presence or manifestation, was not *to him*, but *in him*—in modern phrase, was not objective, but subjective.

From all these passages of Holy Writ we find, then, that Christ's presence—which is not exclusively or most categorically promised in connection with the bread and wine of the Lord's Supper, but is generally and fully promised to two or three believers in their common prayers, and to any loving and obedient disciple—is manifested after a real and spiritual sort; is seen by the mind's eye of faith; in other words, is subjective in the mind of man, not objective in any external matter or substance.

This exposition of Scripture truth might be almost indefinitely enlarged and confirmed; but we must, in this

---

[1] ἀποκαλύψαι τὸν υἱὸν αὐτοῦ ἐν ἐμοί.

branch of our inquiry, content ourselves with a very brief notice of only two more passages whose bearing on the subject is important.

(e.) Matt. xxviii. 16—20.

The Saviour's words to the eleven disciples, on the Galilean mountain (Matt. xxviii. 16—20), urged them to make and baptize disciples of all nations, and to teach the observance of all His commandments; and for this stupendous work, which is still so lamentably far from any adequate fulfilment, the encouragement which Jesus gave was in the words, " Lo, I am with you [1] alway,[2] even unto the end of the world [*till the conclusion of the age.*]" [3] Here is another large promise of Christ's presence, co-extensive, as we take it, with the work of gaining disciples to the Christian faith—co-extensive, such is its own declaration, with the Christian age or dispensation. During all that time, and in all such work, Jesus promises to be *with His disciples.*

How present with them? it must be asked; spiritually and subjectively, or objectively? Was it not even as St. Paul (Gal. iii. 1) reminds his converts, who had never seen Jesus in the flesh or with the bodily eye, that "before" their "eyes Jesus Christ" had "been evidently set forth [4] crucified among you [*in you*]"?[5] Was it not in the same manner, as the same apostle (Col. i. 27) told others of his correspondents, that Christ was *in them* the hope of glory? Was it not in this spiritual and subjective manner, even "in them," and in their minds and hearts, that Christ promised to be with His preachers in all their labours, as long as the dispensation should last? There is no trace or indication that the Saviour, after the ascension, walked *objectively* with Peter, or John, or any other apostle or preacher in ancient or in modern times.

In their minds they (like St. Stephen) might see the heavens open, and Jesus standing at the right hand of God; they might see and know that His occupation there was to inter-

---

[1] μεθ᾽ ὑμῶν.   [2] πάσας τὰς ἡμέρας.   [3] ἕως τῆς συντελείας τοῦ αἰῶνος.
[4] προεγράφη.   [5] ἐν ὑμῖν.

cede for them, according to the will of the Father; they
knew that the sympathy of their great High-Priest was with
them in their every struggle and aspiration; they knew His
Spirit was ever with them as their guide, their comforter, their
exhorter; [1] thus, not corporeally or objectively, but spiritually
and subjectively, they knew Jesus was with them and in them,
and so was fulfilling the promises to common prayer and
loving obedience and life-long efforts to convert all nations.
In these circumstances, as well as at the Table of the Lord,
the generally promised presence of Christ was in them and
with them; but, in all circumstances alike, Christ was present,
quite really and truly, only after a spiritual and subjective,
not after a fleshly and objective, manner.

(f.) Rev. iii. 14—22.

If further evidence in support of all this were wanted, it
might be found in the remarkable passage to be now cited
as bearing on this part of our subject.   In the address of
Christ to the Church of Laodicea (Rev. iii. 14—22), the
pride and sinfulness and peril of that body of believers are
very plainly described by Him who is " the Amen, the faithful
and true witness, the beginning of the creation of God."   The
Saviour counsels that Church to be zealous and repent and
put on the genuine character of Christianity.

Even to this unsatisfactory Church, however, Christ says
(ver. 20), " Behold, I stand at the door, and knock: if any man
hear My voice, and open the door, I will come in to him, and
will sup [2] with him, and he with Me."   Is it, one must ask,
an *objective* door and an *objective* Christ with which we have
here to do?   Is it not, obviously, a *subjective* representation
which is set before the Laodiceans, and (as God is no respecter of persons) before all men in positions similar to
theirs?   Even in the hearts of rebellious, self-conceited, careless men, who are disciples hardly in anything more than
name, Christ, or Christ's Spirit (ver. 22), seeks to awaken
repentance and offers His true riches.

To this extent Christ is present *in and with* the minds

---

[1] παράκλητος.   [2] δειπνή,σω.

even of wicked and backsliding Christians. If they will repent, listen to His exhortations and warnings, soften their hearts, humble themselves, awake to spiritual realities, then they will feel His presence more. That presence will be a delight and a joy, a sweet and familiar companionship to them. It will be no longer as a loving and neglected watchman who warns them against dangers, but as a welcome and beloved friend, that Christ will "sup with them, and they with Him." Thus, even with the wicked He is present, but it is as one standing in the intellect as it were, outside the heart, and asking for admission. With the repentant and obedient, He is still present, but it is as one whose delighted and delightsome Spirit permeates the whole heart and soul and intelligence of the man who has opened to him.

This (Rev. iii. 22) is part of "what *the Spirit* saith to the Churches;" and so there is no room for the question here, whether it is Christ bodily and objectively, or Christ spiritually and subjectively, who says, "I stand at the door and knock." In the minds even of the indifferent and haughty Laodicean Christians—and if in theirs, surely in every Christian mind, however proud, cold, and culpable—Christ is present and is active with admonition, counsel, and entreaty. In the same mind, let us ask, when its mood is changed by repentance and renewed zeal, is Christ *more present?* Can a being, divine or human, or both, be, *objectively, more or less* present in one and the same time and place? Must he not be, *objectively*, either present or absent? But here, in the case of the Laodiceans, He is present as one standing and waiting *outside* the unrepentant heart, and as one admitted *inside* the same heart when it repents.

What is this but to say that, throughout, Christ for His part is present—divinely present, infinitely present, equally present—with the Christian, whether that Christian welcomes Him or not; there is no variation in the degree or measure of Christ's presence, unless indeed the man can make himself to be, at last, utterly rejected,—otherwise, Christ is present with him in all His divine fulness; and the only variation is, *subjectively*, in the man himself? He either realizes or he ignores the presence of the Lord. He either repels or he welcomes Christ. He either grieves the Spirit or he gladly yields to the Spirit's gracious suggestions. He either keeps Christ standing and knocking without, or he opens the door and admits Christ as his revered though familiar guest.

It is not a little remarkable that this demonstrably subjective presence of Christ, varying wholly and only with the variations of the man's mind, should be compared to a "*supping*" with the man, and the man with Christ. Whatever degree of divine and providential intervention any reader may recognise in the composition of Scripture, or even if such intervention be denied altogether, it is a noteworthy fact that whereas the presence of Christ, as we have seen, is far from being exclusively promised in connection with the communion of the Lord's Supper; and whereas such undoubted presence depends, for its guarantee and assurance, upon what is implied in the nature of "communion," and upon the general promises that Christ will be present with those who pray, with those who lovingly keep His word, with those who strive to win souls to Him, and even with those who in their self-deception deeply need His admonition,—one of the most distinct and emphatic promises of that presence of our Lord is given to Christians living an unworthy and deplorable life; and the very presence of Christ, *supping with them*, is assured to those Christians, not on condition of their breaking bread and drinking wine in remembrance of Christ, but on condition of their opening their hearts to the Lord's entreaties that they will "be zealous and repent."

The teaching of Holy Writ is, not that Jesus is in the bread and wine, independently of the communicant's mind and heart; but, on the contrary, our supping with the Lord, and He with us, depends on wholly different conditions. Our supping with Christ, and He with us, rests on this sure and certain ground that, for believers, He is in them and abideth in them. If they grieve Him, by pride and self-conceit and other wrong-doing, still He loves them and rebukes them and chastens them (Rev. iii. 19)—this is His standing at the door and knocking; but, if they desist from their evil ways and turn to righteousness again—this is their "hearing His voice and opening to Him "—He, who has never left them nor forsaken them, will then, whether in the breaking of bread at the Lord's Table or in any other act of Christian life and duty, sup with them and they with Him.

Truly, Christ's presence with us, even His *supping* with us, is not tied to any rite, however solemn—not even to the usages of the communion at the Lord's Table. His presence can be procured and assured to us by no outward and material object. It depends, according to His own promises, on our state of mind and heart.

But now let us, in connection with this remarkable passage of Scripture, test the doctrine of Christ's objective presence in the bread and wine, independently of the recipient's condition of mind, by one more criterion. Let it be supposed for a moment that, in the elements of the Supper, Christ is objectively though indescribably present, and that so He gives Himself to be eaten, and His blood to be partaken of, by the communicants.

On this supposition, what must have been the words addressed to the Laodiceans? Must they not have been to this effect? I wait in the broken bread and in the cup of blessing. If any man hearken to My words, and be zealous and repent, he shall open his mouth ; and, in the bread he eats and in the wine he drinks, I will be present, and he shall sup, not *with* me, but *on* me ?

If an objective presence of Christ in the elements had been intended to be taught by our Saviour and the writers of the New Testament, such a promise as that given to the Laodiceans would have been impossible. How could Jesus be at once objective food in the Supper of His disciples, and, at the same time, a guest partaking of that Supper with the same disciples? If we should be told that there are two Suppers of the Lord, one in which He gives His flesh and blood objectively as food, and another in which He is present subjectively as a guest supping with His followers, then the reply is obvious; namely, that in the institution of the Lord's Supper, at all events, Jesus contemplated, as we have seen, drinking the cup *with His people* (*vide* Matt. xxvi. 29, Mark xiv. 25, Luke xxii. 18) ; and so the alternative is forced upon us— either Jesus contemplated drinking, with His disciples, His own objective blood ; or He spoke of His presence at the Supper, at every Lord's Supper, as subjective, in the mind of the believer, and not as objective, in the elements independently of the believer's mind.

The former of these alternatives is too repulsive—too near profanity—to be dealt with in detail, held in reality, or grappled with at close quarters. And thus, again, in the absence of any trace of Scripture proof for the strange doctrine of an objective presence of Christ in the bread and wine of the Supper, independently of the recipient's spirit—in face of all Scripture references to the Lord's Supper, and its institution and its usage, witnessing against an objective presence as strongly as they witness for a subjective presence— we are necessarily led to the conclusion that, while Christ's command binds us to celebrate the Lord's Supper ; while doubtless grace, even the infinite and manifoldly effective grace of His divine presence, is given to this as to each act of obedience to His word ; yet this presence of Christ is so entirely subjective and contingent upon the recipient's spirit or state of mind and heart, that, if there be a contentious spirit in the recipient, or any other unfitting condition of soul, the bread and wine, though partaken after most solemn blessing and giving of thanks, are to such a recipient, as St. Paul taught the Corinthians, not a Supper of the Lord at all.

§ 7. *Other Scriptures connected with our Subject.*

We now proceed to notice two passages of Holy Writ which require attention, because of their more or less direct and immediate connection with our subject. The first is an episode in the narrative of St. Paul's shipwreck.

(*a.*) *Acts* xxvii. 35.

Some fourteen days had the apostle and his fellow-voyagers passed in anxiety and hunger. Thereupon, encouraged by the vision he had received, St. Paul exhorts them to " take some food." [1] " And, when he had thus spoken," the history proceeds (Acts xxvii. 85, 36), " he took bread, and gave thanks [2] to God in presence of them all : and when he had broken it, he began to eat. Then were they all of good cheer, and they also took some food."

The phraseology of this narrative is strikingly like that which had already, when St. Paul thus acted, become habitual, and well-nigh technical, as appertaining to the Lord's Supper among Christians. There is the " took bread," the " giving thanks " to God for it, the " breaking," the " eating." There is even a parallel to the Christian " gladness " and " fellowship," for St. Paul's companions became " of good cheer," and they also partook of food.

Can we think that St. Paul had in his mind no recollection of the Lord's Supper and its declaring the death of Christ at this solemn time of peril in shipwreck ? Can we think he intended no reference to the blessed Supper for those companions who might, even during the voyage, have become capable of appreciating its consolation, susceptible of its holy encouragement ? Must we not think that, with however much or little comprehension on the part of the different beholders, St. Paul was here commemorating the dying love of Christ ?

On either of the suppositions suggested by these questions, it is noticeable how, in the apostolic age, the most common life, the most secular circumstances, were coloured by the " breaking of bread " and by the " communion " with Christ and with one's fellow-men. Ordinary life was so much of a communion and a Lord's Supper—the communion of the Lord's Supper was so entirely a part of every-day Christian life—that they were blended and became hard to be distinguished. So holy and joyful was the Christian life ; so simple and unceremonial was the communion of the Lord's Supper.

[1] τροφῆς. "Meat," it should be remembered, was old English for food generally, not for flesh in particular, as now.

[2] εὐχαρίστησε—he *eucharized*, or gave thanks for the bread. This Greek verb *eucharize* is, of course, derivatively akin to the noun " *eucharist*," a thanksgiving.

Surely this intermixture of the commemorative Supper with common life has its lesson for those of us who, in the present day, are disposed to draw very strongly marked lines between the Lord's Supper and every other portion of Christian life or worship.

(b.) 1 *Cor.* xiv. 16, etc.

The other passage, to which attention should not fail to be directed, occurs in St. Paul's first Epistle to the Corinthians (xiv. 16). The context treats of the greater usefulness of intelligible speech—preaching, praying, or singing, in words that can be understood—as contrasted with the ecstatic but unintelligible utterances of those who had the gift of "tongues." In this connection the apostle writes, "When thou shalt bless with the Spirit" (that is, in the unintelligible utterance of "tongues"), "how shall he that occupieth the room of the uninitiated[1] say the Amen at thy Eucharist, seeing he understandeth not what thou sayest?"

This text, by reason of the "blessing" named in it, and the "Eucharist" (or giving of thanks), which were both familiar phrases constantly employed by the primitive Christians in connection with the Lord's Supper, is generally interpreted as referring to the breaking of bread. St. Paul's mention of "*the Amen*" is regarded as confirming this interpretation, inasmuch as "the Amen" of the congregation, in its assent to the eucharistic blessing, became a marked and famous characteristic of the Lord's Supper in early Christian days.

Assuming then, as may fairly be assumed, that St. Paul's reference in this text is to the Lord's Supper, we derive from this passage several important lessons. Besides the terms "Lord's Supper," "Communion," "Breaking of Bread," we are here furnished with another designation, "Eucharist" (or "giving of thanks"), for the same holy rite; and, like each of the other designations, this of Eucharist is assuredly full of appropriateness, and rich in suggestive significance. Well

---

[1] ἰδιώτης, not "unlearned" generally, but unacquainted with any particular subject under notice.

may the rite, in which we commemorate Christ's redemptive death, be a Eucharist full of thanksgiving.

But notice, again, that St. Paul here teaches us the inferiority of even miraculously bestowed gifts of unintelligible "tongues," as compared with plain words, in the eucharistic service, such as could be "understanded of the people." Is there no useful instruction in this verse for those who retain a Latin service amongst congregations unacquainted with the Latin language? Nay, for any of us who turn our backs on the congregation, and so make it more difficult for our fellow-worshippers to hear our words and take part in the worship with the understanding, is there not in this text a needful word of admonition? And does not this apostolic warning apply, with still greater force, to those amongst us who, conceiving themselves to be acting vicariously for the people in the Eucharist, deem it permissible, if not desirable, that the voice of the officiating minister should, in certain parts of the Eucharist at all events, be dropped so low as to become a whisper scarcely audible by the congregation?

These questions can hardly fail to elicit a right answer from any thoughtful reader of the verse we have been examining; and that answer will assuredly be in keeping with the apostle's general maxim on the same subject (1 Cor. xiv. 19), "In the Church I had rather speak five words with my understanding, that I may teach others also, than ten thousand words in an [unknown] tongue."

Then there is still another lesson derivable from this passage. Soon after the words immediately under consideration, St. Paul (ver. 23) proceeds, "If therefore the whole congregation [ecclesia, the assembly or church] be come together into one place, and all speak with [unintelligible] tongues, and there come in those that are uninitiated, or unbelievers, will they not say that ye are mad?"

In these words the apostle indicates that the Christian assembly, in his time, was open to the visits of unbelievers as well as of those believers who were as yet but slightly, if at all, initiated into the deeper truths and higher aspirations of Christ's religion. And for these visitors, whether they might be partially acquainted with the Gospel and already almost persuaded to be Christians, or whether they might be only curious and inquisitive unbelievers, St. Paul enjoined that the general usages of the congregation, and especially the observances in the breaking of bread, should be open without reserve, and so intelligible as to appeal to the understanding of all—" edify ' (ver. 17) the minds of the uninformed and convince the judgment of the most sceptical.

This does not look like encouragement, on the part of the apostle, of any esoteric teaching for the select few, to the exclusion of the masses. Exoteric teaching for the multitude and esoteric doctrine for the minority, was the practice of some heathen philosophers, and may have been the delight and the safeguard of priestly confraternities in all ages; but they are diametrically opposed to apostolic usage, which appeals to the reason and the understanding of all men; which, so far as hearers can bear and comprehend the truth, is all anxiety to make that truth known, even to the utmost bounds of what the Father has divulged. Light not darkness, revelation not obscurity, the intelligible not the bewildering, are the aim and object of Christ's teaching and of apostolic exhortation, alike in ordinary worship and in the special ministering of the Eucharist.

The importance and usefulness of this Pauline instruction will become especially apparent when we enter upon an examination of certain opinions and practices of later Church history. Meanwhile, this passage teaches us that, in all parts of Christian worship, our language ought to be simple and intelligible; our appeal should be to the heart through the intellect; we should address ourselves, not to the initiated only, but also to the unenlightened and the unbelieving.

§ 8. *Scripture Light on the Attempt to set the Lord's Supper above all other Acts of Christian Life or Worship.*

An attempt is sometimes made to exalt the communion of the Lord's Supper into the position of the highest act of religious worship, as an observance that more than any other brings the Christian into the very presence of God and the Saviour.

It would be most remote from our wish to do anything that might detract from the true beauty and glory of the Eucharist. But, on the other hand, no injury is ultimately and really more damaging, in any case, than undue and false glorifying, which is sure to be followed by a reaction of excessive depreciation. Already there are not wanting signs of such a reaction with reference to the ritualistic exaltation of the Lord's Supper.

We have seen that, at the institution of the Eucharist, Christ certainly did not say of the wine, "This is My blood," but He did say, "This is the new covenant in My blood;" and similarly, beyond all reasonable doubt, Christ did not say of the bread, "This is My body," but He did say, "This is the new covenant ratified by My body, which is being given for you."

And, yet again, in the great discourse at Capernaum (John vi.), Christ did not speak with any reference to the Eucharist, or its bread and wine; but He Himself did definitely teach (ver. 35) that coming to Him as a disciple was eating His flesh, and belief in Him was drinking His blood, in the sense of that discourse.

And this line of reflection will be further illustrated and enforced by the remembrance that, so far as the presence of God and of our Lord is concerned, that highest privilege and blessing is promised more definitely to the common prayer of believers, or to general fidelity and obedience to Christ's commands, or to labours for the extension of Christ's kingdom, than to the practice of the breaking of bread. Indeed, the greatest assurance of the divine presence with us in the Eucharist rests on the fact that that service is an act of common prayer and praise, is an act of obedience to Christ, is an attempt to declare, by act as well as word, the death of the Lord till His coming again.

Thus far then, if such comparisons must be instituted, the Lord's Supper depends for its highest glory in Christ's presence, not on its own inherent character and the promises connected with itself, but on the fact that such divine presence is promised to prayer, obedience, and preaching; and, to this extent and in this manner, the blessed Eucharist cannot truly be described as superior to common prayer, holier than general obedience, or more assured of Christ's presence and co-operation than such preaching by a disciple as strives to teach the observance of all our Lord's commands.

If, again, we measure the dignity of the Lord's Supper by the dangers attaching to unworthy participation, they are terrible indeed, and they bespeak its high dignity and importance: but they cannot exceed the tremendous peril of unworthy hearing of the Gospel such as makes the Christian preacher "a savour of death unto death" "in them that perish" (2 Cor. ii. 15, 16); they cannot exceed the "certain fearful looking for of judgment and fiery indignation" which attaches to all wilful sinning after that we have received the knowledge of the truth (Heb. x. 26, 27); neither can they surpass, in terribleness, the results of falling away on the part of "those who were once enlightened, and have tasted of the heavenly gift, and were made partakers of the Holy Ghost and have tasted the good Word of God, and the powers of the world to come" (Heb. vi. 4, 5, 6).

Measured by this standard, the vast religious importance of the Eucharist is seen not to surpass that of the ordinance of preaching or of general compliance with Christ's precept of righteousness and holiness.

Some Christian writers have ingeniously, and with no slight argumentative force, contrasted the few and brief references to the Eucharist in the New Testament with the comparatively abundant and copious insistance, in its pages, on the duties of obedience and prayer, and on the practice of Christian teaching and exhortation; and from this line of observation the inference has been legitimately enough drawn that, holy and beautiful as the Eucharist is made to appear in the few passages of Holy Writ in which reference is made to it, still it cannot surpass in dignity or importance those other topics and observances which fill every page of the Christian Scriptures.

§ 9. *The Lord's Prayer and the Lord's Supper in respect of their Direct and Unaltered Descent to us from Christ.*

The assertion is sometimes made that the Holy Communion is the only part of Christian worship which has come down to us direct and unaltered from the very hands of Christ.

That the blessed sacrament, with various additions and alterations, has come down to us from our Saviour, is most true ; and we glory in this truth as affording us an unbroken chain of historical connection and evidence between the table where the Lord presided in an upper chamber at Jerusalem and our present practice. To go beyond this, however, and allege that the modern celebration derives sanctity from its unaltered imitation of our Lord's Supper, or of the apostolic rite, is to ignore the facts of history, and to set one's self in opposition to plain and unmistakable truth.

If we want a part of Christian worship which has come to us direct and unaltered from our Lord, and if the so-called " central act " of Christian worship is to be characterized by this mark, it must not be sought in the sacrament of Communion, but in the form and model of prayer (without the final ascription) as taught us by our Lord, and as handed down by St. Matthew and St. Luke.

We point to this unquestionable truth from no wish to detract from the honour due to the Lord's Supper, but with a desire to give that rite its due place in the economy of grace, while we exalt the Lord's Prayer to its unique and unrivalled pre-eminence in the same system.

§ 10. *Scripture Usage as to " the Body of Christ."*

We close this part of our investigation with the remark that, whereas it is in the highest degree improbable, as has been seen, that our blessed Lord ever called the eucharistic wine His blood, or the eucharistic bread His body, there is something else which apostolic usage constantly designated as the body of Christ. If we look at St. Paul's Epistle to the Colossians, for instance, we find the apostle writing

(Col. i. 18), "He [Christ] is the head of the body, the Church;" and (Col. i. 24), I "now rejoice in my sufferings for you, and fill up that which is behind[1] of the afflictions of Christ in my flesh for His body's sake, which is the Church;" or, passing by other similar expressions in the same epistle, and passing also several instances of the same usage in the Epistle to the Ephesians, let us notice that which occurs in the fifth chapter of that epistle (Eph. v. 30). Through several preceding verses St. Paul has been insisting on the obedience and love which the Church should exercise towards Christ, who is her husband and her head. Then follow the words, " For we are members of His body, of His flesh, and of His bones."

Here is, indeed, transubstantiation and incorporation of believers into Christ. By Christ giving Himself (ver. 25) for the Church, and by that Church being sanctified and cleansed so as to be a glorious Church, not having spot, or wrinkle, or any such thing, but that it should be holy and without blemish (verses 26, 27)—thus are accomplished the union and incorporation of the Church with Christ.

If now we turn to the earliest of St. Paul's extant Epistles to the Corinthians (1 Cor. xii. 12, 13), we find these words, "For as the body is one, and hath many members, and all the members of that one body, being many, are one body: so also is Christ. For by one Spirit are we all baptized into one body." After following up this instruction for a while, the apostle summarizes it thus (ver. 27): "Now ye are the body of Christ, and members in particular."

The same epistle furnishes us with yet another illustration of this usage which, though, like the preceding, it has been dealt with already in this essay in some of its bearings, cannot now be omitted from this concluding line of thought.

The apostle writes (1 Cor. x. 16, 17), " The bread which we break, is it not a communion of the body of Christ? For we, the multitude, are one bread, one body: for we all take part out of the one bread."

In this last passage not only are the multitude of believers

---

[1] τὰ ὑστερήματα, that which is lacking.

declared to be the one body of Christ, but the bread of the Eucharist, which is also named, is defined as, not the body of Christ, but as *a* communion (not "*the*" communion, as the English version renders it), *a* means of fellowship, one of several means, like faith, or baptism, or prayer, or co-operation in works for the saving of souls—one of several such means for ingrafting and incorporating men into the body of Christ.

St. Paul might have been contemplating the errors and disputes of coming ages, when he so frequently teaches, throughout his letters, that men, believing men, are the body of Christ, and His flesh ; or when he insists that there must be no confusion—there must be most distinct discernment—between the bread in the Eucharist and the body which is Christ and His people in all their multitude ; or when He lays down this distinction between us who are the body of Christ and the bread which, worthily received, is a communion or means of participation in that body which is Christ and His people.

§ 11. *Conclusion.*

Thus consistently does Holy Writ avoid giving encouragement to the idea of an objective presence of Christ in the elements of the Lord's Supper.

We have looked to metaphors whose usage preceded and followed the institution of the Eucharist ; we have carefully studied the records of the institution of the Lord's Supper ; we have diligently examined the practice of the New Testament writers on this subject: and everywhere, without exception, we have found irrefragable proofs that the presence of Christ at the Eucharist, as on all other occasions since the Ascension, is subjective, by His Spirit, in men's minds and hearts ; and however prayer, or self-denying work, or a book, or a discourse, or the breaking of bread, may either of them be the instrument and means, with God's blessing, for ingrafting a soul into Christ and Christ into that soul, still it is part of our allegiance to truth—it is our solemn and bounden duty—on pain of being unworthy and bringing judgment on ourselves, to distinguish between the means of grace and the grace itself, between the material and the spiritual, between the objective bread and the objective wine, on the one hand, and the subjective and most real presence of Christ by His Spirit on the other hand. Assuredly, on this subject, if on any, there is wisdom and piety in yielding ourselves to the guidance and instruction of the Saviour and His apostles as those can be found, in their pristine purity and simplicity, only in the writings of the New Testament.

BOOK II.

POST-APOSTOLIC USES OF THE LORD'S SUPPER.

FROM the Scripture record concerning the institution and usage of the Lord's Supper, we pass now to a consideration of the manner in which that simple rite of Christian communion was dealt with in the ages that intervened betwixt the apostles and the Reformation.

CHAPTER I.

PLINY'S MENTION OF THE CHRISTIAN "SACRAMENT."

ON this point some little information may possibly be derived from the famous letter of Pliny the Younger to the Emperor Trajan. The date of this letter is quite early in the second century, within a few years of the death of the last of the apostles. Pliny, as is well known, was governor of a Roman province in what we now call Asia Minor. Under those circumstances he addressed the following inquiry to his imperial master (Pliny's Letters, Book x. let. 97) :—

"It is my custom, sire, to refer to you all points concerning which I am in doubt; for who can better guide my hesitancy or inform my ignorance? Having never been present at the trials of Christians, I know not in what manner, or to what extent, they are wont to be punished or examined. Indeed, I have had no slight doubt whether there ought not to be different modes of procedure in dealing with those of different ages, with the delicate and with the more robust ; whether pardon should not be extended to those who retract, or whether, in the case of one who has ever been a Christian, his having desisted should be of no avail ; and whether punishment should attach to the very profession of Christianity apart from any crime, or whether it should be inflicted by reason of crimes that may co-exist with such a profession.

" Meanwhile, this has been my mode of dealing with those who were accused before me of being Christians. I asked them the question, Were they Christians ? If they confessed, I repeated the question once and again, accompanying it with a threat of punishment. Those who persisted I ordered away to execution. For I entertained no doubt, whatever that might be to which they confessed, that, assuredly, pertinacious and inflexible obstinacy ought to be punished.

" There were others of like foolishness, whose cases I set down for trial at Rome, inasmuch as they were Roman citizens.

" Ere long, the accusations were multiplied by reason of our dealing with them, as one generally finds, and fresh cases were brought under my notice, not only in greater numbers, but marked by new characteristics. There was published an anonymous writing which contained the names of many persons who deny that they either are or ever were Christians. When these, following my example, called upon the gods ; offered prayers, with incense and wine, to your image which, for this very purpose, I had ordered to be set in the midst of the statues of the deities ; and when, moreover, they reviled Christ—actions to whose performance, it is said, real Christians can by no possible means be constrained—I thought they should be discharged.

" Others, who were named in the list, acknowledged themselves Christians. Presently, however, they denied it, saying it was true they had been Christians, but they had ceased to be so—some three years previously, some several years since, some few even so long as twenty years ago. All these also worshipped your image and the statues of the gods and reviled

Christ; and, moreover, they affirmed that the sum of their error or offence, whichever it might have been, had consisted in this :—that on a set day, before dawn, they were wont to assemble and repeat, in alternate parts, a chant to Christ as God; that they then bound themselves by an oath [*sacramento*] not to commit any crime, but to abstain from robbery, theft, or adultery; to avoid every breach of faith; and never to refuse, when called upon, to restore a deposit which had been entrusted to them : and, when these rites had been performed, it was their custom to disperse, and then again to assemble for the purpose of partaking in common a meal of an entirely harmless nature. This last practice, however, they had abandoned after the issuing of my edict in which, according to your commands, I had forbidden the assembling of popular confraternities [*hetærias*].

"And for these reasons I deemed it the more necessary to ascertain, even by means of torture, what might be the truth, in these matters, from two young women who bore the official name of deaconesses [*ministræ*] among the Christians. I found by this means, however, nothing but a perverted and extravagant superstition : and therefore I postponed further inquiry till I might avail myself of thy counsel. For it seemed to me a matter worthy of reference to thee, especially because of the number of those who were in danger of being accused as Christians; for many persons, of every age, of every rank, and of both sexes, are already imperilled and will be so. Nor is it only in towns, but even in villages and in rural districts, that the contagion of this superstition has taken effect; and yet it seems not impossible that the mischief may be stayed and set right. One fact at all events is quite clear, namely, that the temples, which were almost deserted, begin to be once more attended, and the accustomed sacrifices, after long disuse, are being resumed ; everywhere victims are being sold for which, till quite lately, scarce any purchaser was to be found. And from this it is easy to infer what a vast number of people can be won back if opportunity for retracting be afforded them."

In this letter of the unbelieving but acute and philosophical

Roman ruler, there are many points on which one is tempted to dwell; but we must pass by the too notorious cruelty of Roman law, the wide extent to which Christianity had prevailed in a few years, the testimony of Pliny that it had gained a footing in his province twenty or five and twenty years before the date of his letter, the harmlessness and yet the often unlimited zeal which was found in the Christians, the existence of deaconesses in that early Church, the falling away of some Christians under persecution, the faithfulness even unto torture and death of others, the fact that believers were found not only among the poor and miserable but in every rank, and even among those who, as Roman citizens, were persons of sufficient influence and importance to have their cases remitted on appeal to Rome—these and other points, especially the utter unfriendliness and scorn of Pliny, from whom this eulogy of our religion is nevertheless extorted by truth and justice alone,—all these points must be passed by us without further notice, in order that we may fix our attention on Pliny's description of certain particulars in the Christian life and worship of those very early times.

And here we notice that the assembling of the Christians took place " on a set day " (*stato die*), doubtless on the first day of the week, the Lord's Day, of the New Testament writers—the Day of the Sun, as we shall presently find it called by an early Christian author. On this " set day " it had been the practice of the Christians formerly to hold two assemblies—one at a very early hour in the morning; the other, apparently from its exciting Roman jealousy as partaking of the nature of a suspected association, at a late hour, when night was approaching. The early meeting was characterized by the addressing of a chant to Christ as God.

Thus, we have important testimony from Pliny to the primitive belief in our Saviour's divine nature, and to the prevalence of worship addressed to Him as one with the Christian God. An interesting feature in this ancient chant of the Church is its having been sung *alternately* by some two portions of the assembly. Is not this indicative of such a practice, as we find in the oldest extant Liturgies, of the

minister and the flock responding to one another in the
words :—

Minister. The Lord be with you.
People. And with thy spirit.
M. Lift up your hearts.
P. We lift them up unto the Lord.
M. Let us give thanks unto the Lord.
P. It is meet and right so to do.
M. It is very meet, right, and our bounden duty, that we should at all
times, and in all places, give thanks unto Thee, O Lord, Holy Father,
Almighty, Everlasting God.

Supplications and responses like these, together with longer
prayers to which the congregation responded with the Amen,
are found in the still extant Liturgies, which, coming to us
from the fourth or fifth century, bear the names of St. James,
St. Mark, and other venerable men.   Such responsive litanies
and prayers must, in their origin, have been older than those
ancient Liturgies, which all contain them ; and it is highly
probable that they are the echoes of the chant raised, with
some kind of alternation, in the Church described by Pliny.

It is very interesting to notice that the musical intonation
given to those primitive devotions addressed to Christ, or, at
least, the music which was mingled with the prayers and
praises, led the Roman governor to call the service, in great
part, if not wholly, " the singing of a chant[1] to Christ."

And next we have to notice, in Pliny's representation of
Christian worship, his mention of an oath (*sacramentum* in
the Latin) by which, he says, the Christians bound themselves.   Pliny's description of this *oath* strikes us as very
strange and remarkable.   Neither in Scripture, nor in the
post-apostolic writings, do we find anything like this oath in
any ancient delineation of Christian worship.[2]   It is represented as an oath against wrong-doing, robbery, theft, adultery, breach of faith, and abuse of trust.

If we could suppose that the decalogue was recited in the
Liturgy of that very early age, somewhat as it is rehearsed

---

[1] *Carmenque* Christo quasi Deo *dicere* secum invicem.
[2] There is no probability of the baptismal vow having been thus repeated
every week.

now in the Communion Service of the English Church, we might understand some of the characteristics of this oath ; but, then, the introduction of the Ten Commandments into the English Liturgy originated in the sixteenth century, and no direct ancient precedent for this custom is known to us, apart from the letter of Pliny which we are considering.

The Roman governor had evidently taken no little pains to discover as much truth as he could in connection with Christianity. He obviously wished to lay before the emperor as clear an account as possible of all the important facts he had discovered. Irrelevant matter, mere mistaken fancies, something entirely alien from the explanations afforded him by the Christians—such idle representations were not likely to proceed from Pliny, least of all when he troubled a master like Trajan with facts that were to be considered. Careless inaccuracy in such a case would bring disgrace upon the governor if it were detected by the emperor. We may be sure there was something real which led Pliny to name this oath and the details he connects with it.

What was there in the religion of the earliest Christians which might give rise to this part of Pliny's description ? In trying to answer this question, we must bear in mind that the evidence, upon which the description is based, was in part at least extracted by torture from two unhappy deaconesses.

If now we image to ourselves the kind of examination by question and answer implied in this horrid process, it will yield as its most probable results just such testimony as that which Pliny submitted to Trajan.

It is natural to suppose that, without the intervention of interpreters or translators, the unfortunate deaconesses would themselves employ the Latin language in which their wretched jailers would interrogate them amidst their terror and their agony.

What, they would be asked, is done by you at the early meeting of the Christians ?

We chant a service to Christ as our God, they would reply.

What else ? the jailers would demand.

We join in a sacred vow ("*sacrament*," as they would call it in Latin, and as we, people of Western Europe, have learned to call the same holy rite).

To the torturers, this term "sacrament" would not bear the signification it most readily conveys to our minds. To Trajan's contemporaries a "sacrament" suggested *an oath;* and one is obliged to realize to one's self the interest which this word would kindle in the minds of those who were trying to extort from the deaconesses some secret and unacknowledged deeds of evil. "An oath," the torturers would think; yes, now we are coming to the pith and kernel of this hateful superstition. It has seemed harmless enough hitherto; but that, which is done by the Christians in secret, we have never yet elicited. Now we shall discover it. They bind one another by a sacrament, an oath! Well, tell us now the nature of this your secret oath? To what mischief, to what crime, do you pledge yourselves by this oath?

To none, would be the reply of the poor women; and, as Rome's hideous scourge, with its knots of metal, fell upon them, still they would persist in their testimony that the Christian sacrament bound them to no evil deed.[1]

What! do you conspire for no robbery, no theft?

For none, would be their cry; and so this negative, too, finds its place in the record of their examination, as does, presently after, their denial of any violation of the laws of chastity.[2]

The Roman record of the next portion of their confession represents them as saying their sacrament was a pledge against any breach of faith,[3] and against the unjust retaining of anything which had been entrusted to their custody.[4]

These last two particulars seem out of keeping with such an examination under torture—out of keeping with the questions likely to be asked from Christian women at such a time.

[1] Non in scelus aliquod.
[2] Ne furta, ne latrocinia, ne adulteria committerent.
[3] Ne fidem fallerent.
[4] Ne depositum appellati abnegarent.

The natural interpretation of this part of the case we take
to be that the torturers, weary and disappointed at discovering
no heinous crime connected with the Christian oath, changed
the form of their interrogatories at this point.

You deny all crimes as the burden of your Christian " sacrament," they would say; to what then are you bound by this
oath of yours?

To such a query the unhappy victims might well reply,
Our oath binds us never to deny our faith, never to be false
to our religion.

One perceives at once how easily an expression like this,
most common among Christians, would be misapprehended by
Pliny or his subalterns, as if it were intended for the ordinary
Latin phrase which referred, idiomatically, to breach of faith
in general.   The deaconesses spoke of the sacrament as
pledging them not to break faith with Christ. They were
understood to mean that they took an oath against unfaithful-
ness in general.   There is an ineptitude in the latter vow,
whereas the former is most appropriate.   For Christians to
take an oath that they would keep faith generally, looks like
a platitude, making much ado about what would be with
them a matter of course; but to swear fidelity to Christ as
the Captain of their salvation—to take, as it were, a military
oath of fidelity and obedience to Jesus—was just the special
mark and characteristic of a believer.

So do we understand this part of the representation of the
Christian " sacrament; " and, similarly, the next expression
in Pliny's letter makes the Christians bind themselves by oath
to restore honestly, when called upon to do so, whatever might
have been entrusted to their custody. What a strange and
improbable narrowness this gives to the delineation of Christian
character !   Suppose, however, that the deaconesses went on
to say their " sacrament " pledged them faithfully to keep and
guard that good thing—as was St. Paul's expression (1 Tim.
i. 18, vi. 20)—which had been committed unto them. To
the unbelieving Romans this Scriptural and almost technical
phrase would be obscure and unintelligible, and nothing could
be more likely than that Pliny, or those acting under his

order, would misunderstand the Christian oath as pledging
Christ's followers to be faithful in the capacity of trustees and
custodians of property in general, instead of binding them to
be faithful guardians of the deposit of truth and hope and love
committed unto them in the Gospel of Christ.

Thus do we follow, step by step, along the confession
extorted from the two deaconesses. So do they tell us of a
sacred vow ("*sacrament*," or oath) by which their co-religion-
ists were wont to bind themselves at the early gathering of
the Lord's Day morning. It was an oath, not binding them
to any crime, theft, adultery, or the like, but to fidelity
towards their Captain, Christ, and to inviolable constancy in
guarding the good thing committed to their trust by Christ.

Here, then, we have a fresh name, "Sacrament," added to
the list of appellations for the Eucharist, and this is done in
the decade immediately following the age of the apostles.

Nothing can be more probable than that the Lord's Supper
had, by some of the apostles themselves, been called an oath,
as is the signification of this Latin word "Sacrament."

So far as we can trust Pliny's description of the most
salient points in the religion of the early Christians—and his
character and position and obvious painstaking in the matter
combine with the whole spirit of his delineation to assure one
of its trustworthiness—we have here, not only a fresh name
for the Christian "breaking of bread," a name which has
been perpetuated and sanctioned by all subsequent usage in
the Church of the West, but in the very name we have testimony to the effect that, whatever else the communion of the
Lord's Supper might be to Christians, one most impressive
characteristic of it, as it appeared to the minds of the Latin-
speaking peoples, was as the military oath of courage, obedience, and fidelity to Christ and His Gospel.

Pliny fails to make mention of any outward badges, symbols, and tokens connected with the sacrament. To him that
which was, before all things, conspicuous, was that it was
an oath binding men to a course of conduct—a course of
moral action, opposed to evil, and in support of faith and
fidelity.

It is of no small moment that we should observe one or two other points in this part of Pliny's letter. He records that, in the earlier period of his rule in Bithynia, it had been the custom of the Christians to assemble a second time, late in the day, for the purpose of partaking of a harmless meal[1] in common. This was, manifestly, the Supper, in accordance with apostolic usage, as an evening meal, in the course of which was celebrated the eucharistic breaking of bread and drinking of the cup. This later assembling of the Christians had been abandoned, however, in compliance with the command of the emperor and his representative.

It is difficult to imagine that the Bithynian Christians would give up their eucharistic breaking of bread at the same time that they, from political considerations, desisted from the evening meal that had hitherto accompanied it; and thus we find confirmation of our belief that the sacrament of the early morning was, as we have been observing, a celebration of the Eucharist: and, if this be so, we have an instance, probably one of the very earliest instances, of the Lord's Supper being made, no longer part of a meal in common, but a sacrament, with breaking of bread and drinking of the cup only, in the morning ere yet day had well dawned. In later times (for example, in the days of Tertullian) the evening meal of Christians had again come into vogue; but under the rule of Pliny it was, at least for a time, abandoned; and, in obedience to the State, that Church of confessors and martyrs changed even apostolic customs in matters of such small moment as whether the communion was in the morning or the evening, whether it was conjoined with the meal in common, or dissociated from it.

It is fair to say that, though Pliny calls Christianity a " perverted and over-zealous superstition," he gives no facts or proofs which would justify any one in calling the religion of Christ a superstition in the modern sense of that word. We leave those, whose convictions differ from our own, to imagine what Pliny must have written to Trajan, on this aspect of the case, if he had found the Christians in his pro-

---

[1] Ad capiendum cibum, promiscuum tamen et innoxium.

vince believing and teaching that bread and wine, after eucharistic blessing, remained, indeed, to all appearance still bread and wine, but were, in some imperceptible, indescribable, and inconceivable manner, changed into the objective flesh and blood of Christ, whose material body was, nevertheless, described as being in heaven and absent from earth at the same time that it was thus objectively present in the bread and wine of the Lord's Supper.

As wide as the poles asunder, however, is Pliny's representation of the Christian sacrament as an oath from this idea of an objective presence of an absent object.

CHAPTER II.

FROM this heathen representation of the Christian sacrament about the year 110 A.D., we proceed to notice the teaching of certain ancient Christian writers on the same subject. In this connection, of course, the volume of evidence that might be adduced is immense. Apart from any independent investigations that might be instituted, Dr. Pusey and his allies would furnish us with a copious " Catena Patrum " on the one side ; while, on the other side, the late Dean Goode, Dr. Harrison,[1] and those who agree with them, would present the same links in the chain of evidence (and other added links, too) in quite a different light.

Results of somewhat similar divergence would be obtained if we yielded ourselves, on the one side, to the teaching of Daillé's well-known old book on " The Right Use of the Fathers," or to the guidance, on the other side, of the late Professor Blunt.

Instead of attempting to produce many brief quotations concerning the Eucharist from Ignatius or Polycarp, or from other writers of questionable authenticity, we shall endeavour to set before the reader one very complete picture of the Lord's Supper as it was practised in the early Church ; and from this, we think, important conclusions may be drawn that will

[1] John Harrison, D.D. Edin., Vicar of Fenwick, near Doncaster, author of " Whose are the Fathers ?" "An Answer to Dr. Pusey's Challenge," "An Answer in Seven Tracts to the Eucharistic Doctrine of Romanists and Ritualists," etc., etc., etc.

enable us to deal very briefly with the vast mass of citation that has been adduced, and still may be adduced, from the Christian writers of post-apostolic antiquity.

Before proceeding to quote from those great men whose writings, like their fame, have reached down to these modern times from the earliest centuries of the Christian era, it may be well to offer a few introductory remarks.

Apart from the testimony to any writer's power which is furnished by survival through ages, the reader who can contemplate works like those of Justin, Origen, Tertullian, Chrysostom, Jerome, or Augustin, and yet can fail to perceive the depth and originality and force which characterize their pages, is not to be envied by us. We cannot sympathize with him. In genius, and in force of thought and expression, these ancient Christian authors appear to us, from the specimens we have read, not as pigmies, but as giants.

Contemplate their paucity of advantages, the scarcity of manuscripts, the awkward form in which those manuscripts existed, the difficulty attaching to intercourse between the scholars of those ancient days ; and, in view of these obstacles to research, the learning of the early Christian writers is wellnigh as admirable as the ingenuity with which they often handle topics that were then new to the world and to themselves. To these great students and thinkers and writers, the designation "Fathers" has constantly been applied by vast numbers of those who have succeeded them ; and, in respect of much of our present religious thought and nomenclature having been created by the so-called Fathers, there is an appropriateness in the title.

On the other hand, however, it should not be forgotten that there is something, in the very essence and spirit of Christ's religion, which forbids the setting up of any merely human authority as that by which the intellectual freedom of believers is to be limited, or their opinions are to be prescribed and dictated. Not only is the apostolic appeal to individual judgment in such utterances as, "I speak as to wise men ; judge ye what I say" (1 Cor. x. 15) ; or "Prove all things ; hold fast that which is good" (1 Thess. v. 21) ; or "Be ready always to give an answer to every man that asketh you a reason of the hope that is in you " (1 Peter iii. 15); but the very chief of apostles defines the limits of his own authority in such wise as that whilst, on the one hand, neither he, nor any man, nor even an angel from heaven, may change the Gospel of Christ (Gal. i. 8), and whilst he is bound to preach that Gospel and enforce it to the very utmost of his knowledge, wisdom, and power, yet, on the other hand, it is his own emphatic and most noteworthy declaration, " Not for that we have dominion over your faith, but are helpers of your joy " (2 Cor. i. 24). And 'all this apostolic insistency on the necessity and duty of private judgment is in perfect harmony with the teaching of our Lord—indeed, finds its authorization in words like those of the Saviour when He said, " Be not ye called Rabbi : for one is your Master, even Christ ; and all ye are brethren. And call no man your father upon earth : for one is your Father, which is in heaven. Neither be ye called masters : for one is your Master, even Christ " (Matt. xxiii. 8—10.)

Thus distinctly, in the letter of precepts as well as in the general spirit of the New Testament, are we forbidden to constitute the writers of the post-apostolic Church as " Fathers " in the sense of men whose opinions are to bind us with any degree of authority other than that of ordinary Christian advisers or informants. It may be wise, or it may be unwise, to call those writers " Fathers " in the sense of men who originated not a few of the terms and definitions of modern theology; but it is obviously unscriptural and wrong to yield them that venerable name with the idea that they are writers who must be obeyed rather than judged.

It is this injudicious attempt to overstrain patristric authority that has provoked, from those who dislike it, the rejoinder that the post-apostolic writers of the Church's first six centuries were not the " Fathers " but the " children " of Christendom.

It is an old fight of words, and perhaps one not likely to be settled soon, whether the early recipients of any system of teaching are *Fathers* in respect of their handing it down to their successors, or *children* inasmuch as humanity, with the accumulated experience of the intervening ages, is now older and should be wiser than it was in their time.

This vexed question we shall not attempt to decide peremptorily; but, in examining any opinions of the so-called Fathers, we must not forget that while they were men of more than ordinary mental power—while not a few of them were men of extraordinary intellectual gifts—yet their own opinions varied from period to period of their career as writers, and all their opposing variations of thought cannot be accepted as right and true. The habit of rhetorical exaggeration learned by the unbeliever, or the layman, clung to him when he became a Christian and a Churchman. The professional subtlety of the advocate, the dogmatical refinement of the metaphysician, the fancy of the imaginative man, the stern logic of the exact and systematic thinker, the general dignity of the man of lofty mind, the occasional trifling of the wayward or the less strong-minded—all these peculiarities adhered to the several writers with whose opinions we are now concerned. We adduce their testimony and their thoughts, not as of judges to whose decision we must submit, but as the best evidence we can obtain concerning the post-apostolic doctrines and practices in connection with the Lord's Supper.

A. *Justin Martyr's Testimony.*

Probably the earliest extant passages of any length, bearing upon our subject, are to be found in the writings of Justin, the philosopher and martyr. The approximate date of Justin's genuine writings may be taken as about A.D. 150. Justin's Apology or Defence of Christianity is in two parts, which are addressed to different Roman emperors, Antoninus Pius and Marcus Aurelius. This was followed by the narrative of a Dialogue concerning Christianity between Justin and Trypho, the Jew. Justin himself was a native of Samaria, probably not of Jewish extraction. He studied in many schools of philosophy before addicting himself, as a layman, to the wisdom that is in Christ.

(a.) *From the Dialogue with Trypho.*

From his Dialogue with Trypho (pp. 344, 345 of the Paris edition), we cite the following words :—

" The true priestly race of God are we, as God also Him-self witnesseth when He saith that in every place among the Gentiles men bring sacrifices which are pure and well-pleasing to Him. God, however, accepteth sacrifices from men only through His priests. God in the prophets (προλαβών) wit-nesseth that He is well-pleased with all men, therefore, who through the name of Jesus Christ [offer] the sacrifices which He (Christ) enjoined, that is, in the thanksgiving of the bread and of the cup, which sacrifices are made by the Christians in every place upon earth.

" But the sacrifices, which are made by you [Jews] and by those priests of yours, God rejects, saying " (Mal. i. 10), " ' And your sacrifices I will not receive at your hands, be-cause,' as He says, 'from the rising of the sun to his setting My name hath been glorified among the Gentiles, but ye profane it.' And ye ˹Jews˺, in your love of contention, still persist in saying that it was the sacrifices of those then living in Jerusalem under the name of Israelites which God rejected; but that the prayers of the men of that race, who were then in a state of dispersion, God expressly received and called their prayers sacrifices.

" Now, in your assertion that the prayers and thanksgivings [Eucharists], made by worthy men, are the only sacrifices which are perfect and well-pleasing unto God, I entirely agree with you, for these things only have Christians also received for to do even for a remembrance; [1] and in connection with their food, alike solid and liquid, there is a remembrance of God and of the suffering which God suffered through Him " (that is, probably, through, or in the person of, Christ).

(b.) *From the Apology.*

This is an important and interesting quotation from

---

[1] The Greek here is very obscure and the text apparently corrupt. We give the best rendering we can of the words καὶ ἐπ᾽ ἀναμνήσει δὲ τῆς τροφῆς αὐτῶν ξηρᾶς τε καὶ ὑγρᾶς ἐν ᾗ καὶ τοῦ πάθους ὃ πέπονθε δι᾽ αὐτοῦ ὁ Θεὸς τοῦ Θεοῦ μέμνηται.

Justin Martyr; but, before commenting on it, let us produce another passage from the same writer's Apology, that so this entire representation of the Lord's Supper, in the middle of the second century, may lie before the reader at one glance.

In the course of admitting a new member into the Christian assembly, writes Justin (Apol. Prim. ch. xcvii.) :—

"Then, after thus washing[1] the believer, who has taken his place among us, we conduct him to the brethren, as they are called, in the place where they are assembled for the earnest offering of common prayers as well for themselves, as for him who has been enlightened, and for all in every place, that we may be thought worthy, after having learned the things which are true, to be also found good citizens in our works and keepers of the commandments, so that we may be saved with the eternal salvation.

"At the end of our prayers we salute one another with a kiss. Then there is brought to him who presides over the brethren[2] bread and a cup of water and mixture; and the president, upon receiving this, gives praise and glory to the Father of all things through the name of His Son and of the Holy Spirit; and he makes a great thanksgiving for being thought worthy of these things by God. When he has completed his prayers and his thanksgiving, all the people who are present assent to his good words, saying Amen. Now the 'Amen' is a Hebrew word signifying, So be it.

"After this thanksgiving of the president and this assent of all the people, those who are called deacons amongst us give to each of those who are present a portion of the bread and wine and water over which the thanksgiving has been pronounced, and to those who are not present they carry portions away. And this food is called amongst us Eucharist [that is, thanksgiving], and of it only he is allowed to partake who believes the things taught by us to be true, who has washed in the washing for remission of sins and for regeneration, and who so lives as Christ enjoined.

"For we regard not these things as common bread or a common beverage; but in like manner as Jesus Christ our

---

[1] μετὰ τὸ οὕτως λοῦσαι.   [2] τῷ προεστῶτι τῶν ἀδελφῶν.

Saviour was made flesh by the word of God and bore flesh
and blood for our salvation, so have we been taught that the
food over which prayer and giving of thanks have been said
according to His command—(and by this food in its assimi-
lation [its change][1] the blood and the flesh of each and all of
us are nourished)—that this food is the flesh and blood of
that Jesus who Himself was made flesh. For the apostles, in
the memoirs, called Gospels, which were composed by them,
have thus narrated that a command was laid on them when
Jesus took bread and gave thanks and said, This do for
the remembrance of Me ; this is My body : and when, having
taken the cup likewise and given thanks, He said, This is
My blood; and that He gave portions to them only.

"And this, we are told by those who are initiated in the
mysteries of Mithras, is done [among them], the imitation
having been introduced by the wicked demons. For that
bread and a cup of water, with certain added words, have
their place among the rites of him that is initiated, is a matter
which ye either know or can ascertain. But we [Christians]
after these things, for the future, continually remind one another of these things ; and those among us who have possessions give aid to all who are in want; and there is a continual
association amongst us. And for all our food [2] we bless the
Maker of all things through His Son Jesus Christ and through
the Holy Spirit.

"And on the day called Sunday we have an assembly alike
of those who dwell in town or country ; and we read as much
of the memoirs of the apostles and the writings of the prophets
as time permits.

"Then, upon the reader's ceasing, the president admonishes
and exhorts us to imitate their good examples.

"After that we all stand up together and pray, and, prayer
ended, there is brought bread and wine and water ; and the
president lifts up his voice in prayer and thanksgiving to the
best of his power, and the people assent to his good word
with their Amen.

"Then is made the distribution to each individual, an

---

[1] κατὰ μεταβολήν.   [2] ἐπὶ πᾶσι τε οἷς προσφερόμεθα.

the participation by each of the things over which thanks
have been given; and to those who are not present with us
portions are sent by the deacons.

"Those who are well off and inclined to do so, give each
as he likes and determines; and that which is collected is
deposited with the president, and he assists those who are
desolate and in distress."

(c.) *Comments on these Passages.*

Thus have we set out before the reader Justin's full
account of the Lord's Supper as it was administered in his
day, some hundred and twenty years after its first institution
by the Saviour—some fifty or sixty years after the death of the
latest survivors among the apostles. Though we have only
given two extracts from Justin, one from the Dialogue and
one from the Apology, yet it will be observed that these two
passages contain three distinct and more or less complete
references to the "breaking of bread." One occurs in the
Dialogue with Trypho; the second describes the communion
of a newly baptized Christian; and then, immediately upon
that, follows, in the Apology, a description of the Lord's
Supper as it was celebrated on each Sunday by the Christian
congregation.

In later times much reserve was practised by believers
with reference to this sacred rite. They were unwilling to
speak of it in detail or to write about it, except for those who
were already baptized communicants, or were in the way of
speedily becoming so. Of any such reticence, however, no
sign is indicated by Justin. As St. Paul wrote openly on
the subject to the Corinthian Church; as the apostle wished
the uninitiated and unbelievers to be instructed, and impressed, and won by looking on at the Christian Eucharist;
just so Justin, too, makes no difficulty about treating of the
holy Supper with the most entire frankness. Whether he
addresses the unbelieving Jew Trypho, or whether his defence
is made before one or other of Rome's heathen emperors, Justin
lays bare the Christian practice of the sacrament without any

trace of a wish to throw a veil over the whole of the rite, or over any part of it.

If this primitive candour and simplicity had been maintained by later Christians, how much less danger must they have incurred of their doings being misunderstood and misrepresented! If the Christian assemblies had continued open to the inspection of any visitor, there would have been less opportunity for the enemies of the Gospel to disseminate horrible scandals concerning the alleged Thyestean feasts and other abominations which they charged against the Church. As opposed to any attempt or wish to conceal the acts and significance of the Lord's Supper, we should notice Justin's readiness to reiterate his explanation of the eucharistic customs in his day.

The first matter of detail which presents itself to our notice in Justin's words, is his statement concerning the Christian priesthood. The true priestly race, he writes, are "*we*"—I, Justin, who am not set apart as a Christian minister, not ordained; I, a believing layman, and the rest of the believers, alike ministers and people,—"we" are God's true *priests*. We it is who, in every place among all nations, are enjoined by God to offer to Him sacrifices which shall be as well-pleasing as they are pure.

There is a sound and a spirit in these words of Justin which reminds us how St. Peter and St. John (1 Peter ii. 5, 9; Rev. i. 6) had taught that all believers are "an holy priesthood," "a royal priesthood," "kings and priests unto God." Justin makes it plain that, even at the Table of the Lord, however much there may be deacons and presbyters or overseers (bishops), there are no officials of the Church who, any more than the simplest members of that Church, can be called sacrificing priests. On the contrary, Christ being, literally, the one and only Sacrificing Priest or High-Priest, all believers, alike lay and clerical, are in Justin's estimation, even as in the judgment of the apostles, all of them, metaphorically, priests unto God.

Justin's next important point is that all Christians, as priests, must offer sacrifices unto God; and the nature of those sacrifices he proceeds to make clear. They are, he says, none other than "only prayers and thanksgivings made by worthy men;" and among these is included "the thanksgiving [or Eucharist] of the bread and wine."

Justin here calls the thanksgiving over the bread and wine a sacrifice which all Christians everywhere offer to God through the name of Jesus Christ. Observe, it is the thanksgiving through Christ that Justin in this passage calls a sacrifice; and, exactly in the same manner, the apostles taught that we should all offer to God the spiritual sacrifices of praise and thanksgiving and prayer. It is true Scripture never designates the bread and wine of the Supper as "sacrifices." Scripture never brings the bread and wine into such close verbal association with the "sacrifice" of thanksgiving as Justin here does. We should notice this deviation from Scripture usage. New customs of language make room for new ideas; and we shall presently find that, even in the writings of Justin himself, there is a further departure from Scripture precedent to be noticed ere long. Still, in this passage now under review, where the Eucharist of bread and wine is called a sacrifice *only* as being a kind of thanksgiving, it is hard to say that we find anything in plain and direct contravention of the spirit of the New Testament in describing thanksgiving as a proper spiritual sacrifice, whether it be felt and spoken at the Table of the Lord, over bread and wine, or in any other place and under any other circumstances.

It is to be regretted that Justin did not always confine himself to this strictly defined use of the word sacrifice. Elsewhere, he calls the eucharistic elements a sacrifice without limiting his meaning to a spiritual offering of thanksgiving. No doubt he meant that the presentation of bread and wine was an acted thanksgiving, and so was a spiritual sacrifice. This would be a permissible and hardly an unscriptural use of words; but the unguarded and undefined employment of the term "sacrifice" readily lends itself to the upholding of the unscriptural idea that there are other sacrifices for sin besides that once offered by Christ upon the cross.

In the obscure and hardly grammatical words with which

this first quotation from Justin closes, the one thing which impresses itself on the reader is that the Eucharist was regarded, in the middle of the second century, as pre-eminently a *memorial* rite.   In connection with their "food, alike solid and liquid," there is a marked emphasis placed on the duty of associating all nutriment of the body with a remembrance of Christ's sufferings for us.   If the thanksgiving over the bread and wine was a spiritual sacrifice to be offered by all believers, lay and clerical, in their common capacity of priests unto God, all Christians were bound, each time they partook of bread and wine, to commemorate in their minds the one perfect sacrifice of Christ's sufferings.   Thus, on Justin's showing the sacramental bread and wine, in the public congregations were far from being the only reminder of Christ's death Such a recollection was to be called up in the believer's mind by every participation of food, " either liquid or solid."

And now we come to our second quotation from Justin the passage in which he explains to the Roman emperor two parts of Christian life :—

1. The participation of the Eucharist among the brethre by a newly baptized believer.

2. The administration of the Eucharist in the assembl of believers on the Sunday.

In the preface to the earlier of these two descriptions of the Eucharist it is very interesting to observe the sympath of the brethren for their newly admitted member.   Not only should we notice their prayers for him, but for themselv also, and for the universal Church.   Nor is it only the cath· licity of these supplications which is instructive, but the· burthen also while they ask that, as God has deigned to teach us the truth, so we may by our works evince ourselves to ɔ good citizens, good members together of the Christian con· monwealth, and faithful observers of its laws and commar·ments.   So, by knowledge of the truth, by good works s fellow-citizens, and by compliance with Christ's laws, shall e be saved with the eternal salvation.

Next follows a reference to the kiss of peace with wh·h the newly baptized was welcomed among his fellow-citizes.

And then we come to the eucharistic rite itself. Justin
represents some one of the brethren as being their president
and leading their devotions throughout the Supper.   This
president is not designated or characterized in any way as an
ordained person.   He is not represented as a bishop or a
presbyter or a deacon.   He is simply, for the occasion, the
president of the brethren.   Obviously, he might be a Church-
officer; and, if a Church-officer was present, he would most
naturally preside over the brethren : but Justin tells the
emperor nothing about this.   Rather, his representation of
the "president of the brethren" tallies with what we have
seen in some earlier pages of this essay. As the head of each
Jewish family or party presided at the Passover supper ; as
our Saviour in this capacity presided at the Last Supper ; as
heads of families were sure to preside in "the breaking of
bread at home " mentioned in the Book of the Acts of the
Apostles; so here, in Justin's Apology, the picture presented to
us is not of a presbyter becoming, as distinguished from the
congregation, a sacrificing priest, but of one, among a body of
brethren who were all equally priests by reason of their
citizenship in Christ, selected as their president for the occasion or for a longer period.

B. *Principles laid down by Tertullian, Chrysostom, and Augustin
—the last as quoted by Gratian.*

This point which is thus brought out by Justin's use of the
word "president" is insisted upon by several later Fathers.
Thus, Tertullian (De Exhortatione Castitatis, c. vii. p. 522)
teaches, "Are not even we laymen priests ? " Accordingly,
where no ordained ministers are present, he continues, "Thou
offerest [up the thanksgiving over the bread and wine] and
thou baptizest, and thou art a priest, alone, for thyself."
Similarly, Chrysostom (2 Homil. 2 Tim. vol. xi. p. 671, edit.
Benedict.) taught, "I am about to say what may appear
strange, but be not astonished or startled at it. The offering
[of the sacramental thanksgiving] is the same whether a
common man [1] or Paul or Peter offer it." To the same effect

---

[1] κἂν ὁ τυχὼν προσενέγκῃ.

Jerome (Adv. Lucif. vol. ii. p. 141, edit. Basil. ap. Frohn.) alleges the validity of a sacrament administered by a layman on the principle that "as any one receives, so also can he give." Thus, the baptized can give the baptism he has received; the partaker of the Lord's Supper can administer the Lord's Supper. And so, once more, unless Gratian (Corp. Juris Canon. Pars iii. de Consecr. Distinctio 4, c. 21), entirely against his own convictions and predilections, misquotes a letter from Augustin to Fortunatus, that great writer represents this opinion as prevalent in his time when he says, "We are accustomed to hear that even laymen are wont to administer a sacrament which they have received."

This absence of any absolutely distinctive priesthood from men in holy orders; this common character of priesthood in all believers, lay and clerical; this qualification of the Christian layman to administer the Eucharist in the capacity of a president among his fellow-believers, who are all, likewise, priests as much as himself;—this is a line of instruction that is enforced by no lesser men than Justin, Tertullian, Jerome, Chrysostom, and Augustin; and, what is far more important, it is in keeping with the example and teaching of our Saviour and His apostles. Assuredly, it is a line of instruction not without its usefulness and its aptitude, alike for celebrants and communicants, in this later portion of the nineteenth century.

C. Further Comments on Justin.

Justin tells us that the elements employed in the sacrament were bread and a mixture of wine and water. This using water mixed with the wine is so harmless a custom and was so likely to have been the course adopted by our Saviour himself, that we should hardly be surprised if an attempt were made to procure the removal of those legal barriers that now forbid its adoption in the English Church and yet it is a small matter, a point of all but absolute indifference either way; and, in such cases, because of their bearing upon more important matters, it is generally the wisest course to imitate, as nearly as possible, the precis-

example set before us in the Scripture record, rather than to adopt an ideal course of our own. On this principle, as our Lord made no mention of wine and water, but only of wine, in His institution of the Eucharist, it may be wise to "let well alone" in the regulations regarding the cup that now prevail in the Church of England.

Justin goes on to tell us that the president, on receiving the bread and wine, gives praise and glory to God, the Father of all things (thus imitating the custom of the Paschal supper among the Jews), with the characteristic Christian recognition of the Son and the Holy Spirit through whom the Father bestows His blessings. Upon this follows a full and particular thanksgiving to God for deigning to make the congregation partakers of all His gifts and of the sacramental bread and wine.

It is important to notice that, upon the conclusion of his prayers and thanksgivings by the president, great stress is laid by Justin upon *all* the people, who are present, associating themselves in the offering of those spiritual sacrifices by their conjoint[1] and crowning assent in the utterance of the word "Amen," whose significance is "So let it be." True, for the sake of order and comeliness, the president has, so far, been their mouthpiece and spokesman; but it must not be supposed they have been indifferent spectators; it must not be thought the president has been thinking and feeling and making vows instead of them, without their taking an active and intelligent part in all that he has done. So far from this, the time has now come for them, with the grand effect of voice coming from a multitude, to pronounce their hearty assent in the loud Amen, So may it be; So would we have it. It is too common a fault among us, in modern times, to neglect this our conjoint action with the president, this our active part in the priestly and other functions he is discharging as our representative. Such negligence finds no excuse in Justin's picture of the early Christians, or in St. Paul's representation of the apostolic Church.

After repeating his statement that the president pro-

[1] πᾶς ὁ παρὼν λαὸς ἐπευφημεῖ λέγων ᾽Αμήν.

nounced the thanksgiving, and the whole people gave their glad acclaim of assent to it, Justin tells the emperor it was the duty of those who were styled "deacons" among the Christians to give to each member of the congregation a piece of the bread and a portion of the wine and water, and even to any absent members of the Christian body the deacons carried similar portions. There is no failure on Justin's part to inform his readers that the wine of the Eucharist was partaken of by each and every member of the Church just as all partook of the bread.

As we found a verb akin to "Eucharist" employed for the giving of thanks, in the Supper, by St. Paul and by the Lord Himself, so, in this passage, Justin tells us that the noun "Eucharist" was the name among Christians for "this food," as he calls the bread and wine.

Justin's next point is, that no one was permitted to take part in the Eucharist unless he was prepared for such participation by three qualifications:—He must believe in the truth of the things taught by Christians; he must have submitted himself to the washing for putting away of sin and for regeneration; and he must be living in compliance with the injunctions of Christ. Mark, there is no requirement of auricular or any other confession to a Church officer; there is no preparatory penance to be undergone; neither is there any semblance of sacerdotal absolution. Mark again, that attached to the Hebraism for baptism [1] are the spiritual characteristics of putting away sin and being born again into sonship to God; and, besides such baptism, that which is required of communicants in the Supper is belief of the Christian truth and carrying out of the Christian life.

And now we come to a deeply interesting part of this quotation from Justin. However obscure and involved may have been the Greek which Justin here wrote; however corrupt the text of the passage may have become; as matters stand, several points appear to be intended and established by the writer with unquestionable distinctness.

First of all, the Christians of Justin's time did not regard

λουσαμένῳ τὸ λουτρόν, having washed the washing.

the eucharistic elements as "common bread or common beverage." This special estimation of the eucharistic elements may mean very little or it may mean a great deal. How much it meant must depend on the words which follow. Obviously a building, which is hallowed by certain associations that cling to one's mind, is no longer a common building in the thoughts of him who is possessed by those associations. It was the jail in which Bunyan wrote; or it was the house in which Shakespeare courted Ann Hathaway; or it was the birthplace, or the familiar haunt, or the grave of one or other of the men who bear more than kingly sway over our minds. These, and a thousand other hallowing associations, make the cell of a jail, the kitchen of a cottage, or the lowliest spot on earth to be no longer common and like other places for us. So, too, a book or any object, which has been much used and loved by a friend who was very dear to us, is no longer a common book like any other copy of the same work. And, in the same manner, with however infinitely higher associations, bread and wine, which have been hallowed as special tokens and reminders of the death of our Redeemer, can no longer be common and ordinary objects in our estimation.

Such a general sentiment, which lies at the bottom of what Justin is now saying to us, is a feeling in which well-nigh every man must sympathize. Justin, however, proceeds to something more definite than this. He institutes a comparison between the incarnation of our Saviour through the word of God, and the food (whereby our flesh and blood are nourished), but which, through the word of prayer and thanksgiving enjoined by Christ, is,[1] as Christians were then taught, the flesh and blood of the incarnate Jesus.

(a.) *Justin's Adoption of "This is My body," and "This is My blood."*

Before commenting on these words let us see, as Justin continues his line of thought, what is the ground and reason which he assigns for this statement. It is none other than that, in the original institution by our Lord Himself, the

---

[1] εἶναι.

words used over the bread were, This is my body; and those used over the cup were, This is my blood.

Obviously, in certain conditions of Justin's memory, if not in his general and pervading apprehension of Christ's teaching, all trace of the fuller statement, This is My blood of the covenant, has been lost. Still less does he bear in mind that, as we have seen, it is a moral certainty that Jesus did not say, This is My blood of the covenant, but did say, This is the new covenant in My blood; and, similarly, did not say, This is My body, but did say, This is the new covenant in My body.

Here we have the point of bifurcation for Christian thought. Henceforward, if not even from an earlier date than that of Justin, there will be two distinct streams of Christian principle recognisable in well-nigh every thinker and every writer of any eminence. At one time the imperfect and abridged, and paraphrastic version of the Saviour's words, This is My body, This is My blood, will cling to each mind and impress it. At another time the same Christian mind will be under other, and truer, and more spiritual influence; and there will be a powerful reaction against the materializing of spiritual things which is sure to arise out of this curtailed and misleading statement of our Lord's real words as He employed them at the institution of the Eucharist, and as they stand recorded by St. Luke and St. Paul.

Not until a later point in this our essay will it be appropriate to show, in the words of the Fathers themselves, the form and direction taken by this pious and reasonable reaction. Here, and at present, we go not beyond the record of Justin's Apology. He and his contemporaries believed that, as Jesus was made flesh and bore (or took[1]) flesh and blood for our salvation, similarly eucharistic bread and wine "are" the flesh and blood of that incarnate Jesus.

This was their opinion; and, if we can rely on the genuineness of the Ignatian Epistle to the people of Smyrna, it was some half a century older than even Justin's writing, for Ignatius there blames certain heretics in these words,

---

[1] ἔσχεν.

" They [the Docetæ] abstain from the Eucharist and from public prayer because they do not acknowledge that the Eucharist is [1] the flesh of our Saviour Jesus Christ which [2] suffered for our sins and which the Father in His kindness raised." Whether these words were written by Ignatius or not, we have the distinct and definite belief of Justin and his contemporaries—that eucharistic bread and wine were not common nutriment, were not like other ordinary food, because they were in some sense the flesh and blood of Christ.

This important opinion of Justin should by no means be ignored; but neither should we forget that the greatest of the so-called Fathers of the Church explain that when they designate the sign, bread or wine, by the name of the thing signified, body or blood, they do so with no notion of a change of substance, but only to lift men's minds from the low level of the material signs to the high contemplation of the heavenly sacrifice. This we should remember; and, moreover, we should not forget that Justin's opinion, quoted above, was avowedly based altogether on the conception that Jesus said, This is My body, This is My blood; so that, inasmuch as Jesus said something else, according to Luke and Paul, instead of those words, the opinion must vary, or must vanish, together with the varying signification or the entire vanishing of the above reason upon which Justin tells us that it rested.

If Jesus meant in the institution, This cup is the new covenant ratified by My blood which is shed for you and for many, for the putting away of sin, then this would be the true interpretation of Justin's dangerous abbreviation, This is My blood. If Jesus meant and said (as St. Paul, 1 Cor. x. 16, xi. 25, represents him to have said and meant), This cup is a participation [3] of the new covenant in My blood, then this is very different from the signification likely to be put on its abridged form, This is My blood; and to the extent of this, the real utterance and meaning of our Saviour, would Justin's own reason for the belief that was in him compel us to

---

[1] εἶναι.   [2] τὴν ὑπὲρ ἁμαρτίων ἡμῶν παθοῦσαν.

[3] κοινωνία, a communion, a fellowship, a participation, a means of entering into.

modify the bald and literal interpretation of Justin's opinion that the eucharistic bread and wine are the flesh and blood of Jesus.

Because the Lord said, This cup is a means of participation in the new covenant ratified by the shedding of My blood; therefore, on his own showing, Justin, if he had borne those words of the Saviour in mind when he was writing the words of our quotation, would have expressed himself thus : The eucharistic bread and wine is no longer common and ordinary nutriment, because it is hallowed in our memory by association with the death of Christ, because it is a reminder of Christ's giving His body and His blood for our salvation—because, as Jesus taught, it is a perpetually blessed means of entering into and sustaining the fellowship of us all in the new covenant ratified by the shedding of Christ's blood.

If Justin (and perhaps Ignatius before him) and many another writer in the centuries that were to follow, had borne in mind the real words of Jesus and had abstained from unduly curtailing those words, the painful inconsistencies of patristic opinion on this subject would have been avoided; on this point, at all events, there would have been no injurious division in the mind of the Church; on this important topic we should all have been at one among ourselves and with the Saviour.

(b.) Justin's Reference to the "Mysteries" of the God Mithras.

Having thus noticed this belief and the ground on which it rests, we pass on to the next point in our quotation; and in this Justin gives us the strange piece of information that, in the mysteries of the Persian god Mithras, the worshippers partook of bread and a cup of water over which certain formularies were spoken. And this imitation of the Christian sacrament has, in Justin's opinion, been brought about by the suggestion of the evil demons. This ancient idea, of wicked spirits causing spurious imitations of parts of the Christian ritual, puts one in mind of the thoughts which are said to have occurred to the Jesuit missionaries as they discovered, in the religion of Buddha, very close resemblances to the Madonna and Child, the priesthood, the monastic orders, and numerous other portions of their own system.

Possibly, to the intelligent modern reader, far simpler and yet deeper and more instructive explanations of such phenomena will present themselves. We must not, however, dwell upon this subject here. Neither is this the place for a disquisition concerning the extent to which Rome and her empire and her wars made nations acquainted with one another, and brought together, in the capital, specimens of the diverse modes of worship that were in use among the Egyptians, the Jews, the Persians, and countless other tribes. How Justin, in some visit to Rome, may have ascertained the particulars he here mentions, can only be matter of surmise.

Arising out of this reference to the worship of Mithras there is, however, one point quite worthy of notice. We refer to Justin's bringing the "mysteries" of heathen religion into comparison—as it were, into contact—with Christianity, and especially with the sacrament of the Lord's Supper. The participation of bread and wine in the Christian Eucharist has, according to Justin, its counterpart or its imitation in the participation of bread and water by the initiated in the mysteries of Mithras. The one rite is so far like the other, in words of thanksgiving or of administration, as well as in elements to be partaken of, that, however little the resemblance may have been suggested by evil spirits, yet the parallelism is undeniable, and the mysteries of Mithras are clearly and unquestionably, teaches Justin, an imitation of the Christian Eucharist.

We are far from risking the affirmation that never, at any earlier date, had points of analogy been observed between the Lord's Supper and the "mysteries" of heathen religions. We neither say nor think that in every point of comparison there was agreement. Obviously, Justin made no secret of the nature and meaning and mode of celebration attaching to the Eucharist; whereas no worshipper at Eleusis, or at any of the heathen mysteries, would have been willing, or would have dared, to divulge to the Jew Trypho, or to the Roman emperor, the nature and signification and mode of initiation connected with any mystery of a prevailing heathen religion.

In this point of secrecy in the heathen mysteries and of entire frankness in the earliest portraiture of the Lord's Supper, alike by the Samaritan layman Justin and by the great apostle St. Paul, there is an unlikeness between the real Christ and Mithras, between the openly instructing communion of the Lord's Table and the jealously guarded initiation in some obscure shrine of heathendom.

Even of those mysteries of Mithras how little does Justin say! "Bread and water" are employed, "with certain added formularies which ye either know or may learn!" Mithras had his secret only to be told to the initiated; and, however unimportant or however momentous might be the burthen of that secret, it was not to be mentioned to the profane.

As Christianity, in the succeeding centuries, adopted this Greek name,[1] "mystery," as another designation for the Lord's Supper, the Eucharist lost the transparent candour and openness of its early days; and it, too, came to be regarded as a secret rite whose meaning and celebration must be kept hidden from all except those who, as catechumens and as recipients of baptism, had been duly initiated.

Observe, however, that in heathendom, and in the Christianity of the earliest days, men never dreamt that the "mysteries" were an unintelligible secret for the initiated. Contrariwise, those who were not worshippers of Mithras knew and understood little or nothing of the bread and water and the form of words connected with them; but any man who chose to be admitted to the worship of that Persian deity was, in the act of admission and initiation, instructed as to the nature of the outward and visible signs or symbols and as to the meaning, or purport, or intention which was signified by them. Thus, "mysteries," the most solemn and sacred among the heathens—those mysteries whose divulging was profanity, to be visited by the most terrible penalties—were secrets only to the uninitiated. To those who took part in

---

[1] μυστήριον, a secret revealed.

any "mysteries" all was explained. This explanation was "initiation." He who knew not the symbols, bread and water or whatever in each case they might be, or he who knew not the religious significance of those symbols, was not initiated. To strangers and outsiders the "mysteries" were a secret still hidden; but to those who frequented the shrine and gained admission to its *arcana*, the "mysteries" became a secret revealed.

So had the New Testament writers employed the term "mystery." They never, indeed, designated the Lord's Supper as a mystery; but whatever they did call by that name was a secret no longer hidden but clearly revealed. In later ages the opinion grew up that the Christian Eucharist was a terrific subject of obscurity—something to be jealously kept secret from the unbaptized; and in this misconception it is only too easy to perceive a fruitful source of the charges brought against the Church, that her secret observances were abominable, that her kiss of charity was impure, that her Supper of the Lord was preceded by the murder of an innocent and consisted in the eating of its flesh. How near the truth were these false charges! How they would be fostered, and were fostered, by secrecy! How a ray of apostolic light and publicity would have prevented much of the persecutor's cruelty, much of the martyr's suffering.

If in any age, primitive or modern, the Christian sacraments are called "mysteries," it is most desirable that the term should be used correctly, as signifying symbols, like the bread and wine, with a definite and intelligible meaning, according to which they remind us of the redeeming death of Christ till His coming again, and they thus bind and incorporate us into fellowship with His body once given for us, and they also unite and associate us all into membership in His body the Church, into corporate union one with another, each with all.

Let the outward sign and the inward signification be thus apprehended as they were by the Saviour and by His apostles and disciples; and then "mystery," a secret not known to unbelievers, a blessed revelation to all who come to Christ, will be a most appropriate and felicitous title for the Lord's Supper, to be added to those which Scripture and the history of the earliest Christians have already brought under our notice.

So important is Justin's comparison between the Eucharist and the mysteries of Mithras.   So is that comparison an illustration, or, possibly, the origin of the application of the name "mystery" to the Christian breaking of bread.

At a later point in our inquiry it will be necessary to revert to this subject.   For the present these remarks may suffice to guard us against any misapprehension to the effect that the Lord's Supper, because it is rightly called a mystery, is therefore in part or wholly unintelligible even to the most devout of worshippers.

After this allusion to the mysteries of Mithras, Justin points out how completely and persistently the Lord's Supper is an act of communion and fellowship of Christian men, one with another.   The sacrament completed, there is not an end of our communion; but we thenceforward continually remind one another of what was done, and what was promised, and what was meant in the Eucharist : there is a continual interchange of partnership and help between the more wealthy and the more necessitous among us; indeed, we never cease, in the highest and best sense, to be together.[1]

And, as if this prolongation of the Eucharist into a lifelong fellowship with men did not complete Justin's idea of the Christian communion in the Supper, he adds that never do the recipients of that sacrament partake of any nourishment for their bodies without blessing[2] the Maker of all things through His Son Jesus Christ and through the Holy Spirit. So abiding, and continuous, and all-comprehensive alike of God and man, is the union and fellowship which is cemented at the believer's earliest celebration of the Eucharist, and never ceases from that day forward.

But yet, it would seem as if Justin wished to urge upon

---

[1] καὶ σύνεσμεν ἀλλήλοις ἀεί.

[2] εὐλογοῦμεν, the eucharistic term for blessing pronounced over the bread and wine.

the attention of his reader, We do not leave the continuance of this union, between the Christian and his fellow-men and his God, to the general and sustained recollection thus indicated to you; but there is a fixed day in each week, the day especially named after the sun (Sunday, as we moderns call it still), and on that day we hold an assembly of all believers whom we can bring together from town or country.

In this Sunday worship of Justin's contemporaries it is most interesting to notice that the characteristic features were :—

1. Reading the Gospels and the Prophets.
2. A practical discourse by the president of the assembly.
3. Common prayer by all the assembly in a standing attitude.[1]
4. The bringing in of bread and wine, over which the president prays and gives thanks; the people's assent with their "Amen;" the distribution by the deacons to all who are present and to any who may be absent.
5. An offertory in which those who are well off give according to their own wish and deliberate choice; and, the proceeds being deposited with the president, he assists the needy.

The points of resemblance, between this ancient Sunday service and Christian worship in modern times, are happily numerous and conspicuous. It is not necessary to dwell on them at any length.

The "sermon" is represented as highly practical, consisting of exhortations to the imitation of whatever good examples had been set before the congregation in the "Lessons," as we call them, of the prophets and apostles.

In the Common Prayer not only is the standing attitude worthy of observation by us of the English Church, to teach us sympathy in this respect with the Presbyterians, but this attitude of *standing* to pray may be instructive for any who are disposed to fall into excessive practices of prostration in their prayers, particularly in their devotions on approaching

[1] ἀνιστάμεθα κοινῇ πάντες καὶ εὐχὰς πέμπομεν.

the Lord's Table.   Clearly, a very different custom prevailed in the Church which was familiar to the eyes of Justin in the second century.

Very important and very full of instruction for us is the picture of every believer joining heartily in the prayer of that ancient Sunday worship.   The president did not pray in their stead while they were listless, or bore the appearance of being weary; but they stood up and, whether repeating aloud some prearranged supplication, or whether silently listening to their president, or however they expressed their emotion, it was made apparent to Justin and to any observer that every member of the congregation was praying.

In all which follows, concerning the bread and wine, and the president's thanksgiving, and the people's "Amen," and the participation of the elements, and concerning the offertory and its distribution, Justin adds little if anything to that which he had told us in his previous description of the communion of the newly baptized.   Here is nothing calling for special remark over and above what has been elicited by Justin's two earlier descriptions of the Eucharist.

We leave this full and frank portraiture of the sacrament which Justin set before the Jew Trypho and the unbelieving Roman emperor with a distinct impression that, towards the middle of the second century, all Christian lay people were recognised to be as fully and truly priests as any of the clergy.   With regard to *priesthood*, there was no difference between the laity and the president who ministered in the Eucharist.   This marks a point of agreement between Justin and the New Testament, but it marks also a portentous difference between our author and the sacerdotalism of the Middle Ages.

Every worthy recipient of the Lord's Supper did, in Justin's estimation, offer a sacrifice to God, but that sacrifice, though it included the eucharistic elements of bread and wine, still consisted, in strictness, according to Justin's express testimony, "only" of prayers and thanksgivings, the very "spiritual" sacrifices which, in the New Testament, are enjoined upon the entire body of believers.   The whole eu-

charistic service, as represented by Justin, was an appeal to
the intelligent sympathy of the people. Unless they came
"worthy" or "meet" to pray, unless they joined, each and
all of them, in the prayers and thanksgiving, unless their
"Amen" was a hearty and intelligent assent to the president's prayers and thanksgivings, Justin, like St. Paul,
would manifestly have pronounced their coming together to
be no eating the Supper of the Lord.

So far Justin represents to us, in this passage, a simple,
Scriptural, and beautiful picture of primitive worship and
communion.

But we have seen that this is not all. Justin added that,
after prayer and thanksgiving had been said over the elements
in accordance with Christ's command, those elements were no
longer ordinary bread and wine. They were the flesh and
blood of Christ, because the Lord had said, in appointing the
Eucharist for His remembrance, This is My body, This is
My blood.

To what extent Justin and the great writers of Christian
antiquity understood these words literally, to what extent they
limited and modified their meaning and gave them a figurative interpretation, we shall inquire in the sequel ; but, except
in this part of his teaching on the Lord's Supper, there is no
trace of Justin's holding that Christ was objectively present in
or with the bread and wine of the Eucharist.

If, instead of the abridged form, This is My blood,
Justin had kept steadily before his own mind and that of his
readers the fuller and more accurate record of what our
Saviour said and meant, the result, logically, would have been
very strongly marked. His words must then have been to
this effect : The eucharistic bread and wine are the flesh and
blood of Christ, because the Lord said, in instituting the
sacrament, This bread and this cup are a fellowship, or
means of participation, in the new covenant ratified by My
body given and by My blood shed for you and for many for
the putting away of sin.

To argue, from Christ saying the cup was a participation
in the new covenant sealed by His blood-shedding, that that

same cup was the blood of Christ, is as gross and palpable an abuse of reasoning as can well be conceived.

And, be it remembered—even if any reader still remains convinced, in spite of all that has been said in our previous pages, that the very words spoken by Christ were, This is My blood of the covenant—this, however improbable, however morally impossible we may deem such a conclusion, however it may obscure the thoughts and confuse the mind of him who entertains it,—still this version of our Saviour's words cannot alter the logical statement just set out by us, as long as the words of St. Paul and St. Luke remain as the Scriptural, and therefore the only absolutely authoritative, interpretation of what was meant by, This is My blood of the covenant.

For let us state the argument in full, on the supposition that the precise words of Jesus were, This is My blood; and the result will come out thus: This bread and this wine are the flesh and blood of Jesus, because the Lord said, at the institution, This bread and this cup are My body and blood, *meaning* (as we are taught by St. Paul and St. Luke), This bread and this cup are a participation in the new covenant sealed by the giving of My body and by the shedding of My blood for the putting away of sin.

Until any man shall be rash enough to say that St. Paul and St. Luke neither give the words of Jesus, nor express His meaning in the terms which they record as having been spoken by Him, this fatal flaw must remain in the reasoning by which Justin argues that bread and wine are flesh and blood, because Jesus said or meant that they were a participation in the new covenant ratified by His giving His body and shedding His blood.

Wherever this train of reasoning occurs, This bread is My literal and objective flesh, because it is a fellowship in the new covenant ratified by the death of My body, its obvious fallaciousness must surely be apparent, until "flesh" and "participation in a covenant ratified by the death of a body" shall be precisely equivalent and exchangeable phrases.

D. *Occasional Ambiguity the utmost Charge, with reference to materializing Christ's Presence, that can be brought against Justin and the Early Christian Writers.*

Here, then, we find in Justin Martyr what some will regard as traces of two lines of thought, two forms of expression. His prevailing tone of thought, his all but universal mode of utterance, is distinctly opposed to the theories and practices of modern sacerdotalism; but, in two or three of the lines written by him which we have been examining, there is a semblance at least of Justin's having maintained one part of the materialistic theory of the sacrament—that, namely, which teaches that the eucharistic elements are the flesh and blood of Christ.

And this same peculiarity will be found to exist in very many of the "Fathers" of the Church. At one time they give the most spiritual character to the Lord's Supper and to Christ's presence at the Supper. And then, at another time, they seem inconsistent with themselves, and they give an apparent sanction to the idea that, because the abridged form of Christ's words is, This is My body, This is My blood, therefore the bread and wine are, or become, or are transformed into the flesh and blood of Jesus as if He were materially and objectively present on His Table.

To produce examples, in detail, of this twofold teaching of the ancient Christian writers, would extend the length of this essay beyond what our plan permits or requires. Suffice it to say that a string of patristic quotations, with a materialistic comment, may be found in the work of Dr. Pusey; whilst passages of an opposite character, or sometimes the same passages with an entirely different interpretation, may be seen in such books as Waterland's "Review of the Doctrine of the Eucharist," Goode's "Nature of Christ's Presence in the Eucharist," Blunt's "Early Fathers" (especially Lecture xii. of his Second Series), and also in the publications of the Rev. John Harrison, D.D., the present Vicar of Fenwick.

The remark, which applies to all teaching in favour of an objective presence of Christ in the elements, is that which has been already urged on our reader's attention. It is, indeed, surprising to find how invariably the abridged form, This is My body, This is My blood, is made the basis of the enormous theories which spring out of a belief in Christ's objective presence in the bread and wine of the Eucharist. And yet this abridged form is not only interpreted literally, in spite of its obvious and necessarily figurative signification, but this abridged form is, moreover, dealt with, habitually and constantly, by writers who indulge in a materializing tendency, as if it was the only recorded form of what our Saviour said at the institution of the Supper—as if St. Matthew and St. Mark had not recorded that Jesus spoke of " blood of the covenant " (a clearly figurative phrase in itself, one would suppose)—as if St. Paul and St. Luke had not rendered the probably Aramaic words of the Lord by the phrase, " This cup is the new covenant in My blood."

Instead of giving to the reader a string of patristic quotations, some seeming to favour the notion of an objective presence of Christ in the elements, others seeming no less positively to controvert and disprove it, we wish to point out two or three tolerably marked epochs in the history connected with this idea.

E. *Epochs in the History of Sacramental Materialism.*
1. *Justin (and Ignatius ?).*

Whereas we have seen that the New Testament knows absolutely nothing of an objective presence of Christ in the eucharistic elements ; and, whereas Holy Writ represents Jesus, if He used words that could be abridged into the form, This is My blood, yet only to have used them in the sense, and with the meaning, This cup is the new covenant in My blood ; Justin, on the contrary (and possibly Ignatius fifty years sooner), ignore all the modifying addition which Scripture appends to the form, This is My blood—and, still further, they ignore the Scriptural words, This cup is the new covenant in My blood. For them—assuredly for Justin, when he wrote the part of his Apology quoted above— there was no thought of any qualifying terms, or of any fuller explication, in a certainly figurative sense; but only there pressed on his recollection the memorable abridgment, This is My body, This is My blood: and upon this maimed and imperfect quotation of Scripture truth, Justin, like all who preceded or followed him in the idea of an objective presence of Christ in the Supper, based his notion.

Here, then, is the first marked epoch in the history of man's departure from Scriptural simplicity in the doctrine of the Eucharist.

2. *Cyprian.*

Still, in Justin's description of the Supper, the laity are as much sacrificing priests as the clergy; and the only sacrifices are prayers and thanksgivings, and (as appears in one passage[1]) the bread and wine for the Eucharist. Justin, like the New Testament writers, knows nothing of apostles or bishops or presbyters or presidents being sacerdotal, or hieratic, or priestly, in any sense apart from the whole body of believers. By the age of Cyprian, however (A.D. 250), this was changed.

Though there are not wanting passages to show that Cyprian held nothing but a figurative presence of Christ in the eucharistic elements, yet he employs language which has sufficed to give encouragement to the belief that the thank-offering of bread and wine was something more than a thank-offering; that it was an [2] *imitation* of the sacrifice once made by Christ upon the cross; and, accordingly, that the men, who made this imitation of the Saviour's one sacrifice, acted in Christ's stead, were His vicars, and to that extent were sacrificing priests.

Quotations, already laid before the reader, show that long after Cyprian, even in the time of Jerome, Chrysostom, and Augustin, the most eminent teachers of the Church drew no

---

[1] Justin's words are, Προσφερομένων αὐτῷ θυσιῶν, τουτέστι τοῦ ἄρτου τῆς εὐχαριστίας, καὶ τοῦ ποτηρίου ὁμοίως τῆς εὐχαριστίας. J. M. Dial. p. 260. Par. Ed.

[2] " Nam si Jesus Christus Dominus et Deus noster ipse est summus sacer-dos Dei Patris, et sacrificium Patri seipsum primus obtulit, et hoc fieri in sui commemorationem præcepit, utique ille sacerdos vice Christi vere fungitur, qui id quod Christus fecit, imitatur, et sic incipiat offerre quod ipsum Christum videat obtulisse." Cyprian, Epist. 63.

very sharp and exclusive line between the clergy and the laity in respect even of administering the sacraments of Baptism and the Lord's Supper. Their principle was—whatever Christian rite any man, lay or cleric, has received, the same he can confer or administer. One who has been baptized can baptize; one who has been a partaker of the Lord's Supper is competent to administer that holy sacrament to others.

But still, in spite of this subsequent reaction in favour of truth, as early as the time of Cyprian we begin to find distinct marks of the belief that the thank-offering of eucharistic bread and wine was an imitation—*not a repetition, be it observed*—of Christ's one sacrifice of Himself; and that he who presided at the blessing and thanksgiving connected with that bread and wine, was acting in the place of Christ, the one and only real Priest or sacrificing Mediator.

3. *Four Unscriptural Accretions to the Doctrine of the Lord's Supper.*

From the time of Cyprian onward, then, notwithstanding reactions and oppositions, we have four unscriptural factors intermingling themselves around the presence of Christ in the Eucharist.

1. There is an ignoring of every Scriptural modification or interpretation of the words, This is My body, This is My blood.

2. There is based on these Scriptural words, used in a sense different from that of Scripture, a belief in some kind of identity between the bread and wine of the Supper and the body and blood of Christ.

3. There is an idea that the thank-offering of bread and wine is, in some degree, an imitation of the sacrifice of the death of Christ.

4. The inference is in course of being drawn that the president at the Lord's Supper, instead of being a brother among those who are all equally with himself "priests unto God" (Rev. i. 6), is discharging functions analogous to those of the great High-Priest who offered Himself on the cross once for all.

4. *Working of these Accretions.*

Henceforth these four unscriptural elements of thought will be in the Christian Church. Let them be softened and toned down as much as any student may think that Cyprian and others intended they should be ; let them be counteracted, as may be, by the occasional utterance of a Jerome, or a Chrysostom, or an Augustin ; still they must be reckoned with, in future, as important influences in leavening the mass of Christian thought.

They will ere long become entangled with the natural custom of the bishops and presbyters being the " presidents " —to use the phrase of Justin and of Tertullian—whenever they chanced to be present at a celebration of the Lord's Supper ; and so the idea will grow up, that only bishops or presbyters can properly discharge the sacerdotal function in imitation of the Lord. Thus bishops and presbyters will come to be esteemed as priests—sacrificing priests—not in common with all believers, but in contradistinction from the rest of the people. In this manner, instead of all Christians being a royal priesthood according to Scripture, a priestly race according to Justin, there will arise a professional priesthood within the catholic priesthood of the entire Church.

5. *Circumstances particularly favourable to these Accretions.*

These five unscriptural elements of thought must, when once set working in the minds of men, have produced vast results in striking contrast with all that we have seen to characterize the teaching of the apostles on points connected with this entire subject. But when one regards these five elements for producing a revolution in any men's minds, as fostered by all the circumstances that marked the coming centuries of the Church's history, it is no marvel that they turned the world upside down.

Consider how this doctrine, of priests who could alone bless bread and wine so that it should be (in some sense) the body and blood of Christ, must have affected superstitious emperors who, like Constantine, would postpone baptism till the hour of death, that its waters might then effectually and finally wash away all sin. What would such emperors, and their more ignorant and, if possible, more superstitious subjects, be ready and anxious to make of an order of men who could, in any sense, give—or, at their pleasure, withhold—the flesh and blood of the Saviour to be taken into the mouth with the assurance that remission of sins in this life was thus secured, and, in the life to come, endless felicity?

The claiming such power, and the belief in it, must have produced wonderful results among men of any age and country; but the actual circumstances of the Roman empire became more and more favourable to the upholding and propagating of such a system. To those who believed in this system and worked it, there came courage, consolation, and grandest hope of more than mundane victory. To those who were subjected to this system, it brought, if not comfort and hope, at all events an almost stupifying sense of terror, a narcotic influence of rest in obedience to priestly superiors and masters.

Amidst the effeminacy and alarm of Rome's children, as national dissolution came upon the Empire of the West, how must the strength of the Christian priesthood with (in some sense) the body and blood of the incarnate Son of God in their hands, under their control, have been a giant force amidst the weakened pigmies of the human race! How little could these degenerate men retain or recover the glorious liberty which Paul delighted to portray, and which Jesus gave! Here was, indeed, a soil in which the seeds contained in those five unscriptural principles must germinate and flourish.

But this was only the beginning of the circumstances and events that favoured the reception and spread of these same principles of a religion most unlike to that of the New Testament. From every side there came upon the empire invasions of half-savage strangers, under the names of Lombards, or Goths, or Vandals, or Huns. Whether they came direct into Italy, or whether they occupied Gaul, or penetrated into Spain, or made their way along the northern coast of Africa, or from those shores crossed the sea and approached the very citadel of Rome herself, in every direction these savage swarms came crushing in upon Rome and carrying victory with them in every land, in almost every fight.

Well-nigh the only resistance, that opposed them bravely, is typified and represented in the story of the aged bishop sallying forth from the gates of Rome, with his priests and with his sacred things, to arrest the progress of their conquest and their devastation. And this courage produced its effect, impressed the ferocious hearts of the conquerors. So it came to pass that the victorious hordes were subjugated, in their rude minds, by the religion of those whom they conquered. If, frequently, they fell under the influence of Arians on the one side, as frequently, at least, they came under the sway of Rome and her bishops. Ultimately, indeed, the entire movement was in this latter direction; and so the whole Church, or almost the whole, was a mass of effeminate citizens or rude and strong barbarians, leavened most imperfectly by any learning or refinement on the part even of the clergy.

In such a mass of uncultured men nothing could be more certain than that the very religion of Christ itself would be accepted and developed in its least spiritual aspects, in its most sensuous, material, and objective forms.

Of the two texts, "This is My blood," "This cup is the new covenant in My blood," there could be little doubt which would be most acceptable to the unlettered savages and to the ministers who now, as sacrificing priests, wielded a dark and potent spell over the laity. Such a people and such a priesthood would trouble themselves little about the problem of the elements retaining the semblance and the taste of bread and wine. Whatever of the terrible was associated with objectively and materially eating the flesh of the God-man, and drinking His blood, would be in accordance with their predilections. The stranger the phenomenon, the greater the miracle. The less intelligible the process, the more stupendous the power of the priests who wrought out the declared results.

6. *Prevailing Opinion of the Ninth and Tenth Centuries.*

Before the incursion of the northern hordes, men's minds had swayed between the spiritual and figurative eating Christ's flesh by coming to Him, especially in the sacrament, and the grosser idea of eating Christ's flesh by the mere outward act of partaking of the eucharistic elements. The four or five hundred years that followed the downfall of Rome's empire in the West produced a mighty change in this as in so many other respects. By the ninth or tenth century it was most rare to meet with any one, lay or cleric, who doubted the miracle, of daily recurrence, by which bread and wine, in the priest's hands, under the priest's blessing, became the very flesh and blood of Jesus—yea, the flesh and blood, they said, which was born of Mary and which was crucified.

Any figurative interpretation was beyond their power of imagining. For truths and aspirations of a spiritual sort they lacked the needful habit of spiritual discernment.

From all those centuries one can produce no narrative like that of Justin Martyr. When, in the sequel, we come to examine any of the Mass-books that were growing and taking definite form through those centuries, we shall find them to contain more of contrast than of resemblance to the picture of the Lord's Supper in Justin's time—still more of contrast and opposition to all which was practised by the apostles.

Even when the light of intelligence began to be rekindled in Europe once again, doubt and inquiry concerning the miracle of transubstantiation were regarded as inimical to truth, hostile to the powerful array of the priests, offensive in the sight of God. Subtle disputations among the Schoolmen touched the mode and conditions and consequences of the transformation rather than its reality. The inquiry was not, Is the bread changed into flesh, or the wine into blood? And upon what evidence does this allegation rest? The scholastic query was not, Is the change of bread into flesh real and true? but, Assuming its truth, how is the change wrought? The " accidents " and phenomena of bread remain and we see them ; but the " substance," that on which the " accidents "

of colour, form, and taste are superimposed—that "idea"
which, being invisible, underlies all the phenomena—this we
see not. This "substance," this underlying idea, may be
changed and yet we see it not. Thus, the substance of bread
and wine, in the Eucharist, may be changed, by the priest's
words, into the *substance* of Christ's flesh and blood, and yet,
the *accidents* of form and colour and taste and solidity remaining unchanged, we cannot see the transubstantiation. We only
believe it; and the greater the credulity—they called it faith
—the more the merit.

7. *The Neglected Question, Is Credulity a Sign of Reverence?*

Those metaphysicians paused but little to reflect that the
credulity, which believes without evidence or reason, is at
least as presumptuous and as self-conceited as the incredulity
which persists in disbelief in spite of ample evidence and
sufficient reason. Credulity, in their judgment, was a virtue,
the more holy the grosser it was.

If, in the middle of the third century, we found, in Cyprian's
time, traces of the five elements that go to materialize the
Eucharist and set up a privileged priesthood for its administration, it is not surprising that, in seven or eight succeeding
centuries, the effeminacy of Rome's sons, the coarse sensuous-
ness, not to say sensuality, of Gothic barbarians, and the
disputatious metaphysics of men like Paschasius Radbertus,
or Lanfranc, or Anselm, had completely developed and established a system in which bread and wine were miraculously
transubstantiated into flesh and blood. The intervention of a
special order of men called priests was necessary for the
effecting of this miracle; without a share, vicariously or
directly, in this continually repeated sacrifice, there was no
safety for any man either in this world or the next; but, with
such a participation, vicarious or otherwise, the soul of man
was in the stronghold of safety in this life and in the safest
way for the life to come.

Paschasius Radbertus and his fellow-workers inherited the
accumulated errors of four or five centuries when they brought

their logical astuteness to bear upon these topics and, as a consequence, elaborated their doctrine of transubstantiation.

8. Councils (*Fourth Lateran and Tridentine*).

From them it was an easy step for the Fourth Lateran Council to take the subject up and give the stamp of Rome's approval and authority, where the subtle word-fencing of these and other metaphysicians had already given definition. And thus, except for what anathemas the Council of Trent might add, three centuries later, the Roman doctrine of transubstantiation was elaborated and completed.

Instead of This cup is the new covenant in My blood—which Christ either said or meant—the only form reverenced at Rome was the abridgment, This is My body, This is My blood—which, if Christ said it, He meant necessarily in the sense of the fuller form recorded by St. Luke and St. Paul. Instead of all Christians, lay and clerical, being equally and alike priests unto God, and all qualified, on due occasion, to administer the sacrament which had been administered to them, there was a separate order of sacrificing priests railed off from the laity and endowed with a monopoly of power in the sacrifice of the Mass.[1] Instead of a communion and fellowship, in both the bread and the wine, amongst all believers on the common platform of their royal priesthood in Christ, there was often a sacrifice of the Mass celebrated by a priest, who might be alone or might have one attendant with him ; there was rarely a participation in the sacred feast by the laity ; there was never such a participation in the cup of the Lord's Supper. Vast was the change that had come over the simple and beautiful communion of all in bread and wine as enjoined by Christ Himself and as practised by the apostles.

F. *Protests and Opposition on the part of more Spiritual Believers.*

Before we submit to the reader a translation of the later mediæval Mass-book, it is desirable to remind him that, even

---

[1] " Mass," as the communion of the Lord's Supper had come to be called from the concluding words of the Liturgy, " Ite, *Missa* est."

in the dark ages, this materializing of what we saw Christ instituted as a spiritual communion with Himself and with His whole body, the Church—this setting up of a clerical priesthood of some Christians instead of Christ's royal priesthood of all believers—had not gained the ascendancy it held in the thirteenth century without protest and opposition.

Wicliffe and those who came after him were far from being the earliest upholders of a purer worship and more evangelical doctrine.

In the eleventh century Berengarius, a dignitary of the French Church, with whatever vacillation and with however little success, had so opposed the then prevalent doctrine of transubstantiation and of an objective and material presence of Christ in the elements, that he drew down upon himself synodical condemnations and was only rescued from the death of a heretic by the friendship, perhaps the sympathy, of Hildebrand. To say nothing of the opposition, on this question, between the followers of Thomas Aquinas and the disciples of Scotus, the doctrine of transubstantiation, on its first promulgation by Paschasius about A.D. 830, met with no feeble rejoinder from Ratramnus or Bertram, who, in his treatise on the body and blood of the Lord, insisted upon the difference between the sign and the thing signified, the figure and the reality. He urged that the proper end and object of the sacramental mysteries is that men's minds may, by their means, rise from the outward and visible to the inward and invisible. He pointed out that, if Christ's body could be eaten after a material and objective fashion, there would be no exercise of faith, but an employment of the senses only, in such an act. He did not deny that the elements were changed by the eucharistic blessing so that, after that blessing, they were the body and blood of Christ—(observe how the exclusive remembrance of the abridged form, This is My blood, and the ignoring of the more spiritual and fuller form, This cup is the new covenant in My blood, wrought even in such a man as Bertram)—but he insisted that the change was subjective, in the thought and feeling of the recipient, as had been taught by the earliest Christian writers.

G. *The Lord's Supper gradually converted into "The Mass."*

This doctrine of the subjective presence of Christ's body and blood in the sacramental bread and wine, and Bertram's reference to ancient writers, may serve to carry us back from the ninth century to the age of certain much earlier Christian authors.

We have seen that in some of their writings are to be found the beginnings, or something more than the beginnings, of a departure from the simplicity that was in the apostolic " breaking of bread."

They unfortunately lost sight of the duplicate record of our Saviour's words. For them, generally and practically, Christ might never have said, This cup is the new covenant in My blood. For them, in their ordinary mode of thinking and writing, this fuller utterance of the Lord—this only authentic exposition of what the Evangelists meant when they ascribed to their Master the words, This is My blood of the covenant —might never have been spoken by Christ, might never have been written by St. Luke and St. Paul.

For them, as completely as for too many modern Christians, the only words that constantly adhered to their memory, and habitually moulded their conceptions of the Lord's Supper, were an abridgment of an abridgment. Rarely do they mention the words, This is my blood of the covenant. Even this abbreviated form is, by the Fathers, almost invariably abbreviated still further into, This is My blood, as parallel with the other abbreviation, This is My body.

This abbreviation of our Lord's words, and this unintentional, but most deplorable, ignoring of His fuller statement, which contained the unmistakable meaning of His words, were, we cannot doubt, the cause—the first and originating cause—of all the wide difference that separates " the breaking of bread at home," as practised by the apostles, from the sacrifice of the Mass offered by the priest alone in the chancel of the mediæval Church.

But it must not be thought that the change, whose seed lay in the ignoring of Christ's words and their proper signification by Justin, and possibly by Ignatius, sprang at once into full development. Slowly there grew up the practice of a morning Supper, of only a morning Supper, of a morning Supper to be partaken of fasting. Slowly, from the New Testament abstinence from calling the Supper in any sense a sacrifice, there grew the usage of designating the prayers and thanksgivings, and even the elements of the Supper, a sacrifice. From all Christians, as families or as assemblies, breaking bread together without a trace of priestly intervention, except by Christ Himself, there grew up the notion that all Christians engaged in this rite in their capacity of a royal priesthood offering spiritual sacrifice unto God. Then came a confusion between making a gift to the brethren of things required for the love-feast, and making an oblation to God of those same provisions for the love-feast and for the communion of the Lord's Supper.

Then, as the bread and wine came to be identified (at first figuratively and spiritually, in after ages literally and materially) with Christ's body and blood, there gradually crept in the idea that the objective flesh and blood of Jesus were, from celebration to celebration, repeatedly sacrificed in the Church. From the body and blood of Christ having been once for all given upon the cross to put away sin, there sprang, in later times, the notion that the oft-repeated sacrifice of the Mass was effectual, not only to procure pardon for sinners upon earth, but also for the remission of penalties suffered by souls in purgatory.

The Table of the Lord came to be called the altar. To distinguish the ministers at that altar from their fellow-priests, the entire congregation of Christians, there was superinduced an ignoring of the truth that every Christian is a priest; and there was brought in the erroneous idea that some Christians, those, namely, who administered the sacrament of the Lord's Supper in particular, were priests above their fellow-Christians. The latter were the "laity" (merely a Greek term for the people), and the former came to be alone designated as "priests."

All these changes, and many others connected with them

—such as the introduction, on certain occasions, of public confession by notorious sinners and their public readmission to Church privileges; and, in the dark ages, the substitution for this public discipline of private (or auricular) confession and sacerdotal absolution as an indispensable preliminary to communion—these changes sprang up gradually, through the decades and through the centuries, and made the mediæval Mass to be a rite wide as the poles asunder from the original "breaking of bread" as instituted by Christ and practised by the apostles.

The whole complication of such changes, however, had their seed and germ and root in the misconception which not only abridged our Lord's words into This is My blood, but interpreted even that abridged form in senses any and all of which would have been negatived and contradicted by the fuller statement of Christ's words, This cup is the new covenant in My blood.

II. *Opposing and Spiritual Principles laid down by the Greatest of the Fathers.*

As these changes were gradually introduced, some of them colouring the pages of Justin if not of Ignatius, not a few of them observable in the earliest Liturgies, which probably come to us from the fourth or fifth—possibly from the third—centuries, there were misgivings and oppositions in the minds of those believers who felt them to be not only innovations but errors.

It is not our intention to give instances of protest against such errors and innovations in detail; but there are some general principles supplied by men, among the Fathers themselves, who have been ever the most influential and the most universally as well as highly esteemed; and these principles must not be altogether overlooked by us.

One of these important and fundamental truths bears upon the interpretation of expressions used by the Fathers themselves. This principle may be sufficiently exemplified in the following words of Augustin :—

" If the sacraments bore no resemblance to those things of

which they are sacraments, they would not possess the nature
of sacraments at all. From this resemblance, however, the
sacraments are very frequently called by the names of the
things of which they are sacraments."   Thus, " after a
fashion,[1] the sacrament [or outward sign] of the body of
Christ is the body of Christ, and the sacrament of the blood of
Christ is the blood of Christ."—Ep. ad Bonifac., ep. 98.

Again, "Everything which is a sign of another thing
seems, after a fashion,[2] to be personified as that other thing :
just as the apostle said, That rock was Christ, because the
rock spoken of was indeed a sign of Christ."—Aug. De Civ.
Dei, Book xviii. ch. 48.

And yet again, " A thing which is a sign is wont to be
called by the name of the thing of which it is a sign : and so
it is written, The seven ears are seven years ; for it is not
said, They signify seven years : and the seven kine are seven
years ; and there are many examples of the same kind. . . For
it is not said, The rock signifies Christ, but words are used
as if the rock was that which in substance it is not, but which
it only signifies ; and similarly blood, because (on account of
a kind of vital substance in it) it is a sign of life, is, in sacramental language, called life."—Aug. Quæst. in Levit. Book iii.
Qu. 57.

And, in another place,[3] Augustin tells us that the object
of this interchange of names, between the sign and the thing
signified, is that when we look upon the sign—the bread or
wine, for instance—we may be reminded by the change of names
of the things signified, and our minds may be lifted up to contemplate that which is higher than the sign—the gift, for
instance, of Christ's body and blood for us and for all the
world.

Here, then, at the end of the fourth century or the beginning of the fifth, we have a most important principle laid
down that, in speaking of the sacraments, the Christian

---

[1] Secundum quemdam modum.

[2] Quodam modo.

[3] Ideo enim mutata sunt nomina, ut ad mysterii significationem nos excitaret
mutatio nominum. Aug. in Psalm xxxiii., Sermo 1, § 7.

custom was to call the sign by the name of the thing signified—to call bread the flesh of Christ, and wine His blood—
not from any confusion in the minds of those who so spoke;
not because they believed there was any material and objective presence of Christ in or with the bread and wine; not
because they culpably failed to discern the Lord's body in
heaven, or His body the Church, as distinct and different
from the signs or symbols, bread and wine;—not from any
such careless and materializing error as this, but because,
fully recognising that bread and wine were only signs, and
flesh and blood, or the covenant ratified by flesh and blood,
was the thing signified, therefore they called the palpably
unchanged symbols by the name of the holy things they signified, in order that men's hearts might thereby be the more
certainly elevated to the heavenly meaning of the earthly
symbols.

The subsequent history of the Church has shown how
lamentably perilous was this practice of designating sacramental signs by the names of those holier things which they
signified; but it is most instructive and most satisfactory to
find, from the distinct and often repeated testimony of one of
the very greatest of Western theologians, that this usage was
far indeed from originally denoting a confusion in the minds
of Christians between the sign and the thing signified—that,
these two objects being quite distinct from one another, the
anxiety of those who called the one (the sign) by the name of
the other (the thing signified), was to draw away the attention
of worshippers from the lower (the sign, the bread and wine)
to the higher (the thing signified, the body and blood of
Christ).

From these passages we learn how far Augustin was from
believing there was any objective presence of the Lord in the
eucharistic elements: and we also learn that, so far as he was
a competent interpreter of Ignatius, or Justin, or Cyprian,
and the other great writers who had preceded him, he wished
them to be understood, not as materializing in bread and wine
the presence of God who is a Spirit, but as doing their utmost
to lift men's thoughts above the local and material limits of

bread and wine, into association with that eternal Son who, though a Spirit, did, while He tabernacled in flesh on the earth, give His body and His blood for the putting away of the sins of the whole world, and so ratified a new covenant betwixt God and man, and instituted a new communion between man and man, as well as between man and Christ and God.

Here, then, is the first principle for the interpretation of sacramental language, as laid down by that Augustin who, among patristic writers, hardly had a superior.

When the sign is called, as it often is, by the name of the thing signified—bread called flesh, the rock called Christ, kine called years, blood called life, wine called blood—do not think there is any change of matter or substance implied; do not think there is any objective presence of the thing signified in the sign; do not suppose there is, or ought to be, any confusion of these things in the mind of an intelligent teacher; but remember that the misnomer is employed for the very purpose of dissociating your attention and your affection from the lower sign, and directing them to the higher thing signified.

If the abridged form, This is My blood, had always been understood in accordance with this maxim of the great Bishop of Hippo, its curtailment would not have wrought the mischief, produced the misunderstanding, called forth the bitterness, generated the superstition, and caused the schism which have resulted from a forgetfulness alike of the New Testament and of Augustin's rule.

It is marvellous that the variety and number of types or things significant of other things, called by the names of those other things, and yet never confounded with those other things, did not preserve the Lord's Supper from this desecration.

It is marvellous that the way in which Scripture varies the type, by comparing Christ's body much more frequently with the multitude of those who believe in Christ than with the eucharistic elements, did not act as a preservative against the idea of a material transformation or an objective

presence.   Who ever dreams of an assembly of Christians
(Scripturally designated as Christ's body) being transmuted
into the material substance of Jesus ; or of His being objectively and bodily present with them, because spiritually and
subjectively He is always with them ?   Our astonishment, in
this respect, is not lessened when we find the early Christian
writers adopting this variety of things signified by one and
the same sign, and actually carrying it much further than had
been done by the Scripture-writers themselves.   For instance,
in his commentary on 1 Cor. x. 17 (Homil. xxiv. § 2,) in
treating of the words, For we, being many, are one bread and
one body, Chrysostom writes, " What mean I by the word
communion ?   We are that very body itself ; for what is the
bread ?   It is the body of Christ ; and what do the communicants become ?   They become the body of Christ—not
many bodies, but one body : for as the bread is made one by
the putting together of many grains, so that the grains are
nowhere apparent, and yet the grains are there but their
individual granular existence is hidden by their union and
intermixture, so also we are conjoined with one another and
with Christ."

Thus, Chrysostom represents the " body of Christ " to be
the aggregate of believers ; and, to the same effect, Augustin
(Serm. 272), after stating that Jesus ascended into heaven,
and " took up His body thither," presently proceeds, " How is
the bread His body ? and the cup, or its contents, how are
they His blood ?   These things, brethren, are therefore called
sacraments, because in them one thing is seen and another
thing is suggested to the mind.   That which is seen has
a bodily form, that which is suggested to the mind has a
spiritual fruit.   Now, if you wish to know what is meant by
the body of Christ, listen to the apostle saying to believers,
Ye are the body of Christ, and His members.   If, then, ye
are the body and members of Christ, the mystery (or sacrament) of yourselves is placed on the Lord's Table—ye
partake the mystery (or sacrament) of yourselves.   To that
which ye are, ye respond with the Amen, and by responding
ye assent to it ; for thou hearest the words, The body of

Christ, and thou respondest, Amen. Be a member of Christ,
that thy Amen may be sincere. . . . And now, what we are
to understand respecting the cup is evident without further
comment. For, as, in order that there may be the visible
form of bread, many grains are moistened into one mass ; as
that happens which Holy Scripture says of believers, There
was in them one soul and one heart towards God ; so, also,
with respect to the wine. Remember, brethren, from whence
comes wine. Many separate grapes hang upon a bunch, but
their juice is mingled together into one. So also the Lord
Christ hath been our sign or representative, hath wished us
to belong to Himself, hath consecrated upon His Table the
mystery (or sacrament) of peace and of our oneness."

So, again, quite consistently with this representation of
the aggregate of believers as being the bread and the wine
of the Lord's Supper, Augustin says, in another place
(Serm. 229), " Because He suffered for us, He commended to
us, in that sacrament of yours, His body and His blood
which, also, He made even us ourselves to be ; for even we are
made His body, and, by His mercy, we are what we partake.
. . . Now, in the name of Christ, ye are come, as it were,
to the cup of the Lord : and there ye are upon the Table ;
and there ye are in the cup."

Such is the variety of application with which the greatest
of the Fathers use this language.

Precisely as they said Christ's flesh was on the Table, and
His blood was in the cup, and both were partaken by communicants, so, no less definitely and categorically, did they
teach that the aggregate of believers, the entire Church of the
faithful, were " on the Lord's Table," were " in the cup," and
were there " partaken of " by every communicant.

No one pretends that Chrysostom and Augustin believed
there was an objective and material change of all believers
into bread and wine, or into the flesh and blood of Jesus.
Why, then, should it be thought that the early Fathers
believed, any more, in an objective change of the bread and
wine into the material body and blood of our Lord ? No one
pretends that Chrysostom and Augustin believed there was

an objective presence of Christ's body and blood always in the entire aggregate of the faithful which they called Christ's body and blood. Why, then, should it be thought that they believed there was an objective presence of Christ in the eucharistic elements which those Fathers similarly, neither more nor less, designated as Christ's body and blood ?

Here, then, we arrive at a second principle for the interpretation of the Fathers :—When, in sacramental language, the body of Christ and His blood are said to be on the Lord's Table and in the cup, and to be received and partaken of by communicants, this is no more to be understood as implying an objective and material presence of Christ in or with the elements, than such an objective and material presence of all Christians is understood when, no less distinctly, we, like grains for the bread, like juice from the bunch of grapes, are all declared to be "on the Lord's Table," "in the cup," "received" by the communicants. If the presence of the Christian multitude in the eucharistic elements is subjective and spiritual, no less subjective and spiritual is the presence of Christ.

And now we pass on to another most important principle, which is laid down by no less a writer than Augustin, for the interpretation of all Scripture, especially of such passages of Holy Writ as are concerned with the eating Christ's flesh and drinking His blood.

From Augustin's treatise on Christian Doctrine (Book iii. ch. xvi.) we produce the following words :—

" If any precept forbids an evil deed or a crime, or if it enjoins a useful or beneficent action, the language is not figurative. If, however, any precept seems to enjoin an evil action or a crime, or if it seems to forbid a useful or beneficent action, the language is figurative. Except ye eat, it is said, the flesh of the Son of man, and drink His blood, ye have no life in you. A crime or an evil act seems to be enjoined : the language must therefore be figurative ; and the precept really commands us to join one with another in our sympathy with the suffering of our Lord,[1] and to lay up, as a

[1] Præcipiens passioni dominicæ communicandum.

CHAP. II.]   IN THE LORD'S SUPPER.   179

treasure in our memory, the sweet and useful recollection that
His flesh was crucified and wounded for us."

Apart from Augustin's here adding his weight to the
general teaching of the Fathers that the eating Christ's flesh
and drinking His blood, inculcated in John vi., is not primarily,
at all events, sacramental and occasional, but spiritual and
habitual—itself no unimportant illustration of the best
patristic teaching in connection with the general subject of
this essay—we have here a principle of the first importance.
If Scripture, still more if any so-called Father, seems to enjoin
anything immoral, the language cannot be meant in its literal
signification ; it can only be intended to be taken figuratively.

This maxim, in its wide sweep, converts every precept that
would be murderous, cannibalistic, loathsome, in its literal
acceptation, into a figure ; and if more incisive definiteness
could be given to the maxim, it is added in that Augustin
illustrates his principle of interpretation by applying it to
words spoken by our Saviour Himself—and those words such
as are very often misquoted and misrepresented as if they
taught that partaking the eucharistic elements was identical
with eating the flesh of Jesus and drinking His blood.
Piety and common sense must surely yield their assent to
this principle of the great African bishop as soon as it is pro-
mulgated and reflected on.   There needs no argument or
comment in support of it.   Its applicability to our subject is
pointed out by its author himself.   We leave it in its grand
simplicity to convert into the richness of figurative and
spiritual significance every mention, in Scripture and elsewhere, of eating the flesh of Christ or drinking His blood.

For such passages in the Fathers, for such arguments in
the pages of Paschasius, for such decrees of councils—whether
of the Fourth Lateran or of Trent—or for such modern
attempts to resuscitate mediæval ideas, as are irreconcilable
with its sage teaching, this maxim of Augustin must always
remain as a solemn confutation and rebuke.   There can be
no literal and objective eating of Christ's body, or drinking
His blood, even in the eucharistic bread and wine, because
such an act would be evil and criminal.

So, then, we have three great principles of interpretation supplied to us by the Fathers themselves :—

1. It is a common practice to call a symbol by the name of that which it symbolizes without intending to imply any identity of matter or substance between the sign and the thing signified, but only to draw attention to some resemblance or analogy between the two, and especially to direct the reader's mind to the superior importance and interest of the thing signified over its sign. Thus, eucharistic bread and wine are often called the body and blood of Christ, not with any idea of material and objective identity between the elements and Christ, but because there is a resemblance of relations between them, the former nourishing men's bodies and the latter nourishing their souls; and again, there is a hallowed association of thought and feeling, enjoined by Christ Himself, in accordance with which participation in bread and wine should always deepen our grateful sense of communion in the new covenant of love and righteousness ratified by the giving of Christ's body and the shedding of His blood.

2. Our second principle is, The patristic language which thus calls the symbol by the name of the thing signified is so far from being intended to be taken literally, is so thoroughly figurative, that it often varies the metaphor so as, in connection with eucharistic bread and wine, not only to call them Christ's flesh and blood, but to employ them as proper designations for the whole company of Christians.

3. And then our third principle is, Wherever any language, even in the holiest of books, would involve us, if taken literally, in evil or criminal deeds, we must understand such language as figurative; and this with special reference to phrases which speak of eating Christ's flesh and drinking His blood. The literal sense is here abhorrent and criminal, and therefore only a figurative interpretation is admissible.

I. *Translation of the Salisbury Mass-Book.*

And now, from these dominating principles of patristic and eucharistic interpretation, we proceed to lay before the reader a translation of the Latin Mass-book such as it had come to be in England, in the fifteenth and early part of the sixteenth centuries. There were many such Mass-books prevailing in different portions of the Church. That which was in use over a great part of England, and which became to a considerable extent the basis for the English Reformed Liturgy, was the Mass-book of Salisbury, the Sarum Missal; and it is that which we propose now to render into English as an example of what was then the embodiment and substitute for the simple "breaking of bread" of the apostolic Church.

THE ORDER AND RULE[1] OF THE MASS ACCORDING TO THE USAGE OF THE CHURCH OF SALISBURY.

While the priest [2] puts on the sacred vestments for the purpose of saying Mass, let him repeat the hymn,

Come, Thou creative Spirit.
Send forth Thy Spirit:
And Thou shalt refresh the face of the earth.

Prayer.

God, unto whom every heart is open and every desire speaketh, and from whom no secret is hidden; cleanse the thoughts of our hearts by pouring into them Thy Holy Spirit; so that we may merit[3] to love Thee perfectly and praise Thee worthily. Through Christ.

Then let the Antiphon follow,

I will go unto the altar.

The Psalm.

Judge me, O God (Psalm 43).

Then is said the Antiphon,

I will go unto the altar of God, to God who maketh glad my youth.
Lord, have mercy.
    Christ, have mercy.
Lord, have mercy.
Our Father, etc.
Hail, Mary, thou that art highly favoured; the Lord is with thee: Blessed art thou among women, and blessed is the fruit of thy womb, Jesus.

[1] "Canon," a rule.

[2] "Sacerdos," a sacrificing priest, as opposed to "Presbyter" (an elder), from which, by abbreviations, in different times and countries, are derived Preostre (Saxon), Priester (German), Prêtre (French), and Priest (English); so that, derivatively and properly, the English word "priest" has nothing to do with the idea of *sacrificing*, but is simply an abbreviation for the Greek word "Presbyter," which signifies an *Elder*, comparative of *Presbys*, old.

[3] "ut mereamur," that we may deserve, gain, attain; but with the idea of merit conspicuous in every signification of the word.

When these rites are ended, and the office (otherwise called the anthem or the introit) of the Mass is begun, at the first words of the "Glory be to the Father," etc., after the office, let the priest, with his attendants,[1] approach the step of the altar; and with the deacon standing by him on his right hand, and the sub-deacon on his left, let him say his own confession, beginning after this manner:

And lead us not into temptation,
But deliver us from evil.
Confess ye unto the Lord, for He is good:
For His mercy is from generation to generation.
I confess to God, to blessed Mary, to all the saints, and [*turning towards the choir*] to you: I have sinned, too much, in thought, word and deed, by my own fault. [*Then, looking to the altar*] I entreat the holy Mary and all the saints of God, and [*looking to the choir*] you, to pray for me.

Then the choir, looking at the priest, respond,

The Lord be merciful.

Then the choir, turning to the altar, make their confession, as did the priest. Then the priest gives the Absolution:

May Almighty God have mercy upon you, and put away from you all your sins: deliver you from all evil: preserve and confirm you in all goodness: and lead you to eternal life. Amen.
May the Almighty and Merciful God grant you absolution and remission of all your sins, opportunity for true penitence,[2] amendment of life, and grace and comfort of the Holy Spirit. Amen.

Then shall the priest say,

Our help is in the name of the Lord.
Choir. Who made heaven and earth.
Priest. Blessed be the name of the Lord.
Choir. From this time forth and for evermore.
Let us pray.

Then, Prayers being ended, let the priest kiss the deacon and, afterwards, the sub-deacon, saying,

Receive the kiss of peace and love, that ye may be fit to perform the divine services of the holy altar.

These duties having been thus performed, let the candle-bearers set down the candlesticks with the candles at the step of the altar; then let the priest go to the altar, and let him say, in the middle of the altar, with a low voice and with body bowed and hands joined,

Let us pray.
Take from us, O Lord, all our iniquities, that with pure minds we may merit to enter the holy of holies. Through Christ.

Then let the priest raise himself and kiss the altar in its midst, and let him cross[3] himself on the face and say,

In the name of the Father, and of the Son, and of the Holy Spirit. Amen.

Then let the deacon put incense into the censer, having first said to the priest,

Bless [this].

---

[1] Cum suis ministris.   [2] Spatium veræ pœnitentiæ.   [3] Signet se.

And let the priest say,

Lord, may it be sanctified by Thyself, in whose honour it shall be burned. In the name of the Father, and of the Son, and of the Holy Spirit.

Then let the deacon, as he delivers the censer to the priest, kiss his hand; and let the priest cense the middle of the altar and each of its corners,[1] first on the right, then in the middle, and then on the left. Then let the priest be censed by the deacon; and afterwards let him kiss the scripture-book.[2] . . . Then let the ministers (or attendants) draw near, in order, to the altar, first the two candle-bearers walking together, then the incense-bearers, then the sub-deacon, next the deacon, after him the priest. . . . And, when this has been done, let the priest and his attendants betake themselves to the seats prepared for them, and let them wait [thus] till the " Glory be to God on high," and let that, whenever it is said, be begun at the middle of the altar.

Glory be to God on high; and in earth peace to men of good will. We praise Thee, we bless Thee, we worship Thee, we glorify thee, we give thanks to Thee for Thy great glory, O Lord God, heavenly King, God the Father Almighty.

O Lord, the only begotten Son Jesu Christ; O Lord God, Lamb of God, Son of the Father; Thou who takest away the sins of the world, have mercy upon us. Thou who takest away the sins of the world, receive our prayer.[3] Thou who sittest at the right hand of the Father, have mercy upon us.

For Thou only art holy; Thou only art the Lord; Thou only, O Jesu Christ, art most high, with the Holy Spirit, in the glory of God the Father. Amen.

. . These things ended, and having made the sign of the cross on his face, let the priest turn himself to the people, and raising his arms a little and joining his hands, let him say,

The Lord be with you.

Let the choir respond,

And with thy spirit.

Let the priest again turn towards the altar and say,

Let us pray.

Then the Prayer is said. And if there be any special[4] Prayer, let the priest again say, Let us pray, as before. And when there are several Collects to be said, then all the Prayers which follow are begun with one Let us pray, and ended with a single Through our Lord: so, however, that not more than seven Collects be thus blended together, according to the custom of the Church at Salisbury. . . . After the introit of the Mass, let one of the candle-bearers bring the bread and wine and water, which have been set aside for the service of the Eucharist; and let the other bring a basin of water and a towel. . . . At the beginning of the last Collect before the Epistle, let the sub-deacon go through the midst of the choir, to the pulpit, to read the Epistle. . . . While the Epistle is being read, let two boys, in surplices, [pass] through the midst of the choir towards the pulpit, and having bowed towards the altar, on the step of the choir, let them be ready to begin the " Gradual " and to chant their verse. While the verse of the " Gradual " is being sung, let two, in a higher position,[5] put on silken copes, to chant the " Alleluia," and let them go through the midst of the choir near to the pulpit. Let the " Alleluia " come next. After the " Alleluia " let the " Sequence " follow. And at the end of the " Alleluia " or " Sequence " or " Tractus,"[6] let the deacon, before going to read the Gospel, cense the middle of the altar only. . . . Then let him take the scripture-book, that is, the book of the Gospels, and, bowing to the priest who stands in front of the altar, with his face towards the south,[7] let him say,

Bid, sir, that I bless.

[1] Utrumque cornu, each horn.
[2] Textum. "Textum" is subsequently defined as " the book of the Gospels."
[3] Deprecationem.   [4] Si aliqua memoria habenda est.
[5] De superiori gradu.   [6] An anthem so called.   [7] Versâ facie ad meridiem.

Let the priest reply,

The Lord be in thy heart and in thy mouth for utterance of the holy Gospel of God. In the name of the Father, and of the Son, and of the Holy Spirit. Amen.

And so let the deacon go through the midst of the choir, reverently bearing the scripture-book in his left hand, and let him go to the pulpit, preceded by the incense-bearer and the candle-bearer. . . . And let the Gospel always be read towards the north.[1] And when he begins the Gospel, after "The Lord be with you," let him make the sign of the cross with his thumb upon the book, then on his forehead, and then on his breast.

The Gospel according to [etc.]

The Gospel ended, let the priest, in the middle of the altar, begin,

I believe in one God [etc.]

After that :

The Lord be with you.

Let us pray.

Then is said the "Offertory."[2]   After the "Offertory" let the deacon give to the priest the cup (or chalice), together with the paten (or plate) and the sacrifice ; and on each occasion let him kiss the priest's hand. Let the priest, as he receives the cup from the deacon, carefully set it in its appointed place upon the middle of the altar ; and, bowing himself somewhat, let him lift the cup with both hands and offer it as a sacrifice to God, while he says this Prayer :

Receive, holy Trinity, this offering[3] which I, an unworthy sinner, offer in honour of Thee, of blessed Mary, and of all Thy saints, for my sins and offences, and for the salvation of the living and the repose of all the faithful dead. In the name of the Father, and of the Son, and of the Holy Spirit. May this new sacrifice[4] be accepted by Almighty God.

This Prayer ended, let the priest replace the cup and cover it with the cerements ;[5] and let him decorously place the bread upon the cerements in front of the cup which contains the wine and the water, and let him kiss the paten and replace it, on the right of the sacrifice, upon the altar, partially under cover of the cerements. When this is done, let him receive the censer from the deacon, and let him cense the sacrifice . . . and whilst censing it, let him say,

Let my prayer, O Lord, be directed towards Thee like as the incense in Thy sight.

Then let the priest himself be censed . . . and, these things having been thus performed, let the priest go to the right corner of the altar, and let him wash his hands while he says,

Cleanse me, Lord, from all impurity of my heart and body, that I may purely perform the holy work of the Lord.

Then let him return, and standing before the altar, with head and body bowed, and with joined hands, let him say,

In the spirit of humility and with a contrite mind may we be received, O Lord, by Thee ; and may our sacrifice be so offered in Thy sight that it may be accepted this day, and may be pleasing to Thee, O Lord my God.

Then, raising himself, let the priest kiss the altar on the right of the sacrifice ; and, giving the Benediction over the sacrifice, let him cross himself and say,

[1] Versus aquilonem.

[2] The *offertorium* was a verse which was sung at this point in the Liturgy ; and during its continuance the people made their offerings.

[3] Oblationem.

[4] Novum sacrificium.

[5] Corporalia, body-clothes.

[6] Ultra sacrificium.

In the name of the Father, and of the Son, and of the Holy Spirit.

Then let the priest turn towards the people, and say in a low voice,[1]

Pray, brothers and sisters, for me, that my sacrifice, which is yours also,[2] may be accepted by the Lord our God.

Then shall the clergy respond quietly,[3]

May the grace of the Holy Spirit illumine thy heart and lips; and may the Lord receive meetly[4] (or worthily) this sacrifice of praise at thy hands, for our sins and offences.

Then let the priest return to the altar and say his private[5] *prayers according to the number and arrangement of those set forth above before the Epistle, beginning thus,*

Let us pray.

And, when his prayers are ended, let the priest say audibly,

For ever and ever;

Without raising his hands, however, till he says,

Lift up your hearts.

And then let the sub-deacon receive the Offertory and the paten at the hand of the deacon. . . .

After this manner shall all Prefaces to the Mass be begun every day throughout the year, as well on week-days as on festivals:

For ever and ever.   Amen.
The Lord be with you.
And with thy spirit.

Here let the priest lift up his hands, whilst saying,

Lift up your hearts.
We lift them up unto the Lord.
Let us give thanks unto the Lord our God.
It is meet and right so to do.

This Preface is to be used every day [when no special Psalm is appointed]:

It is very meet and right, just and salutary, that we should give thanks unto Thee at all times and in all places, Holy Lord, Almighty Father, eternal God, through Christ our Lord; through whom Angels praise Thy Majesty, Dominions worship, Powers tremble. Heavens and the heavenly virtues and the blessed seraphim unite to celebrate Thee exultingly. And, together with them, let our voices be admitted, we beseech Thee, as with suppliant acknowledgment we say,

Holy, holy, holy, Lord God of Sabaoth. The heavens and earth are full of Thy glory. Hosanna in the highest. Blessed is he that cometh in the name of the Lord. Hosanna in the highest.

Then, straightway joining his hands and raising his eyes, let the priest begin,

Thee, therefore, most merciful Father, we suppliants beseech and pray [*Here let the priest rise and kiss the altar on the right of the sacrifice*

---

[1] Tacita voce.   [2] Meum pariterque vestrum.
[3] Privatim.   [4] Digne.   [5] Secretas orationes.

while he says] that Thou wouldst receive and bless these ✠ gifts, these ✠ services,[1] these ✠ holy and unblemished [2] sacrifices.

And when the crosses have been made over the cup, let him raise his hands and say,

In the first place, which we offer for Thy holy Catholic Church, that Thou mayst deign to give it peace, to guard it, to unite it, and to govern it throughout the entire world, together with Thy servant our Pope *M.* or *N.* and together with our president [3] [that is, their own bishop only] and with our king *M.* or *N.*, and with all the orthodox and all them that hold the Catholic and apostolic faith.

Here let the priest pray, while thinking of the living,

Remember, Lord, thy servants and handmaidens, *M.* and *N.*, and all this congregation, whose faith and devotion are known to Thee, for whom we offer, or who themselves offer, to Thee this sacrifice of praise for themselves and for all their connections, for the redemption of their souls, for the hope of their safety and salvation ; and to Thee, the Eternal God, the Living and the True, they bring their vows :

Whilst we are in fellowship with, and venerate the memory of, first, glorious Mary ever virgin, mother of our God and Lord, Jesus Christ ; but also the memory of Thy blessed apostles and martyrs, Peter and Paul, Andrew, James, John, Thomas, James, Philip, Bartholomew, Matthew, Simon, and Thaddeus ; Linus, Cletus, Clement, Sixtus, Cornelius, Cyprian, Lawrence, Chrysogonus, John and Paul, Cosmas and Damianus ; and all Thy saints ; and to their merits and prayers do Thou grant that in all things we may be defended by the aid of Thy protection. Through the same Christ our Lord.   Amen.

Here let the priest look with great reverence towards the host,[4] and say,

This offering of the service of us and of Thy whole family, we beseech Thee, Lord, that Thou being reconciled [5] wilt accept ; keep our days in Thy peace ; and grant [6] that we, being rescued from eternal perdition, may be numbered with the flock of Thine elect.   Through Christ our Lord.   Amen.

Here, again, let him look towards the host, and say,

And this oblation do Thou, Almighty God, we beseech Thee, deign to make in all things bless ✠ ed, de ✠ voted, [7] rati ✠ fied, reasonable, and acceptable, so that it may become,[8] to us, the bo ✠ dy and bl ✠ ood of Thy most beloved Son, our Lord Jesus Christ :

Here let the priest lift up his hands and join them; and then let him wipe his fingers, and while elevating the host, let him say,

Who, the day before He suffered, took bread into His holy and venerable hands, and lifting up his eyes to heaven [*Here let the priest raise his eyes*], to Thee, His Almighty God and Father, [*Here let the priest bow,*

---

[1] Munera.   [2] Illibata.   [3] Antistite.
        [4] Hostia, a victim, or sacrifice slain.   [5] Placatus.
    [6] Jubeas.   [7] Ascriptam.   [8] Ut nobis . . . fiat.

and then, slightly raising himself, let him proceed] gave thanks to Thee, and bless✠ed, and brake, [*Here let the priest touch the host while he says*] and gave to His disciples, saying, Take and eat of this, all of you ; for this is My body.

These words ought to be spoken at one breath and with one utterance, without a pause. After these words let the priest bow towards the host ; then let him elevate it above his forehead, that it may be seen by the people ; and then let him reverently replace it before the cup after the form of a cross has been made by it. And then let him uncover the cup and hold it in his hands, without separating the thumb from the first finger, except while he gives the blessing only ; and let him thus say.

Likewise, after supper, He took this glorious cup into His sacred and venerable hands ; and, giving thanks [*Here let the priest bow and say*] to Thee, He bless✠ed, and gave to His disciples, saying, Take and drink of it, all of you ;[1] [*Here let the priest elevate the cup a little and say*] for this is the cup of My blood, of the new and eternal covenant, the mystery of the faith, which shall be shed for you and for many for the remission of sins. [*Here let the priest elevate the cup as high as his breast or above his head, saying*] As oft as ye do these things, ye shall do them in memory of Me.

Here let the priest replace the cup, and let him raise his arms after the fashion of a cross, the fingers joined till the words, " of Thy gifts."

Wherefore also, O Lord, we Thy servants, together with all Thy holy people, mindful of the blessed passion of the same Christ, Thy Son our Lord ; mindful also of His resurrection from the lower[2] regions, and of His glorious ascension into the heavens ; offer to Thy excellent[3] majesty of Thy gifts and bounties, a pu✠re host, a sa✠cred host, an imma-✠culate host ; the sa✠cred bread of eternal life and the c✠up of perpetual salvation.

And upon these deign to look with propitious and serene countenance ; and to accept them like as Thou didst deign to accept the offerings of Thy righteous child Abel, and the sacrifice of our patriarch Abraham, and the offering of Thy high-priest Melchisedek, a sacred sacrifice, a spotless host.

Here let the priest, with body bowed and hands interlaced, say,

We humbly beseech Thee, Almighty God, command that these things may be borne by the hands of Thy holy angel to Thine altar on high,[4] in sight |of Thy divine majesty ; so that as many of us [*Here let the priest raise himself and kiss the altar on the right of the sacrifice, and say*] as have, in this participation at the altar, received the sacred bo✠dy and bl✠ood of Thy Son, may [*Here let the priest cross himself on the face, and say*] be filled with all heavenly bene✠diction and grace. Through the same Christ our Lord.   Amen.

Here let the priest pray for the dead.

Remember, also, O Lord, the souls of Thy servants and handmaidens, *M.* and *N.*, who have gone before us with the sign of the faith, and who sleep the sleep of peace. For them, O Lord, and for all who rest in

[1] Bibite ex eo omnes.   [2] Ab inferis.   [3] Præclaræ.
[4] In sublime altare tuum.

Christ, we pray for Thine indulgence [1] in the place of cooling, light, and peace.   Through the same Christ our Lord.   Amen.

Here let the priest smite his breast once and say,

To us sinners, also, Thy servants whose hope is in the multitude of Thy mercies, deign to give some part and association with Thy holy apostles and martyrs ; with John, Stephen, Matthias, Barnabas, Ignatius, Alexander, Marcellinus, Peter, Felicitas, Perpetua, Agatha, Lucia, Agnes, Cecilia, Anastasia, and all Thy saints ; and into their company admit us, we beseech Thee, not weighing merit but bestowing pardon.[2] Through Christ our Lord ; through whom, O Lord, Thou ever createst all these good things, [*Here let the priest make the sign of the cross three times over the cup, and say*] Thou sancti✠fiest them, Thou vivi✠fiest them, Thou bless✠est them, and bestowest them upon us. [*Here let the priest uncover the cup and make the sign of the cross with the host five times*] Through H✠im, and with H✠im, and in H✠im, is all honour and glory to Thee, God the Father Al✠mighty, in the unity of the Holy ✠ Spirit, [*Here let the priest cover the cup and keep his hands upon the altar until the Lord's Prayer is said*] for ever and ever.   Amen.

Let us pray.

Admonished by Thy saving precepts, and fashioned[3] by the divine institution, we are bold to say—

Here let the deacon receive the paten and hold it uncovered, on the right of the priest, with his arm held out upwards, until the Prayer, " Grant propitiously," etc., is said.

Here let the priest raise his hands and say,

Our Father, etc. . . . Lead us not into temptation.

Let the choir respond,

But deliver us from evil.

The priest says by himself,[4]

Amen.

Deliver us, we pray Thee, Lord, from all evils, past, present, and to come ; and, by the intercession of blessed and glorious Mary, ever virgin, mother of God, and by the intercession of Thy blessed apostles Peter and Paul and Andrew, and all Thy saints—

Here let the deacon give the paten to the priest, whose hand he shall kiss, and let the priest kiss the paten ; then let him raise it to his left eye, then to his right ; then let him make a cross with the paten above his head ; and then let him replace it in its proper place, saying—

Grant propitiously peace in our days, so that, assisted by the help of Thy mercy, we may both be always free from sin and also safe from all disquietude.

Here let the priest uncover the cup, and, while bowing, let him take the body and, holding it over the bowl of the cup between his thumbs and forefingers, let him break it into three portions, saying meanwhile,

[1] Locum refrigerii, lucis et pacis, ut indulgeas, deprecamur.
[2] Non æstimator meriti, sed veniæ largitor.
[3] Divina institutione formati.   [4] Privatim.

Through the same our Lord Jesus Christ, Thy Son.

(*Second breaking.*) Who liveth and reigneth with Thee, God, in the unity of the Holy Spirit ;

Here let the priest hold the two fragments in his left hand, and the third fragment in his right, over the top of the cup, saying as follows with an audible voice,

For ever and ever. Amen.

Here let him make three crosses, within the cup, with the third portion of the host, saying,

The peace of the L✠ord be e✠ver with ✠ you.

Let the choir respond,

And with thy spirit.

For the saying of the "Agnus," let the deacon and sub-deacon both come near to the priest, on his right hand, the deacon next him, the sub-deacon further off ; and let them say, each by himself,[1]

Lamb of God, which takest away the sins of the world, have mercy on us.

Lamb of God, which takest away the sins of the world, have mercy on us.

Lamb of God, which takest away the sins of the world, have mercy on us.

Here let the priest make the sign of the cross over the above-mentioned third portion of the host, and let him put it into the sacrament of the blood, saying thus,

May this sa✠cred mixture of the body and blood of our Lord Jesus Christ be made to me, and to all who receive it, health[2] of mind and body, and a salutary preparation for meriting[3] and receiving eternal life. Through the same Christ our Lord. Amen.

Before the giving of the " Pax," let the priest say,

O Lord, holy Father, Almighty and Eternal God, grant me so worthily to receive this sacred body and blood of Thy Son our Lord Jesus Christ, that by this I may merit to obtain[4] remission of all my sins, and to be filled with Thy Holy Spirit, and to have Thy peace. For Thou art God, and there is none other beside Thee, whose glorious kingdom abideth for ever and ever. Amen.

Here let the priest kiss the right side of the cerements[5] and the top of the cup, and then the deacon, and let him say,

Peace be with thee and with the Church of God.
Response. And with thy spirit.

Let the deacon, on the right of the priest, receive from him the " Pax,"[6] and hand it to the sub-deacon : then let the deacon carry the Pax to the step of the choir, to the leaders of the choir : and let these carry the Pax to the choir, each to his own side, beginning with the eldest. After the giving of the Pax let the priest say the following Prayers by himself,[7] before he communicates, holding the host meanwhile in his two hands.

O God the Father, Fountain and Source of all goodness, who, led by mercy, wast willing that Thine only begotten should for us descend into

---

[1] Privatim.   [2] Salus.   [3] Promerendam.
      [4] Ut merear accipere.   [5] Corporalia.
[6] The " Pax " was a picture of Christ.   [7] Privatim.

the lowest parts of the world [1] and should take flesh which I, unworthy, hold here in my hands ; [*Here let the priest bow to the host while saying*] Thee I adore, Thee I glorify, Thee with the whole purpose of my heart I praise : and I pray that Thou wilt not forsake us Thy servants, but that Thou wilt put away our sins ; so that, with pure heart and chaste body, we may merit [2] to serve Thee, the only living and true God. Through the same Christ our Lord. Amen.

O Lord Jesu Christ, Son of the Living God, who, according to the will of the Father, with the co-operation of the Holy Spirit, hast given life to the world by Thy death ; deliver me, by this sacred body and this Thy blood, from all mine iniquities and from every evil : and make me always to obey Thy commands : and suffer me never throughout eternity [3] to be separated from Thee, who, with God the Father and with the same Holy Spirit, livest and reignest God for ever and ever. Amen.

O Lord Jesu, may the sacrament of Thy body and blood, which though unworthy I receive, be not to me for judgment and condemnation, but by Thy goodness [4] may it be profitable for the salvation of my body and soul. Amen.

Let the priest, with lowliness, address the body, before receiving it,

Hail, for ever, holiest flesh of Christ, to me before all things and above all things highest and sweetest. [5] May the body of our Lord Jesus Christ be to me the way and the life. In the name of the ✠ Father, and of the Son, and of the Holy Spirit.

Here let the priest take the body, having first made a cross with the body itself in front of his mouth. Then, with great devotion, let him say to the blood,

Hail for ever, heavenly draught, to me before all things and above all things highest and sweetest. May the body and the blood of our Lord Jesus Christ be profitable unto me a sinner as a perpetual medicine for eternal life. Amen. In the name of the ✠ Father, and of the Son, and of the Holy Spirit.

Here let the priest take the wine; and after taking it let him bow down and say with devotion the following Prayer:

I render thanks to Thee, O Lord, Holy Father, Almighty, Eternal God, who hast refreshed [6] me by the most sacred body and blood of Thy Son our Lord Jesus Christ : and I pray that this sacrament of our salvation, which I an unworthy sinner have received, may not come [7] to me for judgment and condemnation on account of my deservings, but may be for the advancement of my body and soul unto life eternal. Amen.

And when this has been said, let the priest go to the right corner of the altar with the cup in his hands, his fingers still joined as before, and let the sub-deacon draw near and pour wine and water into the cup; and let the priest rinse his hands lest any relics of the body or the blood remain upon his fingers or in the cup. . . . After the first washing or outpouring this Prayer is said:*

That which we have received with the mouth, O God, may we take

---

[1] Ad infima mundi.   [2] Mereamur.
[3] Nunquam in perpetuum.   [4] Tuâ pietate.   [5] Summa dulcedo.
[6] Refecisti.   [7] Veniat.   [8] Resinceret.

with a pure mind ; and of the temporal gift may there be made unto us an eternal medicine.

Here let the priest wash his fingers in the hollow of the cup with the wine that was poured in by the sub-deacon; and, when it has been drained,[2] let this Prayer follow:

May this communion, O Lord, cleanse us from guilt and make us to be partakers of the heavenly medicine.

After taking the ablutions, let the priest set the cup upon the paten in order that, if aught remain, it may drop out; and then, bowing himself, let him say,

Let us adore the sign of the cross by which we have received the sacrament of salvation.

Then let the priest wash his hands; the deacon meanwhile folding up the cerements. The washing of hands ended, and the priest returning to the right corner of the altar, let the deacon hold the cup to the priest's mouth, in case any of that which was poured in should still remain to be consumed. Then, after that, let the priest, with his attendants, say the "Communion."[2]

Then, having made the sign of the cross on his face, let the priest turn himself towards the people, and, with his arms slightly raised and hands joined, let him say,

The Lord be with you.

And, again turning to the altar, let him say,

Let us pray.

Then let him say the post-Communions according to the number and order of the Prayers prescribed above to be said before the Epistle. And when the last post-Communion is ended, and the sign of the cross has been made on his forehead, let the priest again turn to the people and say,

The Lord be with you.

Then the deacon (says),

Let us bless the Lord.

Sometimes, however, the words spoken are—

Go : (the congregation) is dismissed.[3]

As often, however, as the form "Go, the congregation is dismissed," shall be employed, it is always to be spoken by the priest turning towards the people; and when the proper form shall be, "Let us bless the Lord," or "Let him rest in peace," this is said facing towards the altar. After these words, let the priest, with bowed body and joined hands, in a low voice, say this Prayer in front of the middle of the altar:

May the devotion of my service[4] be pleasing to Thee, O holy Trinity ; and grant that this sacrifice, which I unworthy have offered in the sight of Thy majesty, may be acceptable to Thee, and may be a propitiation for me and for all on whose behalf I have offered it, through Thy mercy. Who livest and reignest God, for ever and ever. Amen.

And when this is ended, let the priest arise and, crossing himself on the face, say,

In the name of the Father, and of the Son, and of the Holy Spirit. Amen.

---

[1] Quo hausto—and when it has been quite drunk up.

[2] The "Communion" was a verse, taken from one or other of the Psalms, to be chanted at this time.

[3] Ite, missa est. This participle, "*missa*," came to be used as a noun or name for the whole Communion Service of which it had been the end. This is, of course, the derivative origin of the word "Mass."

[4] Obsequium servitutis meæ.

And so, after bowing, let them return, surrounded by the candle-bearers and the other attendants, in the same order in which they approached the altar at the beginning of Mass. And immediately after (the words) "I render thanks to God," let there be begun in the choir the "Ninth Hour," when it is said after Mass. But let the priest, as he returns, say the Gospel [In the beginning was the Word, etc.].

So ended the service of the Mass according to the usage of Salisbury. We have omitted a few rubrics and some special prefaces for particular seasons. Otherwise the ordinary Mass of Sarum is here literally translated.

J. *Comments on the Salisbury Mass-Book.*

And now it will be necessary to comment, as briefly as possible, upon the salient characteristics of this service, and especially upon any marked points of resemblance or contrast between it and the earliest descriptions of the Lord's Supper as they come to us from the New Testament or from Justin Martyr.

1. *Change of Name.*

At the very outset it is remarkable that, instead of using any of the numerous terms employed in Scripture and in the times nearest the apostolic age, such as Breaking of bread, Lord's Supper, Communion, Eucharist, Sacrament, this Use of Salisbury designates the sacred service of the Lord's Table as "The Mass."

It has been sometimes attempted to show that this term is derived from the Hebrew word, "Missah," signifying a "number." [1] We can attach no weight to this somewhat forced and far-fetched derivation. Ambrose, towards the close of the fourth century, is said to be among the earliest of those who introduced the word "Mass" as a name for the Lord's Supper; and assuredly we should look for a Latin phrase, on the tongue of the great Bishop of Milan, much more

---

[1] Those who adopt this derivation of the word "Mass," support it by reference to Deut. xvi. 10. where the Hebrew word is, not "Missah," a noun signifying "number," but *Missath*, a preposition (as Gesenius shows) signifying "at the rate of, even as." Thus, if "Mass" were derived from the Hebrew, its root idea would require to be, not sacrifice, but number, proportion, and would be as remote as possible from the notion of sacrifice. Other considerations, showing that the idea of sacrifice has no proper place in the meaning of the word Mass, are well stated by Bingham in his "Antiquities of the Christian Church," Book xiii. ch. i. § 4.

readily and naturally than for a word derived from the Hebrew. Be that as it may, however, the changed name for the Christian " breaking of bread " is not without significance.

Here is a new idea made to be most prominent in the service of the Lord's Table. The name " Mass," we take it, is obviously derived from *Ite, missa est*, " Go, you are dismissed ; " and it was, at first, a name applied not only to the Eucharist for communicants, but to all services of the Church, even to those which were open to catechumens or candidates for baptism, and to all other non-communicant members of the congregation.

In process of time, no doubt, the phrase, *Missa catechumenorum*, the Mass or service for non-communicants, was abandoned, and the expression, *Missa fidelium*, the Mass for communicants, remained in use until this service alone came to be designated as " the Mass ; " and by that time sacrificial ideas, not of offering prayers, or praises, or gifts as figurative sacrifices, but of offering Christ slain as a victim (" host ") upon the altar, were connoted by the term " Mass : " and so, instead of a social breaking of bread with holy remembrance of the Lord's body given, and of His blood shed for us ; instead of communion or fellowship with Christ crucified and with the whole body of believers ; instead of thanksgiving— men were taught that the most prominent idea of the Lord's Table was to be that of a sacrifice, apparently other than that of Christ's body once offered, apparently different from the spiritual sacrifice of thanksgiving which all Christians were to offer to God in their common and universal character of "priests." The older notion, attached to the word Mass, had been, as we have seen, that of a service, from which part of the congregation was dismissed—the catechumens, namely, and the excommunicated of the early Church—and so the Mass became a secret service for the initiated only.

Whichever derivation and whatever meaning be adopted for the word " Mass," it can hardly be denied that, in this mediæval word, a new and unscriptural idea of sacrifice, or else a vapid notion of mere change from one congregation to another, is substituted for the Scriptural, simple, and dignified

ideas of the Breaking of bread, the Lord's Supper, the Communion, the Eucharist, or the Sacrament and vow of military
obedience to Christ and fidelity to our fellow-soldiers in the
Church.   Some may say there is little or nothing in a
change of name, but we are disposed to think so pointed an
alteration in the title of a religious act is not without grave
significance.

At all events, the word "Mass" has become very accurately marked as standing for all the Liturgy and all the
rites just set forth above as the Salisbury Missal; and as we
know there are cases in which words are of such importance
that by them, and by our usage of them, we shall be condemned or justified (Matt. xii. 37), so we are convinced that
this substitution of "Mass" for the earlier names of the
Eucharist is nowadays, as it was in the Middle Ages, a
matter of grave importance, of deep significance.

2. *Language of Worship, Intelligible or Unintelligible.*

The next point that should be noticed is that, whereas St.
Paul was so anxious his words in every service of the Church
should be distinct and intelligible, this Latin service of the
Mass was, in the sixteenth century—and is still in the unreformed portion of the Western Church—employed for every
congregation, in all the countries of Europe, although vernacular languages had everywhere come into vogue, and the
Latin tongue had as universally ceased to be understood by all
but the small number of the learned.   Here was, assuredly, a
practice as irrational as it was unscriptural.

3. *The Terms "Priest," "Altar," "Sacrifice."*

Throughout the whole service of the Mass, the "priest"[1]
is the most conspicuous figure in every sense of the term;
and the constantly recurring mention of the "altar" at which
he stands or bends, the frequent reference to the "sacrifice"
which on that altar he offers, and the propitiation he is represented as making—all these acts and facts show abundantly
that he is no priest, in common with the whole body of the

[1] Sacerdos, of the Latin; Ἱερεύς, of the Greek Liturgies.

faithful, offering spiritual sacrifices, of prayer and praise only, to God. On the contrary, and in diametrical contravention of Holy Writ, he is intended to be a mediating priest, offering a sacrifice of propitiation to God, and accordingly trenching upon, and usurping, the rights and prerogatives of that Christ who, in the New Testament, is declared to be the one mediator between God and man (1 Tim. ii. 5), the alone Priest and High-Priest (Heb. iv. 15; vii. 23—27), the one Sacrifice once offered (Heb. x. 12—14).

Such a sacrificing priest, of the Mass, is as opposed to the character of the president among us the true race of priests—to employ Justin's phraseology—as he is diverse from and opposed to the whole catalogue of Christian office-bearers named in the New Testament. They are apostles, prophets, teachers, workers of miracles, healers, helps, governments, speakers with tongues, interpreters (1 Cor. xii. 28, 29); or they are evangelists, pastors (Eph. iv. 11), or bishops, presbyters, deacons, angels—all these designations are given in Scripture to officers in the Christian Church; but by the name of priest no Church officer is ever designated in the apostolic writings. That title, in figurative application, is bestowed, by Peter and by John the divine, upon all Christians equally, upon laity and clergy alike; but, in its exact and literal signification, it is reserved by the truly apostolic Church for Christ and Christ alone.

With respect to the repeated mention of the "altar" in the Mass, where the New Testament would dictate a mention of the Lord's Table, we shall only here remind the reader of what has been written in a former part of this essay, pp. 76—80.

4. "Vestments," etc.

After noticing these important contrasts between the Mass and the apostolic breaking of bread, we proceed to draw attention to the "sacred vestments," so called, that are to be assumed by the priest, or to the "silken cope" which a lesser ministrant is to put on before he chants the "Alleluia." Where is there a trace of such practices in Scripture? How markedly are they absent from the word-pictures of Justin

Martyr! Yet, in the Mass-book, they stand not by themselves. Their æsthetic prettiness is matched by "candlesticks" to be used in daylight; by incense and censers and
censing in abundance; by basins and towels and washings
which are as vapid as those of the Jews, and even more
uncomely because of their publicity.

We pass by the bowings oft; the kissing now of one object
or person, now of another; the transitions from one position
to another; the facing in different directions at different
moments; the reading the Epistle northwards and the Gospel
southwards; the utterance at one breath of a long string
of words; the keeping the thumbs and first fingers in particular positions; the rinsing and draining of the cup, and
holding it up for any drops to fall into the priest's mouth—
these minor matters we pass by with the mere remark, that
the unsophisticated mind can hardly fail to observe the minute
and effeminate character of these practices and prescriptions in contrast with the manly simplicity of the Eucharist
as described by Justin, and, still more, as enjoined and
portrayed by the Evangelists and by St. Paul.

5. *The Idea of "Merit."*

The next point to which we would draw attention is the
manner in which the idea of "merit" is introduced into the
Mass. It is true there are passages in the Mass of exceeding
beauty, in which the idea of human frailty and sinfulness is
most fitly recognised. In such passages, quite in accordance
with the oldest usage, we meet with expressions such as these:—

"O Lord Jesu, may the sacrament of Thy body and
blood, *which though unworthy I receive*, be not to me for judgment and condemnation, but by Thy goodness may it be
profitable for the salvation of my body and soul. Amen."

Or, again, "I pray that this sacrament of our salvation
which I an unworthy sinner have received, may not come to me
for judgment and condemnation *on account of my deservings*,'
etc.

These words have the true ring of Christian piety in them
But there are others, in the same Mass-book, coming doubtless

from a different author and a more corrupt age, whose spirit
is as different from these as is their sound.   For instance, at
the close of the beautiful collect for the cleansing and inspiration of our hearts, we find, in the Mass, these words :—

"So that we may *merit* to love Thee perfectly and praise
Thee worthily.   Through Christ."

Similarly, at the end of the commemoration of Mary and
the apostles and martyrs, we meet with the words :—

"And to *their merits* and prayers do Thou grant that in
all things we may be defended by the aid of Thy protection.
Through the same Christ our Lord.   Amen."

And so, once more, in the prayer over the mixture of the
bread and wine, one supplication is that it may be "a salutary
preparation *for meriting* and receiving eternal life."

How different is all this idea of our merits, and of the
merits of our fellow-beings, from the Christian principle that
when we have done all the possibilities of our infinitely
capable nature, we are still unprofitable servants who have
only done that which was our duty ! (Luke xvii. 10.)

And yet, again, how far short fall these phrases in the
Mass of the pious truth, "Merit lives from man to man, and
not from man, O Lord, to Thee."   Such pleading of human
merit before God is obviously in contravention of Scripture
and natural piety, and even of the better portions of the
Mass-book itself.

6. "*Ave Maria*," etc.

As to the "*Hail, Mary*" of the prefatory portion of the
Mass; as to the declaration, in the collect following the "Offertory," that the offering is made "*in honour of blessed Mary* . . .
for my sins and offences, and for the salvation of the living and
the repose of . . . the dead ;" and, again, as to the pleaded
"*intercession of blessed and glorious Mary, ever Virgin*, mother
of God;"—these appeals and prayers to the blessed mother of
our Lord are in strange opposition to the teaching of Scripture, that while Jesus was loving and dutiful to His mother,
in all things lawful, from the cradle to the cross, yet He failed
not to remonstrate with her forgetfulness that His Father's

work had highest claims upon Him even in boyhood; that the fitting hour for His wondrous works must be patiently awaited at Cana; and that they who heard and did His commands were nearer and more truly akin to Him than His mother after the flesh while she disbelieved his heavenly mission.

Such firm though loving opposition on the part of Jesus to His mother's erring ways is strangely out of keeping with the notion that that blessed woman's intercession in heaven availeth aught. Nor, if we bear in mind how completely Scripture represents Mary as misunderstanding her son and joining in the family cry that His zeal for God and man betokened Him as mad, do we find any ground for the belief that Mary's mind was so intelligently and entirely in harmony with the will of Heaven that her supplication must needs be in accordance with the purposes of God. True, we hope and trust that she has been numbered with all those spirits of the just made perfect who form part of the fellowship of the saints; but this is surely no ground for supposing that Mary has special merit, or any merit, wherewith to intercede for others before God.

No less contrary to Scripture, which speaks of the brothers of our Lord, and carries instruction in the assurance that Joseph knew not his wife "*till* she had brought forth her first-born son," is the address to Mary as "ever virgin."

7. *Confession, in the Mass.*

As to the confession and absolution which are introduced into the Mass, we observe that they are only so far out of keeping with the teaching of Holy Writ as they prescribe confession to "blessed Mary, to all the saints, and to you," the congregation present from time to time, in addition to confession to God. Such confession, however, is not prescribed as a detailed enumeration of one's sins aloud. Neither is it, on the face of the Salisbury Mass-book, a prescribing of private confession to the priest. It may be, if confined to the letter of the Mass, an humbling of one's self before one's fellow-believers, not out of keeping with St. James's precept, Confess your faults one to another. It may be a prelude or an adjunct to some such examining of one's self as that enjoined by St. Paul. In either of these aspects of the matter, the confession of the Mass might be permissible enough. Church history does not fail, of course, to tell us how public confession of notorious sin was part of the severe discipline of comparatively early times. Nor does history leave us uninformed how this terrible and humiliating ordeal was afterwards made easier for penitents by the substitution of private confession to the priest.

These arduous and perilous practices, however, are not directly referred to in the Salisbury Missal. Its general acknowledgments of our sinfulness, with the true and beautiful words "through my own fault" (*meâ culpâ*), are only so far in opposition to the spirit of the New Testament as they harshly and forcibly drag in a mention of the Virgin Mary.

8. *Absolution, in the Mass.*

The form of absolution is not a little remarkable.

It is entirely different from that indicative form, "I absolve thee," which was never used before the twelfth or thirteenth century.[1] It is a prayer, a repeated prayer, for God's forgiveness of the penitent :—

"May Almighty God have mercy upon you and put away from you all your sins ; may He deliver you from all evil; may He preserve and confirm you in goodness ; and may He lead you to eternal life. Amen."

This is a series of supplications of beauty unsurpassable ; and whencesoever Osmund, the compiler of the Sarum Missal, derived it, in the latter part of the eleventh century, its odour is of sanctity, of wisdom, and of apostolic Christianity.

The second prayer is as follows :—

"May the Almighty and Merciful God grant you absolution and remission of all your sins, opportunity for true penitence, amendment of life, and grace and comfort of the Holy Spirit. Amen."

Here, again, is only one exception that can be taken to the words. "Penitence" is but a poor rendering of the word

[1] See Bingham's Antiquities, xix. 2. § 5.

μετάνοια (repentance) in the New Testament. These latter words, in the English and the Greek, denote a weighing again of the judgments of the mind, and a consequent entire change of judgment and of mind. They include, doubtless, more or less of pain ("penitence," penance) at the discovery of one's self in a wrong mind, with wrong judgments; but this element of pain, which is the chief if not the only ingredient in the Latin word penitence, is very far from being all, or the main part, in that repentance, not to be repented of, which is the result of godly sorrow.

To this extent the second part of the absolution in the Mass falls short of the Scriptural ideal; but, otherwise, it is excellent—no mere empty declaration of that which is either useless if the penitent be already absolved in heaven, or untrue if he be no real penitent, but one void of sincere repentance.

The form of absolution in the Mass combines prayer for pardon with no slight instruction as to the way that leads to forgiveness; and this prayerful teaching of Christ as the way, the truth, and the life, for the putting off of sin, is the highest mode of absolution. Only in proportion as this absolution in the Mass treats of "penitence" instead of "repentance," and omits more definite and express reference to Christ as the Saviour, does it fall short of the perfect standard of Scriptural absolution; and, indeed, it ought in fairness to be said that, probably, the poverty of the Latin language in any other term adequately to express the μετάνοια of the Greek, or the "repentance" of our English, may be the cause of part of this faultiness in the Missal's form of absolution.

9. *" Holy of Holies," etc.*

Very different is the feeling with which we bring under notice the next point in the Mass-book. Before the giving of the kiss of peace, we find this prayer :—

"Take from us, O Lord, all our iniquities, that with pure minds we may merit to enter the holy of holies. Through Christ."

This expression, "holy of holies," is here evidently intended to designate that part of the church-building in which lies " the altar" of the Mass; and such an usage of the phrase is thoroughly unscriptural and misleading.   In Judaism, of course, the inmost shrine of the Temple was the "holy of holies"; but in apostolic Christianity that very expressive figure of speech is appropriated to something very different from any part of an earthly building, namely, to that higher world whither (Heb. ix. 12) Christ, by His own blood, entered in once, having obtained eternal redemption.

To designate the site of the Lord's Table in a church as " the holy of holies," is thus obviously as unscriptural a misnomer as to call the Table an altar, or to speak of men's meriting God's grace as is here done.

The whole system must, in the light of Scripture, either stand or fall together.   In the Mass-book one finds abundant mention of the "priest," the " altar," the "holy of holies," the " sacrifice," the " host," or victim slain (*hostia* of the Latin); but in Scripture not one of these terms, not one of the ideas they connote, is ever brought into connection with the sacrament of the Lord's Supper.   The " priest," in apostolic thought, is either every believer offering spiritual sacrifices of prayer and praise, or else it is Christ offering Himself once for all.   The apostolic " altar " is the cross, outside Jerusalem, on which Jesus suffered.   The " sacrifice," or victim slain, or " host " is none other than Christ crucified.   The " holy of holies " is heaven, whither Christ ascended, and where He ever liveth to make intercession for us.

Such is the invariable use of these correlative terms in the New Testament ; and their systematic employment, in other connections of thought and with quite different and, to a great extent, contradictory significations in the Mass-book, cannot fail, we submit, as an obvious matter of logical necessity, to mislead the minds of the unlearned and the unwary by putting other persons and other things and other ideas into the place of those intended by apostolic teaching and example.

10. *The Sign of the Cross.*

We pass by the frequent employment of the sign of the cross, now singly used, now thrice repeated, and now again five times. This symbolic action is, assuredly, harmless enough in itself; but, so often reiterated, it becomes wearisome and vexatious, and is only too apt to degenerate into a series of empty and thoughtless formalities. No trace of such a practice is to be met with in the records of the apostolic Church.

11. *" Corporalia."*

There is meaning, and it is unscriptural meaning, in naming the cloth for covering the bread and wine " corporalia " (cerements or body-clothes); for this name implies that when Christ said, This is My blood, He did not mean, as Scripture teaches, This cup is the new covenant in My blood, but He meant something quite different and inconsistent with that His explication of the words, namely, that the wine was changed objectively into His blood, and the bread into His body. So unscriptural and anti-scriptural is the whole phraseology and the whole underlying idea of the Mass, that it crops out even in such otherwise unimportant terms as this of " corporalia."

12. *The " Pax."*

In the handing round of the " Pax" we have another ceremony which is entirely unknown to the apostolic writers. It is said that the kiss of peace, such as was practised in the time of Justin, gave rise to scandals, and that, therefore, it was abandoned, and the " Pax," a material representation of Jesus, was handed round to be kissed by all the congregation, instead of the members kissing one another. Be that allegation true or not, here is an innovation—a somewhat distracting innovation—for which the earliest Christianity affords no warrant of precept or example.

13. *Bringing in the Elements.*

On the injunction that " after the introit of the Mass " certain officials shall bring in the bread and wine and water,

and a basin of water and a towel, we are constrained to
remark that such an action is calculated to disturb the
solemnity and quiet of religious worship, and is completely
unlike the taking part in a supper and in breaking of bread,
such as that delineated in the writings of the apostles and
Evangelists; and let it not be thought that such points—
even minute points—of dissimilarity are unimportant. So far
from being insignificant, the spirit and meaning of a rite is
constituted by its details. With simple and impressive but
undistracting details, the intellectual and spiritual purport
of the rite is one thing. With a ritual of complicated
gorgeous and distracting details, the rite is quite different in
its effect upon the human spirit. Hence the importance of
observing the numerous and involved details of the Mass in
contrast with the simplicity of the Eucharist as described
in the New Testament.

14. " In the Name of the Father," etc.

From this notice of the bringing in ·of bread and wine and
other things, not before the Lord's Supper, but in the midst of
the service, after what the Mass-book calls the " introit," we
pass on to notice a striking form of words of frequent occurrence in the Mass. Over and over again the priest enunciates
the words, "In the name of the Father, and of the Son, and of
the Holy Spirit." These terms are probably an imitation of
the very ancient practice of ending sermons with an ascription of glory to the Trinity. Used as they are, however, in
the Mass-book (and in certain modern churches of the West
at the beginning of sermons and in many other places),
their aim seems to be, not so much to glorify the Godhead, as
to assert, for the preacher or the priest, that he speaks and
acts in place of the Trinity, and with all the authority of God
Himself. That any single minister of religion should assume
to himself such authority, or should use words capable of
being fairly understood as if he arrogated to himself or to
his office such authority, is, we confess, a phenomenon of
surprising audacity.

Its frequent repetition in the Mass-book forms quite a

characteristic feature in that service, and stands out in marked contrast with apostolic utterances against lording it over God's heritage (1 Peter v. 3), and against the iniquity of one who should so act or speak "that he, as God, sitteth in the temple of God, showing himself that he is God" (2 Thess. ii. 4).

Such audacity, not to use a stronger and perhaps a fitter word, is in very marked opposition to the letter and the spirit of the New Testament.

15. *Inconsistencies in the Mass.*

And next we come to notice certain words of prayer and of apostrophe, in the Mass, connected with the eucharistic elements. These expressions are sometimes hardly consistent one with another. They betoken, in a very interesting manner, the different ages, and the quite opposite conditions of religious thought, out of which the Mass-book grew in its several parts.

From very early times, for instance, and from a frame of mind akin to that of the apostles, must have proceeded the supplication that Almighty God would so bless the oblation of bread and wine "that it may become *to us* the body and blood of" Christ. Notice the difference between praying that the elements may become the body and blood of Christ absolutely, objectively, and in themselves, on the one hand, and praying, on the other hand, that they may become so, relatively, subjectively, not in themselves but to and for us— that we, receiving the bread and wine, may also receive the spiritual benefits that accrue to man from the body of Christ slain and from His blood shed. Here is thought and piety very widely separated from transubstantiation or consubstantiation; and it is not easy to reconcile this prayer for the subjective presence of Christ at the Lord's Supper with the " Hail for ever, holiest flesh of Christ," or with the " Hail for ever, heavenly draught," of another part of the Mass.

It is very interesting and instructive to observe how prayers for the sacramental elements " becoming," relatively to the recipients, a blessing and a means for the reception of Christ and His salvation, abound in the Mass-book. This indicates an earlier origin for such parts of the Mass than the thirteenth century, when the Lateran Council made transubstantiation a doctrine to be believed by the Church.

Nay, those frequent and distinct marks of a belief in the sacramental presence of Christ being in and with the recipients, not in, with, or instead of the elements, betoken that Osmund himself, in drawing up the Salisbury Missal, grafted into it traditional thoughts that were more ancient than Paschasius Radbertus, that probably came down in an unbroken stream from the apostles and from the Lord Himself. Very beautiful are these gleams of truth in the midst of mediæval darkness ; but they become strange and ghastly when we find them in close contrast with the materializing of Christ's eucharistic presence—as, for instance, in the prayer, " May *this sacred mixture of the body and blood* of our Lord Jesus Christ *be made to me, and to all who receive it,* health of mind and body," etc.

Why, surely, if communion with the Lord be a matter of substantial and objective participation, and if the " mixture " be already absolutely and objectively the " body and blood " of Christ, no greater blessing could on that hypothesis be realized, prayed for, or imagined, than physical incorporation and identity with that already present Deity ; and so this supplication would be vain. But the ancient spirit of Christendom breathes through the mediæval error, and supplicates that, over and above any material change believed to have come upon the bread and wine and to have made them " body and blood," there yet may be an effect, in the minds and hearts of all partakers, by means of which the realization of communion with Jesus, and of all the benefits thereof, may accrue to the recipients. And what is this but an acknowledgment, in the Mass-book itself, and that at the very moment of declaring the doctrine of material transubstantiation, that the highest and only effectual and salutary presence of Christ is " to the recipients," relatively to themselves, not in the mere material elements, however changed these may be supposed to be by consecration, but in the minds of partakers—that is, subjectively, not objectively ?

So have we, in the Mass itself, not only the Scriptural idea of Christ's subjective presence; but the unscriptural notion of His material and objective presence is also taught by the same Mass, and sometimes, as in this collect we have just been considering, the two inconsistent and contradictory lines of thought fall into close neighbourhood and conspicuous contrast.

16. *Words of Institution in the Mass.*

And now it will be necessary to look, for a few moments, at the words of institution as they are quoted and engrafted into the Sarum Missal.

Of the words connected with the bread, we will only observe that, in view of the mediæval and pre-Reformation practice of the priest generally communicating in the elements instead of the people, in view of the rare occasions on which the entire congregation partakes of the communion in unreformed Churches, it is very remarkable to find that the Salisbury Mass-book had added to the Saviour's form of institution, connected with the bread, the last three words of the injunction, "Eat of it, *all of you.*"

But let us now look at the words of institution of the wine as they are recited in the Missal :—

"Likewise, after supper, He took the glorious cup into His sacred and venerable hands : and, giving thanks to Thee, He blessed and gave to His disciples, saying, Take and drink of it, all of you; for this is the cup of My blood of the new and eternal covenant, the mystery of the faith, which shall be shed for you and for many for the remission of sins. As oft as ye do these things, ye shall do them in memory of me."

There is no need to dwell at any length upon the epithet "glorious" attached to the cup, or upon the introduction of the word "hands," with the epithets "sacred and venerable" attached to them ; but we cannot help making two remarks on this point.

First, a quotation, we submit, should be made with the least possible alteration of its original form. This holds good with the greater force the more solemn may be the occasion of the quoting; and it -will be confessed on all sides that, whether regard be had to the position and nature of Him who originated the words of sacramental institution, or whether we regard the tremendous results of change in the bread and wine attributed to the repetition of the Lord's words over the eucharistic elements, this is an occasion demanding the most exact quotation.

But, further, we must observe that, in our best judgment of what is comely and dignified, the contrast between "Likewise, after supper, He took the cup," and the more ornate terms imported into the Mass-book—this contrast is like that between the lily as it comes from the hand of God, and the same lily when man has painted over its loveliness.

The next point to be noticed in the words of institution is the introduction of the term "disciples" as the designation of those to whom our Lord gave the cup. This we hold to be unquestionably the correct noun for the filling up of the quotation in this place; but this fair and Scriptural mention of the disciples, as *disciples* and not as apostles, is not a little striking and instructive when we remember that, in the later usage of the Mass-book, the laity were deprived of all participation in the sacramental wine; and one chief argument, in defence of such withholding of the cup, is that Christ gave it to His *apostles* as such, and not in their character of *disciples*.

In the same line of logical thought does the due quotation of Christ's words, "Drink of it, *all of you*," occur to us. Obviously, these words of sacred institution and command could not be expunged or obliterated even after the late mediæval custom had been established of keeping one-half of the Eucharist from the laity in utter and diametrical contravention of the sacred precept, Drink of it, *all of you*. When the priest was left, in the majority of Masses, to partake of the bread by himself or with a mere handful of people from among the spectators, it might be alleged in his defence that he was ready to administer to all, but that the congregation was slow and negligent, and therefore did not partake; but here, in dealing with the cup, the priest was bound to rehearse the Saviour's command, Drink of it, all of you, and yet he would on no account permit the laity—that is, the vast majority of the congregation—to comply with their Lord's freshly recited injunction. Such defiance of apostolic writings and of the divine maxim would seem inconceivable if it were not plain and notorious.

Inaccuracy and the foisting in of strange matter, other than that which Christ appointed, mark the continuation of what should be our Saviour's words of institution.

In none of the four histories of the institution are the words, " This is the cup of My blood," to be found. Nor do those histories qualify the new covenant, in this connection of thought, with the harmless epithet " eternal." Neither do they represent Jesus as calling the cup or any part of the Eucharist " the mystery of the faith." Nor do those histories put any such future tense into the Lord's mouth as that which is here incorrectly quoted by the Mass to the effect that Christ's blood " *shall* be shed." Accuracy of quotation, in the method here adopted of blending all the four records of the institution, would have required the words to stand thus: This cup is My blood, that is, It is the new covenant in My blood ; but then this accurate blending of the Scriptural narratives would have been fatal to the doctrine of transubstantiation and of any objective presence of Christ in the cup. It would have defined and limited the sense in which the cup could be called the blood of Christ as only signifying or symbolizing the new covenant ratified by Christ's blood. The introduction of the word " eternal " is harmless enough, except in so far as it is a painting of the rose.

Still worse, in point of taste, and more characteristically unscriptural, is the Mass-book's dragging in here of the words, " the mystery of the faith," as if Christ had spoken them.

However many things Jesus or the writers of the New Testament may have designated as mysteries or things once secret and unknown, but now revealed and made quite clear to every believer, there is no trace or indication that they ever once applied the name " mystery " to the sacrament of the Lord's Supper; and therefore, in whatever sense, true and wise or false and foolish, the terms "mystery of the faith" are here introduced, they are surreptitious. They are, contrary to all Scripture usage, represented as applied by Christ to this part of the Eucharist.

The object of the futurity which is attributed to the shedding of Christ's blood, as if He had said, My blood which *shall be shed*, instead of pointedly saying, My blood which *is being* shed—the purpose of this deliberate substitution of the Mass's future for Christ's present is, we fear, too obviously, to sustain, in the minds of the heedless or the ignorant, the unscriptural idea that Christ's blood, instead of being shed once for all upon the cross, was often to be poured out in the service of the Mass.

Let it be borne in mind that this recitation of the words of institution is just that which the maintainers of the Mass depend upon as constituting the consecration of the bread and wine. These words of institution, it is, which, on their showing, change the bread and wine into different substances, and make them flesh and blood—these words of Jesus are relied upon as bringing the Lord's objective presence into the bread and wine; and yet observe how these most important words are tampered with, and changed and added to. What we have here is indeed a marvellous reliance upon the words of Christ to work a miracle, while yet those words are not quoted in their integrity, but there is a stupendous and audacious altering and corrupting of them.

17. *Sacrifice for the Dead.*

What a flood of light is thrown upon the mediæval and unreformed use of the Mass as a sacrifice for the dead by the words, "Let him rest in peace," which are prescribed as the termination of the Mass when it is said on behalf of the dead! For this practice there is, of course, no shade or vestige of Scripture warrant. The practice is utterly opposed to apostolic teaching; and whether we think of the abuses which have degraded the Church by reason of this unscriptural practice, or whether we think of the inhuman cruelty of any priest who, having in the Mass a power to lessen and expedite the supposed horrors of a soul in purgatory, should wait to use that power until the widow or the orphan had paid him money for the Mass, the idea is as terrible in its heartlessness as it is monstrous in its unreasonableness, and wholly without the semblance of any support from Holy Writ.

18. *The " Amen."*

Before closing these comments on the Missal of Sarum, there are two or three further points of contrast to which attention should be drawn as distinguishing the Mass of the sixteenth century from the Lord's Supper in the time of Justin Martyr, in the middle of the second century.

We noticed, in examining Justin's description of the sacred rite, with what insistency it was urged that the people—all the people—took part with their president in every portion of the service. The people's " Amen," " the Amen," was a marked feature in the celebration. " The people," says Justin, " assent to his good words with their Amen." So far from this being the invariable practice in the Salisbury Mass-book, several solitary supplications are prescribed, and there is at least one repetition of the Lord's Prayer, that shortly before the breaking of the bread, in which the priest is to say the " Amen " by himself." [1]

No reason can be assigned for thus precluding the people from a privilege and a duty prescribed alike by piety, by reason, and by the practice of primitive and apostolic times, except the mediæval desire to make the distinction more and more marked between the officiating priest and the people or participating priests. This characteristic of the Mass is curious, unscriptural, and anti-apostolical in itself, but we notice it the rather for a reason that will soon become apparent when we enter upon the investigations of our next book.

19. *The " Sermon."*

In Justin's description we noticed that, after reading from " the memoirs of the apostles and the writings of the prophets," " the president admonishes and exhorts us to

[1] Privatim.

imitate their good example ;" in other words, there was a practical discourse, or sermon, made in the midst of the Liturgy, after the reading of the Lessons or the Epistle and Gospel.   Here was an appeal to the reason and judgment of the congregation, and a pious attempt to work upon their will and self-determination through the mind and heart.

The sermon was thus, in primitive times, a very important part of the eucharistic service; but when we come to the Mass-book of Salisbury, among all its copious and abundant rubrics, telling where candles shall be put, how fingers shall be wiped and how they and thumbs shall be held together or apart—amidst a vast complication of such minute injunctions, there is no mention made of any appeal to the heart and conscience of the people by the sympathetic intelligence of him who acts as leader and president in the service.   In other words, while the body is regulated in its every movement, the higher parts of man are left unheeded and uncared for.   It is indeed a contrast and a falling off that has in this respect crept in between the time of Paul or of Justin, and the days of mediæval ignorance.

20. *Participation or Communion.*

In Justin's description of the Lord's Supper it was notice-able how the deacons distributed the bread and wine to all who were present, and how, even to absent members of the Church, they conveyed portions of the eucharistic elements.

What a change had come over this practice when, in the days of Chrysostom, the people dispersed occasionally, after listening to his eloquence, without partaking of the Eucharist; when, in later times, certain councils made communion obli-gatory upon the laity only three times in the year, at Christmas, Easter, and Whitsuntide ; and when, in the thirteenth century, the fourth Lateran Council made such communion, with auri-ular confession, obligatory no more than once a year, at Easter ! So it came to pass that, instead of every member of the Chris-tian Church communicating in both the sacramental elements at least once a week, the vast majority of the congregation were, by the sixteenth century and long before that time, forbidden to participate in the cup at all; and for their hardly more than annual participation in the other element of bread, not a single rubric is to be found in the Mass-book of Sarum.

When, thus, the practice of communion and fellowship in the sacred feast was forbidden, maimed, curtailed, and by implication discouraged, it could hardly be matter of astonishment that the Mass-book well-nigh ignored all mention of "communion," all reference to charitable help for fellow-Christians, and all reminders among communicants—after their communion or away from the place of celebration—that Christian life should be so pure and energetic and self-denying as to be worthy of that high and holy communion with God and Christ and all the saints.

Just as, in spite of the general tone of the Mass-book implying that the whole congregation are to join in the prayers and thanksgivings, yet the people had been taught to leave all or almost all to the priest long before the sixteenth century, so the ancient apostolic idea of communion and fellowship had well-nigh disappeared from the Missal. Its traces were still to be found, indeed, in one or two references to "communion" and "post-communion." Otherwise, Mass was most frequently not a communion at all, but only a solitary and private celebration.

21. *Utter Change, in the Mass.*

The Supper of the Lord, with its joyful communion in prayer and praise and breaking of bread, as instituted by Christ and practised by the apostles and depicted by Justin Martyr, had vanished and passed away; and the thing being changed and gone, language, without perhaps the conscious intention of those who used it, bore its emphatic and honest testimony to the change by substituting for the sacred and significant titles applied to the Communion in primitive times the slight and insignificant name of the Missa, the Dismissal, the Mass.

K. *The Plan of this Essay excludes an Historical Analysis, in detail, of Extant Ancient Liturgies.*

This representation of the contrast between the Communion

of apostolic times and the Mass of the middle and dark ages, might be traced in its growth and development if the plan of this essay permitted or required us to examine the extant Liturgies of the Greek Church, or of the so-called apostolical constitutions; and similar results would accrue to us from an investigation of the ancient sacramentaries of Leo, or Gelasius, or Gregory the Great.

Our object, however, has not been to weary the reader with too many details of history or antiquity, but rather to set before him a distinct picture of the communion of the Lord's Supper in its first institution, in its apostolic simplicity, in its primitive usage. Then we tried to indicate some of the sources whence arose a departure from the Scriptural and primitive practices and doctrines; and, lastly, it has been our endeavour to lay before the reader the actual Mass service of the pre-Reformation period, in order that its points of contrast might be distinctly recognisable in comparison with the memorial breaking of bread enjoined by the Lord as a communion with Himself and with all the members of His body the Church.

L. *Conclusion—the Contrast.*

A more striking contrast—a wider and more substantial difference than that between the Missal in its unknown Latin tongue and the apostolic Communion in words that were intelligible; between the non-sacerdotal presidents of the Communion and the sacrificing priests of the Mass; between the ordinary and unnoticeable costumes of the Communion and the gorgeous chasubles of the mediæval service; between the memorial feast of the apostles and the propitiatory sacrifice of the dark ages; between the humility and self-depreciation of the original breakers of bread and the merits spoken of in the Mass; between the Lord's Table of St. Paul and the high altar of sacerdotalism; between the Scriptural representation of Mary's errors, weakness, and dependence upon Jesus and upon John, and her meritorious intercession as inculcated in the Missal; between the utter absence of utensils and paraphernalia in the Scriptural Communion

and the manifold array of candles and candle-bearers, incense and incense-bearers, choirs and holy of holies, basins
and towels, corporals and sacrifices and hosts, hand-washings
and cup-drainings, " Pax " representations and signs of the
cross, introits and graduals and antiphons and sequences in
the Mass; between the apostolic appeal to man's conscience
and his judgment and the mediæval dictation, " In the name,
of the Father, and of the Son, and of the Holy Ghost ; " between the Lord's command, " Drink of it, all of you," and
the withholding of the cup in the Romish service ; between
the frequent celebration without auricular confession in
apostolic times, and the merely annual celebration with
private confession to the priest in the Middle Ages; between
all the people being priests according to John and Peter
and Justin, and only some of the ministering officials being
priests according to the Mass; between the sermon as an
important feature of the primitive Communion, and the
absence of a sermon in the Use of Sarum ; between the whole
congregation responding to the president and sounding forth
its Amen in antiquity, and the marked discouragement given
to the people's occasional Amen in the Mass; between the
bread and wine being the body and blood of Christ only
inasmuch as they were a communion of the new covenant
ratified in the giving of His body and the shedding of His
blood, as Scripture teaches, and the bread and wine being
verily transmuted into the material or objective body and
blood of Him who was born of Mary and pierced with a
spear on the cross, as is taught by mediævalism;—a more
striking contrast than is presented by this far from exhaustive
catalogue of the differences between Christ's Breaking of
Bread on the one hand, and the mediæval service of the
Mass on the other hand, we submit it would be difficult to
imagine : and so we leave the matter in order to see how this
difference was dealt with in England three centuries ago and
in succeeding times.

BOOK III.

THE LORD'S SUPPER IN THE REFORMED CHURCH OF ENGLAND.

CHAPTER I.

ENGLAND, AN EARLY AND IMPORTANT AGENT IN CHURCH REFORM.

FROM the consideration of the Eucharist as instituted and practised in New Testament times, and as changed between those times and the sixteenth century, we come now to examine the mode of administration prescribed in the existing Church of England.

A very few preliminary words must suffice to remind the reader how early and conspicuous a part had been taken by England in the cry for a reformation of matters ecclesiastical.

If Dante had already sung, in Italy, the lament over corruptions in high and holy places and the consequent need of a return to better and older practices, he was followed, at all events, after no long interval, by Chaucer and "Piers Plowman," who denounced in no measured terms the greed of the clergy and the want of greater purity among the monks. It was in England, too, that Wicliffe and the Lollards translated and studied the New Testament; and in this country it was that they demanded a return, in doctrines and practices—not least in those connected with the Mass—to the model which presented itself to them as they investigated the ancient and original writings of the apostles and evangelists. Huss and his disciples in Bohemia learned their principles from the writings and preachings of Wicliffe, which travelled with the students in their migrations from one University to another— from Oxford to Prague, for instance.

Luther had not carried his inquiries far when he discovered that he was a Hussite, even as Huss had been a follower of Wicliffe. Thus, through two centuries, the Reformation, set on foot in England, moved onwards, till it became one of several influences that urged forward the popular and mighty movement of the monk of Wittenberg, in Germany.

And if, thus, the popular wave of German reform was connected with impulses that came from an English parsonage in the fourteenth century, it is obvious that the more cautious and learned action of Erasmus, with his "Praise of Folly" and his translation of the Greek Testament, was intimately connected with the work of Grocyn and Linacre, Colet and Thomas More, in Oxford and in London.

Apart from the political career of Henry VIII. and Thomas Cromwell and Cranmer, it is not difficult to understand how two independent lines of religious thought and feeling were at work in England in the first half of the sixteenth century. Among the people there was not wanting sympathy with the bold Reformers of the continent; and among the learned there was distinct if not original study and action, following, perhaps, along the lines laid down even in Italy by Pico della Mirandola and Politian and other learned disciples of Savonarola.

CHAPTER II.

So it came to pass that, after translations of the Bible into the vernacular had been made and affixed to public reading benches during the reign of Henry VIII., the opening days of Edward VI. witnessed the attempt, in England, to offer the laity participation in the sacrament of the Lord's Supper in both the elements of bread and wine, and through the medium of the vulgar tongue, which was, at that time, alone " understanded of the people."

This first effort to return to apostolic usage, in the matter of the Lord's Supper, is remarkable, amongst other things, for having been appended to the Latin Mass. The mediæval Mass service was not abolished or even translated. It was left in use; but, at its close, an English service was grafted on to it.

Here it may be well to say that parts of this earliest English Communion Service are derived from a Liturgy which had been drawn up (A.D. 1543) by Bucer and Melancthon for Hermann, Archbishop of Cologne. English translations of this Liturgy were published in the years 1547 and 1548, under the title of " A Simple and Religious Consultation of Us, Hermann, Archbishop of Cologne and Prince Elector," etc.

The points that we should chiefly notice in this first English Communion Service may perhaps be sufficiently indicated without here producing the entire composition.

On the next Sunday or holy-day, or at least one day

preceding the administering of the Communion, the people were to be admonished in a form closely resembling that which now stands in the Prayer-book as the first of the two exhortations to the Communion. From this form were then omitted the words, " Therefore if any of you be a blasphemer," etc., because they occurred in another part of the service. Besides the instructions, still to be found in the exhortation, there was an admonition "requiring such as shall be satisfied with a general confession not to be offended with them that doth use, to their further satisfying, the auricular and secret confession to the priest ; nor those also which think needful or convenient, for the quietness of their own consciences, particularly to open their sins to the priest, to be offended with them which are satisfied with their humble confession to God, and the general confession to the Church."

There is a tone of admirable charity in this part of the exhortation ; but, besides its charity, it contains a principle of very great importance which we ought to notice. The mediæval Mass could not be partaken of until the intending communicant had made a private confession to his priest and received penance and absolution from that priest. Instead of the communicant examining himself and judging himself, as had been the apostolic injunction, mediævalism prescribed that he should be examined and judged by a priest as an indispensable condition to his receiving the eucharistic bread.

Of this thoroughly unscriptural piece of ecclesiastical and inquisitorial despotism these charitable words are a practical abolition. They imply the non-necessity of such confession and penance and absolution, while they enjoin toleration for those who abstain from it. If the practice had been deemed necessary or desirable or expedient, Cranmer and his associates would not have pointedly introduced into their new Liturgy an apology for its disuse. This bringing home of the responsibility of self-examination to the individual communicant is a matter of the highest importance, as distinguishing the modern Church of England from that of the Middle Ages.

It is true these words of exhortation to mutual forbearance

have disappeared in our subsequent liturgies; but, then, it should be remembered that, their principle once having been laid down, and the practice of private sacramental confession having fallen into desuetude, another course of action is now prescribed for the intending communicant, namely, that he should examine himself and only have recourse to a clergyman for friendly and Scriptural advice and information on any exceptional point concerning which he cannot satisfy his own conscience. This will become clearer as we proceed with our essay; but, in the mean while, it may be observed that the omission of the exhortation to forbearance by no means lessens the appeal to private judgment and the assertion of responsibility on the part of each individual communicant.

"The time of Communion" was to be immediately after the priest himself had received the sacrament. Thus, prominence was at once given to the idea of the communion or fellowship of all believers with one another and with Christ's body, the universal Church, as well as with Christ Himself, its head. This restoration of the idea of union and communion to its proper place in the very forefront of the eucharistic service will continue to mark the English Liturgy more and more distinctly as we approach the existing formularies.

"Until other order shall be provided," the consecration of the bread was to proceed as it had been wont to do; but the priest was to "bless and consecrate the biggest chalice, or some fair and convenient cup or cups full of wine with some water put into it;" and of this it is enjoined that he shall "not drink it all himself, but taking one only sup or draught, leave the rest upon the altar covered," and, turning to the intending communicants, shall thus exhort them:—

"Dearly beloved in the Lord, ye coming to this holy Communion must consider what St. Paul writeth to the Corinthians, how he exhorteth all persons diligently to try and examine themselves," etc., and so on, very nearly as in our present exhortation at the time of celebrating the Communion.

Then followed a warning by the priest, very nearly in the terms of our present first exhortation to Communion, "If any man here be an open blasphemer," etc.

Here the priest shall pause awhile, to see if any man will withdraw himself; and if he perceive any so to do, then let him commune with him privily at convenient leisure, and see whether he can with good exhortation bring him to grace : and after a little pause the priest shall say,

You that do truly and earnestly repent you of your sins . . . make your humble confession to Almighty God, and to His holy Church, here gathered together in His name, meekly kneeling upon your knees.

Then shall a general Confession be made in the name of all those that are minded to receive the holy Communion, either by one of them, or else by one of the ministers, or by the priest himself, all kneeling humbly upon their knees.

Almighty God, Father of our Lord Jesus Christ, Maker of all things [etc.].

Then shall the priest stand up, and turning him to the people, say thus,

Our blessed Lord, who hath left power to His Church, to absolve penitent sinners from their sins, and to restore to the grace of the Heavenly Father such as truly believe in Christ, have mercy upon you, pardon [etc.].

These forms of confession and absolution are modelled after those in Hermann's Consultation ; but it has been well pointed out by Mr. Procter, in his " History of the Book of Common Prayer," how wisely the English Reformers, while availing themselves of this model, yet eschewed certain less desirable characteristics thereof. For instance, we may notice that, instead of our sins being attributed, in part at least, to natural and utter depravity and to " Satan the kindler thereof "—as is done in Hermann's form—the first English Communion Service prescribed a simpler form in which sin is acknowledged and deplored in our guilt and responsibility for it, apart from all reference to doctrines which, to some minds, might extenuate man's personal guilt by throwing part of the blame on innate depravity and on Satanic temptation.

No less wise is the English abstinence from language of such high tension as that of Hermann, which describes man as prone to all evils, abhorring all good things, and having transgressed God's holy commandments without end and measure in despising God and His Word, etc.

In that earliest English Liturgy it is observable that confession was made, not only to God, but "to His holy Church" also. The owning of wrong to those against whom it has been done is undoubtedly a duty in its proper time and place; but our sympathies go with the cry of the penitent Psalmist,

"Against Thee only have I sinned," rather than with a practice which should associate even the holiest congregation of men with the Most High God, to whom the self-humiliation of the soul is offered.

In Hermann's form of absolution, after " the pastor " has recited certain comforting texts of Scripture, he proceeds, in the name of the congregation, saying, " I, the minister of Christ and the congregation, declare and pronounce remission of sins, the favour of God, and life everlasting, through our Lord Jesus Christ, to all them which be sorry for their sins, which have true faith in Christ the Lord, and desire to approve themselves unto Him."

This is, beyond all question, a beautiful and harmless modification of the late mediæval indicative form, " I absolve thee ; " but we confess to entertaining a decided preference for that precatory form, " Our Blessed Lord . . . have mercy upon you, pardon and deliver you," etc., which was substituted by our Reformers for the indicative form that had found its way into Hermann's Consultation.

Upon the Absolution there followed the reading of the texts called " The Comfortable Words."

And then came the administration of the elements in the following form :—

The body of our Lord Jesus Christ, which was given for thee, preserve thy body unto everlasting life.

The blood of our Lord Jesus Christ, which was shed for thee, preserve thy soul to everlasting life.

It is curious, and not without interest in connection with the latter part of our present Prayer of Humble Access, to notice here the manner in which the bread is associated with our bodies, and the wine with our souls.

The service concluded with the Benediction, founded upon a verse in the fourth chapter of the Epistle to the Philippians, " The peace of God, which passeth all understanding, keep your hearts and minds in the knowledge and love of God, and in His Son Jesus Christ our Lord.   Amen."

With reference to the administration of the cup it was enjoined that, " If there be a deacon or other priest, then shall he follow with the chalice, and as the priest ministereth the bread, so shall he, for more expedition, minister the wine."

The bread "shall be such as heretofore hath been accustomed; and every of the said consecrated breads shall be broken in two pieces at the least."

If the consecrated wine be not sufficient for all who wish to communicate, "the priest, after the first cup or chalice be emptied, may go again to the altar, and reverently and devoutly prepare and consecrate another, and so the third, or more, likewise beginning at these words [in the Latin Missal] 'Likewise after supper,' and ending at these words, 'which shall be shed for us and for many for the remission of sins,' and without any levation or lifting up."

These rubrics are not without instructiveness. There is admirable common sense in the mode prescribed for administering the cup by a second clergyman so as to economize time. There is an obvious intention that no person, wishing to partake of the wine, shall be hindered from doing so on the plea that all the consecrated wine has been consumed. On the other hand, the wafer-bread was retained; and the term "altar" was still employed as the designation of the Lord's Table.

CHAPTER III.

THE reader will have observed that, in this earliest English service for the Communion, the phrase occurs, "until other order shall be provided." Thus is it intimated that the mixture of a Latin Mass service with an English appendix was only a temporary arrangement. Here was an indication, too, of the importance attached by the Reformers, in the beginning of Edward VI.'s reign, to the laity receiving the Communion in both kinds, and to the employment, without loss of time, of intelligible language in the sacred Liturgy.

Thus it came to pass that in March, 1548, the short English "Order of Communion" was set forth with all due authority; and, by the continued labours of Cranmer and other divines, it was followed and replaced, in June of the next year (1549), by "The Book of Common Prayer." Henceforth it was enjoined that this book, and only this book, was to be used in all common and open prayer and in the administration of the two sacraments.

And now it must be our effort to give as brief a representation as may be possible of the chief characteristics of this book in the part of it having regard to administration of the Eucharist.

At the outset, we observe that the designation set at the beginning of the service was "The Supper of the Lord and the Holy Communion, commonly called the Mass."

Here was a tolerably prominent and conspicuous return to the ancient Scriptural names of the Eucharist; and if the title "Mass" was retained, as a means of identification for the ignorant between the new English service and the mediæval Latin Liturgy, it was marked with the qualifying terms "commonly called," a phrase which indicated pretty clearly the wide prevalence rather than the propriety or validity of the title so described.

Of the rubrics at the head of this Communion Service, the first required all intending communicants to signify their names to the curate "overnight, or else in the morning, afore the beginning of matins, or immediately after."

At present we are apt to think little of a rubric like this; but it should be remembered that, in the middle of the sixteenth century, its importance was very great and its character strongly marked. Hitherto, no man had been permitted to communicate until he had gone to the priest to make an auricular confession, and to receive from the priest penance and absolution. And now, in 1549, instead of this tremendous power of granting or withholding communion being kept in the hands of the clergy absolutely and universally, the right and power of communion is conceded to the laity, and is left to their own judgment and responsibility, subject only to certain limitations laid down in the two next following rubrics.

This, which seems so commonplace a matter to us, Protestant Englishmen, nowadays, was a very practical confirmation and carrying out of the injunction, in 1548, that none should be offended with them who, avoiding private confession to the priest, were "satisfied with their humble confession to God, and the general confession to the Church."

How much power, that might be abused to purposes of tyranny, was thus taken out of the hands of the clergy! How much conscientious responsibility was thus healthily thrown upon the communicants themselves! How much more nearly this system resembled the Pauline command, "Let a man examine himself," than the mediæval prescription, "Let a man be shriven by the priest!"

The two reserved cases, in which some limit is still put to the freedom and responsibility of the communicant, are these :—

(1.) Open and notorious evil livers and wrong-doers are to be called and advertised by the clergyman that they presume not to come to the Lord's Table until they have manifested repentance and amendment and made recompense for wrong done to others. Here is one limitation of the right and duty of each communicant to judge of his own fitness for participation in the sacrament; and, in this instance, the curate's power seems to end when he has given the notorious evil liver or wrong-doer that advice, whether public or private, or both, which is indicated in the phrase, " shall call him and advertise him that in any wise he presume not to come to the Lord's Table."

(2.) The second limitation of the general right to communicate is more definite and absolute. The curate is not to suffer partaking of the Lord's Table by them, betwixt whom he perceiveth malice and hatred to reign. He may admit to communion one of the parties who shall be inclined to reconciliation, while he refuses the Communion to "him that is obstinate."

Here were remnants but, comparatively speaking, very small remnants, of the mediæval power of the priest to grant or to withhold communion in the case of people who had been led to believe that such communion was the chief instrument of divine forgiveness in life and the necessary condition for salvation in death.

Even these traces of the vast power of mediæval sacerdotalism have been rendered still more innocuous in our present Prayer-book, as we shall see in due time. In the mean while, let it suffice to have thus drawn the reader's attention to the return towards apostolic freedom and piety marked by these opening rubrics of Edward VI.'s service for the Supper of the Lord.

In quitting these rubrics, it is quite worth while to contrast their wholesome freedom and encouragement of self-examination with, not only the practice of the unreformed Church of the Middle Ages, but also with the following precept in Hermann's Consultation, "We will that the pastors admit no man to the Lord's Supper, which hath not first offered himself to them ; and after that he hath first made a confession of his sins, being catechized, he receive absolution according to the Lord's word."

So early did the English Liturgy show its native and Scriptural love of liberty and self-responsibity, in comparison with other reformed services as well as with the formularies of mediævalism.

The next rubric in Edward VI.'s first Prayer-book is that which enjoins the dress to be worn by those who minister at the Lord's Table. This matter of costume, in itself of the most infinitesimally small moment, is at present raised into quite abnormal conspicuousness and importance by the contest over it between the sacerdotalists, on the one hand, and the anti-sacerdotalists on the other hand.

The priest, who executed the holy ministry in the Communion, was to wear " the vesture appointed for that ministration, that is to say, a white alb plain, with a vestment or cope."

The " alb " was a white linen garment with somewhat close-fitting sleeves. It was distinguished from the ordinary surplice by these sleeves, by its fitting generally closer to the body, and by its being girdled round the waist.

The " cope " was a semicircular cloak, which was thrown over the shoulders so that its straight edge should be buckled in front, under the chin.

The vestment (or " chasuble ") was a long oval costume, with a hole in the middle through which the wearer's head emerged, while the garment hung, by his shoulders, half in front and half behind him. Its back was decorated with a cross ; its front with an upright line. The latter is said to have symbolized the pillar of scourging.

If this was to be the dress of the chief officiating minister, any priests or deacons, who helped him in his ministration, were to " have upon them likewise the vestures appointed for their ministry, that is to say, albs with tunicles."

The " alb " has been described above.

The " tunicle " was shorter than the alb, with shorter sleeves, and was made of richer, heavier materials than the linen of the alb.   It was not oval, like the chasuble, but was straight-edged at the bottom.

Of these Church dresses, generally, it is interesting to remark that, in their origin, they were—most of them, at all events—not a distinctive, clerical garb; but just as the dress of the Blue-coat School was the ordinary dress of English lads 400 years ago, and has been retained in use in Christ's Hospital after its abandonment in other places, so becoming a characteristic and a peculiarity of that school—similarly, the various clerical garbs were the common dresses of the country and age in which they originated, but have been continued in use until, being out of date if not out of place, they have come to constitute a set of professional and ministerial robes and garments.

After regulating the dress of those who minister at the Lord's Supper, the rubric of 1549 proceeds to enjoin that, at the time appointed for the Communion, "the clerks shall sing in English for the office or introit (as they call it) a Psalm appointed for that day."

It is noticeable how anxious were the compilers even of Edward the VI.'s first Prayer-book that the whole service should be in language intelligible by the people.   Not even the introit (or chant during the approach of the priest to the altar) was to be any longer in Latin.   It must be, like all the service, in English.

Instead of the forty-third Psalm, which, with its magnificent song concerning the approach to God's (Judaic) altar, had been the ordinary "introit" of the mediæval Mass-book, there were henceforth to be employed different Psalms for each day: and so a step was taken towards getting rid of the Middle Age idea that approaching the table of the Lord was identical with "going unto the altar of God."

Those who wish to re-introduce into the English Church the disused term "introit," with its cognate ideas of sacerdotalism, ought to lay to heart such indications of the Reformers' principles as are contained in the abandonment of Psalm xliii. as the "introit," and in the terms of derogation, the "introit (*as they call it*)."

The next portion of the rubric enjoins that "the priest, standing humbly afore the midst of the altar, shall say the Lord's Prayer, with this collect, 'Almighty God, unto whom all hearts,' " etc.

This, as we have already seen, is an exact copy of the opening prayers of the Salisbury Missal's ordinary service of the Mass, the idea of "merit," however, being omitted from the English collect.

Then the priest was to "say a Psalm appointed for the introit;" and, after that, the priest was to "say," or the clerks were to sing :—

> Lord, have mercy upon us.
>   Christ, have mercy upon us.
> Lord, have mercy upon us.

Then the priest, "standing at God's board," was to begin, "Glory be to God on high."

The clerks were to continue the words, "And in earth peace," etc.

Then the priest was to turn to the people and say :—

> The Lord be with you.
> *Answer.* And with thy spirit.
> *The priest.* Let us pray.

Then was to follow the collect of the day, with one of the two collects following for the king: "Almighty God, whose kingdom," etc., or "Almighty and Everlasting God," etc.

The collects ended, the priest, "or he that is appointed," shall read first the Epistle and then the Gospel. After the announcement of the Gospel, "the clerks and people" were to answer, "Glory be to Thee, O Lord." It may be observed how much of ritual is omitted, in connection with the reading of the Epistle and Gospel, as compared with the Missal printed above. The incense, the kissing of the book, the procession with the candle-bearers, etc., and the precise order to read the Gospel facing southwards—these formalities have disappeared even from the pages of Edward VI.'s first Prayer-book; and the change is, we submit, noteworthy and significant.

The next precept of the rubric was that, after the Gospel, " the priest shall begin, ' I believe in one God; ' and the clerks shall sing the rest " of the Nicene Creed.

After the Creed was to follow " the sermon or Homily, or some portion of one of the Homilies as they shall be hereafter divided : wherein if the people be not exhorted to the worthy receiving of the holy sacrament of the body and blood of our Saviour Christ, then shall the curate give this exhortation to those that be mindful to receive the same."

The exhortation was to be that (" Dearly beloved in the Lord," etc.) now employed at the time of celebration of the Communion, only adding the warning (taken from the service of 1548) against open sinners coming to the holy Table. This warning stood after the words, " sundry kinds of death."

In cathedral churches, or other places where there was daily Communion, it was sufficient—proceeded the rubric— that this exhortation should be read once in a month : and in parish churches, upon the week days, it may be left unsaid.

And if upon the Sunday or holy-day the people be negligent to come to the Communion, then shall the priest earnestly exhort his parishioners to dispose themselves to the receiving of the holy Communion more diligently, saying these or like words unto them,

Dear friends, and you especially upon whose souls I have care and charge [etc.]

This exhortation was substantially the same as that which now stands as the first form for giving " warning for the celebration of the holy Communion." It was marked by a few verbal differences from the existing notice. It omitted the reference to " auricular and secret confession to the priest," which stood in the similar exhortation of 1548. And it contained words, omitted now, and not to be found in the form of 1548, to the effect that wrong-doers must make satisfaction and due restitution, or else " neither the absolution of the priest can anything avail them, nor the receiving of this holy sacrament doth anything but increase their damnation."

The idea and much of the language of this exhortation is, as says Mr. Procter, taken from Hermann's Consultation and other foreign services for the Communion. After the exhortation the rubric proceeds : Then shall follow for the offertory one or more of these sentences of Holy Scripture, to be sung while the people do offer, or else one of them to be said by the minister, immediately afore the offering.

In the mean time, while the clerks do sing the Offertory, so many as are disposed shall offer to the poor men's box, every one according to his ability and charitable mind. And, at the offering days appointed, every man and woman shall pay to the curate the due and accustomed offerings.

What is noteworthy here is the entire voluntariness and spontaneity of the offering which the people seem to have gone from their place in church to make to the "poor men's box" in its apparently fixed position. It would, perhaps, have been better if there had been less idea of what was *customary* and *due* in the offerings for the clergy. One can hardly fail to observe the exigency of the Church's mediæval demands exemplified in the latter part of the rubric, while the free, cheerful, and unconstrained gifts of apostolic usage find their illustration in the former part.

The next rubric enjoins that—

So many as shall be partakers of the holy Communion shall tarry still in the quire, or in some convenient place nigh the quire, the men on the one side, and the women on the other side. All other (that mind not to receive the said holy Communion) shall depart out of the quire, except the ministers and clerks. Then shall the minister take so much bread and wine as shall suffice for the persons appointed to receive the holy Communion, laying the bread upon the corporal, or else in the paten, or in some other comely thing prepared for that purpose; and putting the wine into the chalice, or else in some fair and convenient cup prepared for that use (if the chalice will not serve), putting thereto a little pure and clean water: and setting both the bread and wine upon the altar. Then shall the priest say,

The Lord be with you.
And with thy spirit.
Priest. Lift up your hearts, etc.

At this point were introduced the special "Prefaces," for Christmas, Easter, Ascension Day, Whit Sunday, and Trinity Sunday. On the other, ordinary days, the priest proceeded—

Therefore with angels and archangels, etc.

Holy, holy, holy, Lord God of Hosts : heaven and earth are full of Thy glory : Osannah in the highest. Blessed is He that cometh in the name of the Lord : glory to Thee, O Lord, in the highest.

This the clerks shall also sing.

When the clerks have done singing, then shall the priest, or deacon, turn him to the people, and say,

Let us pray for the whole state of Christ's Church.

The very ancient custom of mixing water with the wine is here seen to have been retained in the first Prayer-book of Edward VI. The general observances of the Offertory, and the setting the elements on the altar, are like those of the

Mass-book, but simpler and less ornate. The separation of the men and women at the Communion is an innovation as compared with the Salisbury Missal. Not a little remarkable is the phrase "persons *appointed to receive* the holy Communion." From the rubric, at the end of the service, it appears that "the parishioners of every parish shall offer every Sunday, at the time of the offertory, the just value and price of the holy loaf;" and "some one at the least of that house, to whom, by course, it appertaineth to offer for the charges of the Communion, or some other whom they shall provide to offer for them, shall receive the holy Communion with the priest."

This language makes it apparent that, in 1549, there was difficulty in inducing the people to communicate ; and some, "in course" or turn, were "appointed" as under a constraint to receive the Lord's Supper each Sunday.

It will be noticed by the careful reader that various rites and prayers, which were prescribed in the corresponding part of the Missal, are omitted in the service of Edward VI.

For the rest, this portion of the Liturgy of 1549 is modelled pretty closely upon the Sarum Missal, only that "The Lord be with you," "Lift up your hearts," and the "Holy, holy, holy," are rendered in English instead of being in Latin.

Here followed the longest and most important prayer of the whole service, introduced by the rubric—

Then the priest, turning him to the altar, shall say or sing, plainly and distinctly, this Prayer following.

Almighty and Everliving God, which by Thy holy apostle hast taught us to make prayers and supplications, and to give thanks for all men, we humbly beseech Thee most mercifully to receive these our prayers [etc., as in our present Prayer for the Church Militant, down to the words "in trouble, need, sickness, or any other adversity"].

Then, instead of the present ending of the Prayer for the Church Militant, were added these words :—

And especially we commend unto Thy merciful goodness this congregation which is here assembled in Thy name, to celebrate the commemoration of the most glorious death of Thy Son : and here we do give unto Thee most high praise and hearty thanks for the wonderful grace and virtue, declared in all Thy saints, from the beginning of the wor_{..} to and chiefly in the glorious and most blessed Virgin Mary, mother of Thy, Son Jesu Christ our Lord and God, and in the holy patriarchs, prophets, apostles, and martyrs, whose examples, O Lord, and steadfastness in Thy faith, and keeping Thy holy commandments, grant us to follow. We commend unto Thy mercy, O Lord, all other Thy servants which are departed hence from us, with the sign of faith, and now do rest in the sleep of peace : Grant unto them, we beseech Thee, Thy mercy and ever-lasting peace, and that, at the day of the general resurrection, we and all they which be of the mystical body of Thy Son, may altogether be set on His right hand, and hear that His most joyful voice, Come unto me, O ye that be blessed of My Father, and possess the kingdom which is prepared for you from the beginning of the world : grant this, O Father, for Jesus Christ's sake, our only Mediator and Advocate.

O God, heavenly Father, which of Thy tender mercy didst give Thine only Son Jesu Christ, to suffer death upon the cross for our redemption, who made there (by His one oblation, once offered) a full, perfect, and sufficient sacrifice, oblation, and satisfaction for the sins of the whole world, and did institute, and in His holy Gospel command us to cele-brate, a perpetual memory of that His precious death, until His coming again ; Hear us, O merciful Father, we beseech Thee, and with Thy Holy Spirit and Word vouchsafe to bl✠ess and sanc✠tify these Thy gifts and creatures of bread and wine, that they may be unto us the body and blood of Thy most dearly beloved Son Jesus Christ ; who, in the same night that He was betrayed, took bread, and when He had given thanks, He brake it, and gave to His disciples, saying, Take, eat ; this is My body which is given for you : Do this in remembrance of Me. *Here the priest must take the bread into his hands.*

Likewise after supper He took the cup, and when He had given thanks He gave it to them, saying, Drink ye all of this ; for this is My blood of the New Testament, which is shed for you and for many for remission of sins : Do this, as often as ye shall drink it, in remembrance of Me. *Here the priest shall take the cup into his hands.*

All this prayer, let it be borne in mind, is to be said by the priest still turning to the altar, without any elevation or showing the sacrament to the people.

Quite worthy of observation is such a phrase as "the wonderful *grace and virtue* declared in all Thy saints from the beginning of the world, and chiefly in the *glorious* and most blessed Virgin Mary, mother of Thy Son Jesu Christ our Lord and God, and in the holy patriarchs, prophets, apostles and martyrs." Such words are quite alien from the letter and spirit of the apostolic writings. They are akin to the mediæval doctrine of "merits," as a treasure of super

*rogatory good works wrought by the saints, and placed at
*the disposal of the Pope and his emissaries for transference,
at their discretion, to such penitents as, by purchase of in-
dulgences or otherwise, procure to themselves the good will of
the Pope or his vicegerents. These phrases remind us of the
"glorious Virgin," named in the Salisbury Missal; but this
mention of "wonderful grace and virtue," in the saints, surpasses even the Mass-book. Such phrases occur for the last
time in the Protestant Church of England, though not of
Scotland, in this first Prayer-book of Edward the Sixth; and,
for that reason too, we shall do well to notice them carefully
in this place.

Very beautiful is the commending to God's mercy of all
those "who are departed hence from us . . . and now rest in
the sleep of peace;" but it must be regretted that the feeble
description of the blessed dead as having departed "with
the sign of faith"—meaning an external cross marked upon
them—was not abandoned, and some such noble words as
"departed in Thy true faith," or "departed this life in Thy
faith and fear," substituted for them.

The only other points we deem it necessary to notice, at
present, are those which follow; as, for instance, the retention
of the invocations of the Holy Spirit and the Word upon the
eucharistic elements. These invocations, though they come to
us with the oldest of extant Liturgies, find no place in the
original records of our Saviour's institution of the Supper:
and, as it is most desirable to keep very close to Christ's
example in all things, especially in a sacred rite which has
been so tampered with as the Eucharist, we cannot but think
that these invocations, occurring in the service of 1549, were
wisely omitted in later English services for the Communion.

Especially are we confirmed in this conviction when we
reflect that the invocations were made with a view to the
bread and wine being the body and blood of Christ. It is
true, the prayer was that the bread and wine may be "*unto
us*" the body and blood of Christ; in other words, Englishmen, in 1549, prayed, not for an absolute and objective
change of bread and wine into body and blood, but they

supplicated, as indeed did the mediæval Mass-book also—as we have seen—that relatively to us, subjectively in us, the bread and wine might be the body and blood of Christ. Still there was, in these invocations and in this prayer, the semblance, for the minds of the thoughtless, of a material conveyance of the body and blood in, or by, or instead of, the bread and wine; and therefore we rejoice that, by the omission of these invocations and this prayer, later editions of the Communion Service returned to a nearer imitation of our Lord's example. Obvious enough are the signs of the cross, twice enjoined in the prayer of consecration given above. These signs disappear from later Liturgies; and, whatever may be thought of the harmlessness of the sign in itself, its abandonment is noteworthy, not only as a concession to those who felt scruples at its employment, but as marking progress in the direction which led away from unscriptural rites and ceremonies.   .

And now we revert to the prayer of consecration and oblation of the bread and wine, which proceeded in these terms :—

Wherefore, O Lord and Heavenly Father, according to the institution of Thy dearly beloved Son, our Saviour Jesus Christ, we Thy humble servants do celebrate, and make here before Thy divine Majesty, with these Thy holy gifts, the memorial which Thy Son hath willed us to make : having in remembrance His blessed passion, mighty resurrection, and glorious ascension, rendering unto Thee most hearty thanks for the innumerable benefits promised unto us by the same, entirely desiring Thy Fatherly goodness mercifully to accept this our sacrifice of praise and thanksgiving ; most humbly beseeching Thee to grant that, by the merits and death of Thy Son Jesus Christ, and through faith in His blood, we and all Thy whole Church may obtain remission of our sins, and all other benefits of His passion. And here we offer and present unto Thee, O Lord, ourself, our souls and bodies, to be a reasonable, holy, and lively sacrifice unto Thee ; humbly beseeching Thee, that whosoever shall be partakers of this holy Communion, may worthily receive the most precious body and blood of Thy Son Jesus Christ, and be fulfilled with Thy grace and heavenly benediction, and made one body with Thy Son Jesus Christ, that He may dwell in them and they in Him. And although we be unworthy (through our manifold sins) to offer unto Thee any sacrifice, yet we beseech Thee to accept this our bounden duty and service, and command these our prayers and supplications, by the ministry of Thy holy angels, to be brought up into Thy holy tabernacle before the sight of Thy divine Majesty, not weighing our merits, but pardoning our offences, through Christ our Lord; by whom, and with whom, in the unity of the Holy Ghost, all honour and glory be unto Thee, O Father Almighty, world without end. Amen.

In this prayer, certain of whose phrases are modelled, with improvements, upon the Salisbury Missal, it is only necessary here to remark that, with the omission of the entreaty that angels may carry men's prayers into the tabernacle of the Divine Majesty, this portion of the consecration of 1549 was adopted as the first of the two post-Communion collects in the later editions of the English Liturgy.

After this prayer, for the Church at large and for the consecration and oblation, the priest proceeded :—

Let us pray.

As our Saviour Christ hath commanded and taught us, we are bold to say, Our Father, which art [etc.] . . . and lead us not into temptation.

Then the congregation took up the words, "But deliver us from evil. Amen."

It was Gregory the Great who, about the end of the sixth century, introduced the Lord's Prayer into this part of the sacramental service. A reference to page 188, above, will show us that the strange expression here, "We are bold to say," etc., comes directly out of the Salisbury Mass-book. The mode of saying the Lord's Prayer, in this and other parts of the mediæval Latin services, is not a little curious. The priest says all the early petitions. The choir repeats the last supplication, "But deliver us from evil." And, in the Mass, the priest says the "Amen" *to himself*.[1] This quaint mode of dealing with the Lord's Prayer disappears from the English rubrics after 1549; but, for reasons which will subsequently appear, it is quite worth noticing as having existed in the Salisbury Missal and in Edward's first Prayer-book.

After the Lord's Prayer, the priest was directed to say :—

The peace of the Lord be alway with you.

Choir. And with thy spirit.

The priest. Christ our Paschal Lamb is offered up for us, once for all, when He bare our sins on His body upon the cross; for He is the very Lamb of God, that taketh away the sins of the world : wherefore let us keep a joyful and holy feast with the Lord.

[1] Privatim.

We are not aware whether there was any precedent whatever for the introduction into this part of the Communion Service of this combination of St. Paul's words (1 Cor. v. 7, 8) with those of John the Baptist (John i. 29). Be that as it may, we cannot withhold the tribute of our admiration from the beautiful adaptation of those two texts into the eucharistic Liturgy; but, as there is no shadow of reference to the sacrament of the Lord's Supper either in the apostle's words or in those of the Baptist, it was assuredly an act of wisdom, as it was of courage, to omit this tempting, apt, and beautiful misapplication of Scripture from the editions of the Communion Service subsequent to 1549.

The next rubric directs :—

Here the priest shall turn him towards those that come to the holy Communion, and shall say,

You that do truly and earnestly repent [etc., as in the service of 1548].

Next followed the general Confession. Then was said the Absolution in the same words as are now used. Then followed the comfortable words. The Prayer of Humble Access, in the name of the communicants, was, as at present, in the words, "We do not presume," etc.

Then followed the administration, under the guidance of a rubric, at the end of the service, in these words :—

Although it be read in ancient writers, that the people, many years past, received at the priest's hands the sacrament of the body of Christ in their own hands, and no commandment of Christ to the contrary, yet forasmuch as they many times conveyed the same secretly away, kept it with them, and diversly abused it to superstition and wickedness, lest any such thing hereafter should be attempted, and that an uniformity might be used throughout the whole realm, it is thought convenient the people commonly receive the sacrament of Christ's body in their mouths, at the priest's hand.

The order of administering the elements was, moreover, regulated by this rubric :—

Then shall the priest first receive the Communion in both kinds himself, and next deliver it to other ministers, if any be there present (that they may be ready to help the chief minister), and after to the people.

In this rubric the reason for first administering to the clergy is very noticeable. It is not because the ministers were supposed to stand in any higher honour, but for convenience sake; that they, having partaken themselves, may be ready to assist in administering to the rest of the congregation.

Then follows this further instruction :—

And when he delivereth the sacrament of the body of Christ, he shall say to every one these words,

The body of our Lord Jesus Christ, which was given for thee, preserve thy body and soul unto everlasting life.

And the minister delivering the sacrament of the blood, and giving every one to drink once and no more, shall say,

The blood of our Lord Jesus Christ, which was shed for thee, preserve thy body and soul unto everlasting life.

These forms of administration were not identical with the phrases of the ancient Greek Liturgies, "The holy body," "The precious blood of our Lord and God and Saviour;" neither were they a translation of the forms in the Missal. They had the advantage, however, of being simple and intelligible; and they avoided the appearance of making the bread applicable especially to the body of the communicant, and the wine to his soul, which had been curiously enough done in 1548.

The quaint injunction to give one sup of the wine, and one only, to each communicant is worth observing. It makes sure that there shall be no withholding of the cup from the laity or any one; and it provides against any irreverent or superstitious desire to partake of more than the sip which sufficeth for loving memory, and yet is safe from the peril of indecorum or excess.

While the eucharistic elements were being administered, the clerks were to sing :—

O Lamb of God that takest away the sins of the world, have mercy upon us.

O Lamb of God that takest away the sins of the world, grant us Thy peace.

O Lamb of God that takest away the sins of the world, have mercy upon us.

This English translation of the "Agnus Dei" was to be chanted, from the time of the priest's taking the elements, throughout the entire administration.

Then the clerks were to sing, "every day, one" sentence of the "post-Communion," which consisted of some twenty-two verses selected from the New Testament.

Then the priest was to give thanks on behalf of all the communicants, turning him first to the people and saying—

The Lord be with you.

The people. And with thy spirit.

Priest. Let us pray.

Almighty and Everlasting God [etc., as in the second of our present post-Communion collects].

Then the priest, turning him to the people, shall let them depart with the blessing, "The peace of God," etc.

It was added as a rubric—

When there are no clerks, then the priest shall say all things appointed here for them to sing.

And again,

When the holy Communion is celebrated on the work-day, or in private houses, then may be omitted the Gloria in Excelsis, the Creed, the Homily, and the Exhortation beginning, "Dearly beloved," etc.

Besides the six "Collects to be said after the Offertory, when there is no Communion, every such day one," there stood, at the end of the Communion of 1549, a collect "for rain," and another "for fair weather."

The last point we need notice at present, in connection with the Communion Service of 1549, is that among the rubrics, at the end of the service, stood this injunction:

Yet these days [Wednesday and Friday in each week] (after the Litany ended) the priest shall put upon him a plain alb or surplice, with a cope, and say all things at the altar (appointed to be said at the celebration of the Lord's Supper) until after the Offertory. And then shall add one or two of the Collects afore written, as occasion shall serve by his discretion. And then, turning him to the people, shall let them depart with the accustomed blessing.

Two inferences arise out of this rubric: first, it looks as if, on Wednesdays and Fridays, the Litany might, at least sometimes, be said without the minister having put on a surplice. Else, why the injunction that he should, after the Litany, put on such a garment? We forbear to go into this inquiry because it would lead us into an examination of other services besides that for the Communion.

The second inference, necessarily arising out of this rubric, is that when the priest went to officiate at the altar, even though there was to be then no celebration of the holy Communion, he was instructed to put on especial and peculiar vestments.

How this rubric and the other, at the beginning of the

service, bearing on vestments, still touch the question of garments proper to be worn by the clergy nowadays—or how they
fail so to affect us—may appear in a subsequent part of this
essay.   Meanwhile, we call attention to the minuteness and
insistency with which the matter was regulated in the first
book of Edward VI.

CHAPTER IV.

AND now we proceed to notice, as briefly as possible, the important points connected with the English service for administering the Lord's Supper between the years 1549 and 1662, in which latter year the service was ultimately fixed and arranged as it stands and is used at present.

§ 1. *Demolition of "Altars."*

The first point to be noticed, in this period, is the demolition of all fixed structures made of stone as "altars" in the churches throughout England, and the setting up in their stead of movable, wooden "tables."

This important change was encouraged by Bishop Ridley, and enforced, in 1550, by the Injunctions of King Edward VI.

The object and purpose of the change was clearly expressed, in the words of the martyr-Bishop of London, to be, to "move and turn the simple from the old superstitious opinions of the Popish Mass . . . to the right use of the Lord's Supper."

This distinct abolition and destruction of "altars" in the Church of England, the setting of "tables" in their place, and the avowed object of the change should be carefully borne in mind by every student of our subject—especially by any who have allowed themselves to fall into the habit of designating the Lord's Table as an altar.

§ 2. *Edward VI.'s Second Liturgy.*

While such changes in the material structure of English churches were deemed necessary, and were being executed, i was not to be expected that a Communion Service, like that of 1549, would continue to give satisfaction to the Church ; and accordingly, in 1552, Edward VI.'s second Prayer-book was sanctioned and published.

So far as our present inquiry is concerned, the changes, made by the Communion Service of 1552, may be thus described.

The title of the service was "The Order for the Administration of the Lord's Supper or Holy Communion." Thus all mention and recognition of the "Mass" was at the outset put away and ignored.

A great difference, which marks off the service of 1552 from that of 1549, is the introduction into the former of the Ten Commandments and the prayers for grace to incline our hearts to the keeping of them. This change appears to have been adopted after the example of the services then in use among certain foreign refugees of whom Pullein (Pollanus) at Glastonbury, and John à Lasco in Austin Friars, London, were the leaders and pastors.

The following is a translation of Pullein's Latin service (published in February, 1551) so far as it appertains to our present purpose. Pullein's object, in the part of the service quoted from, is to lead his people to confession and pardon. He thus proceeds :—

"And throughout the whole of this time, let the people most reverently stand or kneel, whichever posture may seem best to each ; and then, after the declaration of the gospel of forgiveness by the pastor, let the people again, led by the choir, rehearse the entire Decalogue.

"Then let the pastor exhort the congregation to pray ; and let him lead them thus : Lord, be present with us that we may make our prayers to God with one accord. O Lord God, merciful Father, who in this Decalogue hast taught us by Thy servant Moses the righteousness of thy law, deign so to write it in our hearts by Thy Spirit, that for the rest of our life nothing may be so cherished and desired by us as to please Thee in all things by perfect obedience through Jesus Christ Thy Son. Amen."

R

Here, then, we see the origin of the Commandments and Responses being introduced into the English Liturgy in 1552.

Besides this addition, certain important omissions were then made. The "introit" disappeared. So did all mention of the Virgin Mary, as well as the thanksgiving for the patriarchs, prophets, apostles, and martyrs, with their wonderful grace and virtue. The sign of the cross was abandoned. So was the invocation of the Holy Spirit and the Word in the consecration of the elements. Water was no longer to be mixed with the wine. The form of administration was entirely changed—the words with the bread being only, "Take and eat this in remembrance that Christ died for thee, and feed on Him in thy heart by faith with thanksgiving;" and with the wine, these only, "Drink this in remembrance that Christ's blood was shed for thee, and be thankful." The long Prayer of Consecration, besides the changes already noted, was broken up into three parts—the Prayer for the whole state of Christ's Church militant here on earth, the Prayer of Consecration, and the first of our present post-Communion collects. For the word "altar" was substituted everywhere, throughout the service, the phrases, "God's Board," "Lord's Table." The Table, at Communion-time, was to stand, with a fair linen cloth upon it, in the body of the church, or in the chancel, where morning prayer and evening prayer were appointed to be said. The minister was to "use neither alb, vestment, nor cope, but, being archbishop or bishop, he shall have and wear a rochet, and, being a priest or deacon, he shall have and wear a surplice only."

"To take away the superstition which any person hath, or might have in the bread and wine," the rubric directed that—

It shall suffice that the bread be such as is usual to be eaten at the table with other meals, but the best and purest wheaten bread that conveniently may be gotten. And if any of the bread and wine remain, the curate shall have it to his own use.

At the end of the service was added a declaration explanatory of the kneeling posture prescribed for communicants during the administration of the bread and wine. Among other things, this declaration stated "that it is not meant thereby that any adoration is done, or ought to be done, either unto the sacramental bread and wine then bodily received, or to any real and essential presence there being of Christ's natural flesh and blood."

Such, in brief, was the Reformed Liturgy of 1552; and it would be difficult to imagine a service whose letter and spirit, alike, were more remote from any notion of an objective change in the eucharistic elements, or from the idea that the body and blood of Christ were conveyed into a man's mouth, together with, or by means of, the bread and wine. The whole doctrine plainly is that, as the eucharistic elements nourish and refresh the body of man, so the spiritual food of Christ's body and blood, received by faith and loving thankfulness, nourish and refresh man's soul. Such was the second Communion Service of Edward VI.; and with forms marvellously like to this, in spite of Laudian and other sacerdotal reactions, has the office for administration of the Lord's Supper come down to us.

§ 3. *Elizabeth's Liturgy and Act of Uniformity.*

The next point to be noticed, in our historical survey of the period between 1549 and 1662, is that, from 1553 to 1558, under the rule of Philip and Mary, there was an entire suspension and undoing of all Protestant Church reform in England. It was an age of martyrs and retrogression.

After these five terrible years, however, Queen Elizabeth came to the throne in 1558, and presently there was issued another Book of Common Prayer, with another Communion Service; and this was upheld and enforced by a new Act of Uniformity.

At the beginning of Elizabeth's Prayer-book stood the following rubrics :—

The order where Morning and Evening Prayer shall be used and said.

The Morning and Evening Prayer shall be used in the accustomed place of the church, chapel or chancel, except it shall be otherwise determined by the Ordinary of the place; and the chancels shall remain as they have done in times past.

And here is to be noted that the minister, at the time of the Communion, and at all other times in his ministration, shall use such ornaments in the church, as were in use, by authority of Parliament in the second year of the reign of King Edward the Sixth, according to the Act of Parliament set in the beginning of this book.

Now, as regards this " Ornaments Rubric " of Elizabeth's Prayer-book, there are certain points to be observed.

It is quite clear that the "authority of Parliament," named in it, is the Act of 1549, which sanctioned the use of Edward's first Prayer-book, and gave authority to all the rubrics contained in that Prayer-book. This point is not only plain on the face of things, but it has been distinctly established by the judgment of the Privy Council, in *Liddell* v. *Westerton* (A.D. 1857).

Elizabeth's "Ornaments Rubric," however, refers also to her Act of Uniformity as the Act set in the beginning of her Prayer-book; and there are two portions of that Act which it may be well here to produce.

Its opening words are :—

"When at the death of our late Sovereign Lord King Edward VI., there remained one uniform order of common service and prayer, and of administration of the sacraments, rites, and ceremonies in the Church of England, which was set forth in one book, intitled The Book of Common Prayer, and Administration of the Sacraments and other Rites and Ceremonies in the Church of England authorized by Act of Parliament holden in the fifth and sixth years of our said late Sovereign Lord King Edward VI., intitled An Act for the Uniformity of Common Prayer and Administration of the Sacraments, the which was repealed and taken away by Act of Parliament, in the first year of the reign of our late Sovereign Lady Queen Mary, to the great decay of the due honour of God, and discomfort to the professors of the truth of the Christian religion.

" Be it therefore enacted, by the authority of this present Parliament, that the said statute of repeal and everything therein contained, only concerning the said book and the service, administration of sacraments, rites, and ceremonies contained and appointed in or by the said book, shall be void and of none effect from and after the Feast of the Nativity of St. John Baptist, next coming. And that the said book, with the order of service and of the administration of sacraments, rites, and ceremonies, with the alteration and additions, therein added and appointed by this statute, shall stand and be, from and after the said Feast of the Nativity of St. John Baptist, in full force and effect, according to the tenour and effect of this statute, anything in the aforesaid statute of repeal to the contrary notwithstanding.

" And further be it enacted by the Queen's Highness, with the assent of the Lords and Commons, in this present Parliament assembled, and by authority of the same, that all and singular ministers, in any cathedral or parish church, or other place within this realm of England, Wales, and the marches of the same, or other the Queen's dominions, shall from and after the Feast of the Nativity of St. John Baptist next coming, be bounden to say and use the matins, evensong, celebration of the Lord's Supper, and administration of each of the sacraments, and all their common and open prayers, in such order and form as is mentioned in the said book so authorized by Parliament in the said fifth and sixth year of the reign of King Edward VI., with one alteration or addition of certain Lessons to be used on every Sunday in the year, and the form of the Litany altered and corrected, and two sentences only added in the delivering of the sacrament to the communicants, and none other, or otherwise," etc.

After some intervening paragraphs, Elizabeth's Act of Uniformity concludes with these words :—

" Provided always, that it be enacted that such ornaments of the church, and of the ministers thereof, shall be retained and be in use as was in this Church of England by authority of Parliament in the second year of the reign of King Edward VI., until other order shall be therein taken by the authority of the Queen's Majesty, with the advice of her Commissioners appointed and authorized, under the Great Seal of England, for causes ecclesiastical, or of the Metropolitan of this realm. And also that if there shall happen any contempt or irreverence to be used in the ceremonies or rites of the Church, by the misusing of the orders appointed in this book, the Queen's Majesty may, by the like advice of the said Commissioners or Metropolitan, ordain and publish such further ceremonies or rites as may be most for the advancement of God's glory, the edifying of His Church, and the due reverence of Christ's holy mysteries and sacraments."

It is interesting to remark that the earlier of these two passages from Elizabeth's Act of Uniformity revived in all its force the rubric of King Edward's second Prayer-book, which enjoined the minister to wear, at the Lord's Supper, neither " alb, vestment, nor cope," but only a rochet if he were a bishop or archbishop, and a surplice if he were a deacon or priest.   Such is the drift of the earlier part of Elizabeth's Act of Uniformity ; but then the proviso of its later part is that the "Vestments Rubrics " of Edward's first Prayer-book shall be so far resuscitated as to permit the wearing of alb, vestment, or cope and tunicle, if those garments or any of them were not only sanctioned by Parliament in 1549, but also were in use in the first year of Queen Elizabeth's reign. This last condition, we take it, is implied in the words of the Act, " shall be *retained* and be in use."

As to the different phrases employed in Elizabeth's Ornaments Rubric and in her Act of Uniformity, it is clear that the statutory expression, " shall be *retained* and be in use," must overrule the mere rubrical direction, " shall use such ornaments as were in use ; " and this is in accordance with the recent judgment of the Privy Council (*Ridsdale* v. *Clifton*).

Meanwhile, how stood the facts in the first year of Elizabeth's reign when this Act of Uniformity was passed ?   In the Romish system, which had been set up again by Mary, there was, of course, a re-introduction in many churches, if not in all, of vestments, copes, albs, and tunicles ; but, over and above the clergymen who had fled to foreign parts in Mary's reign, there would be still remaining, in their English parishes, not a few of the clergy whose predilections, if they dared avow them, were rather with the Protestant reforms of Edward VI. than with the Romish restorations of Mary ; and these clergymen would, on pretexts of poverty and with various similar excuses, delay the acquisition and employment of the costly vestments which had been disused and abandoned in Edward's later days.   Or, if they had been constrained, against their inclination, to resume, under Mary's persecutions, the gorgeous attire of the Roman Mass, they would, on the death of Mary and on the accession of her Protestant rival, Anne Boleyn's daughter, lose no time in laying aside the hated badges of Rome's sacerdotalism and Mary's oppression.

So it would come to pass that, in the very earliest days of Queen Elizabeth, there would be an extensively prevailing disuse, in the parish churches of England, of those vestments which had been enumerated, as lawful, in the rubrics of Edward VI.'s first Prayer-book. And thus we may see the importance of the phrase, in Elizabeth's Act of Uniformity, which sanctions the *retaining*, not the re-introduction, of such "ornaments" as, having been in legal usage in Edward VI.'s second year, were still employed at the time of the passing of Elizabeth's Act of Uniformity.

We lay no great stress on the fact that in Strasburg, Zurich, Frankfort, and other foreign retreats of the English Protestant refugees—and in the secret worship of Protestants still within the realm of England during Mary's reign, or immediately on the accession of Elizabeth—there would be "ornaments," or habiliments for the ministers, of the simplest and least sacerdotal character; because, although the sympathies of the statesmen and prelates of Elizabeth's time were with these Protestants at home and abroad, far rather than with the Romanist clergy left in England by Queen Mary, yet it is only a possibility, not a certainty, that the "ornaments," in use among these Protestant worshippers, were to be a standard of what was intended to be *retained* by Elizabeth's Statute of Uniformity.

On this last line of reflection we do not insist, though it cannot be altogether without weight in determining what was meant by the permission to *retain* such ornaments for the clergy as were in use in the first year of Elizabeth's reign. In view, however, of the absence of chasubles and such-like ornaments from many English parish churches in the first year of Elizabeth, it seems to us that it must be at least an open question whether, under Elizabeth's Act of Uniformity, the vestments of sacerdotalism would have been a legal or a necessary ornament for all the English clergy in administering the sacrament of the Lord's Supper.

Still, in consideration of Queen Elizabeth's reputed proclivities in this matter, and in consideration of the dislike which the Reformers of that day felt and expressed for the pretext afforded, by the possible ambiguity of the Act of Uniformity, for the re-introduction of the chasuble and cope and alb and tunicle, let us suppose, for argument's sake, that Elizabeth's " Ornaments Rubric " and the last clause of her Act of Uniformity did give legal ground for restoring and re-introducing the costume of the Mass into the administration of the Lord's Supper—what then ?   Why, first, we have Archbishop Sandys's letter to Archbishop Parker, in which he remarks upon this ambiguity, or worse, and the possible cloak it affords for reaction towards sacerdotalism.   " Our gloss upon this text," writes Dr. Sandys, " is, that we shall not be forced to use them "—the vestments, namely, of the Mass—" but that others in the mean time shall not convey them away, but they may remain for the Queen."

Then, again, we are assured (for example, by Mr. Procter in his "History of the Book of Common Prayer," p. 59) that "the use of the earlier ornaments was not generally introduced."

§ 4. The " Injunctions" and " Advertisements."

And, yet again, whatever may be the force of Mr. Procter's assertion, or of Dr. Sandys's letter, the "Injunctions" of Elizabeth's first year set on foot a diligent inquiry concerning the vestments, copes, and other ornaments, etc., appertaining to every church throughout the realm ; and, before very long, in 1564, these inquiries were followed by Elizabeth's "Advertisements," in which it was ordered that, "In the ministration of the holy Communion in cathedrals and collegiate churches, the principal minister shall wear a cope, with gospeler and epistoler agreeably, and at all other prayers to be said at the Communion Table to use no copes, but surplices;" and, further, it was enjoined, "That every minister saying any public prayers or ministering the sacraments or other rites of the Church (not in a cathedral or collegiate church) shall wear a comely surplice with sleeves, to be provided at the charge of the parish."

These "*Advertisements*" were so promptly executed that, in 150 parishes of the diocese of Lincoln, in the years 1565 and 1566, there have been published inventories showing that the chasubles and albs had been systematically defaced, destroyed, or put to other uses; and so thoroughly and universally was this putting away of the vestments of the Mass carried out, that, upon evidence produced, the Privy Council (in *Hibbert* v. *Purchas*) draw the general inference thus: "Upon the whole there is abundant evidence that within a few years after the Advertisements were issued the vestments used in the Mass entirely disappeared."

Thus, within a very few years after Elizabeth's accession, if not actually from the beginning of her reign, we find her Prayer-book and her Act of Uniformity in force with the abatement and suspension of any sanction that may, by possibility, have been given in the first year of her reign to the vestments of the Mass.

§ 5. *Comments on Elizabeth's Liturgy.*

The points requiring particular notice in Elizabeth's Communion Service are very few.

"After the Creed," it was prescribed, "if there be no sermon, shall follow one of the Homilies already set forth, or hereafter to be set forth, by common authority."

After such sermon, Homily, or exhortation, the curate shall declare unto the people whether there be any holy-days or fasting-days the week following, and earnestly exhort them to remember the poor, "saying one or more of these" (Offertory) "sentences following as he thinketh most convenient by his discretion."

Then shall the churchwardens, or some others by them appointed, gather the devotions of the people, and put the same into the poor men's box, and, upon the offering days appointed, every man shall pay to the curate the due and accustomed offerings; after which done, the priest shall say [etc.].

In the Prayer for the Church Militant there was no reference to those who had departed this life in God's faith and fear,

but, immediately upon the words, " who in this transitory life
are in trouble, sorrow, need, sickness, or any other adversity,"
there followed the conclusion—" Grant this, O Father, for
Jesus Christ's sake, our only Mediator and Advocate.
Amen."

The two exhortations, which now give warning that, on
——day next, the minister purposes celebrating the Lord's
Supper, stood in Elizabeth's service as addresses, not notices,
either of which the curate was to read to the people as, in his
discretion, he judged to be desirable.

The rubric directed that the general confession should be
said " either by one of" the people, "or else by one of the
ministers, or by the priest himself, all kneeling." This rubric
is interesting, inasmuch as it gave an active and quasi-minis-
terial position in the service to the laity.

The administration of the bread and wine was thus enjoined :—

*Then shall the minister first receive the Communion in both kinds himself, and next deliver it to
other ministers (if any be there present, that they may help the chief minister), and after to the
people in their hands kneeling. And when he delivereth the bread, he shall say [etc.].*

The bread, it will be noticed, was given into the hands of
the communicants. The purpose of administering to the
clergy before the laity continues to be explained as one of
convenience, that they may be free to help in the rest of the
service. It is not intended thereby to show any superior
authority or dignity as appertaining to the ministers.

The words of administration were a combination of the
two forms that had been used in the first and second books
of Edward the Sixth. They only differed from our present
form by the introduction of the word "and," in each form,
after the words "everlasting life."

§ 6. *The Thirty-Nine Articles of Religion.*

Before leaving this part of our subject, it should be mentioned that it was early in Queen Elizabeth's reign, in 1562,
two years before the issuing of the " *Advertisements*," that the
" *Articles*," which had been forty-two in number under Edward
the Sixth, were revised, reduced to the number of thirty-nine,
and re-enacted.

Several of these Articles bear upon our present inquiry.

The fourth Article, for instance, teaches that Christ bodily "ascended into heaven, and there sitteth until He return to judge all men at the last day." Nothing can well be clearer than the inference from this, that Christ cannot be bodily or objectively present in consecrated bread and wine on earth.

The teaching of the twenty-third Article, in connection with the sacraments, is not a little important, and demands at least a passing notice. Only those, that Article tells us, can publicly preach or minister the sacraments in the congregation who have been "lawfully called, and sent to execute the same. And those we ought to judge lawfully called and sent, which be chosen and called to this work by men who have public authority given unto them in the congregation, to call and send ministers into the Lord's vineyard."

Observe that ordination, or due qualification for the holiest ministerial work—alike of preaching and administering the sacraments—is not made to depend on the intervention of the episcopal or any other particular mode of Church government. Some may prefer, as we do, government and ordination by bishops. Some may prefer another mode of ecclesiastical rule. But, however all that may be, our twenty-third Article pledges us to recognise, under God, the congregation as the fountain and source of ministerial qualification in men who are to preach and minister the sacraments.

The first requirement of the Article is a congregation.

Then, in such congregation, public authority is given to certain men to call and send ministers.

Then those callers and senders choose and call others for the work of the ministry.

Those who are so chosen and called we "ought to judge lawfully called and sent."

This idea of Orders, and of the men who are lawfully qualified to administer the sacrament, goes not beyond the teaching of the early Christian centuries, as we have seen, but it is surely suggestive of tolerance and charity and good fellowship towards those who are without the advantage (as we think) of episcopal ordination; and it assuredly throws no little light upon the divergence of principle between the Reformed Church of England and any who say that without priests or deacons, ordained by bishops, there can be no valid consecration and administering of the eucharistic bread and wine.

But we pass on to the twenty-eighth Article, whose words are as follow: " The Supper of the Lord is not only a sign of the love that Christians ought to have among themselves one to another; but rather it is a sacrament of our redemption by Christ's death : insomuch that to such as rightly, worthily, and with faith, receive the same, the bread which we break is a partaking of the body of Christ; and likewise the cup of blessing is a partaking of the blood of Christ."

It should be noticed that the teaching of this part of the Article is—

1. The Lord's Supper is a sign (or sacrament, for a sacrament is an outward sign of some inward grace signified) of the love due from one Christian to another.

2. And the Lord's Supper is even more a sign (or sacrament) of our being redeemed by Christ's death.

3. For consistent believers the eucharistic bread and wine are a means of participation in the new covenant ratified by the body given and the blood shed by our blessed Lord.

Having laid down these statements as to what the Lord's Supper is, the Article proceeds to tell us of something which is not to be found in the Lord's Supper :—

" Transubstantiation (or the change of the substance of bread and wine) in the Supper of the Lord, cannot be proved by Holy Writ; but it is repugnant to the plain words of Scripture, overthroweth the nature of a sacrament, and hath given occasion to many superstitions."

The first and second of these assertions, that transubstantiation cannot be proved by Holy Writ, but is repugnant thereto, are what we endeavoured to make good in the first book of this essay.

That transubstantiation, or the objective transformation of

bread and wine into Christ's body and blood, overthrows the
nature of a sacrament, is obvious upon the consideration that
a sacrament is a sign of something signified—in other words,
a sacrament has two distinct parts, the sign and the thing
signified. In the Lord's Supper bread and wine are the signs,
and Christ's body and blood are the things signified. Suppose
the bread and wine to be changed into the body and blood of
Christ: and you confound the sign with the thing signified;
you do away with one or other of the two essential parts,
and so you destroy the idea of a sacrament or overthrow its
nature.

It lies beyond our purpose to enumerate in detail the
superstitions—from the idea that the priest can create God, to
the notion that by constantly reiterated sacrifices of the God so
created the priest can beneficially affect souls in purgatory—
which have sprung from the doctrine of transubstantiation,
and have been occasioned by it; but the history of the Church
is replete with illustrations of this part of the teaching of our
Article.

The next words of the twenty-eighth Article are:—"The
body of Christ is given, taken, and eaten, in the Supper, only
after an heavenly and spiritual manner. And the mean
whereby the body of Christ is received and eaten in the Supper
is faith."

The three averments of this paragraph are:—

1. The body of Christ is given, taken, and eaten, not, be it
observed, in the bread and wine, but in the Supper, on the
occasion of the eucharistic banquet, in connection therewith.

2. This giving and eating takes place, not after an earthly,
material, and objective fashion, but "only after an heavenly
and spiritual" manner; and that it is also after a *subjective*
manner, is made clear by the remaining declaration of the
paragraph.

3. The means by which Christ is received and eaten, in
the Supper, is not the bread and wine, but is faith. But
faith is, beyond all question, a frame of mind, a subjective
condition of the recipient; and such a mental condition does
not receive and feed upon that which is material and objec-

tive, but only on that which is subjective, heavenly, and
spiritual.

The remaining words of the twenty-eighth Article allege that
"the sacrament of the Lord's Supper was not by Christ's ordinance reserved, carried about, lifted up, or worshipped:" and
this statement rests on the absence of any indication, in Scripture, that the bread and wine were so dealt with; and also rests
on the positive assurance, in Scripture, that our Saviour said to
His disciples, " Take, eat," or " Drink of this, all of you," and
the disciples who were present did accordingly eat and drink :
and so there was an end of that pro-Paschal Supper.

If further proof of the entire subjectivity of participation
in Christ's body and blood—as taught in the Reformed Church
of England—were needed, it might well be found in the twenty-
ninth Article, which has for its heading the words, " Of the
Wicked which eat not the Body of Christ in the use of the Lord's
Supper."   And the Article itself declares that, " The wicked,
and such as be void of a lively faith, although they do carnally and visibly press with their teeth (as St. Augustin
saith) the sacrament of the body and blood of Christ, yet in
no wise are they partakers of Christ : but rather, to their
condemnation, do eat and drink the sign or sacrament of so
great a thing."

Here we have the exchangeableness of the terms " sign "
and " sacrament " put very plainly before us by the last
words of the Article itself; while the entire burthen of the
Article is to show that so distinct are the sign (or sacrament)
and the thing signified, that the former may be partaken of
without its being accompanied by any participation in the
thing signified—nay, so utterly subjective is participation in
Christ's body and blood, the things signified, that though the
wicked partake, ever so much, of the objective signs, bread
and wine, they yet are no recipients of the things signified,
because their minds and hearts are not right within them.

While the Articles of the Church of England are thus
clear in the testimony against what is nowadays called an
objective presence of Christ in the Lord's Supper, they are no
less definite in their opposition to the idea that, in that sacra-

ment, there is any propitiatory sacrifice of Christ. The words of the thirty-first Article, "Of the one Oblation of Christ finished upon the Cross," are these :—

"The offering of Christ once made is that perfect redemption, propitiation, and satisfaction, for all the sins of the whole world, both original and actual; and there is none other satisfaction for sin, but that alone."

This paragraph teaches that, however one looks at sin— whether as that which has, like some stain in the ancestral blood, poisoned the whole race; or as that personal and actual transgression which blasts and enfeebles personal and individual energy and peace—in either view of sin, and in every view of it, the sacrifice of Christ's perfect obedience, culminating in His death on the cross, was the one only and ample means of procuring to man reconciliation with the holy God. "Wherefore," continues the Article, "the sacrifices of Masses, in the which it was commonly said, that the priest did offer Christ for the quick and the dead, to have remission of pain or guilt, were blasphemous fables and dangerous deceits" ("blasphema figmenta sunt, et periculosæ imposturæ," in the no less forcible and authoritative language of the Latin version of the Articles).

Such is the language in which we clergymen have, over and over again, pledged ourselves against the doctrine of the " Mass," with its supposed reiteration of Christ's propitiatory sacrifice. Such is the language by which we stand still pledged so long as we retain benefice, or position, or title, or semblance of English clergymen; and, surely, it behoves those amongst us who are announcing the celebration of "Mass" and "High Mass" in our churches, to take heed how we encourage and perform, under circumstances of the most tremendous solemnity, that which our very profession, as clergymen connected with the English Church, involves us in declaring to be blasphemous figments and perilous impostures.

These Articles of the year of grace 1562 are assuredly no small contribution towards that historical study which can alone give proper force and meaning to the existing Liturgy;

and they are a most important part of the light and significance in which the clergy stand constantly pledged to regard
and use the Communion Service of our existing Prayer-
book.

Thus distinctly and completely was the Church of England,
within four years of Elizabeth's accession, guarded against
any semblance of the doctrine of the mediæval Mass, with its
notion of a repeated sacrifice of Christ upon the altar. Thus
was the Church also guarded against any idea that Christ's
presence, in the Supper, was objective in the bread and wine.
Those elements, it was insisted, might be taken and eaten ;
and yet, unless the subjective condition of individual faith
fitted the communicant for worthily receiving Christ, the
consecrated bread and wine could convey no presence of
Christ to him, but only condemnation for dealing lightly with
the sign of so holy a thing.

This condition of the English Church and her Liturgy
remained unchanged for upwards of forty years. The fixed
stone altars had been demolished and replaced by movable
tables of wood. The Latin Missal had been done away with,
and the English service for the Lord's Supper stood in its
place. The chasuble and alb and cope and tunicle had
been systematically destroyed ; and the surplice, and only
the surplice, besides a tippet and a square cap, remained as
the garment for the officiating clergyman. Ministers of the
English Church were pledged against the sacrifices of the
Mass and against the belief of anything but a subjective
presence of Christ received by the communicant through the
means of faith.

§ 7. *The " Canons " of* 1603–4.

For forty years, and upwards, this condition of the Church
and its teaching had been established when we reach the date
of the Hampton Court Conference under James I., and the
issuing by Convocation, with the king's sanction, of the
Canons Ecclesiastical.

In the Communion Service, as it came forth from the
conference at Hampton Court, the only change to be observed

is the introduction of the words, "to accept our alms," into the opening of the Prayer for the Church Militant.

The Canons of 1603–4 are worth noticing in connection with our present theme, because, if to any one it should appear doubtful how far the Advertisements of 1564, and the action consequent thereon, had been a literal and legal taking order by the Queen, with the advice of her commissioners or of the metropolitan—in such case of doubt, the Canons supply a literal and exact taking other order by the king's majesty, with the advice of the metropolitan.

These Canons know nothing of any "altar" for use in Christian worship, but, in the language of the Privy Council judgment (*Liddell* v. *Westerton*) they "assume the existence in all churches of convenient and decent tables for the celebration of the holy Communion, and provide that they shall be kept in repair," etc.

The twentieth Canon directs the churchwardens to supply "wheaten bread," and this alone is mentioned. Upon these words is based the judgment of the Privy Council (*Hibbert* v. *Purchas*), "If wafer-bread is equally permitted, or the special cakes of Edward VI.'s first book, and of the Injunctions, it is hard to see why the parish is to supply wheaten bread, in cases where wafers are to be supplied by the minister, or from some other source. And if wafers were to be in use, a general injunction to all churchwardens to supply wheaten bread would be quite inapplicable to all churches where there should be another usage."

The Canons sanction the use of the Prayer-book as it issued from the Hampton Court Conference, with the "Ornaments Rubric" in the same form as it had borne in 1559: and they throw no little light upon the sense in which that rubric was then understood by prescribing (Canon 24) the use of a "decent cope" for the principal minister in the holy Communion in cathedrals and collegiate churches, "according to the Advertisements" published in the seventh year of Elizabeth; and by further appointing (Canon 58) "that every minister saying the public prayers, or ministering the sacraments, or other rites of the Church, shall use a decent and comely

s

surplice with sleeves, to be provided at the charge of the parish."

In connection with the Hampton Court Conference, it may be well here to remind the reader that the contest of the Puritans, then and generally, was against the surplice, and not against the chasuble and other vestments, as, assuredly, it would have been if garments like these had then been in use. The silence of the Puritans, about other vestments than the surplice only, may be taken as strong implicit evidence that no other vestment was then in vogue.

The Canons (21 and 22) direct that all parishioners shall receive the Communion thrice in the year at least. They enjoin that ministers shall give warning publicly, in the church, at morning prayer, the Sunday before every time of his administering the holy sacrament. They bid the clergy (subject, of course, to any other laws of the realm bearing upon this point) not to admit to the Communion " notorious offenders," or " schismatics," or " strangers " from other parishes. They (Canon 71) regulate the conditions on which the Communion may be administered " in times of necessity " in private houses; and (Canon 112) they enjoin the exhibiting to the bishop or his chancellor the names and surnames of all parishioners, " as well men as women, which being of the age of sixteen years received not the Communion at Easter before."

This may suffice as a representation of the Canons of 1604 inasmuch as they bear upon our present subject.

In no respect do they countenance the idea of there being any sacrifice of Christ, or any objective presence of our Lord in, with, or instead of, the sacramental bread and wine. On the contrary, the whole bearing of the Canons is against the idea of a priest in gorgeous attire, or of an altar and a propitiatory sacrifice. These inseparable characteristics of the mediæval Mass are as remote as possible from the canonical requirements of a decent and comely clothing for the minister, and setting forth of the Table for communion and not for sacrifice.

§ 8. *The Catechism, on the Lord's Supper.*

This will be the proper place for a notice of Bishop Overall's explanation of the sacraments, in the concluding portion of the Church Catechism, as far as it is connected with our subject. This addition to the Catechism of 1549 was made in the year 1604; and although, in the part of it connected with baptism, certain changes were introduced in the revision of 1662, yet the part concerning the Lord's Supper remains still as it was in 1604.

The introductory questions treat of baptism as well as the Lord's Supper. Let the reader observe that Bishop Overall's first question is, not, How many sacraments are there?— —there may be, and there are, any number of " sacraments " in the classical sense of oaths, or in the later Latin sense of things or signs sacred—but the question of the Catechism has regard to none of those except such as Christ hath ordained (or appointed) in His Church. And to this question the answer is, " Two only;" the word " only " being employed for the purpose of excluding five rites which the Church of Rome has endeavoured, within the last three or four hundred years, to raise to an equality with the two rites which, alone, were instituted by Christ Himself in His Church.

Then follows an important clause in which it is declared that these two sacraments are not absolutely and indispensably necessary to salvation, but that they are generally necessary thereunto.

A thief on the cross, or converts who were not baptized in infancy, and have only turned their hearts earnestly to Christ when the sacraments were out of their reach by reason of their being captives in some heathen dungeon, whence they shall only issue to be put to death—men who, by God's grace, have become believing and repentant in any circumstances where the sacraments are not attainable, are not to despair, neither are their more advantageously situated fellow-Christians to take a despondent view of them as if, without the sacraments, there could be no possibility of salvation. This principle obviously touches the case of infants who die un-

baptized; it bears upon the hope of those who, from education and honest conviction, are persuaded, without any
inclination to disobey our Lord Christ, that baptism and the
Lord's Supper were rites used by Christ, and sanctioned by Him
for a time and under peculiar circumstances, and not binding
upon men in these modern days. It bears on all such cases,
and implies that, as the thief on the cross was, without any
sacrament,[1] assured of his salvation by Jesus Himself; and as
Christian sacraments cannot be less than Judaic rites "of the
heart, in the spirit and not in the letter," or "in the flesh,"
"whose praise is not of men, but of God," (Rom. ii. 28, 29);
so the two sacraments, or either of them, are not absolutely
and under all circumstances indispensable, but are ordinarily
and "generally necessary to salvation."

That these two sacraments are "Baptism and the Supper
of the Lord," we have already assumed, as the answer of the
Catechism proceeds to declare.

The second question of the Catechism asks, "What
meanest thou by this word Sacrament?" And the reply is
important. Observe, the question and answer do not touch
the general and vague meaning of the term. The inquiry is,
What dost *thou*, as a Christian and an English churchman,
mean? And the answer is no less precise; "I"—as a member
of Christ in the English Church—"I mean" by a sacrament:—

1. "An outward and visible sign,"
2. "Of an inward and spiritual grace given unto us,"
3. "Ordained by Christ Himself,"
4. "As a means whereby we receive the same,"
5. "And a pledge to assure us thereof."

If the five alleged sacraments of the Roman Church are
tried by the first three of these items in the definition of a
sacrament, it will be found that they cannot stand the test.

"Confirmation," or the laying on of hands upon those
that are baptized and come to years of discretion, however
it may be an admirable and most useful copying of apostolic

---

[1] We consider the idea of the thief having been baptized by the water from
the spear-wound in Christ's side as quite unworthy of discussion in the present
age.

example, yet as it was not enjoined by Christ, so it fails to be a Christian sacrament.

"Penance," meaning thereby private confession to a priest and absolution pronounced by him, was not, so far as the confession goes, enjoined by Christ; it is, at least, open to grave question whether the "binding and loosing" by "the keys of the kingdom of heaven," and the "forgiving and retaining sins" by "the Spirit" of Christ, are not powers and duties and tremendous responsibilities attaching to the teaching and exemplifying of Christ's Gospel quite apart from, and exclusive of, any official and indicative form such as the sacerdotal *Ego te absolvo,* "I absolve thee," which, as we have already seen, had its origin in the twelfth century. And thus, of the two parts of "penance," it is most improbable that one, priestly absolution, as practised in "penance," was appointed by Christ; and it is certain the other part, auricular or private confession to a priest, was not instituted by Christ. And thus, without insisting on the absence of any divinely appointed outward sign in connection with "penance," it fails to be a sacrament.

"Orders," again, or the laying on of hands for the ordaining men to be ministers of Christ, is an apostolic practice often referred to in the Book of the Acts of the Apostles, and in certain of St. Paul's Epistles; but for its origin with our Saviour Himself no direct and unimpeachable evidence can be produced. The Saviour chose twelve apostles and sent them on certain definite missions, and also sent them to teach and preach the glad tidings of His mercy and love to all nations. He promised to be with them even unto the end of the world (or age or dispensation). He gave to them, in common with all His disciples, the power to bind and loose by the keys of the kingdom of heaven, and to forgive (literally, *to put away*) sins, or to retain them, by the Spirit. All this our Lord did with and for the apostles and disciples, but it is impossible to produce a text in proof that Christ's mode of appointing the apostles, or the seventy, or any one else, was, by laying on of hands; and no less impossible is it to prove that the Saviour appointed any definite, external method, by laying on of hands or otherwise, for the ordaining of successors to the apostles.

Thus, then, "Orders" fails to be a Christian sacrament, not only for want of any outward sign like water in baptism, or like bread and wine in the Lord's Supper, but because there is no record or proof that even the laying on of hands, whether by an apostle or a bishop or a presbytery, was instituted by Christ Himself; but, on the contrary, the absence from the Gospels of any allusion to such an act or ordinance on the part of our Saviour, makes it in the highest degree probable that, as the institution of the order of deacons grew out of the wants of the Church, as shown by experience subsequent to our Lord's ascension, so, too, the laying on of hands, in imitation of ancient Jewish custom (cf. Numb. viii. 10, xxvii. 18), was a result, not of what Christ had directly commanded, but of the requirements of the Church as it grew.

"Matrimony," again, though sanctioned, blessed, and raised to the highest honour by Christ and Christianity, is not an ordinance appointed by Christ. He found the ordinance already in existence. He treated it in a manner calculated to lift it once more to the height of a pure and indissoluble bond of love beyond that between parent and child, even as in the beginning it had been instituted by the Creator Himself. But Christ did not ordain matrimony ; indeed, it is clear that, in certain exceptional circumstances, our Lord, like His apostle, is represented as contemplating the possibility of its being desirable that some individuals should forbear to marry. So far was Jesus from ordaining " matrimony " as a sacrament.

Of "Extreme Unction," the fifth of the rites designated as sacraments by the Church of Rome, it need only be said that there is no trace of Christ having appointed any rite analogous to it ; and the single passage of Holy Writ, on which its vindication is based, is one in which St. James argues for the efficacy of prayer even in the case of a sick man who shall send for the elders of his congregation or neighbourhood, and upon their anointing him with oil in the name of the Lord and praying over him, he shall be healed ("saved," in the Greek), and the Lord shall raise him up, and his sin, if he have been living in sin, shall be forgiven him.

This is obviously a possible and admissible interpretation of James v. 14, 15; indeed, its possibility is fully admitted by these words of the Council of Trent (Sess. 14, Can. 4), " Some-times by means of extreme unction the sick man attains bodily health,[1] where that is expedient for the soul's health; " and if it be even possible that St. James's reference is to salva-tion as a raising of the body in this life, the passage will make but a sorry support for the practice of "extreme unction," a rite, as its name intimates, resorted to by the Church of Rome for the benefit of those who are at the point of death.

Whatever may have been the apostolic practice referred to by St. James, and whatever may be the Tridentine theory of "extreme unction," it is clear that, although we find here an outward sign, there is no certitude of its having been ordained by Christ Himself; and so this rite, like the other four we have examined, fails to be a Christian sacrament.

So much it has seemed necessary to say, with reference to the characteristics of a sacrament in Christ's Church, to point out how these essentials are wanting in the five rites, called sacraments by the Church of Rome, and denied that august title by the Church in England.

We have thus noticed the three first items in the Cate-chism's definition of a sacrament. The two remaining points are that the outward and visible sign, ordained by Christ Himself, is to be "a means whereby we receive " the inward and spiritual grace, and is to be "a pledge to assure us " of our receiving it.

As to the first of these two points, it is necessary to remind the reader that the outward sign is a means of receiving the spiritual grace to those only who rightly, worthily, and with faith, receive the same. To unworthy participants the out-ward sign is so far from being a means by which they receive the inward grace that, in the Lord's Supper, according to the twenty-ninth Article of the Church of England, " The wicked,

[1] Sanitatem corporis interdum consequitur.

and such as be void of a lively faith, although they do carnally and visibly press with their teeth (as St. Augustin saith) the sacrament [or outward sign] of the body and blood of Christ, yet in no wise are they partakers of Christ : but rather, to their Condemnation, do eat and drink the sign or sacrament of so great a thing "—in the language of the twenty-fifth Article, " In such only as worthily receive the " sacraments have they " a wholesome effect or operation : but they that receive them unworthily purchase to themselves damnation, as St. Paul[1] saith."

Thus it appears that the outward and visible sign is a means whereby the worthy and believing communicant receives the inward and spiritual grace ; but, without such fitness and faith on the part of the communicant, it fails to be such a means. Nothing can make the truth more plain that the reception of the inward grace depends on the subjective condition of the communicant. In other words, the inward and spiritual grace of a sacrament is something not objectively combined with, or present in, the outward sign ; but it is something subjective, whose presence, on the occasion of any receiving of the outward sign, depends on the faith, and is vouchsafed to the heart and soul of the recipient.

In like manner, of course, it is only to the faithful that the outward sign is a pledge to assure them of their receiving the inward and spiritual grace ; but to the faithful it is a most comforting pledge—more and more comforting as the mind increasingly dwells upon the unbroken and unquestionable continuity with which the Lord's Supper, for instance, has been celebrated through all the past eighteen centuries and a half, until the thoughtful communicant is carried, through the communion and fellowship of all saints in the intervening ages, into the closest association with Christ Himself, in the upper chamber at Jerusalem, and there learns, from the lips of his Lord, that these pledges mean, and have preached by symbol through all the generations, that Christ's body was once given in the sacrifice of His obedience and death, and

---

[1] St. Paul's word is κρίμα (1 Cor. xi. 29), signifying judgment generally, not " damnation " in the nineteenth-century meaning of that word.

His blood was once for all shed, in propitiatory mercy, to put away sin, even the sin of the whole world.

Such a means, and such a pledge, of receiving the inward and spiritual grace, is the outward and visible sign or sacrament in the Lord's Supper; but it is so, as we have seen, only to those who, by that faith which worketh by love, are subjectively fit for its reception.

The next question and answer in the Catechism merely bring out forcibly the two parts of a sacrament, the "outward visible sign" and the "inward spiritual grace" of which we have just spoken. And then, passing by the next four questions and answers of the Catechism which have reference to baptism only, we come to the query, "Why was the sacrament of the Lord's Supper ordained?" Nothing can be plainer than the answer, "For the continual remembrance of the sacrifice of the death of Christ, and of the benefits which we receive thereby."

These "benefits" will be described in a subsequent answer. Meanwhile, let it be observed that the avowed purpose of the Lord's Supper is not to offer or repeat a sacrifice, but is to keep up, from age to age, from celebration to celebration, a ceaseless and undying recollection of the one sacrifice once for all made by Christ upon the cross.

The next question and answer are in terms as plain and intelligible as possible. "What is the outward part or sign of the Lord's Supper?" "Bread and wine, which the Lord hath commanded to be received."

How the Lord did so command bread and wine to be received, we learned in some detail when, in Book I., we endeavoured to examine the history of the Supper's institution as recorded by the Evangelists and by St. Paul.

It may be well to add here, with reference to the two parts described as appertaining to the sacrament, that the precise language, as to a sign and a thing signified or an inward grace, comes to us from Augustin and other ancient Christian writers, but if we owe the phrases to them, the things themselves are patent, as we have seen, on the pages of the New Testament.

The next interrogatory of the Catechism, regarding the Lord's Supper, is, "What is the inward part or thing signified?" The answer is, "The body and blood of Christ, which are verily and indeed taken and received by the faithful in the Lord's Supper."

Let the reader observe that, although to the thoughtless and inexperienced these words "body" and "blood" may be apt to suggest material things, yet in the Catechism they are definitely limited to an "inward and spiritual" signification. The body and blood of Christ are not here material things at all. They are the inward and spiritual grace of the Lord's Supper. They are so far from being corporeal entities that their presence in the Supper is not attached to, and combined with, the bread and wine objectively, but depends on the faith of the recipient. Still, "by the faithful"—by those who are fit and worthy communicants—this inward and spiritual grace, of Christ's body given and His blood shed, is "verily and indeed taken and received in the Lord's Supper."

Then comes the question, "What are the benefits whereof we are partakers thereby?" And to this the reply is given, "The strengthening and refreshing of our souls by the body and blood of Christ, as our bodies are [strengthened and refreshed] by the bread and wine."

Than this nothing could be more intelligible and Scriptural. Material food nourishes our bodily frame; and, similarly, the soul is nourished by spiritual grace, even by the death and sacrifice—by the body of Christ given and His blood shed—and these are received in the Lord's Supper by faith.

The last question and answer of the Catechism are very important and well worthy of every man's frequent consideration. "What," it is asked, "is required of them who come to the Lord's Supper?" And the well-known answer is, "To examine themselves." There must be no shrinking from the labour and pain and responsibility. Books may instruct us in some particulars, wisely or unwisely. Friends, Christian friends, ordained or unordained, may help us, or try to help us. But, if we are in earnest, if we would reap the full and proper benefits of Christ's ordinance, we must do neither more nor less than what the Catechism, using St. Paul's own language, prescribes.

And, amongst possible lines of self-examination, it would be difficult to suggest any that should be simpler, or more searching and useful, than that recommended in these last words of the Catechism : " To examine themselves,"—

1. "Whether they repent them truly of their former sins ? "

2. Whether they " stedfastly purpose to lead a new life " ?

3. Whether they " have a lively faith in God's mercy through Christ, with a thankful remembrance of His death " ?

4. Whether they " be in charity with all men " ?

Let any man use this prescribed line of self-scrutiny, and he will hardly need the aid of minister or other friend to help him : and though we can never be perfect in our fitness to communicate, or to live, or to die in Christ, yet here is a training and course of preparation which, together with prayer for the guidance of God's Spirit, and accompanied by careful reading of certain definite portions of Holy Writ, is safe as not making the simple and unwary acquainted with sins of which they were guiltless; is sure to lead them to the detection of their sins ; and is certain to direct them to Christ and Him crucified and Him raised and glorified ; and so to fill them with self-abnegation and humility, and yet with hope and sanctity, which may best prepare them for all the realities of life and death and judgment, as well as for a happy participation in the communion of the Lord's Supper.

§ 9. The Scottish Liturgy of 1637.

And now we come to examine the Communion Service in the famous Scotch Prayer-book of 1637, generally known as Archbishop Laud's Book of Common Prayer.

This we examine, not, happily, because it has any legal force or authority over us, but because, in its historical bearings, it throws light upon our English Communion Service. It lies not within the compass of our present essay to refer even cursorily to the immense political results, in Scotland and in England, that sprang out of the publishing of the

Scotch Prayer-book. We simply study it for illustration of the English Communion Service.

At the outset we remark the version of the so-called "Ornaments Rubric" in the Scotch Prayer-book. It purports to direct "where and how" prayer shall be said. "And here," are its words, "it is to be noted, that the presbyter or minister at the time of the Communion, and at other times in his ministration, shall use such ornaments in the church, as are prescribed, or shall be by his Majesty, or his successors, according to the Act of Parliament provided in that behalf."

In this rubric are not a few noticeable points. Instead of the "minister" being spoken of, mention is made of the "*presbyter* or minister;" and this innovation is no accident, or isolated instance of the use of the word "presbyter" in the Scotch Prayer-book. Everywhere, throughout the services, even in the consecration form of the Scotch book, the word "presbyter" stands where, in the English books, the word "priest" occurs. Of course, this was a thoroughly scholar-like and legitimate exchange of terms. Laud was aware, and every competent reader of these books and of the New Testament knows, that the merely human minister of Christianity is not a sacrificing, or sacerdotal, or hieratical priest, but is an elder or "presbyter," whose title has undergone different abbreviations in different languages until it has become "*prêtre*" in France, "*priester*" in Germany, and "priest" in England.

This is known by every tyro in the study of these matters. Still, there is often an ambiguity in the use of the English word "priest." Unfortunately, it is employed sometimes as an equivalent for the hieratical or sacrificing minister; at other times it denotes the elder or presbyter, who is no sacrificer, but merely a president and leader and teacher, whose office is clothed with the venerable attributes of one distinguished by age, with its experience and wisdom, beyond his fellows.

Now, in face of this ambiguity of the English word "priest," it is an immense advantage that Archbishop Laud, bringing his Prayer-book into Scotland, where Presbyterianism was in vogue; where sacrificing priests, other than Christ Himself, were abhorred; should have felt that, in honesty and in scholarship, he could abandon the ambiguous word "priest" and adopt in its stead the term "presbyter."

This is a course of action which should be laid to heart by all students of this subject, especially by any who are inclined to introduce sacerdotalism, or the system of sacrificing priests, into the English service; and they should the rather lay it to heart because they are in general prone to admire Archbishop Laud.

Another noteworthy point, in this Scotch rubric, is the manner in which the presbyter's ornaments in the church are to be regulated by the decision, from time to time, of the sovereign and the Parliament.

It is not on any particular Act of Parliament that we now care to fix the reader's attention; but it is not a little interesting and instructive to notice how entirely the High Church prelate, and those who joined him in framing this rubric, were content to abide, in matters of Church law, by the ruling of those authorities of king and Parliament which it is now too much the custom to designate as "secular," as if God did not set up kings and princes and all rulers just as truly as He sets up bishops or presbyters—as if every body of rulers had not its "secular" aspects in which it must exist and in which it may be regarded, and also its "religious" or "spiritual" aspects from which, even by irreligion, it can make no escape and in which it may be regarded. This point, at all events, was instructively clear to Laud and his cotemporaries, and it may well be contemplated by not a few of us in the present day.

But we pass on to consider Laud's Communion Service itself.

One of the rubrics at the head of the service is in these words :—

The holy Table having at the Communion-time a carpet and a fair white linen cloth upon it, with other decent furniture, meet for the high mysteries there to be celebrated, shall stand at the uppermost part of the chancel or church, where the presbyter, standing at the north side or end thereof, shall say the Lord's Prayer, with the Collect following for due preparation.

What this "other decent furniture" was to be, was a question left open in the mean while. It is a phrase quite unlike any we have found in use among the Prayer-books of the Reformed Church from the time of Edward the Sixth onwards. Much would, of course, depend on the sense attached to the qualifying expression, "meet for the high *mysteries* there to be celebrated." Let "mysteries" signify things that were secret but are now explained, as is their proper meaning, and the furniture meet for such mysteries would be simple indeed; but let "mysteries" mean something different from this intelligibleness of the Gospel, and then the suitable equipment would be in accordance with this character of the "mysteries" —awful if they be awful, dark and enigmatic and symbolic if such be their character.

Notice, too, that, instead of a movable table, which at Communion-time was to be placed in the most convenient part of the church—as had been the direction of earlier English Prayer-books—the Scottish order was that the holy Table should stand in one fixed part of the church or chancel, "the uppermost part" whatever that may mean, and there the presbyter (note well the substitute for our ambiguous term "priest") shall officiate.

It is not a little interesting, in connection with modern controversies, to read that Laud's intention was the "*north side or end*" should be the place for the presbyter to take up his position. Whether the Table stood with its end or its side towards the congregation, it was at the north of the Table that the presbyter was to stand and officiate in this part of the Communion Service.

In the rubric before the reciting of the Decalogue, instead of our present words following "transgression," the Scotch service read, "transgression of every duty therein, either according to the letter, or to the mystical importance of the said commandment." It is a practical and important comment upon the precepts of the Decalogue which is here offered us.

During the reading of the Offertory sentences, the "devotions" of the people were to be collected in a basin, reverently delivered to the presbyter, and by him humbly presented as "oblations" before the Lord, and set upon the holy Table.

'And the presbyter shall then offer up and place the bread and wine prepared for the sacrament upon the Lord's Table, that it may be ready for that service." And then shall he say the Prayer for the Church Militant.

Such was the development of custom since the time when the people put their offerings into the poor men's box. Then came the injunction that the churchwardens were to collect the people's offerings, and put them into the poor men's box. Now, in the Scotch service, the offerings are to be delivered to the presbyter, and made an oblation upon the Lord's Table.

It is a curious and interesting illustration of the progress of custom, but if the idea be confined to offering unto God such thank-offerings, it will be only a return to practices like those which prevailed in the very early Church—indeed, it will be a resort to action which comes within the letter of Scripture itself, which declares that with sacrifices of almsgiving God is well pleased. Only be it remembered those were to be figurative sacrifices, not offered upon an altar or a Lord's Table, but upon the cross of Christ.

Not very important were the words introduced into the Prayer for the Church Militant after the expression, " in holiness and righteousness all the days of their life " :—

[And we commend especially unto Thy merciful goodness the congregation which is here assembled in Thy name to celebrate the commemoration of the most precious death and sacrifice of Thy Son and our Saviour Jesus Christ.]

A rubric enjoined that when there was no Communion, these bracketed words were to be left out.

After the words, " sorrow and sickness, or any adversity," the Scotch Prayer for the Church Militant proceeded :—

And we also bless Thy holy name for all those Thy servants, who, having finished their course in faith, do now rest from their labours. And we yield unto Thee most high praise and hearty thanks for the wonderful grace and virtue declared in all Thy saints, who have been the choice vessels of Thy grace and the lights of the world in their several generations : most humbly beseeching Thee that we may have grace to follow the example of their steadfastness in Thy faith and obedience to Thy holy commandments, that, at the day of the general resurrection, we, and all they which are of the mystical body of Thy Son, may be set on His right hand, and hear that His most joyful voice, Come, ye blessed of My Father, inherit the kingdom prepared for you from the foundation of the world : Grant this [etc.].

Beautiful as is much of this prayer, we cannot help feeling that the idea of man's life being described, before God, as full of " wonderful grace and virtue," is, to our mind, most painful and unbecoming; and we rejoice that such thoughts find no place in the present English service.

Into the midst of the third exhortation, after the words, " sundry kinds of death," were introduced these warnings :—

Therefore if any of you be a blasphemer or slanderer of His [God's] word, an adulterer, or be in malice or envy, or in any other grievous crime, bewail your sins and come not to this holy Table, lest after the taking of that holy sacrament, the devil enter into you, as he entered into Judas, and fill you full of all iniquities, and bring you to destruction both of body and soul.   Judge therefore yourselves [etc.]

Words like these stand now in the first of our warnings that the sacrament is about to be administered on a coming day— like these, we say; and yet surely they are very different, for, instead of enjoining the sinner to bewail his sins *and* not come to the holy Table, the English service warns the sinner to repent him of his sins *or else* come not to the holy Table.

The general confession was to be made " by the presbyter himself, or the deacon, both he and all the people kneeling humbly on their knees."

There is no trace of one of the people leading the congregation even in this part of the Scotch service.

The next rubric enjoins, " Then shall the presbyter (or bishop)" pronounce the Absolution.   We should notice that even here it is a *presbyter*, not a *priest*, who is to read the Absolution.

Similarly, at a later point in the Scotch service, the direction of the rubric is :—

Then the presbyter, standing up, shall say the Prayer of Consecration, as followeth, but the during the time of consecration, he shall stand at such a part of the holy Table, where he may with the more ease and decency use both his hands.

In the midst of the consecration prayer, after the words " we most humbly beseech Thee," was added this supplication :—

And of Thy Almighty goodness vouchsafe to bless and sanctify with Thy Word and Holy Spirit these Thy gifts and creatures of bread and wine, that they may be unto us the body and blood of Thy most dearly beloved Son : so that we receiving them according to Thy Son our Saviour Jesus Christ's holy institution, in remembrance of His death and passion, may be partakers of the same His most precious body and blood : who [etc.].

In this return to the phraseology of the mediæval Mass-book is to be noted, not only the unscriptural prayer that the divine Word and Spirit may come upon the elements objectively, but, moreover, the petition that those elements may be —"to us," no doubt, and so far the presence of Christ is to be subjective—the body and blood of our Saviour. It is this idea, of uniting Christ's presence with the elements, instead of making it altogether dependent upon, and received by, the faith of the communicant, that constitutes the difference between the reformed Communion and the mediæval Mass, as it had constituted the difference between that Mass and the Lord's Supper of apostolic days ; and this re-introduction of the mediæval corruption into the Scotch service is a most subtle instance of the reaction Laud wished to establish amidst concessions like that of abandoning the word " priest," and substituting for it the term " presbyter." Let the act be that of binding Christ, in any way, to the objective elements of bread and wine, instead of subjectively to the soul of the believer, and all the evils of mediævalism will assuredly follow in due course.

Rubrics in the Scotch service directed the officiating presbyter to take into his hands the paten and the cup at the moments of reciting the words of the Gospel which describe the corresponding acts of our Lord.

Immediately after shall be said this memorial, or Prayer of Oblation, as followeth,

Wherefore, O Lord and Heavenly Father, according to the institution of Thy dearly beloved Son our Saviour Jesus Christ, we Thy humble servants do celebrate and make here, before Thy divine Majesty, with these Thy holy gifts, the memorial which Thy Son hath willed us to make, having in remembrance His blessed passion, mighty resurrection, and divine ascension, rendering unto Thee most hearty thanks for the innumerable benefits procured unto us by the same. And we entirely desire Thy Fatherly goodness mercifully to accept this our sacrifice of

T

praise and thanksgiving [etc. as in the first of the two existing post-Communion collects of the English service].

This memorial ended :—

Then shall the presbyter say,

As our Saviour Christ hath commanded and taught us, we are bold to say, Our Father which art [etc.].

It is curious to observe how, in every particular where it seems possible to bring in an imitation of the mediæval forms —even in this mode of beginning the Lord's Prayer, which is so unlike the Scriptural idea of coming boldly to the throne of grace (Heb. iv. 16)—the Laudian party made such an imitation. Doubtless this phrase, about daring or "being bold" to say the prayer which Christ commanded, crept into the Missal as a result of that superstition which made a scruple and a hidden secret of the use of this most blessed prayer.

Then shall the presbyter, kneeling down at God's board, say in the name of all them that shall communicate, this Collect of humble access to the holy Communion, as followeth,

We do not presume [etc.].

Then shall the bishop, if he be present, or else the presbyter that celebrateth, first receive the Communion in both kinds [and then deliver it to any clergymen who may be present] that they may help him that celebrateth; and after to the people in due order, all humbly kneeling. And when he receiveth himself, or delivereth the bread to others, he shall say this Benediction :

The body of our Lord Jesus Christ, which was given for thee, preserve thy body and soul unto everlasting life.

Here the person receiving shall say, "Amen."

The form for administering the wine was similar.

When all had communicated, the celebrant was to "go to the Lord's Table, and cover with a fair linen cloth, or corporal that which remaineth of the consecrated elements, and then say this Collect of Thanksgiving, as followeth :—Almighty and Everliving God," etc.

Then shall be said, or sung, Gloria in Excelsis, in English as followeth.

Then the presbyter, or bishop if he be present, shall let them depart with the blessing.

After the divine service ended, that which was offered shall be divided in the presence of the presbyter and the churchwardens, whereof one half shall be to the use of the presbyter to provide him books of holy divinity ; and the other half shall be faithfully kept and employed on some pious and charitable use, for the decent furnishing of that church, or the public relief of their poor at the discretion of the presbyter and churchwardens.

If the form of administration and the post-Communion as given above, are of interest as showing the tendency of Laudian thought in matters sacramental, this rubric is also worth noticing because of its practical simplicity in allotting half the Offertory to the purpose of buying books of divinity for the presbyter. Evidently he, who drew up this rubric, was deterred by no fear of poverty and semi-starvation before his eyes as the too probable portion of the clergy in his time, and within his experience. With thorough Scottish love of learning, he desired, at whatever cost of penury and pain for the bodies of the presbyters, to procure them the means of adding to their intellectual stores; and thus he seems to have thought he should be providing a blessed means of enjoyment for the clergy themselves, and one of the best and most useful means of union and fellowship betwixt them and the intelligence of their people.

Then, too, the wholesome and proper influence given to the laity, as represented by the churchwardens, is very noteworthy and admirable in this rubric.

Even in the Laudian Liturgy, these points in this rubric give us very practical illustrations of the idea of communion and fellowship which is so important a part of the proper and Scriptural celebration of the Lord's Supper.

Only one other rubric, attached to the end of the Scotch Communion Service, can now be produced by us. It is worded thus :—

And to take away the superstition which any person hath, or might have, in the bread and wine (though it be lawful to have wafer-bread) it shall suffice that the bread be such as is usual: yet the best and purest wheat bread that conveniently may be gotten. And if any of the bread and wine remain, which is consecrated, it shall be reverently eaten and drunk by such of the communicants only as the presbyter which celebrates shall take unto him, but it shall not be carried out of the church. And to the end there may be little left, he that officiates is required to consecrate with the least, and then if there be want, the words of consecration may be repeated again, over more, either bread or wine; the presbyter beginning at these words in the Prayer of Consecration (" Our Saviour in the night that He was betrayed, took bread," etc.).

In this rubric one important point is the difference recognised between the two things called " bread such as is usual," and " wafer-bread." There is no room for question whether Laud, and those who acted with him in this matter, regarded " wafer-bread " as a product which would be included in the general phrase " bread such as is usual." It is clear they held the products to be so different and distinct that, while they gave a general sanction to the use, in the Lord's Supper, of bread such as is usual, they thought it necessary to mention separately, and so to enact, the lawfulness of " wafer-bread." So far as the use of language in the seventeenth century goes, this passage of the rubric is important, and it indicates that if, in those days, "bread such as is usual" had been appointed for the Lord's Supper, without mention of "wafer-bread" as also legalized, the latter would, by such omission, have been left illegal. It would have been "wafer-bread" not sanctioned for the Lord's Supper, as distinct from "bread such as is usual," which was so sanctioned.

Another noticeable point in this Scotch rubric is that, although any remnants of the consecrated bread and wine were to be reverently eaten and drunk by communicants only, and so were not to be applied to common purposes of nutrition, yet Laud and his companions were sufficiently set against such superstitious employment of the consecrated elements as had been too common in the mediæval ages; and therefore the rubric enjoined that the elements should not be carried out of the church.

And now we take leave of this Laudian service for the Communion. It exemplifies for us the spirit which animated a portion of the English clergy in the period betwixt the conferences of Hampton Court and the Savoy. It carried back the Liturgy, in many ways, into closer resemblance to the mediæval Mass-book than had been admissible in England since the death of Queen Mary. Yet its adoption of the term "presbyter," instead of "priest," was a clear testimony to important truth connected with those words.

It is not necessary for us to occupy the reader with a study of those reactionary changes, away from the Laudian tastes and convictions, which prevailed in England under the Commonwealth.

Suffice it to say that the influence of the Puritans and Presbyterians in England, however it failed to alter the Prayer-book as much as may have been desired by those parties, conjointly or respectively, sufficed to prevent the Book of Common Prayer, and its Communion Service, travelling back as far towards the Mass as went this Scotch book of 1637.

§ 10. *The Existing Liturgy of* 1662.

The proof of this, as connected with the Communion Service of 1662, which is that still by law established in England, we now proceed to examine.

"The Order of the Administration of the Lord's Supper, or Holy Communion." Such continued to be the name and designation given to the eucharistic service of the Church of England. With the exception of the words having been "The Order *for*," etc., in earlier times, this had been our Church's name for the rite ever since 1552, when the alternative title of "commonly called the Mass" was abandoned.

(i.) *Introductory Rubrics.*

The first of the four rubrics at the head of the Communion Service is thus worded:—

So many as intend to be partakers of the holy Communion shall signify their names to the curate, at least some time the day before.

It is needless to say that, in modern practice, the requirement of this rubric has fallen into general desuetude. It rests on the conscience and responsibility of each worshipper whether or not he will come to the Communion; and it is a most rare occurrence for any person who intends to communicate to give notice to the clergyman as is enjoined by this rubric. It is interesting to observe that whereas, in the corresponding rubrics of earlier Prayer-books, it had been sufficient that the names should be made known to the clergyman after "matins" on the morning of the Communion-day, in 1662 this was changed. The names must be signified "at least some time the day before." The meaning of this change seems to be that, between 1604 and 1662, the custom had grown up, in the English Church, of reading matins, the Litany, and the Communion Service, or part of it, as one long, continuous service instead of as three distinct services.

It is much to be wished that, while this modern grouping of the services continues, arrangements should be made whereby too frequent repetitions of the Lord's Prayer and the collects for the Sovereign might be avoided.

The next two rubrics may be treated of together. Their words are :—

And if any of those be an open and notorious evil liver, or have done any wrong to his neighbours by word or deed, so that the congregation be thereby offended; the curate, having knowledge thereof, shall call him and advertise him, that in any wise he presume not to come to the Lord's Table, until he hath openly declared himself to have truly repented and amended his former naughty life, that the congregation may thereby be satisfied, which before were offended; and that he hath recompensed the parties, to whom he hath done wrong; or at least declare himself to be in full purpose so to do, as soon as he conveniently may.

The same order shall the curate use with those betwixt whom he perceiveth malice and hatred to reign; not suffering them to be partakers of the Lord's Table, until he know them to be reconciled. And if one of the parties so at variance be content to forgive from the bottom of his heart all that the other hath trespassed against him, and to make amends for that he himself hath offended; and the other party will not be persuaded to a godly unity, but remain still in his frowardness and malice; the minister in that case ought to admit the penitent person to the holy Communion, and not him that is obstinate. Provided that every minister so repelling any, as is specified in this, or the next precedent paragraph of this rubric, shall be obliged to give an account of the same to the Ordinary within fourteen days after at the farthest. And the Ordinary shall proceed against the offending person according to the canon.

In brief, these two rubrics enjoin the curate to withhold the sacrament from notorious evil livers and wrong-doers, and from those who obstinately cling to malice and hatred. This withholding the cup, however, is tantamount to excommunicating the persons from whom it is withheld : and, happily, in our Church and State, excommunication can only be inflicted by a judicial sentence in a proper court; so that, practically, what a clergyman has to do with notorious wrong-doers, who will neither be reclaimed by his pious exhortations, nor will even be restrained by conscience and decorum from profanely communicating in the Lord's Supper, is to give an account of the matter to the Ordinary and leave him to take what further steps his wisdom may suggest and the law require.

Happily, however, proceedings of this sort are very rare ; and the recent action of the law courts, as well as the general tendency of public opinion, will help to restrain prosecutions and excommunications and withholdings of the sacraments, making the appeal rather to the conscience and better feelings of those who may have rendered themselves notorious in sin. Two reflections should assuredly urge themselves on all minds under such circumstances :—

1. Men, set free from clerical judgment and public discipline of the Church, should be the more careful to examine and judge themselves, generally in the way of self-scrutiny, and especially in preparation for the Lord's Supper.

2. The clergy, in proportion as they are the less expected or empowered to exercise public authority in keeping back

those whom they may deem unworthy communicants, are the more bound, in duty before God and man, to use all diligence, alike in the instructions and exhortations of the pulpit, and in what private influence of sympathy and counsel lies within their power, for the reclaiming of sinners and for the further-ance of manly piety and holiness amongst their congregations generally and amongst their communicants in particular.

The last rubric standing at the head of the Communion Service is this :—

The Table, at the Communion-time having a fair white linen cloth upon it, shall stand in the body of the church, or in the chancel, where Morning and Evening Prayer are appointed to be said. And the priest standing at the north side of the Table shall say the Lord's Prayer, with the Collect following, the people kneeling.

Within the recollection of many now living the universal practice was to cover the Table, at Communion-time, with a fair white linen cloth. Now, though the old practice still holds good in many places, it is a not uncommon custom merely to spread a strip of white linen along the top of the Table, leaving all the front and its decorations exposed as at times when there is no Communion. We can only say the old custom is more in keeping with the idea of a table on which a holy banquet is to be spread; while the modern practice savours more of the effort to obliterate the Reform-ation, ignore the New Testament, and bring back the " altar " of mediævalism. Small as this matter is in itself, it is by such symbolic trifles that a system of mediæval rites and mediæval doctrines is being introduced and propagated.

The " Vestments " Question.

This may be a convenient place in which to draw attention, very briefly, to the costume legally prescribed for the minister who celebrates the sacrament of the Lord's Supper. The point has been recently investigated and decided by the Privy Council in the case of *Ridsdale* v. *Clifton*.

The decision of that highest law court of the realm is described as having been unhesitatingly arrived at by the numerous and most distinguished personages, lay and clerical, who took part in the judgment. The eccentricity of one judge, who irregularly expressed his dissent, makes it desirable to bear in mind the readiness and certainty with which the entire body of the Judicial Committee describe themselves as agreeing in their common action: and, indeed, considering that the subject under examination had occupied the Council six years previously in the case of *Hibbert* v. *Purchas;* and remembering that, five years before that, again, in 1866, the subject had been studied, and an opinion had been given to certain bishops, by Lord Selborne, Lord Cairns, and others ; it may be regarded as certain that never was an abler body of judicial men asssembled to give judgment on a point with which their peculiar training and previous studies made them more singularly well acquainted; and these men, after hearing some of our ablest counsel, learned in the law, decided, without any hesitation, that the "Advertisements" of Queen Elizabeth must be read into the Ornaments Rubric of our existing Prayer-book in accordance with the statute of 2 Elizabeth c. 25; that the rubric, with this statutory addition, is confirmed by the Canons of 1604, and is ratified by the Act of Uniformity of 1662. If this line of enactments required confirmation, the Privy Council held that such confirmation was abundant in the practice of the English Church from the year 1662 down to the year 1840. And this contemporaneous and long-continued practice, the Privy Council found, makes entirely in favour of the surplice and against the chasuble.

It is true that, by the strict letter of the "Advertisements" of Elizabeth, the principal ministers, in cathedral and collegiate churches, should, in celebrating the holy Communion, wear a "cope" and corresponding garments—not a "chasuble," be it remarked—but, then, this costume has become obsolete in the course of the last two centuries and upwards, and, though the Privy Council lay it down as legally permissible in cathedrals and collegiate churches, we should not admire the taste, or the discretion, of any dignitaries or others who strove to re-introduce a mediæval garb which has been long laid aside and which is singularly out of keeping with the whole spirit and genius of the English Church. Be that, however, as it may, one thing is clear, namely, that in our parish churches, and in all except cathedral and collegiate churches, the only vestment allowed for the clergy at the Communion is the surplice.

These few words with reference to the vesture of the officiating minister, in the Lord's Supper, we have thought it right here to introduce while treating of the rubric which regulates the covering of the Lord's Table at Communion-time.

Other parts of this rubric, besides that which deals with the fair white linen cloth for the Table, have been even more strangely and entirely neglected and disused. The Table, instead of standing, at Communion-time, in the body of the church or in the chancel, where morning and evening prayer are appointed to be said, is nowadays kept always at the east end of the chancel, as far as may be from the reading pew ; and, moreover, instead of the Table standing with its length parallel to the length of the church, so that its end should be towards the east, and its side towards the north—in which case the clergyman could strictly obey the rubric by standing at the north side of the Table—the side of the Table is now systematically set against the east wall of the church, and so the minister, if he is to comply exactly with the rubric by standing at the *north* of the Table, can only do so by departing, perhaps, from a strict and literal obedience to the rubric's injunction that he shall stand at the north *side* of the Table.

Again we say the matter is, in itself, of infinitely small importance. However, there was justice and historical, as well as rubrical, accuracy on the side of those who recently threatened the sacerdotal innovators with reprisals in the way of obeying this rubric and setting the Table "table-wise," not "altar-wise," according to the phraseology of the old dispute.

Standing at the north side of the Table, the "priest"—for he continues to officiate in England, though Laud proposed to set up the "presbyter" in Scotland, it will be remembered—shall say the Lord's Prayer, with the collect following.

In connection with the Lord's Prayer, in this part of the service, an old custom has prevailed all but universally, that the people shall be silent and let the priest say the Lord's Prayer here by himself. This old custom is in distinct contra-

vention of the rubric before the first Lord's Prayer in the
morning service, where we read—

*Then the minister shall kneel and say the Lord's Prayer with an audible voice; the people also
kneeling, and repeating it with him, both here, and wheresoever else it is used in Divine Service.*

It is probable that this old and general custom, violating
the English rubric as it does, is an imitation of the mode of
dealing with the Lord's Prayer in certain parts of the Mass-
book. There, in the canon of the Mass, and apparently in
other places, the priest was to say the Lord's Prayer down to
" Lead us not into temptation; " then the choir took up the
petition, " But deliver us from evil; " and the priest said the
" Amen " by himself.

Within the last few years the choir and people, in modern
English churches, have learned to be silent during this
" Amen." This is another of those innovations which aim, or
tend, to re-introduce the mediæval Mass instead of the reformed
and apostolic Communion. This innovation is, like the old
custom named above, a distinct violation of the rubric, at the
end of the Absolution in morning prayer, which prescribes
that—

The people shall answer here, and at the end of all other Prayers, Amen.

We have heard this omission of the " Amen " by the
people defended on the plea that the word " Amen " is printed
in type different from the italics of the " Amen " at the end
of the Collect for Purity. They, who employ this argument,
can hardly have observed that a large proportion of the
" Amens " in the Communion Service, and in the morning
and evening prayers, are printed in the same manner as this
one at the opening of the Communion Service; and the
traditional explanation of the matter we have always understood to be that " *Amen*," in italics, is to be said by the people
only, without the minister, and " Amen," not in italics, is to
be repeated both by the people and the minister. Be that as
it may, the letter and spirit of the English Prayer-book know
nothing of the Lord's Prayer to be said by the priest only;
and it is to be regretted that the novelty, of the people being
instructed to be silent at an " Amen," has been also introduced, in defiance of the whole genius of the English Book of

Common Prayer, as well as of common sense and piety, and the practice of primitive and apostolic times.

(ii.) *Exhortations concerning the Lord's Supper.*
(a.) *The First Exhortation.*

And now, before proceeding to consider the Communion Service itself, this seems the appropriate place in which to draw the reader's attention to the two exhortations which are appointed to be read in anticipation of the Lord's Supper.

The rubric introducing the first of these exhortations is this :—

When the minister giveth warning for the celebration of the holy Communion (which he shall always do upon the Sunday, or some holy-day, immediately preceding), after the sermon or Homily ended, he shall read this Exhortation following.

It will, we think, be clear to the attentive student that they, who composed this rubric, did not mean that the exhortation should be used, as part of it very generally is, as a form of notice that the Lord's Supper will be administered on a coming day. Rather what the rubric contemplates and directs is this: On the Sunday or some holy-day immediately preceding the celebration of the Communion, the minister shall, after reading the Nicene Creed, give notice of the Communion in what form of words he thinks proper (as the first rubric after the Creed enjoins). Then he is to preach a sermon or read one of the Homilies (according to the second rubric after the Nicene Creed); and then, after such sermon or Homily ended, he is to read, at his discretion, one or other of the two exhortations we have now in view, unless his sermon or Homily shall have dealt with the subject.

Of course this must have lengthened the service considerably; but, then, it is to be remembered that people were patient with very long occupation in matters of religion in ages when a popular preacher might turn up the hour-glass to give his hearers another hour. Besides, the Communion Service, with its notices and its sermon and its added exhortation, was not intended to be a continuation of Morning Prayer and the Litany. It was not contemplated there should

be one long period of two hours, or two hours and a half, of
attempted religious occupation.

Be all that as it may, however, the order sketched above,
for the giving notice of Communion and for reading one or
other of these exhortations, was the course prescribed by the
rubrics of 1662.

How these exhortations, originated and composed in the
period of the Reformation, have been altered, and how they
were formerly used as part of the service preparatory to the
Lord's Supper, has been perhaps sufficiently shown in some
previous pages of our essay, or may yet appear.

We now proceed to notice the exhortations themselves,
that we may thus learn more exactly the views and aims with
which it is recommended, in our existing Prayer-book, that we
should approach the Lord's Table.

The opening paragraph of the first exhortation reads
thus :—

> Dearly beloved, on ——day next I purpose, through God's assistance,
> to administer to all such as shall be religiously and devoutly disposed the
> most comfortable Sacrament of the Body and Blood of Christ ; to be by
> them received in remembrance of His meritorious Cross and Passion ;
> whereby alone we obtain remission of our sins, and are made partakers of
> the Kingdom of Heaven.   Wherefore it is our duty to render most humble
> and hearty thanks to Almighty God our heavenly Father, for that He hath
> given His Son our Saviour Jesus Christ, not only to die for us, but also
> to be our spiritual food and sustenance in that holy Sacrament.   Which
> being so divine and comfortable a thing to them who receive it worthily,
> and so dangerous to them that will presume to receive it unworthily ; my
> duty is to exhort you in the mean season to consider the dignity of that
> holy mystery, and the great peril of the unworthy receiving thereof ; and
> so to search and examine your own consciences, (and that not lightly, and
> after the manner of dissemblers with God ; but so) that ye may come holy
> and clean to such a heavenly Feast, in the marriage-garment required by
> God in Holy Scripture, and be received as worthy partakers of that holy
> Table.

It should be noticed that what is here proposed to be
administered is the sacrament (or outward sign) of that
inward spiritual food which the soul, through faith working by
love, should derive from Christ's body given for us, and from
Christ's blood shed for the putting away, the forgiveness and
abandonment, of sins.

It should be observed, also, that this sacred rite, instead of being designated "awful" or "terrific," as it sometimes has been, is represented to us, in the English Church, as "the most comfortable" sacrament. Let this word "comfortable" be understood in its common acceptation of soothing, consoling; or let it be taken in its grander and more derivation signification,[1] in which it denotes a binding together all the parts of any system (the human constitution, for instance, of memory, passion, energy, hope, and conscience), and so making that system strong for action as well as for endurance —in both these senses the sacrament is well described by the epithet "comfortable," even as (John xiv. 16, xv. 26) the Holy Spirit is called by the name "Comforter" with like meaning and with similar propriety.

This most consoling and strengthening sacrament is offered to "all such as shall be religiously and devoutly disposed."

"Disposed"—by whom ? By God in His grace, undoubtedly; but that grace is placed at our disposal already and always, while the day of salvation lasts, by Him who says, "Come unto Me, all ye that labour and are heavy laden, and I will give you rest." It is only in the sense in which we dispose ourselves, lay out our own plans, bend our own wills, exert our own energies, and persevere to the end in our own determination, that our disposition is here spoken of as something to which we should give heed. Give heed that, whilst God is urging you to accept His abundant and sufficient grace in Christ, you dispose and turn yourselves in the way of religion or the binding one's self to duty and to God—yea, in the way of devotion, devoting and dedicating one's self, body, soul, and spirit, to Him who, when we were enemies (Rom. v. 10), reconciled us unto Himself by the death of His Son.

To all who, whatever may be their condition of sin at present, shall hearken to the divine call and turn and dispose themselves in the way of religion and devotion, the most comfortable sacrament of Christ is offered. And this offer is made in order that the outward sign of bread and wine may "be

---

[1] It is derived, of course, from *cum*, together, and *fortis*, strong.

received in remembrance of His meritorious cross and passion."

What a remembrance! The wife looks with unutterable fondness upon the portrait of her absent spouse who, for her sake, is bearing hardship, perhaps is facing death; but the believer looks upon the elements, which feed his body, and is reminded of the cross and suffering of the Saviour who, to redeem mankind from sin and self and degradation, faced death and every horror that can be imagined under the idea of the sinless One being made sin (2 Cor. v. 21) for us, and of His being forsaken by His God (Matt. xxvii. 46). Yes, looking on the bread and wine, let us be reminded of that cross and passion with which, as with all Christ's sacrifice of perfect obedience, the Father declared Himself well pleased or satisfied (Matt. iii. 17).

In this was its merit or effectiveness. Herein it was "meritorious," as contenting the very righteousness of God Himself. And it is by this meritorious cross and passion of Christ "alone" that "we obtain remission of our sins, and are made partakers of the kingdom of heaven." Not by the bread and wine, but by that which the bread and wine bring to our remembrance, was reconciliation procured to us; and only that same cross and passion of Christ, which brought us pardon of sin, can so strengthen our inner man that we, having received God's free pardon, may, henceforth and for ever, abandon sin, and so complete the remission or putting away of evil: and thus relieved of sin, the only thing which God hates, we shall be His dear children, and members of that more than world-embracing commonwealth of which God Himself is King—the kingdom of righteousness and peace and truth, that kingdom whose beginning may be on earth, but whose development and expansion reach throughout eternity and the infinite.

And in contemplation of these truths, proceeds the exhortation, "it is our duty to render most humble and hearty thanks to Almighty God, our heavenly Father, for that He hath given His Son our Saviour Jesus Christ, not only to die for us, but" to be the food and sustenance of our souls and spirits in the holy sacrament of the Supper. And as this is "so divine and comfortable a thing to them who receive it worthily "—of course, the epithet "divine" may qualify anything, from a divine ordinance, an ordinance appointed by God, to a Person of the Godhead; and, no less obviously, it is applied to the Lord's Supper in the former of these two senses, as to an ordinance "divine" from its being instituted by God—and as, on the other hand, it is most perilous for any to be rash and profane in receiving the bread and wine which, as they feed the body, are emblems of Christ in that He feeds the soul and spirit; in view of this danger on the one side, and these blessings on the other, it is "my duty to exhort you in the mean season to consider the dignity of that holy mystery, and the great peril of the unworthy receiving thereof."

Here is no advice to abstain from Communion, but, on the contrary, the exhortation is that the mean season, the few hours or days, at most, to intervene between the notice and the celebration, should be so occupied as that any, who to-day are unworthy, may, by Communion-time, have been by God's grace rendered fit for reception of the Lord's Supper.

"Consider the dignity of that holy mystery," says the exhortation. What, indeed, must be the dignity of Christ's Table, and of feeding there, with His mystical body, the whole company of believers, on the spiritual food of His most precious body and blood once sacrificed for us all!

"Mysteries" as a Designation for the Lord's Supper.

In this passage, as in two or three others in our Communion Service, the Lord's Supper is styled a "mystery." Let it be borne in mind that this word is not a translation. It is an actual Greek word. Doubtless, its definition, in Johnson's Dictionary, is—"Mystery, something above human intelligence, something awfully obscure." If, however, we bear in mind that the word is Greek, not English, in its original tongue; and if, accordingly, we seek its definition in Liddell and Scott's Greek Lexicon, we shall there find that "mystery" signifies "a revealed secret."

The Greek history of the word is, that it was derived from a verb signifying "to gag" or close the mouth. Hence it signified something, in the religions of Greece—the Eleusinian and other mysteries—which the initiated must keep secret from those who were not initiated. The secret was revealed, explained, made known to those who were initiated. To them it was made intelligible enough, but they must only speak of it among themselves, with their fellow-worshippers. Such a piece of religious teaching, secret to the uninitiated, clear to the initiated, was any mystery of the heathen Greeks.

It is in this sense, of a secret revealed, and only in this sense, that the word "mystery" is employed in the Greek Testament. To you, says our Lord, it is given to know the mysteries of the kingdom of heaven (Matt. xiii. 11). This was addressed to the "disciples," to those who sought and obtained initiation into Christ's teaching. They were to know and understand its mysteries. In the same way, in many passages of his writings, St. Paul insists that by revelation (or withdrawing the veil) the mystery of Christ had been made known unto him. The burthen of this mystery, which in other ages had not been made known, but now was revealed unto the apostles and prophets by the Spirit (Eph. iii. 3, etc.), was that God loved, not only the Jews, as they had dreamed, but also loved all men in all nations, so that the Gentiles were to be fellow-heirs with the Israelites, and of the same body, and partakers of His promise in Christ by the Gospel. And this mystery, which had been hidden from the foundation of the world, but was now made known, it was St. Paul's declared object and duty (verses 8, 9) to preach among the Gentiles, and to make all men see.

Similarly, in all the numerous passages of the New Testament, in which the word "mystery" occurs, it is invariably used to signify, not a secret still hidden, but a secret clearly revealed and explained. So it is (Rom. xvi. 25, 26) when the apostle says that the preaching of Jesus Christ is "the revelation of the mystery, which was kept secret since the world began, but now is made manifest and . . . made known to all nations." So it is with reference to the same "mystery" (if

that, and not " testimony," be the correct reading in 1 Cor.
ii. 1). There the mystery or testimony of God is " declared."

And, in the same chapter (verses 7, 8, 10), where the
apostle speaks of "the wisdom of God in a mystery, even the
hidden wisdom, which God ordained before the world unto our
glory," he describes this "mystery" as something which,
before Christ, "none of the princes of this world knew ; " but
"now" (ver. 12), he says, " we have the mind of Christ " (ver.
16), and (ver. 10) "God hath revealed" this mystery "unto us
by His Spirit: for the Spirit searcheth all things, yea, the deep
things of God." It is of these same mysteries, as secrets made
known, that St. Paul (1 Cor. iv. 1) declares the apostles are
"stewards " or dispensers. So too, when (1 Cor. xiii. 2) St.
Paul is exalting the grace of Christian love above all other
characters and qualities and gifts, it is with the knowledge or
" understanding of all mysteries " that he compares it. Not
otherwise (1 Cor. xiv. 2, 5) St. Paul pronounces " mysteries,"
spoken in an unknown tongue, without being interpreted, inferior to plain prophesying or preaching, on the very ground
that they are not understanded.

Observe, however, it is not the "mysteries," in themselves,
which the apostle describes as unintelligible, but it is the
unknown language in which they are spoken which he blames.
In other words, the apostle considered an unintelligible
mystery worthless ; but a mystery, as a secret revealed so
that it could be understood, no man valued more highly.

Accordingly, when in the next chapter (1 Cor. xv. 51) St.
Paul is explaining, in the clearest language, certain facts connected with the future advent of Christ, he calls his explanation telling or showing his correspondents a mystery.

It is uniformly of knowing, and understanding, and making
manifest, and speaking, and holding in a pure conscience
with a view to declaring,—that the apostle (Eph. i. 9, iii. 3, 4,
9, vi. 19; Col. i. 26, 27, ii. 2, iv. 3 ; 1 Tim. iii. 9) speaks in
connection with the "mystery " of the Gospel and of Christ.
Never, in a single instance, does he refer to this " mystery "
as obscure or as a subject on which reticence is becoming.
On the contrary, he always names it as something which God

has revealed or unveiled for the express purpose of its being at all costs published, and made intelligible, and believed in all nations and by all men.

Nor is the use of the word "mystery" different in other parts of the New Testament where it is employed to designate something else than the Gospel of Christ. Thus, for instance (Eph. v. 32), where St. Paul urges husbands to love their wives by the example of Christ's love for His spouse, the Church, he carries on the parallel until he says, "We are members of His body, of His flesh, and of His bones." For this union with Christ, a man must give up father and mother and all things, so that "they two shall be one flesh." "This," continues the apostle, "is a great mystery"—a grand secret revealed, something which man would never have imagined or dared to hope, but something which God hath shown and made it possible for us to understand by the mind and spirit of Christ—"this is a great mystery: but I speak concerning Christ and the Church," and their intimate and indissoluble union. "Nevertheless, let every one of you, in particular, so love his wife as himself; and the wife see that she reverence her husband."

The height and depth of this love of Christ is, indeed, past man's understanding, but not so its nature and tendency and purpose. So far as St. Paul designates the love that is from Christ to us, and that should be from us to Christ, "a mystery" he makes it as clear and transparent as anything can well be.

In like manner, when the apostle (2 Thess. ii. 7) treats of "the mystery of iniquity," however much we, after the lapse of eighteen centuries, may have lost the exact historical clue to his meaning, he was speaking what was manifestly quite intelligible to his Thessalonian converts. He may have suppressed names of individuals and written about "the man of sin," "the son of perdition," "the lawless one" (verses 3, 8), in order to lessen the risk of persecution for himself or his correspondents; but when he was with them (ver. 5), he had told them these things. They knew (ver. 6) what withheld the evil influence that was already at work.

In all this there was nothing obscure or unintelligible to the Thessalonians. They possessed entirely the clue we have lost, at least in part, for the understanding of this passage. To them " the mystery of iniquity " was not an unintelligible puzzle. It was a secret to the uninitiated, but to St. Paul's friends and contemporaries it had all been recently explained; and it was thus a mystery in the true Greek sense, a secret revealed.

The next instance in which we should observe St. Paul's use of the word " mystery " is that wherein (1 Tim. iii. 16) the apostle declares that " without controversy," that is, confessedly, " great is the mystery of godliness ; " and then he proceeds to enumerate some of the constituent elements of that grand and glorious secret revealed—namely, the manifestation of God in the flesh, His justification in the spirit, His being seen by the angels who delighted to look upon the spectacle of Christ on earth, His being preached unto the Gentiles as well as to the Jews, His being believed on in the world generally, and His being received up into glory as our High-Priest and Intercessor at God's right hand.

Here is, indeed, an abundant confirmation of St. Paul's statement that the mystery of piety—in other words, the revealed secret of God's Gospel for making men pious—is, not dark or obscure or awful, but great, stupendous, admirable. True, there are many aspects, of each of these constituents of godliness, in which they are at present but partially comprehended by us. We know them—as we know the springing of a blade of grass and all the simplest and most complex objects of our cognizance—only " in part " and not completely or adequately.

Still, it is not these unknown and, perhaps, unknowable parts of the constituents of godliness which are presented to his readers by St. Paul as illustrating the grandeur of the mystery of godliness. Rather, his argument is, Contemplate the facts you know and understand—of the unknown you can form no trustworthy conception—but contemplate the facts already within your knowledge regarding Christ's incarnation, His righteousness of spirit as well as act, His delightsome-

ness to angelic gaze, the catholicity of His announcement
and intended acceptance in the world, even among all nations;
—contemplate these plain facts, and add to them Christ's
departure into heaven's glory, and His merciful occupation
there; and, in these revealed facts, behold the grandeur of
God's Gospel, the mystery or revealed secret for winning
hearts to piety.

Very different would have been the meaning of St. Paul's
words if he had written, Without controversy, dark and awful
is the unintelligible puzzle of godliness. And this contrast
with St. Paul's real words may confirm us in the assurance
that here, as in all his other employments of the word
"mystery," St. Paul used it in its true Greek signification, of
a revealed secret, as opposed to the modern and English corruption of the word into a name for all that is unintelligible
and awful.

And similar is the use of the word "mystery" when St.
Paul shows the Roman Christians (Rom. xi. 25) that blindness
and unbelief are happened unto part of the Israelites until the
swarming multitudes of the nations shall enter the kingdom
of Christ. This revelation or clear statement of fact St. Paul
calls a "mystery."

Precisely similar is the employment of the word by St.
John the Divine in his Apocalypse, where, if he speaks of
"the mystery of the seven stars," he explains (Rev. i. 20)
that "the seven stars are the angels of the seven Churches;"
or, if he employs St. Paul's familiar phrase, "the mystery of
God" (Rev. x. 7), he takes care to explain that this mystery
is the Gospel which God declared to His servants the prophets.[1]
And, yet again, if (Rev. xvii. 5, 7) St. John the Divine mentions "the woman" upon whose forehead was written a name,
"Mystery," he does not fail to describe her further as
"Babylon the great, the mother of harlots and abominations
of the earth," drunken with the blood of the saints and martyrs of Jesus, sitting on seven mountains (v. 9), and con-

---

[1] τὸ μυστήριον τοῦ Θεοῦ, ὡς εὐηγγέλισε τοὺς ἑαυτοῦ δούλους τοὺς προφήτας—
"the mystery of God, as He declared the glad tidings to His servants the
prophets." Dean Alford and Dr. Davidson thus translate the words.

nected with seven kings, of whom five are fallen, and one is, and the other is not yet come, etc.

Now, whether we, in this nineteenth century, have or have not lost the clue for unriddling the enigma of this delineation, certain it is that St. John the Divine considered its meaning would be transparently clear to his contemporaries in the seven Churches of Asia (Rev. i. 4), for he distinctly addresses his book to them as a revelation, an unveiling, a showing of the things that must shortly be. And now we have produced every instance in which the word " mystery " occurs in the New Testament, and invariably, without an exception, we have found that it denotes the very opposite of anything unintelligible; its meaning always is something made clear and revealed.

The attentive reader will have noticed that the term " mystery " is never used, in Holy Writ, to designate the Lord's Supper. There is no trace or sign of such an usage among the apostles.

As, however, the religion of Christ spread itself over the world and became known to those who were acquainted with the mysteries of the Greek and other religions, these last, remembering that there were different external objects employed as symbols of certain definite religious (or irreligious) meanings—outward and visible signs of inward significations —in the heathen mysteries, and finding water in one rite of Christianity, and bread and wine in another rite, similarly employed as symbols of things signified, they called these Christian rites by the name of those heathen observances; and so " mystery," a symbol with a clear and important signification, became the Greek name for each of our Christian sacraments.

How, unhappily, the idea of awfulness was subsequently grafted on to the meaning of this Greek word; how, because the heathen mysteries had been kept secret from all but the initiated, so the Lord's Supper was to be kept unexplained and unknown to all but those who, as catechumens and as baptized, had undergone Christian initiation; how these innovations on the simplicity and frankness of the apostolic usage

of the Lord's Supper brought that holy rite into disrepute
with unbelievers, and caused it to be traduced and blasphemed
as a hideous resort to Thyestean banqueting—these sad
occurrences stand recorded on the pages of ecclesiastical history; but these were accretions of darkness and superstition
which had no proper connection either with the Christian
sacraments themselves or with the Greek name "mystery"
applied to them two or three times in the English Communion
Service.

Whenever, as here in the first exhortation and, subsequently, in the exhortation used at the time of celebration, and in the second of the post-Communion collects, we
find the Lord's Supper called a "mystery," let us remember
the beautiful signification of this Greek word, in the New
Testament and elsewhere, as a secret revealed by God's
mercy; and let us keep our minds clear of those patristic
and mediæval superstitions of awe and unintelligibleness as
connected with any secret which the Lord has opened and
revealed to us.

Thus, as the exhortation bids us, let us consider, on the
one hand, the dignity, honour, and glory of the holy mystery
of the Supper; and, on the other hand, let us bear in mind
the great peril of its unworthy receiving. So shall we be led
to honest searching and examining of ourselves in the sight
of God; and so may we come "holy and clean to such a
heavenly feast." Mark the tone of joy which is in this word
"feast," a tone in thorough harmony with the joyousness
we saw exhibited in the apostolic breaking of bread (Acts ii. 46).
And mark also the cleanness which is insisted on in the reference to the marriage-garment required by God in Holy Scripture—that marriage-garment which consists in putting on
Christ and being righteous as He (1 John iii. 7) is righteous.
This is "the righteousness of the saints[1]" (Rev. xix. 8), an
array of "fine linen, clean and white;" the very marriage-
garment not only of the guests in the parable (Matt. xxii. 11),
but of the bride herself.

This, as teaches the exhortation, is the proper condition

_____
[1] τὰ δικαιώματα τῶν ἁγίων, the righteous acts of the saints.

in which to "be received as worthy partakers at" the "holy Table."

And now the exhortation proceeds to instruct us as to the mode of attaining this condition :—

The way and means thereto is, First, to examine your lives and conversations by the rule of God's commandments ; and whereinsoever ye shall perceive yourselves to have offended, either by will, word, or deed, there to bewail your own sinfulness, and to confess yourselves to Almighty God, with full purpose of amendment of life. And if ye shall perceive your offences to be such as are not only against God, but also against your neighbours ; then ye shall reconcile yourselves unto them ; being ready to make restitution and satisfaction, according to the uttermost of your powers, for all injuries and wrongs done by you to any other ; and being likewise ready to forgive others that have offended you, as ye would have forgiveness of your offences at God's hand : for otherwise the receiving of the holy Communion doth nothing else but increase your damnation. Therefore if any of you be a blasphemer of God, an hinderer or slanderer of His Word, an adulterer, or be in malice, or envy, or in any other grievous crime, repent you of your sins, or else come not to that holy Table : lest, after the taking of that holy Sacrament, the devil enter into you, as he entered into Judas, and fill you full of all iniquities, and bring you to destruction both of body and soul.

Self-Examination.

As to self-examination, the method here recommended is, that we should set up God's commandments—say, the Decalogue of the Old Testament and the two commandments of the New Testament, Love God with all your heart, and Love your neighbour as yourself—as a standard of reference, and then compare our "life and conversation," all our ordinary, as well as extraordinary, doings and sayings and passions, with the spirit—"the mystical importance," as says the Scotch service—of each command. This will, of itself, be an excellent line of self-scrutiny. To give variety, however, and constantly fresh energy to this most important part of Christian devotion, it may be suggested that we should sometimes take the practical parts of an Epistle ; for example, Eph. v. 1—vi. 20, or Rom. xii. 1—21 ; or, again, take the works of the flesh and the fruits of the spirit (Gal. v. 19—23) ; or, again, for the purpose of self-comparison, make a list of the contentiousness and party spirit and other sins blamed by

St. Paul in his first Epistle to the Corinthians; or go thoughtfully, with pious and studious meditation, through the several petitions of the Lord's Prayer, ascertaining how far you attach definite, simple, and yet comprehensive meanings to each supplication, and how far you really and habitually desire, and strive to accomplish, the conditions prayed for in each; above all, have an increasingly intimate and vivid acquaintance with Jesus, the God-man, the carpenter of Nazareth, the beneficent, the patient, the sinbearer—cultivate this intimacy with the Christ of the Gospels and of St. Paul's writings: and in any or all of these exercises, vigorously and prayerfully carried on, the Spirit of God will help you; your self-examination will be close, searching, spiritual, and certain, as the divine promises are certain, to prepare you in such wise that ye may come holy and clean to the heavenly feast.

With reference to sin, in which we shall thus discover ourselves, the counsel of the exhortation is, " there to bewail our own sinfulness," not casting the blame of our offences on circumstances or tempters or our nature, but crying out in the wise piety of the ancient confession, " *Meâ culpâ*," by my own fault, have I done this; and so should we make our confession, it is urged, not to man, but "to Almighty God, with full purpose of amendment of life."

If, however, there be occasion to acknowledge one's sins to any of our fellow-men whom we have wronged, the exhortation provides for this contingency, and enjoins that we shall reconcile ourselves to our neighbours whom we may have injured; that we shall be ready to make restitution and satisfaction, to the uttermost of our powers, for all injuries and wrongs we have inflicted; and, moreover, we must be ready to forgive others who may have injured us, and this with the same heartiness with which we desire forgiveness of our own sins at the hand of God.

Otherwise, continues the exhortation, receiving the holy Communion without such self-examination, without such reparation for wrongs done, without such forgivingness of heart, " doth nothing else but increase your damnation."

What is *meant* by these words is most true, namely, that unrepentant and unloving participation in the sacrament of God's love will increase our judgment, will make us judge ourselves the more deeply and painfully—or, failing that in the mean while, will make us to be the more searchingly and tremendously, though lovingly and healingly, judged by God.

All this, which (as we have seen) is what is said by St. Paul (1 Cor. xi. 29), and, therefore, is what is *meant* by our exhortation, is most true; and the only pity is that the distinctness and moral force of its utterance are marred and obscured by the employment of the word " damnation," which, whatever may have been its popular acceptation 270 years ago, has come now to signify exclusively final punishment in the future life.

To associate this " damnation," or being cast into hell, with a single unworthy participation of the Lord's Supper, or even with many such participations, is as remote as possible from the meaning of Scripture, and, therefore, from the true and intended meaning of the English Liturgy. The very phrase, "*increase* your damnation," shows that the authors of the exhortation had not in their minds an infinite and endless perdition, for that could admit of neither increase nor diminution. The exhortation speaks, not of an *absolute* and infinite and endless misery, but of a *comparative* judgment which may, more or less, be diminished or " increased." It is difficult to measure the superstition and other harm being caused by a misconception of this one word.

From sins of unforgiveness and the like, the exhortation proceeds to enumerate several other grievous sins, whose very enumeration may assist us in examining ourselves. If any be a blasphemer of God, speaking irreverently of the Deity, or taking His holy name lightly on the lips—if any be in the habit of hindering the progress of God's word, in Holy Writ, or in the blessed Son who is the Word; or if any slander and speak ill of that Word ; if any mock and discourage those on whom the Word has, for the time at least, produced a serious and sobering effect—if any be impure or unfaithful in those holiest and tenderest relationships that should subsist between

man and wife—if any be unkindly and unlovingly, or otherwise than sympathizingly and generously, disposed towards all
his fellow-creatures—or if any " be in other grievous crime "
—what then?   What does the English service advise?
"Repent you of your sins;" not merely be sorry for your sins.

Sorrow is an important part of repentance, but it is not the
whole, nor is it even the most important part. The most
important part of repentance is change of mind [1] and heart
and life. If this be in a man, we venture to say that the
sorrow and pain of the process by which such change may
have been brought about, is a very minor consideration. It
is not a question of, How many tears have you shed? how
long has the bitterness of remorse been endured? and so
forth. The great question is, Has the sinner beheld the
beauty of Christ in contrast with the depravity of sin, and has
he been changed, by the renewing of his mind, into some
incipient likeness of the Lord? If this question can be satis-
factorily answered, the sinner is repentant. It is such a
repentance, not to be sorrowed over, that the exhortation here
recommends.

"Or else," without such repentant change of mind and
life, "come not to the holy Table." Well worth noticing,
as was before stated, is the improvement in this part of the
exhortation as compared with its earlier form. Instead of,
Let a man bewail himself *and* come not to the Table, it is
now, Let him repent, let him change his mind, let him give
up his sin, let him take upon him the Lord Christ's likeness
and grace instead of his sin; and so let him come to the
blessed feast. Only in case he will not so repent, is he
warned not to approach the Table.

The exhortation then assumes, we think with much reason,
that Judas, in his avarice and theft, in his hankering after a
kingdom of this world with pomp and wealth for himself, in
his wrath at Christ's approving the "waste" of the precious
ointment, in his double dealing with Jesus and with the
priests who sought the blood of Jesus, in his defiance of
every means by which Christ strove to warn and win him

---

[1] μετάνοια, in the Greek Testament.

from his course of treachery and betrayal—in this terrible disposition the Liturgy represents Judas as having participated in the original Last Supper of the Lord; and the warning is held before those who might be contemplating a thoughtless and unholy participation, that sin often ends in a steep decline. The sinner has trifled with holy things, and set God and conscience at defiance, until there comes forth a lying spirit to deceive him, or until even Christ Himself can no longer endure the hypocrisy of the man who pretends to be His friend but has already sold him, and is only watching for the opportunity of a betrayal already determined. To such an one, Jesus may say the tremendous words, "That thou doest, do more quickly."[1] Thou hast decided to do it. Thou art persisting in that decision. Thou art already *doing it*. Increase not the deliberateness and therefore the guilt by pausing in thine action. "That thou art doing, do more quickly."

And when such a pitch of wickedness is reached, when a man, Judas-like, has so given himself over to the spirit of evil, well may that spirit be represented as entering into the man, and filling him full of all iniquities which must bring both soul and body to destruction. Surely, some such warning against persistent sin, and especially against double dealing and hypocrisy with Christ and in religion, is no unwise or unnecessary part of our exhortation.

At this point we reach the concluding paragraph of the first exhortation :—

And because it is requisite, that no man should come to the holy Communion, but with a full trust in God's mercy, and with a quiet conscience; therefore if there be any of you, who by this means cannot quiet his own conscience herein, but requireth further comfort or counsel, let him come to me, or to some other discreet and learned minister of God's Word, and open his grief; that by the ministry of God's holy Word he may receive the benefit of absolution, together with ghostly counsel and advice, to the quieting of his conscience, and avoiding of all scruple and doubtfulness.

Undoubtedly, a full trust in God's mercy and a quiet conscience are most desirable frames of mind at all times; and, if

---

[1] τάχιον (John xiii. 27), the comparative degree, *more* quickly, not "quickly" only.

we are to enter into special and intimate fellowship with God
and Christ and our brethren in the membership of Christ's
body, at the Lord's Table, it cannot be doubted but that such
trust and such quiet are then particularly "requisite."

Consultation of a Scrupulous Person with a Clergyman.

The attaining such trust and such quiet, in proportion as
it is a great blessing, is sometimes most difficult to achieve,
especially if it be not set about and carried through by coming
to Christ as the author of our faith, and ever coming more
and more to Christ Himself as the finisher, also, of that same
faith and trust and peace.

All the previous instructions of the exhortation have
aimed at a man's preparing himself, by God's grace, to come
to the Communion with such trust and peace of conscience.
But, now, suppose that in any case—that is, in some exceptional instance, not as a rule—any of the congregation
cannot quiet his own conscience by such self-examination as
has been above prescribed, what does the exhortation recommend in such exceptional cases?

The first step prescribed is, that the disquieted individual
shall make choice of any Christian "minister" he thinks
proper. This "minister" is not spoken of as a priest or a
confessor, but in the most general term descriptive of those
who serve the Lord Christ, and serve or minister to Christ's
people for the Lord's sake. This minister need not be one of
the parochial clergy. He may be an entire stranger or a most
familiar friend. He may be chosen entirely at the discretion
of the man whose conscience is unquiet. It is supposed that
what the man wants is "further comfort and counsel;" and,
with a view to obtain that, he is advised to select a "minister"
of whose learning he is assured, and with whose character as
a discreet person he is satisfied.

Having put himself in communication with such a minister,
what is the disquieted soul advised to do next? Is he urged
to *confess his sins* to this priest? No such thing. He is to
"open his grief." Quite possibly, his grief and disquietude
may arise, not from the peculiar nature of his sins, nor

from their number and heinousness. His sorrow may be consequent on his not clearly apprehending the cardinal truth of salvation by Christ only, or it may spring out of a misapprehension of some part of God's glad tidings of mercy. In any such case he is not advised to name a single sin to the minister. It is "his grief," the cause of his disquietude, that he is advised to "open" to the religious friend whom he has chosen for this purpose.

But, if even some ill deed be the ground and cause of his distress, he is not encouraged by the exhortation to deal with it as a sin that must be "confessed," still less as a sin from which he must be absolved by a Church-officer in order to procure pardon from God. Even if his "grief" spring directly out of one or more sins, he is advised to open and explain the grief of his condition, not its wickedness.

And then let us mark what is to follow upon his opening his grief. God's holy Word is to be ministered unto him. Truth after truth, from its sacred pages, is to be laid before his disquieted mind, as the learning and discretion of the selected minister may deem right and necessary. Any clergyman could officially pronounce the twelfth-century form, "I absolve thee," but that is not what the man of unquiet conscience wants and has sought. He requires the learned and discreet ministering of those passages of Scripture, and of those examples of his predecessors in such disquietude, which shall bear upon his particular grief and so give him "the benefit of absolution."

Let the reader bear in mind that, as Bingham has well put it ("Antiq. of the Christian Church," Book xix. ch. 1), whereas the indicative absolution, by the priest's "I absolve thee," was an innovation of the twelfth century only, the best and most ancient absolutions were conferred on men, whether in connection with the sacraments of baptism and the Lord's Supper, or otherwise, by prayer for their pardon and by teaching them the truth and reality and power of God's forgiving mercy as it is revealed in the Gospel.

It is true, in the service for the Visitation of the Sick, in consideration for people who had been accustomed to the

indicative absolution of later mediævalism, there is a rubric
enjoining that if—after all kinds of other prayers and minis-
trations had been essayed—the sick person still felt his
conscience troubled with any weighty matter, he was to be
moved to make a special confession of his sins; and then, if
he humbly and heartily desired it, the priest was instructed to
absolve him after this sort :—

> Our Lord Jesus Christ, who hath left power to His Church to absolve
> all sinners who truly repent and believe in Him, of His great mercy for-
> give thee thine offences : And by His authority committed to me, I
> absolve thee from all thy sins, In the Name of the Father, and of the Son,
> and of the Holy Ghost. Amen.

This "sort" of absolution is prescribed, but no man is
bound to use the precise form of the indicative absolution if
he prefers another form. The old rubric of 1549, enjoining
an absolution "in this form," etc., was, in 1552, softened
down into an absolution "after this sort"—a sort of absolution which has been provided in tender consideration for any
scruples of a sick or dying person ; though it is evidently
not an usage which the English Church recommends, but one
which she, with increasing hesitation, yields and permits by
way of concession.

The Sarum Missal had instructed the priest to say to
the sick person, in the corresponding part of its Visitation
Service :—

> If thou wouldest come to the vision of God, it is altogether needful
> that thou shouldest be clean in mind and pure in conscience ; for Christ
> saith in the Gospel, Blessed are the pure in heart, for they shall see God.
> If therefore thou wouldest have a clean heart and a sound conscience,
> confess all thy sins.
>
>   *Then let the priest absolve the sick person from all his sins in these words* [etc.].

There are remarkable differences between the Salisbury
absolution and that of the Reformed Church of England.
Into an examination of those, however, we must not be
allured. Let the reader compare the Sarum Missal's per-
emptory command that the sick man should confess all his
sins, if he would be pure and would see God, with the English
service's concession of a *special* confession if it should be

desired by the sick man. The confession is exceptional instead of being universal. It is "special" of such sins—such "weighty matters"—as the sick man chooses to divulge. It is not a confession of *all* his sins such as was required by the mediæval service.

Yet one more point should be noticed in connection with this subject. The rubric of 1549 had enjoined that this absolution, of the Visitation Service, should be used, also, "in all private confessions;" but in 1552, and in the later revisions of the Prayer-book, this rubric was pointedly omitted, so that the only case in which the English Church now tolerates and concedes a "special" confession and a "sort" of absolution in any degree like that in the indicative form, is when a sick man, unable otherwise to quiet his conscience, chooses to make a "special" and exceptional confession and desires an absolution.

It thus appears how utterly in opposition to the law and tendency of the English Church is the course of those who encourage, if they do not inculcate, private confession as generally desirable for penitents and as involving sacerdotal absolution in the indicative form.

Our Church's other confessions, at morning and evening prayers, and at the Communion, are general and public acknowledgments of sin; and her absolutions are such as result to the penitent from prayer and declaration of God's Gospel, and not from any authority of the priest to say, "I absolve thee."

So we are brought back to the absolution "by the ministry of God's Word" which is recommended, in the exhortation, for those who, without the minister, cannot quiet their own consciences. Besides this absolution by the promises and mercies of God in Christ, the minister is to afford the man with an unquiet conscience what "ghostly" (or religious) "counsel and advice" he can, out of his learning and discretion; and so, it is hoped, the unquiet conscience may be set at rest and all scruple and doubtfulness avoided.

Any person who, on the strength of this exceptional recommendation that a man of troubled conscience should open his grief and seek absolution by the ministering of God's Word, urges the general practice of private confession and an indicative absolution, so acts in defiance of the fact that the old rubric, which permitted such a course, has been expunged from the English Prayer-book; and he goes counter to the general use of public confession and precatory or evangelic absolution, while he employs for penitents in general a sort of absolution exceptionally conceded to the fears of such of the dying as require it.

(b.) *The Second Exhortation.*

With these remarks we quit the first exhortation, which was taken from Hermann's Consultation, and we proceed to an examination of the second form of exhortation, which was composed by Peter Martyr.

The rubric, introducing the second exhortation, calls for no remark.   Its words are :—

Or, in case he shall see the people negligent to come to the holy Communion, instead of the former, he shall use this Exhortation.

Nothing can be simpler than the opening words of the exhortation :—

Dearly beloved brethren, on —— I intend, by God's grace, to celebrate the Lord's Supper: unto which, in God's behalf, I bid you all that are here present; and beseech you, for the Lord Jesus Christ's sake, that ye will not refuse to come thereto, being so lovingly called and bidden by God Himself.

This is the first occasion on which we have met with the expression "celebrate the Lord's Supper." It is a most happy phrase, however, and quite unobjectionable, whether we regard it as implying that the rite to be "celebrated" is to be publicly honoured and exhibited in its simple glory, or whether we understand it of the multitude of believers who should, at Communion-time, crowd around the blessed Table.

For the rest, the exhortation, basing itself on an observed "negligence to come to the holy Communion," at once takes up the tone of earnest entreaty. The minister not only bids the congregation, in his own name, all to communicate ; but he reminds them that, in such words as, "Do this in remembrance of me," or "Let a man examine himself, and so let him eat of the bread and drink of the cup," there is a most loving invitation from God Himself, bidding all men to the Communion, and joining itself with such assurances as, " Him that cometh unto Me I will in no wise cast out."

This invitation to the sacred and joyous feast is then compared with men's bidding of their friends to a banquet ; and the line of thought is thus carried on :—

> Ye know how grievous and unkind a thing it is, when a man hath prepared a rich feast, decked his table with all kind of provision, so that there lacketh nothing but the guests to sit down ; and yet they who are called (without any cause) most unthankfully refuse to come. Which of you in such a case would not be moved? Who would not think a great injury and wrong done unto him ? Wherefore, most dearly beloved in Christ, take ye good heed, lest ye, withdrawing yourselves from this holy Supper, provoke God's indignation against you.

This part of the exhortation is most noteworthy on account of the thoroughness—we had almost said, the homeliness— with which the comparison between God's bounteous mercy and man's hospitality is set forth, and the latter is made to illustrate the former, even as in our Saviour's parable (Luke xiv. 21, 23).

It is surely a most wholesome thing to have this desire, on God's part, that His Table should be filled, that the room in His mansion should be occupied, that many should be brought in, that all men should come and avail themselves of this and the other means of grace, brought into most distinct view. God's bidding us to His gracious banquet is no empty and abstract argument of cold reason merely. It is the summons issued by man's best Friend, by Him who alone is truly worthy of the epithet good, by the Almighty King of heaven and earth.

Under these circumstances the exhortation bids us take good heed lest, by withdrawing ourselves from the holy Supper, we provoke God's indignation against us.

As to pleas like those advanced in the parable, I have bought a yoke of oxen, I have bought a piece of ground, I have married a wife, and all such hindrances of harmless, worldly occupation, the exhortation speaks in these dignified and fitting terms :—

x

It is an easy matter for a man to say, I will not communicate, because I am otherwise hindered with worldly business. But such excuses are not so easily accepted and allowed before God.

Any man, on the slightest reflection, feels at once that the most harmless and virtuous occupation should not hinder one from hearkening to the divine call, but, contrariwise, God's gifts to us in our property, our work, or our domestic relationships, are so many added motives for our obeying Him, thanking Him, and rendering Him the tribute of our most loving remembrance.

Then, besides these harmless hindrances, another set of obstructions, which keep men from God, are thus brought into view :—

If any man say, I am a grievous sinner, and therefore am afraid to come : wherefore then do ye not repent and amend ? When God calleth you, are ye not ashamed to say ye will not come ? When ye should return to God, will ye excuse yourselves, and say ye are not ready ? Consider earnestly with yourselves how little such feigned excuses will avail before God. They that refused the feast in the Gospel, because they had bought a farm, or would try their yokes of oxen, or because they were married, were not so excused, but counted unworthy of the heavenly feast.

The directness and plain speaking of this remonstrance with the sinner in his wilfulness, and with the ungodly in his carelessness, need no comment.

And, upon this, the exhortation proceeds :—

I, for my part, shall be ready ; and, according to mine Office, I bid you in the Name of God, I call you in Christ's behalf, I exhort you, as ye love your own salvation, that ye will be partakers of this holy Communion. And as the Son of God did vouchsafe to yield up His soul by death upon the Cross for your salvation ; so it is your duty to receive the Communion in remembrance of the sacrifice of His death, as He Himself hath commanded : which if ye shall neglect to do, consider with yourselves how great injury ye do unto God, and how sore punishment hangeth over your heads for the same ; when ye wilfully abstain from the Lord's Table, and separate from your brethren, who come to feed on the banquet of that most heavenly food. These things if ye earnestly consider, ye will by God's grace return to a better mind : for the obtaining whereof we shall not cease to make our humble petitions unto Almighty God our heavenly Father.

In reading this part of the exhortation it should be remembered that, in the sixteenth and seventeenth centuries, the laxity of mediæval times, and the practice of the priest alone receiving the elements instead of the people communicating, had brought things to such a pass that, when the curate read this exhortation, it was often doubtful whether there would be three or four persons to join him in the celebration. Herein is the emphatic force of the words, " I, for my part, shall be ready."

Then, in the spirit of the ambassadors described by St. Paul in 2 Cor. v. 20, the curate proceeds, according to his office, to bid the people in God's name, on behalf of Christ, and for their own salvation's sake, to be partakers of this holy Communion.

Let it be observed, in connection with this entreaty, " As ye love your own salvation," that whilst there is no pledge of salvation materially conveyed with the bread and wine—that pledge being contingent on the subjective condition of the recipient, and being only conveyed to him by his own faith— there is Christ's distinct command that we should eat this bread and drink this wine in remembrance of Him ; and, consequently, to those who recognise the obligation of this command, disobedience is the refusing of Christ and His salvation ; and participation must be at least " generally necessary to salvation."

Very noticeable is the declaration of the Gospel message in the words, " As the Son of God did vouchsafe to yield up His soul by death upon the cross for your salvation ; " and upon this what follows ? No charge to come to private confession and absolution ; no command to receive the body and blood of Christ *objectively* present in the elements of bread and wine ; but a repetition of the Scriptural precept to receive the Communion or sign of fellowship with the Lord and with all His people, in remembrance of the sacrifice of His death, as He Himself hath commanded.

Then follows a warning of the " injury " to God and the 'punishment" to one's self involved in *wilfully* abstaining from the Lord's Table, and separating one's self from the fellowship and encouragement of those brethren who come to feed on the banquet of that most heavenly food. " Heavenly food ! "

Food which is not in the elements on earth, but is in heaven, whither, as the ancient Christian writers and Liturgies delighted to put it, we must "lift up our hearts" if we would really eat His heavenly flesh and drink His heavenly blood.

Most encouraging are the last clauses of this second exhortation. If ye earnestly consider these things, if ye keep your mind fixed on them, and if ye lay them to heart, there is no doubt, uncertainty, or contingency about the matter, but ye will, by God's promised grace and help, return to a better mind. And, for the obtaining of this, the minister will not fail to use the marvellously enjoined privilege of intercessory prayer and humble petitions to Almighty God our heavenly Father.

Instead of anathema or threat, such promise of intercession is a meet conclusion for these exhortations to the Communion.

(iii.) *The Opening Lord's Prayer.*

And now we take up the examination of the service itself. How the Lord's Prayer and the "Amen," at its conclusion, should be repeated by the people, with the priest, we have already learned from the two rubrics standing before the first Lord's Prayer in the morning service of the English Church.

Most appropriately and beautifully is this prayer of prayers appointed as the beginning of the administration of the Lord's Supper.

Our Father, which art in heaven, Hallowed be Thy Name. Thy kingdom come. Thy will be done in earth, As it is in heaven. Give us this day our daily bread. And forgive us our trespasses, As we forgive them that trespass against us. And lead us not into temptation ; But deliver us from evil. Amen.

The first two words, "Our Father," may be regarded as a summary of the whole Liturgy, the keynote of the entire service, for they bring us into communion with the Father, "My Father and your Father" as Jesus called Him after the resurrection (John xx. 17) ; and, by invoking that Father as "*our* Father," they bring us into fellowship and brotherhood with all men as His children. And this, surely, is the very spirit in which we should approach the Table of the

Lord, loving all men as our brothers, the children of our God and Father; and loving supremely Him who made us in His likeness, and who, when we by sin had marred the resemblance, did once again cause us, by Christ and in Christ, to be "created in righteousness and true holiness" (Eph. iv. 24).

This "our Father," we must not forget, is in heaven as well as upon earth; and if we would hold true and worthy communion with Him, we also must in heart thither ascend where Christ ever sitteth at the right hand of God. May we and all men learn to name Him reverently. Thus will reverence be in us and grow; and that reverence, being directed towards the pure and sinless and almighty spiritual Father, manifested in Jesus, will be the first and not least precious of the boons men can seek; " Hallowed be Thy Name."

But this " our Father" is the highest and the best; and, as such, is the eternal King of right. May His kingdom come, and its laws of righteousness be written in our hearts and minds as the perfect law of liberty, which can alone establish and maintain order and peace and goodwill among all men and all creatures. So, in our hearts and in the hearts of all men, may the kingdom of God and of His Christ be set up; " Thy kingdom come."

Not only may the laws of righteousness thus bear sway, but whatever, without being a written or a spoken law of the Most High, is His will, His *wish*, which He will not compel us to perform, but which, if we do it, will make us free indeed—may that His divine wish be done as perfectly, intelligently, and willingly by man and every creature upon earth, as it is done by the angel hosts, by the spirits of the just made perfect, by all the countless inhabitants of the air and of the far-off worlds, yea, even as it is done by planets and suns and all the orbs that move so gloriously and obediently through space by us immeasurable—" Thy will be done on earth, as it is in heaven."

And Thou, " our Father," who hast made and dost sustain us and all these Thy creatures, the tokens, by their resemblances and by their relationships and adaptations, of

Thy unity and of Thy wisdom, Thou art not far from any one of us. Thou knowest our weakness and our necessities; Thou givest us many things—givest us all things richly for enjoyment;[1] and yet Thou teachest us a wisdom that is above luxury, and superior to abundance; Thou teachest us, while we aim at the perfect and labour for the highest, to be content with what we have though it be little indeed: and thus Thou teachest us, and we pray, "Give us this day our sufficing bread."[2]

Thou wilt, in Thy bounty and Thy love, give us this and whatsoever else is needed and is good for us; this wilt Thou do, though we, alas! have, by our wilfulness and our ignorance, broken the fair order of Thy beauteous world, injured our fellow-creatures, and wrought confusion and mischief in those wondrous minds and hearts and consciences with which Thou hast endowed us. Still, these sins, which we have thus committed against Thee, cry out against us on all sides; they accuse and haunt and terrify us; and we exclaim, "Our Father," "forgive us our sins."[3]

And may Thy mercy, which delights in pardon, which sent Christ to seek and to save us and all who were lost and dead in sins—may that divine mercy teach us to forgive to the very utmost those who injure us. Every time we pray for Thy forgiveness of our sins, may we cultivate in ourselves the holiness and the happiness of a forgiving spirit; for so hast Thou, "our Father," taught us to associate our forgiving with our being forgiven, and therefore we implore Thee, "Forgive us our trespasses, as we forgive them that trespass against us."

Thou wilt not tempt us in such wise that we must be overcome. With each temptation Thou wilt make a way to escape that we may be able to bear it (1 Cor. x. 13); but, for our discipline, to train and develop our faith and character, we see that trials and temptations abound in the world. They are very potent and we are very weak. Of ourselves we are not sufficient for these things. And this is known to

---

[1] εἰς ἀπόλαυσιν. 1 Tim. vi. 17.   [2] τὸν ἄρτον ἡμῶν τὸν ἐπιούσιον.

[3] ἁμαρτίας (Luke xi. 4), sins, trespasses.

Thee, "our Father;" and so Thou teachest us, and we heartily pray, "Lead us not into temptation."

But if, for our spirit's growth, we must be tempted and tried, then let Thine almighty arm be our support and our rescue. Evil is very tremendous; and the spirit of evil, within us and without, is very powerful, so again we cry aloud to Thee, as Thou, "our Father," hast taught us, "But deliver us from evil."

So may it be. "Amen."

To us it seems difficult to imagine how either priest or people can be silent while this Lord's Prayer, with thoughts ten thousand times better and richer than any we can suggest, is being uttered, or when the opportunity presents itself for responding with an "Amen."

(iv.) *The Collect.*

As the Lord's Prayer carries us up to the very age of Christ and the apostles, and brings us into communion with them and with all the generations of saints who have since employed its holy supplications, so the Collect for Purity is derived to us from an antiquity of many centuries. It was, as we have seen, in the Salisbury Missal; and there are evidences of its being as old as the time of Alcuin, in the eighth century.

Its words are well-nigh as simple as they are grand :—

Almighty God, unto whom all hearts be open, all desires known, and from whom no secrets are hid ; Cleanse the thoughts of our hearts by the inspiration of Thy Holy Spirit, that we may perfectly love Thee, and worthily magnify Thy holy Name ; through Christ our Lord. *Amen.*

Most appropriate, surely, as the beginning of the Lord's Supper, the service emphatically of self-examination, is the invocation here used which reminds us that the God, with whom we have to do, is not only almighty, but especially is one who seeth in secret, and to whom the darkness and the light are both alike. However much careless sinners may fail to look into their own hearts, God seeth them altogether ; to Him all hearts are open ; to Him all desires, however un-watched by ourselves, however unsuspected by those most

intimate with us, are known; and from Him are hidden
no secrets, however insignificant and insidious they may yet
be, or however masterful and cankerous and disgraceful we
may have already permitted them to become. This Heart-
searcher it is to whom we are led by the collect; and the supplication we address to Him is, "Cleanse the thoughts of our
hearts."

There, at the very spring and fountain of all human
inclination, will, and energy, may the All-seeing begin His
purifying work. While the sin is yet a mere occasional
dream, hovering, cloudlike and undefined, over and almost
apart from the mind, may it be dispersed and expelled;
or if it have grown familiar, if it haunt us in every leisure
moment, and thrust itself intrusive into our busy hours,
or even into our times of prayer and pious meditation,
Thou, God, art almighty—the evil thought, too powerful for
us, is not so strong as Thou. Quench its unhallowed flame.
Stay its murderous life. "Cleanse the thoughts of our
hearts;" and as there can be no void place in nature—as
the unoccupied will soon be held by demons—as only Thy
presence is sweet and potent enough so to cleanse us, let
the blessed purification be effected by the inbreathing of Thy
Holy Spirit, that so we may, not a little only, not in measure
and in part merely, but wholly, devotedly, and perfectly give
our hearts to Thee in the love that knows no limit and can
reach no end. Thus may we be changed; may men take
notice of our altered life and character, and see that we have
been with Jesus and with God; and thus, seeing our good
works, may they glorify our Father in heaven. So may we
"worthily magnify Thy holy Name;" and may all this be
done by the Spirit and the Name and Intercession of "Christ
our Lord."

So may it be. "Amen."

(v.) *The Ten Commandments.*

And then from this general prayer, with admirable judgment does the English Liturgy lead us to the investigation
of details. In general terms, by themselves, lurks danger of

self-deception; but, avoiding private confession to any priest,
it is well to set before men searching particulars for self-
detection and self-recovery: and, accordingly, the rubric
enjoins :—

*Then shall the priest, turning to the people, rehearse distinctly all the Ten Commandments; and the
people still kneeling shall, after every Commandment, ask God mercy for their transgression
thereof for the time past, and grace to keep the same for the time to come, as followeth.*

The only point we wish to notice in this rubric is the
explanation given by it of the responses after each commandment. These, be it observed, are intended to ask God's
merciful pardon of our past transgressions in connection with
each command, and His gracious help in keeping the same for
the time to come.

To the Jews of old, just emerging from the Egyptian land
of bestial gods, about to enter the territory of Phœnician gods
of hateful lust like Ashtoreth, of direst cruelty like Moloch,
the first commandment communicated by Jehovah to his servant Moses for His people Israel was :—

God spake these words, and said; I am the Lord thy God : Thou
shalt have none other gods but Me.

" I," who send forth lightning and thunder, so making the
mountains to burn and smoke, so making the valleys to re-
verberate with the sound of a trumpet—" I," who slew the
animal deities of Egypt by the plagues, who sent Moses to
be your emancipator, who overthrew your enemies in the Red
Sea—" I," who am thus shown to you as the hater of cruelty
and slavery and oppression, as the sender of saviours, as the
judge between right and wrong, as the graver and writer of
commands for your eyes, as the speaker of words to your
minds—" I am the Lord," Jehovah, the being of all time that
was, that is, that shall be, " your God," your mighty one,
your hero, your incomparable and unique. There can be only
one incomparable, unique, supreme. " Thou shalt have none
other gods but Me."

And if, to the Jew, this was the first commandment, surely
its spirit and import should come home to us no less. " I,"
the creator and arranger of all things,[1] from the tiniest

---

[1] Θεός, derived from τίθημι, I set.

animalcule shown by the microscope to the vastest systems
revealed by mathematics or by the telescope—" I," in whom
you live and move and have your being—" I," whose works
you can increasingly study and comprehend because you are
My offspring made in My likeness—" I," whose judgment you
forecast in your discernment between good[1] and evil, between
generous and base, between hateful and lovable—" I," whose
co-eternal Son became the incarnate messenger to man, the
Saviour from sin—" I," not gold, nor man's praise, nor art,
nor even science, none of these nor any creature, but only
" I " am thine Eternal, thy Lord, the Spirit, the one supreme,
unique, thy God.

Well may we respond to this command with a cry for
pardon that we have not always kept it in the past, and with a
supplication that our hearts may be thereto inclined in all the
time to come :—

Lord, have mercy upon us, and incline our hearts to keep this law.

And then the second commandment is to be rehearsed
distinctly by the " minister " :—

Thou shalt not make to thyself any graven image, nor the likeness of
any thing that is in heaven above, or in the earth beneath, or in the
water under the earth. Thou shalt not bow down to them, nor worship
them : for I the Lord thy God am a jealous God, and visit the sins of the
fathers upon the children, unto the third and fourth generation of them
that hate Me, and shew mercy unto thousands in them that love Me, and
keep My commandments.

No image of a thing on earth, in heaven, or in any conceivable locality, shalt thou make to bow down thereto and
worship it. The Eternal Lord, Jehovah, thy supreme and
unique, thy God, will not, in His loving wish that thou shouldst
have only the highest for thine ideal, the perfect for thine
aim and guide—in this His divine and generous love, He will
not give His honour to another, He is a jealous God : and,
moreover, to check and arrest thee in any violation of this or
any other law of His, be it observed and remembered by thee,
that, while " the righteousness of the righteous shall be upon
him and the wickedness of the wicked shall be upon him "

[1] God, a word akin to " good " in our tongue and in all the Teutonic
languages.

(Ezek. xviii. 20), so that there shall be no truth in the idea that the son or the father, if he repent and turn from evil ways, bears the iniquity of the other; yet, still, there is tremendous truth in the saying that, except repentance intervene, sin is cumulative, characters and constitutions degenerate, God visits the sins of the fathers upon the children, from generation to generation, as long as they continue to hate and disobey Him; but let that hatred turn to love, that disobedience to keeping of His commandments, and then His mercy, His forgiveness, His repenting Him of the evil He had said He would do, will show itself in all its divine glory.

If, thus, all spurious imitations of God were forbidden to the Jew, surely not less are they forbidden to us for whom, though the Son of God was once manifested in the flesh, yet now, for eighteen centuries—in order that, in our minds and hearts, we might know His mind and spirit—He has been withdrawn from us in the flesh, so that not even the great apostle (2 Cor. v. 16) could any longer know Christ after the flesh.

For us, then, no less than for the Jew, there must be no making of pictures and images of God to worship them; and even of Christ, it must not be the flesh, not the likeness of His body in its beauty or in its crushed condition, not the " Bambino " or the " Ecce Homo " of the artist, that we must worship; but only the spirit and mind of Him who went about doing good, who blessed when He was reviled, and, so doing, as ever, He showed us the " Father." This Spirit God in Christ, and Him only, must we set up for our worship; and, even so, by constant reference to the original memorials of Him in the Gospels and in the Epistles, we must take good heed lest we image Him even to our minds as otherwise than the one God who is "love," who is "our Father," who is "the Saviour of all men, especially of them that believe " (1 Tim. iv. 10), and yet, once more, who is, for the overcoming and destroying of all evil, " a consuming fire " (Heb. xii. 29).

Forgiveness for the past, and help for the future, may well be supplicated in view of these precepts:—

Lord, have mercy upon us, and incline our hearts to keep this law.

And so we are brought to the study of the third commandment:—

Thou shalt not take the Name of the Lord thy God in vain : for the Lord will not hold him guiltless, that taketh His Name in vain.

Words are the product and utterance of character, so that a man, even among men, may to a considerable extent be condemned or justified by his ordinary and familiar language. And, moreover, harsh and cruel words, or coarse and licentious words, propagate in the society where they are employed the very characters and dispositions which they evince. Rough talk, proceeding from rude breasts, creates in the speaker, and in those conversing with him, a growing rudeness. This observation is apt to hold good even where the rough words are spoken, at first, not in the full intent and significance of their cruelty or licentiousness. Words used "in vain," quite idly, grow familiar, till, some day, their meaning obtrudes itself on the speaker or the hearer, and thus a new realm of evil is exposed to the view of the ignorant and the unwary.

How much wisdom as well as piety is illustrated in the warning not to take God's Name in vain! If that which should be a word often on men's lips, but ever lifting them up to their highest capacities of thought and feeling, yea, ever raising them beyond their own powers into the divine likeness,—if that Name, without such hallowing and elevating associations, be made familiar as an empty phrase, how much is lost to the spirit and character of the man who so speaks of God without being lifted Godwards.

But this mighty Name will not consent to be an idle word, a mere empty sound. It will become, to him who consciously takes it in vain, a root of profanity and blasphemy ; and that sound, whose every repetition ought to be a fresh call to higher life with the Father and the Saviour of our spirits, will be conducive to more and more deadness to God and the things of God, if it be not suggestive of light irreverence and growing irreligion, if it do not become a word by which we verily mock and insult the sanctity of Heaven.

Such a lesson on words and their power and their peril—

especially on words that ought to be associated with God and the things of God, is read to us by the third commandment.

After prayer for pardon of our faults in this respect and for future help in the words,

Lord, have mercy upon us, and incline our hearts to keep this law,

we are brought to the fourth commandment :—

Remember that thou keep holy the sabbath day. Six days shalt thou labour, and do all that thou hast to do ; but the seventh day is the sabbath of the Lord thy God. In it thou shalt do no manner of work, thou, and thy son, and thy daughter, thy man-servant, and thy maid-servant, thy cattle, and the stranger that is within thy gates. For in six days the Lord made heaven and earth, the sea, and all that in them is, and rested the seventh day : wherefore the Lord blessed the seventh day, and hallowed it.

To the Jew this spoke of the seventh day of the week as the sabbath ; and this day he was to " keep holy." At one time Israel as a nation, or the individual Jew, would be in such a frame of mind that the gathering of manna, or the collecting a few sticks on the sabbath day, would be felt as a violation of its sanctity. In such cases God would mercifully provide, and enable the man of scruples to keep the day holy according to the requirements of his conscience ; and woe to that man who dishonoured the day.

At another time, centuries later, a condition of national thought and experience would be reached in which it would be known that the sabbath is not an end in itself, but a means to an end. " Man was not made for the sabbath, but the sabbath for man." Man was not created to carry out certain sabbatical observances, but the sabbath was instituted to give man rest, and to cultivate in him those habits and resolves of piety which are the highest exercises of his spirit and which give an elevation and a sweetness to all his other occupations. When such a time should be come, it would behove the Jew still to " keep holy " the sabbath day, but his proper mode of observing it would not be as a precisionist who could not allow a grain of corn to be plucked without a murmur, but, rather, he would hallow the day of rest by a special remembrance, in all its hours, that God's word is,

"I will have mercy and not sacrifice." Happy the Jew who could rise to this better use of the sabbath, and could employ it for works of healing and beneficence and tolerance— yea, most happy the Jew who, in presence of Jesus as the Messiah, could perceive that he stood confronted by a Son of man who was greater even than the sabbath day.

In whatever sense each Jew, or generation of Jews, knew best to keep the sabbath holy, in that sense—whether in the highest observance like Jesus, or in the lowest like the most scrupulous of the Pharisees—he was in duty bound to keep the day holy; he was to do nothing which could be called "work;" and he was to use his power and influence to extend to man and beast the same blessed period of rest from work, even from that work which was enjoined for him on all the other six days of the week. Observable is the considerateness for servants, and cattle, and strangers of other nations, which is implied and inculcated in this part of the Jewish commandment.

As a ground for this sabbatical observance, the Jew was reminded that all creatures had been brought into existence by the Eternal in six days or periods of time, until, in the seventh period, Jehovah changed His work from that of creation mainly to that of sustaining—we say "changed His work" and so rested, not only because this is the best kind of rest, but also because of the testimony of Jesus (John v. 17), "My Father worketh hitherto, and I work."

By this command the Jew was bound, and a very high and solemn obligation it was for him, whether it rested on God's ceasing from creation in the seventh period[1] of the world's history (Exod. xx. 11), or on considerateness and sympathy for servants who would require rest (Deut. v. 15).

But, for us Christians, the obligation of this Jewish law, in its letter and as a ceremony, is at an end. Like the whole law of Moses, it has decayed and waxen old and vanished away (Heb. viii. 13). In respect of this fourth commandment,

---

[1] We use the words "day" and "period" exchangeably, because in Hebrew, as in English, a period of any duration is styled a "day," as "of small things," etc.

as of all the positive injunctions of Judaism, there has been "a disannulling of the commandment going before, for the weakness and unprofitableness thereof" (Heb. vii. 18). No man is to be allowed to "judge us" Christians "in respect of sabbaths" (Col. ii. 16).

Yet while all this is true, there is another sense in which Jesus came not to destroy the law, but to fulfil it, in part by glorifying it in His own life and in His own sacrifice, in part by giving new life and spirit to its every precept. For, indeed, no sane man would doubt but that a law of the Eternal, once enunciated, must ever contain a germ and principle of wisdom which it would be well for all ages to ascertain and observe.

What, then, shall we say is the principle of this fourth commandment? Surely, the wisdom and duty—experience, in the French Revolution, and in other times and places, teaches us to say *the general necessity*—of man's resting at stated periods from the otherwise exhausting and wearisome routine of his regular work.

And, again, the example of the divine institution for the Jews may well combine with the custom of the Christian Church 'from ancient times, to fix for our rest one day in seven, and that the first day of the week—the Lord's Day, as the day of Christ's resurrection had come to be called before the writing of the Apocalypse (Rev. i. 10)—the Sunday of which Justin Martyr wrote, as we saw above. Furthermore, the principle or spirit of the fourth commandment will lead the Christian to associate the observance of rest from ordinary work on the Lord's Day with remembrance of God and the vast epochs of that creative work whose latest and highest product was man. Nor will the Lord's Day fail to bring to the mind of the Christian happy and thankful remembrance of Christ and His resurrection, and all that is suggested by the Son of man and His victory over death and the grave.

In whatever other ways the Christian may deem it right to re-create his body, soul, and spirit, on the happy day that celebrates, each week, the resurrection, he cannot fail to recognise the duty and the privilege of acts of worship and of beneficence and charity and tolerance ; and if such be felt, for us, to be the abiding spirit and obligation of the fourth commandment, well may we ask for pardon as to past derelictions and for help in future obedience :—

Lord, have mercy upon us, and incline our hearts to keep this law.

And so we come to the fifth commandment :—

Honour thy father and thy mother ; that thy days may be long in the land, which the Lord thy God giveth thee.

Of course, the promise, with which this command closes, was given to the Jews and to them only.   To us, as Christians, there is no possession of an earthly Canaan promised ; nor is the prospect assured to us that, if we honour our parents, we shall live long in this world.   Jesus did not live long Himself; and it is enough for us, the servants, to be as our Master. His kingdom is not of this world ; and we, like Him, must look forward to a recompense and a crown of glory in the future and the eternal.

We do not mean to deny that a life of Christian purity, piety, and freedom tends generally to health of mind and body, and so to longevity ; but this " promise of the life which now is " is not the specific covenanted blessing of Christianity.   A man may, as a good Christian, honour his parents and yet die early, for instance, in battle or in the crash of a railway accident.

But, however this assurance of a prolonged enjoyment of Canaan may have been offered to the Jew only, the injunction of the commandment addresses itself to our common humanity.   It is good for man, instead of slaying the aged and the decrepit as useless and as cumbersome, to cultivate all tenderness in dealing with the infirm.   It is especially good for man to carry on this sanctifying helpfulness and sweetness towards those of his own family and household.   Reverence, in any character, is a source of beauty to those who contemplate it and a source of peaceful delight and strength to those who possess it.

We say nothing of the advantage that must generally accrue to children who so honour their parents and their elders as to be guided and enlightened by foregoing stores of experience. We speak, rather, of the happiness of being reverent towards all men, and especially towards our parents; and we speak of the ripening effect on character, of the lifting up of domestic life and joy, consequent upon cherishing and honouring in their advancing age those parents who watched and guarded us in the feebleness of infancy and amidst the perils of youth. We speak of the golden chain of love and happiness which, by such honouring of our father and mother, shall be made to consecrate and unite the entire course of existence, the whole circle of the family, from the cradle to the grave, from the infant to the aged grandsire.

And yet, again, to Christians, as parents, this command will not fail to bring into remembrance the co-related duties that we owe to our children. How can these be better expressed than in the language of St. Paul? "And, ye fathers, provoke not your children to wrath; but bring them up in the nurture and admonition of the Lord" (Eph. vi. 4).

Alas! for our faults in relation to this, as to each other precept of the Decalogue, we too deeply need to pray:—

Lord, have mercy upon us, and incline our hearts to keep this law.

Of the sixth commandment,

Thou shalt do no murder,

what shall we venture to say beyond drawing attention to the words of Christ Himself, in which He warns us that the spirit of this injunction is woefully violated by us if we be angry with our brother without a cause, or if we indulge in the temper which looks contemptuously on another and is ready to express itself in such utterances as, "Raca," thou empty personage, or "More," thou fool (Matt. v. 22)?

This sixth commandment, read in the right spirit of a Jew and still more of a Christian, would thus banish from the world all unkindly and disrespectful words or thoughts concerning our fellow-men. It would lead us to overcome evil with good; it would establish righteousness and benevolence as the ruling passions and habits of mankind; it would lead us to recognise the image of God in every man, however fallen and marred ; and, so, this command would bring us, as it did the apostles, to uphold and practise the philosophy and religion which lie in such a maxim as, "Honour all men. Love the brotherhood" (1 Pet. ii. 17).

Truly, in face of this precept, we may well exclaim :—

Lord, have mercy upon us, and incline our hearts to keep this law.

Upon this follows the seventh commandment :—

Thou shalt not commit adultery.

To nations and individuals immersed in sensuality and licentiousness, as were the Jews so often in their history, and as were the Romans and those among whom they bore rule, over the whole world, in our Saviour's time, the mere veto of this command was a revelation. Abstinence from the hideous and cruel vices of the harem and other places lifts the abstainers into a new world of manliness, self-respect, and influence. Of this, however, and of the grosser forms of vice touched by this command, Christianity has happily made it impossible for us to treat in pages like these. Wherever the command, as a veto, may still be needed, here, and in the New Testament, it stands in all its simple force.

But to Christians, of the slightest earnestness and intelligence, its spirit addresses a higher tone of admonition. It teaches men to be habitually watchful over every word and thought and act in dealing with the weaker sex. Chivalrous in protecting their peace and purity, we should regard "the elder women as mothers and the younger as sisters" (1 Tim. v. 2) ; and when, in the providence of God, the kindred soul is found, the one woman met who, so long as life lasts, is to be companion, helpmeet, bone of our bone, flesh of our flesh, we two one—then should there be, with thankfulness to God for the holy institution of marriage and for the blessed gift of a wife, entire gentleness, consideration, and watchfulness for that one woman who concentrates in herself all our love and yet causes the chivalrous spirit of beneficence to go forth from us more intelligently, and therefore with better sympathy, towards all the sisters of whom she is the type and the ideal.

A corresponding behaviour of women and of wives is no

less binding upon them, and, in its devotedness, sympathy, and fondness, is beautifully portrayed in Scripture, in many a passage besides that one (Eph. v. 33) which bids the wife see that she reverence her husband.

How such a relationship of man to woman has constituted a chief ingredient in the power of the Teutonic race, is known to every student of history. How it has softened the manners of Europe and of Christendom, and been a main characteristic in the glory of Christianity, is no less indubitable. To what an extent heart-union between the father and mother blesses a home—alone makes a *home*—for the children and for all the household, is a truth familiar to every observer of life ; as is, also, the beneficial moral effect of such a home of sweetness upon all who live in its blessed atmosphere. The physiologist could probably tell of the ill effects on families and races (physically) of the want of pure and fitting love betwixt parents ; and he could bear witness, likewise, of the physical health and robustness that are apt to attach to the progeny which come of loving parentage.

Look at this commandment as we may, its original ordinance, and its enforcement by the religion of Christ, are admirable ; and we must feel, the more we examine it and ourselves and the society which surrounds us, the more need is there for us all to join in the supplication :—

Lord, have mercy upon us, and incline our hearts to keep this law.

Concerning the eighth commandment,

Thou shalt not steal,

we shall say nothing here, because of the simplicity and directness with which it enjoins respect for the property of others, and because the tenth commandment goes still more deeply into the motives that prompt to theft.

When we contemplate the destitution and poverty so widely prevalent in the world, and when we reflect on the spirit too common even among those having abundant possessions, where " much would have more," the necessity makes itself felt by us of joining in the petition :—

Lord, have mercy upon us, and incline our hearts to keep this law.

In no state of society is the precept of the next commandment useless :—

Thou shalt not bear false witness against thy neighbour.

The wisdom, however, of such a maxim, in a condition of
things such as existed among the Jews, is very striking. The
mischief that flows from false witness in courts of law is so ex-
tensive, and the evil results of colloquial scandal and slander
are so subtle and far-reaching, that we should, indeed, examine
well our lives to ascertain that our habitual modes of speech,
alike in the easier and lighter converse of society, and in the
more formal and grave declarations of business and justice,
are truthful and candid and as little as possible injurious to
our fellow-men.

In dealing with this portion of the Decalogue, as, indeed,
with all our duty to our neighbour, it will be most desirable to
test our compliance with each precept by inquiring how far
we carry out its maxims as honestly and heartily in the
interests of other men as we should think it right for them to
do in our interests—whether, in a word, we habitually observe
the golden rule, of doing as we would be done by, in reticence
as to the lesser faults of our neighbours, in speaking out
plainly unfavourable truth concerning them when it is important and, in the judgment of conscience, right that evil
deeds should not be concealed; and whether, generally, we
think and speak the best we truly can of every man.

Here is a field for self-examination that demands much
attention at all times, especially when we are approaching that Table of the Lord where we pledge ourselves to
fellowship with man as well as to communion with God in
Christ. Few, indeed, will there be who, on searching into
their common habits in these respects, will not be compelled
to grieve over many a fall as they utter the prayer :—

Lord, have mercy upon us, and incline our hearts to keep this law.

And now, in prescribing duty and in suggesting a course
of self-examination, the Prayer-book brings us to the tenth
commandment :—

Thou shalt not covet thy neighbour's house, thou shalt not covet thy neighbour's wife, nor his servant, nor his maid, nor his ox, nor his ass, nor any thing that is his.

The literal precept, on the face of it, enjoins that, as we look upon our fellow-man, in the possession of all which is his, we shall keep back and repress any envious desire to dispossess him injuriously, or against his will, of a single thing in order that we may enrich ourselves by its possession. Useful, however, and searching as is this Jewish command—precluding as it does all theft and hard bargaining and over-reaching, or the entertaining a desire to act in any such manner—the Christian will assuredly feel that, in view of his heavenly Father, who bountifully giveth men all things freely to enjoy, and in view of Christ, who, instead of coveting that which belonged to any man, freely gave Himself and His life to all men and for all men, we ought to cultivate within our hearts the generous sympathy which, so far from envying other men's welfare, rejoices in it and contributes to its augmentation by every possible means of gratulation and good wish; thus, actually and in detail, rejoicing with them that do rejoice.

How many a thankless and unjoyous heart might we thus help to appreciate God's gifts, and to delight much more than ordinarily and at present in the abundance of the gifts and in the goodness of the Giver. Assuredly, there is too little gratitude to God for all the good things of nature, talents, and grace that He bestows upon us; and there is far too little joy in the reception and use of those His gifts.

Well will it be for the world generally, and for ourselves also, if, by entering into the Christian spirit of this tenth commandment, we not only rejoice in the welfare and in the possessions of other men, but if we also, as it were, infect them with a spirit of delight in the employment of their gifts and talents, and of gratitude to the bounteous Giver of all good things.

Thus have these commandments of the Decalogue shown us a wide field of duty to God and man which we should explore, in preparation for the Lord's Supper, to ascertain how far we have complied with their letter and their spirit in the past; how far we are resolutely bent on conforming our lives to them, by God's unfailing help, in time to come; how far we are humbled in contrition for our past sins; how far our prayers to God, and our present acts and intentions towards man, are a pledge and a beginning of a new and happy, as well as self-denying, life in Christ and in His Spirit.

Beautiful is the supplication that is prescribed to follow upon all these commands of duty and suggestions of self-scrutiny :—

Lord, have mercy upon us, and write all these Thy laws in our hearts, we beseech Thee.

Not only are we here taught to implore God's forgiving mercy for our bygone transgressions, but the prayer, taking up that harmony of the Old and New Testaments which is produced by the quotation of Jeremiah (xxxi. 31) in the Epistle to the Hebrews (viii. 10), so leads us to beseech that God will write all His laws in our hearts.

Let the communicant weigh well the change, to himself and to the world, if all God's laws, in the spirit and in the letter of them, were thus inscribed upon men's affections so that we might constantly delight in doing God's holy and beneficent will.

This would indeed produce a new heaven and a new earth wherein should dwell righteousness.

With these few and imperfect, but we trust suggestive, remarks we must leave this important part of the Communion Service.

(vi.) *Collects for the Queen.*

It is no new thing for the Christian Church to recognise the duty of making supplications, prayers, intercessions, and giving of thanks for all men, for kings and for all that are in authority, that we may lead a quiet and peaceable life in all godliness and honesty (1 Tim. ii. 1, 2). Accordingly, at this point in the service, there are introduced into the English Liturgy Collects for the Queen, one or other of which is to be used at the discretion of the minister. Such prayers, in longer or shorter forms, were in all the old Liturgies and Mass-books, in some part or other of the service.

In the English Prayer-book they are thus introduced :—

Then shall follow one of these two Collects for the Queen, the priest standing as before, and saying,

Let us pray.

Almighty God, whose kingdom is everlasting, and power infinite ; Have mercy upon the whole Church : and so rule the heart of Thy chosen Servant Victoria, our Queen and Governor, that she (knowing whose minister she is) may above all things seek Thy honour and glory : and that we, and all her subjects (duly considering whose authority she hath), may faithfully serve, honour, and humbly obey her, in Thee, and for Thee, according to Thy blessed Word and ordinance ; through Jesus Christ our Lord, who with Thee and the Holy Ghost liveth and reigneth, ever one God, world without end. *Amen.*

Or,

Almighty and everlasting God, we are taught by Thy holy Word, that the hearts of Kings are in Thy rule and governance, and that Thou dost dispose and turn them as it seemeth best to Thy godly wisdom : We humbly beseech Thee so to dispose and govern the heart of Victoria Thy Servant, our Queen and Governor, that, in all her thoughts, words, and works, she may ever seek Thy honour and glory, and study to preserve Thy people committed to her charge, in wealth, peace, and godliness : Grant this, O merciful Father, for Thy dear Son's sake, Jesus Christ our Lord. *Amen.*

The rubric, it may be noticed, enjoins the priest to stand as before ; that is, instead of " turning to the people," as had been his position while reading the commandments, he is to stand at the north side of the Table as he had done while saying the Lord's Prayer.

Of course, it was not contemplated that these collects should be read in the same congregation which had already taken part in the similar petitions of the Litany, or of Morning or Evening Prayer. The repetitions arise, as we have seen, from throwing what were intended to be several separate services into one : and common sense, if not that which is decorous in piety, would indicate that the officiating clergyman should use, in each congregation, not more than one Collect for the Queen ; and that, when the Prayer for the Church Militant is to be said, no other collect or suffrage for the monarch should be rehearsed. Surely, it needs not to be said that one prayer for her Majesty would be at least as significant of loyalty as two or three, and it would certainly be in other respects more becoming.

The ancient exhortation, "Let us pray," occurring here, is worthy of a passing notice. It was, in certain ages of the Church's history, wont to be called aloud, chiefly by the deacons, as an admonition to the people to be on the alert in their devotions; and, assuredly, its precept should be distinctly spoken, and reverently attended to, in these days. It might not seldom be useful in recalling some wandering thoughts.

The burthen of the first collect is that God, as the ever-lasting and almighty King, will so rule the heart of the earthly monarch and of all her subjects that the Queen may remember she is God's minister, and may seek, above all things, His honour and glory; while her subjects, remember-ing that her authority is derived from God, may faithfully and religiously discharge their part of the relationship.

The second collect, basing itself upon the truth that all hearts are subject to the divine sovereignty, prays that our monarch may be so disposed by God that, in all her thoughts, words, and works, she may ever seek the honour and glory of God, and the preservation of God's people committed to her charge in welfare (the meaning of "wealth" two hundred years ago), peace, and godliness.

(vii.) *The Nicene Creed.*

The Prayer for the Queen being ended, the rubric enjoins as follows :—

Then shall be said the Collect of the Day. And immediately after the Collect the priest shall read the Epistle, saying, The Epistle [or, The portion of Scripture appointed for the Epistle] is written in the —— Chapter of —— beginning at the —— Verse. And the Epistle ended, he shall say, Here endeth the Epistle. Then shall he read the Gospel (the people all standing up) say-ing, The holy Gospel is written in the —— Chapter of —— beginning at the —— Verse. And the Gospel ended, shall be sung or said the Creed following, the people still standing, as before.

Of the "Collects for the Day" it is interesting to remark that, with a few exceptions, and subject to such alterations as it was necessary to make, at the time of the Reformation, in order to clear them of the superstitious and unscriptural accretions of the Middle Ages, they are of great antiquity, coming to us, through the Mass-books of the Western Church, from the fifth and sixth centuries, as is shown by the sacramentaries of Leo, Gelasius, and Gregory.

The selection of the Epistles and Gospels is, generally, of no less antiquity. It is quite worth noticing what a difference of spirit is shown between the simple injunctions for the reading of the Epistle and Gospel in the English service, and the complicated and highly ornate ritual attaching to their reading in the Missal. Such an abandonment of excessive and distracting rites and ceremonies should indicate to all thoughtful persons how averse the English Reformed Church, as by law established in England, is from everything which goes beyond the simplicity of Christ, and the dictates of moderation and good taste.

After the Gospel is to be sung or said "the Creed following, the people still standing." This Creed is popularly called the " *Nicene* " Creed; but, of course, every student of history is aware that the Creed, here recited, is the Nicene with additions.

Of these additions, the largest part come from the Council of Constantinople (A.D. 381). They consist of nearly all the words following "in the Holy Ghost." We say nearly all, because a very important addition, the phrase " *and the Son*," descriptive of the procession of the Holy Spirit, comes from none of the first four general councils, but is derived from quite a different source, namely, from the Spanish Council of Toledo (A.D. 589), the edict of Charlemagne in the ninth century, and the still later decision of Rome (A.D. 1014). However Scriptural and true may be the doctrine of the double procession of the Spirit from the Father *and the Son*, there can be no doubt but that the irregular mode of introducing these words, "and from the Son," into the so-called Nicene Creed, has had a lamentable effect in dividing the Churches of the East and West; and one may be allowed to express a wish that either this innovation might be omitted from the Creed of the West, or that both East and West might agree upon a substitute for it, such as, " Who proceedeth from the Father and is sent by the Son."

As to the general character of the Creed, we may best

describe it as a triumphant song of faith. It is a joyful enumeration of the particulars on which is based the strength of our Christian reliance. Hence, as we think, the appropriateness of the rubrical permission to *sing* the Creed instead of merely saying it.

For the authority on which the Creed rests, and the sense in which it is to be accepted and believed, the eighth of our Thirty-Nine Articles has something very important to teach us, namely, that all the three Creeds should be believed because "they may be proved by most certain warrants of Holy Scripture."

If we were required to understand the numerous portions of the Creed as defined and interpreted by the historical circumstances out of which they sprang, our position would be most trying. It would be necessary for us to study, and keep in memory, the dark and intricate metaphysical disputes of the early post-apostolic Christian centuries. As a result of such studies, very few intellects would arrive at any clear apprehension of the questions then debated. Still fewer would, for any length of time, retain a recollection of the points they had apprehended. And of those who thought they understood the matter, some would rank themselves on one side, and some on the other, to fight over again the distressing word-battles of the Alexandrian and other Churches.

Instead of all this, the English churchman may ascertain the Scriptural sense of each part of his Creed, and with that he may be contented, and may humbly rejoice.

How glorious is it, for instance, to rest, amidst all vicissitudes, upon the assurance that the one all-powerful Creator of heaven and earth, of things which we can see, and of things too minute or too distant to be seen by our eye,—this one Creator is our "*Father*"!

And yet, again, what comfort is there in believing that the man Jesus, who stood in the unique relation to that Father of there having been no time when He was not God's Son and Himself divine, is our Lord and Master and Friend and Saviour, who proves Himself all this by His wondrous birth, by His truly human life with all its temptations and its

sinlessness, by His cruel death under Pontius Pilate, by His
burial, His resurrection, His ascension, by His intercession
for us now at God's right hand, and by the certainty that
He shall one day be our Judge to discern between good and
evil, and our King to establish the reign of endless and infinite right !

To all who struggle, to those who seem worsted, and to
those who only in part triumph in the great war between sin
and righteousness, what solace, strength, and sanctification is
in this portion of our Creed, every word of which is only an
echo of that which apostles and apostolic men teach us in
Holy Writ !

And, moreover, while we can neither see God nor the
blessed Son Jesus, what a joy is it to be assured that a Spirit,
a living, ever-present Power who is above matter, who comes
from the Father by the Son, who is so thoroughly one with
the Father and the Son that they cannot be worshipped and
glorified without His being also worshipped and glorified—
that this Spirit, who was of old, and spake by all the prophets,
is our Lord, and Master, and Friend, and Sanctifier ; yea, is
the Giver of life to every man and every creature which lives
or ever has lived !

Worthy to be appended to this triumph-song of our faith
in God, is the conviction that, for the comfort and salvation
of man, God has instituted one *Kyriake* (which we pronounce
" Church " and the Scotch pronounce " Kirk," which is,
however, a Greek word signifying the whole assembly of men
belonging to the Lord)—and this one kirk, or " Kyriake," or
Church, which was taught by the apostles, and provided by
them with an organization fitted for those times, but free to
be further adapted to the changing necessities of each age
and of all circumstances—this one Church, apostolic alike in
its primitive teaching and in its complete freedom, we believe
that God instituted, not to be national, for a single people
like the Church of the Jews, but to be " catholic," universal, drawing into itself all men in every nation (1 Tim. ii 4 ;
Matt. xxviii. 19 ; 2 Pet. iii. 9).   Thus may we, without
reference to councils or Fathers, that were far from being in

all things trustworthy oracles and guides, declare our happy belief in one apostolic Church which God wishes to make catholic, and which only the sin of man hinders, in the mean while, from becoming all-comprehensive.

Then, again, as to those who already profess and call themselves Christians, it is, according to this Creed, our blessed persuasion that all who have been baptized with water, in the name of the Father, the Son, and the Holy Spirit, are bound together by that one baptism for the putting away—the forgiveness and abandonment—of sins (Eph. iv. 5). Under whatever form of Church government, by whomsoever administered, so this sacrament of baptism be fitly and worthily received, it is an effective sign of the remission of sins ; and it binds the entire body of them that have received it into the deepest and best of unities and brotherhoods that earth can know. Moreover, we believe and anticipate with hope that, in bodies however changed and glorified, still in bodies endowed with personal identity, conscious of the past and capable of recognition, there shall be a rising again of the dead, and for them, as for all who shall not have died when Christ returns to judge the quick and the dead, we believe there shall be a future of that eternal life which con-sists (John xvii. 3) in " knowing the only true God, and Jesus Christ whom He hath sent."

Such is a brief epitome of the meaning of that Creed in which, as we approach the Lord's Supper, we are bidden joy-fully, in song or otherwise, to celebrate the strength of our reliance upon our God and Father in Jesus Christ by the Holy Spirit.

The words of the Creed are these :—

I believe in one God the Father Almighty, Maker of heaven and earth, And of all things visible and invisible :

And in one Lord Jesus Christ, the only-begotten Son of God, Begotten of His Father before all worlds, God of God, Light of Light, Very God of very God, Begotten, not made, Being of one substance with the Father ; By whom all things were made, Who for us men, and for our salvation came down from heaven, And was incarnate by the Holy Ghost of the Virgin Mary, And was made man, And was crucified also for us under Pontius Pilate. He suffered and was buried, And the third day He rose again according to the Scriptures, And ascended into heaven, And sitteth on the right hand of the Father.   And He shall come again with glory to judge both the quick and the dead : Whose kingdom shall have no end.

And I believe in the Holy Ghost, The Lord and Giver of life, Who proceedeth from the Father and the Son, Who with the Father and the Son together is worshipped and glorified, Who spake by the Prophets. And I believe one Catholic and Apostolic Church.   I acknowledge one Baptism for the remission of sins, And I look for the Resurrection of the dead, And the life of the world to come.   Amen.

(viii.) *Rubrics after the Nicene Creed.*

After the Creed there follow these three rubrics :—

Then the curate shall declare unto the people what holy-days, or fasting-days, are in the week following to be observed.   And then also (if occasion be) shall notice be given of the Communion ; and briefs, citations, and excommunications read.   And nothing shall be proclaimed or published in the Church, during the time of Divine Service, but by the minister : nor by him any thing, but what is prescribed in the rules of this book, or enjoined by the Queen, or by the Ordinary of the place.
Then shall follow the Sermon, or one of the Homilies already set forth, or hereafter to be set forth, by authority.
Then shall the priest return to the Lord's Table, and begin the Offertory, saying one or more of these sentences following, as he thinketh most convenient in his discretion.

The first of these rubrics makes this the time for the general giving of notices in church.   We have already observed that the notice of Communion is to be given at this point in the service in the minister's own words—one or other of the longer exhortations, which stand after the Prayer for the Church Militant, being used at the close of the sermon.

In the service of 1662, this was the time appointed for publishing banns of marriage ; but the Marriage Act of 26 Geo. II. (c. 33, s. 1) appointed their publication "immediately after the second lesson" of Morning or (failing that) of Evening Prayer.   "Briefs" were royal letters authorizing a collection for some charitable purpose; and "citations" called upon accused persons to appear, at a given time and place, before the ecclesiastical judge.   "Excommunications" were the sentences of such judges.

It will be observed with what care any notices, except those sanctioned by the Prayer-book, the Queen, or the bishop, are excluded from use in the church ; and how the minister only is to give the permitted notices.   In the sixteenth and seventeenth centuries such restrictions were probably wise and necessary.   Custom, however, has learned to regard them with no slight laxity.

The sermon,[1] which was to be preached at this part of the service, had its parallel, as we saw, in the address of the Church's president as described by Justin Martyr.

No rubric in the mediæval Mass-book provided for such an appeal to the intelligence of the congregation. When in the reformed service the minister was not prepared with a sermon, or was not a licensed preacher, one of the " Homilies " was to be read instead of a sermon. These Homilies, as is well known, are in two books—the former published in 1547, and proceeding in great part from the pen of Cranmer; the latter set forth in 1563, and attributed more or less confidently to the labours of Bishop Jewel. In the thirty-fifth of our Thirty-Nine Articles, the Homilies are described as containing " a godly and wholesome doctrine, and necessary for these times." This, of course, is a general approval of the Homilies, and by no means expresses or implies an entire agreement as necessarily to be yielded to every averment put forth in their pages or to each and every argument adduced in them.

The " Homilies ; " their Doctrine concerning the Lord's Supper.

This may be a convenient point at which to draw attention to the doctrine of the Church of England, concerning the Lord's Supper, as it is set forth in her " Homilies."

In the second book of Homilies there is a discourse, in two parts, on this subject ; and from that discourse we cull the following instructions.

The Eucharist is described as a "public celebration of the memory of Christ's precious death, at the Lord's Table."

It is a " heavenly supper where every one of us must be guests and not gazers, eaters and not lookers, feeding ourselves and not hiring others to feed for us."

"Three things, requisite in him that would seemly, as becometh such high mysteries, resort to the Lord's Table,"

---

[1] In connection with the recent practice of beginning the sermon without a prayer preceding, or with only the mediæval, elliptic utterance, " In the name of the Father, and the Son, and the Holy Ghost," it may be well to remind the reader that such proceedings are without any legal sanction ; whilst the fifty-fifth canon (1604) prescribes that before every sermon the preacher shall use a form of prayer there enjoined, *or some other short prayer to the same effect.*

are—to have "a right and worthy estimation and understanding of this mystery;" to come in sure faith; to have
newness and pureness of life to succeed the receiving of the
same.

Let the reader observe how the Homily urges that this
mystery must be studied, known, and understood by the
communicant.

"We must take heed," says the Homily, "lest of the
memory it be made a sacrifice," etc. "What hath been the
cause of the ruin of God's religion, but the ignorance hereof?
What hath been the cause of this gross idolatry, but the
ignorance hereof? What hath been the cause of this mum-
mish massing, but the ignorance hereof? Let us therefore so
travail to understand the Lord's Supper that we be no cause
of the decay of God's worship," etc.

"To make Christ thine own," in the Lord's Supper, "and
to apply His merits unto thyself . . . thou needest no other
man's help, no other sacrifice or oblation, no sacrificing priest,
no Mass, no means established by man's invention."

The required newness of life is described as consisting of
thankfulness such as is implied in the word Eucharist; unity
wherein they that eat at this Table should be knit together
in love, as was signified by the ancient designation of the
"Agape;" and "pureness and innocency of life."

To ascertain whether we have these requisites of the new
life, "we, and not others, must thoroughly examine, and not
lightly look over, ourselves; our own conscience, not other
men's lives;" and this "we ought to do uprightly, truly,
and with just correction."

If these are some details of the Church of England's
homiletic teaching, it may be instructive, in the present day,
to mention that, whereas the Homilies give eighteen of their
pages to considering "the right use of the church or temple
of God, and of the reverence due unto the same," and to the
"repairing, and keeping clean, and comely adorning of
churches," they devote no less than eighty-three pages to
the three parts of the Homily "against peril of idolatry and
superfluous decking of churches."

Surely such facts are significant. It is not only the details as quoted above, but it is the general spirit of the English Protestant Reformed Church, which breathes through the Homilies, as through all her formularies, that should warn us of the peril of dishonesty in approaching, as ministers and members of her communion, any of the characteristic doctrines and rites of the mediæval and Roman Churches.

And now, in taking up the consideration of the third rubric after the Nicene Creed, it may be observed that no rule has been laid down as to the pulpit or place from which the sermon was to be delivered—unless, indeed, the eighty-third Canon, with the duty and discretion it lays upon churchwardens, and upon the Ordinary of each locality, be regarded as such a rule—but the pulpit was certainly to stand apart from the Communion Table, for the injunction is that, after the sermon, the priest shall " *return* " to the Lord's Table and begin the Offertory, saying one or more of the subjoined sentences as he judges best.

(ix.) *The Offertory Sentences.*

Of the sentences it is only necessary to say that they treat of beneficence and almsgiving in general ; then several of them enjoin the duty of upholding the ministers of the Church ; then there is a special appeal to the rich, that they should be ready to give and glad to distribute ; then there are promises of God's approval of the sacrifices of beneficence and liberality ; then persistence in giving to the poor, either out of great possessions or small, is urged on the strength of two verses from the apocryphal Book of Tobit ; and then two passages from the Book of Proverbs declare the blessedness of providing for the sick and needy, and so lending to the Lord.

These Offertory sentences are as follow :—

Let your light so shine before men, that they may see your good works and glorify your Father which is in heaven.—*St. Matt.* v.

Lay not up for yourselves treasure upon the earth ; where the rust and moth doth corrupt, and where thieves break through and steal : but lay up for yourselves treasures in heaven ; where neither rust nor moth doth corrupt, and where thieves do not break through and steal.—*St. Matt.* vi.

Whatsoever ye would that men should do unto you, even so do unto them ; for this is the Law and the Prophets.—*St. Matt.* vii.

Not every one that saith unto Me, Lord, Lord, shall enter into the Kingdom of heaven ; but he that doeth the will of My Father which is in heaven.—*St. Matt.* vii.

Zacchæus stood forth, and said unto the Lord, Behold, Lord, the half of my goods I give to the poor ; and if I have done any wrong to any man, I restore four-fold.—*St. Luke* xix.

Who goeth a warfare at any time of his own cost? Who planteth a vineyard, and eateth not of the fruit thereof? Or who feedeth a flock, and eateth not of the milk of the flock?—1 *Cor.* ix.

If we have sown unto you spiritual things, is it a great matter if we shall reap your worldly things?—1 *Cor.* ix.

Do ye not know, that they who minister about holy things live of the sacrifice ; and they who wait at the altar are partakers with the altar? Even so hath the Lord also ordained, that they who preach the Gospel should live of the Gospel.—1 *Cor.* ix.

He that soweth little shall reap little ; and he that soweth plenteously shall reap plenteously. Let every man do according as he is disposed in his heart, not grudgingly, or of necessity ; for God loveth a cheerful giver.—2 *Cor.* ix.

Let him that is taught in the Word minister unto him that teacheth, in all good things. Be not deceived, God is not mocked ; for whatsoever a man soweth, that shall he reap.—*Gal.* vi.

While we have time, let us do good unto all men ; and especially unto them that are of the household of faith.—*Gal.* vi.

Godliness is great riches, if a man be content with that he hath : for we brought nothing into the world, neither may we carry any thing out.—1 *Tim.* vi.

Charge them who are rich in this world, that they be ready to give, and glad to distribute ; laying up in store for themselves a good foundation against the time to come, that they may attain eternal life.—1 *Tim.* vi.

God is not unrighteous, that He will forget your works, and labour that proceedeth of love ; which love ye have showed for His name's sake, who have ministered unto the saints, and yet do minister.—*Heb.* vi.

To do good, and to distribute, forget not ; for with such sacrifices God is well pleased.—*Heb.* xiii.

Whoso hath this world's good, and seeth his brother have need, and shutteth up his compassion from him, how dwelleth the love of God in him?—1 *St. John* iii.

Give alms of thy goods, and never turn thy face from any poor man ; and then the face of the Lord shall not be turned away from thee.—*Tob.* iv.

Be merciful after thy power. If thou hast much, give plenteously : if thou hast little, do thy diligence gladly to give of that little : for so gatherest thou thyself a good reward in the day of necessity.—*Tob.* iv.

He that hath pity upon the poor lendeth unto the Lord : and look, what he layeth out, it shall be paid him again.—*Prov.* xix.

Blessed be the man that provideth for the sick and needy : the Lord shall deliver him in the time of trouble.—*Psalm* xli.

(x.) *Rubrics following the Offertory Sentences.*

The rubric, immediately following, prescribes the mode of collecting the alms for the poor and other devotions of the people, as well as the manner of their being presented and placed upon the holy Table by the priest.

Whilst these sentences are in reading, the deacons, churchwardens, or other fit person appointed for that purpose, shall receive the alms for the poor, and other devotions of the people, in a decent bason to be provided by the parish for that purpose ; and reverently bring it to the priest, who shall humbly present and place it upon the holy Table.

Notice, the collection is to be, not only of the alms of the poor, but of " other *devotions* " of the people. These " other devotions " would consist of money devoted by the people to charities recommended by the briefs, or to the maintenance of the church and clergy, or to any other pious purposes. Such gifts of devotion, apart from alms for the poor, would doubtless be the " oblations " of which we shall read presently in the Prayer for the Church Militant.

But first another rubric, thus worded, demands a moment's consideration :—

And when there is a Communion, the priest shall then place upon the Table so much bread and wine, as he shall think sufficient.

After which done, the priest shall say.

Previous to the year 1857, it might have been urged that this rubric, as interpreted by the long prevalent usage of the Reformed Church of England, merely signified that " *when* " (that is, so often as) there shall be a Communion, " *then* " (that is, on those days), and by some agency of himself personally or of his deputy, the clergyman shall place a sufficient quantity of bread and wine upon the Table at some time antecedent to his saying the Prayer for the Church Militant; and it might have been urged that the most convenient and decorous time for this action would be before the beginning of the service.

However, in that year, 1857, in the case of *Liddell* v. *Westerton*, the Privy Council judgment decided that, " no doubt, the true meaning of the rubric " is " that at a certain point in the course of the Communion Service the minister shall place the bread and wine on the Communion Table."

The Privy Council also held that the then usual practice

of placing the elements on the Communion Table before the commencement of the service is certainly not according to the prescribed order.

We confess to the opinion that, apart from this judgment of the supreme court of law, the rubrics on this point would have seemed to us adequately complied with if, on days when the Communion was to be celebrated, the clergyman took care that, at any time before reading the Prayer for the Church Militant, sufficient bread and wine were placed on the Communion Table. That being attended to, and the alms and other devotions collected and placed on the Table, all rubrical requirements would seem to be discharged; and the concluding words of the rubric, "After which done, the priest shall say" the Prayer for the Church Militant, would appear to be in perfect harmony with such ancient practice.

However, in 1857, the innovation of the so-called credence table had been brought amongst us; and, though it had been forbidden by previous decisions of the law courts, "on the ground that" credence tables "are adjuncts to an altar," yet the Privy Council then decided that a credence table "is simply a small side table, on which the bread and wine are placed before the consecration, having no connection with any superstitious usage of the Church of Rome." The Council regarded these side tables as adjuncts, not to an altar, but rather to the Communion Table; and, accordingly, as being analogous to "pews, cushions to kneel upon, pulpit cloths," and other "articles not expressly mentioned in the rubric," but "consistent with, and even subsidiary to, the service," the novel credence tables were sanctioned by the Privy Council.

A point worth noticing here is, that whereas the form of rubric proposed to Convocation, in 1661, contained the words, "The priest shall then *offer up and* place upon the Table so much bread and wine as he shall think sufficient;" the words in italics were deliberately erased so that there should be no pretence for saying that, in our English Communion Service, there is any oblation or offering up of the bread and wine.

The "oblations," named in the next following prayer,

denote, obviously, something else than the elements of bread and wine; namely, the " other devotions," besides alms for the poor, which the congregation is offering as a sacrifice of thanksgiving unto the Lord.

With reference to the modern practice, which has sprung up in not a few churches, of employing the wardens, or the pew-openers, to count with mechanical exactness the number of intending communicants, and then whisper them to one or other of the clergy, with a view to consecrating the precise quantity of bread and wine that will be required, may we be excused if here we express a hope that care will be taken, by those who bear a part in such nice reckonings and in such whisperings, lest the more observant portion of the communicants be disquieted by what may easily assume the appearance of something being wrong and out of order?

(xi.) *The Prayer for the Church Militant.*

And now we proceed to notice the Prayer for the Church Militant :—

Let us pray for the whole state of Christ's Church militant here in earth.

Almighty and Everliving God, who by Thy holy Apostle hast taught us to make prayers, and supplications, and to give thanks, for all men We humbly beseech Thee most mercifully [*to accept our alms and oblations, and*] to receive these our prayers, which we offer unto Thy Divine Majesty; beseeching Thee to inspire continually the universal Church with the spirit of truth, unity, and concord: And grant, that all they that do confess Thy holy Name may agree in the truth of Thy holy Word, and live in unity, and godly love. We beseech thee also to save and defend all Christian Kings, Princes, and Governors; and specially Thy Servant Victoria our Queen; that under her we may be godly and quietly governed: And grant unto her whole Council, and to all that are put in authority under her, that they may truly and indifferently minister justice, to the punishment of wickedness and vice, and to the maintenance of Thy true religion, and virtue. Give grace, O heavenly Father, to all Bishops and Curates, that they may both by their life and doctrine set forth Thy true and lively Word, and rightly and duly administer Thy holy Sacraments: And to all Thy people give Thy heavenly grace; and especially to this congregation here present; that, with meek heart and due reverence, they may hear, and receive Thy holy Word truly serving Thee in holiness and righteousness all the days of their life

If there be no alm. or oblations, then shall the words [o accepting our alm: and oblations] be left out unsaid.

And we most humbly beseech Thee of Thy goodness, O Lord, to comfort and succour all them, who in this transitory life are in trouble, sorrow, need, sickness, or any other adversity. And we also bless Thy holy Name for all Thy servants departed this life in Thy faith and fear ; beseeching Thee to give us grace so to follow their good examples, that with them we may be partakers of Thy heavenly kingdom : Grant this, O Father, for Jesus Christ's sake, our only Mediator and Advocate. *Amen.*

Such a prayer in the Communion Service is common to the English Liturgy and all those of antiquity.

The words "militant here in earth" were added to the introductory call to prayer in 1552, in order to guard against superstitious and mercenary errors concerning purgatory, and in order to dispel the dream that God's just and merciful dealing with the departed can be in any way dependent on the prayers or sacrifices of some priest who traffics in Masses for the dead. This addition is by no means intended to intimate that we have no interest in the memory of the dead. On the contrary, this very prayer ends with a beautiful and most happy reference to those dear ones " gone before."

The prayer opens with an invocation of the Almighty as having taught us by St. Paul (1 Tim. ii. 1, 2), to make supplications, and to give thanks for all men. We are to beseech God to accept our offerings for the poor, " our alms," and our " other devotions," as the gifts for the church, the clergy, and any specific purposes of charity, are called in the rubric noticed above.

These latter " devotions " are here, in the prayer, designated " oblations." Nothing can be more unfounded than the supposition that the " oblations " signify the bread and wine, in spite of the fact that it was vainly attempted to introduce into the rubric, as we have seen above, words implying that the bread and wine were to be " offered up " and so made an " oblation." Whatever " other devotions " may be included in the term " oblations," Convocation refused to describe the bread and wine as being " offered up " and so made an oblation. Besides, there is the express mention of " other devotions," in addition to " alms for the poor ; " and these other devotions just answer to the term " oblations " here. And, together with these sacrifices of alms and other devotions,

God is implored to receive our prayers for the "universal Church."

The reader should not fail to notice the substitution of this synonym for the word "catholic," here and in the Litany, where we ask God to rule and govern His holy Church *universal* in the right way.

A similar usage prevails in the first of the Ember Week collects; and, in the "Prayer for all Conditions of Men," the usage is beautifully illustrated by the employment, indeed, of the phrase "the catholic Church," with the explanation that this catholic or universal Church consists of "all who profess and call themselves Christians," however much they and we may still need to be further "led into the way of truth."

It is surely good for us to be brought, thus early in the Communion Service, into sympathy with the most erring of our fellow-Christians. It is good for us to realize our union with them, and to pray for them as part of the catholic or universal Church of God. And what a prayer it is we are taught to make, on their behalf and our own, for divine inspiration by the spirit of truth, unity, and concord!

Then follows an admirably comprehensive supplication for all Christian kings, princes, and governors. Most important is it to intercede for our own monarch. Upon her depend such vast influences of morality, purity, and religion. Under God, the Queen must lead and set the manners and customs that is, in the widest and most spiritual sense, the morals of the nation.

We do well to pray that God will bless and guide the Queen, the Royal Family, and the Houses of Parliament, for these are, humanly speaking, the wells and sources of those influences which regulate society and the realm.

But, if we would rise to the true grandeur and dignity of this Prayer for the Church Militant, there is a wider common wealth than that presided over by our Queen. The nations especially the Christian nations, are all one in the widest citizenship of Christ and the universal Church. In many an age a quarrelsome ruler has set Europe on fire with the terrible brand of war; or some extravagant empress or queen has introduced the ruinous and demoralizing fashion of people vying with each other as if to see who could live furthest beyond their means.   Or regard, again, the influence of some immoral or profligate ruler, and see the degradation and sensualism made common by such a personage; and in view of this, or of either of the imperial, aristocratic, or plutocratic powers sketched above, reflect how desirable it is to join heartily and intelligently in this petition for *all* Christian kings and rulers.

Godly and quiet government is the burthen of the prayer as it proceeds; and in view of the horrors of war and civil distraction and obstructiveness and revolution, well may we urge this petition at the throne of grace, remembering the old maxim, *Laborare est orare*, which, in this adaptation of it, may be rendered, Man does not really pray for aught till he also toils for its attainment by every means within his reach.

In the same spirit of reasonable and pious loyalty to the government under which we live, the next petition prays that justice may be fairly and impartially, or "indifferently," as the old expression is, administered among us, so that wickedness and vice may be repressed, and true religion and virtue may be upheld.

Neither to this, nor to the next supplication, that all the clergy may both by precept and by example show forth the truth of God's holy Word, the glory of righteousness, and the simple beauty of His sacraments, will it be necessary to claim the attention of any wise or godly man.   The blessedness of such grace from heaven must be obvious to those who give any heed to serious matters.

Nor is the wisdom and piety of the next part of the Prayer for the Church Militant less conspicuous, in which we ask God's heavenly grace for all men, and especially for ourselves and the then present congregation, that all may, with meek heart and due reverence, hear God's holy Word, and not only hear it, but give it a hearty reception, so that it may be a leaven and an influence in our lives, producing the sweet fruits of righteousness habitually.

To those who have earnestly adopted these petitions so far

it will be easy and acceptable now to raise a supplication, on behalf of any who mourn and are in trouble, that our Father will, of His goodness, comfort and succour all such.

We have already referred with delight to the next words of this part of our English Communion Service; and here we must confine ourselves to the reflection how beautiful is this memory of the blessed dead. There is no superstitious allusion to the *sign* of the cross resting upon them, or to any outward and material token, that might be mistaken for a talisman or a magical charm, such as we saw indicated in some of the mediæval rites, but there is a thanksgiving to God for His gifts of inward and spiritual grace, whereby " faith and fear," trust and reverence, have been implanted in the hearts of all those blissful multitudes who already rest in the Lord and are perfected in paradise as the spirits of the just.

How meet is it, too, that we, who love the memory of those dear ones, who delight to think of their amiability, their patience, their sanctified energies, should pray to their Father and our Father, that whereinsoever those, who have entered into their joy, followed in the steps of Christ, we likewise may follow their good examples and so be admitted, with them, into the eternal home with many mansions, whither Jesus has gone before that He may prepare for the reception of all who love Him.

Quite in keeping with the whole of this beautiful prayer is the end, wherein we beseech our Father to grant all this for the sake of Jesus Christ, than whom we have, in the capacity of a sacrificing priest, or in the efficacy of an atoning victim, no other Mediator, no other Advocate.

Assuredly, at this point, it is reasonable and natural that the congregation who have been listening with attention, with sympathy, and with accord, should give utterance to their feelings by a hearty exclamation of "Amen," so may it be.

And now, passing over the warnings of the sacrament as about to be celebrated—which we have already examined, in their logical connection, as introductory to the Lord's Supper —we arrive at the third of the long exhortations beginning with the words, " Dearly beloved."

(xii.) *The Exhortation to Communicants.*

The rubric, at the head of this exhortation, is in these words :—

At the time of the celebration of the Communion, the communicants being conveniently placed for the receiving of the holy Sacrament, the priest shall say this Exhortation.

The first point, indicated here, is that the compilers of our Liturgy anticipated there would be times when this Communion Service, down to the end of the Offertory, would be employed in the assembly of the Church, although there should be no celebration of the Lord's Supper. The same fact might have been gathered from the rubric before the Prayer for the Church Militant, " When there is a Communion," implying other occasions for using the service so far, when there is no Communion. The rubric before the first exhortation implies the same custom, when it directs that " warning for the celebration " shall always be given on the Sunday or some holy-day immediately preceding. What need of this if there was to be a celebration every Sunday, or every holy-day ? With reference to a stated celebration, recurring every week as regularly as the Sunday Morning Prayer, there would be no need of such a warning; but if the celebration was intended and expected to take place three or four times in the year, or even once or twice in the month, then such special notice would be suitable or necessary.

This rubric marks the point of divergence between the English Communion Service properly so called and that which has sometimes been designated the ante-Communion, a part of the service which is intended to be used at other times than when the Communion is to be celebrated. Accordingly, it may be well to notice here the appointed mode of ending the service when there is no Communion.

On this point not a little variety of practice exists in different churches. In many places, the morning service terminates with the sermon, followed by a collect, taken from the six at the end of the Communion, and then by the Benediction—the whole pronounced from the pulpit. This was the all but universal practice forty years ago.

Since then, however, it has become not uncommon for the clergyman to leave the pulpit immediately after the sermon and return to the Communion Table, there to say a collect and the Benediction, sometimes with and sometimes without the reading of the Offertory sentences and the Prayer for the Church Militant.

If we examine the rubrical injunctions on the subject, they may appear somewhat complicated, for, at the head of the six collects at the end of the Communion Service, there is a rubric in these terms :—

Collects to be said after the Offertory, when there is no Communion, every such day one or more.

This injunction, taken together with the prevalent interpretation of the rubrics immediately preceding the Prayer for the Church Militant, that that prayer is to be read only when the minister has just placed the elements on the Table, would make it appear that one or more of the six collects after the Communion Service was intended to be a substitute for the Prayer for the Church Militant on non-Communion days. But then there is, on this supposition, no rubrical provision for ending the non-Communion service with the accustomed benediction ; and, besides, after the six collects before named, there is a rubric to this effect :—

Upon the Sundays and other holy-days (if there be no Communion) shall be said all that is appointed at the Communion, until the end of the general Prayer [For the whole state of Christ's Church militant here in earth] *together with one or more of these Collects last before rehearsed, concluding with the Blessing.*

This makes it appear that, on non-Communion Sundays, the strictly legal and proper rubrical termination of the service is after the sermon, the Offertory ; then the Prayer for the Church Militant ; then one or more of the six collects ; and then the blessing.

Of such a practice, in these days when it is customary to make Morning Prayer, the Litany, and the Communion all into one continuous act of divine service, it must be acknowledged that, apart from the consideration that both mind and body of all but the most robust worshippers will be worn out from fatigue in following so protracted a service, there is the further difficulty that such a service, so composed of the Morning Prayer, the Litany, and the Communion, contains several repetitions of the Lord's Prayer, three sets of Prayers for the Queen, besides many other repetitions of prayers for the sick, the clergy, and for all in authority; and such reiteration can hardly fail to produce weariness and listlessness rather than devotion and godly earnestness.

On these and many other grounds of piety and common sense, it seems most desirable—if the old custom of forty years ago, or if the modern Act for shortening services with the bishop's approval, may permit such a deviation from the exact letter of the rubric—not to re-introduce, or not to continue, the addition of the Prayer for the Church Militant to the already protracted combination of Morning Prayer, Litany, and Communion.

So much has it seemed right to say with reference to the rubric that separates the actual celebration of the Communion from the commandments and other introductory portions of the service on non-Communion days; and if this needs to be considered, how much more is it necessary to apply similar observations to the practice, still prevalent in many of our churches, of adding the complete Communion Service, with its appointed sermon, to the Morning Prayer and Litany.

Nothing but habit, which is often not favourable to vivid impressions of piety and active resolves of devotion—nothing but the passive quiescence of habit enables men to tolerate such a custom; and it is much to be desired that, either by the already legalized separating of Morning Prayer and the Litany and the Communion into distinct services for different congregations meeting at different hours,—or else by procuring the necessary legal sanction for the omission of all repetitions, in continued services, of a prayer which has already been used once in that service,—help might be given to the weakly who wish to join in public worship, and piety might be promoted among all those who, even with the best resolutions, are not at present able to sustain attention to a service not unfrequently lasting for nearly three hours—say, from eleven o'clock in the morning till two o'clock in the afternoon.

So painfully is this evil felt, that diverse methods are

being resorted to for its abatement. In some churches the ancient and very important practice of the preacher giving instruction and exhortation in connection with the Lord's Supper, is set aside on Communion days; and either there is then no sermon or a mere hurried utterance of some ten or twelve minutes. This is surely a most undesirable departure from what we saw, in our first chapter, was the practice of the Church as early as the days of Justin Martyr; and it is also a setting lightly by the apostolic ordinance of preaching, while it depreciates the intellectual appeal to the congregation, the attempt to win their hearts to God by moral suasion, in comparison with the more mechanical and routine portions of church service.

There are thus many motives all tending in one direction, and that for the wise shortening of our religious services, especially of the service for the Holy Communion, by omitting repetitions which are apt to become vain, and by keeping the different services for Morning Prayer, Litany, and Communion, each distinct from the others.

Among the devices for avoiding the evil of too long a service, one, of quite recent introduction, is the frequent omission of the somewhat lengthy exhortation which follows the rubric we have been considering. The aim is praiseworthy, though the method employed for its attainment is illegal. How far it may be wise, apart from the question of legality, to omit this particular exhortation, must depend on the acquaintance possessed by each congregation with the benefits on the one hand, and the dangers on the other hand, attaching to the sacrament of the Lord's Supper.

No doubt, the modern habit of omitting this exhortation finds a sort of sanction in the proposal of the Ritual Commission (page 18 of their fourth report, 1870) to introduce the following rubric on the subject: "*Note.*—This exhortation may be omitted at the discretion of the minister, subject to the control of the Ordinary."

And now let us proceed to examine this exhortation, the words of which are:—

Dearly beloved in the Lord, ye that mind to come to the holy Communion of the Body and Blood of our Saviour Christ Christ consider how Saint Paul exhorteth all persons diligently to try and examine themselves, before they presume to eat of that Bread, and drink of that Cup. For as the benefit is great, if with a true penitent heart and lively faith we receive that holy Sacrament; (for then we spiritually eat the flesh of Christ, and drink His blood ; then we dwell in Christ, and Christ in us ; we are one with Christ, and Christ with us ;) so is the danger great, if we receive the same unworthily. For then we are guilty of the Body and Blood of Christ our Saviour ; we eat and drink our own damnation, not considering the Lord's Body ; we kindle God's wrath against us ; we provoke Him to plague us with divers diseases, and sundry kinds of death. Judge therefore yourselves, brethren, that ye be not judged of the Lord : repent you truly for your sins past ; have a lively and stedfast faith in Christ our Saviour ; amend your lives, and be in perfect charity with all men ; so shall ye be meet partakers of those holy mysteries. And above all things ye must give most humble and hearty thanks to God, the Father, the Son, and the Holy Ghost, for the redemption of the world by the death and passion of our Saviour Christ, both God and man ; who did humble Himself, even to the death upon the Cross, for us, miserable sinners, who lay in darkness and the shadow of death ; that He might make us the children of God, and exalt us to everlasting life. And to the end that we should alway remember the exceeding great love of our Master, and only Saviour, Jesus Christ, thus dying for us, and the innumerable benefits which by His precious blood-shedding He hath obtained to us ; He hath instituted and ordained holy mysteries, as pledges of His love, and for a continual remembrance of His death, to our great and endless comfort. To Him, therefore, with the Father and the Holy Ghost, let us give (as we are most bounden) continual thanks ; submitting ourselves wholly to His holy will and pleasure, and studying to serve Him in true holiness and righteousness all the days of our life. *Amen.*

The persons addressed, it is to be observed, are those who intend to participate in the sacrament. The last rubric had enjoined that they, as "the communicants," should be "conveniently placed for the receiving of the holy sacrament." Whether they were to be in the body of the church, or in the chancel, is not determined, and would depend, apparently, on whether the Table stood in the one place or the other ; and that, again, according to the fourth rubric at the beginning of the service, would depend on the place " where Morning and Evening Prayer are appointed to be said."

Obviously, the Church of England does not aim at saying Morning and Evening Prayer in one part of the church and celebrating the Communion at quite another part of the church. Wherever the ordinary morning prayers were wont to be said, there *inner* in the body of the church or in its chancel, was the Table to stand at Communion-time; and, evidently, near to it were the communicants to be placed for the sake of convenience.

It is quite worth noticing that the rubrics nowhere enjoin any change of place on the part of the communicants from this point of the service onwards. There is nothing to make it appear that the people ought to come to the Communion rails after the Prayer of Consecration.

Rather the whole drift of the rubrics is that the communicants shall, at the beginning of the Communion Service properly so called, be conveniently placed for the receiving of the holy sacrament: and then to them kneeling in those convenient places, in the body of the church or in the chancel, wherever the Table and the service might be, the minister, after communicating himself in both the elements, was to deliver the same to the people also; and then, when "all" had communicated, he was to "return to the Lord's Table" and reverently replace on it the remainder of the consecrated elements.

There is, in all this, no trace of an injunction that the communicants should come to the so-called "Communion rails," either in parties of one or two, or in sections such as could find kneeling room along those rails. Far be it from us to recommend any unnecessary innovation in the accepted and existing practice; but in these days, when not a few people are sticklers for rubrical exactness, it is well to notice that established custom has its important and universally acknowledged part in deciding points of ritual which are not distinctly provided for by the rubrics.

Another point which is brought under notice by the rubrical directions just quoted, and by the opening words of this exhortation, is that the English Communion Service is addressed to those "that mind to come to the holy Communion." They are the congregation who are to be conveniently placed for participation in the elements, and to "all" of whom the bread and wine are to be delivered.

It is true, no provision is made for the withdrawal of non-communicants at any part of the Communion Service ; but it is assumed that there will be a severance of those who communicate, and those who do not communicate, at some period before the beginning of this exhortation.   Otherwise, how could the communicants be " conveniently placed " ?   And if the question be raised whether that severance should be made by the two parties both remaining within the walls of the church, or by the withdrawal of the non-communicants, the answer appears plain when we consider that not a word of the service, from this point onwards, makes any reference to non-communicants as present and onlooking ; and that, contrariwise, the universal practice of the English Church, only a few years since, was for all non-communicants to quit the sacred edifice after a collect and the short benediction had been said by the preacher in the pulpit.

This fact, of the English Communion Service being intended only for communicants, is important, not only as a matter of seemliness and good order, but as making against the modern ritualistic attempt to convert the reformed Communion Service into a gorgeous spectacle, like the mediæval High Mass, which may be contemplated by numbers of non-communicants as well as by those addressed in our third exhortation as minding or intending "to come to the holy Communion of the body and blood of our Saviour Christ."

Whatever authority may be ascribed to the teaching of the Homilies—and the thirty-fifth of our English Articles of Religion does, be it remembered, approve them as containing a godly and wholesome doctrine—they emphatically condemn, as we have seen, the practice of being " gazers and not guests " at the holy Table.

(a.) Benefits of Worthy Participation.

After the opening words, so addressed to communicants only, the object of the exhortation is to produce a lively remembrance of St. Paul's command that men should "examine *themselves*," and should so eat of the bread and partake of the cup.   The bearing of this apostolic precept, against private confession of a sacramental sort, and in favour of energetic self-scrutiny, by the help of the Decalogue, the Lord's Prayer, and various other methods by which a man may detect his own sins and be stimulated, God's Holy Spirit helping him, to vigorous efforts for the abandonment of sin and for the culture in himself of all holy graces and spiritual perfections—this matter has been dwelt upon. in earlier pages of this essay, and shall not be now further enforced. Besides, words can hardly be simpler, or more to the purpose, than those of the exhortation itself, when it calls attention to the benefits of receiving the sacrament (or sign) of so holy a thing, and defines these benefits as consisting in a "spiritual" participation of the flesh and blood of Christ, and treats this "spiritual" eating and drinking as synonymous with our dwelling in Christ and Christ in us, or, again, as synonymous with our being one with Christ and Christ one with us.

Of course, the citation of these figures concerning Christ dwelling in us (1 John iii. 24; Eph. iii. 17; John vi. 56; John xiv. 23), and Christ being "one with us" (John xvii. 11, 21, 22, 23), is most noteworthy. The construction of the service, here, is such that if the oneness with Christ were less in dignity and holy import than the dwelling in Christ, or if either the oneness with Christ or the dwelling in Him were of less importance than the spiritually eating His flesh and drinking His blood, we should be landed in what is called *bathos*, or the intellectual disappointment which is experienced when the mind, having been raised into association with high and lofty themes, is suddenly and unhappily brought down, at an anti-climax, to lower and less glorious topics.

To avoid the discomfort and indecorum of *bathos*, the later terms of such an enumeration, as we have here, must be at least equally important with the earlier terms, if not even more important than they. Thus, spiritually eating Christ, dwelling in Christ, oneness with Christ, must either be equivalent phrases, or the second must be of grander import than the first, and the third nobler than the second.

But observe, in this line of thought, that the third phrase, "oneness with Christ," is taken from Christ's prayer in the seventeenth chapter of the fourth Gospel, and has, in that its proper source, its defining usage, nothing to do, primarily and directly, with the Lord's Supper.

The prayer is that all believers may be one with one another, with Christ, and with God, in a perfect and glorious union of love and holiness; and, such being the non-sacramental significance of our third term, the second is, like it, unconnected with anything especially sacramental in its Scriptural origin, for what the beloved apostle wrote (1 John iii. 24) is, "He that keepeth His" (Christ's) "commandments dwelleth in Him, and He in him." Here the condition of Christ's indwelling is compliance with any and all of our Lord's commands; and this indwelling is no more promised to compliance with the command to break bread than to conformity with any other command. Indeed, the special precepts of the Master, associated by St. John with the promised indwelling, are that we should believe on the name of Jesus Christ, that we should love one another, and that we should cultivate the spirit of Christ. And, similarly, St. Paul (Eph. iii. 17) makes Christ's dwelling[1] in us depend generally on our faith and love, not, in any especial manner, on our partaking of the Lord's Supper. Just so, too, in the famous passage (John xiv. 23), the "abode" or dwelling of God and His Christ with any man is made contingent upon Christ's being loved, and His words kept, generally, without any special reference to the Supper of the Lord. And in the other passage where Christ's indwelling is mentioned (John vi. 56), as we have already seen, the discourse was uttered a year before the institution of the Lord's Supper, and could therefore have no direct and especial reference to that as yet unknown rite. Indeed, as we have also seen, the eating and drinking Christ, spoken of in John vi. 56, are defined (verses 35, 63) to be coming to Christ and believing on Christ; and this, with the distinct assurance that no material union with Christ—not

---

[1] St. Paul uses the verb κατοικῆσαι. In the three Johannean passages the verb μένειν, or one of its derivatives, is employed. This, however, in no way affects our argument.

even the eating of His flesh materially and objectively, if that were possible—would be of any profit, but only the words spoken by Him are spirit and are life, and thus are the spirit that giveth life.

Most important is it to observe that thus, according to the teaching of the English reformed Prayer-book, no less than of Holy Writ, the highest benefits of a worthy reception of the Lord's Supper consist of just such blessings as accrue to man from any and every act of love, faith, and obedience towards our Lord. If a man receive Christ's words, and be influenced by their spirit, he eats Christ's flesh and drinks Christ's blood spiritually; he dwells in Christ and Christ in him; he is one with Christ and Christ with him: and this identification with Christ, and incorporation into Him, takes place just as truly and effectually—according to Scripture as quoted by the Communion Service—whether a believer exercises patience and charity amidst the provocations of fellow-Christians, or whether he gives a cup of water to another in the name of Christ, or whether he achieves some heroic deed of faith and love, or whether, in the Christian spirit of liberty, wisdom, and holiness, he breaks bread and drinks wine in remembrance of the sacrifice of the death of Christ.

It is not for us to say that one holy action—one fruit of the spirit of righteousness—is better than another. We cannot say that the breaking of bread is better than almsgiving, or more important than forgiving an enemy, or grander than resisting unto blood in the strife against sin. Enough for us to know that each such act, and many another likewise, wrought by us through the grace of God and of His Christ, is, as a manifestation of faith and loving obedience, a spiritual eating of Christ, an indwelling of Christ in us, and a becoming, on our part, one with Christ while He is one with us.

If, confronted by these facts, any objector should ask, Why then partake of the Lord's Supper at all, since its benefits may be derived to us through other channels? We rejoin, In God's visible world, various kinds of food are good for the body, though each of them may contain the same ingredients of nitrogen, carbon, and what not: and, no less, in God's

nvisible world, various exercises of Christian grace are good
or us, though each may bring to us the same benefit; or
lse, if it were otherwise, Christ would not have enjoined so
many diverse acts of faith and happy obedience.

(b.) Perils of Unworthy Participation.

Such is the thoroughly Scriptural teaching of the English
Prayer-book as to the benefits of a proper participation in the
Supper of the Lord; and, next, the exhortation admonishes
is concerning the perils of unworthily receiving the holy
acrament.

These perils are tremendous, and we can have no inclina-
ion to depreciate their real importance. Our attention has
)een already engaged in examining some of them when we
vere studying the twenty-seventh and twenty-ninth verses
)f the eleventh chapter of St. Paul's first Epistle to the
Corinthians. This will make it easier for us now to notice
;ach of the dangers enumerated in our exhortation.

The unworthy communicant incurs guilt in connection
vith such holy things as the body and blood of Christ.
Surely, if he have any feeling of reverence or any sentiment
)f compassion, he must desire to hold himself free from
)lame, void of sin, with reference to that body and blood of
Christ which were given to ransom him and all men from sin
and its misery. We appeal to no lower motive of fear, though
hat topic, like many others, may readily be suggested by the
dea of any men so lightly and irreligiously taking part in
his most sacred rite as to be guilty, in it, in connection with
)ur Lord's great sacrifice of reconciliation.

But, while thus we would urge every possible consideration
o deter men from unworthy participation in the holy Com-
nunion, let it not be forgotten that St. Paul laid it down, in
iis teaching (Gal. v. 2, 4, ii. 21), that any man, who trusted
n such ritual observances as circumcision (though that had
)een of divine institution), was frustrating the grace of God,
vas falling from grace, was making Christ of no profit and of
10 effect unto himself.

Verily, it is possible to be guilty in connection with Christ,

and His death, and His body and blood, in other ways besides
an improper partaking of the holy Supper. And, indeed, if
we listen to the words of another apostle (Jas. ii. 20), they
will tell us that "Whosoever shall keep the whole law and yet
offend in one point, he is guilty of all." In St. James's application of these words, they denote that if any Christian
permit his judgment, in some case submitted to the congregation, to be warped by the "vile raiment" of the poor man, or
by the "gold ring and goodly apparel" of the other, then
such a Christian is "partial in" himself and a "judge of evil
thoughts;" and thus, or in any analogous mode, to be guilty,
in one particular, is to manifest a crookedness of character, a
perverseness of mental vision, which, under adequate temptation, would be capable of any sin and so is guilty of all. In
other words, the judge who shows himself a respecter of
persons, or the man who commits any sin against God or
man—who, for instance (1 Tim. v. 8), neglects to make provision for his family—has denied the faith, is worse than an
unbeliever, is morally certain to break any law to whose
violation he may be adequately tempted, is thus guilty of all,
and, no less than the careless communicant, is guilty in connection with the body and blood of Christ.

Terrible is the guilt of unworthy communion; but no less
terrible is the guilt of every sin. The measure of the guilt, in
each case, depends not only on the act done, but on the motive,
intention, and disposition with which it is done. St. Paul
may chide the Galatians as foolish, or the sinless Lord of
mercy may Himself reprove as fools those who were so slow
in believing what the prophets had written; but let like
expressions be employed in a spirit of injurious anger or
malicious scorn, and they make a man *guilty* and in danger of
"the judgment," "the Sanhedrim," "the Gehenna of fire"
(Matt. v. 22).

Similar reflections hold good with reference to the second
peril named in the exhortation.

The word "damnation" is, according to the modern usage
of the term, a most unfortunate mistranslation of the word
"judgment" as written by St. Paul (1 Cor. xi. 29). He that

eats the sacramental bread and does not consider and discern the utter difference betwixt that material element, which can only nourish the body, and the spiritual food of Christ's sacrifice, which can feed the soul and change us from the weakest of sinners into the most heroic of saints—such an undiscerning communicant brings on himself judgment and self-condemnation in that day of the Lord, come when and how it may, when, awakened by one of the many trumpets of God, he shall open his mental eyes and see of what spiritual joy and fellowship he has deprived himself, and how foolishly and culpably he has neglected to cultivate, to the utmost, the spiritual presence and friendship of Christ, which might have been found and realized in the breaking of bread with fellow-believers just as much as, and no more than, in giving meat to the hungry and drink to the thirsty, or in lodging the stranger, clothing the naked, visiting the sick, or going to the prisoners; for, assuredly, he, who thus acts, does it for Christ Himself: and he, who neglects so to act, brings on himself the direst of judgments (Matt. xxv. 34—43).

No act or word is so insignificant, in itself, but it forms a constituent in the character we are stamping on ourselves, in the judgment one day to be pronounced upon us by Christ and by our own conscience at last enlightened by Him who is the light of the world.

Which act in a sinner's career may, in that day, be the blackest and the heaviest, in judgment, no man knoweth. It may be that the real guilt and consequent judgment of the most unworthy communicant will be light when compared with that of some who have thoughtlessly repeated the Lord's Prayer, or some " Pater Noster," while their minds and hearts were set upon acts and intentions of profaneness and devilry.

With regard to the next named peril of unworthy communion, that we thereby "kindle God's wrath against us," it is most wise that this should be named in the exhortation; but every thoughtful man, who hearkens to its utterance, should remember that the apostolic teaching (Rom. i. 18) is that, "the wrath of God is revealed from heaven against

all ungodliness and unrighteousness of men." The measure
of God's wrath, like the measure of man's guilt, varies with
the intention and wilfulness of the agent, rather than with the
nature of the act. But the divine wrath is kindled against
every sin, and not against unworthy participation in the
sacrament alone or chiefly.

Next, the exhortation reminds us that, according to St.
Paul's teaching (1 Cor. xi. 30), unworthy communion at the
Lord's Table "provokes" God "to plague us with divers
diseases and sundry kinds of death." We have already seen
how, with or without miraculous intervention, the man who is
so gluttonous, or such a wine-bibber, as to carry those vices
into the most sacred functions of religion, is morally certain
to practise them so extensively and persistently in other parts
of his life, as to bring upon himself the whole wretched set of
ailments which follow in the track of these sins under the
names of *delirium tremens* and a host of other diseases. This
is a most serious danger attaching to the unworthy communicant; but it was not in connection with this sin that the
horror of death fell suddenly upon Ananias and upon Sapphira
(Acts v. 5, 10), when they were convicted, in their avarice and
their profane lying, by the words of the apostle Peter. And,
moreover, there is truth and wisdom, as all experience proves,
in the words of Jesus which implied that, whereas special sin
cannot always be inferred from special suffering (John ix. 1—3;
Luke xiii. 2—5), yet sin is too often the cause of such suffering;
and sin, if persisted in, is usually certain to bring, in its train
of wretched consequences, "some worse thing," it may be in
the form of direr sickness or of death. So needful is the
admonition not to communicate unworthily for fear of sickness and death; and so no less needful is the same admonition with reference to every sin, whether it be the selfish
carelessness that violates some sanitary law of God, or the
dishonesty that perishes horror-stricken on detection, or the
secret sin that proceeds from bad to worse, with only the eye
of God and the conscience of the transgressor privy to the
evil.

In view of these warnings of our exhortation, let us beware

of the sin and peril of unworthy participation in the Supper of the Lord; but let us be no less on our guard against the superstition which imagines that it is chiefly, if not exclusively, by this sin that such peril is incurred. Rather let us be assured by Holy Writ, and by experience, that when the Christian, at all events, commits, knowingly, any sin, he is guilty in spite of the Lord's body given and the Lord's blood shed for him; he brings on himself the certain judgment of God and his own conscience; he kindles God's wrath against him; he provokes God to plague (that is, to smite) him with divers diseases and sundry kinds of death.

Hereupon, the Prayer-book bids those, who "mind to" communicate, to judge (or examine) themselves; to repent of sins past; to believe, livingly and perseveringly, in Christ our Saviour; to amend their lives; and to be in perfect charity with all men. These particulars, constituting as they do the best and only perfect or adequate preparation for holy Communion, we have already noticed in considering the final answer of the Church Catechism.

So, says the exhortation, shall ye be "meet partakers of those holy mysteries"—partakers, that is, be it well remembered, not of something awfully unintelligible, but of the secret revealed and made clear in Christ, that God so loved the whole world, when that world was dead in trespasses and sins, that He gave His only begotten Son to live amidst the opposition of sinful men, and to die upon the cross as a propitiation for the sins of the whole world, that His life might be a ransom for all men, and that He, being lifted up from the earth, might draw all men unto Him. This is the secret which the princes of the world (1 Cor. ii. 8) could not discover till Christ unveiled it and showed it to all men by His Spirit; and of this blessed revelation of divine love the breaking of bread is an appointed and most precious remembrance—a very means and channel by which sinners, sanctified in heart and mind, enter into closest union of soul and spirit with their Lord, who is for ever interceding for them, according to the will of God, at the right hand of heaven's throne of grace.

Such are the mysteries which, as was pointed out in a former part of this essay, it is given unto all Christians to know and understand.

(c.) *Thanksgiving for the Benefits of Christ's Blood-shedding.*

Well may the exhortation, upon this, proceed to remind us that our Communion is, emphatically and above all, a service of joyful gratitude, as, we have seen, is indeed denoted by its being styled the Eucharist or Thanksgiving. Excellent, though not admitting of being stated in clearer words than those employed in the exhortation itself, is the explanation that our thanks are due to God—as the Father, the Son, and the Holy Ghost—for nothing less than the redemption, or rescuing, of the whole world from the bondage of sin and its miserable results, and for effecting this rescue by such a sacrifice as the death and sufferings of Christ our Saviour, who is both God and man.

Then, still further to quicken our thankfulness, several details of this saving mercy of God in Christ are set forth, as, for instance, the self-humiliation of Christ dying on the cross, that we, miserable sinners, might be lifted up from " darkness and the shadow of death " into the glorious position of God's children, the possessors of eternal life.

Upon this follows a remarkable passage, grand in its simplicity, in which our attention is called to the Lord's Supper as a remembrance of Christ's death, a pledge of His love, and a source of great and endless comfort. The most striking point in this passage is that wherein, after mentioning " the exceeding great love of our Master, and only Saviour, Jesus Christ, thus dying for us," reference is made to "the innumerable benefits which by His precious blood-shedding He hath obtained to us." These words are pregnant with meaning. The holiest saint in heaven may be reminded by them of every sin and every habit of evil from which he was emancipated by the cross. He will know that every new grace, which grew in his heart or mind, sprang from the seed of Christ's self-sacrifice. He will contrast the wretchedness of sin unrepented, unforgiven, persisted in, with the light and glory of his saved condition, and he will be conscious that to him these are some of the benefits procured by Christ's precious blood-shedding.

In the charity of heaven he will look round and see the hosts of the redeemed, and he will praise God because such marvels of redemptive change have been wrought, in a great multitude, out of all nations, too numerous to be counted, by the same precious blood-shedding. The sweetness of the gentle, the courage of the brave, the wisdom of the sage, the perfection of the just, among all the saints, he will attribute only and truly to the same cause.

In like manner, amongst the humblest of the poor on earth, and amongst the wisest of earth's noble-born, the song of each individual believer will be in praise of that precious blood-shedding which brings salvation and growing saintliness to every man who turns to Christ.

Vast themes for reflection have we here, yet far from being all that is suggested by these words. The pious student of history will ask, What influence wrought in Paul, and Origen, and Tertullian, and Augustin, and Chrysostom, and the countless lights of the early Christian centuries? And the answer must be, The precious blood-shedding of Jesus.

Who reproved and arrested the slaughterous cruelty of such an emperor as Theodosius the Great? After his massacre of the five thousand at Thessalonica, who debarred him while unrepentant from the consolations and privileges of the Christian Church? The answer must be, Ambrose, under the influence of the cross of Christ.

Who separated whole companies of men from the absorbing occupations of the chase, the deeds of violence, the savagery of war? Who made those hosts of tonsured brethren great in agriculture, great in literature, great in study, great in self-chosen poverty? Who taught women to seek gentle pious work in beneficence of every kind, and to raise the ideal even of womanhood by their purity and self-denial and usefulness? The answer must be that, in spite of celibacy so practised as distinctly to contravene Scripture, it was the blood of Christ which wrought all the benefits that were, in their early days, effected by the monks and nuns for mankind.

Similarly, if it be asked, What power mingled the East and West, and quickened the vast and beneficent activities of trade and science and renascent learning? The only answer must be, In spite of superstition and greed and treachery, it was the blood of Christ that touched the holy city with that sanctity which moved the Crusaders and set on foot the progress, commercial, literary, and scientific, which through these six hundred years has never ceased to work, if no longer in the Saracen from Arabia, at least in his Jewish congener, and, on a vaster scale, in the far-reaching brotherhood of Christendom.

Such thoughts, and a thousand others, cannot fail to be suggested to the student of history, as he hears of the innumerable benefits obtained to man by the precious blood-shedding of Christ. We do but name the abolition of serfdom and slavery in mediæval and in modern times. We do but name the amelioration of war customs among the more civilized. We do but name the hope, already confessed, in so many places, and by men of highest influence, to be a duty, to make wars cease. We do but name the tenderness of the Christian hospital, the exceeding worth of the ragged school, the Sunday school, the parish school, the Board school. We do but name the source and origin of the grammar schools, and of the colleges in our universities, and of all the vast majority of institutions founded to educate the poor. We do but name the condition of woman, the child, the wife, the mother, in all Christian families. And these are only a few of "the innumerable benefits" obtained for us, directly and indirectly, by the precious blood-shedding of our Saviour Christ.

A truly fruitful root of thankfulness is here touched by our exhortation. Every man can feel, increasingly, the inestimable blessing of salvation from sin for himself and for his neighbours; and whilst the least cultured can experience, ever more and more—it is a culture in itself—this side of the innumerable benefits of Christ's cross, the man of learning and of thought, sharing the peasant's sanctifying joy, will perceive, with every extension of his knowledge, fresh and additional proofs and manifestations how past numbering are the benefits that come to man from the precious blood-shedding of Christ.

Upon this suggestion of inexhaustible food for Christian thought and thankfulness, most appropriately there follow the plain and unmistakable words with which our third exhortation ends :—

To Him, therefore, with the Father and the Holy Ghost, let us give (as we are most bounden) continual thanks ; submitting ourselves wholly to His holy will and pleasure, and studying to serve Him in true holiness and righteousness all the days of our life. *Amen.*

Such is one of the three exhortations bestowed upon the English Service by the Reformation. These three exhortations, like, it is true, to the sermons of Justin Martyr's time, are not only something given us by the Reformation, but they, and the reciting of the Ten Commandments, were introduced as a substitute for the degrading and loathsome practice of private confession, that corrupt innovation which crept into the Church in the darkest days that succeeded the inroads and victories of the untutored Goths.

If the length of our now complicated services, or even of the Communion Service by itself, with the modern numbers of communicants and the still more modern method of repeating the words of administration to each communicant, though they have to be said several hundreds of times, make the service painfully and dangerously protracted, and if we are thus constrained to omit this third exhortation, with its wealth of thought and piety, let us not fail to remind our people frequently of its contents ; and, indeed, it would be difficult to imagine any wiser course for the preacher than often to try and prepare people for the Communion, and for all Christian life, by drawing attention to this exhortation and to the many and various lines of thought suggested therein.

(xiii.) *The Shorter Exhortation to Communicants.*

Upon the third exhortation follows a rubric in these words :—

Then shall the priest say to them that come to receive the holy Communion.

This rubric is only noticeable as implying the absence of non-communicants, for how, if others were still present, could these words be addressed only to a part of the audience ? And how negligent, if not unfeeling, would be the omission, both here and throughout the rest of the service, of all reference, courteous, compassionate, or intercessory, to those who, as able to be present and yet as abstaining from communion, would be declaring themselves in particular need of such intercession or instruction.

The simple words to be addressed to the communicants are :—

Ye that do truly and earnestly repent you of your sins, and are in love and charity with your neighbours, and intend to lead a new life, following the commandments of God, and walking from henceforth in His holy ways ; Draw near with faith, and take this holy Sacrament to your comfort ; and make your humble confession to Almighty God, meekly kneeling upon your knees.

In this invitation the conditions assumed are sorrow for sins, love towards all men, and resolve to live henceforth in holy compliance with God's commands ; and, these postulates being clearly laid down—as, indeed, they have been prepared for, and led up to, by all the previous parts of the Liturgy—the intending communicants are invited to " draw near," evidently not by local and bodily movement, for they have been already " conveniently placed," but with the mind and heart they are to come and draw nigh to God, who, no less in Christ than in nature, is a Spirit and must be approached and worshipped in spirit and in truth.   And this approach, be it observed, is to be made with faith or humble confidence while we receive the sacrament or outward sign of Christ's body and blood to our comfort.

Such faith is to be exercised, and such comfort is to be found, in this as in every other act and part of Christian life and worship, because we have always, in heaven, a High-Priest who (Heb. iv. 16, x. 19—22; Eph. iii. 12), though sinless, can yet be touched with the feeling of our infirmities, and who, through His life and death in the flesh, opened for us a new and living way into "the holies."[1] "*Therefore*," as say the Scriptures, because of this great High-Priest, and because of His one sacrifice (Heb. x. 10, 12, 14) once offered, "let us draw near with a true heart, in full assurance of faith ; " "let us come boldly unto the throne of grace, that we may obtain mercy and find grace to help in time of need."

Thus does Scripture, whence the liturgical expression "Draw near" is taken, teach us that here is signified, no access to an earthly Communion Table, but approach to that "house of God," eternal in the heavens, over which our High-Priest presides, sitting at the right hand of God. Such is the drawing near to Christ in heaven indicated in this part of our Communion Service ; and, so drawing near in spirit to the Saviour, the communicant will assuredly find "comfort," solace, encouragement, and strength in partaking of the appointed symbols to remind him of Christ's death for us.

Upon this, the invitation bids us make our "humble confession to Almighty God," meekly kneeling upon our knees.

The posture is prescribed ; and its becomingness will hardly be questioned by any. Should it, however, be a difficulty or a stumbling-block to others, let us not raise such a matter into fictitious importance, but let each and all strive to set others before ourselves and our own inclinations where, as it seems, no serious point of conscience can be involved.

Far more important, however, is the mental attitude of the communicant. By the whole structure of the service, as well as by the entire genius of the Gospel, and by the special confidence just encouraged, the communicant is supposed to be now "worthy" or fit to receive the signs of Christ's body and blood. Yet this preparation and this fitness or worthiness are so far from endowing him with merit, or making him, in himself and apart from Christ's pardoning mercy, meet to stand before God or to approach God even in worship, that it is just

---

[1] τῶν ἁγίων in the original, Heb. x. 19.

as a sinner, a repentant sinner, needing pardon and grace, that he is invited to come " with faith " and hold communion with Christ and Christ's whole body at the Table of the Lord. So appropriately is this confession of sin introduced at this point in the service.

(xiv.) *The Confession.*

A rubric preceding the Confession is in these words :—

Then shall this general Confession be made, in the name of all those that are minded to receive the holy Communion, by one of the ministers: both he and all the people kneeling humbly upon their knees, and saying.

Such a general and public confession is a remnant of the ancient patristic mode of openly acknowledging and deploring sin, as contrasted with the mediæval demand for private and detailed confession. The injunction of the rubric that clergy and laity should all, alike, join in one audible acknowledgment of sin before God, is a wholesome departure from the later mediæval practice of a private confession of the priest by himself and of the people by themselves.

Priest and people, alike, can only draw near to God as humble sinners and penitents, all equally needing the pardon that comes to each only through the one Mediator. It is well that all should humble themselves in making this acknowledgment openly before God and the congregation, and that the terms of the Confession should be so wide as to embrace all in self-humiliation, and yet so general as to expose none either to the contamination of learning other people's sins or to the degradation of too much looking ourselves, or directing the gaze of others, on a past that should be buried as something for which we are not only grieved but thoroughly ashamed.

The Confession enjoined is in these words :—

Almighty God, Father of our Lord Jesus Christ, Maker of all things, Judge of all men ; We acknowledge and bewail our manifold sins and wickedness, Which we, from time to time, most grievously have committed, By thought, word, and deed, Against Thy Divine Majesty, Provoking most justly Thy wrath and indignation against us. We do earnestly repent, And are heartily sorry for these our misdoings ; The remembrance of them is grievous unto us ; The burden of them is intolerable. Have mercy upon us, Have mercy upon us, most merciful Father ; For Thy Son our Lord Jesus Christ's sake, Forgive us all that is past ; And grant that we may ever hereafter Serve and please Thee In newness of life, To the honour and glory of Thy Name ; Through Jesus Christ our Lord.   Amen.

This wise and searching formulary is derived from several sources.

The part of it, which speaks of provoking God's wrath and indignation against us, is not only Scriptural as an acknowledgment that any sin and all sin, no less than unworthy communion, brings, as we saw above, the wrath of God upon us, but this phrase is found in the confession prescribed and used by Pollanus in the congregation of refugees who found a retreat at Glastonbury, when persecution obliged them to flee from their home at Strasburg.

The words, " by thought, word, and deed," come to us from the mediæval services.

The rest of the Confession, its greater part, we derive from the form which Melancthon and Bucer drew up for Hermann, Archbishop of Cologne ; and in their work those reformers were guided, to a great extent, by the teaching of Luther.

Here, then, in this Confession, as in the general construction of the English Liturgy, we have a most catholic admixture of parts and elements derived from antiquity before the Reformation, as well as from the teaching of the various leaders of the Reformation itself. Well may such facts be remembered by us, and rightly do they teach us to be in loving and intelligent communion with our fellow-Christians in all ages and countries, and in all the different modes of Church government that have prevailed or may prevail.

As to the form of confession, let it be observed that, while its utterance humbles us, duly, in presence of our fellow-worshippers, it is addressed to God and God only, in accordance with that cry of the ancient penitent (Psalm li. 4), " Against Thee only have I sinned and done this evil in Thy sight."

Observe the appropriateness of thus opening our hearts to that God whose forgiving mercy is most conspicuously shown in that He is the Father of our Lord Jesus Christ. So, too, we confess to Him who, as the Maker of all things, knows our hearts, our weaknesses, our temptations, and the grace likewise by which He strengthens us if we will use it.   No less appropriately is it to the Judge of all men, who knows the very secrets of our hearts, that we make confession.   Happy they who flee to that Judge now, for self-detection and amendment, that they may not lay up in store for themselves more tremendous judgment when this day of grace and salvation shall be past.

Before this God in Christ we not only acknowledge our sins, but we bewail them.   The communicant has already, in the theory of our service, reached such a condition of mind that he can truly say, "We do earnestly repent, and are heartily sorry for these our misdoings; the remembrance of them is grievous unto us; the burden of them is intolerable." Already sin, in its injurious effect upon man, in its dishonouring of God, in its bringing about the crucifixion of our Lord, in sight of God's righteous abhorrence of it and of His redeeming sympathy towards the sinner, has become thus painful to us; and more and more we strive and pray to realize the hatefulness of moral evil, spiritual poison, and to deepen our aversion from it and our aspiration after every grace and every virtue that are opposed to it.

In this frame of mind it is that we call upon our most merciful Father to have mercy upon us, and, while He forgives all that is past, to grant us such grace and help that we may ever hereafter serve and please Him in newness and righteousness of life, to the honour and glory of His name, through that blessed Christ by union of our spirit with whom we can do all things, even by our faith overcoming the evil of the world, and constraining men to take notice of us that we have been with Jesus, and in His society have learned to do those good works that so conspicuously glorify the Father.

(xv.)   *The Absolution.*

After the Confession follows this rubric :—

Then shall the priest (or the bishop, being present) stand up, and turning himself to the people, pronounce this Absolution.

Here all that need be observed is the intention of the

Church that the assurance of God's pardon shall be conveyed to the congregation by the most experienced and dignified of the ministers who may be present ; and this, by reasonable supposition, will be the bishop if he be in attendance. It is not, and cannot be, that the words are true in the mouth of one man and not true in the mouth of another. Their realization, in the case of each communicant, or of each man who hears any form of absolution, must depend solely upon the state of each man's heart.

God's wish to save all men in Christ varies not. It is fixed. The only contingent matter is in the sinner. Will he turn and live by using the proffered help of God's Spirit announced in the Gospel; or will he persist in sin and die ? In the latter event, no prelate, or dignitary of the Church, can give him valid absolution. In the former event, he has real absolution direct from God and Christ, whether the terms of pardon, and the fact of pardon, be delivered to him by a layman, or by a deacon, or by a presbyter, or by a bishop, or by no man but only by the written record of God's forgiving or absolving love in Christ.

Who pronounces the blessed conditions of pardon, and the intercessory prayer for pardon, is thus only a matter of decorum, and of hope that the man most eminent in the dignity of the Church on earth will declare the Gospel message of pardon most convincingly, and will make the prayer of intercession most devoutly.

On these grounds it is well that the bishop, if present, should pronounce the following Absolution :—

Almighty God, our heavenly Father, who of His great mercy hath promised forgiveness of sins to all them that with hearty repentance and true faith turn unto Him ; Have mercy upon you ; pardon and deliver you from all your sins ; confirm and strengthen you in all goodness ; and bring you to everlasting life ; through Jesus Christ our Lord. *Amen.*

These beautiful and simple words consist of two parts, and illustrate what, as we have already seen, are the two ancient modes of absolution. The first part declares that it is the promise of Almighty God that He will forgive the sins of all them that with hearty repentance and true faith turn

unto Him.   This is absolution by the ministering of the
divine message of pardon by Christ.   This is the kind of
absolution mentioned, in the "warning" of Communion, as
desirable for the man who cannot quiet his own conscience.
It may be enforced and supported by the wise and skilful
application of passages from Holy Writ, and by the counsels
and instructions of any discreet and learned minister of God's
Word ; but its substance is embodied in the first few words of
the Absolution we are now concerned with.   It is nothing
more or less than a declaration of the gospel of God's mercy
in Christ to every repenting and believing sinner ; and it is
true, whoever speaks it, or even if no man speak it.

The second part of our Absolution is taken from a form
employed at vespers in the Sarum Use ; and it is an exquisite
example of precatory absolution, of prayer for the sinner's
pardon and progress.   Not only does he who uses this form
of absolution pray for God's mercy to pardon all our past
sins, but the supplication is also for deliverance from the
bondage of evil habits, from the power of temptation, from
every inroad of sin : and, moreover, whatever thought or
wish or resolution of goodness has been already given us by
the Spirit of God, the prayer is that it may be confirmed and
strengthened ; and that thus we may, through Christ, be
brought to the perfection of that eternal life which is the
possession of every man that hath the Son, and which will be
a possession ever more and more realized and enjoyed as we
learn and know more of that God and His Christ whom to
know is (John xvii. 3) eternal life.

Such is the Absolution, by ministry of God's truth and
by prayer,—not by the mediæval novelty of *Ego te absolvo*—
which the Church of England enjoins in this her Communion
Service, as well as in her service for daily Morning and
Evening Prayer.   Nothing could be more Scriptural and
beautiful.

(xvi.) *The Comfortable Words.*

The congregation are directed to assent to this instruction as to God's pardon of the penitent, and to make these

prayers, for mercy and confirmation and eternal life, their own by their "Amen;" and "then the priest shall say" the well-known "comfortable words," giving what emphasis he can to each by calling on the congregation especially to "hear" them.

Hear what comfortable words our Saviour Christ saith unto all that truly turn to Him.

Come unto Me, all that travail and are heavy laden, and I will refresh you.—*St. Matt.* xi. 28.

So God loved the world, that He gave His only-begotten Son, to the end that all that believe in Him should not perish, but have everlasting life.—*St. John* iii. 16.

Hear also what Saint Paul saith.

This is a true saying, and worthy of all men to be received, That Christ Jesus came into the world to save sinners.—1 *Tim.* i. 15.

Hear also what Saint John saith.

If any man sin, we have an Advocate with the Father, Jesus Christ the righteous ; and He is the propitiation for our sins.—1 *St. John* ii. 1.

The idea of these texts being introduced, to give force to the teaching of the Absolution, is taken from the Lutheran form drawn up for Archbishop Hermann by Melancthon and Bucer. The texts selected, however, for our service are not wholly identical with those in Hermann's book. The first and last texts are found in both books. Our second and third verses are substitutes for other passages from Acts x. 43 and John iii. 35, 36.

Without attempting to compare the aptitude of these quotations, one thing seems clear, namely, that the opening words are most happily fitting for the wants of sinners who, as the Confession had said, feel themselves under a grievous and intolerable burden in the remembrance of sin.

To men in such a condition nothing can be more appropriate than our Lord's invitation and promise, "Come to Me, and I will give you rest." The catholicity of Christ's redemption is wisely brought under our notice by the second of the comfortable words, which reminds us that it was for "the world" God gave His Son, that all, by believing, might have eternal life. The third indicates not only the truth of

Christ's coming into the world to save sinners, but also the importance of that truth having "all acceptation."[1] And the fourth comfortable word addresses itself to any who, in spite of the Gospel and its blessings, have yet fallen into sin. To them it says that, not the sacrament of the Lord's Supper, not the absolution of a fellow-mortal, but Christ "the righteous" is our Advocate, that is, our Comforter,[2] and the propitiation,[3] or channel of divine mercy, for our sins.

So happily and completely do these comfortable words embrace the entire compass of the Christian's spiritual wants from the time of his being called to come for rest to Christ to the end when he shall cease from liability to sin, and enter into the presence of God and his one Mediator.

(xvii.) "Lift up your Hearts."

After these texts of Scripture the service leads us to the very ancient versicles in which minister and congregation challenge one another to the lifting up of hearts unto God and to the giving Him thanks :—

After which the priest shall proceed, saying.

Lift up your hearts.
We lift them up unto the Lord.
Let us give thanks unto our Lord God.
It is meet and and right so to do.

Let it be noticed how it is the heart whose lifting up is the essential part of this as of all Christian acts of worship. Unless the heart be lifted up to God in fervent thanksgiving, the Eucharist is naught.

Accordingly, at this point, the clergyman reiterates the importance of this duty to which he has already bidden the people and received their assent. The instruction for this part of the service is thus worded :—

Then shall the priest turn to the Lord's Table, and say,

* *These words* [Holy Father] *must be omitted on* Trinity Sunday. — It is very meet, right, and our bounden duty, that we should at all times, and in all places, give thank unto Thee, O Lord, Holy* Father, Almighty, Everlasting God.

---

[1] πάσης αποδοχῆς ἄξιος.   [2] παράκλητος.   [3] ἱλασμός.

The minister turns from the congregation towards the Lord's Table at this point, because the next portions of his duty will be at that Table and in connection with it.

In the words appointed for the priest, here, what is very noticeable is that, instead of setting the Eucharist by itself, as a thanksgiving quite apart from all others, the ground taken is that, at all times and in all places, it is very meet, right, and our bounden duty to give thanks to God.

(xviii.) The Proper Prefaces.

And upon this foundation of general thankfulness to God is based the special worship of the Eucharist. The rubric accordingly enjoins :—

Here shall follow the Proper Preface, according to the time, if there be any specially appointed: or else immediately shall follow,

Therefore with Angels and Archangels [etc.].

Of the "Proper Prefaces," that had been named in the mediæval Mass-book for certain days,—one of them, in honour of the Virgin Mary, having been introduced in 1095 by Pope Urban II.—only five have been continued in the English service ; those, namely, for Christmas, Easter, Ascension Day, Whit-Sunday, and Trinity Sunday.

The five Proper Prefaces stand thus in the English Prayer-book :—

PROPER PREFACES.

Upon Christmas Day, and seven days after.

Because Thou didst give Jesus Christ Thine only Son to be born as at this time for us ; who, by the operation of the Holy Ghost, was made very man of the substance of the Virgin Mary His mother ; and that without spot of sin, to make us clean from all sin. Therefore with Angels, etc.

Upon Easter Day, and seven days after.

But chiefly are we bound to praise Thee for the glorious Resurrection of Thy Son Jesus Christ our Lord : for He is the very Paschal Lamb, which was offered for us, and hath taken away the sin of the world ; who by His death hath destroyed death, and by His rising to life again hath restored to us everlasting life. Therefore with Angels, etc.

Upon Ascension Day, and seven days after.

Through Thy most dearly beloved Son Jesus Christ our Lord ; who after His most glorious Resurrection manifestly appeared to all His Apostles, and in their sight ascended up into heaven to prepare a place for us ; that where He is, thither we might also ascend, and reign with Him in glory. Therefore with Angels, etc.

Upon Whit-Sunday, *and six days after.*

Through Jesus Christ our Lord ; according to whose most true promise, the Holy Ghost came down as at this time from heaven with a sudden great sound, as it had been a mighty wind, in the likeness of fiery tongues, lighting upon the Apostles, to teach them, and to lead them to all truth ; giving them both the gift of divers languages, and also boldness with fervent zeal constantly to preach the Gospel unto all nations ; whereby we have been brought out of darkness and error into the clear light and true knowledge of Thee, and of Thy Son Jesus Christ. Therefore with Angels, etc.

Upon the feast of Trinity *only.*

Who art one God, one Lord ; not one only Person, but three Persons in one Substance. For that which we believe of the glory of the Father, the same we believe of the Son, and of the Holy Ghost, without any difference or inequality. Therefore with Angels, etc.

The Prefaces for Christmas and Whit-Sunday were composed in 1549. The other three are ancient, and date from the times of Pope Gelasius and Gregory the Great. Their subjects are, of course, connected with the special seasons of the Church's year, and, in each case, the event commemorated is made a ground for especial thanksgiving as an appropriate opening of the eucharistic service ; for the " canon," or generally recognised rule and order for this service, is, by some, regarded as beginning at this point. In a sense, all has been preparatory hitherto ; but now, and since the ancient versicles, " Lift up," etc., we deal, they say, with the service of the Lord's Supper and its so-called " canon " proper.

(xix.) *The " Holy, Holy, Holy."*

An earlier rubric has already shown us that, on ordinary Communion days, when there is no Proper Preface, the hymn " Holy, holy, holy," often called the *Tersanctus,* is to follow immediately upon the *Sursum corda* sentences.

On days with Proper Prefaces the direction is :—

After each of which Prefaces shall immediately be sung or said,

Therefore with Angels and Archangels, and with all the company of heaven, we laud and magnify Thy glorious Name ; evermore praising Thee, and saying, Holy, holy, holy, Lord God of hosts, heaven and earth are full of Thy glory : Glory be to Thee, O Lord most high. *Amen*

It is well to notice in this rubric, as in those preceding the

Nicene Creed and the " Glory be to God on high," that the alternative is given either to sing or say these parts of the service.
In this alternative two lessons are contained: first, the
English Church teaches how joyful and bright should be her
Eucharist, lighted up, in contrast with the portions that must
necessarily be read most gravely, by the sweet mirth of pious
song; and, if this be one instruction of these rubrics, the
other is no less important, and certainly not less needed in
the present day.   Here, and elsewhere, the English Prayer-
book teaches us to sing certain parts of our service, unless the
absence of singers compel us to read—for such we willingly
believe is the meaning of the alternative, " shall be sung or
said "—but it is only with these two modes of carrying on
divine worship that our Church is acquainted.   She nowhere
enjoins or permits that mongrel utterance known as " sing-
song," or " intoning "—an utterance which is not singing,
because there is no sweet variety of musical cadence in it, and
which is not reading, because it follows not the natural
pauses and emphases required by the meaning of the words.

Either in singing, then, or, if that cannot be, in reading,
here is to follow the *Tersanctus*.   Efforts are sometimes made
to deter the congregation from joining in this chant until the
words " Holy, holy, holy," are reached.   It is very plain,
however, that the rubric bids us all sing, or say, the entire
clause from " Therefore with angels," onwards.   And, thirty
years ago, such was the general, if not the universal, custom.

Very beautifully does this song attempt to realize the idea
of Christ's catholic or universal fellowship by associating our
praise and thanksgiving with that of the angelic hosts, who
bear God's messages to every part of creation, and with that
of all the company of heaven, including the goodly fellowship
of the apostles and prophets, the noble army of martyrs, and
all the spirits of the just made perfect; including the multitudes out of all nations whom as yet we have not known;
and including, also, our own familiar and dear ones, " not
lost, but gone before."

Surely, if the heathen Cicero, in his treatise on old age for
instance (chapters 21, 22), could anticipate with gladness the

" glorious day when he should enter the council and assembly of minds touched with divinity," we Christians, for whom Jesus has gone before to prepare abiding-places in His Father's many-mansioned home—we Christians, whose apostle could say that to him to live was Christ and to die was gain —we ought, at least occasionally, to kindle our piety and our sense of the unseen sufficiently to enable us heartily to take part with all God's other creatures, everywhere, in lauding and magnifying the holy name of Him who shows omnipotence and wisdom and beneficence on every side, and who, even in pain and all the terrible discipline of death and of moral evil, still teaches us how suffering is calculated and intended to draw forth sympathy and help in the beholders, and, in those who suffer, to quicken effort after amelioration or, where that cannot be in this life, to elicit courage to endure, patience to be ripened in gentleness, and cheerful loving faith that, seeing Christ, looks forward, beyond these agonies, to the rest and glory which remain.

Enough, cries such a soul, that we suffer like our Lord, that we may be crowned with Him; good, that we learn obedience, and be made perfect, by our appointed sufferings as He by His. Thus thinking, thus feeling, we may, either in circumstances of joy or of sorrow, join with intelligent and loving spirits everywhere, in heaven and on earth, in this happy and sanctifying song to the " holy, holy, holy, Lord God of hosts."

(xx.) *The Prayer of Humble Access.*

Next follows the rubric introducing the Prayer of Humble Access :—

Then shall the priest, kneeling down at the Lord's Table, say in the name of all them that shall receive the Communion this Prayer following.

In this rubric there is nothing which calls for particular notice, unless it be that the prayer is to be said " in the name " of all them that shall communicate.

This same expression had been employed in the rubric preceding the Confession—there, however, all who were minded to receive the holy Communion were to join in saying the Confession, while here only the minister is directed to utter the words of the prayer.

Two reflections arise out of this phrase in the two rubrics : first, it will be of no avail for the priest to use these or any words "in the name of" the people unless their hearts are with him in his words. They must confess, and bewail, and pray, earnestly and with their hearts, unless the service is to be, so far as concerns them, in name and in word only, and not in deed and in truth.

What would be thought of a petition made to an earthly potentate in the name of men who were indifferent as to that which was sought in their name ? Would not such a petition be a mockery on the part of the people, and an affront to the potentate ? And, if so, how much more is earnestness of devotion before heaven's King an indispensable condition for this and all our worship.

The other point to be noticed, in connection with both these rubrics, is that if others, besides the communicants, were present in the Church, they, no less, but rather more, than the communicants, would need to confess their sins generally, and particularly their hardihood in attending the Communion as spectators more or less interested, and yet refusing to partake of the bread and wine according to Christ's ordinance. This general consideration, coupled with the fact that no form of confession or of prayer is provided for non-communicants, but only and specifically for them that mind or intend to communicate, is, we take it, a clear indication that the theory and purpose of the English Church is that all shall communicate who are present at the celebration.

And now we come to the Prayer of Humble Access itself :—

We do not presume to come to this Thy Table, O merciful Lord, trust-ing in our own righteousness, but in Thy manifold and great mercies. We are not worthy so much as to gather up the crumbs under Thy Table. But Thou art the same Lord, whose property is always to have mercy : Grant us therefore, gracious Lord, so to eat the flesh of Thy dear Son Jesus Christ, and to drink His blood, that our sinful bodies may be made clean by His body, and our souls washed through His most precious blood, and that we may evermore dwell in Him, and He in us. *Amen.*

This prayer was composed for the English "Order of Com-munion" in 1548. It is unlike any collect known to us in other and older Liturgies, unless, indeed, the following phrase, in a prayer used by Basil, be thought to have suggested part of it. Basil prayed, " Therefore, all-holy Lord, do we Thy simple and unworthy servants, who have been permitted to minister at Thy holy altar, not for our righteousness, for we have done no good thing upon earth, but for Thy mercies and compassions which Thou hast shed on us abundantly, approach Thine altar."

(a.) " Table" not " Altar; " Coronation Service and Coronation Oath.

If this ancient prayer suggested aught, beyond a mere phrase, to the compilers of the English service, it was rather in the way of contrast than of resemblance, of avoidance than of imitation; for in 1549 they purposely omitted the word "altar " from all our services, and in this very prayer their usage varied between the phrases " God's Board," " Holy Table," and " Lord's Table." It is true that, in the service used at English coronations, the Lord's Table is styled an altar; but, then, that service is no part of our Church's authorized formularies. It is a form sanctioned, we believe, in most of its parts, only by the Privy Council of our monarchs, and alterable, in those parts, at the mere discretion of that Council; and, so far is the Coronation Service from any accurate use of ecclesiastical terms, especially as connected with the Lord's Table, that while with one breath it calls that Table an " altar," with the next it describes the Table and the space surrounding it as " the theatre."

It thus appears how popular and inaccurate is the language of the Coronation Service with reference to the Lord's Table, and how little ground it affords for the argument that the Church of England ever sanctions so unscriptural a practice as the speaking of an altar as part of the fittings and appurtenances of a Christian Church. When it can be fairly and truthfully alleged that the Church allows the Table and its surroundings to be called a " theatre," then, and not before then, can the usage of the Coronation Service be adduced to prove that the English Church styles the Lord's Table an " altar."

As, however, this subject of the Coronation Service has been brought under our notice by an unfair use which is sometimes made of part of its language, it may be well here to call attention to the fact that, whereas the general language and arrangement of that service are not, so far as we know, sanctioned by any canon of the Church or any statute of the realm, but rest only on the determination of the Privy Council, there are embodied in the Coronation Service a declaration and an oath to be taken and subscribed by the monarch; and of these the latter is authorized and prescribed by numerous Acts of Parliament—for example, by 1 Will. and Mary, st. i. c. 6; by 5 Anne, st. i. c. 8; and by 39 and 40 Geo. III., c. 67 : and these forms, of declaration and oath, are quite worth quoting in connection with the English Church and its Prayer-book and Communion Service.

Part of the declaration is in these words :—

"I, George the Third, by the grace of God King of Great Britain, etc., Defender of the Faith, etc., do solemnly and sincerely, in the presence of God, profess, testify, and declare that I do believe that in the sacrament of the Lord's Supper there is not any transubstantiation of the elements of bread and wine into the body and blood of Christ at or after the consecration thereof by any person whatsoever ; and that the invocation or adoration of the Virgin Mary or any other saint, and the sacrifice of the Mass, as they are now used in the Church of Rome, are superstitious and idolatrous. And I do solemnly, in the presence of God, profess, testify, and declare that I make this declaration, and every part thereof, in the plain and ordinary sense of the words read unto me, as they are commonly understood by English Protestants, without evasion, equivocation, or mental reservation whatsoever, and without any dispensation already granted me for this purpose by the Pope, or any other authority or person whatsoever," etc.

If these be the words of the declaration, no less stringent and important are the terms of the oath, the third part of which is thus arranged in the way of question and answer :—

"*Archbishop.* Will you to the utmost of your power maintain the laws of God, the true profession of the Gospel, and the Protestant Reformed Religion Established by Law? And will you maintain and preserve inviolably the settlement of the Church of England and the doctrine, worship, discipline, and government thereof as by law established within the kingdoms of England," etc.?

"*King.* All this I promise to do.

"Then the king . . . laying his right hand upon the holy Gospel," says "these words: The things which I have here before promised, I will perform and keep. So help me God.

"Then the king kisseth the book and signeth the oath."

Now, about this declaration sanctioned by this oath, there is no room for excusable misunderstanding. The whole matter is appointed and required, as we have seen, by many most important statutes of the realm. This oath and the declaration, except in so far as they may be limited and modified by Parliament, are of the very essence and substance of the English constitution and monarchy.

And it is in this sense, and as bound by this declaration and its oath, that each English monarch receives from every English clergyman, at his ordination, a pledge of allegiance in the terms of the article in the thirty-sixth Canon (of 1604), to the effect that—

"The King's Majesty, under God, is the only supreme governor of this realm, and of all other his Highness's dominions and countries, as well in all spiritual or ecclesiastical things or causes, as temporal."

And, as if that canonical form were not distinct enough, the law requires that every candidate for deacon's and priest's orders, and every incumbent on taking possession of his church, shall take the following oath :—

"I, *A. B.*, do swear that I will be faithful and bear true allegiance to her Majesty Queen Victoria, her heirs and successors, *according to law.* So help me God."

Thus is every clergyman bound by oath, so long as he does not resign his cure and renounce the essential conditions of his ordination in the English Church, to bear faithful, true, and lawful allegiance to the English sovereign as the declared

and sworn opponent of the superstitious and idolatrous sacrifices of the Mass, and as the equally declared and sworn
defender and upholder of the Protestant Reformed religion
established by law.

There is, we say, no reasonable excuse for ignoring these
oaths of the clergy and of the monarch; and it is to us simply
amazing to find clergymen, like the editor of the *Directorium
Anglicanum* and numbers of others among the Ritualists and
those with Ritualistic proclivities, retaining the *status* and
often the cures and preferments of English clergymen, and
yet reviling the name of Protestant, denouncing the Reformation, decrying the "Established" Church, and denying the
authority of the Queen in Council; while, at the same time,
they practise, to the utmost of their power, the rites of the
Roman communion and inculcate the doctrines of the "sacrifice of the Mass!"

Surely, those clerical defamers of the Protestant Reformed
Church, by law established, must have forgotten their own
repeated oaths and must be ignorant of the most elementary
principles of the English constitution. It is charitable to
hope they are thus oblivious and thus ignorant; but, then,
similar forgetfulness or ignorance of law would not exculpate
the coiner, or the forger standing at any criminal bar of the
country.

How the anti-Protestant section of the Ritualistic clergy
can satisfy their own consciences, or free themselves from the
charge of perjury in this matter, we are at a loss to imagine.
At all events, however that may be, this study of the Coronation Service, so often quoted by Ritualists, has taught us that,
until we are prepared, in strictness of language, to call the
chancels of our churches "theatres," we must not depend on
the popular language of portions of the Coronation Service to
justify us in styling the Communion Table an "altar;" and,
moreover, the same study of the graver and more important
parts of the Coronation Service has brought distinctly under
our observation the unquestionable fact that every clergyman
is bound, by oath after oath, to render lawful obedience to the
Queen in Council as, under God and Christ, the very head of

the English Church: and, yet again, every English clergyman is equally pledged loyally to uphold and conform to
the Protestant Reformed Church as by law established.

That other grounds no better support the name of "altar"
as misapplied to the Table of the Lord, we have already seen;
and therefore we rejoice that, in the Prayer of Humble Access,
as in every part of the Church's formularies, that unscriptural
and misleading term, "altar," has been avoided or abandoned,
and the true name of the Lord's Table has been employed.

Good, in this respect, is the contrast between Basil's liturgical prayer and this part of the English service.

(b.) *The Prayer itself.*

Most happily does our Prayer-book disown all merit, or
meritorious worthiness, in our approach to the sacrament.
Not trusting in anything we have done, even when we have
striven to make our lives most righteous, but casting ourselves wholly on the divine mercy and forgiveness and sanctification in and by Christ—so only do we come to the holy
Table. Calling to mind the history of the Syro-Phœnician
woman (Mark vii. 27, 28), we acknowledge ourselves as de-
serving a position even lowlier than that which she took to
herself; for, whereas she aspired to the privilege of picking up
such crumbs of divine help as fell under the Jewish table,
neglected by the Jews, we own ourselves unworthy even of
such crumbs.

It is most desirable that we should notice how, in this
history of our Lord's dealing with the Canaanite woman, the
help she asks, in the way of healing for her daughter, is styled
"bread" and "crumbs" of bread. So natural and Scriptural
is the idiom which designates all manner of coming to Christ
and believing on Him and partaking of any benefits from
Him, as eating His "bread," the "bread" which God has
prepared for His children. In this, as in so many other
illustrations in our first book, we see that eating the bread of
God and of Christ is very far from signifying exclusively, or
most frequently, a participation in the sacrament of the Lord's
Supper. Happy they who seek to eat the bread of Christ in

every way, sacramental and non-sacramental; and happy they who come to Christ with the same persistent earnestness and the same humility which characterized the Syro-Phœnician. Well for us if, with such thoughts and such purpose, we adopt this self-abasement of the Prayer of Humble Access.

Then, in contrast with our unworthiness, is set forth the unchanging beneficence of God and of His Christ, "the same yesterday, to-day, and for ever," and the property or character of whose unchangeableness is "always to have mercy." To this God it is that we raise the supplication, Grant us so to eat the flesh of Christ, and to drink His blood—that is, so to come to Him, and so to believe on Him, generally in all life and worship, and particularly in this sacrament, that, both in soul and body, we may be cleansed and benefited by the sacrifice, once made and once for all finished, of His precious body and blood.

This supplication for benefits, both for our souls and bodies—both, that is, for our minds, with their infinite aptitudes and capacities, and for our bodies with their many infirmities, and yet with such wonderful interdependence between them and our minds—this supplication is, in the Prayer of Humble Access, quaintly arranged so that, for the thoughtless, there is need to be warned against imagining that it is by the flesh rather than by the blood of Christ that "our sinful bodies" are to be made clean, and by His blood rather than by His flesh that our "souls" are to be "washed." In reality, no such superstitious idea is meant to be countenanced by the Prayer-book: but just as, in the existing forms of administration, the prayer is that the body and blood of our Lord may preserve our bodies and souls unto everlasting life; and, just as in Scripture (1 Thess. v. 23) St. Paul prays that men's spirits, souls, and bodies may be preserved blameless unto the coming of Christ; so, in like manner, this prayer, notwithstanding its quaint arrangement, asks that, through the perfected sacrifice of Christ, we may be washed and cleansed both in body and soul. To this the entreaty is added, that so, in the pre-sacramental language of the fourth Gospel (John vi. 56), we may evermore dwell in Christ and He is us.

How this blessed indwelling is promised (John xiv. 23) to all who keep Christ's commandments generally, and who love Christ, we have already seen. Happy we if we intelligently and earnestly keep the particular command to break bread in grateful remembrance of Christ and in loving fellowship with all believers, that we may so procure to ourselves that the Father and the Son shall come and make their abode with us. Amen; so let it be.

(xxi.) *The Prayer of Consecration.*
(a.) *The Rubric.*

And now we proceed to consider the rubric which introduces the " Prayer of Consecration : "—

When the priest, standing before the Table, hath so ordered the bread and wine, that he may with the more readiness and decency break the bread before the people, and take the cup into his hands, he shall say the Prayer of Consecration, as followeth.

The clergyman is here directed to stand " before the Table," previous to saying the prayer, in order that he may so arrange the elements that his taking the paten and the cup into his hands, during the prayer, may be the more readily and devoutly done " before the people."

In regard to this rubric several points have been established by the recent judgment of the Privy Council in *Ridsdale* v. *Clifton.*

" Before the Table " is a position, their lordships hold, which may denote the clergyman's standing either on the north side of the table, looking south, or on the west side, looking east, while he arranges the bread and wine for consecration. On whatever side of the table the minister may stand, however, their lordships declare the words " before the people " to be equivalent in meaning, in this rubric, to " in the sight of the people." " They have no doubt the rubric requires the manual acts to be so done, that, in a reasonable and practical sense, the communicants, especially if they are conveniently placed for receiving of the holy sacrament, as is presupposed in the office, may . . . see them." Whatever position the minister may assume, "he must," in the opinion of their lordships, "stand so that he may, in good faith, enable the communicants present, or the bulk of them, being properly placed, to see, if they wish it, the breaking of the bread and the performance of the other manual acts mentioned. He must not interpose his body so as intentionally to defeat the object of the rubric and to prevent this result."

The general view of the Privy Council is that, "if it were necessary[1] that there should be extracted from the rubrics a rule governing the position of the minister throughout the whole Communion office, where no contrary direction is given, or necessarily implied, the rule could not . . . be any other than that laid down in *Hibbert* v. *Purchas;* and they entertain no doubt that the position which would be required by that rule—a position, namely, in which the minister would stand at the north side of the Table, looking south—is not only lawful, but is that which would, under ordinary circumstances, enable the minister, with the greatest certainty and convenience, to fulfil the requirements of all the rubrics."

Thus explicit is the lawful obligation on every clergyman to say the consecration prayer at the north end of the Table, looking south. Still, notwithstanding this distinct interpretation of the rubric by the Queen in Council, numbers of the clergy continue to consecrate the bread and wine with their backs to the congregation. The only plea we hear advanced in defence of this procedure is, that the bulk of the communicants can, nevertheless, see the manual acts of the clergyman.

This is an allegation that can most easily be tested. Let a man, in his surplice, stand before the Table with his back towards the people, and from the points of the Table reached by his hands, as he performs the manual acts, let lines touching the sides of his garments be drawn till they reach

---

[1] By this phrase, "if it were necessary," the Privy Council only imply that such a necessity was not laid upon them in the case of *Ridsdale* v. *Clifton*, because the defendants had not brought this point adequately under the notice of the court. By no means do their lordships declare, in the way of anticipation of any future case, that such a rule could not then be necessary, and might not now be most useful.

the walls of the chancel; and is it not clear that, in the vast majority of churches, three or four communicants on the right hand of the clergyman, and three or four on his left, will be the utmost number of those who can, by any possibility, witness the manual acts? If this be so, will six or eight persons constitute "the bulk" of the communicants in our ordinary churches?

Well, then, what must be the result of a future decision in the Privy Council when, in the phraseology of the late judgment, the evidence on this point is brought before the court with precision? Given the width of a man's elbows covered with a surplice, the distance in front of him of his hands when engaged in the manual acts; and with these two data and a drawing to scale of his church and its chancel, together with evidence as to the average number of his communicants and the parts of the church or chancel generally occupied by them during the Prayer of Consecration—and with these simple points ascertained, a large proportion of our sacerdotal clergymen would be proved to be constantly violating the law by interposing their bodies between the bulk of the congregation and the sacramental elements in one of the most sacred acts of religious worship. This, we submit, is not a dignified position to be taken up by any man; it is not edifying for the Christian people; and, as pursued by those whose religious and social duties should make them conspicuous in the observance of all law and order, it is anything but decorous. We trust that a wise policy—to say nothing of higher motives —will induce the Ritualists so to change their attitude in this respect, that further litigation, turning as it would on a mere question of geometrical measurement, may be avoided.

Meanwhile, the legal interpretation of the rubric is clear. The minister must so stand, and so arrange the bread and wine, that the bulk of the communicants shall be able, if they desire it, to see the performance of the manual acts prescribed in the Prayer of Consecration; and, for this end, the lawful and convenient position for the clergyman is at the north end of the Table, with his face towards the south.

(b.) *The Prayer of Consecration itself.*

And now we proceed to examine the form of consecration itself. In doing so it may be convenient to notice that the prayer consists of three parts : The invocation ; The supplication ; and The rehearsal of Christ's words.

A. *The Invocation.*

The invocation is thus worded :—

> Almighty God, our heavenly Father, who of Thy tender mercy didst give Thine only Son Jesus Christ to suffer death upon the cross for our redemption ; who made there (by His one oblation of Himself once offered) a full, perfect, and sufficient sacrifice, oblation, and satisfaction, for the sins of the whole world ; and did institute, and in His holy Gospel command us to continue, a perpetual memory of that His precious death, until His coming again——

The prayer is thus addressed to our Almighty Father in heaven. He is our Father and will withhold no good thing from us. Let us approach Him in loving confidence. He is all-powerful, and His benevolent inclination is limited by no lack of ability to accomplish all that He sees to be for our real advantage. Let us come to Him in full assurance of faith. Yea, let us remember that such is our Father's tender mercy towards us, that, when we were in bondage to sin and evil habits and influences, He gave as our ransom, to buy us back from that bondage, His only-begotten Son Jesus Christ.

And this blessed ransomer, proceeds the invocation, made upon the cross one oblation of Himself once offered ; and thereby achieved a full, perfect, and sufficient sacrifice, oblation, and satisfaction, for the sins of the whole world.

Let it be observed that here is an echo of the Scriptural teaching that Christ was the ransom for all men (1 Tim. ii. 4, 6), in accordance with the divine wish[1] that all men should be saved by coming to the knowledge of Christian truth.

---

[1] ὃς πάντας ἀνθρώπους θέλει σωθῆναι—who *wishes* all men to be saved. The divine *will* is irresistible. The divine *wish* appeals to man's volition for its accomplishment.

And, moreover, we should notice the accumulation of terms here used to signify every possible aspect of Christ's one sacrifice, in its presentation or offering up unto God; in its entire and absolute fulness of perfection; in its satisfactoriness or, in Scripture phrase (Matt. iii. 17), its well-pleasingness[1] to God. Not only did our blessed Lord finish the work which the Father (John xvii. 4) had given Him to do; not only did He most truly exclaim, as the sacrifice of His death was ending, "It is finished," (John xix. 30); not only was there thus made a propitiation for the sins of the whole world (1 John ii. 2); not only was it thus made manifest, in act, as well as word, that God was unwilling any should perish, and would have all men come to repentance (2 Peter iii. 9); but, in this invocation, the Scriptural teaching of the Protestant Reformed Church of England stands in marked contrast with the doctrines of the Church of Rome, and of those amongst us who wish to re-introduce mediæval ideas on this subject. For, whereas the language of the mediævalists treats of the sacrifice of the Mass as being daily repeated in many Churches on earth, our prayer, in harmony with the New Testament, knows only one sacrifice once made upon the cross: and whereas the mediæval notion was of Christ as perpetually offering up His sacrifice in heaven, the Prayerbook and the apostolic writings distinctly teach (Heb. vii. 27) that Jesus "needeth not daily . . . to offer up sacrifice; . . . for this He did once when He offered up Himself;" and, again (Heb. ix. 24, 25, 26, 28), it is declared of the object of Christ's entrance into heaven that it was not "that He should offer Himself often . . . but now once, in the end of the world,[2] hath He appeared, to put away sin by the sacrifice of Himself. . . . Christ was once offered to bear the sins of many."

Thus, alike in the English Prayer-book and in Holy Writ, is Christ, in contradistinction from the many sacrifices of the

---

[1] οὗτός ἐστιν ὁ υἱός μου ὁ ἀγαπητός, ἐν ᾧ ηὐδόκησα: This is My beloved Son, in whom I am well pleased.

[2] "The end of the world," or "the last days," was a well-known designation of the whole Christian or Messianic dispensation.   •

Mass, our one sacrifice ; and, in contradistinction from the mediæval doctrine of His continual offering of Himself in heaven, He made one oblation or offering of Himself once for all. He still, of course, retains the dignity and designation of our High-Priest who has passed into heaven ; but His position in heaven, it should never be forgotten, is, not on the altar, but at the right hand of the throne of God.   Even in the Apocalypse, where an altar in heaven is named several times, (Rev. vi. 9, viii. 3, 5, ix. 13, xi. 1, xiv. 18, xvi. 7) it is not Christ, but the prayers of saints and heavenly incense, which are offered on that altar; and it is not Jesus, but an angel, who ministers at that altar.

In the Apocalypse, as elsewhere in Scripture, the heavenly position of Jesus, the Lamb, the Lion of the tribe of Judah, the Root of David, is " in the midst of the throne of God " (Rev. v. 6), or, in the more usual language of Scripture, He has overcome and is seated with His Father on His throne (Rev. iii. 21).

Our High-Priest in heaven "hath by one offering perfected for ever[1] them that are being sanctified."   "This Man, after He had offered one sacrifice for sins completely [or for ever],[1] sat down on the right hand of God, from thenceforth awaiting till His enemies be made His footstool" (Heb. x. 12, 13).   He is our Priest and High-Priest over the House of God in heaven and on earth ; but it is as having once for all offered Himself as the one sacrifice for sins upon the altar of the cross (Heb. xiii. 10, 12), and as now sitting, a Prince, at God's right hand, that He bears this name.   His present function is as our Intercessor according to God, like the Holy Spirit (Rom. viii. 26, 27, 34) ; as our Advocate, Comforter, Paraclete— again like the Holy Spirit (1 John ii. 1 ; John xiv. 16, 17) ; as the sole Mediator between God and man (1 Tim. ii. 5) ; as one who can be " touched with the feeling of our infirmities " (Heb. iv. 15) ; as one who is " able to save them to the uttermost that come unto God by Him " (Heb. vii. 25).

All these functions and characters are ascribed in Scripture

---

[1] εἰς τὸ διηνεκές, completely, thoroughly, to the utmost in point of efficiency, and for ever in regard to duration.

to our great Priest and High-Priest, but there is no hint in Holy Writ—nay, rather, there is direct, reiterated, and emphatic contradiction of the idea—that Jesus continues, or perpetually offers up, His one sacrifice which was once for all made, offered, and accepted.

Surely, this most important and comforting truth should be no less firmly grasped by us, and no less clearly held fast, than it is distinctly inculcated in the sacred volume and in the English Prayer of Consecration.

The concluding words of the invocation are an historical statement of the fact that Christ, in the Gospel, instituted a memory of His precious death, and appointed that this "memory" should be constantly perpetuated until His coming again.

B. *The Supplication.*

Upon this follows the supplication of our prayer in this form :—

Hear us, O merciful Father, we most humbly beseech Thee ; and grant that we receiving these Thy creatures of bread and wine, according to Thy Son our Saviour Jesus Christ's holy institution, in remembrance of His death and passion, may be partakers of His most blessed body and blood.

No words can be simpler. There is a fresh appeal to the Father whose mercies in Christ had just been dwelt upon ; and to Him the humble petition is raised, that He will hear us, and grant that while, in remembrance of Christ's sufferings and death, and in obedience to His command, we partake of God's "creatures" of bread and wine, our minds and hearts may be so fed with Christ as to enhance our oneness with Him, and His with us.

Most noteworthy is the expression, "*creatures* of bread and wine." Of course these "creatures" are thus characterized as wholly different and distinct from the begotten and un-created Son of God. They, the bread and wine, even at the time when, after their consecration, we shall receive them, are still to be and to be received—so we pray—as *created* whilst He, the Son, is ever *uncreated*.

Another point, well worthy of notice in this supplication, is that we beseech God to grant that our reception of these His creatures of bread and wine may be in accordance with our Saviour's holy institution; that our participation, that is, in the sacred rite, may not be encumbered by the additions of thoughts and acts which had grown up around the sacrament in the dark ages; but that, in all the joyous simplicity and pious devotion of the evangelic and apostolic breaking of bread, we may comply with our Lord's command, and do this in remembrance of Him and of the benefits derived to us from His sufferings and death. Not only do we thus pray that our communion may be in harmony with the original institution, but the English Prayer-book teaches us to single out, especially, this one characteristic of the Eucharist, and pray that it may affect us as a memorial of Christ.

Then, omitting the petition of the Mass, that the Holy Spirit may descend upon the bread and wine and make them unto us the body and blood of the Lord, the Liturgy prays that, in this sacrament, we may, in every spiritual sense, be partakers of Christ's most blessed body and blood. How completely all idea of a participation of the Saviour's objective and material flesh and blood is avoided in this phrase, we have seen abundantly, while examining the teaching of Holy Writ on this point, so that it is not necessary to attempt to show further, at present, that as to all eating of Christ's flesh and drinking His blood, alike sacramentally and non-sacramentally, the flesh and the objective presence could profit nothing, but only the words, the meaning and feeling of Christ, are spirit and are life.

C. *The Rehearsal of the Institution.*

And then, from this beautiful prayer, not that the elements may be changed in any way, but that we, while receiving them in obedient memory of Christ, may be in spirit partakers of His body and blood, the consecration passes on to its third part, in which the history of the institution is thus recited:—

Who, in the same night that He was betrayed, [1]took bread ; and,

[1] Here the priest is to take the paten into his hands.
[2] And here to break the bread.
[3] And here to lay his hand upon all the bread.
[4] Here he is to take the cup into his hand.
[5] And here to lay his hand upon every vessel (be it chalice or flagon) in which there is any wine to be consecrated.

when He had given thanks, [2]He brake it and gave to His disciples, saying, Take, eat, [3]this is My body which is given for you : Do this in remembrance of Me.   Likewise after supper He [4]took the cup ; and, when He had given thanks, He gave it to them, saying, Drink ye all of this ; for this [5]is My blood of the New Testament, which is shed for you and for many for the remission of sins : Do this, as oft as ye shall drink it, in remembrance of Me.   *Amen.*

Except in the " Amen " of the congregation there is not a word of prayer in all this.   It is a rehearsal of what Jesus did and said in giving the bread and wine to His disciples at His Last Supper with them ; and the manual acts of taking the paten and the cup into the minister's hands, of breaking the bread and laying the hand upon it and on the wine—all these acts are obviously intended to call up before the minds of the communicants a more vivid recollection of our Saviour's procedure than would be produced by the mere words.

It was a very ancient custom, as appears from the old Liturgies which remain to us, to introduce more or less of the words of institution into the act of consecration ; and this ancient usage has been retained in the Church of England.

After the full examination, attempted above, of these and all the other words of institution, it is needless here to repeat their exposition in detail ; but the most interesting means of illustrating this part of our service, and at the same time accentuating its apostolic significance, will perhaps be employed if we reproduce this rehearsal with what St. Luke and St. Paul show to have been its alternative and equivalent expressions.

For instance, if one of St. Paul's accounts of the meaning of the institution be adopted (1 Cor. x. 16, 17), the rehearsal will stand thus :—

Who, in the same night that He was betrayed, took bread ; and, when He had given thanks, He brake it and gave to His disciples, saying, Take, eat, this bread is a communion or fellowship or participation [1] of My body in the sense of the many believing members of which I am the head : Do this in remembrance of Me.   Likewise after supper He took

[1] κοινωνία.

the cup; and, when He had given thanks, He gave it to them, saying, Drink of this, all of you; for this cup is a communion or fellowship or participation of My blood which was shed for you and for many for the remission of sins: Do this, as oft as ye shall drink, in remembrance of Me.

Or, yet again, if we adopt St. Paul's record of the words actually spoken over the cup (1 Cor. xi. 25), and, accordingly, of the words suggested for the bread, we shall have the rehearsal as follows:—

Who, in the same night that He was betrayed, took bread; and, when He had given thanks, He brake it and gave to His disciples, saying, This is the New Covenant in My body which is for you: This do for My remembrance. Likewise after supper He took the cup; and, when He had given thanks, He gave it to them, saying, This cup is the New Covenant in My blood: This do, as oft as ye drink, for My remembrance.

Now, these two alternative forms are either of apostolic writing, or they are of apostolic suggestion; and they must necessarily be, therefore, the best and most authentic expositions of the words, as they stand in our Liturgy, taken from the shorter forms supplied by St. Matthew and St. Mark.

How free these fuller forms are from all semblance of a doctrine which implies any change in the objective nature of the bread and wine must be obvious. They represent the sacramental elements as pregnant with significance. The bread suggests many grains of wheat made into one loaf; the wine suggests many grapes pressed into one cup; and both suggest, accordingly, the body and blood of Christ in which all believers constitute that one body of which Christ is the head.

Nor is this all the genuine and Scriptural significance of the sacramental bread and wine, for the bread is also the new covenant ratified by Christ's body given, and the wine is the new covenant ratified by His blood shed for man's redemption.

All this rich significance will be brought before our minds by the Prayer of Consecration, each time we hear it used, if we take Scripture as the best interpreter of Scripture—if, instead of confining ourselves to the shortest and most condensed and epitomized record of St. Matthew and St. Mark, we allow the light to be thrown by St. Luke and St. Paul upon those shorter forms.

One very plain effect of thus bringing the simple teaching of Scripture to bear upon the subject is, that all ground for believing in any transubstantiation, or insubstantiation, or any other material and objective change of the bread and wine, vanishes, and we see that the sense in which Christ said the bread was His body, and the wine His blood, was in so far as each represented the Christian covenant ratified by the sacrifice of the Saviour, or in so far as each represented the union betwixt all believers with one another and with Christ as their head. And this, taken with what has been said in earlier parts of this essay, must suffice for our exposition of the consecration prayer; except, indeed, that we ought to notice the omission, from the existing English Liturgy, of all opportunity and excuse for converting this breaking of bread into a sacrifice for the living or the dead, as was the custom of the Middle Ages, especially at this part of what they called the " canon " of the Mass.

(xxii.) *Rubric on Administration.*

And now we proceed to the rubric concerning the administration of the elements :—

Then shall the minister first receive the Communion in both kinds himself, and then proceed to deliver the same to the bishops, priests, and deacons, in like manner (if any be present), and after that to the people also in order, into their hands, all meekly kneeling. And, when he delivereth the bread to any one, he shall say.

That the clergy shall themselves first communicate, before administering to the people, is an ancient custom, though it does not appear so early as Justin Martyr, and there is no trace of it in the New Testament. However, it is convenient as a matter of order and decorum; and, so far as it gives priority of reception to the clergy, this was explained, in the older English Liturgies, as being done in order that the clergy might be free to assist in administering the elements to the rest of the communicants. There is nothing to make it appear that, in the Liturgies either of the sixteenth or seventeenth centuries, this practice was intended to give greater honour to the clergy as compared with the laity; and, if not in the earlier Liturgies of the Reformed Church, assuredly not in the present Communion Service is such merely sacerdotal precedence likely to have been contemplated or countenanced.

We take the rubric, therefore, to enjoin that the *officiating* clergy shall first communicate, and then all the rest of the communicants, whether lay or clerical, in such order as may be convenient, irrespective of whether any be in Holy Orders or not.

For any non-officiating clerics to be communicated before the laity, and especially apart from the laity, seems to us to be a forgetting of the principle and purpose of the rubric in a somewhat too exact observance of its letter; and if such priority on the part of non-officiating clergymen seem too like priestly assumption on the part of those who claim or encourage it, it is almost needless to say what obviously lies against the practice, adopted in some churches, of administering the elements to unordained members of surpliced choirs after the clergy, indeed, but at the rail by themselves before the rest of the communicants are called up.

The people are meekly to kneel and receive into their hands the Communion in both kinds. This is all very plain in its signification; but there are the further words, "in order;" and for these words we know of no authoritative definition, unless, indeed, we be content, as it seems wisest we should be, with the now universal practice of the communicants going to the "rails" to kneel and receive the elements there in an orderly fashion.

Whether, again, the people should be left free to go to the rails at their own discretion, or whether they should be invited, by a church-officer, to come in convenient numbers and with such an alternation from different sides of the church as shall produce the least crowding and unseemliness or discomfort—these are all points which appear to lie fairly within the meaning of the words "in order;" and the clergyman, and his wardens, in each church, may surely be permitted to manifest their tact and judgment in so arranging these matters as shall best suit the structure of their church and the requirements of their people.

The rubric, which regulates the administering of the wine, is so far identical with the corresponding rule for delivering the bread, that it will be best here to quote it and then to consider it together with its companion rubric :—

And the minister that delivereth the cup to any one shall say [etc.].

Just as the bread is to be *delivered* to any one, so, too, the cup is to be *delivered*. One would think these words were incapable of being misunderstood. They obviously signify that the cup, no less than the bread, is to be given and set free in the hands of each communicant. Yet one may occasionally meet with clergymen who so far forget their duty of obedience to the rubric, and of courteous compliance with the reasonable expectation of communicants, that they retain the cup in their hands while putting it to the lips of the people. Such a practice, like the occasional making of crosses in the air with the cup or with the bread, is much to be deplored, not only as a marked and superstitious departure from the general meaning and spirit of our Protestant Reformed Church, but also because of the pain and indignation which it must create in the minds of many pious but thoughtful persons who come to the English Lord's Table in expectation of what habit, education, and law entitle them there to find, and, instead of this their legal and accustomed right of communion, are presented with an imitation of abolished mediæval forms and doctrines. For, as all parties of any thoughtfulness are agreed, the ceremonies would be unimportant if it were not for the doctrine they symbolize and imply.

Thus, on grounds of law and of Christian considerateness and charity, we appeal to the clergy to abstain, at least in this part of the service, from crossings and from such partial withholding of the cup, as are morally certain to offend not a few communicants. And if it be replied that some would be offended if there were no making of crosses in the air and no retaining of the cup in the minister's hand, the rejoinder is, we think, clear and fair, that those, to whom we appeal, can easily, as being the innovators in the English Church, and as having the law against them, instruct their friends not to expect at the English Communion Table rites which have either been pointedly omitted from the reformed service or else are actually opposed to both the letter and the spirit of our Church.

Isolated or Conjoint Administration.

And now we come to the last point which requires to be noticed in these two rubrics. Certain words are to be said by the minister that delivereth the bread or the cup " to any one." Over the interpretation of these words, much heat has been engendered in recent days. Only a few years ago it was the custom, the general if not the universal custom, for as many communicants, as conveniently could kneel at the Communion rails, to come to those rails together : and then to them, so kneeling, the minister addressed the appointed words of administration ; and, that done, he delivered the bread to each. The same practice was adopted in giving the cup. Then those communicants went to their places in the church, and others filled the rails, to whom the words and the elements were similarly spoken and given ; and so, in due order, all the people communicated.

Now, with reference to this mode of administering, it could not be said that any one who was minded to communicate went away without the minister, who delivered the bread or the wine, saying to him the appointed words.

Mark, the rubric does not enjoin that the words shall be said to each communicant separately, nor to each communicant as he communicates, nor by the minister each time he administers. The rubric merely declares that the minister who delivers the elements " to any one " shall say—it may be, shall say once ; it may be, shall say six times ; it may be, shall say any number of times ; but, at least, once he shall say the words of administration.

When the clergyman pronounces any benediction, he says it to the whole assembly, and no one can go away and truly say that the benediction, pronounced on each and all, was not said to him. Similarly, whether in the administration of the sacramental elements the singular form, as it is printed in the English Liturgy, be retained, or whether the plural form be adopted as is sometimes done, assuredly the words, if only once said by each officiating minister, *are said;* and this is what the rubric enjoins: and even though only once said, they can be taken, and ought to be taken, by each communicant heartily to himself.

Thus, we submit, the custom of forty years ago, and of many a decade anterior to that time, was an adequate compliance with these rubrics.

If any one shall object, that the singular form in the words of administration necessarily implies the words are to be said to each communicant separately, it may suffice to remind such an objector that, sometimes, the English Prayer-book addresses several, or even many, persons in the singular number where it is intended that each person, so collectively and yet singularly addressed, shall very emphatically take to himself, and lay to heart, the words so spoken to each of more people than one.

A case in point may be found in the very next service that occurs in the Prayer-book. There, in the office for the public baptism of infants, the god-parents or sponsors—never less than three in number, and much more numerous, of course, where several baptisms are administered at the same time—are accosted in the singular number: " Dost thou, in the name of this child, renounce," etc.; "Dost thou believe," etc.; " Wilt thou obediently keep," etc.

In view of this purposely singular form for these questions —standing out as it does in marked contrast with the permitted alterations in other parts of the same service, where the sex or number of the children baptized requires such alteration—it will be impossible for any fair and intelligent reader to deny that the singular form of administration, in the Lord's Supper, *may* be addressed to several, or to many, communicants with the intention that each, as in the baptismal service, shall take the words very heartily to himself.

So much for the permissibleness of the words being said to many communicants at once instead of to each separately.

But now we must inquire whether there are any cogent reasons why the words of administration should be addressed to each communicant separately.

We cannot better commence the answer to this question than by considering the allegations, in support of an affirmative answer, set forth by three learned and right reverend personages in their appendix to the fourth report of the Ritual Commission (1870).

The Commission recommends that, when convenience requires it, administration shall be with the saying of the words once to several of the communicants conjointly.

To this three bishops object, inasmuch as they wish the words of administration to be spoken to each communicant separately.

In support of this their wish, they allege :—

The Order of Communion, previous to Edward VI.'s first Prayer-book, and in that book itself, enjoined the priest to "*say to every one the words following.*" It is acknowledged that this injunction was omitted in Edward's second Prayer-book, and in the Liturgies of Elizabeth and James I. ; but it is argued that the twenty-first canon, of 1604, says, "*The minister shall deliver both the bread and the wine to every communicant severally.*"

We ask, Is it not plainly apparent that the omission of the rubric of Edward's earliest Liturgies from all later English Prayer-books is very significant as an argument against the subsequent revisers having intended to compel the saying of the words to each and every communicant separately?

Surely, what the twenty-first Canon requires is that the bread and wine, instead of being passed from one communicant to another—a practice which might lead to certain obvious unseemlinesses and irregularities—should be handed back by each recipient to the minister, and should then by him be delivered to each communicant separately and in turn. Not a syllable does the Canon say about the words being spoken to each communicant separately.

So far the argument of the objectors makes against themselves. But they add, The Presbyterians at the Savoy Conference prayed that the minister might not "be required to deliver the bread and wine into every communicant's hand, and to repeat the words to each one in the singular number; but that it might suffice to speak them to divers jointly, according to our Saviour's example."

Against this Presbyterian request our three episcopal objectors quote the bishops' answer, at the Savoy, to the effect :—

"It is most requisite that the minister deliver the bread and wine into every particular communicant's hand, and repeat the words in the singular number, forsomuch as it is the propriety of sacraments to make particular obsignation to each believer; and it is our visible profession that, by the grace of God, Christ tasted death for every man."

To this we rejoin, Granted, it is desirable the minister should give the elements into each communicant's hand; granted, it may be permissible that, departing from the letter of Christ's example, we should adopt Archbishop Whitgift's favourite form, *Take thou, Eat thou*; granted, with all our hearts, that Christ died for all men, and that every possible means should be employed to carry home this blessed and satisfying conviction of universal redemption to every heart;— granted all this; but where do the Savoy bishops, even with their attention freshly drawn to the subject by the Presbyterian request, say aught about the necessity of the words of administration being repeated, not only in the singular number, but to each communicant separately?

We have felt it right and respectful thus to examine the argument[1] of the modern bishops who object to their brother

---

[1] One other argument, urged by the three bishops, is that it was "frequently made a subject of episcopal and archidiaconal inquiry" whether all the words of administration were said to every communicant, or whether they were said "but now and then, to many" communicants at once? To us this inquiry shows that there was a not uncommon—we say, a prevailing—practice of saying the words but now and then, to many communicants at once. The inquiry being "frequently," but not always or even generally, made, shows that repetition of the words, to each communicant, was a thing desired by some bishops and archdeacons, but not wished by all. And, moreover, the absence, under such circumstances, of any rubric positively enjoining this practice, intimates that, though it was known as a favourite idea with some churchmen, it was neither sanctioned nor required by the majority speaking in the sacred name of law.

Commissioners' report; but we confess that, so far from finding any force in that argument, we leave it with a conviction that, if such learned men could adduce no more cogent reasons for saying the words of administration to each communicant separately, the case must be weak indeed; and moreover, our three bishops have directed our attention to the fact that the revisers of 1662, with all the statements for and against repetition of the words to each individual communicant fresh in their recollection, have left no more stringent injunction than that "the minister, who delivereth the bread (or the wine) to any one, shall say" certain words once or more times at his discretion.

Custom, for nearly two centuries, ruled that the words should be said to as many communicants as could kneel at the rail. If the revisers of 1662 had meant something different from that custom—if they had meant what our objecting bishops think, why did they not draw up some such rubric as this, The minister shall say to every communicant separately the words following ?

But we proceed to more important considerations.

Does any one think that Jesus spoke the blessing and the thanksgiving and the administration to each disciple by himself? No; there is no trace of anything of the sort in either of the histories. On the contrary, the words of our Saviour were, "Take ye, eat ye . . . given for you: Do ye this," etc. ; "Drink ye all," etc. The example of our Saviour clearly favours a conjoint administration, and even the plural form. If greater love or sympathy, or more tender anxiety to bless, could be demonstrated by the words being addressed to each communicant, one by one, surely that mode would have been employed by Jesus, who was all compassion.

This consideration, of our Lord's example, ought to suffice to lead every man to use such conjoint administration as the law of the Church has been shown clearly to permit. As against this divine and most loving example, we know no single argument of any weight or moment in favour of the practice of isolated administration. Indeed, as isolation is the very opposite of communion and fellowship, so this quite

modern innovation, in the Church of England, rather breaks
and injures, if it does not destroy, the beautiful symbol which
should, at the Lord's Table, remind us that, though many, we
are one—one body of all believers with one only head, the
Lord Jesus Christ.

Before considerations such as these, lesser conveniences
fall into insignificance ; but, still, it may be well to remember
that the repetition of the words of administration several
scores of times, not seldom several hundreds of times, must
generally tend to weary, not only the clergy engaged in those
repetitions, but also the people who are called to hear the
reiterated sounds or to await their being ended.

In not a few ways is this irksomeness of the service on
Communion Sundays manifesting itself. Sometimes a communicant is to be seen quietly leaving the church before all
have partaken and before the comely end of the service has
been duly reached. Sometimes the exhortation is omitted, so
as to curtail the intellectual portion of the service, and give
ampler time for these unbidden, if not unhallowed, repetitions.
Perpetually, the sermon is cramped and shortened—even
where the preacher has a message from God and Christ to
deliver—in order that this unnecessary lengthening of the
service, by isolation where there should be fellowship, by
repetitions of what Christ said only once, may be imported
into the English Church.

We trust that all who read these words, unless their force
can be annulled, will set themselves intelligently and piously
against a practice which is inconvenient, injurious to communion, and contrary to the example of our Saviour.

(xxiii.) *The Words of Administration.*

And now we come to the words of administration themselves :—

The body of our Lord Jesus Christ, which was given for thee, preserve
thy body and soul unto everlasting life. Take and eat this in remem
brance that Christ died for thee, and feed on Him in thy heart by faith
with thanksgiving.

The blood of our Lord Jesus Christ, which was shed for thee, preserve thy body and soul unto everlasting life. Drink this in remembrance that Christ's blood was shed for thee, and be thankful.

The words used by our Saviour, in giving the bread and wine, were as we have seen above. They became shortened in the course of the first few Christian centuries, so that, instead of complete sentences directing men to take and eat, or to drink of the cup, detached phrases, elliptical expressions, such as, "The body of Christ," "The holy body," "The precious blood of the Lord our God and Saviour," "The blood of Christ, the cup of salvation," were the forms of administration in common use some four hundred years after Christ.

The inconvenience of these elliptical phrases is obvious, for how would they be filled up by the unlearned? How could they escape being abused, corrupted, and filled up with meanings quite alien from their original sense as first employed in fuller forms by our Lord?

It appears that this inconvenience must have been so strongly felt of old that, in various Churches, there was a return to definite grammatical sentences which were to accompany the reception of the elements. For instance, at Rome, in the time of Gregory the Great, towards the close of the sixth century, the Latin words, spoken on giving the bread, were equivalent to, May the body of our Lord Jesus Christ preserve thy soul.[1]

The Use of Hereford employed Latin words signifying, May the body of our Lord Jesus Christ be the medicine (*sit remedium*) of my soul unto eternal life. Amen. May the blood of our Lord Jesus Christ preserve (*conservet*) my soul unto life eternal. Amen.

Various other forms, like these, came again into vogue. The Latin language was not understood by the people. Otherwise, there was thus some return to intelligible words; and they took the form of prayer that Christ's body and blood might preserve men's souls unto eternal life.

Of course, the further significance even of these prayers would vary as men came to believe in an objective presence of Christ's body and blood in, or with, or instead of the bread

---

[1] Corpus Domini nostri Jesu Christi conservet animam tuam.

and wine, or as they retained the evangelic truth that whilst the bread and wine were symbols and memorials of Christ and His death, the body and blood of Christ were in heaven at the right hand of God.

In the Communion Service of 1549, the English Church adopted, as its form of administration, the words:—

The body of our Lord Jesus Christ, which was given for thee, preserve thy body and soul unto everlasting life.

The blood of our Lord Jesus Christ, which was shed for thee, preserve thy body and soul unto everlasting life.

In King Edward's second book (1552), these forms were abandoned, and, in their place, came to be read the words:—

Take and eat this in remembrance that Christ died for thee, and feed on Him in thy heart by faith, with thanksgiving.

Drink this in remembrance that Christ's blood was shed for thee, and be thankful.

In Elizabeth's reign (1559), these two forms were combined, as we now have them in our Prayer-book, so that, as has been well remarked, we are in communion, here again, with the Reformers of the sixteenth century, who loved the latter part of our present forms of administration, while we are also in harmony with the more ancient Christians, who employed words closely resembling the first halves of our forms.

Well for us if we are, moreover, in unison with the Lord, and with His apostles, who employed their words with a distinct conviction that the bread and wine must be distinguished from the body and blood of Christ—that, for participation in the former, our bodily organs sufficed; but, for receiving the latter, our souls must be lifted up to God and heaven, and so fed with the spiritual food of Christ's sacrifice.

Very beautiful are our existing forms of administration, and full of important meaning; but they are so transparent in signification, and their phrases and doctrine have been, as we proceeded, so fully dwelt upon in previous pages of this essay, that it is now only necessary to draw attention to a very few points connected with them.

Well worthy of notice is the fact that the first half of each form is in terms as general as they can be. The prayer is not, May *this* body, or *this* blood, of Christ preserve thee. Neither is it, May the body, or the blood, of Christ, *present in this sacrament,* preserve thee. But it is, May the body, and the blood, of Christ, which are well known from Scripture to be in heaven, preserve thee. And, to diminish the peril of such superstitious errors, as those just disclaimed, entering the minds of communicants, the words, " Take and eat this," " Drink this," are such that their very signification denotes that the elements are severally to be given to the communicants at the point where those second parts of the administration are spoken. After the general prayers that the body and blood of Christ may preserve us, follow the quite distinct commands, Take and eat *this,* Drink *this.*

What are the things we are to receive and eat or drink ? None other, obviously, than those " creatures of bread and wine " which, in the Prayer of Consecration, we besought our heavenly Father we might rightly receive. The fuller meaning of these later portions of the administration is thus seen to be, Take and eat this creature of bread; Drink this creature of wine.

Other points which should be noticed in the English forms of administration are, that it is in the heart, and by faith, that we are to feed on Christ. The hand by which His body and blood are to be taken is faith. As the ancient Christian writers were wont to put it, not by the teeth is Christ to be pressed, as is the consecrated bread, but by faith ; and not into the mouth is Christ to be taken, as are the consecrated bread and wine, but in the heart and spirit of the believer is He to be thought of and loved, and His blessed will made supreme.

Thus free from all the modern and mediæval materialism which believes that Christ is, in some manner, objectively present in the bread and wine, and objectively taken into the mouth of man, is our English Communion Service, even in those parts where, if such materialism were to be found at all, it would be most likely to manifest itself. Rightly and Scripturally does the Prayer-book, alike in the consecration and in the administration, distinguish between the bread and wine, which are objects for our senses to deal with, and the flesh and blood of Christ, which are subjects only to be thought of and loved in our minds and by our spirits.

(xxiv.) *Rubric for Additional Consecration.*

And now let us examine the first rubric which follows the administration :—

If the consecrated bread or wine be all spent before all have communicated, the priest is to consecrate more according to the form before prescribed; beginning at [Our Saviour Christ in the same night, etc.] for the blessing of the bread; and at [Likewise after Supper, etc.] for the blessing of the cup.

This is an interesting part of our subject. It enjoins that if the bread or wine fail in the administration, more of either element is to be blessed or consecrated. So far, all is as one would expect; but the rubric describes the manner of such " blessing " or " consecration ; " and here is something that was not to be looked for. The bread is, according to this rubric, to be blessed, without a word of blessing, and to be consecrated, without any prayer, by merely reciting over either element the condensed and abbreviated narratives of our Lord's original administration of that element alone, whether it be bread or wine.

We know no precedent in the Church before the Reformation for such a practice as this. Indeed, if the rubric (composed in 1662) were not in tolerably close agreement with that introduced into the Scottish Communion Office in 1637, we should be inclined to think that, by an oversight, the compilers, in 1662, had omitted to enjoin the use of the precatory part of the consecration prayer, together with the appropriate portion of the historic rehearsal. No such injunction, however, was given ; and, as the present English practice agrees substantially, in this respect, with the Scottish Liturgy, we are obliged to believe that the compilers of our Liturgy, in 1662, were convinced that the mere recitation of some of our Saviour's words and acts constitutes a sufficient blessing or consecration of sacramental bread and wine.

This fact is important as showing how little formalism in this particular case was thought necessary by the English

Church in the seventeenth century, and how the mere thought of Christ's institution, and of its meaning, in connection with bread and wine, sufficed to hallow those creatures for a compliance with the command of Jesus, Do this in remembrance of Me.

How far may such a principle be carried? Does not the mere loving thought, that associates Christ and His death, and the benefits we receive thereby, with common bread and wine, anywhere and at any time, bless and consecrate these creatures of God and constitute the homely meal of those who so partake of ordinary meat and drink a very communion with Christ and His people?

Such a line of reflection springs out of this rubric; and, whether its suggestion was intended, or not, by those who wrote the rubric, it carries us back to certain ideas of evangelic simplicity which, in an earlier page of this essay, we noticed as resulting from our Lord's mode of instituting the Supper in a private house and at a family gathering.

(xxv.) *Second Rubric after Communion.*

The second rubric after the administration is in these words :—

When all have communicated, the minister shall return to the Lord's Table, and reverently place upon it what remaineth of the consecrated elements, covering the same with a fair linen cloth.

There is, in this rubric, little that need detain us. It appears to us, we confess, as if the words directing the minister to "return to the Lord's Table," after all have communicated, implied his having been away from the Table throughout the entire administration, as if he had been beyond the "Communion rails" or the "chancel screen," administering the elements to the people in those parts of the church where they had, before the exhortation, been "conveniently placed for receiving of the holy sacrament."

There is something striking and instructive, we think, in the utter ignoring by the English Prayer-book, as well as by the New Testament, of all such divisions between places for the clergy and places for the laity, between the greater sanctity of one part of a church and the lesser sanctity of another part of the same church; and in these days, when, in avowed imitation of pre-Reformation or mediæval customs, attempts are systematically made to draw these lines more markedly, and to invest the whole subject in symbolism, as though the chancel, with its surpliced choristers, typified heaven, and the space within the "rails" typified some higher part of heaven in which Christ is present—in days distinguished by such unscriptural and anti-Reformation endeavours to drag into England's Protestant Church false analogies of Judaism and its Temple, and no less false ideas of an earthly house of prayer being divided into sections corresponding to earth and heaven and heaven's higher regions—it is well to notice that, whatever may be the exact meaning of the minister's being enjoined, in this rubric, to return to the Lord's Table, the English Church in her Prayer-book recognises no such distinction of parts in the house of prayer; but, on the contrary, while having nothing to tell us about "chancel screens" or "Communion rails," she appoints that the sacrament of the Lord's Supper shall itself be celebrated, not at any east end, far off from the congregation and the reading-desk, but rather her injunction is that "The Table, at Communion-time having a fair white linen cloth upon it, shall stand in the body of the church, or in the chancel, where Morning and Evening Prayer are appointed to be said." The English Church thus directs that the Lord's Supper shall be celebrated, not in quite a remote part of the Church, but near the reading-desk and in either part of the edifice where the people are wont to assemble for their other public prayers. The English Church thus teaches, like her Master, that, in Christianity, the sanctity and acceptance of worship depend on no particular place, building, or part of a building, but rest only on the worship being offered, anywhere, in spirit and in truth.

But while this freedom from superstition, as to so-called sacred places, distinguishes the English Church, we should observe how she prescribes that all things, in divine worship, shall be done decently and in order. So, here, in this rubric the minister is instructed "reverently" to place on the Table what may remain, after all have communicated, of the consecrated bread and wine; and, so, he is to cover it with a fair linen cloth.

(xxvi.) *The Lord's Prayer.*

And then follows a third rubric to this effect :—

Then shall the priest say the Lord's Prayer, the people repeating after him every petition.

Our Father, which art in heaven, Hallowed be Thy Name. Thy kingdom come. Thy will be done in earth, as it is in heaven. Give us this day our daily bread. And forgive us our trespasses, as we forgive them that trespass against us. And lead us not into temptation ; But deliver us from evil: For Thine is the kingdom, The power, and the glory, For ever and ever. Amen.

On the Lord's Prayer we have already offered such brief comments as seemed appropriate in a work like this. Here it is only necessary to remark further that, as a matter of taste, we greatly prefer the saying of the Lord's Prayer after the reception of the sacrament rather than between the consecration and the administration, as was the mediæval custom of the Mass.

In the rubric we ought to notice the direction that the people shall repeat every petition after the priest. This is intended to give particular emphasis to the general rule of the English Church, that the people are to repeat the Lord's Prayer with the minister *wheresoever it is used in divine service,* and that the people shall answer "Amen" *at the end of all prayers.*

At this place in the service such special emphasis required to be laid on the general and universal rules quoted above, because, as we saw, the custom of the Mass-book here was that the priest should say the Lord's Prayer down to the words, "Lead us not into temptation ;" then the people should respond, "But deliver us from evil;" and then the priest should say the "Amen" by himself.

Against such complicated and mischievous maiming of the holy prayer the English Church warns her people by this rubric, which denotes, not that here only are the people to join in the Lord's Prayer and the "Amen," but that here, as well as in all other places, they are so to join in the prayer and the

"Amen," notwithstanding the Mass-book's precepts and practice to the contrary.

(xxvii.) *Post-Communion Collects.*

After the Lord's Prayer come two post-Communion collects, either of which it is optional with the clergyman to use at his discretion.

After shall be said as followeth.

O Lord and heavenly Father, we Thy humble servants entirely desire Thy Fatherly goodness mercifully to accept this our sacrifice of praise and thanksgiving ; most humbly beseeching Thee to grant, that by the merits and death of Thy Son Jesus Christ, and through faith in His blood, we and all Thy whole Church may obtain remission of our sins, and all other benefits of His passion. And here we offer and present unto Thee, O Lord, ourselves, our souls and bodies, to be a reasonable, holy, and lively sacrifice unto Thee ; humbly beseeching Thee, that all we, who are partakers of this holy Communion, may be fulfilled with Thy grace and heavenly benediction. And although we be unworthy, through our manifold sins, to offer unto Thee any sacrifice, yet we beseech Thee to accept this our bounden duty and service ; not weighing our merits, but pardoning our offences, through Jesus Christ our Lord ; by whom, and with whom, in the unity of the Holy Ghost, all honour and glory be unto Thee, O Father Almighty, world without end. *Amen.*

Or this.

Almighty and everliving God, we most heartily thank Thee, for that Thou dost vouchsafe to feed us, who have duly received these holy mysteries, with the spiritual food of the most precious body and blood of Thy Son our Saviour Jesus Christ ; and dost assure us thereby of Thy favour and goodness towards us ; and that we are very members incorporate in the mystical body of Thy Son, which is the blessed company of all faithful people ; and are also heirs through hope of Thy everlasting kingdom, by the merits of the most precious death and passion of Thy dear Son. And we most humbly beseech Thee, O heavenly Father, so to assist us with Thy grace, that we may continue in that holy fellowship, and do all such good works as Thou hast prepared for us to walk in ; through Jesus Christ our Lord, to whom, with Thee and the Holy Ghost, be all honour and glory, world without end. *Amen.*

The first of these two collects was appended to the consecration prayer in the English book of 1549 ; and it still holds a corresponding place in the Scottish and American Liturgies.

The part which prays God not to weigh our merits, but to pardon our offences, is to be found in the Salisbury Mass-book.

The second of the collects is a form of thanksgiving, drawn up for the English Liturgy in 1549, not without the adoption into it of parts of the priest's thanksgiving after Communion as it is to be found in the Sarum Mass-book. Thus, here again, as so often before, we find our Prayer-book embodying much of what was good in the mediæval and ancient books, and so bringing us into intellectual and pious harmony with the saints of all bygone ages.

In examining these two post-Communion collects, the first point, which requires attention, is the prayer that God will accept "this our sacrifice." What then, it will be asked, is the English Lord's Supper a sacrifice after all? Observe the completion of the phrase. It is no sacrifice of atonement or reconciliation; it is no repetition or continuation of Christ's one sacrifice; it is not even what has been called, with strange inconsistency of language, a commemorative sacrifice; but it is "a sacrifice of praise and thanksgiving," one of those "spiritual sacrifices" (1 Pet. ii. 5) which laity and clergy are all equally enjoined to offer to God as acceptable through Jesus Christ. Such a sacrifice of "the fruit of our lips" (Heb. xiii. 15) is it, with which, as with beneficence and helpful fellowship, "God is well pleased." This kind of thank-offering is the Eucharist; and by no means is it, as we have seen throughout our study of Scripture and the Prayer-book, a substitute, or a repetition, or a renewal of the great High-Priest's one sacrifice once slain, once offered, and once for all finished, perfected, and accepted.

In opposition to any such baneful error follows the very next petition of the collect, that, through faith in the obedient and well-pleasing (or meritorious) sacrifice of Christ's death, we and all believers, God's whole, or catholic, or universal Church, may obtain pardon and all the other countless benefits which accrue to man, not from his own sacrifices of any kind, but from the sufferings, or "passion," of the Lord.

Then, resuming and completing the idea of our sacrifice of praise and thanksgiving, the collect leads us, according to the words of St. Paul (Rom. xii. 1), to offer and present, not money and not bread and wine, but ourselves, our bodies

and souls, to be a reasonable, holy, and lively sacrifice unto
God.   Quite worthy of being borne constantly in mind is this
devotion of ourselves to the wisest, best, and happiest of purposes in general ; and especially noticeable is the protest
against all vain and superstitious worship that lies in the
Prayer-book's adoption of the epithet "reasonable;" whilst
by the term "lively," or active, energetic, and true to nature,
every wicked vow of celibacy, or of any protracted self-seclu-
sion, is condemned.

Next comes a petition that—instead of imagining we must
have received either utter "damnation" or Christ and all
His benefits because we have partaken of the consecrated
elements—we may, as we have taken a step in the right
direction in obeying the Saviour and approaching His Table,
also proceed along the path of righteousness and be "fulfilled" and perfected with Christ's grace and heavenly
blessing.

Then, remembering our sins and deploring our unworthiness to bring to God even such a sacrifice as this of thanks
and self-devotion, we entreat the acceptance of what we
were bound in duty, obedience, and gratitude to tender,
through the mercy of that God in Christ who far rather
pardons sins than weighs offences.

With an ascription of glory and honour to the Father,
Son, and Holy Spirit, the collect ends, and the people respond
with their "Amen."

The second of the post-Communion collects is a thanksgiving to God, who, if we have rightly, obediently, and faithfully partaken of the holy mysteries—that is, of the secrets
revealed of God's love to all men in Christ—has graciously
fed us, not with Christ's objective and material flesh and
blood, but with the food for our spirits which comes from a
vivid and sanctifying remembrance of the one sufficient divine
sacrifice of that body and blood which are now in heaven at
God's right hand.

Then the collect calls to our remembrance that God is
not changeable ; but, as He has just shown us His mercy in
making us partakers of this sacred "memory" of Christ, so

He therein pledges His consistency as our assurance that He is full of favour and goodness towards us, and that we are parts and portions of that figurative body which consists of all believing people, and has Christ for its head.

Thus one with Christ and with all the holiest of men for whom He died, how can we fail to inherit that eternal kingdom which is part and parcel of the rich benefits procured to us by the one sacrifice of our Lord?

But, then, in the midst of all this " assurance " and joy and thankfulness, we are wisely reminded of our weakness, our proneness to go astray, even after all God's goodness to us; and so the collect teaches us to pray that the divine grace may help and strengthen us steadfastly to persevere in our association with the good fellowship of Christ and His people, and continually to do all such good works as God has prepared [1] for us to walk in.

Then follows the supplication that all this which we have asked, and which lies so far beyond our unaided powers, we may be enabled to accomplish by the spirit and in the character of Christ who strengtheneth us, so that through Him we can do all things, even as, in Him, God bestoweth upon us all good gifts.

Upon this the collect ends with the ascription of honour and glory to the Father, Son, and Holy Spirit, and with the " Amen " of the congregation.

(xxviii.) *" Glory be to God on High."*

Most appropriately is the hymn "Glory be to God on high" introduced at this period in the Communion. Its place, in the early mediæval Liturgy, had been at the beginning of the service; but even apart from the fact that the English Liturgy now begins with an act of self-abasement in contemplating the laws of God which we have too often broken, and that there would be a painful inconsistency between that self-humiliation and the joy of this hymn, there is something particularly felicitous in the introduction at this point of the *Gloria in*

---

[1] The marginal translation " prepared " (Eph. ii. 10) is the correct rendering, of course, of προητοίμασεν in the original.

Excelsis, just when the communicants have celebrated the blessed memory of the Lord, have joined in His holy prayer, have rendered thanks for all this grace bestowed by God upon them, and so have their hearts attuned to join in singing, or, if need be, saying, this hymn of pious gladness :—

Its well-known words are :—

Glory be to God on high, and in earth peace, good will towards men. We praise Thee, we bless Thee, we worship Thee, we glorify Thee, we give thanks to Thee for Thy great glory, O Lord God, heavenly King, God the Father Almighty.

O Lord, the only-begotten Son Jesu Christ ; O Lord God, Lamb of God, Son of the Father, that takest away the sins of the world, have mercy upon us. Thou that takest away the sins of the world, have mercy upon us. Thou that takest away the sins of the world, receive our prayer. Thou that sittest at the right hand of God the Father, have mercy upon us.

For Thou only art holy; Thou only art the Lord ; Thou only, O Christ, with the Holy Ghost, art most high in the glory of God the Father. *Amen.*

This exquisite song of highly wrought Christian feeling scarcely admits of being expressed in plainer language, so it needs no lengthened comment. Its making use of the angels' song [1] (Luke ii. 14) is an adaptation, not a translation, and therefore need not be vindicated.

Only two remarks will we venture to make with reference to this high song of saintly praise. First, it is in keeping with our Saviour's own example that song should follow on the celebration of the Lord's Supper (Matt. xxvi. 30) ; and, next, for joining in this hymn, though the intellect should not be dormant, but, contrariwise, should be on the alert to remember and meditate upon the blessed history of Christ, as well as upon all His gracious dealing with our own individual souls, yet it is with the heart, by the sympathies of loving and grateful affection, that we can at all fitly take part in this true "joy in the Holy Spirit" (Rom. xiv. 17).

(xxix.) *The Blessing.*

And so we approach the end of this wise and beautiful Liturgy :—

---

[1] Δόξα ἐν ὑψίστοις Θεῷ, καὶ ἐπὶ γῆς εἰρήνη ἐν ἀνθρώποις εὐδοκίας : Glory to God in the highest, and upon earth peace among men of well-pleasingness.

Then the priest (or bishop if he be present) shall let them depart with this Blessing.

The peace of God, which passeth all understanding, keep your hearts and minds in the knowledge and love of God, and of His Son Jesus Christ our Lord : and the blessing of God Almighty, the Father, the Son, and the Holy Ghost, be amongst you and remain with you always. *Amen.*

After such high thought, and such tension of holy feeling, how could the service end without a painful diminution of interest ? Only one termination can we conceive which would meet the requirements of the case ; and that is, that, with words of solemn benediction, the most dignified and, as is to be supposed, the most experienced and most sympathizing of those present, the bishop or, in his absence, the officiating presbyter, shall let the people depart, as is the precept of the rubric.

As to our form of benediction, not much need be said. It is a product of the Reformation, and, like well-nigh all the results of that great epoch, is, we venture to think, a most happy production.

Marked is the contrast between this English end of the sacrament and the *Ite, missa est,* " Go, ye are dismissed," of some mediæval services ; or between our blessing and the frequently long benedictory prayers of the Greek Church ; or between our end of the service and the strange and unsatisfactory elliptical utterance at the close of the Roman Mass, *In nomine Patris et Filii et Spiritus Sancti,* " In the name of the Father, and of the Son, and of the Holy Ghost."

Our Benediction is made up obviously of two parts. The first clause, derived from St. Paul's Epistle to the Philippians (iv. 7), was introduced into the English Communion in 1548. The second clause was added in 1549. It probably came to us from Hermann's Consultation, like other parts of our service ; but Latin benedictions, in much older services, are so similar to it that they would seem to have originated both our form of blessing and that of Hermann.

The significance of the Benediction, however, is of far greater moment than its origin.

May the peace which comes from God, and which, in its calm delight, in the strength it gives to the inner man, in the victory conferred by it over all external circumstances, in its difference from any peace the world can give, in the impossibility of its being taken away, in its enduring for ever like God Himself—may this peace, which surpasses all that the mind of man could originate or hope for, so keep and guard your affections and your thoughts, that the latter may be engaged with the knowledge of God and of His Christ, and the former with the love of the same divine Being. And, springing out of this peace, yea, over and above even this peace, may the general blessing of the all-powerful God —alike of Him who is the awe-inspiring and unapproachable Source of all things, and of Him, that Father's Son, our sympathizing Brother, and of Him, the breath of both, who penetrates and permeates all things, and gives to all light and life and comfort and exhortation and guidance—may this God of blessing not only be amongst you from time to time, but may He abide and remain with you always. "Amen;" the last word of this sacred communion and fellowship, in which the people accept for themselves and reciprocate to the minister that of which they and he are equally in need, the boon of God's eternal benediction.

The Six Collects.

As a sort of appendix to the Communion Service, and in conformity with the practice of pre-Reformation books, six collects are printed immediately upon the close of the Communion. They are introduced by a rubric thus worded :—

Collects to be said after the Offertory, when there is no Communion, every such day one or more; and the same may be said also, as often as occasion shall serve, after the collects either of Morning or Evening Prayer, Communion, or Litany, by the discretion of the minister.

On this rubric we have already offered a few remarks on an earlier page of this essay, and so we proceed at once to the six collects :—

Assist us mercifully, O Lord, in these our supplications and prayers, and dispose the way of Thy servants towards the attainment of everlasting salvation ; that, among all the changes and chances of this mortal life, they may ever be defended by Thy most gracious and ready help ; through Jesus Christ our Lord. *Amen.*

O Almighty Lord, and Everlasting God, vouchsafe, we beseech Thee, to direct, sanctify, and govern, both our hearts and bodies, in the ways of

Thy laws, and in the works of Thy commandments ; that through Thy most mighty protection, both here and ever, we may be preserved in body and soul ; through our Lord and Saviour Jesus Christ. *Amen.*

Grant, we beseech Thee, Almighty God, that the words, which we have heard this day with our outward ears, may through Thy grace be so grafted inwardly in our hearts, that they may bring forth in us the fruit of good living, to the honour and praise of Thy Name ; through Jesus Christ our Lord. *Amen.*

Prevent us, O Lord, in all our doings with Thy most gracious favour, and further us with Thy continual help ; that in all our works begun, continued, and ended in Thee, we may glorify Thy holy Name, and finally by Thy mercy obtain everlasting life ; through Jesus Christ our Lord. *Amen.*

Almighty God, the fountain of all wisdom, who knowest our necessities before we ask, and our ignorance in asking ; We beseech Thee to have compassion upon our infirmities ; and those things, which for our unworthiness we dare not, and for our blindness we cannot ask, vouchsafe to give us, for the worthiness of Thy Son Jesus Christ our Lord. *Amen.*

Almighty God, who hast promised to hear the petitions of them that ask in Thy Son's Name ; We beseech Thee mercifully to incline Thine ears to us that have made now our prayers and supplications unto Thee ; and grant, that those things, which we have faithfully asked according to Thy will, may effectually be obtained, to the relief of our necessity, and to the setting forth of Thy glory ; through Jesus Christ our Lord. *Amen.*

It is almost superfluous to say that these collects are of exquisite beauty, and have become household words of piety among us. The first two, and the fourth, were translated. and remodelled, from old forms found in mediæval books. The third and the two last were composed for the English Prayer-book in 1549.

In what words could we better supplicate divine assistance in finding and keeping the way of eternal salvation, amidst life's many changes and chances, than in those of the first collect.

With hardly less felicity of expression does the second collect pray for divine guidance, sanctification, government, and protection for our bodies and souls in the way of God's laws.

The third collect, for the engrafting and fruitfulness of pious instructions which have been just heard, is of universal acceptance.

2 E

No less familiar, because no less approved by the common judgment of believers, is the fourth collect, in which we ask that God's grace may precede and accompany us through life, so that we may glorify His name and, at the last, obtain the perfection of life in Christ.

In the fifth collect we are most wisely led to cast ourselves, with our ignorance and infirmities and unworthiness, upon the compassion of God, that, in the love of Christ, He may give us what we know not how to ask.

The last of these collects is based upon those sayings of Jesus which teach that whatsoever we ask in the name (that is, in the spirit and character) of Him who never besought earthly boons except with an "If it be possible"—with "Thy will, not mine, be done"—and who knew that God's will was the sanctification and salvation of all men, and that, therefore, He would be heard in whatever He thus sought according to the will of God,—whatever we so ask in the name of Jesus, this collect teaches, shall be granted ; and, therefore, it implores God's mercy to bestow what we have thus asked in the service at which the collect may be used.

In all these collects it is remarkable, considering their position in connection with the service for the Lord's Supper, that there is no reference to that holy rite. Assuredly, this ought to show that, in the estimation of the English Church, prayers, apart from the Lord's Supper, are as prevailing as they can be when connected with that sacrament ; and that it is not the "breaking of bread" which gains acceptance for any prayer, but the name and spirit and character of Jesus in which, at any time and in any place, the prayer may be offered.

At the Communion, or away from it, if prayer be made, even in the name of Jesus, but without His spirit and disposition in the man who prays, there is no promise of success ; but, on the contrary, the terrible reply to such prayer may be, "Jesus I know, and Paul I know; but who are ye?" (Acts xix. 15, 16). On the other hand, let prayer be made, in the Communion or away from it, in the spirit and with the disposition of Jesus—so, truly and honestly, in His name—

and whatsoever we ask in this faith, it shall be granted unto us.

Many other instructions might be suggested by these collects—for instance, a lesson about not contemning the reading of Scripture or the preaching of God's Word, in comparison with the sacrament, might be especially drawn from the third collect—but these truths are, and will be, obvious to the thoughtful worshipper.

Rubrics at the End of the Liturgy.

We must proceed now to notice the rubrics that are placed at the end of these six collects.

The first of those rubrics needs only to be quoted here, as it, like that preceding the collects, has been already commented on by us :—

Upon the Sundays and other holy-days (if there be no Communion) shall be said all that is appointed at the Communion, until the end of the general Prayer [For the whole state of Christ's Church militant here in earth] together with one or more of these collects last before rehearsed, concluding with the Blessing.

The next two rubrics are directed against such solitary, or all but solitary, celebration of the Lord's Supper as had been too common in pre-Reformation times, destroying as it did, by its solitude, the very nature and idea of the communion and fellowship of many members with each other and with the Lord :—

And there shall be no celebration of the Lord's Supper, except there be a convenient number to communicate with the priest, according to his discretion.
And if there be not above twenty persons in the parish of discretion to receive the Communion; yet there shall be no Communion, except four (or three at the least) communicate with the priest.

Then follows a rubric directing, at least, a weekly Communion in cathedral and such like establishments where there ought to be a sufficient number of communicants always prepared to participate. Even amongst them, however, the rubric admits of exceptions where there is "reasonable cause" for less frequent celebrations :—

And in cathedral and collegiate churches, and colleges, where there are many priests and deacons, they shall all receive the Communion with the priest every Sunday at the least, except they have a reasonable cause to the contrary.

The next rubric treats of the kind of bread that is to be used at the Lord's Supper. It is thus expressed :—

And to take away all occasion of dissension, and superstition, which any person hath or might have concerning the bread and wine, it shall suffice that the bread be such as is usual to be eaten; but the best and purest wheat bread that conveniently may be gotten.

It is clear that wheaten bread is here sanctioned for use in the Lord's Supper; but attempts have, within the last few years, been made to bring back amongst us "wafers" for use in the Communion; and it was argued that, while bread might "suffice," wafers would be better. Against this the Privy Council judgment (*Ridsdale* v. *Clifton*) has recently decided that a wafer, or a "composition of flour and water rolled very thin and unleavened," is made illegal by this rubric, because such "wafer" is not "bread such as is usual to be eaten;" and this rubric (1662) was framed to put an end to "dissension," which had previously existed, as to whether wafers or bread should be employed. To leave the question open between "bread" and "wafers," would by no means put an end to the dissension; and so the words, "it shall suffice," are authoritatively, and as it appears most justly, ruled to mean that nothing but ordinary "bread" shall be required by either clergy or laity in the Communion. "Bread" "shall suffice" and wafers are illegal. It is well that dissension, on so infinitely small a matter, should be ended.

The next rubric is interesting :—

And if any of the bread and wine remain unconsecrated, the curate shall have it to his own use ; but if any remain of that which was consecrated, it shall not be carried out of the church, but the priest and such other of the communicants as he shall then call unto him, shall, immediately after the Blessing, reverently eat and drink the same.

The first clause of this rubric carries the mind back to early Christian times, when all the communicants brought contributions, as each could, for the *agape* or love-feast, and the quantity provided, over and above what was wanted for the sacrament, was worth being considered and allotted to the minister. It is well to observe that portions of the rubrics are out of date, in order that, while we accept their general significance and spirit, and abstain from what they manifestly are intended to discountenance or forbid, we may not be enslaved to the letter even of those useful rules.

As to the remainder, if any, of the consecrated elements, it was not to be carried out of the church, as had been the ancient custom, because mediæval superstitions had rendered that practice dangerous.

For the same reason, namely, to prevent superstitious abuses, and also, because this consecrated bread and wine, though not changed in substance or in objective nature, had been devoted to a sacred purpose, it was therefore comely that it should be "reverently" consumed by the clergy and other communicants.   Hence this wise rubric.

What a contrast between the manly and decorous conduct it prescribes and the ablutions and rinsings and drainings which were enjoined by mediævalism, and which, alas, we now sometimes see re-introduced as far as possible, even in the Church of England, where Ritualists and their imitators wipe up the last fragments of invisible crumbs by pressure of the thumb as it is made to sweep round the empty paten, or where, after the cup has been fairly drained, water is poured into it, and then that water is drunk.

No such practice is enjoined by our rubric, but, on the contrary, such a superstitious and unmanly custom is out of keeping with the whole English service, and can only find any reasonable justification in theories of an objective change, or a kind of transubstantiation, which are, as we have seen, wholly inconsistent with the letter and spirit alike of Scripture and of the English Liturgy.

The next rubric is thus worded :—

The bread and wine for the Communion shall be provided by the curate and the churchwardens at the charges of the parish.

This simple rule has taken the place of the ancient custom of every communicant bringing a contribution for the love-feast.   It was preceded by rubrics, in our older Prayerbooks, enjoining that the parishioners should, in a certain order, one after the other, provide the bread and wine for the sacrament ; and, in 1549, it was contemplated that they who, on any occasion, provided the elements, should likewise be sure themselves to be among the number of the communicants on such occasion.   As the primitive contribution, from each and all of the communicants, had fallen into desuetude, and as the custom of families providing the elements, in a certain order, was inconvenient, the rubric in its present form became desirable.

The next rubric is as follows :—

And note, that every parishioner shall communicate at the least three times in the year, of which Easter to be one. And yearly at Easter every parishioner shall reckon with the parson, vicar, or curate, or his or their deputy or deputies; and pay to them or him all ecclesiastical duties, accustomably due, then and at that time to be paid.

With reference to the latter portion of this rubric, it may be observed that, by some persons, it has been maintained that, as tithes were wont to be paid on a man's property, so there should be some similar payment on account of his person. Some have even fixed the amount of such payment at twopence (or more) for each individual by the year. Dating from the reigns of Henry VIII. and Edward VI., there are statutes which refer to the four annual seasons for making and paying offerings to the parson or his deputy; and if payment was not made at these times, then it was appointed to be made at the Easter next following.

Out of those ancient laws and customs have sprung the latter part of this rubric and the usage, which still prevails, of collecting voluntary Easter offerings for the parochial clergyman.

The first words of the rubric are, perhaps, more important and interesting to the majority of readers. They may well call back to our memories a time when the apostolic "breaking of bread" was "daily" and "from house to house." Then came a time when all members of the Church were accustomed to "break bread" in the congregation once a week, on the Lord's Day. Then, in the days of Chrysostom, for instance, the complaint was raised that at Communion-time the church was "in a manner empty and deserted." Later still, say between the Council of Agde (A.D. 506) and the time of Charlemagne, canons of the Church accepted this falling off of the frequency of communion as a fact, and enjoined that the laity, on pain of excommunication, should communicate at least three times in each year, namely, at Christmas, Easter, and Whitsuntide.

Matters had not improved when the fourth Lateran Council (A.D. 1215) decreed that every believer, after attaining to years of discretion, should secretly (*solus*) confess all his sins to his priest at least once a year, should diligently perform the penance enjoined him, and should humbly receive the sacrament of the Eucharist at least at Easter—that is, *once a year.*

It was the endeavour of the Reformers to amend this state of things which led to the rubric which directs every parishioner to communicate at least three times in the year, of which Easter shall be one.

How far the people were deterred from communion by such language as Chrysostom sometimes used in describing the Table of the loving Saviour as an " awful "[1] place, and the like, it is plain to remark; and similar superstitions, as they grew and multiplied through the Middle Ages, would have an increasingly deterrent effect, until the people had learned, even from motives of piety misunderstood, to prefer that the priest—in violation of the idea of fellowship and in defiance of Christ's command that all should communicate in remembrance of Him—should partake and, for the most part, consecrate in solitude.

Such historical facts are well worth consideration at all times, and especially now, when the attempt is made, by numbers of the English clergy and laity, to surround the Table of the Lord with mediæval practices which symbolize, and are intended to symbolize, mediæval doctrines.

The same causes, nowadays, will ultimately lead to effects similar to those of the pre-Reformation times if, instead of making the Lord's Table a simple and joyous place of Christian memory and thankfulness, we convert it into a terrible part of the church where, by means only of a privileged caste of priests, there is to be manufactured a talisman, or magic material charm, whose reception shall be safety and salvation to those approved by the priest, and danger or damnation to all others.

If the Protestant Reformed Church of England, in the nineteenth century, suffer herself again to fall into these errors, it will be a strange defiance of the proverb which says, In vain is the net spread in the sight of any bird.

And now we come to the last of the rubrics :—

After the Divine Service ended, the money given at the Offertory shall be disposed of to such pious and charitable uses, as the minister and churchwardens shall think fit. Wherein if they disagree, it shall be disposed of as the Ordinary shall appoint.

[1] φρικτός.

In connection with this rubric for the distribution of the Offertory, all that need be here remarked is, that, instead of any iron rule for dispensing the money collected in the church in certain compulsory manners, its spending and apportionment are left to the discretion of the clergyman and church-wardens, with appeal, if they cannot agree, to the bishop. This is, surely, a plain and convenient arrangement.

Perhaps the most important point in this rubric is the recognition therein given by the Church to the laity as represented by the wardens. The two wardens are to have a voice, together with the clergyman, in dispensing the money of the people. Here is a principle which it will be for the advantage of all parties to keep in mind and to uphold. The Church is not made up of the clergy alone or chiefly. It is the whole body of believers, alike lay and clerical. All are alike and equally made by Christ kings and priests unto God. None can offer a sacrifice to put away the sin of another. None can so assume to himself, or intrude upon, the functions of the one Mediator. So far as there is any difference between the clergy and the laity, it is in that we, the clergy, are the ministers or servants of the laity for Christ's sake; and, if we would attain to honour in this our service and ministry, it must not be by lording it over God's heritage, but by walking in the Master's steps and doing good with meekness, while we win many souls to Christ and righteousness. It must be by remembering, and showing quite unmistakably, that even in our office of teachers, and guides, and watchmen, and stewards, and evangelists, we labour patiently in such noble work, as the apostle says was his custom (2 Cor. i. 24), not as having dominion over men's faith, but as helpers of their joy.

So will laity and clergy work best together for the sanctification of their own souls, for the edifying of the Church and the world, and for the glory of our God and Christ.

To the Communion Service, and to the rubrics we have been considering, is appended the following declaration :—

Whereas it is ordained in this Office for the Administration of the Lord's Supper, that the Communicants should receive the same kneeling ; (which order is well meant, for a signification of our humble and grateful acknowledgment of the benefits of Christ therein given to all worthy Receivers, and for the avoiding of such profanation and disorder in the holy Communion, as might otherwise ensue ;) yet, lest the same kneeling should by any persons, either out of ignorance and infirmity, or out of malice and obstinacy, be misconstrued and depraved ; It is hereby declared, That thereby no adoration is intended, or ought to be done, either unto the Sacramental Bread or Wine there bodily received, or unto any Corporal Presence of Christ's natural Flesh and Blood. For the Sacramental Bread and Wine remain still in their very natural sub-stances, and therefore may not be adored ; (for that were Idolatry, to be abhorred of all faithful Christians;) and the natural Body and Blood of our Saviour Christ are in Heaven, and not here ; it being against the truth of Christ's natural Body to be at one time in more places than one.

This declaration is like, though not identical with, that which was introduced into Edward VI.'s second book in 1552. Having been omitted from the Prayer-book in Elizabeth's reign, it was re-introduced in 1662, with the words, "corporal presence of Christ's natural flesh and blood," instead of the phrase which had previously stood in the corresponding place, "real and essential presence there being of Christ's natural flesh and blood."

The declaration is concerned with the practice of kneeling to receive the sacrament, as it is enjoined in the rubric imme-diately before the forms of administration.

First, we are told that such "kneeling" is appointed for two purposes :—

1. In humble and thankful acknowledgment of the benefits proceeding from Christ, and given, in the sacrament, to all worthy communicants.

2. To avoid profanation and disorder.

Then, in a most praiseworthy effort to make even the ignorant and infirm, or the malicious and obstinate, aware of the danger of misunderstanding and depraving this attitude of kneeling at the sacrament, the declaration proceeds to warn us of two perils which should be avoided in this matter :—

1. Any adoring of the sacramental bread and wine.
2. Any adoring of a corporal or objective presence of Christ's natural body and blood.

Hereupon follow reasons in support of men's avoidance of these perils :—

1. The sacramental elements remain, after consecration as before, merely and substantially, or objectively, God's creatures of bread and wine, and to adore them would be abhorrent idolatry.
2. The natural body and blood of Christ are not on our Communion Tables or in any place on earth, but they are in heaven; and it is against the truth of Christ's natural or objective body to be at one time in more places than one.

This declaration is as binding on the clergy—and on the laity, too, as intelligent members of the English Church—as any other part of the Book of Common Prayer. To put its statements and warnings more distinctly than the English Church puts them in this declaration seems impossible. In support of the reasoning of the declaration, we have endeavoured throughout this essay to produce the evidence of Scripture, reason, faith, and history.

To prolong this effort would not be difficult; but it might defeat our object, which is to lay before the earnest and intelligent reader enough to make him safe, with God's blessing, against the errors now rife and rampant in the Church, and to give him a Scriptural, unsuperstitious, and pious manual, such as may assist him to come happily and profitably to the Table of the Lord particularly, and to the throne of grace generally, in that and all its other adaptations to the wants of the human soul.

GENERAL CONCLUSION.

At this point our investigations reach their limit. Throughout their course, we have desired, we have strenuously laboured, that the dangerous errors, which now hang about the doctrine of the Lord's Supper, should be exposed, traced to their source, and brought under the light of Christ and of the sacred records concerning Christ.

Unless we have wholly failed in this our endeavour, it will have appeared how the belief in an objective presence of the Saviour, in the sacramental elements, took definite form in the centuries of ignorance intervening betwixt Paschasius Radbertus and the fourth Lateran Council. It will have been seen how the ground for this erroneous dogma was prepared in the ambiguities and vacillations of writers earlier than the ninth century; and how these ambiguities themselves sprang from a misapprehension of certain abbreviated forms derived from Holy Scripture. It will have been apparent that, instead of saying or meaning what these abbreviated forms have been misunderstood to imply, Jesus really did say and mean something entirely different from any materialistic doctrine of His objective presence in the bread and wine. It will have been seen that the apostolic "breaking of bread" was a most simple and spiritual rite; that it was one mode—neither the only mode nor the super-eminent mode—of holding communion with Christ, of being made one body with the Lord and with His people, of entering spiritually and subjectively into the very presence of Christ, having Him to dwell and abide in us, while we dwell and abide in Him, making Him one with us and ourselves one with Him.

All this, unless our effort has quite failed, will have been apparent; and, moreover, it will have been clear and unmistakeable that, whereas there was a marked advance in the simplicity and apostolicity of the service for the Lord's Supper, as shown between the first and second Prayer-books of Edward the Sixth, it was the second, or far more simple and evangelic of those two Prayer-books, that was once again solemnly sanctioned by the Act of Uniformity of Queen Elizabeth.

In so far as there may have been any semblance of an exception to this, in respect of the vestments of the clergy, we have seen that, by reason of a clause in that Act of Uniformity, by reason of Elizabeth's "Advertisements," by reason of the Canons of 1604, and by reason of contemporaneous and continued usage, there must be "read into" the Vestments Rubric of Edward's first Prayer-book the less sacerdotal prescriptions of later and modern law.

Thus have we seen every omission of ritual details from the mediæval Mass-book emphasized by the successive editions of the English Prayer-book. Such a course, it is obvious, indicates, not that the rites, prescribed in the Book of Common Prayer, are a *minimum* which may be added to in accordance with mediæval practice, but, rather, this course of history shows that the rites, permitted by the existing Liturgy, are a *maximum* beyond which the law suffers us not to stray. The tendency of English law and of the English Liturgy is altogether in the opposite direction, and aims at carrying us back—without unnecessarily deviating from the customs of any portion of the universal or catholic Church—into nearer and closer conformity with the best and purest antiquity—that, namely, of the apostolic Church in all its simplicity and in all its freedom from minute rites and complicated ceremonies.

In a word, the history of the English Prayer-book, and of its Liturgy, is a striking example and illustration of the principle that Holy Writ is, under God and with conscience, the highest appeal, not only for such lesser matters as those of ritual, but for the far weightier matters of doctrine and truth of which, confessedly, ritual is but the trapping and the sign.

Above all, and throughout all, we have striven to make it

plain that whereas Christ is ever in all men as the Light which lighteth every man that cometh into the world; and whereas the Lord ever abideth especially with and in all His disciples; yet, such is our weakness, we are not able at all times to realize His presence: but there are sent to us, nevertheless, times of refreshing, means of grace; and so it comes to pass that in prayer or praise, in joy or sorrow, in baptism or the eucharist, in some deed of benevolence or in some period of self-abasement—in either of these events, or in any of a thousand other modes of God's dealing with us, there is an awakening on our part; we become conscious of Christ's indwelling; the electric spark of divine love makes us aware of His presence; and this occasional consciousness, whether it be connected with the Lord's Supper or with aught else, is a real, true, and subjective evidence of Christ's presence. No material object has come into our mind; but the spirit of Christ, ever present there, has moved and quickened some nerve of our spiritual and subjective life.

Unless we have ascertained these facts, and pointed to not a few inferences that flow from them, our pages are, indeed, a failure. Unless we have learned from Holy Writ that, in the sacrament, as in all Christian life and worship, the letter killeth and only the spirit giveth life, the flesh profiteth nothing, but only the words and spirit of Christ are truth and are life, vain indeed has been our effort. However, we hope, and pray, for better things; and so we commend this essay to the patient study of the reader, and to the mercy of Almighty God in our Saviour Christ.

PRINTED AT THE CAXTON PRESS, BECCLES.

A LIST OF

C. KEGAN PAUL & CO.'S
PUBLICATIONS.

THE

NINETEENTH CENTUR`

A Monthly Review.

EDITED BY JAMES KNOWLES.

Price 2s. 6d.

———————

VOLUMES I. & II., PRICE 14s. EACH, CONTAIN CONTRIBUTIONS BY

1 *Paternoster Square*,

London.

A LIST OF

C. KEGAN PAUL & CO.'S

PUBLICATIONS.

ABDULLA (*Hakayit*)—AUTOBIOGRAPHY OF A MALAY MUNSHI. Translated by J. T. THOMSON, F.R.G.S. With Photo-lithograph Page of Abdulla's MS. Post 8vo. price 12s.

ADAMS (*A. L.*) *M.A., M.B., F.R.S., F.G.S.*—FIELD AND FOREST RAMBLES OF A NATURALIST IN NEW BRUNSWICK. With Notes and Observations on the Natural History of Eastern Canada. Illustrated. 8vo. price 14s.

ADAMS (*F. O.*) *F.R.G.S.*—THE HISTORY OF JAPAN. From the Earliest Period to the Present Time. New Edition, revised. 2 volumes. With Maps and Plans. Demy 8vo. price 21s. each.

A. K. H. B.—A SCOTCH COMMUNION SUNDAY, to which are added Certain Discourses from a University City. By the Author of 'The Recreations of a Country Parson.' Second Edition. Crown 8vo. price 5s.

ALLEN (*Rev. R.*) *M.A.*—ABRAHAM; HIS LIFE, TIMES, AND TRAVELS, 3,800 years ago. With Map. Second Edition. Post 8vo. price 6s.

ALLEN (*Grant*) *B.A.*—PHYSIOLOGICAL ÆSTHETICS. Crown 8vo. 9s.

ANDERSON (*Rev. C.*) *M.A.*—NEW READINGS OF OLD PARABLES. Demy 8vo. price 4s. 6d.

CHURCH THOUGHT AND CHURCH WORK. Edited by. Second Edition. Demy 8vo. price 7s. 6d.

WORDS AND WORKS IN A LONDON PARISH. Edited by. Second Edition. Demy 8vo. price 6s.

THE CURATE OF SHYRE. Second Edition. 8vo. price 7s. 6d.

ANDERSON (*R. C.*) *C.E.*—TABLES FOR FACILITATING THE CALCULATION OF EVERY DETAIL IN CONNECTION WITH EARTHEN AND MASONRY DAMS. Royal 8vo. price £2. 2s.

ARCHER (*Thomas*)—ABOUT MY FATHER'S BUSINESS. Work amidst the Sick, the Sad, and the Sorrowing. Crown 8vo. price 5s.

ASHTON (*J.*)—ROUGH NOTES OF A VISIT TO BELGIUM, SEDAN, AND PARIS, in September 1870-71. Crown 8vo. price 3s. 6d.

1,78.

BAGEHOT (*Walter*)—THE ENGLISH CONSTITUTION. A New Edition Revised and Corrected, with an Introductory Dissertation on Recent Change and Events. Crown 8vo. price 7s. 6d.

LOMBARD STREET. A Description of the Money Market. Seventh Edition. Crown 8vo. price 7s. 6d.

SOME ARTICLES ON THE DEPRECIATION OF SILVER, AND TOPIC CONNECTED WITH IT. Demy 8vo. price 5s.

BAGOT (*Alan*)—ACCIDENTS IN MINES. Crown 8vo. cloth. 6s.

BALDWIN (*Capt. J. H.*) *F.Z.S. Bengal Staff Corps.*—THE LARGE AND SMALL GAME OF BENGAL AND THE NORTH-WESTERN PROVINCES O INDIA. 4to. With numerous Illustrations. Second Edition. Price 21s.

BARTLEY (*G. C. T.*)—DOMESTIC ECONOMY : Thrift in Every-Day Life Crown 8vo. 2s.

BAUR (*Ferdinand*) *Dr. Ph., Professor in Maulbronn.*—A PHILOLOGICAL INTRODUCTION TO GREEK AND LATIN FOR STUDENTS. Translated and adapted from the German. By C. KEGAN PAUL, M.A. Oxon., and th Rev. E. D. STONE, M.A., late Fellow of King's College, Cambridge, and Assistant Master at Eton. Crown 8vo. price 6s.

BECKER (*Bernard H.*)—THE SCIENTIFIC SOCIETIES OF LONDON Crown 8vo. price 5s.

BENNIE (*Rev. J. N.*) *M.A.*—THE ETERNAL LIFE. Sermons preached during the last twelve years. Crown 8vo. price 6s.

BERNARD (*Bayle*)—SAMUEL LOVER, HIS LIFE AND UNPUBLISHED WORKS. In 2 vols. With a Steel Portrait. Post 8vo. price 21s.

BISCOE (*A. C.*)—THE EARLS OF MIDDLETON, Lords of Clermont and of Fettercairn, and the Middleton Family. Crown 8vo. price 10s. 6d.

BISSET (*A.*)—HISTORY OF THE STRUGGLE FOR PARLIAMENTAR' GOVERNMENT IN ENGLAND. 2 vols. Demy 8vo. price 24s.

BLANC (*H.*) *M.D.*—CHOLERA : HOW TO AVOID AND TREAT IT Popular and Practical Notes. Crown 8vo. price 4s. 6d.

BONWICK (*J.*) *F.R.G.S.*—PYRAMID FACTS AND FANCIES. Crown 8vo price 5s.

BOWEN (*H. C.*) *M.A., Head Master of the Grocers' Company's Middl Class School at Hackney.*

STUDIES IN ENGLISH, for the use of Modern Schools. Small crown 8vo. price 1s. 6d.

BOWRING (*L.*) *C.S.I.*—EASTERN EXPERIENCES. Illustrated with Maps and Diagrams. Demy 8vo. price 16s.

BOWRING (*Sir John*).—AUTOBIOGRAPHICAL RECOLLECTIONS OF SIR JOHN BOWRING. With Memoir by LEWIN B. BOWRING. Demy 8vo. price 14s

BRADLEY (*F. H.*)—ETHICAL STUDIES. Critical Essays in Mora Philosophy. Large post 8vo. price 9s.

MR. SIDGWICK'S HEDONISM : an Examination of the Main Argument of 'The Methods of Ethics.' Demy 8vo. sewed, price 2s. 6d.

BROOKE (*Rev. S. A.*) *M.A., Chaplain in Ordinary to Her Majesty the Queen, and Minister of Bedford Chapel, Bloomsbury.*

LIFE AND LETTERS OF THE LATE REV. F. W. ROBERTSON, M.A., Edited by.

I. Uniform with the Sermons. 2 vols. With Steel Portrait. Price 7*s*. 6*d*.
II. Library Edition. 8vo. With Two Steel Portraits. Price 12*s*.
III. A Popular Edition. In 1 vol. 8vo. price 6*s*.

THE FIGHT OF FAITH. Sermons preached on various occasions. Third Edition. Crown 8vo. price 7*s*. 6*d*.

THEOLOGY IN THE ENGLISH POETS.—Cowper, Coleridge, Wordsworth, and Burns. Third Edition. Post 8vo. price 9*s*.

CHRIST IN MODERN LIFE. Eleventh Edition. Crown 8vo. price 7*s*. 6*d*.

SERMONS. First Series. Ninth Edition. Crown 8vo. price 6*s*.

SERMONS. Second Series. Third Edition. Crown 8vo. price 7*s*.

FREDERICK DENISON MAURICE: The Life and Work of. A Memorial Sermon. Crown 8vo. sewed, price 1*s*.

BROOKE (*W. G.*) *M.A.*—THE PUBLIC WORSHIP REGULATION ACT. With a Classified Statement of its Provisions, Notes, and Index. Third Edition, revised and corrected. Crown 8vo. price 3*s*. 6*d*.

SIX PRIVY COUNCIL JUDGMENTS—1850-72. Annotated by. Third Edition. Crown 8vo. price 9*s*.

BROUN (*J. A.*)—MAGNETIC OBSERVATIONS AT TREVANDRUM AND AUGUSTIA MALLEY. Vol. I. 4to. price 63*s*.
The Report from above, separately sewed, price 21*s*.

BROWN (*Rev. J. Baldwin*) *B.A.*—THE HIGHER LIFE. Its Reality, Experience, and Destiny. Fourth Edition. Crown 8vo. price 7*s*. 6*d*.

DOCTRINE OF ANNIHILATION IN THE LIGHT OF THE GOSPEL OF LOVE. Five Discourses. Second Edition. Crown 8vo. price 2*s*. 6*d*.

BROWN (*J. Croumbie*) *LL.D.*—REBOISEMENT IN FRANCE; or, Records of the Replanting of the Alps, the Cevennes, and the Pyrenees with Trees, Herbage, and Bush. Demy 8vo. price 12*s*. 6*d*.

THE HYDROLOGY OF SOUTHERN AFRICA. Demy 8vo. price 10*s*. 6*d*.

BROWNE (*Rev. M. E.*)—UNTIL THE DAY DAWN. Four Advent Lectures. Crown 8vo. price 2*s*. 6*d*.

BURTON (*Mrs. Richard*)—THE INNER LIFE OF SYRIA, PALESTINE, AND THE HOLY LAND. With Maps, Photographs, and Coloured Plates. 2 vols. Second Edition. Demy 8vo. price 24s.

CARLISLE (*A. D.*) *B.A.*—ROUND THE WORLD IN 1870. A Volume of Travels, with Maps. New and Cheaper Edition. Demy 8vo. price 6*s*.

CARNE (*Miss E. T.*)—THE REALM OF TRUTH. Crown 8vo. price 5*s*. 6*d*.

CARPENTER (*W. B.*) *LL.D., M.D., F.R.S., &c.*—THE PRINCIPLES OF MENTAL PHYSIOLOGY. With their Applications to the Training and Discipline of the Mind, and the Study of its Morbid Conditions. Illustrated. Fourth Edition. 8vo. price 12*s*.

CHILDREN'S TOYS, and some Elementary Lessons in General Knowl
which they Teach. With Illustrations. Crown 8vo. price 5*s.*

CHRISTOPHERSON (*The Late Rev. Henry*) *M.A.*—SERMONS.
an Introduction by John Rae, LL.D., F.S.A. First Series. Crown
price 7*s.* 6*d.*

    SERMONS. With an Introduction by John Rae, LL.D., F
Second Series. Crown 8vo. price 6*s.*

CLODD (*Edward*) *F.R.A.S.*—THE CHILDHOOD OF THE WORLE
Simple Account of Man in Early Times. Third Edition. Crown
price 3*s.*
    A Special Edition for Schools. Price 1*s.*

    THE CHILDHOOD OF RELIGIONS. Including a Simple Account o
Birth and Growth of Myths and Legends. Third Thousand. Crown
price 5*s.*
    A Special Edition for Schools. Price 1*s.* 6*d.*

COLERIDGE (*Sara*)—PHANTASMION. A Fairy Tale. With an I
ductory Preface by the Right Hon. Lord Coleridge, of Ottery St. Mary
New Edition. Illustrated. Crown 8vo. Cloth, price 7*s.* 6*d.*

    MEMOIR AND LETTERS OF SARA COLERIDGE. Edited by her Daug
With Index. 2 vols. With Two Portraits. Third Edition, Revised
Corrected. Crown 8vo. price 24*s.*
Cheap Edition. With one Portrait. Price 7*s.* 6*d.*

COLLINS (*Mortimer*)—THE SECRET OF LONG LIFE. Dedicated
special permission to Lord St. Leonards. Fourth Edition. Large crown
price 5*s.*

COLLINS (*Rev. R.*) *M.A.*—MISSIONARY ENTERPRISE IN THE F
With special reference to the Syrian Christians of Malabar, and the R
of Modern Missions. With Four Illustrations. Crown 8vo. price 6*s.*

CONWAY (*Moncure D.*)—REPUBLICAN SUPERSTITIONS. Illustrate
the Political History of the United States. Including a Correspondence
M. Louis Blanc. Crown 8vo. price 5*s.*

COOKE (*Prof. J. P.*) *of the Harvard University.*—SCIENTIFIC CULT
Crown 8vo. price 1*s.*

COOPER (*T. T.*) *F.R.G.S.*—THE MISHMEE HILLS : an Account
Journey made in an Attempt to Penetrate Thibet from Assam, to open
Routes for Commerce. Second Edition. With Four Illustrations and
Post 8vo. price 10*s.* 6*d.*

CORY (*Lieut.-Col. Arthur*)—THE EASTERN MENACE ; OR, SHADOW
COMING EVENTS. Crown 8vo. price 5*s.*

COX (*Rev. Samuel*)—SALVATOR MUNDI ; or, Is Christ the Saviour o
Men ? Second Edition. Crown 8vo. cloth, price 5*s.*

CROMPTON (*Henry*) — INDUSTRIAL CONCILIATION. Fcap.
price 2*s.* 6*d.*

CURWEN (*Henry*)—SORROW AND SONG ; Studies of Literary Stru
Henry Mürger—Novalis—Alexander Petöfi—Honoré de Balzac—Edgar J
Poe— André Chénier. 2 vols. crown 8vo. price 15*s.*

DANCE (Rev. C. D.)—RECOLLECTIONS OF FOUR YEARS IN VENEZUELA. With Three Illustrations and a Map. Crown 8vo. price 7*s.* 6*d.*

DANVERS (N. R.)—THE SUEZ CANAL : Letters and Documents descriptive of its Rise and Progress in 1854–56. Translated by FERDINAND DE LESSEPS. Demy 8vo. price 10*s.* 6*d.*

DAVIDSON (Rev. Samuel) D.D., LL.D. — THE NEW TESTAMENT, TRANSLATED FROM THE LATEST GREEK TEXT OF TISCHENDORF. A New and thoroughly revised Edition. Post 8vo. price 10*s.* 6*d.*

CANON OF THE BIBLE : Its Formation, History, and Fluctuations. Second Edition. Small crown 8vo. price 5*s.*

DAVIES (G. Christopher)—MOUNTAIN, MEADOW, AND MERE : a Series of Outdoor Sketches of Sport, Scenery, Adventures, and Natural History. With Sixteen Illustrations by Bosworth W. Harcourt. Crown 8vo. price 6*s.*

DAVIES (Rev. J. L.) M.A.—THEOLOGY AND MORALITY. Essays on Questions of Belief and Practice. Crown 8vo. price 7*s.* 6*d.*

DAWSON (Geo.), M.A.—PRAYERS, WITH A DISCOURSE ON PRAYER. Edited by his Wife. Fifth Edition. Crown 8vo. 6*s.*

SERMONS ON DISPUTED POINTS AND SPECIAL OCCASIONS. Edited by his Wife. Second Edition. Crown 8vo. price 6*s.*

DE KERKADEC (Vicomtesse Solange)—A CHEQUERED LIFE, being Memoirs of the Vicomtesse de Leoville Meilhan. Edited by. Crown 8vo. price 7*s.* 6*d.*

DE L'HOSTE (Col. E. P.)—THE DESERT PASTOR, JEAN JAROUSSEAU. Translated from the French of Eugène Pelletan. With a Frontispiece. New Edition. Fcp. 8vo. cloth, price 3*s.* 6*d.*

DE REDCLIFFE (Viscount Stratford) P.C., K.G., G.C.B.—WHY AM I A CHRISTIAN? Fifth Edition. Crown 8vo. price 3*s.*

DE TOCQUEVILLE (A.)—CORRESPONDENCE AND CONVERSATIONS OF, WITH NASSAU WILLIAM SENIOR, from 1834 to 1859. Edited by M. C. M. SIMPSON. 2 vols. post 8vo. price 21*s.*

DOWDEN (Edward) LL.D.—SHAKSPERE : a Critical Study of his Mind and Art. Third Edition. Post 8vo. price 12*s.*

DREW (Rev. G. S.) M.A.—SCRIPTURE LANDS IN CONNECTION WITH THEIR HISTORY. Second Edition. 8vo. price 10*s.* 6*d.*

NAZARETH : ITS LIFE AND LESSONS. Third Edition. Crown 8vo. price 5*s.*

THE DIVINE KINGDOM ON EARTH AS IT IS IN HEAVEN. 8vo. price 10*s.* 6*d.*

THE SON OF MAN : His Life and Ministry. Crown 8vo. price 7*s.* 6*d.*

DREWRY (G. O.) M.D.—THE COMMON-SENSE MANAGEMENT OF THE STOMACH. Fourth Edition. Fcp. 8vo. price 2*s.* 6*d.*

DREWRY (G. O.) M.D., and BARTLETT (H. C.) Ph.D., F.C.S.—CUP AND PLATTER : or, Notes on Food and its Effects. Small 8vo. price 2*s.* 6*d.*

EDEN (Frederick)—THE NILE WITHOUT A DRAGOMAN. Second Edition
Crown 8vo. price 7s. 6d.

ELSDALE (Henry)—STUDIES IN TENNYSON'S IDYLLS. Crown 8vo. cloth
price 5s.

ESSAYS ON THE ENDOWMENT OF RESEARCH. By Various Writers.
> *List of Contributors.* —Mark Pattison, B.D.—James S. Cotton, B.A.—Charl
> E. Appleton, D.C.L.—Archibald H. Sayce, M.A.—Henry Clifton Sorb
> F.R.S.—Thomas K. Cheyne, M.A.—W. T. Thiselton Dyer, M.A.—Hen
> Nettleship, M.A. Square crown 8vo. price 10s. 6d.

EVANS (Mark)—THE STORY OF OUR FATHER'S LOVE, told to Childre
being a New and Enlarged Edition of Theology for Children. With Fo
Illustrations. Fcp. 8vo. price 3s. 6d.

A BOOK OF COMMON PRAYER AND WORSHIP FOR HOUSEHOLD Us
compiled exclusively from the Holy Scriptures. Fcp. 8vo. price 2s. 6d.

THE GOSPEL OF HOME LIFE. Crown 8vo. cloth, price 4s. 6d.

FAVRE (Mons. J.)—THE GOVERNMENT OF THE NATIONAL DEFENC
From the 30th June to the 31st October, 1870. Translated by H. CLAR
Demy 8vo. price 10s. 6d.

FOLKESTONE RITUAL CASE : the Arguments, Proceedings, Judgment, an
Report. Demy 8vo. cloth, price 25s.

FOOTMAN (Rev. H.) M.A.—FROM HOME AND BACK ; or, Some Aspec
of Sin as seen in the Light of the Parable of the Prodigal. Crown 8vo. price

FOWLE (Rev. T. W.) M.A.—THE RECONCILIATION OF RELIGION AN
SCIENCE. Being Essays on Immortality, Inspiration, Miracles, and the Bei
of Christ. Demy 8vo. price 10s. 6d.

FOX-BOURNE (H. R.) — THE LIFE OF JOHN LOCKE, 1632–170
2 vols. demy 8vo. price 28s.

FRASER (Donald)—EXCHANGE TABLES OF STERLING AND INDI
RUPEE CURRENCY, upon a new and extended system, embracing Values fr
One Farthing to One Hundred Thousand Pounds, and at rates progressing,
Sixteenths of a Penny, from 1s. 9d. to 2s. 3d. per Rupee. Royal 8vo. pr
10s. 6d.

FRERE (Sir H. Bartle E.) G.C.B., G.C.S.I.—THE THREATEN
FAMINE IN BENGAL : How it may be Met, and the Recurrence of Famines
India Prevented. Being No. 1 of 'Occasional Notes on Indian Affair
With 3 Maps. Crown 8vo. price 5s.

FRISWELL (J. Hain.)—THE BETTER SELF. Essays for Home Li
Crown 8vo. price 6s.

GARDNER (J.) M.D.—LONGEVITY : THE MEANS OF PROLONGI
LIFE AFTER MIDDLE AGE. Fourth Edition, revised and enlarged. Sm
crown 8vo. price 4s.

GILBERT (Mrs.)—AUTOBIOGRAPHY AND OTHER MEMORIALS. Edited by Josiah Gilbert. Third Edition. With Steel Portrait and several Wood Engravings. Crown 8vo. price 7s. 6d.

GILL (Rev. W. W.) B.A.—MYTHS AND SONGS FROM THE SOUTH PACIFIC. With a Preface by F. Max Müller, M.A., Professor of Comparative Philology at Oxford. Post 8vo. price 9s.

GODKIN (James)—THE RELIGIOUS HISTORY OF IRELAND : Primitive, Papal, and Protestant. Including the Evangelical Missions, Catholic Agitations, and Church Progress of the last half Century. 8vo. price 12s.

GODWIN (William)—WILLIAM GODWIN: HIS FRIENDS AND CONTEMPORARIES. With Portraits and Facsimiles of the Handwriting of Godwin and his Wife. By C. KEGAN PAUL. 2 vols. Large post 8vo. price 28s.

THE GENIUS OF CHRISTIANITY UNVEILED. Being Essays never before published. Edited, with a Preface, by C. Kegan Paul. Crown 8vo. price 7s. 6d.

GOODENOUGH (Commodore J. G.) R.N., C.B., C.M.G.—JOURNALS OF, during his Last Command as Senior Officer on the Australian Station, 1873–1875. Edited, with a Memoir, by his Widow. With Maps, Woodcuts, and Steel Engraved Portrait. Second Edition. Post 8vo. price 14s.

An Abridged Edition. With Portrait. Crown 8vo. price 5s.

GOODMAN (W.) CUBA, THE PEARL OF THE ANTILLES. Crown 8vo. price 7s. 6d.

GOSPEL (THE) OF HOME LIFE. Crown 8vo. cloth, price 4s. 6d.

GOULD (Rev. S. Baring) M.A.—THE VICAR OF MORWENSTOW: a Memoir of the Rev. R. S. Hawker. With Portrait. Third Edition, revised. Square post 8vo. 10s. 6d.

GRANVILLE (A. B.) M.D., F.R.S., &c.—AUTOBIOGRAPHY OF A. B. GRANVILLE, F.R.S., &c. Edited, with a Brief Account of the Concluding Years of his Life, by his youngest Daughter, Paulina B. Granville. 2 vols. With a Portrait. Second Edition. Demy 8vo. price 32s.

GREY (John) of Dilston.— MEMOIRS. By JOSEPHINE E. BUTLER. New and Revised Edition. Crown 8vo. price 3s. 6d.

GRIFFITH (Rev. T.) A.M.—STUDIES OF THE DIVINE MASTER. Demy 8vo. price 12s.

GRIFFITHS (Capt. Arthur)—MEMORIALS OF MILLBANK, AND CHAPTERS IN PRISON HISTORY. With Illustrations by R. Goff and the Author. 2 vols. post 8vo. price 21s.

GRIMLEY (Rev. H. N.) M.A., Professor of Mathematics in the University College of Wales, and Chaplain of Tremadoc Church.

TREMADOC SERMONS, CHIEFLY ON THE SPIRITUAL BODY, THE UNSEEN WORLD, AND THE DIVINE HUMANITY. Second Edition. Crown 8vo. price 6s.

GRUNER (M. L.)—STUDIES OF BLAST FURNACE PHENOMENA. Translated by L. D. B. GORDON, F.R.S.E., F.G.S. Demy 8vo. price 7s. 6d.

GURNEY (Rev. Archer)—WORDS OF FAITH AND CHEER. A Mission of Instruction and Suggestion. Crown 8vo. price 6s.

HAECKEL (Prof. Ernst)—THE HISTORY OF CREATION. Translation revised by Professor E. RAY LANKESTER, M.A., F.R.S. With Coloured Plates and Genealogical Trees of the various groups of both plants and animals. 2 vols. Second Edition. Post 8vo. cloth, price 32s.

THE HISTORY OF THE EVOLUTION OF MAN. With numerous Illustrations. 2 vols. Post 8vo.

HARCOURT (Capt. A. F. P.)—THE SHAKESPEARE ARGOSY. Containing much of the wealth of Shakespeare's Wisdom and Wit, alphabetically arranged and classified. Crown 8vo. price 6s.

HAWEIS (Rev. H. R.) M.A.—CURRENT COIN. Materialism—The Devil — Crime — Drunkenness — Pauperism — Emotion — Recreation — The Sabbath. Crown 8vo. price 6s.

SPEECH IN SEASON. Third Edition. Crown 8vo. price 9s.

THOUGHTS FOR THE TIMES. Eleventh Edition. Crown 8vo. price 7s. 6d.

UNSECTARIAN FAMILY PRAYERS for Morning and Evening for a Week, with short selected passages from the Bible. Square crown 8vo. price 3s. 6d.

HAYMAN (H.) D.D., late Head Master of Rugby School.—RUGBY SCHOOL SERMONS. With an Introductory Essay on the Indwelling of the Holy Spirit. Crown 8vo. price 7s. 6d.

HELLWALD (Baron F. Von)—THE RUSSIANS IN CENTRAL ASIA. A Critical Examination, down to the Present Time, of the Geography and History of Central Asia. Translated by Lieut.-Col. Theodore Wirgman, LL.B. With Map. Large post 8vo. price 12s.

HINTON (J.)—THE PLACE OF THE PHYSICIAN. To which is added ESSAYS ON THE LAW OF HUMAN LIFE, AND ON THE RELATIONS BETWEEN ORGANIC AND INORGANIC WORLDS. Second Edition. Crown 8vo. price 3s. 6d.

PHYSIOLOGY FOR PRACTICAL USE. By Various Writers. With 50 Illustrations. 2 vols. Second Edition. Crown 8vo. price 12s. 6d.

AN ATLAS OF DISEASES OF THE MEMBRANA TYMPANI. With Descriptive Text. Post 8vo. price £6. 6s.

THE QUESTIONS OF AURAL SURGERY. With Illustrations. 2 vols. Post 8vo. price £6. 6s.

LIFE AND LETTERS. Edited by ELLICE HOPKINS. Crown 8vo.

H. J. C.—THE ART OF FURNISHING. A Popular Treatise on the Principles of Furnishing, based on the Laws of Common Sense, Requirement, and Picturesque Effect. Small crown 8vo. price 3s. 6d.

HOLROYD (Major W. R. M.)—TAS-HIL UL KALAM ; or, Hindustani made Easy. Crown 8vo. price 5s.

HOOPER (Mary)—LITTLE DINNERS: HOW TO SERVE THEM WITH ELEGANCE AND ECONOMY. Thirteenth Edition. Crown 8vo. price 5s.

COOKERY FOR INVALIDS, PERSONS OF DELICATE DIGESTION, AND CHILDREN. Crown 8vo. price 3s. 6d.

EVERY-DAY MEALS. Being Economical and Wholesome Recipes for Breakfast, Luncheon, and Supper. Second Edition. Crown 8vo. cloth, price 5s.

HOPKINS (M.)—THE PORT OF REFUGE ; or, Counsel and Aid to Ship-masters in Difficulty, Doubt, or Distress. Second and Revised Edition. Crown 8vo. price 6s.

HORNE (William) M.A.—REASON AND REVELATION : an Examination into the Nature and Contents of Scripture Revelation, as compared with other Forms of Truth. Demy 8vo. price 12s.

HORNER (The Misses)—WALKS IN FLORENCE. A New and thoroughly Revised Edition. 2 vols. Crown 8vo. Cloth limp. With Illustrations.
VOL. I.—Churches, Streets, and Palaces. Price 10s. 6d.
VOL. II.—Public Galleries and Museums. Price 5s.

HULL (Edmund C. P.)—THE EUROPEAN IN INDIA. With a Medical Guide for Anglo-Indians. By R. R. S. MAIR, M.D., F.R.C.S.E. Second Edition, Revised and Corrected. Post 8vo. price 6s.

HUTTON (James)—MISSIONARY LIFE IN THE SOUTHERN SEAS. With Illustrations. Crown 8vo. price 7s. 6d.

JACKSON (T. G.)—MODERN GOTHIC ARCHITECTURE. Crown 8vo. price 5s.

JACOB (Maj.-Gen. Sir G. Le Grand) K.C.S.I., C.B.—WESTERN INDIA BEFORE AND DURING THE MUTINIES. Pictures drawn from Life. Second Edition. Price 7s. 6d.

JENKINS (E.) and RAYMOND (J.) Esqs.—A LEGAL HANDBOOK FOR ARCHITECTS, BUILDERS, AND BUILDING OWNERS. Second Edition, Revised. Crown 8vo. price 6s.

JENKINS (Rev. R. C.) M.A.—THE PRIVILEGE OF PETER and the Claims of the Roman Church confronted with the Scriptures, the Councils, and the Testimony of the Popes themselves. Fcap. 8vo. price 3s. 6d.

JENNINGS (Mrs. Vaughan)—RAHEL : HER LIFE AND LETTERS. With a Portrait from the Painting by Daffinger. Square post 8vo. price 7s. 6d.

JONES (Lucy)— PUDDINGS AND SWEETS ; being Three Hundred and Sixty-five Receipts approved by experience. Crown 8vo. price 2s. 6d.

KAUFMANN (Rev. M.) B.A.—SOCIALISM : Its Nature, its Dangers, and its Remedies considered. Crown 8vo. price 7s. 6d.

KING (Alice)—A CLUSTER OF LIVES. Crown 8vo. price 7s. 6d.

KINGSFORD (Rev. F. W.) M.A., Vicar of St. Thomas's, Stamford Hill; late Chaplain H. E. I. C. (Bengal Presidency).

HARTHAM CONFERENCES ; or, Discussions upon some of the Religious Topics of the Day. 'Audi alteram partem.' Crown 8vo. price 3s. 6d.

KINGSLEY (Charles) M.A.—LETTERS AND MEMORIES OF HIS LIFE. Edited by his WIFE. With Two Steel Engraved Portraits, and Illustrations on Wood, and a Facsimile of his Handwriting. Eleventh Edition. 2 vols. Demy 8vo. price 36s.

ALL SAINTS' DAY, and other Sermons. Edited by the Rev. W. HARRISON. Crown 8vo. price 7s. 6d.

LACORDAIRE (Rev. Père)—LIFE : Conferences delivered at Toulouse. A New and Cheaper Edition. Crown 8vo. price 3s. 6d.

LAMBERT (*Cowley*) *F.R.G.S.*—A Trip to Cashmere and Ladak. With Illustrations. Crown 8vo. price 7s. 6d.

LAURIE (*J. S.*)—Educational Course of Secular School Books for India :—

The First Hindustani Reader. Stiff linen wrapper, price 6d.

The Second Hindustani Reader. Stiff linen wrapper, price 6d.

The Oriental (English) Reader. Book I., price 6d. ; II., price 7½d. ; III., price 9d. ; IV., price 1s.

Geography of India ; with Maps and Historical Appendix, tracing the Growth of the British Empire in Hindustan. Fcap. 8vo. price 1s. 6d.

L. D. S.—Letters from China and Japan. With Illustrated Title-page. Crown 8vo. price 7s. 6d.

LEATHES (*Rev. S.*) *M.A.*—The Gospel Its Own Witness. Crown 8vo. price 5s.

LEE (*Rev. F. G.*) *D.C.L.*—The Other World; or, Glimpses of the Supernatural. 2 vols. A New Edition. Crown 8vo. cloth, price 15s.

LENOIR (*J.*)—Fayoum ; or, Artists in Egypt. A Tour with M. Gérome and others. With 13 Illustrations. A New and Cheaper Edition. Crown 8vo. price 3s. 6d.

Life in the Mofussil ; or, Civilian Life in Lower Bengal. By an Ex-Civilian. Large post 8vo.

LORIMER (*Peter*) *D.D.*—John Knox and the Church of England. His Work in her Pulpit, and his Influence upon her Liturgy, Articles, and Parties. Demy 8vo. price 12s.

LOTHIAN (*Roxburghe*)—Dante and Beatrice from 1282 to 1290. A Romance. 2 vols. Post 8vo. cloth, price 24s.

LOVER (*Samuel*) *R.H.A.*—The Life of Samuel Lover, R.H.A. ; Artistic, Literary, and Musical. With Selections from his Unpublished Papers and Correspondence. By Bayle Bernard. 2 vols. With a Portrait. Post 8vo. price 21s.

LOWER (*M. A.*) *M.A., F.S.A.*—Wayside Notes in Scandinavia. Being Notes of Travel in the North of Europe. Crown 8vo. price 9s.

LYONS (*R. T.*) *Surg.-Maj. Bengal Army.*—A Treatise on Relapsing Fever. Post 8vo. price 7s. 6d.

MACAULAY (*J.*) *M.A., M.D. Edin.*—The Truth about Ireland : Tours of Observation in 1872 and 1875. With Remarks on Irish Public Questions. Being a Second Edition of 'Ireland in 1872,' with a New and Supplementary Preface. Crown 8vo. price 3s. 6d.

MACLACHLAN (*A. N. C.*) *M.A.*—William Augustus, Duke of Cumberland : being a Sketch of his Military Life and Character, chiefly as exhibited in the General Orders of His Royal Highness, 1745-1747. With Illustrations. Post 8vo. price 15s.

MAIR (*R. S.*) *M.D., F.R.C.S.E.*—The Medical Guide for Anglo-Indians. Being a Compendium of Advice to Europeans in India, relating to the Preservation and Regulation of Health. With a Supplement on the Management of Children in India. Crown 8vo. limp cloth, price 3s. 6d.

MANNING (His Eminence Cardinal) — Essays on Religion and Literature. By various Writers. Third Series. Demy 8vo. price 10s. 6d.

The Independence of the Holy See. With an Appendix containing the Papal Allocution and a translation. Crown 8vo. cloth, price 5s.

The True Story of the Vatican Council. Crown 8vo. cloth, price 5s.

MARRIOTT (Maj.-Gen. W. F.) C.S.I.—A Grammar of Political Economy. Crown 8vo. price 6s.

MAUGHAN (W. C.)—The Alps of Arabia; or, Travels through Egypt, Sinai, Arabia, and the Holy Land. With Map. Second Edition. Demy 8vo. price 5s.

MAURICE (C. E.)—Lives of English Popular Leaders. No. 1.—Stephen Langton. Crown 8vo. price 7s. 6d. No. 2.—Tyler, Ball, and Oldcastle. Crown 8vo. price 7s. 6d.

MAZZINI (Joseph) — A Memoir. By E. A. V. Two Photographic Portraits. Second Edition. Crown 8vo. price 5s.

MEDLEY (Lieut.-Col. J. G.) R.E.—An Autumn Tour in the United States and Canada. Crown 8vo. price 5s.

MENZIES (Sutherland)—Memoirs of Distinguished Women. 2 vols. Post 8vo. price 10s. 6d.

MICKLETHWAITE (J. T.) F.S.A.—Modern Parish Churches: Their Plan, Design, and Furniture. Crown 8vo. price 7s. 6d.

MILNE (James)—Tables of Exchange for the Conversion of Sterling Money into Indian and Ceylon Currency, at Rates from 1s. 8d. to 2s. 3d. per Rupee. Second Edition. Demy 8vo. Cloth, price £2. 2s.

MIVART (St. George) F.R.S.—Contemporary Evolution: An Essay on some recent Social Changes. Post 8vo. price 7s. 6d.

MOCKLER (E.)—A Grammar of the Baloochee Language, as it is spoken in Makran (Ancient Gedrosia), in the Persia-Arabic and Roman characters. Fcap. 8vo. price 5s.

MOFFAT (R. S.)—Economy of Consumption: a Study in Political Economy. Demy 8vo.

MOORE (Rev. D.) M.A.—Christ and His Church. By the Author of 'The Age and the Gospel,' &c. Crown 8vo. price 3s. 6d.

MORE (R. Jasper)—Under the Balkans. Notes of a Visit to the District of Philippopolis in 1876. With a Map, and Illustrations from Photographs. Crown 8vo. cloth, price 6s.

MORELL (J. R.)—Euclid Simplified in Method and Language. Being a Manual of Geometry. Compiled from the most important French Works, approved by the University of Paris and the Minister of Public Instruction. Fcap. 8vo. price 2s. 6d.

MORSE (E. S.) Ph.D.—First Book of Zoology. With numerous Illustrations. Crown 8vo. price 5s.

MUSGRAVE (Anthony)—STUDIES IN POLITICAL ECONOMY. Crown 8vo. price 6s.

NEWMAN (J. H.) D.D.—CHARACTERISTICS FROM THE WRITINGS OF. Being Selections from his various Works. Arranged with the Author's personal Approval. Third Edition. With Portrait. Crown 8vo. price 6s.

　*** A Portrait of the Rev. Dr. J. H. Newman, mounted for framing, can be had price 2s. 6d.

NICHOLAS (T.)—THE PEDIGREE OF THE ENGLISH PEOPLE. Demy 8vo. cloth.

NOBLE (J. A.)—THE PELICAN PAPERS. Reminiscences and Remains of a Dweller in the Wilderness. Crown 8vo. price 6s.

NORMAN PEOPLE (THE), and their Existing Descendants in the British Dominions and the United States of America. Demy 8vo. price 21s.

NOTREGE (John) A.M.—THE SPIRITUAL FUNCTION OF A PRESBYTER IN THE CHURCH OF ENGLAND. Crown 8vo. cloth, red edges, price 3s. 6d.

ORIENTAL SPORTING MAGAZINE (THE). A Reprint of the first 5 Volumes, in 2 Volumes. Demy 8vo. price 28s.

PARKER (Joseph) D.D.—THE PARACLETE : An Essay on the Personality and Ministry of the Holy Ghost, with some reference to current discussions. Second Edition. Demy 8vo. price 12s.

PARR (Harriet)—ECHOES OF A FAMOUS YEAR. Crown 8vo. price 8s. 6d.

PAUL (C. Kegan)—WILLIAM GODWIN: HIS FRIENDS AND CONTEMPORARIES. With Portraits and Facsimiles of the Handwriting of Godwin and his Wife. 2 vols. Square post 8vo. price 28s.

　THE GENIUS OF CHRISTIANITY UNVEILED. Being Essays by William Godwin never before published. Edited, with a Preface, by C. Kegan Paul. Crown 8vo. price 7s. 6d.

PAYNE (Prof. J. F.)—LECTURES ON EDUCATION. Price 6d. each.

　I.　Pestalozzi : the Influence of His Principles and Practice.
　II.　Fröbel and the Kindergarten System. Second Edition.
　III.　The Science and Art of Education.
　IV.　The True Foundation of Science Teaching.

　A VISIT TO GERMAN SCHOOLS: ELEMENTARY SCHOOLS IN GERMANY. Notes of a Professional Tour to inspect some of the Kindergartens, Primary Schools, Public Girls' Schools, and Schools for Technical Instruction in Hamburgh, Berlin, Dresden, Weimar, Gotha, Eisenach, in the autumn of 1874. With Critical Discussions of the General Principles and Practice of Kindergartens and other Schemes of Elementary Education. Crown 8vo. price 4s. 6d.

PENRICE (Maj. J.) B.A.—A DICTIONARY AND GLOSSARY OF THE KO-RAN. With Copious Grammatical References and Explanations of the Text. 4to. price 21s.

PERCEVAL (Rev. P.) — TAMIL PROVERBS, WITH THEIR ENGLISH TRANSLATION. Containing upwards of Six Thousand Proverbs. Third Edition. Demy 8vo. sewed, price 9s.

PESCHEL (Dr. Oscar)—THE RACES OF MAN AND THEIR GEOGRAPHICAL DISTRIBUTION. Large crown 8vo. price 9s.

PIGGOT (J.) F.S.A., F.R.G.S.—Persia—Ancient and Modern. Post 8vo. price 10s. 6d.

PLAYFAIR (Lieut-Col.), Her Britannic Majesty's Consul-General in Algiers.

Travels in the Footsteps of Bruce in Algeria and Tunis. Illustrated by facsimiles of Bruce's original Drawings, Photographs, Maps, &c. Royal 4to. cloth, bevelled boards, gilt leaves, price £3. 3s.

POOR (H. V.)—Money and its Laws : embracing a History of Monetary Theories &c. Demy 8vo. price 21s.

POUSHKIN (A. S.)—Russian Romance. Translated from the Tales of Belkin, &c. By Mrs. J. Buchan Telfer (née Mouravieff). Crown 8vo. price 7s. 6d.

POWER (H.)—Our Invalids : How shall we Employ and Amuse Them ? Fcp. 8vo. price 2s. 6d.

PRESBYTER—Unfoldings of Christian Hope. An Essay shewing that the Doctrine contained in the Damnatory Clauses of the Creed commonly called Athanasian is Unscriptural. Small crown 8vo. price 4s. 6d.

PRICE (Prof. Bonamy) — Currency and Banking. Crown 8vo. price 6s.

PROCTOR (Richard A.) B.A.—Our Place among Infinities. A Series of Essays contrasting our little abode in space and time with the Infinities around us. To which are added Essays on 'Astrology,' and 'The Jewish Sabbath.' Third Edition. Crown 8vo. price 6s.

The Expanse of Heaven. A Series of Essays on the Wonders of the Firmament. With a Frontispiece. Third Edition. Crown 8vo. price 6s.

RANKING (B. M.)—Streams from Hidden Sources. Crown 8vo. price 6s.

RIBOT (Prof. Th.)—English Psychology. Second Edition. A Revised and Corrected Translation from the latest French Edition. Large post 8vo. price 9s.

Heredity : A Psychological Study on its Phenomena, its Laws, its Causes, and its Consequences. Large crown 8vo. price 9s.

RINK (Chevalier Dr. Henry)—Greenland : Its People and its Products. By the Chevalier Dr. Henry Rink, President of the Greenland Board of Trade. With sixteen Illustrations, drawn by the Eskimo, and a Map. Edited by Dr. Robert Brown. Crown 8vo. price 10s. 6d.

RUSSELL (Major Frank S.)—Russian Wars with Turkey, Past and Present. With Maps. Second Edition. Crown 8vo. price 6s.

RUSSELL (W. C.)—Memoirs of Mrs. Lætitia Boothby. Crown 8vo. price 7s. 6d.

ROBERTSON (The late Rev. F. W.) M.A., of Brighton. — LIFE AND LETTERS OF. Edited by the Rev. Stopford Brooke, M.A., Chaplain in Ordinary to the Queen.

I. Two vols., uniform with the Sermons. With Steel Portrait. Crown 8vo. price 7s. 6d.

II. Library Edition, in Demy 8vo. with Two Steel Portraits. Price 12s.

III. A Popular Edition, in 1 vol. Crown 8vo. price 6s.

SERMONS. Four Series. Small crown 8vo. price 3s. 6d.

NOTES ON GENESIS. Crown 8vo. price 5s.

EXPOSITORY LECTURES ON ST. PAUL'S EPISTLES TO THE CORINTHIANS. A New Edition. Small crown 8vo. price 5s.

LECTURES AND ADDRESSES, with other Literary Remains. A New Edition. Crown 8vo. price 5s.

AN ANALYSIS OF MR. TENNYSON'S 'IN MEMORIAM.' (Dedicated by Permission to the Poet-Laureate.) Fcp. 8vo. price 2s.

THE EDUCATION OF THE HUMAN RACE. Translated from the German of Gotthold Ephraim Lessing. Fcp. 8vo. price 2s. 6d.

The above Works can also be had, bound in half-morocco.

*** A Portrait of the late Rev. F. W. Robertson, mounted for framing, can be had, price 2s. 6d.

RUTHERFORD (John) — THE SECRET HISTORY OF THE FENIAN CONSPIRACY: its Origin, Objects, and Ramifications. 2 vols. Post 8vo. cloth, price 18s.

SCOTT (W. T.) — ANTIQUITIES OF AN ESSEX PARISH; or, Pages from the History of Great Dunmow. Crown 8vo. price 5s.; sewed, 4s.

SCOTT (Robert H.) — WEATHER CHARTS AND STORM WARNINGS. Illustrated. Crown 8vo. price 3s. 6d.

SENIOR (N. W.) — ALEXIS DE TOCQUEVILLE. Correspondence and Conversations with Nassau W. Senior, from 1833 to 1859. Edited by M. C. M. Simpson. 2 vols. Large post 8vo. price 21s.

JOURNALS KEPT IN FRANCE AND ITALY. From 1848 to 1852. With a Sketch of the Revolution of 1848. Edited by his Daughter, M. C. M. Simpson. 2 vols. Post 8vo. price 24s.

SEYD (Ernest) F.S.S. — THE FALL IN THE PRICE OF SILVER. Its Causes, its Consequences, and their Possible Avoidance, with Special Reference to India. Demy 8vo. sewed, price 2s. 6d.

SHELLEY (Lady) — SHELLEY MEMORIALS FROM AUTHENTIC SOURCES. With (now first printed) an Essay on Christianity by Percy Bysshe Shelley. With Portrait. Third Edition. Crown 8vo. price 5s.

SHILLITO (Rev. Joseph) — WOMANHOOD: its Duties, Temptations, and Privileges. A Book for Young Women. Crown 8vo. price 3s. 6d.

SHIPLEY (Rev. Orby) M.A. — CHURCH TRACTS: OR, STUDIES IN MODERN PROBLEMS. By various Writers. 2 vols. Crown 8vo. price 5s. each.

SHUTE (Richard) M.A. — A DISCOURSE ON TRUTH. Post 8vo. price 9s.

SMEDLEY (M. B.)—BOARDING-OUT AND PAUPER SCHOOLS FOR GIRLS. Crown 8vo. price 3s. 6d.

SMITH (Edward) M.D., LL.B., F.R.S.—HEALTH AND DISEASE, as Influenced by the Daily, Seasonal, and other Cyclical Changes in the Human System. A New Edition. Post 8vo. price 7s. 6d.

PRACTICAL DIETARY FOR FAMILIES, SCHOOLS, AND THE LABOURING CLASSES. A New Edition. Post 8vo. price 3s. 6d.

TUBERCULAR CONSUMPTION IN ITS EARLY AND REMEDIABLE STAGES. Second Edition. Crown 8vo. price 6s.

SMITH (Hubert)—TENT LIFE WITH ENGLISH GIPSIES IN NORWAY. With Five full-page Engravings and Thirty-one smaller Illustrations by Whymper and others, and Map of the Country showing Routes. Third Edition. Revised and Corrected. Post 8vo. price 21s.

SOME TIME IN IRELAND. A Recollection. Crown 8vo. price 7s. 6d.

STEVENSON (Rev. W. F.)—HYMNS FOR THE CHURCH AND HOME. Selected and Edited by the Rev. W. Fleming Stevenson.
The most complete Hymn Book published.
The Hymn Book consists of Three Parts :—I. For Public Worship.—II. For Family and Private Worship.—III. For Children.
*** Published in various forms and prices, the latter ranging from 8d. to 6s. Lists and full particulars will be furnished on application to the Publishers.

SULLY (James) M.A. — SENSATION AND INTUITION. Demy 8vo. price 10s. 6d.

PESSIMISM : a History and a Criticism. Demy 8vo. price 14s.

SYME (David)—OUTLINES OF AN INDUSTRIAL SCIENCE. Crown 8vo. price 6s.

TELFER (J. Buchan) F.R.G.S., Commander R.N.—THE CRIMEA AND TRANS-CAUCASIA. With numerous Illustrations and Maps. Second Edition. 2 vols. Royal 8vo. medium 8vo. price 36s.

THOMPSON (Rev. A. S.)—HOME WORDS FOR WANDERERS. A Volume of Sermons. Crown 8vo. price 6s.

TRAHERNE (Mrs. A.)—THE ROMANTIC ANNALS OF A NAVAL FAMILY. A New and Cheaper Edition. Crown 8vo. price 5s.

UMBRA OXONIENSIS—RESULTS OF THE EXPOSTULATION OF THE RIGHT HON. W. E. GLADSTONE, in their Relation to the Unity of Roman Catholicism. Large fcp. 8vo. price 5s.

UPTON (Capt. Richard D.)—NEWMARKET AND ARABIA. An Examination of the Descent of Racers and Coursers. With Pedigrees and Frontispiece. Post 8vo. price 9s.

VAMBERY (Prof. A.)—BOKHARA : Its History and Conquest. Second Edition. Demy 8vo. price 18s.

VYNER (Lady Mary)—EVERY DAY A PORTION. Adapted from the Bible and the Prayer Book, for the Private Devotions of those living in Widowhood. Collected and Edited by Lady Mary Vyner. Square crown 8vo. cloth extra, price 5s.

WELLS (Capt. John C.) R.N.—SPITZBERGEN—THE GATEWAY TO THE POLYNIA ; or, a Voyage to Spitzbergen. With numerous Illustrations by Whymper and others, and Map. New and Cheaper Edition. Demy 8vo. price 6s.

WETMORE (*W. S.*)—COMMERCIAL TELEGRAPHIC CODE. Second Edition. Post 4to. boards, price 42s.

WHITE (*A. D.*) *LL.D.*—WARFARE OF SCIENCE. With Prefatory Note by Professor Tyndall. Crown 8vo. price 3s. 6d.

WHITNEY (*Prof. William Dwight*)—ESSENTIALS OF ENGLISH GRAMMAR for the Use of Schools. Crown 8vo. price 3s. 6d.

WHITTLE (*J. L.*) *A.M.*—CATHOLICISM AND THE VATICAN. With Narrative of the Old Catholic Congress at Munich. Second Edition. Crown 8vo. price 4s. 6d.

WILBERFORCE (*H. W.*)—THE CHURCH AND THE EMPIRES. Historical Periods. Preceded by a Memoir of the Author by John Henry Newman, D.D. of the Oratory. With Portrait. Post 8vo. price 10s. 6d.

WILKINSON (*T. L.*)—SHORT LECTURES ON THE LAND LAWS. Delivered before the Working Men's College. Crown 8vo. limp cloth, price 2s.

WILLIAMS (*A. Lukyn*)—FAMINES IN INDIA ; their Causes and Possible Prevention. The Essay for the Le Bas Prize, 1875. Demy 8vo. price 5s.

WILLIAMS (*Chas.*)—THE ARMENIAN CAMPAIGN. A Diary of the Campaign of 1877 in Armenia and Koordistan. Large post 8vo. cloth, price 10s. 6d.

WILLIAMS (*Rowland*) *D.D.*—LIFE AND LETTERS OF ; with Extracts from his Note-Books. Edited by Mrs. Rowland Williams. With a Photographic Portrait. 2 vols. large post 8vo. price 24s.

PSALMS, LITANIES, COUNSELS, AND COLLECTS FOR DEVOUT PERSONS. Edited by his Widow. New and Popular Edition. Crown 8vo. price 3s. 6d.

WILLIS (*R.*) *M.D.*—SERVETUS AND CALVIN : a Study of an Important Epoch in the Early History of the Reformation. 8vo. cloth, price 16s.

WILSON (*H. Schütz*)—STUDIES AND ROMANCES. Crown 8vo. price 7s. 6d.

WILSON (*Lieut.-Col. C. T.*)—JAMES THE SECOND AND THE DUKE OF BERWICK. Demy 8vo. price 12s. 6d.

WINTERBOTHAM (*Rev. R.*) *M.A., B.Sc.*—SERMONS AND EXPOSITIONS Crown 8vo. price 7s. 6d.

WOOD (*C. F.*)—A YACHTING CRUISE IN THE SOUTH SEAS. With six Photographic Illustrations. Demy 8vo. price 7s. 6d.

WRIGHT (*Rev. David*) *M.A.*—WAITING FOR THE LIGHT, AND OTHER SERMONS. Crown 8vo. price 6s.

WYLD (*R. S.*) *F.R.S.E.*—THE PHYSICS AND THE PHILOSOPHY OF THE SENSES; or, the Mental and the Physical in their Mutual Relation Illustrated by several Plates. Demy 8vo. price 16s.

YONGE (*C. D.*)—HISTORY OF THE ENGLISH REVOLUTION OF 1688 Crown 8vo. price 6s.

YOUMANS (*Eliza A.*)—AN ESSAY ON THE CULTURE OF THE OBSERVING POWERS OF CHILDREN, especially in connection with the Study of Botany. Edited, with Notes and a Supplement, by Joseph Payne, F.C.P., Author of 'Lectures on the Science and Art of Education,' &c. Crown 8vo. price 2s. 6d.

FIRST BOOK OF BOTANY. Designed to Cultivate the Observing Powers of Children. With 300 Engravings. New and Enlarged Edition Crown 8vo. price 5s.

YOUMANS (*Edward L.*) *M.D.*—A CLASS BOOK OF CHEMISTRY, on the Basis of the New System. With 200 Illustrations. Crown 8vo. price 5s.

THE INTERNATIONAL SCIENTIFIC SERIES.

. THE FORMS OF WATER IN CLOUDS AND RIVERS, ICE AND GLACIERS. By J. Tyndall, Ll.D., F.R.S. With 25 Illustrations. Seventh Edition. Crown 8vo. price 5*s.*

I. PHYSICS AND POLITICS; or, Thoughts on the Application of the Principles of 'Natural Selection' and 'Inheritance' to Political Society. By Walter Bagehot. Third Edition. Crown 8vo. price 4*s.*

II. FOODS. By Edward Smith, M.D., LL.B., F.R.S. With numerous Illustrations. Fourth Edition. Crown 8vo. price 5*s.*

V. MIND AND BODY: the Theories of their Relation. By Alexander Bain, LL.D. With Four Illustrations. Fifth Edition. Crown 8vo. price 4*s.*

7. THE STUDY OF SOCIOLOGY. By Herbert Spencer. Sixth Edition. Crown 8vo. price 5*s.*

7I. ON THE CONSERVATION OF ENERGY. By Balfour Stewart, M.A., Ll.D., F.R.S. With 14 Illustrations. Third Edition. Crown 8vo. price 5*s.*

7II. ANIMAL LOCOMOTION; or, Walking, Swimming, and Flying. By J. B. Pettigrew, M.D., F.R.S., &c. With 130 Illustrations. Second Edition. Crown 8vo. price 5*s.*

7III. RESPONSIBILITY IN MENTAL DISEASE. By Henry Maudsley, M.D. Second Edition. Crown 8vo. price 5*s.*

X. THE NEW CHEMISTRY. By Professor J. P. Cooke, of the Harvard University. With 31 Illustrations. Third Edition. Crown 8vo. price 5*s.*

C. THE SCIENCE OF LAW. By Professor Sheldon Amos. Second Edition. Crown 8vo. price 5*s.*

CI. ANIMAL MECHANISM: a Treatise on Terrestrial and Aerial Locomotion. By Professor E. J. Marcy. With 117 Illustrations. Second Edition. Crown 8vo. price 5*s.*

XII. THE DOCTRINE OF DESCENT AND DARWINISM. By Professor Oscar Schmidt (Strasburg University). With 26 Illustrations. Third Edition. Crown 8vo. price 5*s.*

XIII. THE HISTORY OF THE CONFLICT BETWEEN RELIGION AND SCIENCE. By J. W. Draper, M.D., LL.D. Tenth Edition. Crown 8vo. price 5*s.*

XIV. FUNGI: their Nature, Influences, Uses, &c. By M. C. Cooke, M.D., LL.D. Edited by the Rev. M. J. Berkeley, M.A., F.L.S. With numerous Illustrations. Second Edition. Crown 8vo. price 5*s.*

XV. THE CHEMICAL EFFECTS OF LIGHT AND PHOTOGRAPHY. By Dr. Hermann Vogel (Polytechnic Academy of Berlin). Translation thoroughly revised. With 100 Illustrations. Third Edition. Crown 8vo. price 5*s.*

XVI. THE LIFE AND GROWTH OF LANGUAGE. By William Dwight Whitney, Professor of Sanscrit and Comparative Philology in Yale College, Newhaven. Second Edition. Crown 8vo. price 5*s.*

XVII. MONEY AND THE MECHANISM OF EXCHANGE. By W. Stanley Jevons, M.A., F.R.S. Third Edition. Crown 8vo. price 5*s.*

XVIII. THE NATURE OF LIGHT. With a General Account of Physical Optics. By Dr. Eugene Lommel, Professor of Physics in the University of Erlangen. With 188 Illustrations and a Table of Spectra in Chromo-lithography. Second Edition. Crown 8vo. price 5*s.*

XIX. ANIMAL PARASITES AND MESSMATES. By Monsieur Van Beneden, Professor of the University of Louvain, Correspondent of the Institute of France. With 83 Illustrations. Second Edition. Crown 8vo. price 5*s.*

XX. FERMENTATION. By Professor Schützenberger, Director of the Chemical Laboratory at the Sorbonne. With 28 Illustrations. Second Edition. Crown 8vo. price 5*s.*

XXI. THE FIVE SENSES OF MAN. By Professor Bernstein, of the University of Halle. With 91 Illustrations. Second Edition. Crown 8vo. price 5*s.*

XXII. THE THEORY OF SOUND IN ITS RELATION TO MUSIC. By Professor Pietro Blaserna, of the Royal University of Rome. With numerous Illustrations. Second Edition. Crown 8vo. price 5*s.*

Forthcoming Volumes.

Prof. W. KINGDON CLIFFORD, M.A. The First Principles of the Exact Sciences Explained to the Non-Mathematical.

Prof. T. H. HUXLEY, LL.D., F.R.S. Bodily Motion and Consciousness.

W. B. CARPENTER, LL.D., F.R.S. The Physical Geography of the Sea.

Sir JOHN LUBBOCK, Bart., F.R.S. On Ants and Bees.

Prof. W. T. THISEL? Form and Hab?

Mr. J. NORMAN Spectrum Anal?

Prof. MICHAEL F? plasm and the (

H. CHARLTON BA? The Brain as a?

Prof. A. C. RAMS Earth Sculpture tains, Plains, R were produced been destroyed.

Prof. J. ROSENTHA? of Muscles and

P. BERT (Professor Forms of Lif? Conditions.

Prof. CORFIELD, ? Air in its Relat?

MILITARY WORKS.

*ANDERSON (Col. R. P.)—*VICTORIES AND DEFEATS : an Attempt to explain the Causes which have led to them. An Officer's Manual. Demy 8vo. price 14*s.*

ARMY OF THE NORTH GERMAN CONFEDERATION : a Brief Description of its Organisation, of the Different Branches of the Service and their *rôle* in War, of its Mode of Fighting, &c. Translated from the Corrected Edition, by permission of the Author, by Colonel Edward Newdigate. Demy 8vo. price 5*s.*

*BRIALMONT (Col. A.)—*HASTY INTRENCHMENTS. Translated by Lieut. Charles A. Empson, R.A. With Nine Plates. Demy 8vo. price 6*s.*

BLUME (Maj. W OF THE GERMA from Sedan to 1870-71. Wi Journals of the Translated by Maj. 20th Foo Sandhurst. D?

BOGUSLAWSKI TICAL DEDUC? OF 1870-1. ? Sir Lumley Gr? (Royal Irish) ? tion, Revised ? 8vo. price 7*s.*

CLERY (C.) Cap With 26 Maps ? revised Edition price 16*s.*

DU VERNOIS (*Col. von Verdy*)—
STUDIES IN LEADING TROOPS. An
authorised and accurate Translation by
Lieutenant H. J. T. Hildyard, 71st
Foot. Parts I. and II. Demy 8vo.
price 7s.

GOETZE (*Capt. A. von*)—OPERATIONS
OF THE GERMAN ENGINEERS DUR-
ING THE WAR OF 1870-1. Published
by Authority, and in accordance with
Official Documents. Translated from
the German by Colonel G. Graham,
V.C., C.B., R.E. With 6 large
Maps. Demy 8vo. price 21s.

HARRISON (*Lieut.-Col. R.*) — THE
OFFICER'S MEMORANDUM BOOK FOR
PEACE AND WAR. Oblong 32mo.
roan, elastic band and pencil, price
2s. 6d. ; russia, 5s.

HELVIG (*Capt. H.*)—THE OPERATIONS
OF THE BAVARIAN ARMY CORPS.
Translated by Captain G. S. Schwabe.
With Five large Maps. In 2 vols.
Demy 8vo. price 24s.

TACTICAL EXAMPLES : the Battalion.
Translated from the German by Col.
Sir Lumley Graham. With nearly
300 Diagrams. Demy 8vo. cloth,
price 15s.

HOFFBAUER (*Capt.*)—THE GERMAN
ARTILLERY IN THE BATTLES NEAR
METZ. Based on the Official Reports of
the German Artillery. Translated by
Captain E. O. Hollist. With Map
and Plans. Demy 8vo. price 21s.

LAYMANN (*Capt.*) — THE FRONTAL
ATTACK OF INFANTRY. Translated
by Colonel Edward Newdigate. Crown
8vo. price 2s. 6d.

MIRUS (*Maj.-Gen. von*) -- CAVALRY
FIELD DUTY. Translated by Major
Frank S. Russell 14th (King's)
Hussars. Crown 8vo. cloth limp,
price 7s. 6d.

PAGE (*Capt. S. F.*)—DISCIPLINE AND
DRILL. Cheaper Edition. Crown
8vo. price 1s.

PUBLIC SCHOOLBOY : the Volunteer, the
Militiaman, and the Regular Soldier.
Crown 8vo. cloth, price 5s.

SCHELL (*Maj. von*)—THE OPERATIONS
OF THE FIRST ARMY UNDER GEN.
VON GOEBEN. Translated by Col.
C. H. von Wright. Four Maps.
demy 8vo. price 9s.

THE OPERATIONS OF THE FIRST ARMY
UNDER GEN. VON STEINMETZ.
Translated by Captain E. O. Hollist.
Demy 8vo. price 10s. 6d.

SCHELLENDORF (*Major-Gen. B. von*)
THE DUTIES OF THE GENERAL
STAFF. Translated from the German
by Lieutenant Hare. Vol. I. Demy
8vo. cloth, 10s. 6d.

SCHERFF (*Maj. W. von*)—STUDIES IN
THE NEW INFANTRY TACTICS.
Parts I. and II. Translated from the
German by Colonel Lumley Graham.
Demy 8vo. price 7s. 6d.

SHADWELL (*Maj.-Gen.*) C.B.—MOUN-
TAIN WARFARE. Illustrated by the
Campaign of 1799 in Switzerland.
Being a Translation of the Swiss
Narrative compiled from the Works of
the Archduke Charles, Jomini, and
others. Also of Notes by General
H. Dufour on the Campaign of the
Valtelline in 1635. With Appendix,
Maps, and Introductory Remarks.
Demy 8vo. price 16s.

SHERMAN (*Gen. W. T.*)—MEMOIRS OF
GENERAL W. T. SHERMAN, Commander of the Federal Forces in the
American Civil War. By Himself.
2 vols. With Map. Demy 8vo. price
24s. *Copyright English Edition.*

STUBBS (*Lieut.-Col. F. W.*) — THE
REGIMENT OF BENGAL ARTILLERY.
The History of its Organisation, Equipment, and War Services. Compiled
from Published Works, Official Records, and various Private Sources.
With numerous Maps and Illustrations.
2 vols. demy 8vo. price 32s.

STUMM (*Lieut. Hugo*), *German Military
Attaché to the Khivan Expedition.*—
RUSSIA'S ADVANCE EASTWARD.
Based on the Official Reports of.
Translated by Capt. C. E. H. VINCENT,
With Map. Crown 8vo. price 6s.

VINCENT (Capt. C. E. H.)—ELEMEN-
TARY MILITARY GEOGRAPHY, RE-
CONNOITRING, AND SKETCHING.
Compiled for Non-commissioned Offi-
cers and Soldiers of all Arms. Square
crown 8vo. price 2s. 6d.

WICKHAM (Capt. E. H., R.A.)—IN-
FLUENCE OF FIREARMS UPON TAC-
TICS : Historical and Critical Investi-
gations. By an OFFICER OF SUPE-
RIOR RANK (in the German Army).
Translated by Captain E. H. Wick-
ham, R.A. Demy 8vo. price 7s. 6d.

WOINOVITS (Capt. I.) — AUSTRIAN
CAVALRY EXERCISE. Translated by
Captain W. S. Cooke. Crown 8vo.
price 7s.

WARTENSLEBEN (Count H. von.)—
THE OPERATIONS OF THE SOUTH
ARMY IN JANUARY AND FEBRUARY,
1871. Compiled from the Official
War Documents of the Head-quar-
ters of the Southern Army. Trans-
lated by Colonel C. H. von Wright
With Maps. Demy 8vo. price 6s.

THE OPERATIONS OF THE FIRST ARMY
UNDER GEN. VON MANTEUFFEL.
Translated by Colonel C. H. von
Wright. Uniform with the above.
Demy 8vo. price 9s.

WHITE (Capt. F. B. P.)—THE SUB-
STANTIVE SENIORITY ARMY LIST—
MAJORS AND CAPTAINS. 8vo. sewed,
price 2s. 6d.

POETRY.

ABBEY (Henry)—BALLADS OF GOOD
DEEDS, and other Verses. Fcp. 8vo.
cloth gilt, price 5s.

ADAMS (W. D.—LYRICS OF LOVE,
from Shakespeare to Tennyson. Selected and arranged by. Fcp. 8vo.
cloth extra, gilt edges, price 3s. 6d.

     Also, a Cheaper Edition. Fcp.
8vo. cloth, 2s. 6d.

ADAMS (John) M.A. — ST. MALO'S
QUEST, and other Poems. Fcp. 8vo.
price 5s.

ADON.—THROUGH STORM AND SUN-
SHINE. Illustrated by M. E. Edwards,
A. T. H. Paterson, and the Author.
Crown 8vo. price 7s. 6d.

AURORA : a Volume of Verse. Fcp. 8vo.
cloth, price 5s.

BARING (T. C.) M.A., M.P.—PINDAR
IN ENGLISH RHYME. Being an Attempt to render the Epinikian Odes
with the principal remaining Fragments of Pindar into English Rhymed
Verse. Small 4to. price 7s.

BAYNES (Rev. Canon R. H.) M.A.)—
HOME SONGS FOR QUIET HOURS.
Third Edition. Fcp. 8vo. cloth extra,
price 3s. 6d.
     This may also be had handsomely
bound in morocco with gilt edges.

     Also, a Cheaper Edition. Fcp.
8vo. price 2s. 6d.

BENNETT (Dr. W. C.)—BABY MAY
Home Poems and Ballads. With
Frontispiece. Crown 8vo. cloth ele-
gant, price 6s.

BABY MAY AND HOME POEMS. Fcp
8vo. sewed, in Coloured Wrapper
price 1s.

NARRATIVE POEMS AND BALLADS
Fcp. 8vo. sewed, in Coloured Wrapper
price 1s.

SONGS FOR SAILORS. Dedicated by
Special Request to H.R.H. the Duke
of Edinburgh. With Steel Portrait
and Illustrations. Crown 8vo. price
3s. 6d.
     An Edition in Illustrated Paper
Covers, price 1s.

SONGS OF A SONG WRITER. Crown
8vo. price 6s.

BOSWELL (R. B.) M.A., Oxon. -
METRICAL TRANSLATIONS FROM THE
GREEK AND LATIN POETS, and other
Poems. Crown 8vo. price 5s.

BRYANT (W. C.) — POEMS. Red-line
Edition. With 24 Illustrations and
Portrait of the Author. Crown 8vo
cloth extra, price 7s. 6d.
     A Cheap Edition, with Frontis
piece. Small crown 8vo. price 3s. 6d

BUCHANAN (Robt.)—POETICAL WORKS
Collected Edition, in 3 vols. with Por
trait. Crown 8vo. price 6s. each.

MASTER-SPIRITS. Post 8vo. price 10s. 6d

BULKELEY (Rev. H. J.)—WALLED IN, and other Poems. Crown 8vo. price 5*s.*

COSMOS : a Poem. Fcp. 8vo. price 3*s.* 6*d.*

CALDERON'S DRAMAS : the Wonder-Working Magician—Life in a Dream—the Purgatory of St. Patrick. Translated by Denis Florence MacCarthy. Post 8vo. price 10*s.*

CARPENTER (E.)—NARCISSUS, and other Poems. Fcp. 8vo. price 5*s.*

COLLINS (Mortimer)—INN OF STRANGE MEETINGS, and other Poems. Crown 8vo. cloth, price 5*s.*

CORY (Lieut.-Col. Arthur) — IONE : a Poem in Four Parts. Fcp. 8vo. cloth, price 5*s.*

CRESSWELL (Mrs. G.)—THE KING'S BANNER : Drama in Four Acts. Five Illustrations. 4to. price 10*s.* 6*d.*

DENNIS (J.)—ENGLISH SONNETS. Collected and Arranged. Elegantly bound. Fcp. 8vo. price 3*s.* 6*d.*

DE VERE (Aubrey)—ALEXANDER THE GREAT : a Dramatic Poem. Small crown 8vo. price 5*s.*

THE INFANT BRIDAL, and other Poems. A New and Enlarged Edition. Fcp. 8vo. price 7*s.* 6*d.*

THE LEGENDS OF ST. PATRICK, and other Poems. Small crown 8vo. price 5*s.*

ST. THOMAS OF CANTERBURY : a Dramatic Poem. Large fcp. 8vo. price 5*s.*

ANTAR AND ZARA: an Eastern Romance. INISFAIL, and other Poems, Meditative and Lyrical. Fcp. 8vo. price 6*s.*

THE FALL OF RORA, THE SEARCH AFTER PROSERPINE, and other Poems, Meditative and Lyrical. Fcp. 8vo. 6*s.*

DOBSON (Austin) — VIGNETTES IN RHYME, and Vers de Société. Third Edition. Fcp. 8vo. price 5*s.*

PROVERBS IN PORCELAIN. By the Author of 'Vignettes in Rhyme.' Third Edition. Crown 8vo. price 6*s.*

DOWDEN (Edward) LL.D.—POEMS. Second Edition. Fcp. 8vo. price 5*s.*

DOWNTON (Rev. H.) M.A.—HYMNS AND VERSES. Original and Translated. Small crown 8vo. cloth, price 3*s.* 6*d.*

DURAND (Lady)—IMITATIONS FROM THE GERMAN OF SPITTA AND TERSTEGEN. Fcp. 8vo. price 4*s.*

EDWARDS (Rev. Basil) — MINOR CHORDS ; or, Songs for the Suffering : a Volume of Verse. Fcp. 8vo. cloth, price 3*s.* 6*d.*; paper, price, 2*s.* 6*d.*

ELLIOTT (Ebenezer), The Corn Law Rhymer.—POEMS. Edited by his son, the Rev. Edwin Elliott, of St. John's, Antigua. 2 vols. crown 8vo. price 18*s.*

EROS AGONISTES : Poems. By E. B. D. Fcp. 8vo. price 3*s.* 6*d.*

EYRE (Maj.-Gen. Sir V.) C.B., K.C.S.I., &c.—LAYS OF A KNIGHT-ERRANT IN MANY LANDS. Square crown 8vo. with Six Illustrations, price 7*s.* 6*d.*

FERRIS (Henry Weybridge) — POEMS. Fcp. 8vo. price 5*s.*

GARDNER (H.)—SUNFLOWERS : a Book of Verses. Fcp. 8vo. price 5*s.*

GOLDIE (Lieut. M. H. G.)—HEBE : a Tale. Fcp. 8vo. price 5*s.*

HARCOURT (Capt. A. F. P.)—THE SHAKESPEARE ARGOSY. Containing much of the wealth of Shakespeare's Wisdom and Wit, alphabetically arranged and classified. Crown 8vo. price 6*s.*

HEWLETT (Henry G.)—A SHEAF OF VERSE. Fcp. 8vo. price 3*s.* 6*d.*

HOLMES (E. G. A.)—POEMS. Fcp. 8vo. price 5*s.*

HOWARD (Rev. G. B.) — AN OLD LEGEND OF ST. PAUL'S. Fcp. 8vo. price 4*s.* 6*d.*

HOWELL (James)—A TALE OF THE SEA, Sonnets, and other Poems. Fcp. 8vo. price 5*s.*

HUGHES (Allison) — PENELOPE, and other Poems. Fcp. 8vo. price 4*s.* 6*d.*

INCHBOLD (J. W.)—ANNUS AMORIS Sonnets. Fcp. 8vo. price 4*s.* 6*d.*

KING (*Mrs. Hamilton*)—THE DISCIPLES: a New Poem. Third Edition, with some Notes. Crown 8vo. price 7s. 6d.

ASPROMONTE, and other Poems. Second Edition. Fcp. 8vo. price 4s. 6d.

KNIGHT (*A. F. C.*)—POEMS. Fcp. 8vo. price 5s.

LADY OF LIPARI (THE) : a Poem in Three Cantos. Fcp. 8vo. price 5s.

LOCKER (*F.*)—LONDON LYRICS. A New and Revised Edition, with Additions and a Portrait of the Author. Crown 8vo. cloth elegant, price 6s.

Also, a Cheaper Edition. Fcp. 8vo. price 2s. 6d.

LUCAS (*Alice*)—TRANSLATIONS FROM THE WORKS OF GERMAN POETS OF THE 18TH AND 19TH CENTURIES. Fcp. 8vo. price 5s.

MORICE (*Rev. F. D.*) *M.A.* — THE OLYMPIAN AND PYTHIAN ODES OF PINDAR. A New Translation in English Verse. Crown 8vo. price 7s. 6d.

MORSHEAD (*E. D. A.*)—THE AGAMEMNON OF ÆSCHYLUS. Translated into English Verse. With an Introductory Essay. Crown 8vo. cloth, price 5s.

NEW WRITER (*A*)—SONGS OF TWO WORLDS. By a New Writer. Third Series. Second Edition. Fcp. 8vo. price 5s.

THE EPIC OF HADES. By the Author of 'Songs of Two Worlds.' Third Edition. Fcp. 8vo. price 7s. 6d.

NICHOLSON (*Edward B.*) *Librarian of the London Institution*—THE CHRIST CHILD, and other Poems. Crown 8vo. cloth, price 4s. 6d.

NOAKE (*Major R. Compton*) — THE BIVOUAC ; or, Martial Lyrist. With an Appendix : Advice to the Soldier. Fcp. 8vo. price 5s. 6d.

NORRIS (*Rev. Alfred*) —THE INNER AND OUTER LIFE POEMS. Fcp. 8vo. cloth, price 6s.

PAYNE (*John*)—SONGS OF LIFE AND DEATH. Crown 8vo. cloth, price 5s.

PAUL (*C. Kegan*)—GOETHE'S FAUST. A New Translation in Rhyme. Crown 8vo. price 6s.

PEACOCKE (*Georgiana*)—RAYS FROM THE SOUTHERN CROSS : Poems. Crown 8vo. with Sixteen Full-page Illustrations by the Rev. P. Walsh, cloth elegant, price 10s. 6d.

PENNELL (*H. Cholmondeley*)—PEGASUS RESADDLED. By the Author of ' Puck on Pegasus, ' &c. &c. With Ten Full-page Illustrations by George Du Maurier. Fcp. 4to. cloth elegant, 12s. 6d.

PFEIFFER (*Emily*)—GLAN ALARCH : His Silence and Song : a Poem. Crown 8vo. price 6s.

GERARD'S MONUMENT and other Poems. Second Edition. Crown 8vo. cloth, price 6s.

POWLETT (*Lieut. N.*) *R.A.*—EASTERN LEGENDS AND STORIES IN ENGLISH VERSE. Crown 8vo. price 5s.

RHOADES (*James*)—TIMOLEON: a Dramatic Poem. Fcp. 8vo. price 5s.

SCOTT (*Patrick*) — THE DREAM AND THE DEED, and other Poems. Fcp. 8vo. price 5s.

SONGS FOR MUSIC. By Four Friends. Square crown 8vo. price 5s. Containing Songs by Reginald A. Gatty, Stephen H. Gatty, Greville J. Chester, and Juliana Ewing.

SPICER (*H.*)—OTHO'S DEATH WAGER : a Dark Page of History Illustrated. In Five Acts. Fcp. 8vo. cloth, price 5s.

STONEHEWER (*Agnes*)—MONACELLA: a Legend of North Wales. A Poem. Fcp. 8vo. cloth, price 3s. 6d.

SWEET SILVERY SAYINGS OF SHAKESPEARE. Crown 8vo. cloth gilt, price 7s. 6d.

TAYLOR (*Rev. J. W. A.*) *M.A.*—POEMS. Fcp. 8vo. price 5s.

TAYLOR (*Sir H.*)—Works Complete in Five Volumes. Crown 8vo. cloth, price 30s.

TENNYSON (*Alfred*) — HAROLD : a Drama. Crown 8vo price 6s.

QUEEN MARY : a Drama. New Edition. Crown 8vo. price 6s.

TENNYSON (A.)—Works Complete :—
THE IMPERIAL LIBRARY EDITION.
Complete in 7 vols. demy 8vo. price
10s. 6d. each; in Roxburgh binding,
12s. 6d. (See p. 31.)

AUTHOR'S EDITION. In Six Volumes.
Post 8vo. cloth gilt ; or half-morocco.
Roxburgh style. (See p. 31.)

CABINET EDITION. 12 Volumes. Each
with Frontispiece. Fcp. 8vo. price
2s. 6d. each. (See p. 31.)

CABINET EDITION. 12 vols. Complete
in handsome Ornamental Case. (See
p. 31).

Original Editions :—
POEMS. Small 8vo. price 6s.

MAUD, and other Poems. Small 8vo.
price 3s. 6d.

THE PRINCESS. Small 8vo. price 3s. 6d.

IDYLLS OF THE KING. Small 8vo.
price 5s.

IDYLLS OF THE KING. Complete.
Small 8vo. price 6s.

THE HOLY GRAIL, and other Poems.
Small 8vo. price 4s. 6d.

GARETH AND LYNETTE. Small 8vo.
price 3s.

ENOCH ARDEN, &c. Small 8vo. price
3s. 6d.

IN MEMORIAM. Small 8vo. price 4s.

SELECTIONS FROM THE ABOVE WORKS.
Super royal 16mo. price 3s. 6d. ; cloth
gilt extra, price 4s.

SONGS FROM THE ABOVE WORKS.
16mo. cloth, price 2s. 6d.

POCKET VOLUME EDITION. 13 vols.
in neat case, price 36s.
Ditto, ditto. Extra cloth gilt, in case,
price 42s.

SHILLING EDITION OF THE POETICAL
WORKS. In 10 vols. pocket size,
1s. each, sewed.

TENNYSON'S IDYLLS OF THE KING, and
other Poems. Illustrated by Julia
Margaret Cameron. 2 vols. folio.
half-bound morocco, cloth sides, price
£6. 6s. each.

TENNYSON FOR THE YOUNG AND FOR
RECITATION. Specially arranged.
Fcp. 8vo. 1s. 6d.

TENNYSON BIRTHDAY BOOK. Edited by
Emily Shakespear. 32mo. cloth limp,
2s. ; cloth extra, 3s.

THOMPSON (Alice C.)—PRELUDES : a
Volume of Poems. Illustrated by
Elizabeth Thompson (Painter of 'The
Roll Call'). 8vo. price 7s. 6d.

THOUGHTS IN VERSE. Small crown 8vo.
price 1s. 6d.

THRING (Rev. Godfrey), B.A.—HYMNS
AND SACRED LYRICS. Fcp. 8vo.
price 5s.

TODD (Herbert) M.A.—ARVAN ; or, the
Story of the Sword. A Poem. Crown
8vo. price 7s. 6d.

TODHUNTER (Dr. J.) — LAURELLA,
and other Poems. Crown 8vo. price
6s. 6d.

TURNER (Rev. C. Tennyson)—SONNETS,
LYRICS, AND TRANSLATIONS. Crown
8vo. cloth, price 4s. 6d.

WATERFIELD (W.) — HYMNS FOR
HOLY DAYS AND SEASONS. 32mo.
cloth, price 1s. 6d.

WAY (A.) M.A.—THE ODES OF HORACE
LITERALLY TRANSLATED IN METRE.
Fcp. 8vo. price 2s.

WILLOUGHBY (The Hon. Mrs.)—ON
THE NORTH WIND—THISTLEDOWN :
a Volume of Poems. Elegantly bound,
small crown 8vo. price 7s. 6d.

LIBRARY NOVELS.

AYRTON (J. C.)—A SCOTCH WOOING.
2 vols. crown 8vo.

BLUE ROSES ; or, Helen Malinofska's
Marriage. By the Author of 'Véra.'
Fifth Edition. 2 vols. cloth, gilt tops,
12s.

BUNNETT (F. E.)—LINKED AT LAST.
Crown 8vo.

CADELL (Mrs. H. M.)—IDA CRAVEN :
a Novel. 2 vols. crown 8vo.

CARR (Lisle)—JUDITH GWYNNE. 3 vols.
Second Edition. Crown 8vo.

CHAPMAN (*Hon. Mrs. E. W.*) — A CONSTANT HEART : a Story. 2 vols. cloth, gilt tops, 12s.

CLAYTON (*Cecil*)—EFFIE'S GAME ; How She Lost and how She Won : a Novel. 2 vols.

COLLINS (*Mortimer*)—THE PRINCESS CLARICE : a Story of 1871. 2 vols.

SQUIRE SILCHESTER'S WHIM. 3 vols.

MIRANDA : a Midsummer Madness. 3 vols.

CONYERS (*Ansley*) — CHESTERLEIGH. 3 vols. crown 8vo.

COTTON (*R. T.*)—MR. CARINGTON : a Tale of Love and Conspiracy. 3 vols. crown 8vo.

DE WILLE (*E.*)—UNDER A CLOUD ; or, Johannes Olaf : a Novel. Translated by F. E. Bunnett. 3 vols. Crown 8vo.

EILOART (*Mrs.*)—LADY MORETOUN'S DAUGHTER. 3 vols. crown 8vo.

FAITHFULL (*Mrs. Francis G.*)—LOVE ME, OR LOVE ME NOT. 3 vols. crown 8vo.

FENN (*G. M.*)—A LITTLE WORLD : a Novel. In 3 vols.

FISHER (*Alice*) HIS QUEEN. 3 vols. crown 8vo.

FOTHERGILL (*Jessie*) — ALDYTH : a Novel. 2 vols. crown 8vo. 21s.

HEALEY : a Romance. 3 vols. cr. 8vo.

GRAY (*Mrs. Russell*)—LISETTE'S VENTURE : a Novel. 2 vols. crown 8vo.

GRIFFITHS (*Capt. Arthur*) — THE QUEEN'S SHILLING : a Novel. 2 vols.

HAWTHORNE (*Julian*)—BRESSANT : a Romance. 2 vols. crown 8vo.

IDOLATRY : a Romance. 2 vols. cr. 8vo.

HAWTHORNE (*Nathaniel*) — SEPTIMIUS : a Romance. Second Edition. Crown 8vo. cloth, price 9s.

HEATHERGATE : a Story of Scottish Life and Character. By a New Author. 2 vols. crown 8vo.

HOGAN, M.P. : a Novel. 3 vols. cr. 8vo.

HOCKLEY (*W. B.*)—TALES OF THE ZENANA ; or, a Nuwab's Leisure Hours. By the Author of 'Pandurang Hari.' With a Preface by Lord Stanley of Alderley. 2 vols. crown 8vo. cloth, price 21s.

INGELOW (*Jean*) — OFF THE SKELLIGS. (Her First Romance.) 4 vols. cr. 8vo.

KEATINGE (*Mrs.*)—HONOR BLAKE : the Story of a Plain Woman. 2 vols. crown 8vo.

LISTADO (*J. T.*)—CIVIL SERVICE : a Novel. 2 vols. crown 8vo.

LOVEL (*Edward*)—THE OWL'S NEST IN THE CITY : a Story. Crown 8vo. price 10s. 6d.

MACDONALD (*G.*) — MALCOLM : a Novel. 3 vols. Second Edition. Crown 8vo.

ST. GEORGE AND ST. MICHAEL. 3 vols. crown 8vo.

MARKEWITCH (*B.*)—THE NEGLECTED QUESTION. Translated from the Russian by the Princess Ourousoff. 2 vols. crown 8vo. 14s.

MARSHALL (*H.*)—THE STORY OF SIR EDWARD'S WIFE : a Novel. Crown 8vo. price 10s. 6d.

MORLEY (*Susan*)—AILEEN FERRERS : a Novel. 2 vols. crown 8vo.

THROSTLETHWAITE : a Novel. 3 vols. Crown 8vo.

MARGARET CHETWYND : a Novel. 3 vols. crown 8vo.

MOSTYN (*Sydney*) — PERPLEXITY : a Novel. 3 vols. crown 8vo.

MY SISTER ROSALIND : a Novel. By the Author of 'Christiana North,' and 'Under the Limes.' 2 vols.

SAUNDERS (*John*) — ISRAEL MORT, OVERMAN : a Story of the Mine. 3 vols. crown 8vo.

SAUNDERS (*Katherine*) — THE HIGH MILLS : a Novel. 3 vols. crown 8vo.

SHAW (*Flora L.*)—CASTLE BLAIR : a Story of Youthful Lives. 2 vols. crown 8vo. cloth, price 12s.

SHELDON (*Philip*)—WOMAN'S A RIDDLE ; or, Baby Warmstrey : a Novel. 3 vols. crown 8vo. cloth.

STRETTON (*Hesba*)—HESTER MORLEY'S PROMISE. 3 vols. crown 8vo. cloth.

THE DOCTOR'S DILEMMA. 3 vols. crown 8vo. cloth.

TAYLOR (*Colonel Meadows*) C.S.I., M.R.I.A.—SEETA : a Novel. 3 vols. crown 8vo.

A NOBLE QUEEN. 3 vols. crown 8vo.

THOMASINA : a Novel. 2 vols. cr. 8vo.

TRAVERS (*Mar.*)—THE SPINSTERS OF BLATCHINGTON : a Novel. 2 vols. crown 8vo.

VANESSA. By the Author of 'Thomasina' &c. a Novel. 2 vols. Second Edition. Crown 8vo.

WAITING FOR TIDINGS. By the Author of 'White and Black.' 3 vols. cr. 8vo.

WEDMORE (*F.*)—TWO GIRLS. 2 vols. crown 8vo.

WHAT 'TIS TO LOVE. By the Author of 'Flora Adair,' 'The Value of Fosterstown.' 3 vols. crown 8vo.

YORKE (*Stephen*)—CLEVEDEN : a Novel. 2 vols. crown 8vo.

WORKS OF FICTION IN ONE VOLUME.

BETHAM-EDWARDS (*Miss M.*) KITTY. With a Frontispiece. Crown 8vo. price 6s.

CLERK (*Mrs. Godfrey*)—'ILÂM EN NÂS : Historical Tales and Anecdotes of the Times of the Early Khalifahs. Translated from the Arabic Originals. Illustrated with Historical and Explanatory Notes. Crown 8vo. cloth, price 7s.

GARRETT (*E.*)—BY STILL WATERS : a Story for Quiet Hours. With Seven Illustrations. Crown 8vo. price 6s.

HARDY (*Thomas*)—A PAIR OF BLUE EYES. Author of 'Far from the Madding Crowd.' Crown 8vo. price 6s.

HAWTHORNE (*N.*) — SEPTIMIUS : a Romance. Second Edition. Crown 8vo. price 9s.

HOWARD (*Mary M.*)—BEATRICE AYLMER, and other Tales. Crown 8vo. price 6s.

IGNOTUS—CULMSHIRE FOLK: a Novel. New and Cheaper Edition. Crown 8vo. price 6s.

MACDONALD (*G.*)—MALCOLM. With Portrait of the Author engraved on Steel. Fourth Edition. Crown 8vo. price 6s.

MEREDITH (*George*) — ORDEAL OF RICHARD FEVEREL. New Edition. Crown 8vo. cloth, price 6s.

PALGRAVE (*W. Gifford*)—HERMANN AGHA : an Eastern Narrative. Third Edition. Crown 8vo. cloth, price 6s.

PANDURANG HARI ; or, Memoirs of a Hindoo. With an Introductory Preface by Sir H. Bartle E. Frere, G.C.S.I., C.B. Crown 8vo. price 6s.

REGINALD BRAMBLE : a Cynic of the Nineteenth Century. An Autobiography. Crown 8vo. price 10s. 6d.

SAUNDERS (*John*) — ISRAEL MORT, OVERMAN : a Story of the Mine. Crown 8vo. price 6s.

SAUNDERS (*Katherine*) — GIDEON'S ROCK, and other Stories. Crown 8vo. price 6s.

JOAN MERRYWEATHER, and other Stories. Crown 8vo. price 6s.

MARGARET AND ELIZABETH : a Story of the Sea. Crown 8vo. price 6s.

TAYLOR (*Col. Meadows*) C.S.I., M.R.I.A. THE CONFESSIONS OF A THUG. Crown 8vo. price 6s.

TARA : a Mahratta Tale. Crown 8vo. price 6s.

CORNHILL LIBRARY of FICTION (*The*). Crown 8vo. price 3s. 6d. per volume.

HALF-A-DOZEN DAUGHTERS. By J. Masterman.

CORNHILL LIBRARY of FICTION.
THE HOUSE OF RABY. By Mrs. G. Hooper.

A FIGHT FOR LIFE. By Moy Thomas.

ROBIN GRAY. By Charles Gibbon.

ONE OF TWO ; or, The Left-Handed Bride. By J. Hain Friswell.

CORNHILL LIBRARY of FICTION.
GOD'S PROVIDENCE HOUSE. By Mrs. G. L. Banks.

FOR LACK OF GOLD. By Charles Gibbon.

ABEL DRAKE'S WIFE. By John Saunders.

HIRELL. By John Saunders.

CHEAP FICTION.

GIBBON (Charles)—FOR LACK OF GOLD. With a Frontispiece. Crown 8vo. Illustrated Boards, price 2s.

ROBIN GRAY. With a Frontispiece. Crown 8vo. Illustrated boards, price 2s.

SAUNDERS (John)—HIRELL. With Frontispiece. Crown 8vo. Illustrated boards, price 2s.

ABEL DRAKE'S WIFE. With Frontispiece. Illustrated boards, price 2s.

BOOKS FOR THE YOUNG.

AUNT MARY'S BRAN PIE. By the Author of 'St. Olave's.' Illustrated. Price 3s. 6d.

BARLEE (Ellen)—LOCKED OUT: a Tale of the Strike. With a Frontispiece. Royal 16mo. price 1s. 6d.

BONWICK (J.) F.R.G.S.—THE TASMANIAN LILY. With Frontispiece. Crown 8vo. price 5s.

MIKE HOWE, the Bushranger of Van Diemen's Land. With Frontispiece. Crown 8vo. price 5s.

BRAVE MEN'S FOOTSTEPS. By the Editor of 'Men who have Risen.' A Book of Example and Anecdote for Young People. With Four Illustrations by C. Doyle. Third Edition. Crown 8vo. price 3s. 6d.

CHILDREN'S TOYS, and some Elementary Lessons in General Knowledge which they teach. Illustrated. Crown 8vo. cloth, price 5s.

COLERIDGE (Sara)—PRETTY LESSONS IN VERSE FOR GOOD CHILDREN, with some Lessons in Latin, in Easy Rhyme. A New Edition. Illustrated. Fcp. 8vo. cloth, price 3s. 6d.

D'ANVERS (N. R.)—LITTLE MINNIE'S TROUBLES : an Every-day Chronicle. With 4 Illustrations by W. H. Hughes. Fcp. cloth, price 3s. 6d.

PIXIE'S ADVENTURES ; or, the Tale of a Terrier. With 21 Illustrations. 16mo. cloth, price 4s. 6d.

DAVIES (G. Christopher)—MOUNTAIN, MEADOW, AND MERE : a Series of Outdoor Sketches of Sport, Scenery, Adventures, and Natural History. With Sixteen Illustrations by Bosworth W. Harcourt. Crown 8vo. price 6s.

RAMBLES AND ADVENTURES OF OUR SCHOOL FIELD CLUB. With Four Illustrations. Crown 8vo. price 5s.

DRUMMOND (Miss)—TRIPPS BUILDINGS. A Study from Life, with Frontispiece. Small crown 8vo. price 3s. 6d.

EDMONDS (Herbert)—WELL SPENT LIVES : a Series of Modern Biography. Crown 8vo. price 5s.

EVANS (Mark)—THE STORY OF OUR FATHER'S LOVE, told to Children ; being a New and Enlarged Edition of Theology for Children. With Four Illustrations. Fcap. 8vo. price 3s. 6d.

FARQUHARSON (*M.*)

I. ELSIE DINSMORE. Crown 8vo. price 3*s.* 6*d.*

II. ELSIE'S GIRLHOOD. Crown 8vo. price 3*s.* 6*d.*

III. ELSIE'S HOLIDAYS AT ROSELANDS. Crown 8vo. price 3*s.* 6*d.*

HERFORD (*Brooke*)—THE STORY OF RELIGION IN ENGLAND : a Book for Young Folk. Crown 8vo. cloth, price 5*s.*

INGELOW (*Jean*) — THE LITTLE WONDER-HORN. With Fifteen Illustrations. Small 8vo. price 2*s.* 6*d.*

KER (*David*) — THE BOY SLAVE IN BOKHARA : a Tale of Central Asia. With Illustrations. Crown 8vo. price 5*s.*

THE WILD HORSEMAN OF THE PAMPAS. Illustrated. Crown 8vo. price 5*s.*

LEANDER (*Richard*) — FANTASTIC STORIES. Translated from the German by Paulina B. Granville. With Eight Full-page Illustrations by M. E. Fraser-Tytler. Crown 8vo. price 5*s.*

LEE (*Holme*)—HER TITLE OF HONOUR. A Book for Girls. New Edition. With a Frontispiece. Crown 8vo. price 5*s.*

LEWIS (*Mary A.*) —A RAT WITH THREE TALES. With Four Illustrations by Catherine F. Frere. Price 5*s.*

LITTLE MINNIE'S TROUBLES : an Every-day Chronicle. With Four Illustrations by W. H. Hughes. Fcap. price 3*s.* 6*d.*

M'CLINTOCK (*L.*)—SIR SPANGLE AND THE DINGY HEN. Illustrated. Square crown 8vo. price 2*s.* 6*d.*

MAC KENNA (*S. J.*)—PLUCKY FELLOWS. A Book for Boys. With Six Illustrations. Fourth Edition. Crown 8vo. price 3*s.* 6*d.*

AT SCHOOL WITH AN OLD DRAGOON. With Six Illustrations. Third Edition. Crown 8vo. price 5*s.*

MALDEN (*H. E.*)—PRINCES AND PRINCESSES : Two Fairy Tales. Crown 8vo. cloth.

NAAKE (*J. T.*) — SLAVONIC FAIRY TALES. From Russian, Servian, Polish, and Bohemian Sources. With Four Illustrations. Crown 8vo. price 5*s.*

PELLETAN (*E.*)—THE DESERT PASTOR. JEAN JAROUSSEAU. Translated from the French. By Colonel E. P. De L'Hoste. With a Frontispiece. New Edition. Fcap. 8vo. price 3*s.* 6*d.*

REANEY (*Mrs. G. S.*)—WAKING AND WORKING ; or, From Girlhood to Womanhood. With a Frontispiece. Crown 8vo. price 5*s.*

SUNBEAM WILLIE, and other Stories. Three Illustrations. Royal 16mo. price 1*s.* 6*d.*

BLESSING AND BLESSED : a Story of Girl Life. Crown 8vo. cloth, price 5*s.*

SUNSHINE JENNY and other Stories. 3 Illustrations. Royal 16mo. cloth, price 1*s.* 6*d.*

ROSS (*Mrs. E.*), ('Nelsie Brook') — DADDY'S PET. A Sketch from Humble Life. With Six Illustrations. Royal 16mo. price 1*s.*

SADLER (*S. W.*) R.N.—THE AFRICAN CRUISER : a Midshipman's Adventures on the West Coast. With Three Illustrations. Second Edition. Crown 8vo. price 3*s.* 6*d.*

SEEKING HIS FORTUNE, and other Stories. With Four Illustrations. Crown 8vo. price 3*s.* 6d.

SEVEN AUTUMN LEAVES FROM FAIRY LAND. Illustrated with Nine Etchings. Square crown 8vo. price 3*s.* 6*d.*

STRETTON (*Hesba*), Author of 'Jessica's First Prayer.'

MICHEL LORIO'S CROSS and other Stories. With Two Illustrations. Royal 16mo. price 1*s.* 6*d.*

THE STORM OF LIFE. With Ten Illustrations. Sixteenth Thousand. Royal 16mo. price 1*s.* 6*d.*

THE CREW OF THE DOLPHIN. Illustrated. Thirteenth Thousand. Royal 16mo. price 1*s.* 6*d.*

STRETTON (*Hesba*), Author of 'Jessica's First Prayer.'

CASSY. Thirty-fourth Thousand. With Six Illustrations. Royal 16mo. price 1*s.* 6*d.*

THE KING'S SERVANTS. Thirty-eighth Thousand. With Eight Illustrations. Royal 16mo. price 1*s.* 6*d.*

LOST GIP. Fifty-fourth Thousand. With Six Illustrations. Royal 16mo. price 1*s.* 6*d.*

*** *Also a handsomely bound Edition, with Twelve Illustrations, price* 2*s.* 6*d.*

DAVID LLOYD'S LAST WILL. With Four Illustrations. Royal 16mo. price 2*s.* 6*d.*

THE WONDERFUL LIFE. Twelfth Thousand. Fcap. 8vo. price 2*s.* 6*d.*

A NIGHT AND A DAY. With Frontispiece. Eighth Thousand. Royal 16mo. limp cloth, price 6*d.*

FRIENDS TILL DEATH. With Illustrations and Frontispiece. Twentieth Thousand. Royal 16mo. price 1*s.* 6*d.*; limp cloth, price 6*d.*

STRETTON (*Hesba*), Author of 'Jessica's First Prayer.'

TWO CHRISTMAS STORIES. With Frontispiece. Fifteenth Thousand. Royal 16mo. limp cloth, price 6*d.*

MICHEL LORIO'S CROSS, AND LEFT ALONE. With Frontispiece. Twelfth Thousand. Royal 16mo. limp cloth, price 6*d.*

OLD TRANSOME. With Frontispiece. Twelfth Thousand. Royal 16mo. limp cloth, price 6*d.*

*** Taken from 'The King's Servants.'

THE WORTH OF A BABY, and How Apple-Tree Court was Won. With Frontispiece. Fifteenth Thousand. Royal 16mo. limp cloth, price 6*d.*

SUNNYLAND STORIES. By the Author of 'Aunt Mary's Bran Pie.' Illustrated. Small 8vo. price 3*s.* 6*d.*

WHITAKER (*Florence*)—CHRISTY'S INHERITANCE. A London Story. Illustrated. Royal 16mo. price 1s. 6*d.*

ZIMMERN (*H.*)—STORIES IN PRECIOUS STONES. With Six Illustrations. Third Edition. Crown 8vo. price 5*s*

A LIST

OF THE COLLECTED EDITIONS OF

MR. TENNYSON'S WORKS.

THE IMPERIAL LIBRARY EDITION,

COMPLETE IN SEVEN OCTAVO VOLUMES.

Cloth, price 10s. 6d. per vol. ; 12s. 6d. Roxburgh binding.

CONTENTS.

Vol. I.—MISCELLANEOUS POEMS.
II.—MISCELLANEOUS POEMS.
III.—PRINCESS, AND OTHER POEMS.

Vol. IV.—IN MEMORIAM and MAUD.
V.—IDYLLS OF THE KING.
VI.—IDYLLS OF THE KING.
VII.—DRAMAS.

Printed in large, clear, old-faced type, with a Steel Engraved Portrait of the Author, the set complete, price £3. 13s. 6d. *‚* The handsomest Edition published.

THE AUTHOR'S EDITION,

IN SIX VOLUMES. Bound in cloth, 38s. 6d.

CONTENTS.

Vol. I.—EARLY POEMS and ENGLISH IDYLLS. 6s.
II.—LOCKSLEY HALL, LUCRETIUS, and other Poems. 6s.
III.—THE IDYLLS OF THE KING, complete. 7s. 6d.

Vol. IV.—THE PRINCESS and MAUD. 6s.
V.—ENOCH ARDEN and IN MEMORIAM. 6s.
VI.—QUEEN MARY and HAROLD 7s.

This Edition can also be had bound in half-morocco, Roxburgh, price 1s. 6d. per vol. extra.

THE CABINET EDITION,

COMPLETE IN TWELVE VOLUMES. Price 2s. 6d. each.

CONTENTS.

Vol. I.—EARLY POEMS. Illustrated with a Photographic Portrait of Mr. Tennyson.

II.—ENGLISH IDYLLS, and other POEMS. Containing an Engraving of Mr. Tennyson's Residence at Aldworth.

III.—LOCKSLEY HALL, and other POEMS. With an Engraved Picture of Farringford.

IV.—LUCRETIUS, and other POEMS. Containing an Engraving of a Scene in the Garden at Swainston.

V.—IDYLLS OF THE KING. With an Autotype of the Bust of Mr. Tennyson by T. Woolner, R.A.

Vol. VI.—IDYLLS OF THE KING. Illustrated with an Engraved Portrait of 'Elaine,' from a Photographic Study by Julia M. Cameron.

VII.—IDYLLS OF THE KING. Containing an Engraving of 'Arthur,' from a Photographic Study by Julia M. Cameron.

VIII.—THE PRINCESS. With an Engraved Frontispiece.

IX.—MAUD and ENOCH ARDEN. With a Picture of 'Maud,' taken from a Photographic Study by Julia M. Cameron.

X.—IN MEMORIAM. With a Steel Engraving of Arthur H. Hallam, engraved from a picture in possession of the Author, by J. C. Armytage.

XI.—QUEEN MARY: a Drama. With Frontispiece by Walter Crane.

XII.—HAROLD: a Drama. With Frontispiece by Walter Crane.

‚ *These Volumes may be had separately, or the Edition complete, in a handsome ornamental case, price 32s.*

THE MINIATURE EDITION,

IN THIRTEEN VOLUMES.

CONTENTS.

Vol. I.—POEMS.
II.—POEMS.
III.—POEMS.
IV.—IDYLLS OF THE KING.
V.—IDYLLS OF THE KING.
VI.—IDYLLS OF THE KING.

Vol. VII.—IDYLLS OF THE KING.
VIII.—IN MEMORIAM.
IX.—PRINCESS.
X.—MAUD.
XI.—ENOCH ARDEN.
XII.—QUEEN MARY.

VOL. XIII.—HAROLD.

Bound in imitation vellum, ornamented in gilt and gilt edges, in case, price 42s
This Edition can also be had in plain binding and case, price 36s.

LONDON : PRINTED BY
SPOTTISWOODE AND CO., NEW-STREET SQUARE
AND PARLIAMENT STREET

www.ingramcontent.com/pod-product-compliance
Lightning Source LLC
Chambersburg PA
CBHW052336110726
47901CB00005B/1247